Harlequin is proud to present
of a classic from best selling author

Heather Graham

and
a brand-new romance from rising star
Julia Justiss

Acclaim for Justiss's previous titles:

My Lady's Trust
"With this exceptional Regency-era romance,
Justiss adds another fine feather to her writing cap."
—*Publishers Weekly*

The Proper Wife
"Justiss is a promising new talent and readers
will devour her tantalizing tale with gusto."
—*Publishers Weekly*

The Wedding Gamble
"This is a fast-paced story that will leave you
wanting more…you won't want to put it down!"
—*Newandusedbooks.com*

HEATHER GRAHAM

A master storyteller, Heather Graham describes her life as "busy, wild and fun." Surprisingly, with all her success, Heather's first career choice was not writing, but acting on the Shakespearean stage. Happily for her fans, fate intervened and now she is a *New York Times* bestselling author. Although Heather and her family enjoy traveling, southern Florida—where she loves the sun and water—is home.

JULIA JUSTISS

wrote her first plot ideas for twenty-seven Nancy Drew stories in the back of her third-grade spiral and has been writing ever since. After publishing poetry in college, she served stints as a business journalist for an insurance company and editor of the American embassy newsletter in Tunis, Tunisia. She followed her naval-officer husband through seven moves in twelve years, finally ending up in the Piney Woods of east Texas, where she teaches high school French. Her Regency historical novels have finaled in or won several contests, including the Romance Writers of America's Golden Heart for Regency, *Romantic Times* magazine Best First Historical, the Golden Quill's Best Historical of the Year and Romance Readers Anonymous's Favorite Historical of the Year. She lives in a Georgian manor with her husband, three children and two dogs, and welcomes mail from readers. Reach her at 179 County Road 4112, Daingerfield, TX 75638 or www.juliajustiss.com.

HEATHER GRAHAM

JULIA JUSTISS

Forbidden Stranger

HARLEQUIN®

TORONTO • NEW YORK • LONDON
AMSTERDAM • PARIS • SYDNEY • HAMBURG
STOCKHOLM • ATHENS • TOKYO • MILAN • MADRID
PRAGUE • WARSAW • BUDAPEST • AUCKLAND

ISBN 0-373-83565-5

FORBIDDEN STRANGER

Copyright © 2003 by Harlequin Books S.A.

The publisher acknowledges the copyright holders
of the individual works as follows:

FORBIDDEN FIRE
Copyright © 1991 by Heather Graham Pozzessere

SEDUCTIVE STRANGER
Copyright © 2003 by Janet Justiss

This edition published by arrangement with Harlequin Books S.A.

® and TM are trademarks of the publisher. Trademarks indicated with
® are registered in the United States Patent and Trademark Office, the
Canadian Trade Marks Office and in other countries.

Visit us at www.eHarlequin.com

Printed in U.S.A.

CONTENTS

FORBIDDEN FIRE
Heather Graham

This book is dedicated to "Sister T"—
Teresa Sutton—
with lots of thanks, affection,
very best wishes
and good things, always.

PROLOGUE

Yorkshire, England
March, 1895

THE FIRST TIME Marissa saw the stranger, she was not quite ten years old. But she knew from the moment she saw him that she'd never forget him.

It was cold that day. It was always cold in the small coal-mining town, for the fires were meager, and they never seemed to warm the little one-room hovels where the miners lived. Or maybe it was cold because there was no glass in the windows—they were covered in the winter and spring with whatever newspaper or sacking could be found.

And spring had brought heavy rain that year. But not even the rain could wash away the continual pall of black that seemed to hang over the town. The coal dust from the mines seemed like a miasma that clouded just the land that belonged to the mine. To Marissa, the very color of the air was different, and where the black cleared away was freedom. A different world. And her whole meaning in life came to a longing to escape the cloud of black.

The rains merely turned coal dust to mud.

On that day she saw the stranger for the first time, she had donned a clean dress and a pinafore she had studiously scrubbed herself, determined that it would be white. And she had brushed and braided her hair. It was wild hair, a deep red blond in color. Uncle Theo said it was like a sunset, but when she had first come to the coal-mining town, the children had laughed and called her carrot top. She was as tough and determined as any of them, and they'd eventually come to respect her, but they resented her, too. She was an outsider, and she could read and write to boot. She'd put on airs, Uncle Theo had told her.

Well, she'd had the right. She was the daughter of a Church of England minister, and she'd spent her early years in a far different life. She'd seen enough of the great manors to know that she longed for the life of a lady. Longed for it with every breath of her being. Marissa clung to her pride and her dreams as if they were floats and she were adrift in a vast ocean.

On the day she met the stranger she had just been coming from Petey Quayle's house. His mum had been down with the ague, and Uncle Theo had sent her over with his special chicken soup. Mrs. Quayle had been grateful and very kind, but Petey had determined to plague her silly. She had barely walked out of the house before he had come running up behind her calling out her name. Turning, she knew that he meant to knock her into the mud, and so she had started to run.

It was all the stranger boy's fault. It was, it really was. He came striding around the corner of the pony shed, and Marissa barely had a moment to glance at him before she plowed straight into him. But that one glance burned itself on her memory. He was so perfect. A boy, but a very tall one. Years older than she was. Maybe even a man. He was certainly tall enough. Tall, but very slim. Perhaps eighteen or nineteen. And impeccably dressed in clean fawn trousers, a cranberry vest and a light brown jacket.

She was running too fast to stop, but just before she hit him she met his eyes. He might have been young, but they were a curiously disturbing blue. A blue that stared and probed, and looked into the heart. And his hair was black. Jet black.

"My word!" someone at his side snapped.

Marissa didn't see who it was at first. She had lost her balance and was falling straight into the mud that she had been trying so very hard to avoid.

"Here, let me help you up!" the boy said, reaching for her.

She glared up at him, knowing how filthy the mud had made her. "You knocked me over!"

"I most certainly did not, young lady! You ran straight into me."

"Out of the way, you little coal rat! How dare you speak to a young gent so!" the other voice snapped. It was Mr. Lacey, the manager of the mines. Short and portly, he was also excessively cruel. She sensed that his cruel treatment of a people doomed to work the mines from birth stemmed from his hatred of the wealthy shareholders he was forced to report to.

Lacey and the young man were not alone. They were accompanied by an older man, white-haired and genteel, with the same blue eyes the boy had.

"Here, here, Lacey!" he protested. "There's no cause to bring the child grief!"

He seemed a nice man, but Marissa saw a pity in his eyes that cut her to the quick.

"I'm no coal rat!" she seethed, determined to rise on her own. As she did so, she made certain that the mud flew and that a few big globs hit Lacey. Lacey swore vehemently.

"Father," the boy protested, "I think this man's language quite unnecessary before a child."

"She's a trouble-causing coal rat, whatever her airs!" Lacey insisted. "And if you cause any more trouble with these fine people here, I'll take a switch to you myself tonight. And see that old uncle of yours thrown out!"

The white-haired man stiffened. "The girl can cause no more trouble. I'll not invest here. I'll not invest in human misery!" He walked away.

Lacey stared at Marissa furiously, then ran after the man. "Wait, sir," he called.

But the boy stayed. There was pity in his eyes, and Marissa couldn't help it, she hated him for it.

He tossed her a coin. A small gold one.

It would have probably fed them for a year.

"Buy yourself a new pinafore," he said.

He turned his back on her. Dismissing her.

After all, she was only a coal rat, needing a handout.

"Take this back!" she spat furiously, and she threw the coin at him. She fled home, very nearly in tears.

That night, when she went out to get water from the well, Mr. Lacey had caught hold of her. Before she could struggle free, he'd thrown her over his knee and given her several good stripes with a hickory switch.

With tears in her eyes, she bit him. Bit him hard. He screamed, and she was free.

Marissa never told her uncle.

Neither did Lacey.

And Marissa didn't even hate Lacey anymore than she already did. She understood Lacey. He was certainly no better than she was.

But she hated the boy.

She hated him for being impeccable. And she hated him for being handsome. And she hated him for his deep, rich voice with its American twang.

She hated him because he was free from the black miasma that hung over the town.

September, 1904

THE SECOND TIME she saw him was almost ten years later. She recognized him immediately, even though he had changed immensely. But it would be nearly another whole year before she would know his name.

And his place in her own destiny.

She had changed, too, of course. She was full grown. And she was no longer living in the coal village.

The thing she would remember most was his impatience. He was impatient even before he entered the house.

Leaving the squire's library with a tea tray, Marissa heard

a thunder of horse's hooves on the driveway leading to the house. She had known that an important American acquaintance was coming to see the squire, but she had expected him to arrive in a carriage, or perhaps one of the new motorcars so popular among the fashionable and the rich. She certainly hadn't expected him to come tearing along upon the back of a big brown horse.

She paused to look through the ancient bay window of the manor house, and so she first saw him. He was very tall, and sat the horse well, and dismounted from the animal with an equal flare. His dark well-cut hair was wild from his ride. A waving lock of ebony curled over his forehead as he dropped the reins of the horse and nodded curtly to the squire's stable boy. He headed for the house with long, confident—no, arrogant!—strides, and his impatience was also visible in those strides. He was handsomely dressed, hatless, but wearing tight fawn riding breeches, a crimson vest and navy riding frock along with his high black boots. Marissa stared at him, remembering him, until he disappeared from her view as he leaped up the porch steps and rang—no, attacked!—the doorbell.

Katey, the squire's slim, elderly housekeeper, arrived to open the door. Marissa was left standing in the shadows outside the sliding doors of the squire's library. Poor Katey was nearly swept from her feet as the stranger stormed in. She stepped back hurriedly, and still he did not pause.

"Sir Thomas is expecting me," he said, his accent very much that of a Yank.

Marissa didn't wonder at that, for Sir Thomas had a multitude of friends and associates who were Americans, many of whom came to see him at the manor, but most of his friends were older men. This stranger was not old. Even his voice indicated that he was in his prime. It was deep, rich. The type that when spoken low still seemed to reverberate and take command.

And somehow enter into the body and soul. Marissa felt

that voice, deep and masculine, as if it touched her like a fingertip, rippling along her spine.

It was the boy, she realized. The boy from the coal town. He, too, had grown up. He was very much a man, and had been for many years, it seemed.

As he strode past Katey, she must have moved in the wrong direction or made some other fateful mistake, for a second later, he was plowing into her. The tea tray went flying, and Marissa was thrown against the wall.

She cried out in distress, knowing the cost of the Chinese porcelain tea set.

Damn the man! He seemed ever to be her downfall!

She expected him to push past her, but he didn't. He paused, reaching not for the tea set, but into the shadows to touch her arm and pull her out into the light.

She stared into his eyes. As she remembered, they were very blue. Dark blue. Startling, striking, against the strong, tanned planes and angles of his face. A clean-shaven face, with a hard-set jaw, and a curious fire burning deep in the centers of those eyes. Eyes that roamed over her hastily, from head to toe, assessing her, she thought, as he would soon assess the tea service.

For damage only.

"Are you all right?" he demanded crisply. There was no recognition of her in his eyes. Who would remember a little coal rat from all those years ago?

And now she was merely the maid.

She nodded, jerking her arm free from his touch, suddenly nonplussed. Her heart was beating too rapidly, her breathing was coming too quickly, and although he was showing her— the maid—a definite courtesy, she resented that very concern.

Or did she hate the fact that he was looking at her with such detachment? Or that she was wearing a starched white apron over a very plain gray day dress and that what she considered to be her crowning glory—that carrot red hair turned into a headful of wild, red-gold hair that tumbled to her waist in long, thick waves—was completely hidden by her matching starched white cap?

She resented the very beating of her heart, the way his hand had felt upon her arm, hot, strong. She didn't understand any of her feelings, but she resented him from the depths of her heart for them all. For the way that his eyes flickered over her with that curious fire. For the way that they, like his voice, seemed to touch her, and send a lap of fire racing down the length of her spine.

Pride, she thought mournfully. Everyone told her she had too much of it. Her father had said so, her uncle, Sir Thomas, even Mary, who could find fault with no one.

"I'm fine!" she snapped. She realized that his gaze was locked with hers. He seemed, at least, intrigued with her eyes. To her discomfort, she flushed. She had been told that she had fine eyes. Green eyes, cat's eyes, so said Sir Thomas. Eyes with a startling rich color, darkly lashed and just slightly tilted. Eyes that demanded a second glance, Mary had once informed her. Far too imperious and flashing for a maid, and far too...well, sensual, Mary had also commented. Eyes that could arouse far too many emotions, too many passions, Sir Thomas had warned her.

Well, not in this man. Aye, he still stared at her. But there was nothing other than that flicker of fire and impatience in his own gaze. The lean, rugged planes of his face remained hard.

Then for a moment, it seemed that something flared between them. Something hotter than the fire that lurked in the deep recesses of his blue stare. Something that left her completely breathless, trembling, and angrier than ever.

No, she thought, and she didn't know what it was exactly that she denied.

But it didn't matter. Something harsh and cold and perhaps even anguished extinguished the fire in his gaze. He stepped back.

He has changed, she thought. The boy had not been so hard. This man was steel.

Despite herself, she wondered what had changed him.

Then she worried about herself once again.

She knelt to pick up the tea service. To her surprise, he knelt beside her and impatiently began picking up the pieces along with her. He was brisk. Before she had loaded up two pieces, he had the tray nearly loaded.

"I shall inform your employer that this was my fault," he said.

It was something, Marissa admitted grudgingly. But it *had* been his fault, completely, and she thought that she detected just a bit of condescension in his tone. She should have said thank you. She did not.

"As well you should," she said softly.

He had started toward the doors again. He turned and stared at her. Into her eyes, maybe really seeing them for the first time. Then he laughed. "Perhaps they do breed little tigresses here in the old English countryside, too. You should be in America, girl."

That blue gaze swept over her, then dismissed her, and then he was gone, striding into the library, closing the sliding pocket doors behind him.

Marissa swore softly beneath her breath and swung around with the shattered tea service. She paused, as did Katey, as they heard the stranger's voice rise and then fall. Katey smoothed her hands over her apron. Marissa offered her a wry smile, one that condemned the stranger. No one had a right to argue with the squire. No kinder man existed on the earth.

The exchange between the two men continued heatedly.

The doors slid open once again with a vengeance. "All right, all right! Have it your way—it will be as you wish!" the stranger exclaimed.

Now he was angry as well as impatient. He swept past Katey and Marissa without a backward glance, then paused in the hall, stiffening his spine and squaring his shoulders. He strode to the open doors of the library and stared in at the squire. His voice lowered, but none of the passion had left it. "All right, Sir Thomas. As God is my witness, I'd never cause you distress. But I warn you, sir, that you have gained little in your bargain. Little but the bitter shell of a man."

"I have gained you, my friend," the squire replied, his voice very light. "And that is all that I ask. I know the man." He smiled. "I'll see you at the club before you leave."

The stranger started to speak again, exploded with an impatient oath, then grinned. "Take care, you old goat," he said, and there was affection in the tone. He swiveled and was gone, out the beveled glass double front doors.

Katey and Marissa stared after him.

He left the door open and mounted the brown horse in a leap, that curl of ebony hair still haphazardly hung over his forehead.

And then his eyes touched Marissa once again. He inclined his head gravely, and a taunting smile seemed to curve his lip.

She wanted to scream. She wanted to race to the doorway and swear that she'd not end her days as a maid to be so easily disdained. She'd rise above them all, above everything. She'd die a lady, greater than any they had ever seen.

"Marissa, my dear. Come here, please. I'd dearly love it if you would read to me now. Something from Dickens, I think."

It was the squire calling her. The one man who could make her swallow her pride and bitterness and her longing.

"Aye, Sir Thomas. I shall come," she agreed quickly. But she was still staring at the door as Katey closed it.

Her lips tightened. Aye, she would die a lady, she swore it. She had already come far, she assured herself, and she brought her fingers before her face. Her hands were clean. They were not covered by the coal dust that had left her dearly beloved uncle hacking away night after night. She lived in the manor where brass and wood shone. Where the air was clean.

And she read. She read the classics, and she knew the great operas, and she could speak in a voice to mimic any woman who claimed to be her better.

"Marissa?"

Katey came for the tea tray and Marissa smiled gratefully. Then she entered Sir Thomas's study.

She tried to unwind her clenched fingers, to smile. But somehow, the stranger had left daggers in her heart. She wanted nothing more than to find some form of retaliation for the way he had made her feel.

I will rise above him, I swear it! she promised herself. I will be a lady so great that I can secretly smile and laugh at his discomfort.

But neither before nor after the time she spent reading with him did the squire mention the stranger. And by bedtime, when she could allow her lashes to fall over her eyes, she could still see his eyes upon her, the handsome bronzed and arrogant face. The curious touch of pain that had so briefly come to his gaze.

I will show him, she thought.

She was as determined as she had been as a child.

But in the morning, she smiled at her own foolishness. She'd never show him anything. She'd most probably never see him again.

But she would. Fate was destined to bring him back into her life.

And indeed...

She would show him.

CHAPTER ONE

London, November, 1905

"HE'S COMING!" Mary cried with distress. She allowed the heavy velvet drape to fall into place over the window and looked anxiously at Marissa. Mary's pretty face was pale, and her warm brown eyes seemed huge against the narrow contours of her face. She had lost too much weight, Marissa thought.

It had been a terrible time for Mary, for the squire had died just a month previously after a long, painful illness. Both girls had spent endless hours at his side, doing whatever they could to ease his discomfort.

No matter what their differences, Mary had loved her father. Marissa, too, had loved the squire. They both missed him.

We loved him, we miss him! Marissa thought wryly. And here we stand, determined to undo his dying wish.

"Oh, my God!" Mary moaned, nervously lacing her fingers together. "Are you sure you will be all right?" she anxiously asked Marissa.

Marissa wasn't sure at all. Her breathing was coming too hard and too fast, and butterflies the size of the Jabberwock were flying pell-mell through her stomach. But she'd faced far harder tasks in her life, she was certain. And she had been told that for a brief and shining season, her mother had begun to rise as a young actress upon the London stage. Marissa knew she was a gifted mimic. The act she played today would be for Mary's benefit.

"I'm going to be fine," Marissa assured her friend.

She caught a glimpse of herself in the hotel suite's elegant free-standing mirror.

She would be fine. She certainly looked the part of the lady today. She was clad in one of Mary's beautiful white silk dresses. The tiny buttons were shimmering little pearls that ran from hem to throat and from wrist to elbow. Her skirt was floor length and in the height of fashion, narrow, conforming handsomely to her figure. Her petite boots were beige leather, and buttoned all along her ankles.

Her hair was swept up off her neck and held in place just above her nape by a gold barrette that matched the brooch at her throat.

She was elegant in the most casual way. Mary knew clothing.

Marissa folded her hands negligently and managed to smile at Mary. A tea service was already set on the oak coffee table for her convenience at the arrival of their guest. And she and Mary had played at tea for a long time now.

A very long time.

When Marissa's father, the Reverend Robert James Ayers, had been alive, Mary and Marissa lived close to one another. Robert Ayers had been the vicar at the beautiful old medieval church in the squire's parish.

Marissa had loved and admired him greatly. He had been destined for the coal mines like his brother Theo, but he had proven such a promising child that the vicar of Leominster parish, twenty miles away, had taken him in. Robert had loved to study, and he had grown to love the church, so he had taken his benefactor's place when Father Ridgefield died.

As the child of the local vicar, Marissa had enjoyed many advantages. She had been brought to the manor house for tea on her sixth birthday. Poor Mary had been forced to entertain her. Marissa had presented herself as Miss Katherine Marissa Ayers of Leominster Parish House, and had grown furious when she had seen the other girl laughing. She had hopped up, ready to forget all about being a lady and tearing out a bit of her hostess's hair, when Mary giggled anew and held out her hand in protest of violence.

"I'm not laughing at you," she said. "Truly, I'm not! It's just funny, that's all. You see, I'm really Katherine, too, Katherine Mary Ahearn. Oh, don't you see. Our names are so very alike."

Marissa tossed her head. "I'm known as Marissa."

"And Father calls me Mary, so we shan't have a bit of confusion. Please, I'm really glad that you've come. I'm so very lonely so often."

Marissa had played with Mary often enough, but then her father had died. And with his death she also lost Mary, for she had gone to live with Theo in the mining town. She had hated her new life, but she had loved Theo, a wonderful man, uneducated, unable to read, but with a charming smile, laughing eyes and a way of telling a small girl a story that could make her smile and fall asleep curled into his strong arms.

Life was much worse for other children, Marissa knew that well. Especially orphans. Many of them were beaten and abused by their relatives or stepparents. She had known nothing but kindness.

Kindness…and coal dust.

She had wanted to repay her Uncle Theo in any way she could. And so she had swept and cleaned and cooked, and had done her very best to keep his clothing laundered and mended, and to make their small cottage a home. But when her lessons ended she had known she would soon be sent off to work, for there was no other way for a child of her class.

During the days, though, she had dreamed.

Especially after she had seen the strange boy with his impeccably clean clothing.

She had dreamed of the grand manor where she had studied

with Mary. And she had remembered Mary's delicate white hands, and the furniture that never reeked of coal dust.

And then one Sunday, when Uncle Theo and she had been able to borrow a pony cart and had taken the long drive to Leominster instead of attending the small chapel in the coal town, she had seen Mary again. Standing by the squire's side, she was tall and lovely with her burnished brown hair and warm brown eyes and her beautiful fur-trimmed winter coat. She had grown up. They had both grown up, into young women. They were nearly fifteen.

Marissa looked at her hands, curled around her prayer book. Her nails were broken and ugly, her hands chapped.

And she knew that Mary's hands would still be small and elegant and lovely.

When the last blessing was bestowed, Marissa turned to flee. She did not want to see Mary.

But it seemed that the squire had seen her, for she had barely exited the ancient church with its spires and saints and gargoyles when his hand fell warmly upon her shoulder.

"Why, 'tis you, Marissa, child! We were heartily bereaved at the death of your father. And we missed you dearly, Mary and I. How have you been keeping yourself?"

"Quite well, Squire, thank you," Marissa murmured, wishing she could run. But Mary was behind him. Marissa thought she would lift her elegant nose and turn away from the coal child Marissa had become. But Mary stepped forward and hugged her enthusiastically. "Marissa!"

Before the day was out, Marissa and Uncle Theo had been taken to the manor for tea. Uncle Theo had stared around uncomfortably, and he had spilled his tea and used all the wrong silver, and the blackness of coal that the years had etched into his long bony fingers was glaringly dark against the Ahearns' elegant china, but it didn't seem to matter. Marissa could remember having tea as a child, and then she was ashamed that she could judge an uncle who had been so very kind to her. And seeing Sir Thomas and Mary, she swallowed hard and thought she had truly learned a lesson. Class and elegance did not lie in upturned noses, but rather in the graciousness inherent in these people. When she said thank you and goodbye to Mary and the squire, Marissa came as close to being humble as she had in all her life.

Three days later, the squire visited them in the squalid little coal town, and he suggested that Marissa should come to live in the manor house. Theo refused charity, but Sir Thomas promised that she would be a maid and earn her keep—and her education.

"I cannot give me niece away," Theo said with deep emotion.

"And would you have her grow to womanhood here, marry a miner and watch him die of the black lung only to struggle on to raise an army of little ones herself? I don't ask you to give her away, good man. I ask you only to give her a wee bit of opportunity. I say it from my heart, for my daughter and myself. And in memory of your good brother.

"Good Lord, man! Would that I had authority over this place! I despise the way it is run. But Ayers, man, I can help your girl. Perhaps I haven't the power to change the mine, but I do have the power to change her life. And we are still close enough that she can see you often. She loves you, and she will not be far."

Theo hesitated for only a moment, seeing the earnest appeal in Sir Thomas's eyes. "Go on out, Marissa," Uncle Theo told her. "The squire and I have much to discuss."

When she came back, a bargain had been struck. She would live at the manor during the week, she would work, she would receive a salary, and she would resume her education.

There was nothing like it. Nothing like it on earth. She moved into the manor, into a room in the attic. It was a small room, but it was hers—all her own. Six days a week she worked and studied, and on the seventh, the Sabbath day, she went to church and then she went home to her uncle. She never went empty-handed. Thanks to the squire, she brought hams and fowl and fruit and vegetables and fresh-baked breads. And Uncle Theo would have his friends over, and they would all share in the largesse. She would read to Theo and his cronies, and sometimes she would try to teach some of the little blackened urchins of the other mine families, and she knew that her uncle was very proud of her, and she was proud herself.

She had escaped the coal dust.

Living with the squire and Mary was easy, despite the fact that she worked very hard and studied even harder in her determination to become a lady. Most of the time, she was happy. Very happy. Mary was her employer, but she was also her very best friend. They dreamed together, Mary of love, Marissa of riches grand enough to feed the entire mining population. Marissa learned her mannerisms from Mary, and she copied Mary's accent. She excelled Mary in their history classes, mostly because she loved the tales of brave seafarers and pilgrims and the London Company and all those others who had set out to forge a new life. She was also exceedingly quick with mathematics, since math was useful with money, and she knew that little could be done without that commodity.

She had always thought that the town by the manor was so big, compared with the small community of the village. With Mary, she traveled farther, to the county seat of York. She was fascinated to see the wall that the Romans had built still standing, and she marveled at the magnificent York Minster Cathedral, awed by the age and grandeur, so close to the squalor in which she had lived.

It was as if the cloud that hung over the coal village had been a prison of a kind. It had kept her from viewing anything beyond it.

The years had passed, and most of the time she was pleased. And proud.

Most of the time...

Marissa frowned, wondering what uncomfortable thought hovered in the dark corners of her mind. Only upon occasion did she feel any less the lady than Mary herself. She could hold her head high in any company, and she had been attending the opera and the theater with Mary and certain acquaintances to perfect her current masquerade.

But every once in a while...

Then she remembered. Blue eyes touching her, racing over her, seeming to see her for what she really was. A British maid graced with a burning will to succeed, and a kindhearted employer and the friendship of his daughter. Those eyes had made her feel so uncomfortable. Vulnerable and naked, as if they could strip away every pretense. They had done so to her when she had been a child, and when she had been a woman. They had made her feel hot and flushed and uneasy. And even now, when she most needed her confidence, they seemed to intrude upon the moment.

"Mary, maybe we're making a mistake! Maybe this fellow is kind, and we should be honest and truthful. Maybe he wants a ward even less than you want a guardian! You should deal with this man Tremayne yourself," she murmured suddenly.

Mary's dark warm eyes clouded with pain. She hurried anxiously across the handsome Victorian parlor of their suite. "Guardian! And I'm nineteen already. How could my father have done such a thing!"

"He loved you very much, Mary," Marissa supplied gently. "Truly, I don't think that he meant to hurt you. Mary, your health has never been good, and you've always been so kind and compassionate. I'm certain that your father was afraid that perhaps a fortune hunter might take advantage of that very loving nature of yours. And he might have swindled all your money from you. And left you. Oh, Mary, he was mistaken, but he was a good man. And he did love you!''

"If only I had told him the truth!''

Marissa didn't think that it would have helped any for Mary to have told her father the truth.

Mary was in love, and she had been in love for well over a year. The problem was that she was in love with a young Irish clerk named Jimmy O'Brien.

Marissa liked Jimmy, very much. If she hadn't liked him so much, and liked him from the very beginning, she wouldn't have helped Mary this far.

Though indeed, there were times when Marissa still considered Mary to be a fool.

Jimmy was a fine man. He was a struggler, a survivor, like Marissa was herself. He had left Ireland with little more than a good head for figures and a determination that no more potatoes could be eked from his meagre portion of land. He had a sense for fine wools, and he had managed to obtain a good, decent job with a fine merchant. He bought for his employer, and his eye was keen, and the merchant's shop was doing much better under Jimmy's care.

Mary and Jimmy had met, and fallen in love. The words of warning that her father would never accept the hardworking young merchant had not done a thing to turn Mary aside from her reckless affair. She had never told her father about Jimmy O'Brien, and Marissa had covered for her again and again when she had left the house in sunshine or twilight to carry on her liaison.

"Mary!'' Marissa had warned her repeatedly. "You've grown up with everything you might wish handed to you on a very elegant silver platter! You're accustomed to servants and ease. Mary!'' She had grabbed Mary's small delicate hands with their silk-soft flesh. "Mary, life cannot be so easy if you elope and marry this man!''

"You don't understand what it is to be in love, Marissa,''

Mary had assured her. "I would work for him, I would die for him!"

Such vehemence and passion from shy Mary were quite impressive. But Marissa merely replied, "And you don't know what it is to watch children starve."

Their argument became moot, for it was then that they discovered the squire was ill. And it was not too long before the doctors informed Mary that there was no hope, her father was going to die.

That night she and Marissa had grown closer than ever, crying, hugging one another through the night for what little comfort they could offer one another.

Mary never told her father about Jimmy O'Brien. There was no need to distress a sick man so. When the squire had whispered his last goodbye and Mary had learned to live with the loss, then someday she would marry Jimmy. And in the meantime, Jimmy O'Brien stood by her side. In those weary hours when Mary's father's illness was greatest, Marissa would tend to the squire, and Mary would disappear with her lover. He gave her a comfort that not even Marissa could provide.

Squire Ahearn breathed his last on a beautiful late summer morning. The sun was shining; the daffodils were in full bloom. Both Mary and Marissa had sat beside him at the huge bay window, and he had breathed in the fresh scent of the day, closed his eyes and died.

And three days later, after a very proper funeral, he had been laid to rest in the bosom of his ancestral tomb. Despite the knowledge of certain death, Mary and Marissa had grieved deeply, barely managing to speak to one another for days.

Marissa's Uncle Theo had been heartily worried about her, and so, when Sir Thomas had been dead about ten days, she had left to spend time with Theo at his cottage. She had cleaned away more coal dust, and she had convinced him that Mary was raising her to an income so high that Theo no longer needed to work in the mine. His cough was bad, hacking, almost a continual thing, and Marissa could not bear it. She had just watched Sir Thomas die and she was not about to let Theo follow him. She knew that she told the truth. Mary would be a wealthy woman now, and she could provide for herself and Jimmy and, in truth, offer Marissa a very fine salary, indeed.

But when Marissa had come back to the manor, she had discovered Mary as pale as death, sitting before the fire in her father's library, staring at the flames but not seeing a thing. She had rushed to her friend in fear, and had found Mary's flesh as cold as ice despite the warmth of the fire. Marissa had cried out, hurrying for the sherry. She had forced a sip through Mary's lips, and her friend had looked at her at last, huge teardrops forming in her eyes and falling down her cheeks.

"Oh, Marissa!"

"What, Mary, what is it? I am here!"

"Oh, my God, Marissa! How could he!"

"How could who do what?"

"Oh, Marissa!"

"Mary, Mary, calm down now. Please, you must tell me what has happened! It's Jimmy, is it? What has he done? Why, if he's hurt you—"

"Jimmy would never hurt me!" Mary cried.

Marissa breathed a sigh of relief. "Mary, then please, what has happened?"

"It's father."

But the squire was dead and buried, and Marissa could not begin to understand what had happened.

"Mary—"

"Oh, how could he have done such a thing to me!"

"Mary, what in God's name has he done!"

And at last Mary began to talk, trying to explain the substance of her father's will. Mary had not yet reached her majority. And so her father had arranged for a guardian, someone to control her fortune until she had reached her twenty-fifth birthday. Someone Mary did not even know, one of his American associates. And there was even more to it than that.

"What?" Marissa demanded blankly, trying to assimilate everything Mary was saying.

"He betrothed me to this man!"

"No one can force you to wed this man, Mary."

Mary groaned anew, burying her face in her elbow where it lay upon the arm of the chair. "Marissa, if I do not wed him, he is free to control my money until my thirtieth birthday! He will be free to take over the house—everything!"

"It can't be so!" Marissa assured her, and Mary looked to her with hope. "We'll talk with your father's solicitors and they'll fix things for you."

"No, they won't! They'll be loyal to my father. I don't even know any of his solicitors. Father never involved me with business, and I never worried about it."

"We'll fix things."

"I can't talk to his solicitors."

"I can. I'll call them, and say that I am you!"

Marissa did so, and she was heartily disturbed. Everything that Mary had told her was true. They were in a desperate situation.

The squire had even arranged for a special marriage license from the Archbishop of Canterbury. No banns needed to be cried if Mary chose to marry her guardian. The deed could be done immediately so that the man need hardly stay away from his business in America.

To Jimmy O'Brien's credit, he swore that night that the money meant nothing to him, nothing at all. He loved Mary. His place was nothing but a hovel now, but he would work hard, so hard, and he would save the money to buy his own shop. He would live with Mary anywhere, and with their faith in their love, they would survive.

The two held hands before the fire in the squire's library and stared into the flames, bliss in their eyes. Marissa, with her own problems facing her, left the two of them alone.

But by the next week, Mary had caught a fever. She was desperately ill, and Marissa spent all her time at her bedside, bargaining with God, pleading, promising that she would do anything to save her. Jimmy, too, sat by her bedside.

Mary had not just rescued Marissa from the coal dust. She had been her friend. Marissa had never forgotten the bitterness of those years, or ceased to long for something better for the poor people there. She was afraid that she would carry some of the bitterness and hatred to her grave. But Mary had given her hope, and allowed her dreams to fly.

There was little that Marissa would not do for her.

Mary took a turn for the better. The doctor warned Marissa then that Mary was not strong, that she needed to take the gravest care. She must avoid chills, she must not work too hard.

Jimmy and Marissa were desolate. Jimmy did love Mary, enough to give her up. There was no way for Mary to go and live in a hovel—whether love flourished or no.

"I can't have her, and I can't give her up," Jimmy said, his freckled face lean and haggard and anguished. "I can't leave my Mary!"

"I can get a new job, I can do something—" Marissa began.

"And support us all?" Jimmy scoffed. "Ah, Marissa, you are spirit and strength and wonderful courage and beauty, and I love you as deeply as does Mary. But Marissa! You've your uncle to care for. There's nothing left to be done. Aye, but there is! I shall wait for Mary if needs be until we both be forty, fifty or sixty! I'd wait until my grave!"

Marissa almost smiled, he was so earnest and so dramatic.

"Jimmy, that much waiting would do in us all! No, there has to be some way, something that we can do!"

They didn't come up with any conclusions that night. And Marissa went to bed wondering once again how the squire could have promised his young and beautiful daughter to some old and withered crony, no matter how wealthy and prominent the man might be.

It was the next day when the idea—outrageous as it was—occurred to Marissa.

Mary lay in her bed, silent, her face pale, her cheeks gaunt. Jimmy idly stood by the fireplace, teasing the flames with the poker, and Marissa sat by Mary's bed, silent, too, no longer pretending to read.

"Mary! I can do it!"

"What?"

"I can be you!"

"Oh, my Lord!" Mary breathed. Jimmy stared at them as if Mary's fever had caused them both to go daft.

"Oh, my God! Could we pull it off?" Marissa demanded.

"I know we could. I've never met this man. He's a Californian, or something American like that."

"But everyone here would know us—" Marissa began, then she laughed. "Mary! The solicitors already think I'm you. Oh, we can do this! We'll plan very carefully. We'll go to London! We'll meet him in London."

"Can we…"

"Yes! We'll start right away. We'll agree to the terms with the solicitors. We'll sign everything here, in York. And then we'll keep the solicitors out of it when we meet this American in London!"

"And our names are so very close!" Mary laughed. "How convenient!"

"What are you two saying?" Jimmy demanded.

"Marissa will take my place!" Mary explained happily.

"No, we can't have Marissa marry some ancient old being for ourselves, Mary. We can't," he said. And he was firm.

"I don't have to marry him, Jimmy," Marissa said calmly.

"Just be a dutiful ward. Mary's allowance will be released to me until her thirtieth birthday. And then Mary will receive her inheritance and everything will be fine."

"Will it?" Jimmy demanded, walking over to Marissa. "And what of you? Will you spend ten years of your life alone? What of love for yourself, Marissa? What happens when you meet the man who can give you all that your heart desires?"

Marissa felt a coldness seal itself around her heart. "Jimmy—"

"You know nothing of love, as yet," he interrupted her softly.

"I know a great deal about hunger and death," she reminded him. "If I can take care of Theo, then I will be fine. And, Mary willing, we can even provide a small school there so a few other children may escape. Jimmy, I will be fine!"

Jimmy never was pleased with the plan. He fought it night and day. But Mary and Marissa had made up their minds, and the plan was put into action.

When they received the first correspondence from old Ian Tremayne—a short, curt missive to inform Mary when he would be coming—they were ready with their reply. Mary and Marissa composed it together, and Marissa wrote out the note in her flowing script. They had decided it would be necessary for Mr. Tremayne to become accustomed to Marissa's writing. Miss Katherine Ahearn fully understood the conditions of her father's will and was ready to abide by them upon her guardian's arrival.

The solicitors were informed that Miss Ahearn would abide by all her father's wishes, and Marissa and Mary learned that it wasn't necessary for Mary to sign papers—only Ian Tremayne's signature was necessary to release her funds. Mr. Tremayne already had her funds in his trust, and all other papers.

The solicitors indicated that they were more than willing to be present for her first meeting with Mr. Tremayne, as they fully understood the awkwardness of the situation.

They were impressed with the calm, cool maturity of the young lady who informed them that it would not be necessary at all.

And that was how they came to this day...now...waiting.

There was a knock at the door. Mary stared at Marissa in pure panic, and Marissa managed to smile at last. "It's all right, I promise, Mary. Think about it. I have always been able to charm old men. Mary! We made it past the solicitors! Now go on with you, get into the bedroom."

Mary sped past her, still white.

The knock came again, louder. There was an impatient note to it.

Then Marissa heard the voice. Deep, resonant, confident, the kind of male voice that spoke of authority and power. The kind that could enter the lower spine and send spirals racing up and down the back.

"Miss Ahearn! Are you there?"

The first twinge of unease seized her. She knew the voice. Knew it very well. It had even haunted her dreams, it had intruded upon her spinning her golden webs of aspirations, her hopes of glory.

She did not touch the door, but suddenly it burst open.

Him...

The tall stranger with the startling deep blue eyes. The eyes that touched her the way his voice touched her. Raking over her with a blaze of fire.

Arrogant, powerful, sharp. How could she possibly play out a deception upon this man with his hardened gaze, his determined manner, his ruthlessness? No anger or impatience with herself could quell the trembling at the pit of her stomach.

It was the surprise, she assured herself. The surprise and the fear. He would know her, he would remember.

"Miss Ahearn! I am Ian Tremayne."

Impatience flashed through his cobalt gaze when she still failed to reply. "I have come to fetch you home. Is something wrong? Are you all right?"

No, no, no! She was not all right at all! This was not an older gentleman to be twisted and swayed to her own will.

This was the lad who had carelessly tossed a coin her way. The brash man who had sent her tray crashing to the floor, who had laughed and told her that she should come to America.

This was the stranger who had broken into her dreams and reminded her that beneath her veneer she was a little coal rat.

The stranger had a name at long last.

Ian.

Ian Tremayne.

And already, his sharp blue eyes were narrowing. With recognition? She could not tell. Oh, no! He could not remember her! She had been a child that first time! And later, she had been a maid in a shadowed hallway. He could not remember, he could not!

"Miss Ahearn?"

"Yes, yes! I—I am Katherine!" she said, having found her voice at last. She struggled for a smile, but it eluded her. She managed to raise her hand, and he lifted it to his lips and brushed it with a cordial kiss.

A kiss that burned her fingers. That brushed and yet seared her flesh.

"Please sit down, if you will, ma'am. We've much to discuss of your father's will. We shall try to handle this all amicably since I guarantee you it was none of my own doing."

She was still standing in front of the settee. She seemed unable to move. Suddenly his hands were upon her shoulders, pressing her down to the settee. Then his voice came so close to her ear that the whisper of his breath touched her flesh. "It was not of my doing, but I gave Sir Thomas my word that I would carry out his wishes. And I intend to carry them out, my dear, I feel obliged to tell you. And I will do so, Miss Ahearn. I promise, I will do so.''

CHAPTER TWO

HE WAS SITTING beside her, easily, relaxed, staring at her pointedly, rudely, with no apology. She might still be trembling inwardly, but Marissa would be damned if she would let him intimidate her again. She lifted her chin slightly to speak. She remembered the mannerisms of every one of Mary's rich and imperious friends, and she spoke softly, yet with her own form of arrogance.

"Mr. Tremayne, no one was more shocked than I that my father should have made such an arrangement. We were very close. Obviously, I have no wish for a guardian. Any more than you, sir, seem to have a wish to be one. With a minimum of effort, I'm sure we can reach an amicable understanding."

His brows arched with a certain amusement, then the curl of a smile suddenly faded and he was frowning. "Didn't we meet before?"

"No, Mr. Tremayne, we did not. I was not at the manor the day you called."

"How do you know I called?"

"I—I assumed you called upon Father some time—he had not left this country for years before his death."

"Ah," he murmured. Then he was up, striding the small parlor once again. "I shall wish to return to San Francisco as quickly as possible. Is that agreeable with you?"

She shrugged. "If it's necessary. Of course, I understand that a young woman could be quite a burden to you. If you wish, I've no problems with the idea of your administering the estate from America while I remain in London."

He smiled again, slowly, and for a moment, there was a

certain tenderness about his gaze that softened the rugged planes of his face and made him appear very handsome. "My dear Miss Ahearn," he murmured softly, "I did not wish this responsibility, yet I take it very seriously. I would not dream of leaving a young lady of your tender age in such a city unattended."

"I would not be unattended. I have very good friends."

"So I imagine," he said wryly. Then he paused once again. "Are you sure we have not met?"

"Quite sure," Marissa said, locking her teeth against the sudden bitterness that filled her. No, he would not remember her. She had simply been the dirtied child in the mud. The maid with her hair pulled back and her face in the shadows. She was safe.

But a small tremor shook her, and she lowered her lashes quickly. "I can assure you, Mr. Tremayne, that I am a very responsible young woman, independent and able to care for myself. You could leave me with all good conscience."

"No," he said flatly. She raised her eyes to his cobalt blue ones and found them hard and emphatic. She suddenly longed to throw something at him. He brooked no opposition to his will—indeed, he would not even listen to reason!

But that was all right. They had all agreed that they would move to America if necessary. Jimmy could start up his business in California. They could live very near; it would work out!

"If you intend to argue with me further, Miss Ahearn, please save us both the time and effort. I had not expected a wayward child, yet if you persist..."

He was threatening her! she thought. His tone was low and pleasant, but there was definite threat behind it. If she persisted, what? she wondered indignantly.

Once again her chin rose. She wanted to argue for the sake of argument, just to prove to him that she'd be damned if she was about to follow some Yank's orders.

But it probably wasn't the time for an argument. Discretion, Sir Thomas had assured her, was often the better part of valor.

"I had thought to make this as convenient as possible for both of us," Marissa said sweetly. "But if that is not your wish…"

"Girl, this hasn't been convenient from the start," he said impatiently, then exhaled slowly and apologized. "I'm sorry. I'm sure that this is a shock for you. You have recently lost your father and been informed of a guardian. And of course the terms of his will were quite stringent." Once again, there was a slight glimmer of compassion and tenderness in his eyes, yet it seemed quickly to be gone. Once again, despite her own predicament, Marissa found herself wondering about the man. What had given him that edge of hardness, and even ruthlessness, when he could be so gentle at times?

Times when he was not crossed, she reminded herself. She would have to take great care with him.

She found herself studying him again. He was tall, very tall, and well built, with broad shoulders and lean hips. He wore his clothing with a casual flair. Today he was in black boots, form-hugging black riding breeches, crisp white pleated shirt, black velvet jacket, silk vest and cravat. His body, she was certain, was well muscled beneath the fabric, yet it was his face that made him so imposing a man. His features were handsome, well-drawn and well-defined. He was clean-shaven with arched, clean dark brows, and his chin was firm while his cheekbones were high and well set. His mouth was generous and full, a sensual mouth when it curled to a smile, a forbidding one when it was set in a line. His eyes were his greatest power. They seemed to carry endless years of wisdom. Sometimes weary, sometimes as cold as ice, sometimes alive with a hint of humor, but mercurial, ever changing. He was somewhere around thirty years old, she thought, yet his eyes were much, much older.

"Stringent, indeed," Marissa murmured.

"And I repeat, very definitely not of my choosing," he said. His gaze left her. With his hands locked together at the base of his spine, he paced the room once again. "I cannot be gone long. My business concerns are varied and demanding, and it was not easy to get away. I plan to head back as soon as all necessary arrangements are made. You will be more at your leisure, and I do understand that you might need time to say your goodbyes to friends, to close up the manor and—and to move to a place nearly half a globe away. I think, however, that once you have made the move, you will find yourself pleasantly surprised. My house is large and spacious, I am nearly never around, and when I am, I have a tendency to keep to myself." The last was said somewhat bitterly, and again she found herself wondering about the man. "There is nothing I can do about the fact that none of your money is to be released to you unless the terms of the will are carried out exactly—"

"What?" Marissa was instantly on her feet. "What are you talking about?"

"I thought you understood. Your funds are to be held in trust until your twenty-fifth birthday should you agree to the marriage, and held until your thirtieth birthday if you should not."

"Yes, yes, I do understand that! But there was to be an allowance!"

He shook his head impatiently. "The allowance holds true only if you choose to marry. I'm sorry. I thought you understood that. But I am a wealthy man, Katherine, and I do not intend that you should suffer."

Taking anything from him would be suffering, she was certain of it. She was already deceiving him. If he ever discovered the truth...

She sat, suddenly so weary that she could not stand it.

What now of Jimmy? He was a good man. With a little

help, he could have been a fine merchant, perhaps a wealthy man in his own right.

And what of Uncle Theo?

And Mary... Oh, dear God, could Mary bear another shock?

"There must be something wrong. Terribly wrong. I have seen the lawyers—"

"You must see them again if you still do not comprehend the will," he said, irritation touching his tone. "I shall try to explain it very simply. If you agree to the marriage, your allowance is to begin upon the date of the nuptials, and you will receive the bulk of your inheritance upon your twenty-fifth birthday. If you choose not to marry, then your allowance will begin upon your twenty-fifth birthday, and the bulk of the inheritance will become yours upon your thirtieth birthday. Do you understand?"

"I cannot live like that!" she gasped.

He paused, staring at her, and one of his ink dark brows raised high. "You will have to, Miss Ahearn."

"But I cannot! I've my personal expenses—"

"You will be provided with a home, and I shall, of course, do my best to see to your needs."

"I don't want your charity!" she exclaimed. "Oh, dear God!" she murmured suddenly, and sank back to the settee. That she had even tried to be decent to this man when everything was a disaster! She looked up at him sharply. "We must break the will!"

"There is no way to break the will, I assure you," he said calmly. "The squire was entirely of his right mind throughout his entire life."

"How could he have done such a thing!" Marissa whispered.

Ian Tremayne sighed, and she thought that he was very carefully swallowing his impatience and irritation. He came to the settee and sat beside her. He took her hands in his and for one wild moment she wanted desperately to snatch her fingers free. There was so much power in his touch, so much heat. And he was close beside her, his knees touching hers, his breath once again fanning her face with warmth, his eyes seeming to blaze through her and read her heart. Could he see the deception there?

Did it matter anymore?

"I believe, Katherine, that your father thought you were involved with a rather inappropriate young man. He was worried about you. He felt that your health was weak, that you might destroy your own life."

"He knew!" she gasped, and then she colored, because he was staring at her again, and she realized that he thought *she* had been involved in an affair with an inappropriate man.

Well, it wasn't her, and Jimmy was far from inappropriate! Fury filled her because she was quite certain that he was condemning her with his dark blue gaze.

He dropped her hands and stood. "Yes," he said wryly, "I believe he knew something. Is your affair over?"

Her cheeks flamed once again. It was none of this man's business.

Well, at least she could tell the truth.

"That is none of your business whatsoever, Mr. Tremayne."

"If not now, Miss Ahearn, it will certainly be so once we travel to the States."

She didn't respond, but sat stiffly. "I don't believe that we shall be doing so now," she said at last.

"I beg your pardon, Katherine?"

"Marissa," she said. She smiled tightly. "It is Katherine, initial M, Mr. Tremayne, and I am known as Marissa."

"Marissa," he murmured. She was surprised at the soft way her name whirled upon his tongue.

"There is no reason for me to come with you," she said wearily.

"There is every reason for you to do so. I am your guardian. And I command it."

She looked at him with a certain amusement. "And do you intend to shackle me to your side, Mr. Tremayne? To pull me across the ocean in chains?"

"Trust me," he said pleasantly. "I shall see to it that you come, one way or another. It seems ever more important that I attend to your father's trust in me."

"I cannot go!" she whispered almost desperately.

Once again, he spoke gently. "It will not be so bad. As I have told you, I am scarcely about. I've my own past to live with, and I am not a man anxious for company. I will see to your needs—"

She was on her feet once again. "How could you ever agree to such a setup!" she demanded furiously.

She heard the sharp intake of his breath and saw the angry narrowing of his eyes. "I agreed to take on a guardianship. I knew nothing of the stipulations of the will. Yet I have told you—"

"You agreed to a betrothal."

"Yes, I did, for your father seemed desperate. But he knew that I had no intent of marrying again, that I wanted nothing to do with a new wife. Perhaps that was why the stipulation. He assumed you would be quite safe in my care until you reached your own maturity. And as I have said, it is inconsequential. I can provide—"

"But you cannot provide!" she interrupted him on a husky note, and then she fell silent as his sharp gaze queried her. She could not tell him that she didn't want to accept his charity with one breath and then inform him with the next that she was afraid his charity would not be sufficient to cover her needs.

What in God's name was she going to do? It seemed they were all doomed. Even playing this elaborate pretense had not altered their situation.

"Miss Ahearn," he said, suddenly very impatient, "I am afraid that I am tiring of hearing what you can and cannot do. I have stated the facts to you and they are what they are. Dear Lord, but this could have been easy, and here I am bickering with a whining child—"

"I have never, never whined in my entire life!" Marissa spat out, her hands clenched at her side. And then she realized how close she had moved to him, and felt again the sizzling heat that seemed to emanate from the man. She saw the furious tick of his pulse against the hard cords of his throat and felt the cobalt blaze of his eyes hard upon her. She wanted to back away. She dared not show such a sign of defeat, and yet she wished desperately that she had managed to handle things with more cool dignity and much less drama and passion.

"Nor," she said softly, "am I a child."

"Well, we shall see, won't we?" he asked her quietly. "I pray that you are right."

"And what, exactly, does that mean, sir?" she demanded coolly.

"It means that you are exasperating me beyond all sensible bounds, young woman. I have business in the city. And at this moment I'm afraid I need to bind you to my side as I go about it, for my fears concerning you—Sir Thomas's fears— seem quite justified."

She realized suddenly that he was serious, that he seemed to think she might be ready to run off with the lover she had seemed to admit that she had. She shook her head vehemently.

"You need fear nothing concerning me."

"Needn't I?" He walked around her once again, and she felt his eyes surveying her as he did so. "What guarantees do I have that you will not run the moment my back is turned?"

"There is no guarantee," she said softly, uneasily, whirling to face him. Then she smiled bitterly. "Truly, I have nowhere left to run."

"Make things difficult for me, Miss Ahearn," he said in a

tone so soft it might have been gentle, "and I swear, I shall hunt you down. I've neither the time nor the inclination for this, and if you force my hand, I swear that it can be a ruthless one."

"Of that I've no doubt," Marissa murmured.

"Good," he said after a moment, "then we are understood." He headed for the door and paused before opening it. "I will be back tomorrow evening. We will finalize our plans then."

He did not say goodbye. He exited, closing the door firmly behind him.

Seconds later Marissa heard Mary's cry of anguish coming from the bedroom, then her friend rushed out, pale, nearly hysterical.

"Oh, Marissa! What shall we do now? There is nothing left to do. Dear Lord, I must find Jimmy! I must marry him immediately before he finds out! I don't care about the future, oh, I swear! I can live anywhere, I can do anything. I can find a position as a governess. That would not be too taxing upon my health. I will live in a cottage or a hovel or a one-room flat, I will scrub it, I will—"

"Die in it, most likely," Marissa said bluntly, wearily. "Mary, stop. Take hold of yourself. You are barely over your last bout of fever. You are talking nonsense, and Jimmy loves you far too much to allow it."

"I won't let him know!" Mary cried passionately, her warm brown eyes glistening with the hint of tears. "I love him, Marissa! There is nothing else to do!"

"Mary, listen to me! Your health—"

"No, Marissa, you listen to me!"

"You've lost touch with the realities of life—"

"No, Marissa, you have! Life cheated you when you were a child, so now you would cheat it. You truly don't understand what it is to love someone. Oh, Marissa! I would rather have one moment of ecstasy with Jimmy than a lifetime of mediocrity with any other man. Oh, don't you see that!''

Mary sank down on the settee facing Marissa. The tears streamed down her face. ''There is nothing left, nothing left at all!'' she said.

Marissa found herself patting Mary's shoulder as her friend sobbed.

''We've lost,'' Mary groaned. ''We've lost everything.'' Then she added passionately, ''I hate my father, oh, God, I hate my father!''

''Mary, hush! The squire is dead, and you loved him dearly.''

''I might as well be dead.''

''Don't say that!''

''It's true.''

''No, no, there is a way out of this, I know it,'' Marissa assured her. But Mary was so desolate that Marissa sought desperately for some further words of encouragement. ''We must call the solicitors again in the morning. I'm sure Tremayne must be wrong about this allowance stipulation.''

''Father knew about Jimmy!'' Mary whispered. ''And he had no faith in me!''

''Let's have a sherry, shall we?'' Marissa said. ''And we'll work on this in the morning.''

It took her some time, but she coaxed Mary into taking a drink, and then into bed. Late that night the proprietress of the hotel tapped on the door to say that there was a phone call for Miss Katherine Ahearn downstairs.

Marissa checked to see that Mary slept peacefully, then she hurriedly descended the stairs to reach the establishment's single phone. The connection was very bad, but at length Marissa heard Jimmy's voice.

And she lied. She told him that things were fine, she had met Tremayne. She told Jimmy that the man was young and gentle and very kind, and that she could foresee no difficulties. "I can take care of things, Jimmy, I promise," she vowed.

Then she wondered what she had done, for there was no truth to her words.

"You mustn't sacrifice so much for us, Marissa Ayers," he warned her firmly.

"Jimmy, I'm not sacrificing anything." He didn't believe her. "My Uncle Theo is at stake here, too, Jimmy. My own livelihood."

He laughed softly. "I don't think so, Marissa. You've incredible strength and will. You put the lot of us to shame. And I will not have you doing anything to hurt yourself, and neither would Mary."

"I won't do anything to hurt myself," she said.

"You don't owe us this."

"But I do," she murmured. Jimmy might not understand. Maybe there was no one who could understand.

Mary and Sir Thomas had taken her away from the coal mines. She owed Mary everything. "Jimmy, please be patient. I'll be in touch soon," she promised vaguely.

She stood against the wall, the ear piece still in her hands. For a moment she glanced at it, marveling at the ingenuity of Mr. Bell, who had invented the amazing piece of equipment.

Then she replaced it and grew amazed at herself instead.

Why had she lied to Jimmy?

Because she could not bear that they could not make things work. Nor could she listen to Mary's dreams of ecstasy. She was the one living in the real world, and she knew it.

She had seen the brutal cruelties of that real world often enough, and it seemed that the best way through them was to keep one's gaze ever upward and climb over them.

She sighed and closed her eyes. There had to be a way to make it work.

Moments later she opened her eyes and resolutely made her way up the stairs.

Aye, indeed, there was a way to make it work. And so help her, she would see that it did.

She had to. She loved Mary; she loved Jimmy.

And she could already smell the scent of coal dust sweeping around her ankles.

IT WAS VERY late when Ian Tremayne at last rode through the almost silent streets near Hyde Park to reach the boardinghouse where he was staying. Most carriages were already off the road, and he hadn't seen a single motorcar.

The vehicles hadn't caught on as quickly in London as they had in the States. Of course, in the States, things were still in a mess because of the growing number of horseless carriages and more traditional transportation. Just before he had left home there had been quite an accident on the street down the hill when a horseless milk truck had collided with a horse-drawn ice cart. Suddenly every vehicle on the street—whether motor-powered or animal drawn—had collided into something. Motors had died, horses reared, and ice had melted all over the place. Once it was ascertained that no one had been injured, the spectacle had been rather amusing. Ian smiled with the memory. Diana would have loved the sight. She would have laughed with delight.

But then his smile faded as he dismounted from his rented mare before the boardinghouse and walked her to the gas-lit carriage house. It was a typical London night, filled with fog. And the fog somehow seemed to shroud his heart, letting more painful memories rush upon him.

It had been like this the night Diana had died. A night when the fog had rolled in from the Bay. He had sat with her upon his lap, and they stared out their balcony window, watching the mystic beauty of the fog. She loved San Francisco as deeply as he did, and in those moments, it seemed that their souls touched. She pointed out the stars, disappearing in the fog. And he said that it seemed they sat in heaven, where they were. She rested her head upon his shoulder and sighed softly, and it was several moments before he realized that she had breathed her last. Diana, so fair and fragile, with her delicate features and soft gray eyes. Listening to him build his dreams, listening when he ranted and raved about his buildings and his frustrations with the city. Always there, his support, his life, beside him.

Beside him no more. She was gone, and had been gone nearly two years. Though he would never forget her, never stop loving her, he knew that he had to find a way to keep her from haunting his dreams and his thoughts. She was with him almost always. And the pain of her loss was with him always, too.

Except tonight.

Well, he had to give credit to Sir Thomas's wayward daughter. She was so proud, so damned argumentative and so sure-fire irritating and troublesome that she had made him forget—if only for a little while.

Ian unsaddled and unbridled the mare and led her into her stall. Absently he checked her feed and water, patted her nose, then left the carriage house. He paused outside, his hands on his hips as he surveyed the night. He could scarcely see the park down the street. The fog was coming in, ghostly, eerie.

But he saw no ghosts as he quietly entered the pleasant boardinghouse and strode to his room. There he closed the door carefully behind himself, stripped off his jacket, cravat and tie, and loosened his shirt before falling into the comfortable armchair behind the wide oak sailor's desk. He opened the bottom drawer, drew out the brandy and took a swig.

Indeed, she had intrigued him, this child of his old friend. Those eyes...

He could swear that he had seen them before. Green eyes, haunting eyes, eyes that flashed fire and warning and pride. Spitfire eyes.

He leaned his head against the chair. She was very beautiful, he thought. And despite his impatience with her—and his annoyance that the task of guardian should have fallen into his hands—he had wanted to see the hunted, haunted look disappear from her eyes. Well, he had tried, damn it. Really, he had tried to be courteous, sensitive and patient. The girl simply didn't allow for it.

Anger stirred within him again as he remembered how the wily old Sir Thomas had extracted his promise to care for her. He had harped upon his friendship with Ian's father, he had reminded him that he had stood behind his decision to become an architect, then he had coughed and reminded him that he was going to die.

Ian hadn't really believed him at the time. And it had been his turn to remind Sir Thomas of a few things. Such as the fact that he had so recently lost his wife. That he was an American, with no desire to be anything other. That he must take a young woman far across the sea if he was to be of any assistance to her at all.

And he had reminded Sir Thomas that he had become a harsh and cold and bitter man, and Sir Thomas had merely smiled. "You will promise me, Ian. You will promise me."

And somehow, he had promised.

So now here he was in London, when he should have been home.

Oh, it didn't hurt to come to England. The Tremayne stores always cried out for English goods. But Ian's interest was not in the stores.

The Tremayne dynasty had been founded by Ian's grandfather, a wily Scot who had spelled his name the old way, Iain. He had made his fortune in the gold rush, and had started the emporium. His son James had inherited the Scots business acumen, and the stores had prospered.

James had assumed that his son Ian would love the business as he did. But another fire burned within the son, the fire to build. He loved his city, loved the Bay, loved the fogs that rolled in, loved the coolness and the rugged, beautiful terrain.

It had been Sir Thomas who had written to James over fifteen years ago that he'd be a fool not to allow his son to follow his dream. There was no reason that Ian could not keep the family fortune in balance with the stores and study this new trade.

So there was much that Ian owed Sir Thomas. And his own father, he thought affectionately. James had succumbed to pneumonia five years ago, but he had lived long enough to admire some of Ian's projects. He had lived long enough to meet Diana, and to believe that his father's dreams of a great merchant empire would live through his progeny.

No more, Father, he thought. I have lost her, and there will not be another.

A few women entered into his life, but none that he allowed to touch his heart. San Francisco could be a very progressive city, and he had discovered after the first bitter grief had faded into the depths of his heart that he was still alive, still healthy and still in need of physical companionship.

It always seemed to be available. And he was careful never to whisper words that he did not mean or to issue promises he would never keep. He drove himself with his work, he knew it. But it seemed to be all that was left for him. The child he and Diana had both so longed for had died with her, and he had cast himself into not just the dream of a particular building, but into a dream of building a city.

He meant to pull out a glass for his brandy; he did not. He drank deeply from the bottle, leaning back. His thoughts, which had been on his wife, strayed.

Damn the girl with her green cat's eyes. She was trouble. He didn't dare leave her here on her own. He'd meant to make arrangements and hurry back without her. She could come over at her leisure. Now he didn't dare. As her father had feared, there was clearly a lover in her life. And she seemed willing, no matter what her promises, to throw away her inheritance to have this man.

Ian swallowed deeply again, then set down the bottle and leaned back. He felt the liquor sweep warmly through him. He closed his eyes.

He did not open them again that night. He stretched his legs out on top of the desk, loosened his shirt and dozed with the sheer exhaustion that came from traveling from continent to continent.

HE HEARD THE rap on the door, but he had told the proprietor of the boardinghouse often enough that he did not wish to be disturbed. He opened his eyes and stared evilly at the door, but he did not hasten to rise, nor did he reply.

To his amazement, the door opened.

And to his further amazement, he saw that his early morning visitor was none other than his new, wayward ward.

She was elegant this morning, more beautiful than she had appeared last night in the gaslight of the prim Victorian parlor.

She wore a soft blue day dress with a low-cut bosom and a small, very fashionable bustle. She carried a parasol, wore immaculate white gloves and small elegant boots that just peeked out from beneath the hem of her gown. A matching brocade jacket covered her shoulders, but was fetchingly cut to offer both modesty—and the hint of a very fine cleavage.

She wore no hat, nor had she pinned her hair up, and it fell over her shoulders in sweeping waves like the rays of the sun. It was wonderful hair, hair that rippled and cascaded and fell to her waist, red and gold, fascinating.

She entered the room, and her eyes widened as she saw him at his desk with the brandy bottle before him, his shirt opened all the way down the front and his legs carelessly tossed upon the desk.

He did not bother to move. "Well, well," he murmured. "To what do I owe this honor?"

"I need to speak with you," she murmured.

"Obviously."

She didn't make a move, but seemed frozen against the door. He smiled slowly, wondering if he admired her or disliked her intensely.

No, he did not dislike her, he realized. He disliked what she was doing to his life. He wanted her to be passive and well-behaved and to follow him home and live quietly in her room, so docile that he could forget her.

Cared for, yes, cared for well. But so quiet and well-mannered that he scarce need know she was there.

He would know she was there, he thought. He would always know she was there. She was beautiful, and she must be well aware of it. She had already cast herself into the disgrace of a lover, and in honor of Sir Thomas's memory, he must make certain that she not do such a thing again. She was hardly quiet, and the furthest thing in the world from docile.

Those eyes...

She could tempt and taunt like the most practiced vixen, he thought, and was startled to realize that she had annoyed him last night and annoyed him now because she need only stare at him with those fascinating eyes and he felt the stirrings of longing, hot and pulsating, within his groin. He inhaled sharply, and exhaled, and spoke to her far more harshly than he had intended.

"What? You've come. You've entered unbidden. Speak!"

Green eyes flashed with fury. He was certain that she was going to turn and leave the room. And then he would have to chase after her.

But she seemed to stiffen and lock her jaw. She did not move. Her gaze swept over him scornfully. Her eyes locked upon his bare chest, then rose once more to meet his. She appeared to fight for nerve, then found her courage. She raised her chin, and once more her gaze was imperious.

"I wish to follow my father's will to the letter, Mr. Tremayne. I wish—" She hesitated only the flicker of a second. "I wish to—to marry you."

CHAPTER THREE

"YOU WHAT?" Ian's feet hit the floor. His eyes narrowed sharply, and his voice rang with surprise.

For a moment, Marissa couldn't quite catch her breath. The man seemed to be more formidable than ever. No, he had made a promise to Sir Thomas, and he was merely irritated with her attempts to thwart him. His voice could be gentle; he could be every inch the gentleman.

He didn't look much the gentleman at the moment. He looked every inch the rogue. His chest was nearly naked, very hard muscled and thickly matted with crisp dark hairs against which a gold medallion of St. Luke rested. He was scowling crossly, and a lock of his near ebony hair was dangling haphazardly over his forehead. He had spent the evening drinking brandy, so it appeared.

He was still a gentleman, she assured herself, despite his appearance.

After all, Sir Thomas had trusted him with his daughter's future.

And still...

Deep within her, tremors had begun. To her dismay, she discovered that she was frightened, but also excited. There was something decadently tempting about the taut muscles that formed his chest. Something that made her long to touch...

And then start to tremble anew.

No, no, she didn't want to touch anything. She had to make that clear. Abundantly clear. But just thinking about it made her feel a curious unease.

He didn't want to marry. He had said that he had no intention of marrying again. So he had been married. She had to convince him that...that they could marry one another and lead separate lives.

"I want to marry you," she managed to repeat.

"Whatever for?" he demanded crossly.

"That's entirely obvious, isn't it, Mr. Tremayne?" she said with exasperation. "I need my allowance."

"I am willing to care for you."

"I don't want charity. I want what is mine."

"You don't want charity—but you're willing to marry a stranger for your allowance?" A single dark brow was raised high with incredulity. "Excuse me, Miss Ahearn, but I would think that marriage to a near stranger would have to be less appealing than the simple acceptance of the stranger's largesse." He was amused again. He was not in the least taking her seriously.

"Mr. Tremayne, this is important to me."

"It seems that our newly entwined futures must be important to us both. I am serious, too, Marissa. Marriage is a contract, legal, binding."

"Yes, I know."

"It is also much, much more," he reminded her sharply.

"It wouldn't have to be like that," she said hastily.

"Like what?" he demanded. He was taunting her, she knew. Baiting her, purposely. He was angry, and he meant to draw blood.

She pushed away from the wall, moving into the room at last. But then she paused, for he was now standing. He moved around to the front of the desk, crossing his arms over his chest.

Awaiting her.

She was silent, and he sat back comfortably on the desk, smiling suddenly. "Pray, do enlighten me, Miss Ahearn."

Enlighten him! She longed to smack the amusement from his face.

An ill choice of action, she decided, if she was to coerce him to her will.

She swallowed her anger and tried to speak intelligently and with dignity. "My father's will has devastated me, Mr. Tremayne. There are certain—charities to which I am deeply committed, and I would use my own funds for these expenses. You—you said that you did not intend to marry again. If we marry one another, then you will not have to marry again."

A quizzical expression passed over his face, then he laughed outright. "Obviously. I shall be married to you."

"But not really."

"You cannot collect your inheritance by going through a pretense of marriage."

"No, no, I will marry you, really—"

"I don't wish to marry."

Marissa exploded with a sharp oath of impatience that brought amusement to his eyes, and both his brows shot up. "Mr. Tremayne, you have told me that you are not averse to accepting certain advances from certain women. I can only assume this to mean a certain kind of woman, sir. Harlots and whores, Mr. Tremayne, if I do comprehend your words correctly. I—"

"And dance-hall girls, Miss Ahearn," He added. "We do have some very fine establishments in San Francisco."

"Excuse me. And dance-hall girls. They can be very amusing, I'm certain—"

"Oh, much more than amusing."

"But what of the nights when you might wish to entertain at home? When you need someone to welcome important associates? When you wish to play the gentleman, Mr. Tremayne, which I do assume you do upon occasion!"

"And you are the epitome of graciousness!" he snapped suddenly.

She was silent for a moment, then murmured, "And you, Mr. Tremayne, seem capable of being a master of cruelty."

He sighed softly. "Marissa!" Curiously, her name sounded almost like a caress. "I am sorry, truly. I never meant to be cruel. I wanted this all to be as easy as it could be."

Marissa lowered her lashes, unnerved by his sudden gentleness. "There is no way to make this easy!" she whispered vehemently.

"Do you know what you're asking me?" he demanded.

"Yes!"

"I don't want a wife," he said harshly.

"You don't wish a wife to whom you would be obliged to offer affection!" she corrected him.

His startled look gave her a sudden advantage, and she determined to pursue it. "That is why it is all so perfect!" she exclaimed passionately. And once again, she stood before him. Too closely before him. Her hands rested upon the desk and she stared into his eyes, nearly pleading. He was still smiling. "Oh, don't you see!" she moaned.

"I do apologize, but your logic simply eludes me."

"I wouldn't expect you to—I wouldn't expect you to behave as a husband."

"Ah. And how does a husband behave?" he queried her.

She pushed away from the desk and strode with agitation across the room. Then she realized that she was facing his bed and she swung around, her cheeks flaming. He was taunting her. He knew darned well what she was saying.

"Mr. Tremayne, we could form a marriage in name only. I could receive my inheritance, and in turn—" She paused.

"Yes, well, it's that part I am interested in hearing about," he said dryly.

"I could protect you."

"You could protect me?"

"From unwanted advances."

He burst into laughter. All the grimness left his mouth, and a sizzling sparkle touched his eyes. If nothing else, she had amused him.

"You're being very rude," she informed him coolly.

"Oh! Do forgive me, Miss Ahearn. It's just that, though I do not wish to marry again, there are certain, er, advances that I rather welcome, if you know what I mean."

Her cheeks flamed and she willed herself to betray no emotion, no anger, no embarrassment. She tried her very best to stare at him with nothing more than scorn and to speak as softly as she could. "You would be more than welcome to your diversions, Mr. Tremayne. That is my whole point. You could wander at will, and be plagued by no woman, for you would already have a wife. A wife to whom you owed nothing at all, a wife who would stay out of your way, I might add, and in her gratitude, make your life as comfortable as possible."

"Comfortable?"

She gritted her teeth. "I make a very good hostess for business dinners and all social occasions," she assured him primly.

"Oh, I'm sure that you do!" he said.

She had no further arguments for the moment, and he was still staring at her without replying.

"Well?" she prompted him irritably.

"Well?"

"Have you an answer?"

"I'm thinking," he told her.

"You at least knew something of this arrangement!" she reminded him with a flare of anger.

"But I knew nothing about acquiring a wife," he murmured. "And if I am about to find myself with this wonderful hostess and entertainer who will boldly stand guard against all mamas who wish their daughters married, I am still afraid that I might have a few requirements of my new paragon of virtue."

"Such as?"

"Well," he drawled softly, his blue gaze sweeping over her with a lazy regard, "I would like her to be just that—a paragon of virtue."

Marissa gasped, infuriated. "Just as you are a paragon of virtue, Mr. Tremayne."

"Sorry. I am afraid that it is still required much more of the female in this day and age."

She swirled around, heading for the door. He watched her without protest. Her fingers closed over the knob.

She turned, quivering with anger, but very aware that she was the one playing for the high stakes—he really did not want a wife.

"What do you want out of me?" she demanded.

"The truth."

"Why?"

"You're asking me to marry you," he said harshly. "I want to know something about my future wife."

"Such as?"

"What of your young lover? I'll have no man trailing after you to my home. And I'll be damned if I'll ever give any woman my good name for her to make a cuckold of me by playing at any game with another." She realized then that he was amused, but he was also angry. Very angry. The open shirt displayed the pulse against his throat, and muscles bulged on his naked chest as his arms almost imperceptibly tightened over one another.

She leaned against the door and moistened her lips. Her eyes met his.

"I have never had a lover, Mr. Tremayne," she said flatly.

"You admitted it when I spoke of your father's fears," he reminded her.

"No." Her eyes fell from his, and she shook her head. "I admitted that I knew a man, but..." She forced her eyes to meet his. To offer the honesty that was still a lie. "He was never my—lover."

He rose from the desk and walked to the door. She was tempted to throw it open and run.

She held her ground. His arms came around her as bars on either side of her head, his hands flat against the panels of the door. "I wonder if you are telling the truth. I wonder if you are capable of telling the truth."

"What difference would it make?" she cried out passionately. "I want no real marriage. We could put it in writing, we could—"

"No!" He seemed to thunder out the word, sharp and savage. "You are not listening, my lady. I'll not have my name abused. And I'll have no contract for pretense written down upon paper. And neither will I make any damned agreements about what a marriage will or will not be. One a hostess, the other the provider of an income."

"It is my own income!"

"Not without me."

Oh, please! she thought. She could not face him much longer without screaming. His sudden change from laughter to passion and anger was unnerving. She could not bear it.

"I have told you the truth, I swear it!" she cried suddenly. "There is no man, there has never been a man. I plan to play no games, I just wish to live with a certain dignity—"

"And what, pray tell," he demanded savagely, "if you should discover yourself falling in love again elsewhere?"

"I will not fall in love elsewhere."

"Ah, how assured you are for one so young!"

"Well, you are certain you've no wish to marry again, and you are not yet decrepit!"

"Ah, but I have known love, my lady, and there's the difference," he said, his tone suddenly, deceptively soft.

"Please—"

"What are these charities of yours?"

"They are personal."

"Perhaps a young man is included in them?"

"No!"

He pushed away from the door, turned and paced across the room. A moment later he pulled out the chair at his desk and sank into it. "How strange. I don't see you being such an incredible philanthropist, Marissa."

"I told you—"

"Spell it out!"

"I—I have a maid. No, she is no longer really my maid. But she wishes to be married. They are both young and poor and her health is failing, and I want to bring them both with me. She has been a dear friend all her life. And there is a small mining town I wish to help—"

"And certain miners?" he inquired politely.

"I tell you, sir, that my intentions are entirely honorable!"

"Are they?" he mused, and he sat at the desk, idly tapping his fingers against the wood as he stared at her. He threw up his hands. "Lady, you did not want a guardian, and yet you would accept a husband!"

"I have explained—"

"Ah, yes, well then, let me explain." He leaned forward, folding his hands upon the table, his eyes seeming to impale her as his temper rose with his every word. "I am not an easy man, Miss Ahearn."

"You said that you are often gone—"

"But when I am home, I can be a tyrant. I am demanding and exacting, and I have a horrible temper."

"Indeed? What a shock!" she said with wide eyes and sweetly dripping sarcasm.

"You are asking for this," he reminded her.

"Pray, go on, Mr. Tremayne."

"Bear in mind that I've no wish to marry."

"So you've informed me."

"That I shall go my own way."

"That, sir, will give me the greatest pleasure."

A long finger was suddenly pointed in her direction. "While you, my dear, will be that wonderful paragon you have promised. And you will be at my beck and call for whatever social amenities I might require."

Her heart was hammering. It was a devil's bargain, made in hell. But she had already known that she would pay nearly any price to make this work.

She had paid part of the price, for the lie she was already living was agonizing.

"You make it sound like torture," she murmured, her lashes falling over her eyes.

"On the contrary, I do not beat or abuse women, Marissa." The harshness in his voice had suddenly faded, and she opened her eyes to his once again. "I have merely tried to show you your folly."

Again she moistened her lips to speak. "I came here, sir, with my mind set."

"There are times," he said quietly, "when you may think I resent you just because we are married."

She frowned. "I don't understand—"

"Never mind. There is no way to explain." He rose suddenly. "And I make no promises, no agreements. That is understood?"

She wasn't sure; she really wasn't sure what he meant at all, but she nodded, wondering if he was going to agree, or if this was all a charade to humiliate her.

He stared at her hard. Then he muttered a harsh, "Damn you, girl!"

And he reached for a handsome overcoat, and touched her at last, taking her arm to draw her away from the door.

"Where are you going?" she cried.

He turned to her. Once again, his blue eyes seemed to impale her beneath the rakish fall of the black lock upon his forehead. "I am going for a registrar, my lady. If we're going to do this thing, we'll do it now, and be done with it all. I've got a license. All we need is a registrar.''

The door swung shut in his wake. Marissa gasped. Her knees were beginning to buckle and she braced herself with her hands against the door.

What had she done?

He had agreed. He had agreed too swiftly! He had given her no time to plot and plan, to find a way to make it all false or to make it all real.

But he had agreed. He was coming back with a registrar, and she must do something, she must...

Marry him.

A coldness settled upon her, and the words kept repeating hauntingly in her mind. Help me, God! she thought. But surely God would not help a liar playing such a deception as she played.

There was no choice, she assured herself. No choice at all. She had won, she had come here wanting this, and now, surprisingly, she had gained what she wanted.

But very soon, she knew, he would come to the room with a registrar. And she would stand there and vow to be his wife. His wife. Irrevocably tied to the man.

She started to tremble and closed her eyes. She didn't dare keep thinking, and yet she could not stop. What would happen if she were found out? The knot was tangling more viciously with every turn....

Maybe he didn't mean to go through with it. Perhaps he had gone out to order a tray of tea and crumpets. He did not really mean to marry her; he just wanted to agree to give her the chance to realize what she was saying, to back out of it herself.

Which she could do. If she and Mary were caught perpetrating this deception it would be disaster.

He was letting her escape.

Perhaps she did block out her thoughts, for it seemed that

he had barely left before he was back. At his side was a stocky little man with wispy gray hair. Behind the man were two women—a small, pert maid in a white cap and apron and an older woman, also in a cap and apron.

"My dear," Ian said, still appearing very much the rake, his shirt opened at the neck, his coat haphazardly over his shoulders and a night's stubble upon his cheeks, "this is Mr. Blackstone, the registrar. And this is Meg, and she will witness the ceremony for me. And this is Lucy, who will also witness the marriage. We *do* want it to be legal."

He was not letting her escape.

Marissa tried to smile. She needed to be gracious, to extend her hand to the two women. She couldn't speak. She had barely managed to move away from the doorway at their return. She stared at Ian with wide eyes.

His mouth was set in a grim line, and his eyes were hard upon hers. He said nothing to her, but she knew what he was thinking. She had started this. And now he would finish it.

He would give her exactly what she wanted.

"It will be just a minute here now," Mr. Blackstone was saying, setting his briefcase upon the desk. "I need the proper legal documents and my seal. Mr. Tremayne?"

Ian went to the desk and produced the license.

"Oh, this is so exciting!" Meg said.

"Thrilling," Ian agreed wryly.

"Did you wish to, er, tidy up a bit, sir?" Mr. Blackstone asked Ian.

Ian rubbed his cheeks. He offered Marissa a smile that didn't touch the fire in his eyes. "No, thank you, Mr. Blackstone. My wife will be seeing this Yankee mug every morning of her life from here on out. She doesn't mind it a bit, do you, my dear?"

Marissa smiled at last, as sweetly as she could manage. She touched his stubbled cheek and assured Mr. Blackstone. "I can't tell you just how charming I find Mr. Tremayne to be.

Kind, solicitous—absolutely charming. With or without the stubble. It's such a noble face.''

"She adores me,'' Ian told Mr. Blackstone.

Meg sighed. Lucy giggled. Mr. Blackstone seemed uneasy.

Ian snatched Marissa's hand and drew her to his side. "Can we get on with this?"

"Yes, yes, of course. My papers are now all in order. I think…''

He started to speak the words. Slowly, very slowly. Marissa did not hear them. She felt Ian Tremayne's hand locked around hers, large, warm, powerful.

She was building prison walls around herself, she realized. This was very real. She would have to travel across the globe with him. Live in his house. Answer to his beck and call.

"And do you, Ian Robert, take this woman to be your lawfully wedded wife, to have and to hold, to love and to cherish, from this day forward, till death do you part?''

Marissa couldn't breathe. He would protest now. He would say that it had all been a lark and that he hadn't the least intention of marrying her.

"I do,'' he said firmly.

"And do you—'' The registrar paused for a second, squinting at a paper.

"Katherine Marissa, Mr. Blackstone,'' Ian supplied dryly.

"Yes, yes, of course. Now do you, Katherine Marissa, take this man to be your lawfully wedded husband, to have and to hold, to honor and obey, from this day forward, till death do you part?''

Death? she thought vaguely. It seemed drastic. He hadn't stopped it; she had to do so.

She almost cried out at the sudden pressure upon her hand as his fingers wound tightly around it in warning. "I do!'' she gasped.

Then Mr. Blackstone was talking again, and she really couldn't hear a word he was saying. Moments later Ian was raising her hand, and something cold and way too large was slipped upon her finger.

Mr. Blackstone pronounced them man and wife, and nervously suggested that Ian might like to kiss his bride.

"Kiss my bride," he muttered, and she wanted to wrench away at the bitterness that tinged his voice. For a moment she thought he meant to thrust her far from him. He did not. His hold upon her was very firm. And she was suddenly pulled tight within his arms, and her mouth opened in protest as she saw the intent within his eyes.

No sound escaped her.

His lips touched hers. She expected violence from the way he held her.

But there was none.

His mouth formed over hers with a fierce demand and pressure, but there was something more. Perhaps it was something practiced...something innate within the man.

Whatever it was, she could not think once his lips molded so securely over hers. She felt the brush of the stubble of his beard, she felt his hold, his pressure, his undauntable determination. And yet she felt the seduction. The slow, almost lazy coercion. Her lips were parted beneath his, the startling, damp, heady warmth of his tongue filled her mouth, tasted and explored. Leisurely, and yet with such purpose. The fingers of his left hand entwined with the hair at her nape, holding her still to his thorough exploration. His other hand lay upon the small of her back, holding her close to him, so very close that she felt the pulse and tension of his body, the hardness of his build, and the heat that lay within, simmering, fusing, touching her in a way she had never imagined being touched before.

The tip of his tongue skimmed over her lips, delved deep within her mouth once again, endlessly deep. Her fingers wound into his shirt, for she was certain that if he moved, she would fall. All the fire had seemed to enter into her from his body. And a trembling that was rich with newborn sensations, making her both hot and cold, furious and...

And fascinated.

She should protest.... ·

She could not.

Dimly she heard Mr. Blackstone clear his throat; Meg and Lucy sighed very softly in unison.

And then, at long last, Ian Tremayne moved his dark head, lifting his mouth from hers. His cobalt eyes seared into hers for a long moment, and she could not draw her gaze from his. He touched her lip with his thumb, rubbing the remaining moisture from it. And still his gaze touched hers, yet she did not know what emotion lurked in his eyes. She thought that he was still furious with her for testing his hand. Yet he was the one with the sudden determination at the end. He had taken her course of action and flown with it. In a sudden impetuous heat? She was sure of it, for already she sensed a withdrawal. His touch fell from her face, and he was gazing at Mr. Blackstone again.

"Well, the papers, then," he said flatly. "We should keep this legal."

"Yes, Mr. Tremayne! Most certainly."

Mr. Blackstone pushed the license across the desk. Ian Tremayne leaned low over it and scrawled his name. It was barely legible.

He thrust the pen into her hand. She stared at him. The anger was back with him. "Sign it," he told her. She kept looking at him. "For the love of God, Marissa, sign the damned thing."

She hesitated a second longer. Which name did she sign? Mary's? Would things be legal then? Perhaps not. But if they weren't legal, things would be better if they were caught!

"Marissa!" Her name seemed to be an explosion of impatience. She started to write with trembling fingers, scrawling out her name in a far worse manner than he had done.

She stared at it. It was very nearly illegible. But she knew what she had signed. Katherine Marissa Ayers. At the last moment, she had signed her own name. He would never know. "Ahearn" and the "Ayers" were close enough when written with fingers that trembled as violently as hers had done.

Meg and Lucy stepped forward and signed the wedding license, then Mr. Blackstone did the same, and blotted all the signatures.

"Shall I get some champagne?" Meg suggested, and Mr. Blackstone looked up eagerly.

"Champagne?" Ian mused. Marissa bit her lip in silence. "Champagne. By all means. What is a wedding without a toast?"

"My own sentiments exactly," Mr. Blackstone agreed jovially.

Meg left the room for the champagne and Mr. Blackstone sat behind the desk, finishing with the forms. Marissa and Ian stood in silence. Waiting.

Then Meg burst through the door. Ian took the tray with champagne from her, setting it upon the desk. He observed the label with a critical eye, then shrugged and popped the cork. Champagne bubbled out, and he quickly began to pour it into the five flutes upon the tray.

He handed one to Marissa. Her fingers curled around it. He smiled, grimly. "Till death do us part," he said.

"Hear, hear!" Mr. Blackstone agreed. He lifted his glass and sighed. "To many years of marital bliss!"

"Oh, many years," Ian said wryly.

"To a huge, full, wonderful family! Strong, handsome sons and beautiful daughters!" Meg cried, well into the spirit of the thing.

Did neither she nor Mr. Blackstone see the hostility that lurked in Ian Tremayne's eyes?

They did not, but Marissa did. In silence, she sipped her

champagne, then tossed her head back and swallowed the contents in a gulp. Ian's lip curled as he watched her, and he poured her another portion of the vintage, then added to Mr. Blackstone's proffered flute.

"Well, then!" Blackstone said with a sigh as he swallowed his down and set the glass upon the tray. "The very best to you both. To you, good sir, and you, too, Mrs. Tremayne."

Marissa's head jerked up. Blackstone locked his briefcase and lifted it from the table. Ian Tremayne opened the door for him. Blackstone bowed to Meg, and the little maid smiled and said goodbye and good luck once again and left. The more sedate Lucy followed quickly behind her. "Again, the best to you both," Blackstone said, bowing just before he exited the room.

Ian closed the door behind them. He leaned against it and stared at her.

Once again, she saw the curl of a mocking smile touch his lips. "Ah, yes. Don't look so startled, love. You are, you realize, Mrs. Tremayne. Just as you wished."

She started as he pushed away from the door and came toward her, catching her wrists, pulling her hard against his well-muscled form. "Yes, my dear, you've gotten exactly what you came for. Marriage. Are you happy?"

She tugged uneasily upon her wrists, frightened by his sudden hostility. "Mr. Tremayne—"

"So very formal, Mrs. Tremayne."

"But I'm not really—"

"Oh, yes, you see, that's where you are mistaken. You are really my wife, Marissa. My wife," he repeated softly.

Then he dropped her wrists and headed for the door, pausing with his hand upon the knob. His crooked smile curved his mouth and he repeated the words once again. "I've a wife. Dear God, whatever possessed me? May heaven help us both."

And then, with no explanation, he was gone.

CHAPTER FOUR

"YOU DID WHAT!" Mary gasped with horror.

Marissa, hearing the tone of Mary's voice at her casual announcement that she had gone ahead and married Ian Tremayne, grimaced. She was in the parlor of their suite, trying very hard to be calm and casual while her heart beat a rampant pulse of uncertainty.

Ian Tremayne hadn't returned. He would have to do so eventually, Marissa was certain, because he had left all his things. But she had paced his room for half an hour, trying not to look at those things that seemed to be so personal to the man, growing more and more restless. The room made her uneasy. The desk was filled with business papers, with letters, some addressed in smooth, flowing scripts that could only be feminine. There was his bed. And there was his shaving equipment, a fine ivory brush and cup, his razor and strop.

She couldn't wait any longer. She didn't know if he had expected her to wait, he had slammed out so quickly. She had left the boardinghouse, hailed a hansom and returned to Mary's suite.

There she found Mary awake and pacing the floor, worried about her.

"I married him," Marissa repeated, sinking down on one of the stiff needlepoint chairs that faced the settee over a heavy Persian rug. "We married him, I guess. I don't know. I used my own name. I signed my own signature. I think that makes it legal. The marriage, at least."

"Oh, Marissa!"

Mary hurried to her side and hugged her tightly. "What

made you do such a thing? You shouldn't have. We would have survived somehow.''

"Mary, nothing is really any different.''

"Nothing is different!'' Mary exclaimed. "Oh, Marissa! Don't you know what married people do?''

Marissa cast her a quick, narrowing glance. "Of course I know what married people do!'' she said indignantly. Honestly, Mary could be terribly annoying. "But it's not going to be that kind of marriage.''

Mary sniffed. "Any marriage is that kind of marriage. Oh, of course, he is very good looking.''

"How do you know?''

"I was peeking out the bedroom door last night. He's handsome. Very attractive, really.''

"He had you in fits last night.''

"Oh, but that's because I couldn't begin to deal with such a man. He's such a tremendous presence, demanding. But I think he could be charming.''

"Charming. That's the word,'' Marissa said sweetly.

Mary stared at her, hurt. "I only meant—''

"He is charming, Mary. Completely,'' Marissa lied. And he could be charming. When he wasn't snapping and snarling. "Mary, it's an arrangement, nothing more. If you were peeking last night, you must have been listening too. He was married before. He didn't want to be married again. So I'm really just going to be a guest in the house, and then, because he's already married, no one will bother him to get married. Understand?''

"You made him understand this?'' Mary said, confused.

"Yes. Mary, it's going to be all right.''

"No, it's not! And I can't believe that you went off and married him without a word! Marissa, you didn't give yourself time to think! Maybe we could have come up with something else—''

"With what, Mary?'' Marissa asked wearily.

"I don't know. Something."

"Mary, I didn't think he'd really do it. I had all these won-derful plans and arguments. Then I assumed that if I did get him to agree, we'd make plans for later. The next thing I knew, a registrar was in the room, and we were married."

"Oh, Marissa!"

Mary hugged her tightly, then released her. She stared at her with such mournful, miserable eyes that Marissa patted her hand and rose, determined to cast aside her own fears to reassure her friend. "Mary, you musn't forget that I have my uncle to care for. Actually, it's everything I've always wanted. Mr. Tremayne's home will be very grand, I'm certain. I'll see the opera, the theater, and I'll be a gracious hostess for count-less balls and dinners. I'll be in my glory."

Mary looked at her with a sad wisdom that was unnerving. "A house doesn't mean anything, Marissa. It's brick and stone and wood. And you've entrusted your fate to this man—"

"Our fates, Mary. We'll be together, at least."

"We've traded places, remember?" Mary murmured softly. "He's not going to let you choose your friends from among the poor immigrants."

"We're going to America, Mary. The land of opportunity! And equality."

"Equality takes a long time in coming," Mary said softly.

"Don't worry. He's not going to rule my life! Oh, Mary, don't you see, it will be all right. He didn't want a wife. I'll be an ornament upon occasion. And when I'm not, nothing will change. You'll have a beautiful little home nearby, Jimmy will work, and I'll help you with whatever you need. It is going to work out. It's going to be exactly like we planned. There was really just a minor hitch to our plans, and that was it."

She hiccuped suddenly. Mary stared at her.

"Champagne," Marissa offered. She grimaced. "We celebrated."

"You celebrated!"

"Of course. Remember, I told you," Marissa said blandly. "He's charming. Completely charming." She smiled. "Like a wolf!" she muttered beneath her breath.

"What?" Mary demanded.

"Nothing. Really. Nothing at all."

There was a soft rap on the door. Mary hurried over to it and opened it, then gasped.

Jimmy O'Brien was standing there.

"Jimmy!" Mary said.

"Aye, love, I'm here."

"But you were going to stay away until—"

"Until, love, that was the problem," Jimmy said, taking her hand and moving into the room. His young freckled face was serious, his eyes were grave. He nodded to Marissa then told Mary, "I have to admit, I did not trust the two of you. I was afraid that you might do something foolish, and I am the man here. Mary, I will provide, and I'll care for you both somehow, I mean it."

A soft smile curved Marissa's lips as she listened to the passion and vehemence of his speech. That was Jimmy. He could not really even hope to take care of himself and Mary, but he was willing to promise to care for her, too.

"'Tis too late, Jimmy," Mary murmured. "Marissa's gone off and married the Yank."

"What!" Jimmy exclaimed, horrified.

Marissa sighed. "Jimmy, it's all right—"

"You've married the old bloke!"

"He's not old, Jimmy."

"He's still a strange Yank!"

"Whatever, Jimmy, the die is cast."

"We'll annul it!" Jimmy announced.

Marissa stood and faced them both. "We'll do no such

thing. I barely managed to get what I wanted, and now that I've got it, we're going to live with it. I imagine—''

She broke off because there was another knock at the door, crisp and hard this time. Shivers danced over her spine because she was certain that it was Ian.

Jimmy, unaware, headed for the door. "Wait!" Marissa called out, but it was too late. Jimmy had already opened the door, and it was, indeed, Ian standing there.

He had bathed and changed. And shaved. His hair was damp, the dark wave still rippling over his forehead. He wore an off-white suit that enhanced his dark good looks.

Dark and glowering. He looked at Jimmy with his jaw set at a harsh angle, his blue eyes shooting off sparks, and yet with a harsh, cold control about him. Then his gaze fell upon Marissa across the room, and it was condemning to such an extent that she had to grip the back of the needlepoint chair to keep from visibly shivering.

She could not let him intimidate her so! she told herself fiercely.

"What the hell is going on here?" he demanded, his voice a low, warning growl.

Jimmy backed away from the door, and Marissa bit hard upon her lip, willing him her strength. Tremayne was probably ten years Jimmy's elder, taller and broader, a formidable man. But Jimmy moved back, she knew, because of Ian's dress and confidence. Jimmy was accustomed to poverty, and to giving way to the rich. And she was suddenly very angry for Jimmy, and angry that Tremayne was assuming Jimmy was the lover she had denied she had.

"I am entertaining friends, Mr. Tremayne!" she snapped.

"Lady, you had best not be entertaining—"

"Mr. Tremayne, if you don't mind!" she managed to murmur with incredible presence, her head raised regally. And then before she knew it, a lie was upon her lips. "I thought

I'd lost you," she said. "Please, do come in. I'd like you to meet my very good friends, Mary and Jimmy O'Brien."

His gaze went quickly from her face to Jimmy's, then to Mary's. Jimmy seemed to be frozen. When Ian looked at Mary, his gaze grew more gentle. It had to be something about Mary's face, Marissa thought, and she wondered if she resented Mary for having this effect upon others, or whether she should be grateful for it. There was a gentleness about Mary's beauty. She had the look of a Madonna, as if nothing more than kindness lived in her heart. Her smile was always genuine.

Mary stepped forward, taking his hand in a firm shake. "How do you do, sir. It is indeed our pleasure."

Ian smiled suddenly, bending over her hand. He brushed it with a kiss. "Forgive me, Mrs. O'Brien. I am afraid that I am still fatigued from the journey here, and not in the best of temper."

"Sir, we are not offended."

Yes, we are! Marissa wanted to cry. But Ian's gaze had moved to Jimmy.

Jimmy had removed his cap. He wound it uneasily in his hands. He wanted to speak, Marissa knew, but he was tongue-tied.

"Jimmy, dear!" Mary persisted. "Come meet Mr. Tremayne."

Jimmy stepped forward and shook hands with Ian. Marissa watched as Ian Tremayne quickly assessed the man, and to her surprise seemed to like what he saw.

"Mr. O'Brien, Mrs. O'Brien. The pleasure is mine." He looked across the room at Marissa. "No, my dear, you did not lose me. I simply had some arrangements to make. But I see that I should have waited. I assume that these are your friends?"

"Yes, my very good friends," Marissa admitted without moving. "They—they wish to come to America, too."

His gaze fell upon Mary, and Marissa was certain that he read her ill health in a matter of seconds. "It's a long journey," he said.

"I know," Mary told him.

"What do you do, Jimmy O'Brien?" Ian asked.

Mary cleared her throat. She was standing behind Marissa, and gave her a light prod. "You must ask your husband to sit down, Marissa. And offer him a drink."

"Of course!" She had promised to be such a wonderful hostess and she seemed as incapable of movement as Jimmy. After the angry way that Ian had left her, he seemed calm enough. He seemed almost charming. Once he had decided that the door hadn't been opened by her supposed lover, he had seemed to acquire a keen interest in her friends.

"Mr. Tremayne, please do have a seat. Would you like a whiskey or a brandy, sir? Would—"

Mary was prodding her again, then whispering at her ear. "You've married the man, Marissa. You must call him by his given name, not 'Mr. Tremayne' or 'sir'!"

Ian was staring at them both, smiling. She thought again that at the very least, she seemed to amuse him often enough.

"A brandy would be fine," he told her, lounging comfortably upon the settee. "Mr. O'Brien, join me. Tell me about yourself."

Jimmy was wringing his cap in his hands once again but he moved tentatively to the settee. He sat, or perched, near Ian. Then he seemed to realize that the man had a genuine interest in him. "I'm already an immigrant, to be sure," he said. "Irish," he explained, as if his name and looks didn't give him away in a second.

Ian's grin deepened. "There's plenty Irishmen in San Francisco, Jimmy. What do you do?"

"I was a farmer, but…" he shrugged. "Well, it seemed we were all tryin' to make a livin' from potatoes where there was no living to be made. And I'd always wanted to be a shopkeeper. I could read and write and cipher fair enough, for the village priest, he did see to that. He said that we'd not throw off the yoke of the English if we didn't concentrate on the like.'' He flushed suddenly, realizing that he was in England.

"It's all right, Jimmy, go ahead," Ian encouraged. "So you wanted to be a shopkeeper."

"Aye."

"But it takes capital," Ian said.

"Aye, that it does."

"Well, Jimmy, if you're sure you and your wife have the will and determination to come to America, I think that I can help you."

"I can't take your money—"

"And I don't intend to give it to you," Ian said. He took his brandy glass from Marissa without looking at her, and she felt curiously like the downstairs maid again even as she watched the hope dawning in Jimmy's face.

"You see, Jimmy O'Brien, my father and grandfather were shopkeepers. They had years and years to build up, to gain experience. We've a really fine family emporium in the heart of San Francisco. I don't spend the time there that I should. I'm not a merchant at heart. I'm a builder. But if you're willing to take the time to learn my business and gain some experience, well, I'm certain that we could arrange a salary that would provide you with the savings to open your own place after a while."

Mary gasped with pleasure, her eyes glowing. Jimmy stared at the man as if he had just handed him a thousand pounds in gold.

"Well, Jimmy?"

"I'd work hard, Mr. Tremayne, I swear it! You wait and see, sir!"

"I know you will."

"I expect to start down at the bottom, sir—"

"And that you will, too. In the basement. It's the stock-room, and everyone has to learn the stock."

"I'll learn it upside, downside and all around, sir!" Jimmy vowed.

Ian smiled again. "I'm sure you will." He gazed past Jimmy to Mary, who stood behind him, her hands resting upon his shoulders. His voice grew more gentle. "You will enjoy San Francisco, Mary. It's one of the most beautiful places on earth. I don't think you will miss your home too keenly."

"I cannot miss my home, Mr. Tremayne," Mary said. "Where Jimmy goes is home. And of course, we will be near Marissa. That is all the home that I need."

Ian rose, studying her. Marissa bit her lip, thinking that Ian admired and liked Mary very much. Perhaps they all might have been much better off if they had never planned to deceive him.

But as she had said, the die was cast.

She was the one who had lied and deceived him.

And married him.

"Marissa."

She grated her teeth at the sharp sound of her name upon his tongue. He spoke to her as if she were a child. As if she were still the downstairs maid. And yet he was as polite and gentle to Mary as a man could be.

She gave him her attention, waiting, but did not reply. He stood. "I'd have a word with you alone, madam."

"Oh!" Mary murmured. "Really, Jimmy, dear, we must be going. Mr. Tremayne and Marissa must have an awful lot to discuss."

Jimmy stared at her blankly.

"Jimmy, come on."

"But—"

"I'll make your travel arrangements and advise you of them, Jimmy," Ian told him. He shook Jimmy's hand, then bent his head low over Mary's. "We'll meet again soon enough."

"Yes, of course, and thank you! Thank you so much for everything, Mr. Tremayne."

"Ian, please. We are to be friends."

Mary smiled slowly, beautifully. "Ian, then." She withdrew her hand from his. "Jimmy, come, please."

Marissa watched them depart, Mary determined, Jimmy dazed. As the door closed upon the two of them she was painfully uncomfortable once again, face to face with the man she had married.

"I had thought that we should both leave within the next few days—" he began.

"But I can't!" she interrupted him. It was one thing to play the grand lady in London. But she couldn't just leave the country. She had to say goodbye to Theo, and she had to convince him somehow that she had fallen in love and married and that her husband was very rich and that she would send him checks every month. And then she had to try to convince him to come to America eventually, but that could wait. Maybe she could even travel back for him herself. Beautifully bedecked, magnanimous, a heroine to the mining community where she would see that a school was set up....

That was all in the future. At the moment, she had the piper to pay.

"Admittedly, madam, I have not up until now trusted you," he told her. "This morning, I would have said no."

"But?" she murmured, watching him.

"But I find your friends very responsible, and therefore perhaps I misjudged you."

Resentment flared inside her, but she kept her lashes lowered, determined not to argue. "So you will give me some time?" she said.

"Yes. You and your friends can come on the liner *Lorena*.

She leaves London ten days from now. That should be sufficient for you.''

"Ten days!" she murmured in dismay.

"It is unusual enough, Marissa, that a newly married man should return without his wife. Ten days is what I can give you. The *Lorena* will take you to New York. From there you will take the train to California and San Francisco. It is a long journey. You will be on the ship for about a week and the train for as long again. It would have been much better if you could have prepared to travel with me.''

No! She was tremendously grateful that she would not have to travel with him. They would eventually have to establish some kind of relationship, she knew. But she was willing, very willing, to play for time.

She raised her eyes to his. "Sir, I am competent, even if you've little faith in me. I will manage the journey, with transfers and pitfalls, I promise you.''

He smiled slowly. "Yes, I believe that. You don't lack courage, or strength. For a young woman of your birth and privilege, you're really quite extraordinary.''

Marissa wasn't at all sure that it was a compliment, not the way he gazed at her. But then he turned away, pacing the small parlor. "I do apologize for my manners this morning. You caught me quite off guard.'' He spun and stared at her. "After all, you went from attempting to remain in England to insisting upon marriage. Quite a difference.''

"Perhaps,'' she murmured, watching him uneasily. Mercurial seemed to be the best word to describe him, from the depth of his dark blue eyes to the tone of his voice to his energy. He was constantly in motion. He accused her of change, yet one moment his manner verged upon tenderness, and the next moment the air could be rife with hostility.

"Well, it is no matter now. The deed is done. I'll admit that the haste of the situation was born of impatience and anger. I walked the city for some time after, wondering what I had allowed you to goad me into doing.''

"So it is all my fault!'' Marissa cried in protest.

He laughed. "Fault? No. I'm still not so terribly sure that you really knew what you wanted. No, if there is fault, I think that I take it myself. But it is done now, you see. And I thought that I should tell you a few things.''

Marissa walked uneasily around the settee, using it as a barrier between them, though he offered her no physical harm. She still could not forget the wedding kiss he had bestowed upon her. She would never forget it, she thought, or the way it made her feel.

And with him, alone, she discovered herself watching his mouth and remembering far too much about it. She scarcely knew him, and already she was learning far too much about him. She could close her eyes and remember the curve of his smile. Remember the mockery, remember a gaze of tenderness. She could close her eyes and see his eyes upon her. She knew she would walk down a busy street and remember the timbre of his voice. And the touch of his hands.

Her memories made her grow warm. She swallowed slightly, afraid that he would touch her again and somehow afraid that he would not. It occurred to her that he had never really made any agreement about their marriage; she had no idea of what it was to be like.

"You've already told me quite a few things,'' she murmured coolly, seeking a refined distance between them. "You don't want a wife, you think it's amusing that I might protect you, and there is no such thing as an unwanted advance since you admittedly and eagerly seek the company of—'' She paused, the word "whores'' upon her tongue. She amended her words with a bitter note. "Dance-hall girls. San Francisco does have the finest.''

His lip curled, but he was neither amused nor pleased with

her recitation. "My dear Mrs. Tremayne, but you've got a quick and dangerous tongue!"

"I'm repeating what I've heard," she said tartly.

"I didn't come here to fight with you," he said easily enough. With a lazy stride, though, he was moving toward her. "However, madam, I do find it tempting to remember my deep and solemn vow of guardianship and see to the mending of your reckless ways."

"Oh! And what did you intend?" Marissa gasped, but she thought it wise to move quickly, even while challenging him.

"Oh, something mild. A sound thrashing, perhaps."

"You most certainly can't be serious!" she assured him.

"Can't I?" he demanded. His arm snaked out and his fingers wound around her wrists, and she suddenly found herself drawn tight against him. He was taunting her, she knew, but he was also tense with anger. "Take care, Marissa, for you do not know me at all. I do not always know myself. Take this morning. I certainly had not intended to wed, and you began to speak and I found myself engaged in the deed."

"You said—"

"I said that it was my fault, most assuredly. For no man can be so twisted and manipulated unless he allows it to be so. But I will not be twisted or manipulated any longer. Still, I did not mean to tell you that."

"Please," she murmured suddenly, twisting her wrists in his grasp. She could not bear to be so close to him; she had discovered that this morning. Warmth seemed to leap and sizzle from his body into her own, and she felt too keenly the form and shape and strength of his body. And she felt the rivers of warmth that invaded her, entering her blood, her limbs. The racing fires left her weak and uncertain, wanting to escape, wanting to fling her arms around his neck so she could continue to stand.

"Marissa, I wanted only to tell you that you would find the city beautiful, and my house an easy one to dwell within. You may take the later ship, as I have told you. It will be an easy enough life for you, I daresay. Leave me to my peace and remember I cherish my name and would harshly revenge the misuse of it, and we may get on better than most.''

Her head fell back as she ceased to struggle. She was suddenly caught by the deep blue command of his eyes, and she could fight no more. Nor could she speak.

And he fell silent, too. He was gazing into her eyes. She did not fight him, but neither did he let her go.

Then suddenly he released her, turning away. "I shall see you again directly before I leave. I'm taking the *Princess of the Seas* the day after tomorrow. I shall have all your necessary travel papers and instructions on how to reach San Francisco prepared for you. Oh,'' he added. ''And for your friends, of course.''

She nodded. Now he was brisk and cool once again, all business. He reached the door, and suddenly she found herself moving after him. ''Mr. Tremayne!'' She hesitated as he turned. ''Ian,'' she said softly.

''Yes?''

''I—I didn't thank you.''

''For what?''

''For Mary and Jimmy. For accepting them so cordially. For—for giving him a job.''

He shrugged. ''He seems a likeable enough lad. And he's wed himself a true lady. I'd not make your life a living hell, madam, no matter what your beliefs on the matter.''

He turned and started to leave again.

''Ian!''

She was startled when she called him back a second time. He held the doorknob somewhat impatiently and awaited her words.

His given name still felt so strange upon her tongue, she was amazed that it had slipped from her lips so easily.

''I—I do not wish to make your life miserable, either, sir.''

She thought that she detected a hint of a smile just barely curving his mouth. ''Well, thank you for that,'' he told her. ''Good night.''

He left for good this time, closing the door firmly behind him.

She did not call him back.

She leaned against the door and closed her eyes, thinking that she had survived the day.

And then she remembered that she had married him. Legally married him.

She remembered his kiss, and her fingers brushed over her lips. She felt a swift, searing warmth sweep along her spine.

She tried to close her mind to the memory, to the feel of his hands upon her, to the power within them. He could be very kind...

But he also had a sharp and mercurial temper.

And she had lied to him. She had more than lied to him. She had played a monstrous pretense upon him.

If he ever discovered the deception...

She didn't dare dwell upon the thought. She pushed away from the door with resolution and poured herself a very small sherry, sat down and began to daydream of the trip to see Uncle Theo, when she could tell him that he would never have to step foot inside a mine again.

It was all going to be worth it. Everything. She could do so very much. She had succeeded in the charade. She had learned her lessons well. Everyone was going to be so very happy.

She swallowed more sherry.

If that was the case, then why did she see visions of his searing blue gaze upon her every time she closed her eyes?

And why did she remember so constantly the feel of his hands, the warmth of his touch...

And tremble?

CHAPTER FIVE

THE LONDON FOG was rolling in, but it didn't disturb Ian. He was accustomed to fog, and he loved it. A lot of London reminded him of home—the sight of an expanse of bridge, the swirl of the mist and the coolness of the night against his face.

He had met with a Scottish wool merchant for dinner, and had chosen to walk to the boardinghouse rather than take a hansom cab. He was enjoying himself. There was a great deal of beauty and elegance here in the heart of the city. He paused before a new house going up and critically studied its lines. It would be a beautiful home.

He frowned then, thinking of the postponed meetings he was going to have to reschedule when he returned home. He'd been hired to design an office building. The site was to be upon some of the newly reclaimed land in the marina area, and he was having a hell of time convincing the owners that if they chose to build there, their costs would go up. He felt uneasy about building on the land—it was all fill. Deep pilings would be necessary, and a great deal of steel. And it would also have to be a building capable of sway. Tremors often swept the city, and a certain amount of sway was necessary to keep the structures from cracking. He had been watching buildings go up ever since he was a boy. And he had known even then that more than anything else in the world, he wanted to build. And he had hated the store for standing in the way of that dream.

It was late, he realized, really late. He started to walk in the direction of Hyde Park, and as the moon flared its soft light upon him to join with the glow of the gas lamps, he suddenly raised his hand to note the thin white band around his pinkie where he had removed the signet ring in the middle of his wedding ceremony.

He stopped cold, feeling ill, feeling a heat sweep over him. For what seemed like the thousandth time that day he demanded harshly of himself just what in hell he had done.

And why, in God's name, had he done it?

He paused and leaned against a fence and closed his eyes tightly. He had vowed on the day when he had stood in the drizzling cemetery and watched as Diana's coffin was sealed into the family mausoleum that he would never marry again, never call another woman his wife. They had loved one another too deeply, too fiercely. She had been the most gentle woman he had ever met, so gentle that she had left life behind her with barely a whisper.

It had been a long time before he had managed to touch another woman, and then, perhaps, he had managed to rationalize things in his mind. It was all right to find women entertaining and amusing, and it was even all right to form certain relationships, as long as they were kept in their proper perspective. As long as the women were never his wife, as long as he need never rouse himself to offer love.

And he had been managing just fine....

Now there was this chit of a girl in his life. He had accepted the responsibility that Sir Thomas had begged of him, but he had never expected this.

His mouth set in a grim line of anger. She wanted her inheritance enough to beg and plead. She had sold herself, just as surely as the finest courtesan in London or the most jaded street girl in San Francisco. She'd used logic, indignation, a touch of pathos and even fury, and somehow, she had sparked something dark and dangerous in his heart. He had said no, he had meant no. And then suddenly he had been out pounding the streets in a state of total dishabille, digging up the Honorable Mr. Blackstone—

And exchanging wedding vows.

What was it that she did that could cause him to feel such a passion of fury in his heart and soul? He didn't want to hurt her. By God, she was Sir Thomas's daughter.

No, he didn't want to hurt her. He didn't want to be near her. He had just wanted to go on living, allowing her to roam his house and giving her the freedom of her own life. And she, in turn, should have politely avoided him, stayed out of his way, and behaved graciously and kindly to guests within his home. It could have worked.

But he'd lost his temper and married her...

He pushed away from the fence, still furious with himself as he strode down the street, heading for his room.

He hated her, suddenly and intensely, and what she had goaded him into doing.

He paused again, inhaling, exhaling. No, he didn't hate the girl. He hated his reaction to her. He hated the curiosity she drew from him when he looked into her eyes. She could appear so haunted. As if she was desperate to reach out and grasp things, and hold them tightly, simply because they had always eluded her.

She could have a look about her, as if she had witnessed serious nightmares.

She had just lost her father, he reminded himself. And yet there was more. She could be regal and supreme, she could speak with a voice that rang cool and imperious, and yet, caught unaware, there could be that beautiful and haunting appeal in her eyes. Those cat's eyes, green cat's eyes, proud, spirited, beguiling.

His wife, he reminded himself, and tasted the bitterness on his tongue.

At least she was beautiful. Maybe she had a point. She would be an asset to his home and to his business. He imagined that she could throw an elegant dinner party, and wear mink or silver fox to the opera with panache.

It could be a bargain well met.

And along with her came that young Jimmy O'Brien. Ian was impressed with the lad. Oh, he was, raw, but his eyes held honesty, and he was earnest. And he was seeking the American dream, something that Ian believed in deeply. No kings, no queens, no royalty. Just a tough but beautiful land where hard work and ambition and dreams could be realized. O'Brien could be trusted, he felt.

And O'Brien could save Ian a great deal of time. Ian knew he could have sold the emporium, but it would have seemed like a betrayal. His father and grandfather had loved the store.

And if Diana had survived, and their child had been born, perhaps his own son or daughter would have loved the merchandising business, too.

But now there would be no children, no heirs, ever, he promised himself. He could sell the bloody business.

But he would not.

He had returned to his lodgings, and he quietly let himself in the front door of the boardinghouse.

Just as he reached his room on the second floor, he heard a sound and looked down the stairs. A woman was standing there. A tall, handsome blonde with a full figure and proud carriage. She was dressed in red silk with a matching feather-ornamented hat. Her name was Molly, and she played the piano and sang at the Gray Friars, a pub down the street. She could be elegant, and she could be discreet, and he had shared a pint or two with her during trips to London. He had even mentioned vaguely that he might see her when he had first arrived two nights ago.

She smiled slowly, and he was tempted to call her up. But before he could open his mouth, he felt as if he were suddenly blinded by a pair of flashing green eyes. He could hear Marissa's voice, painfully scornful and dignified despite the very sweetness of her tone, as good as telling him that he was welcome to his harlots and his whores and his dance-hall girls.

Desire seemed to surge within him, along with a sizzling of fury. But when he looked at the tall, handsome blonde he felt only weariness.

"Good evening, Molly," he called to her.

"Mr. Tremayne!" she murmured.

Ian knew she expected more, but he merely said, "Good night, Molly," and entered his room.

He sat at his desk. He had spent last night with the brandy bottle to warm him. It seemed that tonight he would do the same. And he would drink until he could drown out the sight of those haunting emerald eyes.

His wife's eyes.

He groaned and took a long, long swallow of the burning liquor.

Then he leaned his head back and prayed for a decent night's sleep.

AT TWO-THIRTY the following afternoon Marissa stood before the altar at Saint John's to witness Mary's and Jimmy's wedding.

They had both come to the hotel not long after dark the previous night, blushing, happy, so blissful that they appeared to be a pair of fools. And they had announced their wedding to Marissa. Apparently Jimmy had seen a minister the moment they'd come to London. The banns had already been called.

Marissa had been startled and hurt that they had kept it a secret from her, but then she realized that Mary had not wanted her to know, had not wanted Marissa to feel that added pressure.

Jimmy and Mary both hugged her fiercely, thanked her again—and then assured her that they both thought the very world of Ian Tremayne.

Marissa said tartly that that was quite nice, since Mary really should have been the one married to the man, but they were so very happy that she couldn't put a damper on their tremendous enthusiasm.

She loved them both, and she was delighted that it was because of her they could be so very happy. But watching them that night gave her the first pang of emotion regarding all that she had given up.

Mary and Jimmy sat together on the sofa, held hands and gazed into one another's eyes. And there was such a look of adoration between them that she felt as if she was an intruder, and then she realized that she was. She retired quickly and left them alone.

In bed she lay awake staring at the ceiling and relived every moment of her own hasty wedding, then thought about the man she had married. He was definitely not Jimmy, she thought with a sigh. He would never sit before a fire, gazing adoringly into her eyes.

And yet she could not forget his touch, his kiss. And the more she remembered their encounters, the warmer her thoughts made her grow, the more she felt a quaking within, a sizzling of apprehension…

Of excitement.

In the morning, Mary seemed more beautiful than she ever had before. Her eyes sparkled and shone, her cheeks were flushed, and there was no sign left of the fever that had so seriously plagued her just weeks before.

She had dressed in a day dress of soft ivory satin with an elegant Spanish veil that had been left to her by her mother. Her enthusiasm and happiness were contagious, and Marissa could not resist her good humor. They very decadently decided to order champagne for breakfast, and by the time Jimmy came for them in a hansom cab, they were both giggling and giddy.

"So you have to be tipsy to marry the likes of me, eh?" Jimmy teased Mary, but she laughed and uninhibitedly reached her long fingers around his neck and dragged his head down to hers and kissed him so long and sweetly that Marissa finally had to clear her throat to remind them of her presence.

Jimmy laughed a little huskily, and he offered an arm to each girl. They arrived at the church and spoke to the reverend, and Jimmy checked that all their papers were in order. The minister's plump and beaming wife came out to play the organ and sing, and she did both beautifully.

And then the ceremony began, with Marissa and the minister's wife as witnesses. It was small, as small as her own pretense of a wedding had been.

But it was different. So different.

Marissa thought that she had never seen such love in anyone's eyes as that which shone in Mary's and Jimmy's eyes. She had never seen a couple so devoted.

Their vows were barely whispered, but their hearts were in their whispers. When the minister told Jimmy to kiss his bride, and Jimmy did so, Marissa felt she was about to cry. She didn't understand why; weddings did not usually make her want to cry. She realized that she was witnessing something she had never considered might exist. Something that was far, far out of her own reach.

And then some curious inner sense made her turn around. She inhaled sharply, feeling a cold shiver sweep over her.

Ian Tremayne was at the back of the church, leaning against one of the huge white pillars. Casually, comfortably. She had the feeling he had witnessed all of the ceremony.

The blood drained from her face. What was he doing there? How had he come upon them?

She had lied to him, introducing Mary and Jimmy as man and wife. And now here he was at the back of the church, watching the ceremony.

He was standing in the shadow. She could not see his eyes; she could not begin to fathom his thoughts.

But she knew he was staring at her. And she seemed frozen, unable to tear herself away from that gaze.

"Mrs. Tremayne!" the minister called to her. "If you will, please, we need your signature!"

Those words propelled her into action. Mary's real name was on those papers. She had to get them signed and put away. What if Ian should chance to see them?

She sped down the aisle to the side pulpit and quickly scratched out her name, K. Marissa Tremayne. Ian was walking down the aisle.

Mary caught Marissa's eyes and realized that they didn't dare allow Ian to see the papers. She rushed forward, blocking Ian.

"Mr. Tremayne!"

"It was a lovely wedding, Mary. Really beautiful," he told her.

"Thank you. If I'd known you were planning on coming—"

"Well, Mary, I wasn't planning on coming. It was my understanding that you and Jimmy were already wed."

Mary blushed furiously. "Ah, that's Marissa! She was trying to—defend us."

"Defend you?"

"Well, it must have appeared that we…" She let her voice trail away delicately with a note of distress. "She did not wish you to think ill of us."

"Oh, Mary, I did not think ill of you or your young man for a moment," Ian said smoothly. He looked up and smiled crookedly at Marissa over Mary's shoulder. "I did not think ill of you at all."

Jimmy was rolling his set of papers into his jacket while the minister shuffled his. Jimmy, flushing, paid and thanked the minister and his wife, then he, too, hurried down the aisle.

Marissa remained by the pulpit, stiff and straight.

Ian congratulated Jimmy, and Jimmy began to stammer. Ian

waved a dismissing hand in the air. "You did nothing wrong, Jim O'Brien. And I did truly enjoy witnessing the ceremony."

"How did you come to be here?" Mary asked him at last.

"The parlor maid from the hotel sent me here when I arrived at Marissa's room with your traveling papers. Since I did make arrangements for a Mr. and Mrs. O'Brien, I'm glad to see that you are man and wife in truth."

He stepped past them and walked down the aisle to the pulpit where he faced Marissa. He didn't say a word to her, but his eyes were hot upon her and she felt the simmering anger within him.

He wasn't mad at Mary or at Jimmy. He was furious with her. She had lied to him.

He reached out to take her arm. She almost flinched from his touch, but managed to refrain.

"Ah, so this must be Mr. Tremayne!" the minister said jovially. "Elizabeth, had we known Mrs. Tremayne's good husband was going to be here, he could have served with his wife as witness!"

Marissa paled slightly, thinking of the trouble they would have been in if Ian had seen papers that joined James O'Brien and Katherine Mary Ahearn. Ian greeted the reverend and his wife solemnly, adding, "I'd really no idea that I was attending the wedding—my wife did not invite me."

"Oh!" the minister murmured, distressed.

Ian offered him the slight curl of a smile. "It was quite a service, though, and I am very glad that I did not miss it. Good day to you, sir."

He doffed his hat and spun Marissa around. She wanted to wrench free from his hold, but it was firm, and she was swept along without making an effort to escape him.

In the middle of the aisle they reached Jimmy and Mary. "Well, it seems we've quite an occasion here," Ian murmured. "Would you be so kind as to accept a wedding supper from your new employer, Mr. O'Brien?"

Jimmy's mouth worked for a moment without sound. Then he managed to speak. "Sir, it's kind, but I can't accept more from you—"

"Nonsense. Any man can accept a wedding dinner from another. Come along while the night is young. Neither Marissa nor I would want to intrude upon too much of this special time, yet neither would we have you begin this new life without proper celebration. Eh, Marissa?"

Was he serious, or was he taunting her? What was his game? His eyes were still filled with fury when he touched her. His grip was tight with tension.

"Marissa?"

"Of course," she murmured.

He was always in control, she thought. On the street he quickly hailed a cab and asked the driver to take them to an exclusive but expensive club near Parliament, one that was patronized by members of the royal family. Jimmy did not know the name. Mary's eyes widened. "Mr. Tremayne, you needn't—"

"Mary, indulge me," he said.

Soon they were at the club. The doors to the hansom were opened for them, and Ian was lifting Marissa down. A doorman swept them into the club, greeting Ian by name. He spoke with the maître d', and they were quickly led to a table in a private room.

Potted palms adorned the room. The chairs were huge, elegant with carved lions' feet. The table was covered in snowy white linen, and the flatware upon the table was golden while the wineglasses were of the finest crystal. Soft light shimmered from candles in a chandelier.

Ian seated Marissa. Jimmy did a fair job of imitating him as he seated Mary. Ian ordered rack of lamb from the waiter, who obviously knew him. And champagne.

When the champagne came, Ian lifted his glass to Mary and Jimmy.

"To a lifetime of health and happiness!" They all sipped champagne.

"Aye, and thank you!" Jimmy exclaimed, leaping to his feet to toast in kind. "And to you, sir, and to Marissa! A lifetime of—"

He choked at the end, realizing that there was really little to wish them. The slow, taunting curve came to Ian's lip, and he lifted his glass to Marissa. "A lifetime of wealth," he murmured, "and health and happiness, too, of course."

Marissa smiled coolly. "Thank you so very much."

He turned from her with a shrug and spoke to Jimmy. "I'll be leaving tomorrow morning." He reached into his jacket pocket and produced a parcel of documents, which he handed to Jimmy. "Tickets, transfer points, the address and phone number for my home in San Francisco, everything you might need, I hope. I plan on being at the train station when you arrive, but should something prevent me, a carriage or a car will meet you."

Jimmy nodded gravely, accepting the packet. "Thank you, Mr. Tremayne. Thank you."

"Ah, another toast!" Ian said. He lifted his glass again. "To a long and prosperous business relationship between us!" he said.

"Hear, hear!" Mary cried, delighted.

Ian filled the glasses. Marissa discovered that she was acquiring quite a taste for champagne. It went down so easily, and it smoothed out the rough edges of discomfort and unease.

And fear! she thought unhappily. He had come so very close to seeing the name on Mary's wedding papers today!

Ah, but he hadn't really thought to look at them. He didn't suspect. He thought he remembered Marissa at times, but he didn't realize she had been the maid in the shadows or the child in the mining village. And still, tonight, each time he glanced her way, she knew he was condemning her for the one minor lie he had caught her in...

Her glass was empty. He filled it. She felt the sharp probe of his blue eyes, and lowered her lashes to study her crystal glass.

The food was brought and it was delicious. Marissa was saved from much conversation, for Ian questioned Jimmy, and Jimmy talked about Ireland, and wool—he knew wool very well. Ian told him how alike San Francisco and London could be at times, blanketed in fog, mysterious, beautiful. And through the fog you could see the bridge and the bay, and the houses with their gingerbreading and pastels and colors, and they were beautiful. Marissa listened to him, and was suddenly afraid again.

She didn't want to leave England. She didn't want to sail the distance of an ocean, then travel across a continent.

She looked up. Ian was watching her again. She flushed slightly, and her lashes lowered.

She toyed with dessert. The check was signed, and they were soon out on the street. "I'll hail you a cab," Ian said to Jimmy. "And see Marissa to her rooms."

She glanced up, startled, then realized that Jimmy and Mary were married. Legally. Naturally Ian presumed that Mary would be staying with Jimmy. But the thought of being left alone with Ian terrified her.

"Oh, but it's early yet!" she said hurriedly. "Perhaps they'd like to return to my suite for a while."

"For more champagne?" Ian asked politely.

How much champagne had she already swallowed, she wondered. Not enough. She felt dizzy, and guessed she would have a headache later, but at least she felt a little more capable of dealing with him.

"Champagne, sherry, conversation—" she began.

"They are *true* newlyweds, my dear. And surely seek their privacy," he said. He lifted his hand and flagged down a hansom.

There was nothing Marissa could do. She quickly hugged

Mary, not wanting to let her go. She kissed Jimmy, and perhaps clung to him too long.

Ian's arms disentangled her. "I'll see you in America!" he called to Jimmy.

"Aye, sir, in America!" And the bay horse pulling the cab clip-clopped into the night.

"Come on," Ian said roughly. He tugged Marissa's arm and she saw that a second cab was awaiting them.

"I can see myself to the suite," she said with what casual aplomb she could manage.

"You can scarcely walk," he said flatly, "and I wouldn't dream of allowing my dear wife to travel the streets of London alone."

He lifted her up and set her into the cab, then climbed up beside her, calling the address to the driver. They didn't speak but she felt the warmth of him beside her, the flex and movement of his every muscle. She felt the tension that had stayed with him, no matter how smooth his manner, since he had seen her in the church.

They came to her suite. When she had entered the parlor she tried to turn swiftly and thank him for the meal and for escorting her back.

He none too gently pressed her forward, entering determinedly behind her, then closing the door behind himself.

Marissa swept off her cape and moved into the room, dropping the cape upon the settee. Ian leaned against the door, his blue gaze searing.

She fought the champagne, for it was making her dizzy, and her vision was blurry. Perhaps it was for the best, when he stared at her so.

No! She needed her wits to deal with him.

She yawned extravagantly. "Really, Mr. Tremayne, it is late—"

"You were just saying that it was early."

"But I am suddenly so exhausted."

"Well, exhausted or no, Mrs. Tremayne, you've an explanation to make, haven't you?"

"Have I?"

"About your newlywed friends."

She shrugged. "I don't—"

"You lied to me about them."

"It seemed easier to introduce them as man and wife. I knew they were marrying the next day. Why on earth are you so angry about them?" she demanded, determined not to show her fear.

"Oh, I'm not angry about them at all," he said softly.

"Then?" she murmured.

He moved into the room at last. He was stalking her, she thought. She moved back. A quivering seized her. She was angry; she was uncertain.

And she knew that he was going to touch her, corner her and touch her and hold her to his whim. It was in his stride, in his eyes. And she shivered because she did not know if she despised the idea...

Or anticipated it.

"Then...?" she repeated on a note of desperation.

"Then..."

She was backed against the wall. He laid a hand flat on either side of her head, imprisoning her without touching her, except with that blue fire in his eyes.

"What I want to know, my dear Marissa, is just what else you've lied about to me."

"Really, there's nothing—"

"I will have the truth, Marissa. And I will have it tonight."

CHAPTER SIX

"I HAVEN'T LIED TO YOU about anything else!" Marissa protested. She slipped away quickly, moving around the room to keep a distance between them. Coming to the little silver tray with the decanters of brandy and sherry and whiskey, she paused, pouring out a snifter of brandy. She needed to be very calm. "Would you like something?" she asked him politely.

"Yes, I'd like the truth."

She sipped the brandy, studying him over the rim of the glass. "Your Yankee manners are atrocious, Mr. Tremayne."

He moved toward her. She swallowed the contents of the brandy glass, and it was suddenly plucked out of her hands. "Have I married a little drunkard as well as a cunning little liar?"

"A drunkard!"

"Lady, you've had enough champagne today to sink a ship."

"How dare you! You Yankee—"

"Yeah, yeah, us Yanks. It's been like this ever since we finally won that war in 1812."

She tried to move away, but he caught her arm. His touch was forceful, but not painful. She could feel his determination. She wasn't going to escape him again.

"Let's talk," he said flatly.

She didn't have much of an opportunity to resist; she found herself sitting on the settee with him beside her. Close beside her. His eyes blazed into hers.

"Let's have it, Marissa."

She raised her eyes to his. He was so damned determined! She suddenly wanted to spit out the truth and beg for mercy.

No. She wouldn't let him intimidate her. The truth could do nothing for any of them now.

Jimmy and Mary were legally wed.

And she was wed to this man.

She shook her head, allowing her lashes to fall over her eyes. Dear God, she should have left the brandy alone. The champagne had been bad enough. And she needed so desperately to be in control.

Especially tonight. Some fierce fever burned in Ian Tremayne tonight. His eyes seemed ringed with it, both fire and ice, burning hot one minute and cold the next. She'd seen him gentle, tender, amused and angry, but never so tense as this.

All because she had lied to him.

But the life she was living was a lie, and there was no way out of it, no way to tell him the truth. There was nothing to do but play her part, that of the spoiled and willful child of a very rich man.

She stared at him, chin high, eyes level. "I'm sorry that you are so affronted over such a very minor thing as the precise hour and date of a marriage."

"A lie is never a minor thing, Marissa."

"This one was," she insisted. "I knew that Jimmy and Mary would be married, and I wanted you—to accept them as man and wife. I couldn't have left here without them, you see."

"Your lives are so entwined, then? I'm curious. How?"

His eyes were maddening. So dark, so blue, so demanding. She felt pinned to the settee. Desperate. She didn't like the feeling. The warmth emanating from his body encompassed her. The clean scent of his soap hinted warmly of the man's masculinity, and the soft feathering of his breath when he spoke touched upon her face. The sensations were pleasant.

She suddenly wanted to laugh and touch his face, no matter how hard and forbidding that face.

It was the champagne, she thought. Do not touch, for he bites!

She closed her eyes and rested her head against the settee.

"Tell me about these very good friends of yours, Marissa."

"I can't. I'm quite exhausted. I need you to leave. I shall explain everything that you desire at some later time."

"Will you?"

"Indeed."

"I think not."

He caught her hands and pulled her up. Her eyes flew open, blazing with fury. "If you were any kind of British gentleman—"

"Well, I'm not. I'm not British at all. What I am is a Yank, remember, and therefore, according to you, my manners are by nature atrocious."

"All right, all right!" She snatched her hands free from his and leaped to her feet. There was a sudden blackness before her and she wavered. She caught hold of an oak table to remain standing. "Her father, Mary's father, was the vicar of our parish. As children, we were very good friends. And not long after her father died, she came to live with us. It's very simple, sir!" she announced scornfully.

"And Jimmy?"

"And Jimmy?" Marissa found that she was smiling slowly. "Why, she met him, and she fell in love with him. There's no mystery there, Mr. Tremayne."

"Ah, but your life seems to be shrouded in mystery, Mrs. Tremayne," he taunted softly.

"It's quite amazing that you should feel so, sir," she said sweetly.

"I want to know what else you've lied about," he returned.

"I've told you—"

"And I've warned you," he snapped.

She meant to walk by him very smoothly. Chin high, shoulders square—with a firm upper lip. But she had barely moved from the table when the swamping dizziness came over her again. She tripped—she was rather certain that she tripped right over his foot. The next thing she knew she was falling and, reaching out, she came in hard contact with his chest.

He half rose to catch her, then her impetus threw them onto the settee, her fingers curled into his starched white shirt, her body draped across his lap. His arms had wrapped instinctively around her to break the fall. Startled, she gazed into the blue depths of his eyes. She meant to jump quickly away, but she could not. She suddenly seemed to be enveloped in the strength and scent of the man, and in the power of his eyes. She did not move at all, but met his gaze. Heat seared through her. A sweet trembling began in her stomach and traveled like wildfire to her limbs. Delicately she moistened her lips with the tip of her tongue, seeking to speak, to break the curious hold.

And she was suddenly certain that he meant to speak, too. But he did not. Not really. Instead an oath shattered the air, and he bent down to her. He was going to kiss her again, she thought. She should rise, protest.

Instead she awaited the touch of his mouth. The sensations were again spiraling wildly through her. Something molten, something delicious, churned deeply within her. She had felt his kiss before. And she anticipated it now.

It was the champagne. Or the brandy. She could not think. Or perhaps…

It was just the man.

And then his lips touched hers, forming over them with a practiced and fierce demand. Hot and moist and so very sure, they drank in the fullness of her mouth, touching, invading, exploring, eliciting more fervent sensations to swirl and play wickedly within her blood. She felt again the urge to touch him, and this time she did, her fingers uncurling from his shirt front to touch his cheek and feel the texture of his bronzed flesh. She pressed closer against him, instinctively responding to the overwhelming sensuality of the man. Some small voice warned her that she was catapulting into danger with a stranger, with the enemy. But intelligent thought had long since eluded her. She felt only the sweep of his tongue, the molding of his lips, the pressure of his hands, holding her leisurely to his will.

His lips parted from hers.

"Indeed, madam, what other lies have you spoken?"

She fought his grip suddenly, furious, her head reeling.

"None!"

She struggled to rise, slamming her fist against his chest. "None! I am weary, I am exhausted, and you plague me endlessly while you pretend that we can live amicably in the same house. Please! I am too tired—"

"You are too drunk," he said dryly.

"Oh! And you didn't drink champagne as if it were water yourself!"

"I did not drink champagne out of fear."

"I am not afraid of you."

"You are afraid of some truth, and yes, Marissa, therefore you are afraid of me. Very much afraid of me."

"Oh!"

He released her and she leaped to her feet, pointing dramatically at the door. "Tremayne, we shall speak of this some other time, I tell you!"

She started for the door, but he stood and caught her arm. "We'll speak of it now! And take care, madam, that you never again show me a door before we are finished."

She heard his words, but she was suddenly too weary to fight him. She fell into his arms. Her eyes closed and she clung to his shoulders. She groaned softly. "Please, I cannot stand."

"You will stand. It's all a trick with you!"

"No!" she whispered. "No. This is no trick."

He carried her to the settee and set her down on it. He leaned over her, and though she had allowed her eyelashes to drift softly closed over her eyes, she was suddenly aware that he was concerned. She had told him the truth, her knees had buckled, and she had been able to stand no longer. But now she realized that perhaps this was the best game to play with him.

Her lashes fluttered open and she discovered that he was studying her intensely. She found herself returning his gaze, unable to look away. His left hand lay upon her hip while his right hand sat upon her shoulder and his face was close, bronzed, tense, close. She inhaled the clean scent of the man and felt the sudden rush of his breath against her cheek. She wanted to look away; she could not. A sweet cascade of sensation suddenly ran throughout her limbs, hot where he touched her and hot where his eyes seared into hers. It swept her breath away, and caused her heart to quicken its pace until she could feel the maddening pulse within her mind.

"Leave me—" she started to murmur, but her voice broke off for she realized that he was going nowhere.

His mouth was slowly descending upon hers.

His kiss was not gentle. No, not gentle at all.

His lips seared hers with a simmering anger just barely held in check. He did not hurt her, nor did he allow her any room for escape. There was force behind his touch, and still...

And still, somewhere within it, was the sweetness of seduction, of coercion. His left hand lay upon her hip while his right one caught her cheek, his thumb stroking her flesh while his kiss found its own haunting leisure. Her heart began to pound more fiercely. She didn't know if it was the sweet fire of the champagne or of the man entering into her blood, warming her, filling her with the same anger.

And the same passion.

She meant to protest. But instead her lips parted to his fierce demand, and she felt the intimate foray of his tongue, tasting her lips, delving into the dark and secret crevices of her mouth and seeming to enter into her soul. She felt the fascinating sweep of his tongue with her own. Her heart pounded. Darkness seemed to descend. The clean male scent that swept evocatively around him touched and stirred new sensations within her.

Her hands lay against his chest. She needed to push him away. She did not. She let her fingers roam over the fabric of his vest and felt as if she held tight while some whirlwind caught her. Then his lips raised from hers at last, and his eyes were upon hers again, sizzling with anger and fire, and she realized that no tenderness or pity had stirred his actions. Furiously, she shoved with all her strength against him and got to her feet.

"It's time for you to leave, Mr. Tremayne!" she gasped, shaking, wiping his kiss from her lips with the back of her hand as if she could erase the passion between them.

He didn't move. "I still haven't gotten an answer," he told her. "Or perhaps I have."

"I don't know what you're talking about. Now get up and get out."

"You are a rotten little liar," he told her softly.

"Meaning?"

"That was no innocent kiss."

"I did not kiss you."

"Ah, but you see, you returned the touch."

"I was trying to be polite."

"Polite!" he exclaimed, then he burst out laughing. "Dear Lord, how often are you polite? And with just how many men?"

"Oh, you are horrid!"

"Merely American."

"Is it one and the same?"

"I'm wounded, deeply."

"No, dear sir, you wound others deeply."

His voice remained light, but there was underlying danger in his tone. "I'm seeking the truth, my love."

Desperate, she cried out to him. "I haven't lied to you! Oh, dear Lord, help me! I'm trying to tell you—"

She broke off. He was on his feet at last, and heading toward her. Then she realized that he only meant to sweep past her on his way to the door. She inhaled quickly with relief, and he turned.

"I—I haven't lied to you!" she cried, but she faltered. And then she suddenly panicked as his hands came to rest upon her shoulders. She slammed her fists against his chest. "Damn you! Can't you just leave it be! You want your life; I want my privacy!"

But even as she spoke, her lips were still burning where his had touched them, and she shook with tremors from the intimacy they had shared. She hated him, and yet she longed to touch his face. She wanted to feel the contours of that hard, angry jaw. She wanted to soothe the anger away and see him smile with tenderness.

His voice thundered with anger. "You'll have your privacy when you've answered all my questions, Marissa, damn you!"

"You'll leave now!" she snapped. And then dizziness burst within her mind just as he pulled her into a hard embrace. She tried valiantly to straighten and free herself, but she fell into his arms. Her anger drained from her suddenly. Her eyes, wide and uncertain, stared into his. "Ian, please, I—"

"Ah, yes, you are falling again!" he taunted. "Poor sweet innocent! It is the champagne. You need nothing more than to be left alone. Out of the clutches of your cruel guardian— and husband."

She looped her arms around his neck, protesting. "Truly. It is the champagne. I should not have drunk so freely."

"That damnable champagne is there whenever you want it,

Marissa. You are not so inebriated as to act out whatever role you choose to play. I want the truth.''

"What truth?'' she cried out. She was within his arms, held there easily as he stared at her. She returned his gaze, fascinated by the color of his eyes, by the rugged planes and angles of his face. She wet her dry lips with the tip of her tongue and felt a sizzling tremor streak through her. She wanted to taste his kiss again. It was amazing, for she resented him, she could not care for him, and yet she did. "Ian," she murmured, and no other word would leave her lips.

Suddenly he was smiling, and some of his anger drained away.

"Perhaps I shall just discover the truth for myself," he said.

The truth about her, he thought. There was one way to know if she had entertained a lover before. And with the blood seeming to shimmer in his veins and the pounding in his head, he knew that discovering more about her was suddenly necessary to him. He had never wanted a woman more. "If I'll not have something from you in words this night, then by God, lady, perhaps I will have a wife! My manners are already considered rude, and as you claim the champagne, sweet, so can I claim the brandy!''

He unerringly found the route to the bedroom, long strides bringing them into the darkened room. She knew where they traveled. Winds created by his impetus stirred over her face, and she was vaguely aware of what she was doing. It was insane. So were the fires that stirred within her body and soul. She longed to taste his lips again, to know again the fever of his arms.

And more.

"You really must put me down," she told him.

"I intend to," he promised.

They entered the darkened bedroom, and he laid her down upon the bed, then sat beside her as glimmers of moonlight played in the room. She felt her breath coming quickly, but

she did not close her eyes. She sought his in the strange surreal light, and found he was looking at her hair.

It was splayed upon the pillow in the moonlight, shimmering like a thousand fires. His fingers moved quickly within it,
removing the few pins she had used to secure it from her face.
And when it stretched in burning, golden cascades around
them, he lowered his face to hers, catching her chin softly
between his two hands. "Earth and fire," he whispered softly.
"Passion, tension, spirit. God forgive me, for I'll not forgive
myself."

His words stirred a great unease within her soul, but his
kiss quickly wiped that unease away. In the darkness it was
suddenly magic. He tasted the rim of her mouth, and plunged
and delved deeply within it. He whispered against her throat,
against the lobe of her ear.

And then his hands were moving expertly over the tiny
pearl buttons of her elegant blouse. She barely felt the sheath
of silk whisper against her flesh as it was whisked away.

His kiss burned a sweetly forbidden fire against the length
of her throat, delicately, erotically pausing at the point where
her pulse beat wildly.

This was what a woman did when she was madly in love,
Marissa thought vaguely. Lose all sense and reason, and hunger for a man. She was not in love. She was wary, as an
intelligent lamb might be of an experienced, sometimes world-
weary wolf...

No, she was not in love. But she was fascinated, as she had
always been fascinated by him. Angry and fascinated. Careful
and suspicious and fascinated. Furious and fascinated.

Taunted and seduced and fascinated...

Taken in by the spell of his gaze upon her, by his very
touch. The subtle, masculine scent of him was stirring fires
and hungers within her soul. She was fascinated by the gentle,
callused brush of his fingers, by the strength within them, by
the power of his hands. Stirred and tempted and challenged

by the dark lock of hair that fell over his forehead in the mystic near darkness of the room. She was aware of what she did, of where they were, of where this new intimacy would take them. And it was wrong.

But it was also right. Something had been awakened within her. Something secret and beautiful, something of the dreams that Mary had spun, the dreams in which she had never believed. In the shadows, in the night, there was something beautiful and exciting. Something growing that she could not deny. She wanted to hold him, and hold him tight, and pretend that he did love her, to know just a taste of an emotion so rich and fine.

But this was not a dream! She struggled to remember that, but she felt drugged. She slipped into danger, and she saw the flames, yet resisting the sear of the fire seemed impossible. She had to stop him. She had to remind him that theirs was not the customary marriage.

That he did not want her...

She inhaled on a sweet shudder as his fingertips moved over her breast, untying the silken ribbons of her chemise, releasing the ties of her corset. She felt her breasts spill free of the restraint and the burning pressure of his lips low against the valley between them. She had let this go too far, oh, way too far. No, she had not let it, she had encouraged it, she had brought him here, to her.

Ian felt the first protest on her lips when he kissed her again, but he thought it more of her taunting, more of her game. He didn't understand what core of anger had burned so brightly within him, except that she had tricked him, she had lied, and he was suddenly damned sure that she had lied about more.

There *was* a lover. She had married Ian, perhaps planning all the while to turn to her lover. Perhaps to bring him with her across the ocean.

And he wondered what it mattered, there was so little that he could give her. He shouldn't be so angry, he should understand. He couldn't love her; he couldn't give her tenderness; he didn't even want to be near her. She was his wife, not a dance-hall girl.

But there was more to it than that. At least this night there was. There was that never-ending challenge in her beautiful green eyes, and there was the firelight that played within her hair. There was the impudence in her voice, the spirit, the anger, the laughter. The tilt of her chin. And now...the softness of her skin, the sweet taste of the champagne upon her lips, the subtle scent of her perfume.

Yes, the scent of her perfume.

He groaned aloud, taking her breast into the palm of his hand, gently covering the shadow-haunted peak with his mouth, curling his tongue over the nipple as his palm caressed the fullness of the mound. Again he felt her shudder, felt the faint murmurings of protest upon her lips. But even as she murmured, a fire of desire and longing stronger than her words, stronger than his own denial, swept raggedly through him. And again he kissed her lips, kissed them hungrily, angrily, then tenderly, bathing away any little hurt he might have inflicted with the stroke of his tongue.

He moved his fingers along the smooth silk of her stocking from her ankle to the lace of her drawers just above the knee, and there his fingers found the sleek softness of her bare thighs beneath the fabric. He teased her flesh, feeling her body move against his. And he felt again the protests bubbling to her lips, and silenced them with his tongue. He was not unaccustomed to women's finery, and easily found the ties to loosen the lace, and in seconds he had stripped the garment from her.

Alive with the fire of desire, he paid little heed to any other barriers between them. He seared her flesh with the hungry force of his kiss as he briefly adjusted his own clothing, then moved his weight against her body, between her thighs. She had ceased to protest, but trembled incredibly in his hold. Her pulse beat frantically at her throat when he touched it with his tongue. And when he paused, stroking her cheek to look down upon her, her eyes were emeralds, brilliant, stunning against the darkness, both dazzling and dazed. Her lips were parted softly, damp with his kiss, and her hair, that majestic hair, was still splayed in fire and splendor across the pillow. Her throat was long and white and elegant, and her breasts, bared and yet framed in lace and silk, were glorious, rouge peaked in the near darkness, shadowed, and still as tempting as original sin. Her eyes met his with some sudden and strange recognition, and she suddenly inhaled and cried out. ''Ian, I did not intend—''

He did not know what she intended—he knew only that he did not intend to let her speak. There was a mystique in the darkness. He had ceased to think or reason or remember. He threaded his fingers through her hair, holding her to his will as he forcefully kissed away her words.

And as his tongue invaded her mouth, he found the sweet petals of her sex, teasing first with the thrust of his desire, then plunging hard with the spiraling depths of his need. Then he stopped, stunned, waiting.

Not even his kiss could drown out her cry.

Tears stung Marissa's eyes, and she bit hard on her lip against the sudden pain.

Ian had grown still, dead still.

The magic of the night had slipped away, the beauty of the shadows, of the dreams within the room. Suddenly he was very real, and flesh and blood, a man, and not a dream of love. Marissa realized that she had brought him here, that she had been seduced, perhaps, but that she had seduced in turn. And his hand lay against her face, his thumb moving over her cheek.

And feeling the dampness of the tear that lay against her flesh.

"Marissa!" She felt the warmth of his whisper there, and she wouldn't allow him compassion or pity, not now.

"Dear God, don't!" she cried.

And he grew still again, but the pad of his thumb moved gently over her face, smoothing away the dampness. Then his lips touched where his thumb had been, ever gentle. And she longed to scream, to cry out, to toss him from her.

But he did not leave her. He kissed her again and again. Finding her brows, her throat, her lips, her earlobe, her lips again.

And then he moved.

Slowly, so slowly, she was barely aware of his thrust at first.

And she was keenly, achingly aware, because slowly, so slowly, the magic was evoked once again.

She didn't know when she fell within the twilight swirl, not when she felt the budding excitement begin anew. It eased the burning at the apex of her thighs, yet created fire all over again. It came like lava, lustrous, sleek, sweet, moving through her limbs. It stretched out like lightning from the center of her being, and it warmed her, and returned again to that center, making her rise ever higher with the growing wonder of sensation.

And then the softness was gone, the slowness of his motion cast away. He moved like lightning, hard, fast, demanding. His arms were tight around her, and she realized that sounds were escaping her again, no longer protests, but exhalations and sweet, sweet moans. And he urged her to rise against him, and she did, arching to meet his every thrust, twisting, undulating, thinking that she could bear no more, take no more...yet ever reaching for the stars.

And then it seemed that those stars exploded above her and around her. The darkness was shattered with light, and then the light was plunged into darkness. She felt him, hard and powerful, driving deeply into her and shuddering as a hot lava seemed to fill her again. Tremors had seized her, too. Little tremors, bringing again the wonder, the stars, the darkness and the light. And when they left her at last, she was shivering.

It was cold, for he had lifted his weight away. And even as the magic she had barely glimpsed began to fade from her grasp, she realized that he was leaning upon an elbow, staring at her.

And the darkness was no cover against the probe of his eyes. She was in complete dishabille; he still wore his elegant jacket.

She turned aside, groping blindly for the covers, swept into a tempest of emotion. She wanted to hate him, but she knew that she did not. And that was a bitter thought, for she felt again the nagging pain of what she had done, what they had done, and it tore at her heart.

"Why didn't you tell me?"

His voice was a rasp. He seemed so angry still. He seemed angry! It was surely her place.

"Tell you what?" she snapped.

"I assumed—"

"You assumed!"

His hand touched her shoulder, and she wished that she dared to turn, to look into his eyes. But she lay there rigidly, her shoulders tense.

"I'm sorry," he said simply.

"Please, don't be."

An impatient oath escaped him. "Marissa, I did not force you—"

"No!" she cried, flinging back the covers, then swearing as she tried to rise and tripped over the shambles of her clothing. "You did not force me."

He rose quickly, which did not please her, for he appeared so respectable. The disarray of his hair, that dark lock lying over his forehead, was the only sign of all that had passed between them. He was coming around the bed to her, she realized. She wrenched the cover from the bed and swept it regally around herself like a cape. And she backed away, trying to escape him, but he quickly caught up with her, taking her arm.

"What do you think you're doing?"

"I'm leaving—"

"It's your room, you little fool."

"But—" She tried to break free from him. He released her, much to her surprise. Off balance, she fell against the wall.

And she was in his arms once again. And then she saw his eyes, blue, burning into hers. "Damn you!" he said softly. "It's the champagne, right?"

"Oh! Leave me alone!"

"I will."

He laid her upon the bed, but made no move to join her again. "Go to sleep," he told her harshly.

"Sleep! I cannot sleep—"

"You wanted to be alone. I'm leaving you alone. Cherish the privacy, my love. And sleep!" he snapped.

"You must leave—"

"Come the daylight, I am leaving. On a ship across the ocean, remember?"

"With any luck, you will be swallowed within it!" she hissed, trembling.

He paused. "Ah, but luck does not seem to be with you lately, does it my love?" He did not seem to expect an answer. He turned on his heel and left the room.

For long moments she lay there, numb.

Then Marissa felt again the burning that would not ease completely from her body. She closed her eyes, and remembered his kiss, his touch.

And it seemed that her flesh burned everywhere as she remembered the sweetness that had invaded her, the ecstasy. The sounds that had escaped her, the way they had been. She was angry with herself, unable to believe what she had done with her eyes wide open.

I tried to protest! she told herself.

But she had not. Not really. Perhaps she could not have gotten him to leave her rooms, but she could have stopped him from this.

It was the champagne...

No, she had clung to the champagne. It had been an excuse, and she could not deny it.

She wanted to scream. She wanted to claw at his face. She wanted so badly to hate him. And then she realized that her cheeks were damp again, that she had been crying.

And she had been crying because she did not hate him at all.

She craved things she had never imagined wanting before.

A home. A husband, a real husband. Happiness.

And more.

She wanted love.

CHAPTER SEVEN

IAN STRODE to the parlor of the suite and poured himself a generous portion of brandy. The heat of the liquor burned his throat and seemed to shudder its way through him, and still he felt at a loss. He sank down on the settee, studied his glass and swore softly to the night.

What the hell had he done?

Well, you wanted to know if she was lying, he reminded himself. You wanted the truth about the lover the squire had said would destroy her life.

And while she might have lied about half a dozen other things, she had definitely never bedded with the boy.

And that was what you wanted to know, wasn't it? he asked himself mockingly.

And now he knew. Now he had touched and tasted and entered into the realms he had forbidden himself. She had goaded him into it, damn her. Damn her a thousand times over.

His fingers constricted so tightly around his empty brandy glass that it shattered within his hand. Absently he began to pick up the pieces, scarcely aware that he had cut himself, that his palm was bloody.

He dropped the pieces of glass on the table and stared at his hand. Then he swore suddenly, feeling the ragged pain that tore at his heart.

He had betrayed Diana, and he had betrayed himself.

Damn the girl. She had goaded him.

But he couldn't really blame her, he realized, closing his

eyes against the headache that was beginning to pound at the base of his skull.

No, he couldn't blame her.

He had breathed in the sweet scent of her perfume, he had touched the softness of her flesh. And he had fallen into the green fire of her eyes, and there had been only himself to blame. He had wanted her.

She was his wife, he reminded himself. And she had given him what he so rarely found these days. Moments of forgetfulness. More. She had poured over him like a gentle balm, and she had given him a taste of fire. She had eased him in a way that he could not remember being eased. They had made love in a tempest, and the tempest had been good and sweet.

There could even be peace between them.

He swore violently, raking his hair as he came to his feet. No, there could be nothing between them. Nothing at all. Tonight was a mistake that would not happen again.

He heard a soft rustling and rose quickly, turning toward the bedroom door.

Marissa was there. She had changed to a very prim and concealing nightdress, white cotton with blue flowers and a high laced Chinese collar. She seemed composed, and he almost smiled, for it seemed that whatever happened, she held her chin high. Her eyes mirrored the fire in her hair. He swallowed, feeling his fingers clench into fists at his sides, the whole of him constrict with tension. She was very beautiful, willful but proud, and he realized that he admired her. A curious tenderness tempered his rage. Perhaps the anger would not be so great if she did not elicit such a staggering desire. In all men, he imagined, not just himself.

But he had misjudged her; he knew that now.

Words hovered on her lips as she met his eyes, then her gaze lowered. A frown puckered her brow, and she seemed to have forgotten what she had intended to say.

"Your hand!" she exclaimed.

He looked and saw that tiny drops of blood were falling from his clenched fist onto the elegant Persian carpet beneath his feet.

He lifted his hand against his chest. "It's nothing."

But she walked to him and took his hand. Her touch was electric, and he nearly wrenched his hand from her grasp.

Why the hell wasn't she angry with him? Screaming again that he had to get out?

She had been angry, he realized. Furious. Until she had seen the blood. Then it seemed as if some instinct of caring had set in. What a complex creature she was! Cold as ice, hard as nails when she was determined to have her way. Soft at times, capable of laughter.

And still, though he knew her innocent now of certain things, he was still convinced that she was hiding something from him. Every once in a while the emerald fire would leave her gaze, and he would know that she was afraid of some discovery.

But now her gaze was innocent. There was no anger in it, no fear, and for once, no defensive challenge. Her eyes were wide as they touched his, wide and surprised.

"My God, you've really cut it quite severely," she murmured.

"It's nothing," he said curtly, but she had already headed for the bedroom, only to return with a white swatch of bandage and a pharmacist's bottle.

"You might need stitches," she said. He stared at her blankly. "Will you give me your hand, please?"

"I don't need—"

"It will sting, but not that badly," she said. "Give me your hand. Do you want an infection in it? A fever?"

He gritted his teeth and stuck out his hand. She opened his fingers, surveying the cut.

"If you're so anxious for me to sink to the bottom of the

ocean, why not choose a deadly infection instead?'' he asked
wryly.

"Too slow, and not nearly dramatic enough," she returned
quickly. She dabbed at the cut delicately.

"Not true at all. I could die slowly and painfully, and at
the last moment, you could rush to my bedside, hold my hand
and be a virtuous, loving wife for all to see.''

"Um...but I should have to come to America for that. If
you disappear to the bottom of the sea, I won't have to leave
at all.''

"And the money will be all yours.''

She looked up at him, startled. "If you—if you were to
pass away—my inheritance would fall to me?''

He smiled slowly and leaned against the settee, watching
her. "Planning my demise?''

"Maybe.'' She liberally applied the red stuff, and caught
off guard, he let out a gruff oath. "Oh, come!'' she cried.
"Children are painted day and night with this medicine, and
they do not protest.''

"Really? I think that you are planning my demise.''

"Um. Death by iodine solution.'' She deftly wound the
white bandage around his hand, tucking it in neatly. He stared
at his hand, somewhat surprised that she had learned to tend
to minor injuries so competently and swiftly in the secure
world of her father's manor. He looked from his hand to her
face, and their eyes met. And her cheeks were suddenly
flooded with red, reminding him that it had been only minutes
since they had met upon the most intimate level possible.

Marissa leaped to her feet and Ian realized that their
thoughts had traveled like paths. He was startled by the rise
of heat that swept through him when he recalled her touch.
Thoughts came unbidden to his mind. Sweet carnal thoughts
of the volatile pleasure she had created, though she knew very
little. Thoughts of her softness and her beauty. Of mist and
shadows and forgetfulness. Given time, given tenderness, she

could be a lover like no other with her firebrand hair a tangle
to entwine them...

No. He tightened his jaw against the heat and the anger and
the pain that knotted and twisted inside him. He stood also,
and she backed away, and he smiled, glad that she had done
so. Things were becoming too easy between them. Laughter
had come too easily. And there had been a curious closeness
between them when she had tended his hand. He didn't want
it; he had to break it.

"Marissa, I apologize for this night. My American manners
were truly faulty. But you needn't fear. Such an evening will
never occur again."

Something flickered in her eyes, but other than that, her
expression did not alter. She scarcely seemed to breathe.
"Marissa, did you hear me? I said that I was sorry."

"I heard you."

"Well?"

"What does it matter? The harm is done."

He exhaled impatiently. "I'm telling you that—"

"I don't care what you're telling me. It doesn't matter.
Weren't you leaving?"

"I had left you alone, my love. You followed me out here."

"I wanted to see that you were gone."

"Well, I'm not." He was anxious to leave. Why did she
bring out everything perverse in him? "It's nearly morning
now. I might as well wait for the day."

"You can't stay here!" she protested.

He arched a single brow in challenge. Her eyes narrowed.
They both knew she hadn't the strength to throw him out.

She circled behind him. He heard her voice at his back,
innocent, soft. "Is it true, Mr. Tremayne, that if you do sink
to the bottom of the ocean—or die that long and painful death
of infection—that my inheritance falls straight to me?"

A smile curved his lips. "So I believe." He turned quickly,

catching her hand. "Would you add murder to your other sins, my love?"

She snatched her hand away. "Surely, never, sir! But then again, you do not know me well—"

"Well enough," he interrupted smoothly, and was rewarded with a slight coloring in her cheeks again.

"You'll have to wonder, won't you?" she said sweetly.

"My eye will ever be upon you," he promised pleasantly enough.

Her lashes lowered demurely. "I'm sure that will be entirely unnecessary. I shall pray for divine retribution instead."

"Ah, but I am truly curious. Which of us is it that the divinity might bring retribution against?" he queried softly.

Again her cheeks colored softly. "Perhaps we both need to thank the divinity that it will be quite some time before we meet again." She turned regally and headed for the bedroom.

Thank God, indeed, he thought, wincing as tension seized him. He knotted his fingers into fists again, bringing a fresh wave of pain to his hand. She was too adept at whatever game she played.

And too damned superior. He had expected tears and fierce repercussions. He had meant to remind her brutally that it had been as much her fault as his own.

But she had never implied that it had been anything other than something they had both created. She had kept her dignity beautifully.

"Don't think, Marissa, of changing any of the plans I have made for you. You will arrive via the transportation I have arranged, on the proper date."

She paused and looked at him, surprised. "I hadn't intended to change anything. I will arrive just as you have commanded."

"Ah, yes, I imagine that you must. You'll be wanting your allowance."

"Yes."

"What a pity! The sacrifices you must make for money!"

She shrugged, and something about the way she stood ignited his anger and his passion. The challenge was alive in her eyes, just as the fire burned in her hair. "I had nearly decided that you were not so crude and terrible a man."

He found himself walking swiftly toward her and taking her by the shoulders. He wanted to shake her. Fighting for control, he realized that he wanted to do much more than shake her, that he wanted to drag her into his arms again, taste her lips, force his way to her very soul.

He did not shake her; he defied the violence within himself. He merely held her, his eyes dark and narrowing. "Don't deceive yourself, my love. I am very crude, and terrible. Don't ever deceive yourself otherwise!"

She did not flinch, but returned his stare, her head, as always, high, her eyes dazzling, moist, as if there might have been a hint of tears within them.

No, she would not cry.

He released her, fighting the urge to shove her from him. He turned and strode angrily toward the door, but once there, he paused. He did not turn to her.

"I will meet your train when it arrives, my love. See that you are on it."

He flung open the door and strode out.

And he wandered into the depths of the London fog, wondering just what web it was that she could spin that could evoke such a tempest of emotion within a man.

He walked in the fog to forget.

But when he stripped down in his own room for what remained of the night, he was haunted with dreams.

Dreams of Diana.

But Diana's face faded away, and new dreams came to haunt him. Dreams in which he held her—Marissa—and met her emerald gaze. Touched her naked flesh.

And felt the whisper of her words against his flesh. A whisper so soft he could not hear the words...

No.

He tossed in his sleep, and the whispers became louder. Whispers of tenderness, of love.

He would never love again.

He could never touch her again.

She was his wife.

He jerked up, covered with sweat, and slammed his fists into his palm. He inhaled sharply as pain assailed him, and he was glad of the pain, for it released him.

Thank God it was morning. He would soon be on a ship headed for home. Feeling the ocean breeze, letting it cool his head.

And his loins.

He would forget her, forget the night they had shared. By God, he would.

"You look grand, Marissa!" Theo told her. He stared at her with obvious pride as he looked her over, still holding her shoulders after the hug with which he had greeted her. "So very grand. I can't seem to get over just how wonderful you look!"

Marissa smiled at him as the cool morning breeze lifted the tendrils of hair at her forehead and set them gently upon her face. It was a beautiful day. The sky was a radiant blue with just a few puffs of clouds. It was Sunday, so there was no dynamiting to be heard. The world seemed quiet, and the landscape, with its mauves and greens and browns, rolled in the gentle silence. Sheep and cattle grazed the fields that stretched beyond the ramshackle cottages of the village. The few creatures that added substance to the life eked out by the miners.

But then she turned toward the cottages, small, one-room residences for the most, pathetically reaching toward respectability as the miners' wives placed what fall flowers they could find upon the windowsills.

Grand. Theo thought she looked grand.

And here, perhaps, she did.

She had spent money on herself. Mary had warned her not to appear in San Francisco without a proper wardrobe, and had convinced her that they couldn't keep on sharing a wardrobe. "You've sacrificed your soul for the money—and for us, of course!" she had reminded Marissa. "You should have something for yourself."

Mary would never know all that she had sacrificed, Marissa thought wearily, for Marissa would never tell her, no matter how close they were. But she did need clothing, so she had allowed Mary to guide her to the shops in London, but she had used her portion of the inheritance allowance very carefully. She had been far more careful of price than she had been of style, yet still, she had managed to select some very elegant pieces at very reasonable prices. Today she wore a simple cotton dress with a crocheted collar, but the designer had created a very elegant bustle just the right size for fashion, and she had found a charming bonnet with an egret feather that perched at an angle upon her forehead.

And perhaps, she thought, she appeared grand because there was no hint of coal dust upon her person....

She had no right to be ashamed of the coal dust, she told herself. The miners were good people.

Far better than she. Most of them would probably look upon her deceit with horror.

She couldn't think about that now. She linked her arm with her uncle's, her smile still firmly in place, and started walking toward the house. "Uncle, I'm going to America with Mary."

"America!" He stopped on the pebbled path and stared at her. "Marissa, so very far! Why, child! I'll never see you again."

"Don't say that!" Marissa cried. She couldn't bear to hear

such words. His slim face, haggard and worn and yet beautiful in the love and wisdom within the lines and crevices, was very dear to her. "You'll come to be with me soon enough." It was a lie; he couldn't really be with her. Not for years.

Unless Ian Tremayne did sink to the bottom of the sea. And despite the tangle of emotions she felt for the man, she realized that she did not really wish his demise—by fair means or foul.

Just thinking of him brought color to her cheeks, and tremors raced along her spine. She lowered her face and quickly spoke. "You're to retire, Uncle, and I mean it. Mary has given me a fantastic salary, and I've more than enough to spare for you."

"You're not to take care of me, child," Theo told her, pushing open the door to his cottage. Marissa preceded him in and sat at the rough-hewn table before the cooking fire. A black pot sat above the flames, and a kettle sat upon a heated rock. Water for the kettle came from an outside well. There were no conveniences here.

Nothing elegant, nothing fine, she thought, but her eyes were stinging with tears. Except love, for Theo loved her, and wasn't that worth more than anything elegant or fine?

She exhaled, pulling off her gloves, and smiling at her uncle. She meant to keep him alive to love her, she reminded herself. He was staring at her worriedly, and she was suddenly afraid that she had changed somehow, that all the things she had done were emblazoned upon her features. No, that couldn't be, she assured herself. "Uncle Theo, be reasonable. You cannot continue in the mines."

"Marissa—"

"Uncle Theo, do you love me?"

"Marissa, you know that I do!"

"Then you'll stay alive, for me."

He made a sound of impatience, then his cough seized him and he doubled over, wheezing for breath. Marissa jumped to her feet and patted his back, then quickly poured him a glass of cool water from the clay pitcher on the table. He sipped it gratefully, eyeing her all the while. She made him sit. "Theo, you must listen to me. I mean to set up a little school. I went to see the new young curate about it and he assured me that I had provided amply to bring in a teacher. And they said that the old storage building could be suitably made over, but the teacher will need help with the people here, and with odds and ends and such. Uncle Theo, you must be the one to give the help, to be my representative, don't you see?"

He was still wheezing, and it took him several minutes to answer. "So you are moving to America," he finally said softly.

"But you will come soon!" she insisted.

He didn't say anything, and she knew suddenly that he didn't want to come. This was his home, despite the soot and poverty. His friends lived and worked and had died here, and he had always thought to do the same.

Well, he wasn't going to die. And there had to be a better life for the others here.

"Uncle, you will come soon enough," she said.

He nodded, and she squared her shoulders. One day she would have to find a way to come back for him.

"There's rumblings of protest against the shareholders, you know, Marissa," Theo said. "The men are trying hard to find a way for better conditions."

"And so they should," Marissa agreed. "But, Uncle Theo, you're out of it now. Protest is for the young men."

"Wait until the shareholders learn about your school," he warned her.

"The vicar will not let the school be closed," she said, praying that it was true. Not even Mr. Lacey dared defy the vicar, who had caused tremendous havoc when a lad of ten had died from overwork in the tunnels a few years past. "Uncle Theo, you have to make sure that the vicar hears about any trouble Mr. Lacey might decide to cause.''

Uncle Theo sat and stared at her, then sighed. "All right, my girl,'' he promised softly. "I'm out of the mines, and living on your charity.''

"It's not my charity! What is mine is yours, Uncle.''

"Ah, but you work to earn it!''

"Working for Mary is no hardship,'' she said uneasily.

"And glad I am that you're her companion, so fine and sweet a lady. At least I rest assured that she asks nothing difficult or ill of you, lass. She's indeed a great and moral lady, and I rest easy, knowing you're in her company.''

Marissa folded her hands in her lap and looked at them, feeling a burning sensation invade her once again. Mary was a very fine lady. And no, Mary would never ask anything ill of her.

The lies and deceit were all her own. And so was the night in which she had cast away her pride and innocence. For a stranger. A stranger she had married in a massive lie.

A stranger who seemed to hate her. Ever more deeply since the tempest and tenderness...

"Marissa, are you all right? You're pale as death!'' Theo exclaimed.

She looked at him in dismay. "No, I'm—I'm fine, Uncle, honest.'' She smiled quickly. "I'm simply famished, and the pot is sending off the most delicious aroma! Come, let's eat! You always could create the most wonderful meals from so very little. And, oh! I've got to get the coachman to bring in the things I've brought from the manor.''

"Ah, Marissa, did you take more from Miss Ahearn on my poor behalf?''

"We'll be leaving, Uncle. The larder was overstocked. You sit now, and I'll serve our supper.''

"Marissa—''

"Come, Uncle, please? I'll not be able to be with you for

months and months now. Please, sit down and tell me the gossip and let me serve the soup!''

So coaxed, Theo sat, and as Marissa dished up the soup and made tea, he entertained her with stories about the mines and miners and their children. He told her about the day they had managed to ''accidentally'' knock over a bin of coal dust right on Mr. Lacey's head. ''He was madder than a hornet, he was! But he couldn't find no one to blame, could he, and so we all had a good laugh at his expense!''

Marissa laughed, too, imagining Mr. Lacey's fat jowls covered in coal dust. Then she managed to give Theo more pounds sterling than he usually saw in a year, and his awe as he looked at the money suddenly made everything she had done seem worth it all. And there would be more. There would be a school that might save some child from this life, just as Mary had saved her.

No matter how tragic or humiliating her life might prove to be, it would all be worth it.

She sipped her tea, finding that her hand was shaking. Ian was gone, she reminded herself. He was somewhere on the Atlantic right now, and she still had weeks before she would have to see him again.

But there were so many things she couldn't forget! So many things that plagued her! Even now, sitting here, in Uncle Theo's cottage, she could see Ian's face. His eyes alive with fire in the shadows and the darkness. Sizzling with the heat as he moved within her...

She couldn't breathe, and she forced herself to see another picture. His eyes with the fire of fury within them as he warned her, ''Don't ever deceive yourself. Don't ever deceive yourself. I am a crude and terrible man...''

She'd married him; she'd bedded with him. For money? What did that make her?

She felt as if she was going to be sick.

"Marissa, you're as pale as a ghost again. You can't be going to America if you're ill—"

"I'm not ill, I swear it! And I'll write, every week, I promise, Uncle Theo. Oh, Uncle! I do love you so much!" She threw herself into his arms and hugged him fiercely, and willed the memories away. She had done what she had to do, and nothing more.

"And I love you, child. Oh God, I do love you, more dearly than you shall ever know!" he promised. His gnarled hands moved over her hair tenderly, and she suddenly wished that she had never known a different life, that she could stay with him, sheltered in his arms and by his love.

She yearned to close her eyes and pretend that she had never gone to London with Mary, never seen Ian there. Never married him, and never been—touched by him.

But she could not. The die was already cast. And no matter what his anger toward her, she knew he would come after her if she did not arrive in San Francisco.

She could not betray Mary or Jimmy or her uncle.

"What is it, Marissa? What's wrong?" Theo asked her gently.

"Nothing. Just me, Uncle Theo. Hold me tightly, please." He held her until night fell and it was time to go.

Alone in Mary's handsome coach then, she waved goodbye until Uncle Theo was only a speck in the darkness. Indeed, all the mining village was nothing but a speck in the night...

Like a particle of coal dust.

And then she wept, silent tears streaming down her cheeks. She wept for Theo, for the village and for herself. And then she remembered again the first time she had seen Ian Tremayne, the very first time, here in this same dingy, little town fast disappearing into the night.

She remembered her fury, and her thoughts.

She would be a great lady. She would show him.

Ah, yes! She would show him!

She dried the tears from her cheeks and sat straight in the carriage.

And by the time she reached Mary and Jimmy and the manor, no sign of her distress remained.

She would show Mr. Ian Tremayne. She would never shed another tear.

ONE WEEK LATER, at the appointed time, she, Mary and Jimmy stood by the ship's rail.

And this time, it was England's shore she watched disappear.

Mary cried softly. But Marissa was true to herself. She did not shed a tear.

She looked away. Toward the west.

To America.

And to the new life.

CHAPTER EIGHT

San Francisco
January, 1906

A TAP SOUNDED on the door to Marissa's compartment, and she paused in the act of pinning her hat at a jaunty angle that defied the dread in her heart. When she did not respond to the knock, the porter called out cheerfully, "San Francisco! Next stop San Francisco! Five minutes now, Mrs. Tremayne."

Five minutes, Marissa thought, a mere five minutes, and a journey that had seemed epic in its length and scope would be over. She had crossed the mighty Atlantic Ocean, traveling first class on a great ocean liner. Then she had boarded the first of the several trains that had taken her across the entire American continent.

There had been so very, very much to see, to assimilate. She was English, and proud of England.

But this country...

There could be nothing like it. A land of such startling contrasts and beauty. Earth that was green and covered with forests, and then deserts that were orange and gold and mauve and fascinating.

And then there were the people. Everyone seemed to live here. Everyone. German, Dutch, Scandinavian. Black, red, yellow. Oh, London was a melting pot, but this...

She felt such an excitement for the country. She loved each new day.

Until the end.

Today had brought them to the Bay, and to the train ferries, which had brought them into the city. Five minutes and they would arrive. And Mary and Jimmy would set up housekeeping in marital bliss, and she...

She had cast herself into a prison of her own making with a man who never ceased to infuriate...

And fascinate...

She closed her eyes. It was difficult to breathe.

She hadn't cared, she reminded herself. She had sworn to Mary that she wanted nothing more than security. That she had no patience with sentiment. And she had received all she wanted. Theo would be well, a school was under way, she was dressed in silks and laces, and she had traveled the North Atlantic and the great width of America, all in style.

And still, she could feel the bars of her prison closing in on her now. She could almost hear the clang of iron and feel the reverberation as it trembled deep within her soul.

Soon, very soon.

Her time of payment would begin.

MADAM LILLI'S was unique, even among the endless supply of waterfront dance halls that graced some of the lesser streets of the city.

The house had been there since before the gold rush. With the Victorian era, fine gingerbreading had been added to the quaint Colonial architecture. And Lilli, being fond of colors, had added paint and trim until the house stood out like a gilded lady herself, both tarnished and beautiful.

Lilli, arrayed elegantly upon a settee, twitched a feather boa over her shoulder and studied Ian with wide gray eyes as he stared out the window. "That's the third time you've pulled out your watch, Ian. And you haven't paid the slightest heed to a single word that I've said."

He spun around, pocketing his watch, and leaned against the windowsill. "You're the one who said you had no need of conversation,'' he told her, far more sharply than he had intended.

She seemed to flinch, and he was sorry. He swore inwardly once again at the wife arriving at the station this evening.

The wife who had best be arriving, he reminded himself. He wouldn't put it past her to fail to appear. And then what would he do? He'd have no choice. He'd have to find her.

"I don't recall asking a lot of you," Lilli said evenly, the hurt evident in her voice. "I don't mind your Nob Hill mistress, and I don't expect to go to the opera or the theater with you. However, I do appreciate it when you at least pretend that you care who you are with."

He exhaled slowly. "Sorry, Lilli."

Lilli nodded, her lashes sweeping low over her face. He had hurt her, and he knew it, and felt the worse for it. There were no pretenses about Lilli. She was a showgirl with a place to run. She was careful when she selected her lovers, but she made love with a rare talent that bespoke her experience.

She wasn't anything like Diana. Indeed, she was the farthest thing in the world from Diana, with her voluptuous figure and tinted red hair. But it was the very fact of the difference and her forthright honesty that had brought him to Lilli—and the fact that she asked nothing of him, not even simple caring.

"Why do you keep pulling out your watch?" she queried softly. "It's none of my business, of course, and I'm not demanding conversation—"

He strode away from the window and kissed her on the top of the head. "My wife is arriving today."

"Your wife!" She swept the boa around her and leaped up, stunned. "Wife?" she said again. Then she started to laugh, sinking down on the crimson day bed. "You're meeting your wife this evening and you came to see me this afternoon?"

"She's not a wife for real, Lilli," he said flatly. He lifted an arm, looking for an explanation. "She's—she's a ward, really. I'm her guardian."

"So you married her?" Lilli said, fascinated. "It can't be money, you've plenty of your own. I admit—I don't begin to understand."

"Neither do I," he muttered.

She smiled broadly. "Not that I mind. But the charming widow, Mrs. Grace Leroux, is going to mind terribly. In fact, I think I shall enjoy the way she will mind. Hmm. Guardian. Ward. How—how European. Tell me, what's she like? I con- jure up images of a schoolgirl with pigtails. And perhaps buck teeth."

"No, I'm afraid not. In fact, she's quite stunning."

"You've a stunning wife arriving, and you're here?" Lilli said, her voice suddenly very soft.

He was here *because* his wife was arriving, he realized. Because he was damned determined he wasn't going to change his life. His voice hardened again.

"It was an arrangement, Lilli, nothing more. You know my feelings about marriage."

"Yes, I know them," she said, smiling ruefully. "But you see, I never expected you to marry me. Now Grace, she is going to have her problems. She's never believed that you wouldn't marry again. And of course, she was right, since you've a wife arriving. It's just that she assumed that she was going to be the wife."

"Well, she shouldn't assume things, should she?" Ian said. To his annoyance, he realized that he had drawn out his pocket watch again. Irritated, he shoved it back where it be- longed.

"It's all right—you can run out," Lilli told him.

"I'll be damned if I'm running anywhere," he said.

"You'll be late."

"Then I'll be late," he said flatly. He'd be as late as he

wanted. He'd while away the evening with Lilli's sweet brand of forgetfulness.

But he hadn't come today for forgetfulness, he realized.

He'd come because he didn't want to remember the feel of the golden-haired girl in his arms. He wanted to assure himself that he'd never fall beneath her spell again. There were other women to make love to. Women like Lilli.

"Tell me," Lilli said huskily, sweeping him into her embrace as he sat beside her on the day bed, "is the new Mrs. Tremayne aware of this open marriage? Does she, too, intend to find her own brand of entertainment?"

He stiffened. "What?"

"Ian, I was teasing you."

He stood and straightened his cuffs, suddenly impatient to be on his way. He kissed Lilli's cheek and strode toward the door.

"Ian!" Lilli called after him anxiously. "I've a new show opening Saturday night. Will you come? Please? Your patronage brings in so many others."

"Yes, surely, if you think that it will help," he promised. Then he paused. "No. I'd wring her pretty little neck."

"What?" Lilli said.

"No, she's not part of any open marriage, Lilli. I'd wring her neck."

Lilli laughed softly. Ian walked out the door, closing it quietly behind him. Then Lilli's smile slowly faded. A quiet ache formed within her heart. No, she had never deceived herself. She could have never been his wife. His feelings, what he gave her, had been real enough, but he was deceiving himself now.

The marriage meant more than he was willing to admit, it seemed. Far more than he was willing to admit.

A wife was one thing. A wife who mattered was quite another.

And so the ache in her heart.

She sighed softly and rose and walked to the window and looked out at the fog as it rolled in.

She'd still stand by him, as a friend.

She smiled slowly. It might even be amusing to see the very grand Mrs. Leroux meet the new Mrs. Tremayne.

Lilli spun around quickly, calling for her maid. She was suddenly very determined to see the new Mrs. Tremayne herself. Maybe she would even meet her.

Ah, the girl wouldn't want to meet a woman from her husband's past. But she should, for Lilli was not the real competition. And if the girl seemed to warrant it, Lilli just might be willing to offer her a certain assistance when she met the real dragon lady in her husband's past.

MARISSA inhaled sharply. The train was braking. They were pulling into the station.

Mary burst into the compartment, breathless, her cheeks flushed. "This is it! We're here!"

They stared at one another for a minute, then they hugged fiercely. "Oh, Marissa! You've done so much for us!" Mary said.

Afraid that she was going to choke or cry, Marissa answered quickly. "Don't be silly. I'm the one living in the lap of luxury. And I'm afraid that we'll all sink if we're ever caught."

"Don't you be silly," Mary protested. "This is America. We're never going to sink."

Marissa nodded. She should have been the one so determined.

Jimmy burst through the narrow doorway. "Ladies, come on, we're here!" He was carrying Mary's small travel bag and picked up Marissa's. Smiling, Mary turned to follow him as he hurried down the train aisle. He moved with confidence, Marissa thought. Both he and Mary had changed over the long journey. They'd found a new strength in one another.

And she had been losing her own determination in silly daydreams.

She squared her shoulders, dreading the moment when she would see Ian Tremayne again, yet curiously longing to do so, too. He had said that he would come to meet them. Had he done so? Or had he forgotten the wife he had not wanted?

She hurried after Jimmy and Mary. It was a new world. And she'd sworn to herself once that she would show Mr. Tremayne her mettle.

At the steps to the platform she paused for a moment. Twilight and fog were falling over the city. There was little she could see beyond the station, but as her eyes adjusted to the gaslight and the coming night, she became aware of the man standing on the platform.

He was framed in light and shadow, and she saw nothing but his silhouette at first, tall and dark. Even the shadows became him, enhancing the breadth of his shoulders, the leanness of his hips, the fit of his clothing.

She didn't need light to realize that he had not forgotten her. He had come to the station.

Her heart began to pound too quickly, and she was furious with herself. Yet she could not move for a long moment, but remained frozen at the top of the steps.

He must have seen her, for he stepped forward into the light. A hat sat rakishly low on his forehead. It was cream-colored like his suit, and the color contrasted with the black ribbon tie around his throat. As he walked toward her she realized that he was being followed by a young Chinese couple. The man was handsome, the woman extraordinarily beautiful with perfect skin, sleek raven hair to her waist and huge, dark eyes with an exotic, sensual twist. Both were dressed in loose trousers and orange silk Chinese jackets.

Marissa looked at Ian, meeting his eyes. They seemed to sizzle with the same blue fire that had ruled them the night he had left her. The night he had touched her, and somehow destroyed the blind determination that had brought her through a lifetime. She still wanted to hate him. And instead she felt a dizzying heat sweep through her, then tremors seized her and she stiffened, determined to show him no weakness. He was an autocrat, she reminded herself. He was the man who had knocked into a simple maid, heedless of the destruction he had caused.

Even then he had told her to come to America.

Well, then, she was here.

"Mrs. Tremayne?"

The porter was waiting to help her down the steps. She smiled, blushing, and took his hand at last, reaching the platform just as Ian reached her.

He made no pretense of a loving—or even polite!—greeting. He walked straight to her, staring at her still. "So you've made it," he said.

She stiffened her spine and smiled sweetly. "And so have you."

"I promised I would be here."

"And so did I."

"Perhaps I had reason to doubt you."

"I have very great reasons to doubt you," she reminded him, far more sharply than she had intended.

They were barely a foot apart. Marissa suddenly realized that the small space of air between them was thick with tension and that Mary and Jimmy and the porter and Ian's servants were all staring at them wide-eyed, trying to read the innuendo and cool reproach in the words they shot at one another. Perhaps Ian came to the same realization, for he turned to Mary with the smile that could be entirely charming when he wanted it to be. "Welcome to San Francisco. I hope your journey was not too difficult."

"It was wonderful," Mary assured him.

Then Ian remembered his companions and quickly brought the couple forward. "Marissa, Mary, James, may I introduce

John and Lee Kwan, who tend my house. John, Lee, my—''
he paused, then continued evenly enough ''—my wife, Marissa, and her friends, Mary and James O'Brien. Mr. O'Brien
is going to come to work for the emporium.''

Marissa wasn't sure what she expected, but she was surprised at the Chinese man's melodious, accentless speech as
he greeted them. ''I, too, would like to give you all welcome.
Welcome to my city. You will see, she is one of the most
beautiful on earth.''

Then the woman spoke, and her voice was soft with a mu-
sical flow to it. ''Indeed, we welcome you. Anything that you
might require, you've only to ask.'

''Thank you,'' Marissa said, then she realized that the girl's
beautiful, exotic eyes were nowhere near as warm as her
voice. She seemed nearly as hostile as Ian.

''I'll get the bags,'' John said. ''If someone will direct me
to the proper pieces?''

''Aye, of course,'' Jimmy quickly volunteered. ''And
there's plenty of them, I am afraid.'' He grimaced at Ian.
''Women, sir, you know.''

''I know, and I imagine that it will take the three of us,
Jimmy,'' Ian said, flashing him a quick, easy smile. It was a
captivating smile, Marissa realized. Mary was watching him
with a curious affection and admiration, and when Marissa
studied the beautiful and exotic Lee Kwan, she saw that the
Chinese girl was staring after him, too.

He had his charm, indeed. She had discovered that herself.
It was in his manner, and in his eyes, and even in his anger.
She should know. She had fallen prey to it easily enough.

But she would not fall again, she promised herself, feeling
her temper sorely tested. The girl kept his house, indeed. She
gritted her teeth and reminded herself for the thousandth time
that she had received everything she wanted from the bargain.

But she felt the clang of iron and steel again. And she
thought that her prison might well be a torture chamber.

"We shall go to the carriage," Lee told her and Mary. "Come, I'll show you the way."

Marissa and Mary followed Lee through the crowded station and out to the street beyond. Leaving the station behind, Marissa paused. The cool air, rich with fog, touched her cheeks. The remaining daylight was dim, yet it made the scene all the more enchanting.

She could see the hills that looked down upon the bay, and the magical, beautiful homes that sat atop the hills. Painted in soft and rich hues, the city seemed filled with elegance. Victorian row houses, enchanting in their gingerbreading, lined some streets. More elegant grande dames looked down from rich, tree-laden properties. Gas lamps burned with a yellow glow against the growing darkness, and the fog gave it all a picture book quality. It might have been a fairy-tale land. She inhaled quickly, a deep breath, heedless of people passing by her.

It was beautiful. So beautiful. She had been awed by sophisticated New York, and had wondered at bustling Chicago, but here she felt a sweet trembling of excitement deep within her heart. This felt like home. This beauty was soft and enchanting, like the gaslight glow. It beckoned to her and seduced her. She loved the very feel of the air, the color of the night, the kiss of the fog.

She felt someone behind her, but paid no heed.

"It's magnificent!" she whispered.

"Indeed, she's a very great lady," said a rich, husky voice.

She spun around. Ian stood there, carrying a bag in either hand. His gaze had lost something of its anger as he watched her; his eyes were probing hers. She could not speak as he stared at her. "Come on. You've had a very long trip. I'll see you all settled for the night. Tomorrow will be time enough for you to see something of the city." He indicated that she should proceed, and she hurried ahead to his carriage. It was a large, handsome vehicle, drawn by two matching black horses with hides that shone under the lights as beautifully as Lee Kwan's hair.

A horn honked nearby, and an automobile chugged by in the street. A horse drawing an ice cart suddenly reared in fear of the motorized carriage. The auto veered onto the sidewalk. Another horse reared, and a cart of apples and produce went spilling into the street. The automobile sputtered to a halt.

"Progress!" Ian laughed.

"I believe greatly in progress, and I adore automobiles," Marissa told him.

He watched her for a moment. "Good. May we go now? I'd like to get home."

She hurried toward the carriage. She would have ignored him, but he set her bags down, and before she could mount the step, he had set his hands on her waist and lifted her up. John Kwan helped him with the bags, then Ian was beside her.

His scent was rich with leather and soap and his own masculine mystique. She was startled at the vehemence with which memories of a closer time between them returned to haunt her. She caught her breath, determined not to look his way, not to feel the heat and strength of his thigh so tight against hers.

"Ian, the city is wonderful," Mary said. "Which way do we go?"

He pointed in the night. "Nob Hill." He smiled at her. "The city *is* wonderful. There will be a lot for you to see and to learn."

"Why is it called Nob Hill?" Mary asked.

He smiled, and Marissa felt his gaze upon her once again. "Some say that it's from the word 'snob.' But it's not—it comes from the Indian 'nabob.'"

Marissa gazed at him. His eyes were inscrutable, but she felt laughter in his tone, as if he thought she belonged in a place called snob hill!

She was determined to ignore him. Her eyes met his. "I'm sure I shall be very happy upon your Nob Hill, Mr. Tremayne."

"Will you, my love?" he queried politely. "Well, we can only hope."

Marissa started to turn, then thought she saw someone in the crowd watching them. She frowned, staring hard through the fog. She was right; someone was watching them.

It was a woman. Tall, with blazing red hair. She was dressed in a fashionable blue velvet gown whose well-cut lines hugged her stunning body like a glove. The woman realized Marissa was watching her, and she seemed to start. Then she smiled. It was a surprisingly warm smile.

Beside Marissa, Ian turned. Marissa looked at him and saw him frown when he noticed the woman. "Lilli!" he murmured. "What on earth is she doing?"

"A friend of yours?" Marissa asked sweetly. Oh, yes, a friend! Marissa thought, and she wondered why she should be so infuriated.

Because one of her husband's mistresses had come to the station to study her!

She felt a flush of red climbing up her cheeks and she wanted so badly to swallow her bitterness. Why should she care? She wanted nothing from him except a chance at a new life for herself and Jimmy and Mary. And that chance was now hers.

But he'd seduced her, then been furious with her because of it. It had devastated her life, taken over her dreams and her every waking moment. And it had meant nothing at all to him.

She suddenly wanted to tear out his hair.

"A friend?" she repeated.

"A friend," he agreed flatly, staring at her hard.

Marissa turned and waved to the woman. "Lilli, hello!" she called cheerfully.

"What the hell do you think you're doing?" he demanded tensely, for her ears alone.

"Inviting your friend to the house. You do want to keep her, I imagine," Marissa said innocently.

He swore, heedless of Mary, Jimmy and the Kwans. "Lady, you don't invite anyone to my house, do you understand? You don't know who the hell you're talking to!"

"A dance-hall girl, I imagine. But then, this is America. Land of opportunity—and equality," she told him. His fingers were knotting, she realized. He was probably longing to wind them around her throat, and was just barely controlling the urge to do so.

"But I shall ask into my house those whom I choose, madame, not you!" he returned. His voice was soft but his tone warning, near savage. She fought the urge to draw away, and remembered her own fury.

"Do forgive me," she whispered. "I merely wanted to show your—friend—that I intend her no harm. Mistresses are not always fond of the arrival of—"

"Wives. But then you are not the customary wife, are you, my love? No," he answered himself. "Certainly not customary. My dear, dear lady."

Not a lady at all, Marissa thought. A brat from the coal mines, with less financial potential, surely, than the red-haired woman who stood and watched her.

The anger within her grew. Perhaps he wanted to throttle her. She longed to give a good cut to the hard angles and planes of his face.

But Mary was staring at her.

"Not customary at all, I promise you," she told Ian.

And he swore softly, then gritted his teeth and called out to John. "Let's go, please. Just circle around the confusion up ahead."

The carriage jerked as John Kwan flicked his whip in the air and the fine matched blacks started up at a trot.

"Head straight for home, John," Ian instructed, leaning past Marissa.

She closed her eyes, catching her breath. Home. It was his home.

But her home now.

No, his home. To which he could invite whom he chose when he chose. It would not really be her home. He had made that very clear.

She felt a strange fluttering in her heart.

The bars were closing tightly around her prison.

It would be a beautiful prison, she thought. The city had found a place in her heart already.

But still...

No matter how beautiful a prison it might be, it would still be a prison. She would live shackled by the agreement she had forced, furious with Ian Tremayne, fascinated by him.

Jealous.

No! Her eyes flew open. She felt him watching her. She turned quickly to him, and saw she was right. Bright against the darkness, his gaze was hard upon her.

Her jailer...

A shudder touched her soul.

Her jailer, her husband. A husband who did not want her here.

She turned and looked toward the station. The beautiful red-haired woman was still standing there. She lifted her hand and waved.

Fury entered her heart. He had told her he had women in his life. He had made it very clear.

But that was before he had touched her.

She wanted to be away from him! She had barely seen him again, and it seemed that already the night and her life were filled with tempest and pain. Oh, it was a lie, it was all a lie, and she had created it.

And there wasn't anything she could do.

It was time to begin living the lie.

CHAPTER NINE

THE HOUSE WAS MAGNIFICENT.

Jimmy and Mary had been left at the entrance to the grounds, where a caretakers' cottage had been done over for their privacy until they chose to find their own home. John and Lee Kwan had quietly disappeared on their arrival at the grand Victorian entryway, and Marissa was alone with Ian when she walked up the steps to the huge elegant porch with its engraved and beveled windows. He said nothing, but merely opened the front door, allowing her to enter first. And she did so, drawing her gloves from her fingers as she stared at the foyer. It was huge, with a grand chandelier hanging from a high ceiling. The ceiling allowed for the entire length of the extraordinary stairway of hewn and curved wood. The flooring was a light marble, taking away any sense of heaviness that might have been found in the elegantly carved doors leading to other parts of the house.

Marissa stared at the stairway, then realized that Ian was standing behind her, watching her.

"Will it suffice?" he asked.

She swung around to look at him. What was he expecting from her? Maybe she had forced the issue, but she couldn't see offering him eternal gratitude.

Not when she could still remember the woman at the station all too clearly.

He was proud of this house, she thought. And he had a right to be; it was elegant, it was beautiful, and it was still warm. He couldn't have built it himself, for it was far too old a structure, but he had probably added to it.

If she hadn't seen the redhead at the station, she might have been tempted to praise the house, to tell him with warmth and laughter and enthusiasm just how wonderful a house it was.

But she had seen the woman at the station.

He warned you! she taunted herself. And she stepped farther into the room, playing for time. She had fallen prey to him once. She would not do so again. She wasn't sure what she had expected from him, but not this distance and coldness. She was surprised at the way it hurt, and she was suddenly furious again over the last night she had seen him in England. If only he had never touched her!

"Yes," she said quietly, without looking his way. "It will suffice."

"I am so glad," he told her. And the resonance of his voice showed her she had touched some chord deep within him.

She turned to meet his dark and enigmatic gaze. "It's been an extraordinarily long journey. Perhaps you'd be good enough to show me to my private quarters?"

A dark brow shot up, and his lip curved in a hard smile. "Your private quarters?"

"I should remind you, sir, that you were the one so insistent that your private life should not be disturbed in any way."

"Very true. But may I remind you, my love, that you were the one so very insistent on marriage."

"Indeed. And you were so very—kind—as to agree to marriage on my behalf. Yet you were very careful to remind me that you did have your own life. A fact you managed to demonstrate most amply this evening, and therefore I shall be incredibly happy to see that you are not disturbed in any way."

"How very kind," he murmured dryly, and indicated that she should precede him up the stairway. Above her, a stained-glass window graced the landing. It was dark now, but by the gaslight of the chandelier and the hall candles she could see the colors within it, beautiful blues and reds, then the white of a rearing unicorn that seemed to look down upon the stairway.

She reached the landing, with Ian upon her heels. His hand touched the small of her back and he urged her to the right where the hall split in two directions. He paused before a set of carved double doors and pressed the brass handle downward, opening one door. He turned up a wall lamp and soft light filled the room.

It was huge. A massive bed against one wall was covered with a white, gold-trimmed spread and set against a beautifully painted bed frame. The high ceilings were molded, and the walls were papered in a light yellow and mauve print. The hardwood floor was enhanced by an elegant Persian rug in complementary colors. One corner of the room was a hexagonal turret set with windows. A glass table and several chairs covered in a rich gold brocade had been comfortably arranged there. And there was a fireplace. With a marble mantel, two armoires, and a beautiful Art Nouveau dresser and elegant brocade-covered seat. There were two doors within the room, leading to opposite sides.

Tears suddenly stung her eyes. The single room was far larger than the entire cottage she had shared with Theo. The bedspread alone was worth more than Theo made in a year.

Ian pointed to one door. "There's a dressing room and bath beyond, and beyond that, a library, office or sitting room, whatever you choose. All are your private quarters. But by the way, madam, just what is it that I so amply demonstrated this evening?"

Marissa was startled by the sudden question. He hadn't seemed to notice her words downstairs. Apparently he had chosen to ignore them until now. And while it had been easy enough to set little barbs into conversation downstairs, she was annoyed to discover herself at a loss up here.

"As I said before, it was a very long journey—"

"Therefore I suggest you talk quickly," he said politely, only a hint of warning to his words.

She walked over to the Art Nouveau dresser, studying her image as she unpinned her hat and set it down. Her hair was coming loose in wild strands and tendrils, and she suddenly wished she'd left the hat alone. Then she saw Ian's face in the mirror behind her, his handsome features taut, his eyes dark and demanding upon hers. A lock of black hair hung loose over his forehead as he, too, removed his hat, tossing it on the bed. "I've all evening," he told her.

"Ian," she said, speaking to his mirrored image, "if you'd be so kind—"

"Well, I wouldn't be. We've gone through this before. I'm an American, crude, no gentleman. So let's finish this."

She swung around furiously. "Yes, indeed, let's. You poor dear thing! You're mourning your wife, your one and only real wife. And so you want your complete freedom to play with your whores. We agreed to that. I just thought that perhaps you might have better manners than to bring them to the station on the night you were to meet me!"

She had never imagined a man could go so white, or that every muscle within him might tauten and flick with such violence and fury. He took a sudden swift step toward her, his hand raised as if to strike her. Marissa cried out, suddenly and regretfully aware that she had gone a step too far. She had wanted to wound him. She had done so. Swiftly, precisely and well.

"No!" she gasped, ducking low, feeling the blood drain from her own face.

He paused. His hand fell. She saw the long, deadly fingers close into fists, and she tried to run past him.

He caught her, and his fingers threaded through her hair, pulling her to him. She cried out in pain, her eyes stinging with tears. Caught against him, she looked into his eyes that seemed obsidian, and though he hadn't said a word, she found herself apologizing. "I'm sorry! I'm sorry! I didn't mean—"

"Don't ever, ever mention my past again!"

"Let me go! I didn't mean to mention your past! It's your present I find offensive!"

His eyes narrowed sharply. His fingers, entwined in her hair, tightened upon her upper arms. "Why, you little witch! I told you from the very beginning—"

"Let go!" she insisted, pounding against his chest. She could feel his heartbeat, and his heat. The situation was becoming all too reminiscent of an earlier one. She didn't want to be so close to him as a man. It evoked new hatreds and furies, and longings.

"I told you—"

She tossed her head, meeting his gaze with flashing eyes. "Who do you think you are! Don't you think that anyone else has ever been hurt before? I'm sorry about your wife. I'm damned sorry about your wife. But you with your grand house and your store and your building and your disgusting money, you don't begin to understand what real hurting can be. You—"

He shook her suddenly, and she broke off, horribly aware of everything she had been saying.

"What the hell are you talking about?" he demanded heatedly. "What hardship have you ever known? Threatened with a world in which you would have to survive on your own, you married me for money. So don't you ever—"

"I'll not spend my life tiptoeing—"

"What are you talking about!" he thundered.

"I lost my father!" she snapped. "And I—" Again she broke off, not because he touched her harshly or with violence, but because his gaze was so very probing, because it felt as if the room were stifling hot. Pressed so close to his chest, she felt each slam of his heart against her breast. She couldn't breathe, and she wanted more than anything to escape him. But he was staring at her so intently that she thought he could see through the sham of her elegant clothing, that he knew everything that lay beneath. Had she given herself away?

"Tell me!" he thundered. "Tell me what the hell gives you the right to judge me. What hardship have you ever known?"

He no longer accused her of having a lover; the truth of that had been given to him on that night in London. But in her anger she had given much more away, and she was still doing so. "I've seen—I've seen Mary's life. I've seen the miners where she lived cough away their lives, and I've seen their children dressed in rags, starving, no more than skin and bone and wide eyes. I've seen children so covered in mud and smut that they were unrecognizable!"

Oh, Lord! She had to pray, and pray fervently, that she had been unrecognizable. He didn't remember her as the muddied waif in the village, did he? He would never, never associate his wife with that poor creature! Or would he?

She was shaking, her teeth chattering, and her eyes fell from his. "You're not the only one who has ever been hurt!" she repeated.

He didn't move. He was silent, staring at her for so long that she began to feel the pain of his knotted grip upon her.

Finally he released her, but she cried out as he turned away, for tendrils of her hair were still entangled about his fingers. To her surprise he did not jerk free from her, but paused to carefully untangle every last hair. Then he strode toward the door opposite the dressing room and bath. When he spoke, his voice was level and flat, curiously detached.

"John will soon bring your belongings," he said, "and Lee will bring you something to eat. There's a tub with hot and cold running water in the bathroom. If there's anything you need, you've only to ask Lee or John. There's other help in during the day, but only the Kwans live in the house. They've an apartment on the third floor should you need them at any time.''

"I'm usually quite self-sufficient, thank you," Marissa said. She watched as he walked to the door and opened it. She could just see a large room past it, completely different from her own. There was a huge bed within it, covered in dark black and crimson pattern. The floor there, too, was hardwood, and covered with a beautiful Oriental rug in lighter shades to ease the darkness of the bed and draperies. The fixtures were in brass, and a very heavy long oak desk stood before one window.

"My God!" she gasped suddenly. "That's your room."

He paused, turning to her. "It is."

"There's a lock on the door, I assume."

His lip curled with taunting humor. "My dear Mrs. Tremayne, I thought you were distressed because of my, er, friends. Yet knowing that I have those friends would seem to keep your private quarters quite safe from unwanted visits. And if I do recall correctly, just this evening you invited one certain friend into this house!"

"I don't mind your friends," she assured him.

"Then just what is your difficulty?"

"That you—" she began, then paused, inhaling deeply. "I mind that you had that woman at the station."

"I didn't have her there. It is a free world, remember?"

"Will you please just get out so I can lock the door?"

He smiled pleasantly. "Yes, by all means, lock the door. But remember, Marissa, it seems that you are fond of attacking me and my life. You say that it is my present that disturbs you, but you felt it right to comment on my past. So bear in mind that this is my home. My door, my lock. And if for any reason I felt the need, I would shatter the wood from the door to enter any room in this place."

"That wasn't the agreement—"

"No!" he snapped, dispassion gone. "I made no agreements, and no promises. Bear that in mind, lady, and if you would have your precious privacy, then I warn you most strenuously—stay away from me, and keep your judgments and opinions to yourself!''

He stared at her one moment longer, then turned.

The door slammed in his wake, so hard that it seemed the wood already shattered.

She stared at the closed door, swore softly, then sank down on the foot of her bed, alarmed as she felt the threat of tears sting her eyes.

This was a new world, her new world. She already loved the city, and she would have respectability here, for she was the wife of a very rich man. She had so much here.

And she wasn't going to let him ruin it!

She blinked furiously and hurried through the door to her bath and dressing rooms. Each was as elegant as the bedroom. The huge bathroom offered a large white porcelain tub with lions' claw feet, racks of snowy white towels, lovely Dutch tiles on the walls. She opened a cabinet to find soaps and lotions and a large pink bottle of French bubble bath. She closed the cabinet and leaned against it. She couldn't wait for her bags to arrive, for total privacy, to sink into the tub.

She hurried on to explore the next room—her study, library, sitting room, whatever she chose it to be.

She pushed open the connecting door and stared blankly.

My God, she could house half of the miners and their families in these few rooms! If only Mary were with her here!

But Mary wasn't with her. And she wouldn't even be at the caretakers' cottage for long. She and Jimmy would be moving on to their own household.

She was alone here. With Ian too close and too far away all in one. And with John Kwan and the beautiful Lee, who already stared at her with hostility.

Did the exotic Chinese girl offer her master more than domestic services?

As she taunted herself, Marissa felt her face burn. She pressed her hands against her cheeks. She didn't want to know, she told herself.

But she did. With a dread fascination, she wanted to know everything about Ian. Even the things that seemed to pierce so sharply into her heart.

Impatient with herself, she went into the room. It was set up as a library, and she thought that she liked it very much that way. There was a desk with a swivel chair, and there were two leather armchairs set before the fireplace. In the far corner, by a set of bookshelves, was a beautiful day bed, covered in a blue damask set off by the dark brown leather of the armchairs. It was a handsome room with the rows of books, and in a far corner, another turret set with a comfortable blue armchair and needlepoint footrest. The windows took the upper portion of the wall and were etched and set with brass. She imagined that in the day the light would pour in, and that it would be a wonderful place to curl up with a book. And if it rained, and if the wind blew, and the weather turned cold, there was always the fire to come in to.

She had curled into one of the leather chairs when she felt a presence behind her. Holding back a scream, she turned to see that the woman, Lee Kwan, was standing still and silent behind her.

"I startled you, madam. I am sorry."

Marissa leaped up. "You might have knocked," she said, unnerved by the woman's appearance.

"The doors were open. I just wished to let you know that John has brought your things, and I have left you a covered tray. Shall I unpack for you?"

She shook her head, then realized that she did not want to be enemies with Lee Kwan. Not until she knew more about her home, at least.

"Uh, no, thank you. I appreciate the offer, but I prefer to unpack myself."

Lee Kwan's inscrutable dark eyes lowered as she bowed to Marissa. "As you wish."

She was going to turn and leave, Marissa knew, and she was startled when she called the woman back. "Thank you for bringing the tray," she said quickly. The woman nodded, offering Marissa nothing more. "Have you and your husband been with Mr. Tremayne long?" she asked.

"My husband?" Lee asked.

"Yes, John."

"Oh." Lee's lashes flicked over her dark eyes. "He is not my husband. He is my brother. Is there anything else that I can do for you, Mrs. Tremayne? May I draw you a bath?"

"No, thank you." She wanted a bath but she wanted Lee Kwan gone more. "I'll take care of myself this evening, thank you."

"It was a long journey for you," Lee offered.

"Very."

Lee bowed again and turned to leave. Marissa did not call her back.

And when the woman was gone, Marissa followed her to the bedroom, locking the double doors to the hallway. She did not want to be surprised again. It would probably be a long night. As tired and travel worn as she was, she would probably never be able to fall asleep here tonight. In his house.

She stretched out on the bed, running her fingers over the beautiful gold and cream spread. It was such a wonderful house. Or it could be, she thought, if it could be brought to life.

She closed her eyes and tried to imagine what Ian's first wife would have been like. Maybe a very delicate blonde, with no hints of red within her hair. And her eyes would have been a soft blue, and she would have been really beautiful, a lady in every sense of the word. And they would have reigned here together with love and laughter, and then the house would have been truly alive.

She sighed softly. Life would be good here for Jimmy and Mary. Jimmy would flourish at Ian's emporium. He was smart, he could work tirelessly, and he loved Mary with all his heart. Mary would be happy.

It was her own life that would be so very empty.

She wouldn't allow it to be, she told herself. She was going to wallow in the luxury. And write long letters to Uncle Theo, and to the vicar, and she was going to be certain that everything went well with her school.

Uncle Theo and the school were across a continent and an ocean. And life stretched out long before her here.

She was exhausted, she thought. That was why she continually felt the hotness of tears behind her eyelids. She was going to start with luxury, an endless bath with sweet-smelling bubbles in the huge porcelain tub. Then she could put her things away, her beautiful new things, and it would begin to feel like home.

But she never took her long bath that night, never glanced at the tray of food that she had been brought. She didn't even take her shoes off. She closed her eyes, stretched out on the silky cover.

She had no trouble sleeping in her new home, Ian's house, at all.

Nor did dreams trouble her. She wasn't aware when the door between the two rooms, the door she had not remembered to bolt after demanding to know if it could be locked, opened.

Ian walked in quietly and stared at her face for a long moment. He sighed softly, unlaced her shoes and pulled them from her feet. Sweeping back the covers, he laid her upon a pillow and started to loosen her blouse.

The act was too reminiscent of one he had performed before. He felt the muscles tighten in his jaw and despite himself, he smoothed his knuckles over her cheek. She seemed so innocent, sleeping. Beautiful, with her fair skin, softly parted lips, flawless oval face and lovely features. The passion within her was silenced now, but he remembered with discomfort the vehemence of her attack upon him. He turned away from her, lowered the gas lamp and returned quietly to his room.

He stood overlooking the downtown area of the city far below. Lights flickered and gleamed, and the fog was softly swirling in, like a magical dragon, from the bay.

What hardships had he known? he taunted himself. He'd been a fighter, he told himself, always a fighter. He'd gone his own way, he'd fought to build homes and offices that would be both beautiful and safe. He'd never taken the rich man's way out, and despite his father's advice, he'd enlisted in the Navy.

He'd fought for Diana, fought as long and hard as any man could fight.

But he hadn't really known hardship. Marissa was right. Not the way she had made him see it so briefly. But she was a child of privilege, too. How could she bring the suffering so vividly to life?

And why did she have such an effect upon him?

He sighed and kept his eyes upon the city he loved. It wasn't late. By the waterfront, the dance halls and theaters and bars would be going strong. He should don his coat and escape this house tonight.

But he didn't. He continued to stare at the magical city within the magical fog. And when he turned from the windows at last, it was to strip off his clothing, turn down the lamps and crawl into his bed.

He had wanted to hold her tonight, he thought gravely, fingers laced behind his head as he stared at the darkness of the ceiling. It had been something different than the raw desire that had sparked him in London, something deeper than the sexual desire that could still plague him because of her beauty. He had wanted to hold her, to ease away the hurt.

And for the first time, he realized, he had been startled from his depression. He was not the only man to suffer a loss. From the tone of her voice, he had sensed a loss, a pain, different perhaps, but as deep as any pain he had ever known.

She had lost her father recently.

But the anguish he had seen in her eyes seemed to go deeper than that. As if she had truly understood a different world.

He has seen that world himself, and it had, indeed, been dismal. Once investors had encouraged his father to buy into the mine. The squire had warned James Tremayne that he would despise the place, and James had indeed despised all he had seen. Life was hard for the common worker. It was a lesson Ian had learned that day.

But even in that darkness, there had been a curious beauty. And pride. He suddenly remembered the little girl he had seen there. She had been so clean and white. So determined. So different from the other black-faced waifs, covered in dirt and grime and coal, who had reached out small grubby hands for any little pittance that might come their way. She had been angry, and proud. He smiled. It was strange. She'd had eyes like Marissa's, startling, vivid green eyes. Or maybe he was just remembering the child as having his wife's eyes, because both had been determined to give him battle.

The village had been a terrible place. He had sensed death, and pain, and a raw struggle to survive.

Marissa must have felt for her friend greatly.

And tonight, Ian had wanted to hold Marissa, to smooth her hair. To give her security against…

He didn't know.

Shrugging, he ground his teeth together hard and turned over with a vehement twist, pounding his pillow. He was tired; he should sleep. He had a meeting with the men tomorrow about the new buildings for the waterfront district. And he had to show his new wife and her friends something

of the city. And there was young James to see settled in at
the emporium. He was weary; he should sleep.

But he did not.

Ian was the one to lie awake most of the night.

It taunted him to know that Marissa lay just beyond the
door.

A door she had not remembered to lock against him, despite
her words.

There had been something about her, that night in England.
Something that still teased and haunted his senses, something
that made the present seem suddenly more important than the
past. Something in her eyes had challenged him, something
in her heart had awakened him. Something in her innocence
still laid claim to him.

And she had not locked the door. It was his house, he had
told her, his door. And he'd never made any promises or
agreements.

She was so close. All he had to do was step through the
door.

He turned again, closing his eyes tightly. She could not take
Diana's place. He would not let her. He could not let her be
a wife in truth. And if his flesh burned and if his dreams were
fraught with images of her, he would learn to get past them.
That was why he had gone to see Lilli.

But Lilli, even with her pretty face and stately form, could
not compare with Marissa. The lift of her chin, the emerald
blaze of her eyes, the cascade of her hair. Her passion, so
visible in her anger...

So sweet when she allowed it to flow and undulate in his
arms. He could not forget the scent of her skin, the silk of
her hair, entangling him.

Desire... It was natural, for she was beautiful, and she was
young. The sparks of fury that flowed between them could so
easily become more.

But tonight...

Tonight he had listened to her cry out to him. And she mocked him and railed against him.

But her words had been true, and she had awakened more in him than desire. He'd never intended to be a self-pitying monster. He had just missed Diana with all his heart.

He'd married Marissa; he'd made no promises. He had only to burst through the door, lift her into his arms and carry her in here, to his bed. He'd not force her. He'd make love to her, and her protests would die softly away as they had before. And he would ease the rage in his loins and the tension in his limbs.

He rose, sleek and naked in the night. He took two steps toward the door between them, then paused.

He might ease the tension and desire, but he'd create a new tempest in his heart. He could not bring her to this bed, for it had been Diana's bed. He could not sweep Marissa into any world he had shared before.

He had married Marissa. He still could not allow her to be his wife.

The fog settled over the city, and the moon rose high above it to create a soft, surreal glow.

And Ian stood there, muscles knotting, his head cast back. He nearly cried out as pain and longing knotted together within his soul.

Minutes passed, long, aching minutes. He padded to the window and looked out again on San Francisco. He inhaled and exhaled slowly. It seemed that he stared out at the city forever.

A foghorn sounded and he started, then smiled, with just a hint of tenderness curling his lip.

She had just arrived. She was close, and it was his own fault. When she had still been endless miles away, he had not thought that having her so near could wreak such havoc upon him.

She slept in exhaustion. So innocently.

No, he thought wryly. He would not disturb her sleep, no matter what decision he had made within his heart.

He would leave her be.

He realized suddenly that light was breaking through the fog. He had stayed awake for hours, staring into the night.

He laughed ruefully.

He'd leave her be...

Maybe.

And then again...

Maybe he'd let her live in just a bit of the tempest that was nearly driving him to distraction!

CHAPTER TEN

MARISSA AWOKE with a sense of disorientation. She opened her eyes to see her fingers stretched over embroidered cream sheets. Across the room, she could see the door to the bathroom slightly ajar. The morning light was streaming through the etched and beveled windows, and the entire room was cast in a soft glow.

The night's sleep had done her a world of good, and she smiled slowly. This was all hers. These rooms were her domain. With their soft and subtle beauty, they were where she lived.

She rose, frowning for a moment as she tried to remember taking off her shoes, then she shrugged. She had been so very tired, she couldn't even remember falling asleep.

Her bags were still on the floor at the foot of the bed. She rose, found her overnight case and searched diligently for her toothbrush and cosmetics, then headed into the bath. She doused her face and scrubbed her teeth and smiled to the image in the mirror over the porcelain sink. "A prison not so tortuous, I think!" she told herself. She was ready to wrestle with Ian once again this morning. With a vengeance.

She turned on the gold spigots for the tub, thinking of home. This house offered everything. At Uncle Theo's, a bath had been a time-consuming chore. She had to heat endless pots of water, drag out the tub, fill the tub, empty the tub! Even at the manor there had been no running water. There had been several "necessary" rooms, but nothing like this.

She took bubble bath from the cabinet and added it liberally to the water. Then she quickly disrobed and stepped into the tub, luxuriating in the heat.

The bubbles rose around her and she was delighted. She sank down as the water rose, drenching her hair, rubbing her scalp. She inhaled the sweet rose scent of the bubbles and doused herself again, feeling like a child. Then, with a soft sigh, she settled back, her head resting on the edge of the tub, her arms elegantly draped over the sides.

"Not so horrid a prison," she murmured. And she lifted a hand, pointing as she might to make something clear to a schoolboy. "Mr. Ian Tremayne will be made to see that it cannot be had both ways, and then I think that I shall settle in very nicely! He will be put in his place, I swear it!"

"Really?"

The quiet, amused challenge of his voice coming from behind her was the greatest surprise of her life. She almost bolted from the bubbles, then managed to twist around beneath them to stare at him where he leaned against the door frame, his arms casually crossed, brows arched as he stared at her. He was dressed for business in a pin-striped suit with a gray silk vest and white pleated shirt beneath. Hatless, and with the errant lock of hair falling over his forehead, he was striking. Her heart began to pound, and she forgot for a moment that she was ready to wrestle with him. He was definitely one of the most handsome men she had ever seen. Yet it wasn't just his looks that made him so arresting; it was that air of confidence, the energy, the tension. There was danger in his eyes, in the fire within them. And despite her pride, it was far too easy to flicker close to the flames burning there.

She remembered her pride at last. "What are you doing in here?" she demanded sharply.

"Oh, just listening to how you'll put me in my place," he replied with a casual smile.

Flames crept to her cheeks, but she remembered she was

the one with the right to be indignant. "These are my private quarters—"

"I knocked, but you didn't answer."

"Then you weren't given leave to enter!"

"You might have been drowning here, my love. I had to make sure you were all right. Indeed, I thought at first that you *were* drowning, since your head was lost in the foam."

"Well, I wasn't drowning, and I'm quite all right, and you've no business in here at all!"

"I own the house."

"But you gave me the bath!"

"I did not give it to you!" he protested. "I loaned it to you." He took two long strides into the room and knelt beside the porcelain tub. Marissa tried to maintain her dignity by drawing the bubbles around her.

They were breaking up at an alarming pace.

She narrowed her eyes. "Out!" she told him sharply.

"I really don't understand your distress," he said, a leisurely smile curling his lip. "We're adults, man and wife—be honest here! I've seen in the naked flesh all that you would hide behind those elusive bubbles—"

"In the dark, in London, a long time ago—and during a mistake, which you yourself apologized for!" she interrupted, her temper growing. He was so near. And the curve of his smile and the humor in his eyes were nearly akin to tenderness.

He touched her, drawing a soft line from her throat to her shoulder. "It was not so dark, what matters the city, not so long ago, and an apology would do nothing to alter my memory of every piece of your—of you. Dear Lord, those bubbles do not last long when you want them to, do they?"

If she was losing them anyway, Marissa determined in a flash of fury, she might as well use them well. She dipped a hand into the water and sent a spray of bubbles flying onto his face and chest. She was rewarded with a sharp oath and a sea of sputtering. "Marissa, you little witch—"

She leaped up, thinking to escape, remembered she was naked, and decided she had best run anyway.

He caught her just as she reached the bedroom. His hands slid over the length of her flesh, but she eluded him, for the soap that remained on her was slick and slippery. "No!" she shrieked, torn between panic and laughter.

"You've destroyed my suit!" he thundered.

"You destroyed my bath, and my privacy!" she retorted. The bed was behind her. She turned to grab the sheet, but he was moving again, striding quickly across the room. He caught her with an energy that sent them both flying down upon her beautiful bed. She was soft and slippery, the essence of the bubbles still upon her flesh.

"Off!" she commanded. "Ian, you rake—"

"Ah, but you were well warned to stay away!"

"I was in my own bath!"

"You saw fit to wage war."

"I saw fit to defend myself!"

She had entered this marriage knowing everything.

But the texture of his tongue upon her flesh was rough and sleek and exciting, and the flames that had touched his eyes were growing to burst into a fire at the center of her being. She could not allow this.

This was too much like falling in love with him. She seemed to need the laughter in his eyes, the curve of his smile. She hated him because he had others in his life, and not because of the way he had manipulated her own life.

His kiss moved lower. His tongue tasted a patch of bubbles that remained high upon her breast. His fingers curled over hers and entwined, and his kiss moved farther down. Slowly. So slowly. The tip of his tongue just moving over her naked flesh, lower and lower upon her breast.

"You—you do not want me," she reminded him.

His face lay within the valley of her breasts. He paused, pressing a kiss there, running his tongue lightly over that valley. She ached for more. Longing to have him take her deeply into his mouth. She wanted to run her fingers into the darkness of his hair and draw his face to hers and kiss his lips. And she wanted to strip away the soaked pin-striped suit and feel the naked tension of his body.

She swallowed hard and repeated her words, "You do not want me here, Ian. Ian!" She tried to escape his hold, twisting in a fury. But she could not fight his weight and his hold, and he had not released her. As she twisted she was only wedging herself more closely to him. His lips were pressed deeply against her breast, and the fire raged more deeply between her thighs. "Ian!" Taut and still, she called his name.

He was silent for a long moment. Then the husky, muffled velvet of his voice came to her. "Ah, but I do want you," he murmured.

"Let me go!"

"Is that what you want?"

His head rose above hers. There was no laughter in his eyes, only darkness. His features were tense, his jaw hard as his gaze sought hers.

"Ian—"

"What of you, Marissa? Do you want me?"

She caught her breath, unable to speak. His eyes were dark and demanding upon hers. This time they were not doing battle, nor were they jesting. And yet she was too afraid to answer him. She could not spill out her feelings, even if she could completely understand them herself. Then they came clear to her.

Love me! she wanted to cry out. For I have fallen in love with you, in love with a memory, perhaps. And even in love with the anger and the challenge and the arrogance. For I've seen the care, and the tenderness, too. And I've seen the beauty of what can lie between two people, and I never knew that my heart ached for that loving, too.

But he could not love her. He was in love with a ghost, and he made love with faceless women who did not count.

And she couldn't say she loved him, for she was living a lie. She wasn't the woman he thought he had married.

And still she wanted to touch his face, to draw it to hers, to taste his lips upon hers.

She did. She reached out, her fingertips falling upon the curve of his cheek and the bronzed contours of his face. Then she cried out, alarmed at herself, incredulous that she could forget her pride.

"No!" She twisted from beneath him, and he let her go. She sat with her back to him, her spine straight but her head lowered. "No!" she said, and the sound was more desperate than angry.

Not when you long for a dead woman! she added silently. Not when I would be nothing more than a dance-hall girl. She couldn't say those things to him.

"And I meant to taunt you!" he murmured.

She looked at him. He was propped on one elbow, watching her with a wry smile.

"Pardon?"

He shook his head. "Nothing." His eyes closed, and a ragged shudder swept his body. He stood, and to her amazement he stripped the cover from the bed with a fluid motion and set it around her shoulders. "Breakfast is a buffet downstairs. We do share the dining room, since I haven't two, I'm afraid. We need to get started, it's a busy morning. Meet me there as soon as you can."

She rose uncertainly, holding the cover around her. He grinned, came to her and stared into her eyes, then gave her a firm smack on the derriere. "Get cracking, lady. I'm American nouveau riche, a Yank, remember, not British gentry. I have to work to maintain my bank accounts."

He didn't wait for her answer, but left her, slipping through to his own room. She rose and followed him, meaning to lock the door. But she hesitated and did not touch the lock.

She turned pensively instead, and walked slowly to the bathroom to dress.

TEN MINUTES later she found him in the dining room.

A walk down the curving stairway brought her to the entry. She discovered, by walking to her left, that the dining room was there, beyond a large parlor with huge bay windows looking down the lawn to the street. Ian was sitting at the end of the table with a cup of coffee and a newspaper. He looked up when she arrived. He had changed into a navy suit with a paisley vest, and his errant hair had been combed.

"Biscuits and eggs are on the buffet," he told her, and he reached across the table, where a place had been set for her, and picked up her cup. A coffee urn was sitting before him, and he looked at her before pouring from it. "Would you prefer tea?"

She shook her head and slid into her seat. "Coffee is fine, thank you."

He poured her coffee. "You need to eat something. We'll be out all day."

"I'm not very hungry—"

"You need to eat. Lee, would you kindly fix Mrs. Tremayne a plate?"

Marissa started, unaware that the Chinese woman had been standing in the corner. Lee came forward to do as she was bidden, and Marissa stood, determined that she wouldn't require any help from Lee.

"Thank you, Lee. I can manage myself."

Exotic dark eyes touched her for a moment, their hostility still evident, then they fell as Lee bowed her head. "As you wish, Mrs. Tremayne."

Marissa walked to the buffet and helped herself to fried

eggs and biscuits and bacon and sat at the table. She had come down intending to be as mature and reasonable as she could. She had wanted to talk, to form some kind of a livable relationship between them.

But with Lee in the corner of the room, she couldn't talk. She sipped her coffee, which was delicious, and bit gingerly into a piece of bacon.

"I'll try to show you and the O'Briens something of the city this morning," Ian said, glancing at his paper as he spoke. "But I'll need to bring James into the emporium after lunch, and I've an appointment myself. John will be at your disposal to drive you around should you choose."

Lee cleared her throat, as if waiting for permission to speak. Ian glanced her way curiously.

"Perhaps Mrs. Tremayne and her friend would prefer exploring on their own. The cable cars are wonderful."

"Yes, Lee, they are. But perhaps they should become a little more familiar with their surroundings before exploring on their own. It's a beautiful city—it can be a dangerous one, too."

Marissa buttered a biscuit, smiling sweetly as a touch of resentment rose within her. "Um. I understand that the Barbary Coast offers all manner of entertainment, theaters and the like."

"I think you are mainly thinking of years past, when brothels were thicker than flies, my dear."

"They've all gone then?" Marissa queried innocently.

His eyes were hard. He sipped his coffee, then set his cup down. He leaned forward with a pleasant smile. "Not at all. But then, my love, I mean to show you the finer sights of your new city. Are you ready?"

She wasn't ready at all, but it was apparent that he was determined to go. He was on his feet, pulling her chair out for her. "Tell John to meet us at the emporium around two, Lee, to pick up Mrs. Tremayne and Mrs. O'Brien."

Lee nodded. "Will you dine at home, Mr. Tremayne?"

"Yes, we'll be home for dinner, thank you. Come on, Marissa, let's go."

He caught her hand and led her to the foyer, then frowned. "You'll need a cloak of some kind. The weather here changes quickly. Hurry."

She raced up the stairs and dug in her bags for a lightweight cape, then swept up her small reticule with her comb and money. She couldn't have moved faster, but when she reached the entry, he was pacing.

He pushed open the front door and led her down the steps. "If you'll wait here, I'll bring out the car."

"The car?" she asked. He'd picked her up in a carriage. In all her life, she'd never been in a motorcar.

He smiled. "You're not afraid of automobiles?"

"No, no, of course not." She hurried after him, almost crashing into his back when he stopped.

"I said I'd pick you up."

"I know, but I'm anxious to see it."

"It?" He smiled. "Them, my dear." He started walking again, around the main house to the carriage house. The doors were open. To the left were stalls with horses, among them the matching blacks that had drawn the carriage that had come for them at the station. Near the stalls were several different carriages from a row of three motorcars, all shining even in the dim light.

She stared at them until he beckoned to her. "Do you know much about them?" he asked her.

She shook her head.

Ian caught her hand and took her to the rear of the carriage house, to an automobile painted a deep green. It barely resembled a carriage, and had a huge nose. "She's French," he told Marissa. "A Levassor-Panhard, with her Daimler motor here in front." Marissa paused to study the vehicle, but he was already moving on to the next. She followed after him. "This is a Renault, also French. And in front of us is an American car, a 1901 Olds.'' He opened the passenger door and took her hand, helping her up. She smiled with excitement. Perhaps her smile was contagious, for he laughed. "Had I only known you would have come here without the slightest argument if I had commented on the automobiles!''

He cranked the engine. Marissa jumped as the auto burst into life, then chugged its way out of the carriage house and down the driveway. The breeze swept by her and she turned to him. "It's wonderful! But how very odd! I had thought that you were such an avid horseman. Why, you were riding when I saw you—''

She broke off quickly, hoping he did not remember the time she was thinking about, when he had come riding up so heatedly to the Squire's the year before the Squire died. She tried desperately to remember if he had ridden to meet her in the city of London, but her mind had gone blank, and she could feel a nervous flush rising to her cheeks.

"Was I riding?'' he said.

"Oh, maybe I was wrong. I don't remember,'' she said quickly, looking at the road.

"I do love horses. And I've a few magnificent animals in my stalls.''

"I know. The blacks are gorgeous.''

"I've riding horses, too.'' He shrugged. "I love horses, but I do see motor vehicles as the way of the future. Eventually, I daresay, the cars will outnumber the horses.''

They had come to the caretakers' cottage. Mary appeared at the front door, waved, then reappeared with Jimmy behind her. Both were as awed with the Olds as Marissa had been, and Ian allowed them the time to walk around it as he answered Jimmy's questions about fuel and speed and mileage. Then the two crawled into the back, and Ian told them they had a little time, and he'd show them all he could of the city of San Francisco.

From Nob Hill they drove to Union Street and Pacific Heights, then by Russian Hill and Telegraph Hill. They took a detour through Chinatown, then headed toward the waterfront. Along the road, Ian stopped the car atop a hill where they could look down on much of the city. They left the car to stand on the cliff, and Marissa was startled when Ian's hands fell on her shoulders and he pointed out at the city, lightly dusted in fog this morning. Marissa felt a glow of warmth. The morning had been pleasant, she thought. Her excitement over the Olds had pleased him, it seemed. It almost had seemed as if they might be friends this morning. But she couldn't let that happen. She was too haunted by the life he had led, by the things she didn't know—and by the things she hadn't told him.

"It's so beautiful!" Mary said, slipping her arm around Jimmy's waist.

Ian released Marissa and turned to the car. "Think you'll adjust?" he asked Jimmy jovially as they all got back in.

"Aye, that I will. It's a wonderful place, and you're proud of it, I think, Mr. Tremayne," Jimmy replied.

A slow smile curved Ian's lips. "That I am indeed, Jimmy. She's a grand place, never too hot, never too cold."

"Paradise," Marissa murmured.

"Yes, except for—"

He broke off, frowning.

Except for the tremors that sometimes shook the earth, he added silently.

He shrugged. He didn't know why he had avoided mention of the quakes that had shaken the city in 1865. Except that his meeting this afternoon was with the businessmen who wanted to build by the waterfront, in the landfill area.

"Except for what?" Marissa asked him.

"There are no exceptions," he said.

"But you just said—"

He was suddenly curt and impatient. "It's late. We must hurry if you want lunch before going to the emporium."

Marissa fell silent. Ian was quiet as they drove down the hill, then entered the city traffic. Horse-drawn conveyances vied for space with the autos, and Marissa saw her first trolley car. Then Ian pulled up by a curb, and they exited the car. She didn't need him to point out the emporium—it couldn't be missed.

It was a large three-storied building with "Tremayne's" written across the bricks of the top floor in large black letters. But Ian took her arm, guiding her away from it. "We'll lunch here."

There was a large building in front of them. One window advertised the telegraph company, another advertised a bank. Between them was a doorway leading to Antoine's. Ian led them in.

A stairway went to an elegant basement dining area. Snowy white cloths adorned the tables, and candles were set in glass and brass holders. There was rich carpeting on the floor, and the aromas that mingled in the air were appealing. The diners were more arresting in their finery than the restaurant. Ladies in silks and taffetas with elegant little feathered hats sat across from men in their business best. A pianist played soft music from a dais, and the black-jacketed waiters were as proper as the clientele.

The maître d' knew Ian well, and led them to a table by a railing overlooking the piano. He greeted Ian by name, and didn't try to hide his excitement at seeing Marissa.

"Madame Tremayne, *je pense, monsieur?*"

"Yes, Jacques, this is my wife. Marissa, Jacques. And Mr. and Mrs. O'Brien. If you're ever wandering around and in need of a meal, come see Jacques. He will see that you are well cared for, whatever the rush. Isn't that right, Jacques?"

"Oh, *mais oui!*" Jacques agreed. The handsome little Frenchman was smiling widely, with a keen sense of humor and excitement about him. As he seated them and handed them menus, he added, "Madame Tremayne is very young, and very beautiful. *Elle est très belle!*"

Marissa felt a soft blush touching her cheeks as Ian looked at her, too, as if debating the Frenchman's words.

"Yes," he agreed wryly. "She's young."

Marissa had thought that Jimmy might plunge in with something complimentary in her defense, but Jimmy was still busy staring around the restaurant, while Mary was studying her menu.

"Jacques, what on earth is going on with you today?" Ian demanded, exasperated.

"Nothing, nothing," Jacques said quickly. "Monsieur Tremayne, Raoul will wait on you today. I shall send the wine steward immediately, also, yes? Raoul!"

The man was quickly at their side, and seemed as fascinated by Ian's wife as Jacques had been. Marissa was wryly glad that she did not seem to disappoint, yet she was truly curious at the air of excitement she was causing.

"May I order for us all?" Ian asked politely. He was impatient, she realized. He had taken her around the city on her first day, and now he was anxious to get lunch over with and move on to business.

"Please, do," she said, and Ian looked at Jimmy.

"Oh, aye, please do!" Jimmy said quickly, after a moment.

The wine steward poured burgundy into their crystal glasses, which Ian tasted and approved. Marissa noted with a smile that Jimmy had studied his every move, and that Mary watched Jimmy fondly as he sought to learn. Ian ordered and started to tell them about Golden Gate Park, which they had not seen. "A Japanese tea garden was erected there during the Exposition of 1894," he said. "Perhaps the ladies will want to make an excursion one day—"

He broke off suddenly. Marissa turned to discover why.

A woman was walking toward them. She was tall and slim,

with fine, delicate features, large, dark-fringed eyes, and hair so deep and lustrous a brown it was like sable. She smiled, and her chin was held elegantly high. She was dressed in mauve, and a fashionable feathered hat sat jauntily upon her head. She was elegant and sensual, and it was apparent Ian knew her very well.

And it was equally apparent that she was no dance-hall girl.

Ian stood as she approached. He did not seem wary or distressed, and Marissa felt her cheeks burning despite her determination that they should not. Ian had made no promises to her.

"Hello, Grace," he said as the woman approached.

"Ian, dear!" The woman took his hands and rose on her toes to delicately kiss both his cheeks. Her eyes were warm, and she seemed as gentle and fragile as an angel.

Then she turned to Marissa, and her gaze was deadly.

"You must be the new Mrs. Tremayne...child. What a lovely girl, Ian. My congratulations. Oh, I am sorry. Ian has horrid manners at times, doesn't he? Well, perhaps you don't know him quite as well as I do yet. I'm Grace Leroux. We're old friends."

The woman at the station had been one thing—this woman was another. Marissa forgot that at one time she couldn't have cared less what Ian Tremayne did with his life. She wasn't anyone's child, and she wasn't about to let this sweet-faced harpy best her in any way.

She rose, offering Grace Leroux her hand, and smiling serenely. "Very, very old friends, I can see," she said sweetly. "And indeed, my husband's manners can be quite atrocious." She flashed Ian what she hoped was an adoring and intimate smile. She gritted her teeth, hoping he would not step in and make a fool of her.

He did not. His brows rose, his lip curled and he watched her with growing amusement as she continued.

"Mrs. Leroux—or is it Miss?"

"Mrs.," said the woman, her dark eyes narrowing, the hint of a hiss in the word.

"Mrs. Leroux, my friends, Mr. and Mrs. James O'Brien. Mary, Jimmy, Ian's very old friend, Mrs. Leroux."

Jimmy was already on his feet. Mary smiled demurely. Marissa cast a quick glance at Ian, and discovered that he seemed annoyed with the situation.

"Grace, are you staying? Would you like a chair brought?"

"Yes, what a lovely idea," Grace agreed. Ian motioned to their waiter, who quickly brought a fifth chair and seated Grace. She nodded across the table. "Mr. and Mrs. O'Brien," she acknowledged with little interest. She turned her back on Marissa. "Ian, the picnic for the Orphan's Fund is next week, or have you forgotten? Our most influential businessmen will be coming during the day. I do hope that we can count on you to attend." She turned to Marissa. "Oh, dear, it really isn't for wives. Ian, you will be there, I hope?"

"I always support the Orphan's Fund," Ian said with a sigh of impatience. "Of course I'll be there."

"Why isn't it for wives?" Marissa asked with a mock innocence.

"I'm curious myself," Ian murmured, crossing his arms idly over his chest as he watched Grace.

"Well, it's rather a workaday thing, dear. Boring, if you're not involved. And it's a traditional thing, really. Ian has been very involved. He usually escorts me. I am so sorry, dear," Grace purred to Marissa. "You will forgive me for stealing your husband?"

"If I allowed you to steal my husband, I would have to forgive you," Marissa said pleasantly. She folded her hands on the snowy white tablecloth and smiled at Mary. "Mary and I were longing to see the park, so I imagine that we'll explore it on the same day. That way you won't have to feel guilty about my husband, and we won't disturb your tradition."

Grace was still smiling, but the effort seemed to be growing difficult. She stood swiftly. "Well, we shall see," she murmured. "Ian, dear, we'll speak later. It was such a—surprise, meeting you," she told Marissa. Then she waved elegantly and left the table. Marissa noted that she turned and stared at Ian moments later, and that there was cold fury in her eyes. But Ian was not paying any heed, for the waiter had brought their food.

Marissa found herself very quiet during the meal, until the subject of the picnic came up again. Mary asked about the Orphan's Fund. Marissa watched Ian, and was startled when he suddenly turned his head and caught her in the act.

"Should we see the Golden Gate Park that day?" she asked him.

He shrugged, but didn't look away. "If you choose. I've no idea what Grace's tradition is. There is no reason you shouldn't both attend, you and Mary. I plan to have Jimmy busy at the emporium by then."

Marissa lowered her eyes quickly, not wanting him to see that she was inordinately pleased with his words.

Yet when they left the restaurant and Jimmy and Mary preceded them down the street, she could not help but challenge him again.

"You mentioned to the maître d' that you were married. Yet I had the feeling that Mrs. Leroux had no knowledge of me until we met."

He shrugged. "I made luncheon reservations for myself, my wife and friends. I had no reason to inform Grace."

"Yet you almost defended me against her."

He case her a long, dry look. "You seemed to be defending yourself, my love. I've acquired a cat with claws, so it seems."

Marissa stopped in the middle of the sidewalk, and Ian turned impatiently. "I've an appointment this afternoon—"

"She is your mistress, isn't she?"

"Marissa, I told you—"

"You didn't bother to tell your mistress that you'd acquired a wife?"

"It's really none of her business, is it?" he asked her smoothly.

"But it is. I like to be aware of the situations I find myself cast into."

"She's an old friend." He grinned. "Very old, as you were so quick to tell her."

Marissa flushed, but she felt her temper growing. "I don't care to have lunch with your intimate old friends."

"I didn't invite her. Now, would you please come on?"

She didn't move, and he suddenly caught her arm. "Come on!"

She had little choice, for he was nearly dragging her down the street. And when she would have balked again, he paused and turned to her in a sudden fury. "Damn you, girl, you're the one determined on your private quarters!"

"Which you ignored!"

"Ask me in, then." His eyes burned, seeming to bore into her and sweep away the rest of the busy world around them. "I told you, my love, I want you. It was a wretched discovery, but a damned true one. So my affairs, or lack of them, are quite up to you."

"It's not enough!" she cried, trying to shake free of him.

"What?"

"I want—" she began. "I want more than just to be wanted!" she cried out in a rush. She jerked free and hurried ahead, leaving him standing on the sidewalk, reflective, furious.

Then a slow smile crossed his face, and finally he laughed out loud.

CHAPTER ELEVEN

THAT NIGHT Marissa sat at the dining table alone. She picked at an expertly prepared duck à l'orange, and wondered if it was true that Ian had been detained on business.

He had been quick to desert them that afternoon. Well, perhaps he hadn't deserted them. He had turned Mary and Marissa over to one of his clerks, a freckle-faced girl named Sandy O'Halloran, and he had disappeared with Jimmy. Sandy had a natural friendliness and enthusiasm that was instantly endearing, and Marissa felt immediately comfortable with her.

She was the first woman Marissa had met in San Francisco who seemed honestly pleased to meet Ian's wife.

And she obviously loved the emporium. She spent the first hour dragging them from department to department. The emporium seemed to sell absolutely everything from furnishings to garden tools, foodstuffs to recreational paraphernalia. There were bicycles and baseballs, canned goods, the latest in chemises and nightwear, spades and hoes, fine English Chesterfields.

And in the basement there was a cafeteria where the employees had their meals. Though they had already had lunch, Marissa and Mary had tea with Sandy and watched as the employees went through the line for their meals. The cafeteria seemed busy and productive, and the employees were relaxed, talking among themselves as they ate. Marissa caught the occasional covert glance at herself, but she felt that the interest was friendly and open enough, and she smiled in return when she could.

"What do you think?" Sandy asked, seeing Marissa's interest as she surveyed the area.

"I think it's very active!" Marissa laughed.

"Oh, well, then, you should see it on Sunday mornings!" Sandy told her.

"Why?"

"The children from St. Kevin's have their breakfast here after church."

"What is St. Kevin's?" Marissa asked.

"Well, St. Kevin's is the Catholic church, and there is an orphanage, too. Sundays are wonderful."

"You work on Sundays?"

"Oh, no. It's strictly volunteer service, but I do love the children. There are about fifty of the little hooligans. I'm the oldest of twelve, you see, but my sisters and brothers are all back in Ireland. I miss them, and I make up for it on Sundays. Mr. Tremayne supplies all the food, and whoever cares to shows up to help see that it's all ladled out. The children love it. There are griddle cakes and ham and huge sausages and fish—it's a wonder for the children, it is, all the jelly and sweet maple syrup they can eat!"

"Is it in connection with the Orphan's Fund?" Marissa asked her suspiciously.

Sandy gave a little sniff. "No. Mr. Tremayne started his Sunday breakfast long ago. Her Highness Leroux just started with her charity appeals after she learned that Mr. Tremayne—"

She broke off in distress, her eyes very wide as she realized that she was gossiping about her employer's mistress to her employer's wife.

"It's quite all right, Sandy," Marissa said smoothly. "I'm anxious to see this Sunday breakfast. We'll meet you again, I'm certain."

Marissa realized soon after that Mary was wan and exhausted. John Kwan had come for them. Jimmy was busy in the offices, they learned, and Ian had gone to his afternoon meeting.

Marissa accompanied John to see Mary home, but she was determined to explore more of the city herself.

"If you'll bring me downtown, John, I can take a cable car," she told him.

He seemed uncomfortable. "May I show you some of the homes on our hill, Mrs. Tremayne? It will grow dark soon today. Tomorrow you could explore in the morning."

"And you've been told not to let me out of your sight, right?" she asked him wryly.

She could see no reason to cause John distress, so she smiled and agreed to see more of the hill. And after they drove down the hill, where he showed her the magnificent Fairmont Hotel, not yet completed, on the brink of Nob Hill, overlooking the Bay. She was surprised to have thoroughly enjoyed both the impromptu tour and John.

But when she had returned to the house, she discovered that Ian had sent a message home; he would not be there for dinner. And so she was left in the huge dining room alone, with Lee Kwan—whom she did not one bit enjoy—serving her dinner in a stilted silence.

Lee liked her no more than she liked Lee, Marissa realized.

Marissa hovered downstairs as late as she could, but Ian did not return. Finally, when the clock had struck eleven, she gave up and went to bed. Ian still had not returned.

Nor did he disturb her in the morning. She awoke late and found that he had left the house long before she came down to breakfast.

She and Mary spent the afternoon taking a cable car ride. Mary sat on one of the seats, but Marissa could not help but hang on at the entryway, holding her hat on her head as they moved up and down the hills. The cool wind fanned her cheeks. Staring around her with fascination, she decided she loved the city more and more.

On Saturday morning, she awoke once again to find herself alone except for Lee in the beautiful Nob Hill house. More hurt than she was willing to admit, even to herself, she left the house, not mentioning a destination to Lee inside or John by the carriage house. She determined to walk downhill.

She had almost reached the nearly completed Fairmont Hotel when the sound of horse's hooves close behind her startled her. To her surprise, Ian, mounted upon a huge bay, had reined in just behind her.

"Where in God's name do you think you're going?" he said with a frown.

She stepped back, surprised that her heart should hammer with such vehemence. "I am going for a walk. And don't you speak to me that way."

He arched a brow, then leaned low over the horse's neck. "I'll speak to you however I choose, my lady. You scared me half out of my wits."

"I scared you? I do beg your pardon! You're the one who came pounding down upon me."

"I didn't pound—Jinx here trotted."

"Then Jinx here can trot away!" she retorted pleasantly and turned to keep walking.

Jinx didn't trot away. Ian leaped from the horse's back and halted Marissa with an arm around her waist, turning her to face him. His voice had a rough edge to it. "You didn't tell anyone where you were going."

"I didn't know I was required to tell anyone where I was going," she said smoothly, lifting her chin and raising her eyes to his in an emerald challenge. "You never do," she reminded him flatly.

"I'm hardly likely to be the victim of kidnappers or thieves!"

She wished her heart would not pound so loudly, and that the whisper of excitement would not sweep so heatedly throughout her just because he was near, because he touched her. She swept her lashes over her eyes, fearful suddenly that she would give away too much of that excitement.

"Thank you for your concern. Now that you've voiced it and you know I'm out for a walk, I'll thank you to let me proceed."

He stopped her before she had taken a step. "You'll not proceed, young woman!" he snapped. "What foolishness is this? You don't know a thing about the city. You just presume yourself above it all, and you go strutting off not knowing if you're waltzing into danger—"

"Danger!" she taunted him. "Here? On Nob Hill? I hardly think I'm walking through dens of cutthroats and thieves!" She laughed, but her laughter faded at his murderous glare. She slipped free from his arm and backed away. "Ian—"

"Get over here, Marissa."

"I will not!"

"You will!" He promised, taking a step toward her.

"I will not!" He was still coming. She took another step, both dreading and fascinated by the blue fire in his gaze. "You don't bother to speak to me for two days, and then you come riding down upon me like some hound from hell! I will not tolerate it, I'm telling you right now that I simply won't tolerate it!"

"You could have told Lee—"

"I needed air! And I owe nothing to Lee, it is none of her affair—"

"But it is my affair!"

"No, it is not! Not when—"

She broke off with a cry. He had wrapped his arms firmly around her and was setting her up upon the bay with such vehemence she was afraid she would go right over the other side of the horse. But before she could do so he was quickly behind her, and his arms were around her as he took up the reins. Her skirt was not made for riding, and she was forced to fall between his thighs upon the English saddle or lose her balance. Her shoulder rested firmly against his chest, and as he nudged the horse into a smooth canter, she gasped and put her arm around his waist.

"Where are you taking me!" she cried out.

He leaned low. His whisper mingled with the rush of the wind. "You said you needed air!"

And she certainly received it. She could not say that he was careless, for he was an excellent horseman. Yet he rode with a certain recklessness, a wildness, that was exhilarating and exciting. She could feel the heat and energy of the stallion and the man as they rode pell-mell down the street. The wind tore at her hair and plucked at her skirt, chilled and caressed her cheeks. Where his arms touched her, though, she was warm, and deep within her, she felt a rising heat. Tiny laps of fire kissed the base of her spine and radiated like the sun's warmth through her loins to her heart.

She didn't know where they traveled; she didn't care. She closed her eyes and immersed herself in the grace of the animal and the strength of the man. She felt the beat of the horse's hooves. They slowed at last, and the horse moved at a more moderate pace.

As they walked, she opened her eyes and realized that he was staring at her, intently studying her face.

"Where are we going?" she asked him softly. She didn't move her cheek from his chest or her hand from where it lay against his jacket.

He smiled slowly. "For air."

Then he reined in, and, regretfully, she straightened. They were in the midst of a busy world, on a road where the trolley moved, where cars honked, where carriages jangled past.

"The Palace Hotel," he said, indicating the handsome structure before him. His voice had a whimsical quality to it. "General William T. Sherman and President Ulysses S. Grant have stayed here, among others. Caruso will come here on tour soon." He leaped down from the horse and reached up, his hands warm and firm around her waist as he lifted her down beside him. "But there is much, much more to make her great."

He was clearly talking about something that mattered to him, and Marissa was surprised he was doing so to her. He took her hand and walked closer to the hotel, sweeping out an arm to include all of the construction. "She is built on massive pillar foundations that go twelve feet deep, and iron-reinforced brick walls are two feet thick. There's a huge tank of water in the basement, and there are seven more tanks upon the roof. One hundred and thirty thousand gallons of water to fight fires, and five miles of piping to distribute it. Each of the eight hundred rooms is fitted with a fire detector that triggers an alarm in case of fire, and watchmen patrol every floor every thirty minutes. There have been a number of small fires here, and all successfully fought." He fell silent.

Marissa, her fingers curled in his, knew nothing at all about building. But it suddenly mattered very much to her.

"Ian, how do you know all this?" she asked softly.

He shrugged. "It's my business to know." His hand still holding hers, they strolled along the street. "I'm just so damned frustrated. This is the way things should be built. In San Francisco, at least. And those fools who have asked me to design their offices on the waterfront don't seem to realize that. They don't mind paying for an architect, but when I start telling them about pilings and hoses and water tanks, they start crying poverty."

He fell silent, and Marissa walked quietly beside him. "What are you going to do?" she asked at last. "They couldn't possibly—compromise you."

He stopped and turned to her with one of the slow, lazy smiles that had captured her heart when she had not been aware. He brushed a stray strand of hair gently from her forehead with the back of his free hand. "No, Marissa. They will not—compromise me," he said with a soft laugh that held a stirring note of curious tenderness. "I won't build the damned thing for them unless they're willing to do it my way."

He was suddenly in a hurry again, full of energy. She had to run to keep up with him as they hurried back. A doorman held the horse at the entrance to the Palace Hotel. Ian lifted her up by the waist and leaped expertly to his seat behind her. They trotted with the traffic to the rise of Nob Hill, and there Ian gave the horse free rein so that they raced again.

Marissa closed her eyes and leaned against him. When Ian reined in the horse she opened her eyes with a start.

They were not far from his house, but it was a different home they had come to. It, too, was large and beautiful, with stained-glass windows and moderate gingerbreading, two matching turrets, and graceful ells that gave the house both size and beauty.

"It's one of mine," Ian said simply.

"You built it?"

"Yes. Do you like it?"

"It's—wonderful," she admitted.

"Thank you," he told her. He nudged the bay, and they walked in silence to the house.

Marissa had never known that she could be both excited and content at once. Her veins still seemed to leap when he touched her. But it was comfortable, so very comfortable, to rest in his arms.

But her contentment wasn't meant to last. When they reached the house, John was out front waiting for Ian. "What is it?" Ian asked, still mounted upon the bay and holding Marissa close against him.

"A problem with—logistics, Mr. Tremayne," John said. He glanced at Marissa. "Mrs. Leroux says there's an emergency with the finances for the new children's wing at St. Kevin's. They need you immediately."

Marissa's spine stiffened. She pulled from Ian's hold and leaped down from the bay.

To her distress, her skirt caught upon the saddle. She nearly catapulted over, but Ian caught her. She wrenched angrily at her skirt.

He released it for her.

"Marissa!" he called as she strode toward the house. She didn't answer him.

And to her growing rage, she heard his laughter follow her to the house.

That afternoon she lay carelessly in a steaming bubble bath. She leaned back and closed her eyes, despising Grace Leroux, the woman at the train station, Lee Kwan—and herself. Once upon a time it had been easy to despise Ian, too. But now, though her temper simmered and steamed, she could find no outlet for it. She wanted to shake him and hurt him...and make him look at her. She wanted to share things as they had this afternoon. He had dreams, too. Perhaps he had buried the art of loving someone when he had buried his first wife, but he still knew how to dream. And he loved something. He loved building—with a passion.

She started as she heard a door slam. She thought quickly— she was certain that she had locked the door to the hall. She had no intention of being surprised by the silent Lee Kwan.

But she hadn't locked the door between hers and Ian's rooms. And he was coming in now, still in his riding clothes.

A flush that had nothing to do with the heat of the bath flooded her features as she frantically swished the water to make more suds. She wanted him, yes. She was falling in love with him, yes.

But she was not going to let him know it.

Heat pressed behind her eyelids and she felt ridiculously as if tears would sting her eyes again.

Not unless he fell in love with her. Not unless he could rid his life of the Grace Lerouxs and the dance-hall girls and the Lee Kwans...

She looked up, and saw he was carrying a silver tray with two teacups and a beautiful samovar.

Marissa stared at him blankly, then swore with a sudden fury. "What are you doing?"

"Bringing my darling young wife tea," he said. His tone was pleasant, but his eyes carried a satyr's gleam.

She sat up, trying to hold on to her bubbles. "I don't want tea."

"Certainly, you do."

He set the tray upon a wicker stool, poured the tea and brought her a cup. She clung to her bubbles, glaring at him. "I do not want tea."

"Suit yourself." He leaned against the wall and sipped the tea.

"Would you please leave?"

"I came with a gesture of goodwill."

She leaned back, smiling sweetly. "How's Grace?"

"Aha! So there we are. That sweet edge of jealousy!"

She wished he weren't quite so appealing with the gleam in his eyes, the rakish fall of his hair, even the laughter within him.

"I'm not jealous," she said demurely. Her bubbles were popping quickly.

"You're not?"

He was so darned sure of himself. It seemed time to test her own power.

She stretched out a leg prettily, soaping it with an oversize bath sponge. "Not a bit," she said. "Why should I be jealous? This marriage is in name only, right?"

"It's what you've said you want."

She lowered her leg slowly and gracefully, watching it. Then she met his eyes. "You don't want a wife," she reminded him very softly.

He set his cup down on the tray and strode to the tub, staring at her. "Perhaps I've changed my mind."

She smiled, stretching her arms out elegantly before her. "Oh, I think not."

"And why not?" He lowered himself, hunching down beside the tub, his fingers idly moving over the water.

She watched the play of his hands, thinking how very close they were to her naked flesh. She caught her breath, watching him, unable to answer at first. Then she met his eyes again. "You were too eager to run to the beck and call of—" she hesitated a minute, then finished sweetly ":—that old bat."

He burst into laughter, and the spark of fire remained in his eyes as he continued to swirl his hand through the water. "Not jealous?" he murmured.

"I merely call a spade a spade," she said innocently.

His laughter faded, and his ink-dark lashes covered his eyes. "But you see, I didn't leave my wife to run to that old bat. The wife, you see, went huffing off without a single question, giving the husband no recourse."

She gently but firmly pushed his straying hand to the edge of the tub. "No recourse but to run to the old bat?"

"Indeed, I saw the er, old bat. But it was necessary to talk to a friend and assure him he needed to spend his money for a new wing for the children. I had to convince people that all we needed to do was come up with the price of the materials and labor, since my services would cost nothing. And they would all be praised for their generosity, with so little needed!"

She smiled. "I don't believe you."

"It's God's own truth, I swear it," he told her.

"The lady is only a friend?"

A slight curl touched the corner of his lip. He reached out, setting his thumb beneath her chin so that her eyes met his. "Not always. I would be a liar to assure you that nothing ever was. I painted you no half truths in London. But I do admit, the old bat pales mightily in comparison to the young vixen."

She could not draw her eyes from his. She started to smile

at his words, then her smile suddenly faded for he had stood up and was drawing her to her feet.

When she was standing, still in the tub with the water and the bubbles sluicing from her body, he wound his arms around her and his lips met hers. His kiss was hot and filled with a passion that invaded her being just as his tongue invaded her mouth and all the sweet crevices within.

His fingers moved over her naked spine as he kissed her. And he pressed her close against him as his lips deserted hers to roam over the arch of her throat, to find the pulse that beat heedlessly there, to linger, to roam again.

She caught his cheeks between her hands. She felt the masculine texture of them, somewhat rough and exciting, and she met his eyes again. And she stood on tiptoe to press her lips against his, to taste the rim of them, to delve within them herself, shyly taking the initiative at first, then boldly pressing forward.

The scent of him swept her. A rich scent of leather and fine brandy and man. And then she could no longer hold him to her for his kiss was pressed against her shoulders. The searing heat of his mouth curled around her breast as his passion plucked at one rouge crest. Then his lips were buried in the valley between them before moving on.

He fell to his knees, and the flickering motion of his tongue moved in and out of her navel. Then he turned her and a gasp escaped her as his kiss centered upon the base of her spine, as the fire of his tongue moved up and then down again, until a fire seared all the flesh of her buttocks, and she was certain she would fall.

He turned her yet again, and now his kiss was searing the center of her being, boldly, intimately, completely. Shock and excitement wrapped her, and she grasped desperately for his shoulders. She was going to fall. She could not fall. Sensations she could not endure began to sweep through her. Sweet, so

sweet, hot and sweet and so unbearable that she could
surely die.

She cried out, she had to protest. But it was no cry of
protest that left her lips. The cry was sweet with growing
wonder, growing desire...

Then startling, shattering knowledge. So quickly, so won-
derously, so heatedly, a startling, shimmering lava burst
within her. She cried out again, stunned, shivering, gasping,
almost falling.

He swept her into his arms, and his lips touched hers, and
she was so stunned with the wonder that had seized her, she
could not kiss him. She was barely aware that he carried her
into the bedroom, barely aware that she lay on the bed,
stretched out, waiting for him.

And then he was with her. Naked this time. He crawled
atop her and found her lips again. And suddenly she was
clinging to him, shivering. Her eyes met his, he smiled, she
closed her eyes, and he kissed them, then kissed her lips. And
her arms went naturally around him.

And as he kissed her she began to explore his flesh. Her
fingertips moved over his naked shoulders and back. She
heard the sharp inhalation of his breath as she touched him.
And touched him.

She shivered, awakened anew as his weight sank between
her thighs. She buried her face against his shoulder as he
teased her with his touch, creating a new rise of desire, of
heat and dampness. She wanted to cry out, but she could not.
He brought her fingers down and wound them around him,
and she started at the pulse and boldness of his body. She
cried out as he wedged himself hard between her thighs, then
entered deep within her in a slow, sensual thrust.

The rhythm of the world took flight. In his arms, she soared.
She felt the fullness of him within her, she felt the texture of
his thighs, the caress of his hands, the heat of his whisper.
And she felt, too, the wonder, the soaring...

And the final caress of the magic. Deep and shattering, filling her body, coursing through her. Stars seemed to burst, and disappear, and there was nothing but blackness, and she was drifting...

Until she heard her name, the whisper of her name, upon his lips.

She opened her eyes, and he smiled. The slick dampness of their bodies was still hot between them. He had not moved, but remained deeply imbedded within her even as little tremors remained to touch their bodies.

The tremors faded away, and still their eyes met. And he spoke to her again at last.

"I have learned something, Marissa," he said, his voice amazingly tender. "I have learned that I do, after all, want a wife. I want her very much."

Her heart seemed to slam against her chest. And she started to smile, and he caught her lips in another deep and shattering kiss.

And with that kiss, she surrendered all.

CHAPTER TWELVE

MARISSA WOULD REMEMBER little that was precise about that afternoon. Rather she would remember the sensations. There had been sweet comfort in the quiet between them when ecstasy faded to gentle bliss and she lay beside him, her hair a tangle upon his shoulders and chest. There was the sound and the cadence of his words as he spoke to her. He never said he loved her. She wouldn't have expected him to do so. It didn't matter. She had more than she had dreamed, for he wove a future for them. He spoke of the opera, of the ballet, of the waterfront. Of sunsets and sunrises, trips to Sausalito and Carmel, of riding along the coast to see the majestic sights.

Then the quiet and the comfort faded as passion was rekindled. And in the next sweeping wave of fire, she began to learn to explore herself. She began to dare new things, to discover the man. To run her fingers through the soft, dark hair upon his chest, to touch and stroke…to tempt. She was amazed at the laughter between them, at the breathlessness, at the closeness that blanketed them as her inhibitions were shed.

Twilight came, and a soft fog wafted over the city. It seemed to enter the windows, to wrap them in something mystical. Marissa could almost feel it, cool and caressing against her naked flesh. Within its embrace she rose over Ian, smiled and met the curious fire in his eyes. Then leaning low against him she sensually swept the soft length of her hair slowly over his chest, following each silken sweep with the damp heat of a lazy, luxurious kiss. And so she made her way down his body, delighting that he could tremble so beneath her, until he caught his breath in amazement and excitement, going rigid beneath her bold touch. He swore softly, then lifted her above him to impale her swiftly and surely.

The gentle fog tempered her cries and whispers, and caressed her still when she lay exhausted and sweetly sated and amazed once again.

Marissa drifted into sleep, curled by his side, her hair blanketing his chest, her fingers resting lightly upon his naked flesh. She heard a rapping sound, as if far away. Then she started, for the hard-muscled cushion beneath her head moved. "What is it?"

"Lee is at my door," he said. He rose, sleek and handsome in his nakedness. He found his trousers and started for the connecting door.

Then the rapping came at Marissa's door. In the hazy twilight that blanketed the room, Ian cast her a wry grin that caught at her heart. He opened her door.

Lee was there. Marissa heard her softly spoken words, but could not understand them.

Ian closed the door and came to the foot of the bed. His hair was dark and tousled over his forehead, and the shiny dampness of his chest enhanced the muscled structure of it. Marissa started to stretch out on the bed, heavy-lidded, lazy and luxurious.

"Oh, no!" Ian told her with a laugh, snatching up the sheet. "We've company."

"Company!" She bolted up. She was a mess, hair everywhere, naked, and slick with a slight sheen of perspiration.

He smiled easily at her panic. "Take your time—you've at least five minutes. I'd forgotten, Sullivan and Funston are here for supper."

"Who?" she gasped.

"Dennis Sullivan, the fire chief. And Frederick Funston, Brigadier General Funston, that is, acting commander of the

Presidio. He and his wife, Eda, have a beautiful home here
on Nob Hill. I'm afraid you caused it to completely skip my
mind, but they're downstairs now. Lee will serve drinks, I'm
sure.''

''We've company, and you're standing there like that!'' she
gasped.

He laughed and headed for the door to his room. ''I'll be
back in five minutes.''

''No, I can't dress in five minutes and meet people! Ian,
you must wait—''

But he was already gone. Hastily she went to the bathroom.
Biting her lip, she doused herself with cold bathwater then
dried off furiously. She raced to her room, rummaged through
several drawers to find underclothing and proper attire, then
tried to brush, arrange and pin her hair.

Her hair was civilized, she decided, staring into the mirror.
Her eyes were still very wild.

She heard a low whistle and turned. Ian was back, dark,
handsome, immaculate in black. His blue gaze took in her
appearance from head to toe. She had chosen a white ruffled
silk blouse with a high collar and a watered silk skirt. The
white of her outfit was offset by the jet beads and drop ear-
rings she had chosen, and the fine black brocade jacket.

''Am I all right?'' she asked anxiously.

''Positively—virginal,'' he told her. She flushed, and he
arched a brow with a curious smile. ''It's just Dennis and
Freddie and Eda,'' he said, ''not royalty.''

She glanced at him quickly and remembered that although
it had seemed that she had been changed completely and forever by their lovemaking, she hadn't been. She might be in
love with him, but that didn't change the fact that she was
living a lie. She could tell he was thinking that she was accustomed to meeting the upper crust of British society.

She looked at the dresser. Not even the lie really mattered

now. She was a good actress, and she had learned her role well. "They are your friends, aren't they?"

"Yes."

"Then they are very important to me," she said softly.

He was across the room to her with a few long strides, raising her chin with his thumb and looking into her eyes. He studied them carefully and slowly smiled. "My love, you are such an enigma. So very proud and determined, fighting all the way. And yet when you choose, the pride is stripped away, and the heart can be laid bare, and it is a beautiful heart."

"Don't!" she whispered.

"Don't?"

"It is not so beautiful a heart," she murmured quickly. She backed away from him. "You've been very good to my friends." She stood still, then raced to him, throwing herself into his arms and looking into his eyes. "Ian," she began hurriedly, "I started things badly, I forced this on you, but I mean to try to make things work, I want very badly to be what you want—"

"Shh!" he whispered, puzzled, as he caught her face between his hands and kissed her gently. "Marissa, if I had been completely against the idea of marriage to you, I wouldn't have married you, no matter what. I could not have been forced to do so. And since I met you, you've been surprisingly many things that I want, many."

She flushed, her lashes lowering.

"Modesty now?" He chuckled, then moved his thumb gently over her lower lip. "Marissa, you caught my heart the other day. You made me see that I was creating my own hell. Marissa…"

He pulled her against him and held her close. Then he broke away, his eyes sparkling. "Our dinner guests await." He caught her hand and led her from the bedroom, down the the stairway and to the dining room, where their company awaited them.

A short red-haired man stood beside a lively little woman with dancing blue eyes. By the buffet, which was doubling as a bar, was a taller man with a lean face and a haunted gaze.

"Eda, Frederick, Dennis, welcome," Ian said quickly, drawing Marissa around. "My wife, Marissa. Marissa, I give you the true heartbeat of San Francisco and Nob Hill, Mrs. Eda Funston, and her husband, Freddie. And by the buffet, Dennis Sullivan."

The gentlemen assessed her silently; Eda's blue eyes sparkled as she greeted her effusively. "So this is the new bride that has the city abuzz!" Eda said. "Marissa, welcome, welcome. What a lovely addition you are to this house. It has not seemed quite so alive in positively ages."

"Thank you so much," Marissa told her, glancing at Ian. Eda was wonderfully warm. She felt very welcomed, indeed.

Lee appeared. She remained silent until Ian noticed her, then she announced that dinner was ready.

They were soon seated. Lee returned to serve the soup, and Ian poured wine, and the conversation remained casual. Then Dennis Sullivan almost curtly asked Ian, "Have your clients received the permits for the new buildings from City Hall?"

Ian stared at Dennis, then lifted his glass and stared at his wine. Then he looked at Dennis again. "Yes, the permits were received."

The fire chief slammed a fist upon the table and the dishes rattled. He apologized profusely, but he was still vehement when he looked at Ian again. "I'm telling you, this is more corruption! Those codes are insane! It's Mayor Schmitz and that kingmaker of his, Reuf, collecting under-the-table money on these things. Just like the Barbary Coast, feet from our door! Reuf makes money every time he hands out a license for a French restaurant!"

Marissa had no idea what was going on. Eda Funston gently put a stop to the conversation. "Gentlemen, we are at the dinner table!"

"Yes, we are at dinner." Ian offered Marissa a wry smile, then looked at the fire chief. "Dennis, I have turned the project down in no uncertain terms. They'll have to find themselves another builder."

Eda turned the conversation, chatting easily about the upcoming tour of the Great Caruso and his famed temper. When the meal ended and the gentlemen had disappeared into the study for cigars and business, Eda and Marissa wandered across the entry to the parlor, and Marissa asked Eda what was going on.

Eda sighed, taking a seat before the window. "Corruption, my dear. I'm afraid this city is filled with it! My dear Freddie and Dennis and your Ian are quite disgusted with all of it."

"But what, precisely, is going on?" Marissa demanded.

"There's not so very much that we can prove, but we know licenses and permits can be bought. The insurance underwriters have given us reports. It's amazing—and entirely through the diligence of the fire department, they have said—that the city has not burned to the ground. Dennis wanted to train men to use explosives to fight the fires, and he thought a supplementary saltwater system to fight fires was necessary. The War Department in Washington was willing to send men to the Presidio to be in readiness to help with the fire department. All they wanted was for the city to provide a thousand dollars to build a brick vault on the Presidio grounds to house the explosives. Mayor Schmitz managed to thwart his plans."

"But if the city has been warned—"

"The board cannot enforce changes, only recommend that they be made."

"What is wrong with a license for a French restaurant?" Marissa asked her.

"Oh, my dear!" Eda said, and laughed softly, a look of mischief in her eyes. "The restaurant is usually there, all right. Downstairs. And then upstairs...well, French restaurants are often the facade for…well, for bordellos. Er, houses of ill repute. Do you understand?''

"Yes, I understand," Marissa told her, hiding a smile. She understood quite clearly. She might not have known the names of such places, but from the first time Ian had discussed his life with her, she had been well aware that he knew the location of many a dance hall and house of ill repute.

"And the building codes?" she said to Eda.

"Building permits can be bought, you see. But Ian has never been fooled by Mayor Schmitz. He is far too brilliant a builder not to love the quality of his work. I knew he would never agree to work unless his own codes were met!"

She smiled proudly at Marissa, then added softly, "Of course, it is a shame. Someone will be willing to build using those permits. Then heaven help us all if there ever should be a problem!"

Marissa was startled to feel a curious little tremor seize her heart. She shrugged it aside. Whatever happened, Ian would not be involved. And that was all that seemed to matter.

"Well, now, that's settled. Now, tell me more about your life in England, dear. You've the softest, loveliest accent! You're from the country, and your father was a squire, and now you're here. So, does that make you Lady Tremayne?''

Marissa lowered her head quickly. Guilt riddled her. "I'm Mrs. Tremayne, Ian's wife," she said. That, at least, was true. She managed to describe the manor in England, and to avoid any other direct questions.

Eda was sweet and pleasant, and Dennis Sullivan and Freddie Funston were charming when they joined them in the parlor.

And she knew she did well. The evening should have been a triumph.

But listening to Eda talk, Marissa realized bleakly that, for her, every night of conversation might be a tightrope walk. She would always have to lie and hedge and take care.

It was a sorry thought.

She glanced up and realized that Ian, standing by the fire, was studying her very carefully. Something of her unease must have shown on her face, and it seemed as if he was reading into her soul. She was betraying her own guilt.

She looked away from him quickly, her heart thundering.

She was coming to know him so very well. His eyes were still upon her.

And even when someone asked him a question and he turned aside, she knew that he had not forgotten what he had seen in her face.

And later, there would be a reckoning.

SHE WASN'T expecting it as soon as it came.

She was the last at the door, saying goodbye to Eda, when their company left. Returning to the parlor, she felt at first as if her heart were warmed despite the cool winter night. There had been the wonderful afternoon, when she had begun to believe that she could be cherished. And then there had been the evening, when she had begun to believe that she could really become a part of her husband's life.

But as soon as she walked into the small parlor and saw the way Ian looked at her as he stood before the mantel, she was forced to remember that she was living a lie.

She wanted to run for the stairway, to escape to her room, slam and lock the door. Just fighting for the courage not to do so kept her heart hammering hard.

Perhaps cowardice would serve her well at the moment. It was strange how she had once dreaded being too close to him. Now she longed to be close. A passionate kiss could spark the magic to make them both forget that secrets lay in her eyes.

He was staring at her darkly and broodingly. She opened her mouth to speak, but words would not come. She picked up an elegant little pillow from the sofa and plumped it, seeking easy, casual words.

"Your friends are very nice. I enjoyed them thoroughly."

He didn't say a word. "It does seem a shame that you've got this beautiful city and then problems in the City Hall."

He still didn't speak, and she felt her nervousness growing. She set the pillow down. "Well, it seems very late. I think I'll retire for the evening—"

"I think not," he interrupted softly.

There was nothing soft about his gaze.

Marissa straightened her shoulders, swiftly deciding that indignation would be the best way to play the scene, with perhaps a touch of pathos. "Really, Ian," she said very quietly. She lowered her lashes to flutter over her cheeks. "After everything, that you can still accuse me—"

"I'm not accusing you of anything," he said flatly. "And yet that you answer so quickly and defensively disturbs me." His gaze was hard and penetrating still. "And you are not guilty. Then what?" he demanded.

"I don't know what you're talking about!" she snapped.

A wry, suspicious smile curved his lips. He left his stance at the fire and strode toward her.

"I'm going to bed!" she announced haughtily, spinning around, but too late. She knew him; she should have known he wouldn't have allowed her such an arrogant retreat.

He grabbed her by the shoulders, and then his fingers were raking through her hair, holding her head so that her eyes met his relentless blue stare.

"Ian, really—" she began impatiently.

"Yes, really, my love. Tell me what it is that you keep from me?" His voice was low, but intense and passionate. She felt a trembling begin within her, and she shook her head.

"Damn you, there's nothing!"

"There's nothing," he repeated softly.

"Bloody nothing!"

"Ah, but then why is your gaze so haunted? You can no longer fear me, I am certain."

"I never feared you!"

"So what is it that you do fear?"

"Nothing!"

She bit her lip, meeting his hard, hostile gaze.

He couldn't have ceased to want her so quickly! she told herself.

She had not ceased to want him!

If only he would hold her close, kiss her hard, let it be! She longed to cry out, to sweep her arms around him, to forget that she lived a lie. She wanted so badly to tell him the truth at that moment.

But she couldn't. Not now. Maybe the time would come. Perhaps she could earn his trust, his affection, even his love.

"Marissa?"

"There's nothing!" she repeated, trembling. And then she wrenched away from him, certain that he would come after her. And then she would hold him, and make him forget his demands upon her.

But he didn't follow her. He walked to the tall mirrored hall tree by the doorway and picked up his black cape and top hat. "We'll discuss it when I return," he told her briefly. "Have an answer by then." He tipped his hat to her and turned.

Startled, she stared after him. He strode through the beautiful entryway to the front door.

Marissa forgot she was on the offensive and tore after him. "Where are you going?" she asked in amazement.

He smiled. "Out, my dear," he said, and threw open the front door, then headed toward the carriage house.

Marissa felt a blush rush to her cheeks. She couldn't believe the pain and jealousy that seared through her. After the time they had spent together, after the uninhibited abandon she had learned, he was leaving her!

Heading for the Barbary Coast. And French restaurants!

She caught the front door before it could close and followed him out in absolute fury and indignation. "Ian! Ian Tremayne!" she called from the beautiful Victorian porch.

He stopped and spun around.

"Don't dare think to question me again!" she warned him, her eyes alive with an emerald fire. "Don't think to question me—don't come home, for that matter!" she snapped, forgetting that it was his home. Before he could respond, she turned and slammed her way into the house. She leaned against the front door. She couldn't believe it! She was about to burst into hysterical tears. How could he leave her? She had fallen in love, and she had given everything to him, and it had meant the world to her, but nothing to him!

She heard horse's hooves upon the drive, and she knew he was gone.

Marissa glanced up just in time to see Lee Kwan slipping from the entryway to the dining room. She didn't know what the girl had seen or heard, but embarrassment suddenly rippled into her pride just as viciously as pain had torn into her heart.

She turned and slammed out of the house. She would walk down to the caretakers' cottage and see Mary and Jimmy, she thought.

But she didn't really want to see Mary. She didn't want to bare her shattered heart or pride.

She walked into the night. She was startled when the door opened and closed quickly behind her. She spun around to see that Lee had followed her out.

Lee, with her exotic beauty and mysterious face! Marissa felt even more battered.

"Mrs. Tremayne! Please."

"Please what, Lee?" she responded, watching the woman with wary suspicion.

"It's late. Sometimes men—drunk men—wander this way

from the dance halls. We are perhaps too close, as the Funstons think. You must come back in the house!''

Marissa smiled suddenly. ''Where is he going, Lee?''

Lee's dark lashes covered her exotic eyes. ''Just for a ride.''

''You're lying. Why do you bother to defend him from me? I could have sworn that you hated me.''

Lee looked straight at her then, and slowly smiled. ''I did hate you,'' she admitted.

''You did? Meaning that you don't anymore?'' Marissa demanded.

''No, I do not hate you anymore,'' Lee said quietly.

''Well, I admit to being confused. But then, you know where he has gone, don't you? And I do not.'' It was a wild shot, but it seemed that her conversation with Ian's servant had taken a curve that her heart demanded she follow.

''Yes, I know where he has gone.''

''To see the woman by the train.''

''He is doing nothing that will hurt you.''

Marissa threw up her hands, ready to laugh, and ready to cry. ''How can you possibly know what will hurt me?''

Lee shook her head and lifted her chin. ''I know him better than you.''

''Obviously. At least, you have known him longer.''

Lee shook her head again, vehemently. ''You are wrong, Mrs. Tremayne. Your husband has never made me his concubine, though I might well have been willing. He has always been a friend to John and me. He treats us as people, when many blame the Chinese for every ill within the city. We had nothing, we starved. We worked for pennies a day, and John was ill when Ian found us in Chinatown and gave us jobs here. So, yes, I love him. But not as you think. I hated you when I believed that you meant to hurt him. Now, if I am not mistaken, you are in love with him. And you will not hurt him. So I bear you no ill will.''

Marissa stared at the Chinese woman for a long moment, amazed. Lee was not speaking as a serving girl was supposed to speak to her mistress.

But then Marissa had been a serving girl herself, and she had never forgotten her own pride. Lee had much of it. She stood with the gentle evening breeze just plucking at her turquoise silk shirt and black pants. Her fabulous black hair moved in the wind, as inky dark as a raven's wing. Her chin was lifted; she was prepared for anything.

"You have the right to dismiss me now," Lee told her.

Marissa shook her head. "Dismiss you?" Then she laughed, and she almost wished that she could tell Lee the truth about herself. "I have no desire to dismiss you, Lee. And if I did," she admitted, "Ian would certainly not tolerate the act!" She walked toward the woman, smiling, and offered Lee her hand. Lee hesitated, then took it.

"Thank you," Marissa told her.

Lee nodded after a moment.

"But where did he go?" Marissa asked her. Lee was quiet and Marissa said again, "He went to see that woman. The one at the train station."

"There is a show opening tonight. He has gone to support the show, and nothing more."

"How can you know that?"

Lee shrugged. "I know, that is all." Marissa wanted more, and Lee knew it. "Because he cares for you now. I believe he went because his patronage helps her business. So he will go to see the show."

"Why didn't he tell me?"

Lee smiled. "It will take him time," she said. "He is his own master."

On an impulse Marissa laughed and hugged Lee. For a moment the Chinese woman was stiff, then she warmed and hugged Marissa in return.

"Thank you!" Marissa said, then she fled to her bedroom.

The hour was very late. Marissa changed to a nightgown, then began to pace the room. In a sudden fit of anger, she locked the door between the rooms.

And then she paced the floor again.

She curled up at the foot of her bed and ran her hand over the spread. Lee had been in the room, it seemed. She had managed to serve dinner and clean the room.

Marissa hugged her knees to her chest and wondered if Lee was right, if Ian had come to care something about her. She smiled, beginning to weave dreams.

Then she gasped and leaped to her feet as the door between the rooms suddenly seemed to thunder, then came bursting open.

Ian had returned.

She stared at him, and at the door, and he offered her a wry, challenging smile. "It's my house, my door. I warned you, remember?"

She met the challenge with fury. "Your house, your door. My determination for privacy!"

He stripped off his cape, and tossed his hat aside and came striding into the room. She cried out, determined to escape him, but he was too quick. His fingers had already laced around her arms. She began to shake, furious, yet glad that he had come at last. Wanting to shake him, and wanting to hold him.

"How dare you!" she whispered vehemently, fighting his hold. "How dare you go running to your brothel and come back to me!"

He swept her into his arms. "I went to no brothel!" he swore, and tossed her hard upon the bed. She started up, but his weight came down upon her too quickly, pinning her there. And his blue gaze was full of both ice and fire.

"Don't—" she began, but equally vehemently, he challenged her.

"How dare you, madam!"

"How dare I what!" she cried indignantly. She felt the power of his arms, of his thighs. Beneath his trousers she could feel the heat of his body, and more. Against the flimsy fabric of her gown, she could feel the pulse of his desire, growing, insolent, demanding...exciting.

"Lie to me," he whispered.

"I did not run to another!"

"Nor did I."

He caught her lips in a passionate kiss. She surged against him, trying to escape. She was desperate that he understand he could not go to other women and have her, too. She twisted and tossed, and only managed to come closer against him, to become more aware of the promise that lay so boldly between them. She broke free of his kiss. "Ian, I'll not—"

"By God, would you still fight me!" He gazed at her with a fire in his eyes that sent her mind reeling and her heart drumming. A pulse ticked hard in his throat, and she felt the rigid pressure of his muscles.

"I'm not fighting you!" she gasped suddenly. "I'm fighting her!"

"Her?"

"That woman."

"Madam, there is no one to fight."

She believed him. She wanted to believe him. "And—" she whispered.

"By God, and what!" he thundered in sudden torment.

"The questions," she said softly, meeting his eyes.

A breath escaped him. His head fell back, then he stared at her again. "Damn the questions, Marissa. Just hold me. Let me make love to you."

A soft cry escaped her. She wound her arms around him, and when his lips caught hers again, she parted her own beneath him and gave way to the passion of his arms.

CHAPTER THIRTEEN

IN THE DAYS that followed, Marissa made no further mention of Ian's night out. And Ian did not haunt her with questions.

It was a fascinating time for them both, a time for discovery, a fragile time in which they wanted to relish the amazement and wonder of one another. In her wildest fantasies, Marissa had never imagined what it could be like to love such a man. There were wonderful, tempestuous times in bed, and there were times of laughter, too, such as the occasion he crawled fully suited into a tub with her. And there were the gentle times, the slow, lazy, sensual times when they would sip champagne and eat tiny bites of fruit and cheese in bed.

There were evening rides, when Marissa discovered more of the city she was coming to love so very much. And there were the times they would go to the emporium. Marissa loved the store, she was terribly proud to see how very well Jimmy was doing, and she and Mary both became good friends with their one-time guide, Sandy, very quickly. Marissa was particularly fascinated with the orphans at the Sunday meal, finding that the little urchins with their feisty pride reminded her very much of herself when she was a child.

The more she learned about her husband, the greater the pride she came to feel for him. Perhaps he lived on Nob Hill, and perhaps he was welcome among the very best of society. But Ian drew his friends from people he liked. They included builders and policemen as well as the most influential businessmen. He abhorred the politics at City Hall, and would have no part in the bribery that went on there.

He was as willing to sip tea at the caretakers' cottage with Jimmy and Mary as he was to attend the most elite function.

As much as he loved San Francisco, he was not immune to the dangers within the city. One night when they rode, he showed her how close the wildness of the Barbary Coast lay to the quiet of Nob Hill.

"It's a city in which to take grave care," he warned her. They had reined in atop the hill to look down upon the city below. "Murder can be bought for the price of a cheap bottle of whiskey," he told her. "The police have started using automobiles now to patrol the city better, and it seems we have a decent chief in at last, but this is a place where there is a certain amount of crime. Shanghaiing occurs daily—"

"What's that?" she asked him.

He glanced her way quickly. "Ah, my love, you are an innocent! Shanghaiing is kidnapping. Young men and women are taken, sometimes to work on ships—more often to enter the brothels of the Orient. That's why the Barbary Coast is a place you should definitely avoid. I imagine that you'd be worth a fortune, with your hair and eyes, to some potbellied old geezer out there."

"Well, I like that! I'd be worth a fortune only to a potbellied old geezer?" she demanded.

He laughed then, huskily, and the bay pawed the ground as Ian moved his horse closer to hers. "No, my love, though I don't think I'd dare tell you what your value is to me. It might be dangerous information in your hands, and it might well go to your very pretty head."

Marissa smiled, pleased with his response. Their marriage still seemed fragile, but it was enough for now.

"Then you must stay away from the Barbary Coast, too," she said sweetly.

"But there are certain pursuits there to be enjoyed by gentlemen."

"My curiosity is awakened. Since it is not safe for me to

go alone, I shall have to come in your company when you next seek your pursuits.''

"You, madam, are going to have to learn your proper place as a lady and a wife.''

"And you as a gentleman.''

"A Yankee,'' he reminded her.

She sniffed, but after a moment she met his eyes and asked him softly, "Are you then resigned to having a wife once again?'' Then she wished she hadn't spoken, for shadows seemed to cross his features.

"I'm sorry,'' she said quickly. "I didn't mean to cause you pain.'' She nudged her horse and started off at a trot toward the house. Seconds later he was pounding up beside her, then he caught her horse's reins. Startled, she looked at him.

"I am much more than resigned to having a wife,'' he told her. "I am grateful, for you made me see that I lived in a dark cavern of self-pity. You have given me the delight of the sun once again.''

"Oh!'' she murmured, stunned by his words.

"I'm delighted to have a wife. Indeed, come along quickly. Let's return to the house, and I will show you just how delighted.''

Ian smiled at the soft flush that touched her cheeks. He was amazed at the change she had wrought in him.

From the first she had appealed deeply and sharply to his senses. And then she had wedged her way into his soul with her haunting passion and mystery.

He was in love again. Sometimes it was painful, because he felt that he betrayed Diana. But there was something more, for Marissa had taken him from his misery, and now, though he had not ceased to love the memories of his first wife, he had discovered that he had something to offer the new.

She had made his life full again.

And now, as he watched her, he felt the familiar hunger gnawing at his loins. She was part witch, he decided, part vixen to best the harlots of the Barbary Coast, part angel to spread her heavenly hair across the sheets and still blushed a virgin's rouge when she read his mind. He could not remember ever being so sated and content, then so aroused and thirsting from the sound of a whisper or a brush of her cheek.

"Come on—home!" he said, and nudged the bay, and suddenly they were both racing pell-mell for the house. He called to John to take the horses as they neared the carriage house, then he swore suddenly. "I gave them the evening off!" he said. "Ah, well!" He leaped down and helped Marissa from her sidesaddle. She followed him as he led the horses to their stalls. The light in the carriage house was muted as he closed the stalls. The scent of the new hay was sweet.

She had swept off her elegant little bright green riding hat with its dashing feather, and her hair was neither pinned nor tied, but streaming free and wind-tossed down her back in a cascade of gold and flame. In the dim light, her eyes were a beautiful emerald fire. She was very proper in her green riding habit, yet the excitement in her eyes and the curve of her smile were anything but innocent.

She stood several feet from him, watching him, waiting for him. He leaned against the stall door, and allowed his gaze a leisurely stroll down the length of her.

"Ever made love in the hay?" he asked her.

"No," she told him, warily backing away.

"We can correct that."

"No, no, I'm not starting now. You can wind up with hay in your hair and hay in your clothing and—"

She broke off. He had caught up with her and crushed her into his arms. His mouth closed on hers and he tasted the sweetness of it. He buried his face against the streaming silk cascade of her hair, and the lilac scent of her shampoo evocatively pervaded his system.

He lifted her into his arms and carried her into the carriage house, to the rear left corner, where fencing hid the loosened hay. He set her down and swept off his riding cape, laying it over the hay. Throwing himself down on it, he looked at her, certain that he was going to have to do a bit more coaxing.

He was not.

The simple light bathed her. She had cast aside the green jacket and skirt already. She wore only stockings and a silk chemise and pants, fabrics that molded to her body.

Her eyes met his, and she stepped toward him, smiling beautifully. He rose to his knees and circled his arms around her waist. Again, her sweet scent assailed him. He laid his face against her belly, holding her close. Then he kissed her stomach, teasing the soft silk over her body. He drew her down and closed his mouth over her breast, teasing the hardened pink crest beneath the silk, running his tongue over it again and again. She moaned at his touch. He felt the quiver of her heart, the movement within her, felt her surge to his touch. Her lashes had fallen over her eyes. He kissed them, then laid her down, his hands finding the hem of the chemise to pull it over her head. Her breasts, pale and glimmering as perfectly chiseled marble, came free in the night. He touched and caressed her, and found the ribbons of her pants. He pushed them down slowly, and as he bared her flesh to his eyes he bathed it with leisurely kiss after leisurely kiss. Beneath him, she moved more erotically with every teasing flick of his tongue. Mesmerized he watched her. Watched her head toss lightly in the hay, her hair like tangled fire. Watched the rhythm of her hips, her growing impatience, her growing desire.

Then he stripped away his pants, and settled between the sleek temptation of her thighs. He paused to gaze at the beauty of her face. "Marissa, open your eyes," he commanded her. And when she did so, he teased no more but boldly kissed and caressed the heart of her womanhood. With each cry and surge against him, he felt the hammering of his desire rise hard and hungry. She begged him to come to her, to take her then. He did not. He loved her as she quivered and trembled and whispered until the whole length of her exquisite body tightened and shuddered, and seemed to explode like quicksilver. Until she cried out with ecstasy and anguish. And only then did he shed the rest of his clothing in the hay and come to her.

She had risen to her knees. Hungry for him. Eager to hold him, to press kisses against his shoulders. To nip at them lightly...run her tongue against him. To bring sweet ecstasy and anguish to him as he had brought to her. He groaned, casting back his head as she caressed and teased and tormented his body, her tongue like sweet laps of burning honey, her hands and fingers deft and demanding. She slid lower and lower against him until the longing was something he could bear no longer. He cried out, lifted her and laid her flat upon her back. He parted her thighs and sank deep, deep within her.

She wrapped him in her arms and thighs. The glory of her hair entangled them both in a golden cloud. She gave everything, and he marveled at her beauty even as the shattering passion rose to strip away thought. He felt her movement, felt her rise against him, meet him, dance with him, accept and caress him. He whispered words of longing to her, and told her graphically how she made him feel. He rose to a volatile, shuddering climax, pulled away from her, then sank deep, deep within her once again, and there he held.

And as the night cooled them, he thought that he loved her indeed, and the words were on his lips, but he could not say them. Not yet. For now, it had to be enough to hold her, to love her in the silence of the night.

But then he fell to her side, and he heard the soft sigh of her whisper. ''Ian?''

''Yes?''

''I...''

''What?''

"I..."

What was she going to say? He rolled over her, supporting his weight upon his hands. "What is it, Marissa?" he persisted.

Her lashes shielded her eyes. "I like making love in the hay," she said at last.

He smiled, but he felt the disappointment in his heart. Had she been about to whisper softly of love?

No, it would have been deeper than that. She would have told him why that haunting misery so often came to her eyes when she did not know he was watching.

He lay down, holding her. He couldn't press her. It would do no good. When she was ready, she would tell him.

And she would whisper that she loved him.

THE NEXT afternoon Marissa sat upon a blanket on the grass next to a lovely little pond in Golden Gate Park. There were people everywhere, Ian among them. Mary and Jimmy sat beside her, Mary busily throwing dry bread to the ducks in the pond and Jimmy watching Mary while he chewed on a blade of grass, a look of absolute adoration on his face.

They'd met a number of people, among them the mayor, Eugene Schmitz, the man she had heard so much about already. He had been charming, absolutely charming. But his smile did come a little too easily, she thought.

And then Grace Leroux had discovered their little haven on the blanket, and she had most pleasantly managed to take Ian away.

Marissa hadn't minded watching the ducks for a minute or two, for it was a beautiful park and a wonderful day, but when Ian didn't return, she grew restless. "Oh, she is so much trouble!" she whispered in a sudden fury to Mary.

"Shh!" Mary told her. Marissa had never said much about the change in her relationship with Ian. There had been no need for her to do so. Mary had watched the changes in her.

"You mustn't let anyone know that she bothers you in the least."

"Why not? I'd like to rip her dyed hair out!"

Jimmy laughed and brought his opinion into the conversation. "You must not let anyone know that she bothers you, Marissa, because she wants to bother you, don't you see that?"

"But she is so pointedly after Ian!"

"She can't have Ian unless Ian agrees, and that's a fact, Marissa."

That was true enough, Marissa decided. "It seems like there are just so darned many of them!" she murmured, thinking that he had left her once to see a show with Lilli. She had learned a little about the woman from Lee, and she had also learned that Lee liked Lilli a lot more than she liked Grace Leroux. "Why are men always so fooled?" she said to Mary.

Mary, looking over her shoulder, suddenly turned a dark shade of red. Marissa swung around to see that Ian had returned at last. "I don't think that they're so easily fooled," he said, smiling as he settled down beside her. "It just depends on what they want at the moment."

Marissa arched a brow at him. "I wonder what you were wanting when you met our dear Mrs. Leroux." Her voice had a purr in it. Even Jimmy laughed.

"She has a way about her," Ian said.

"Um. As does a black widow," Marissa agreed pleasantly.

"I can see this is heading us nowhere good," Ian said with a laugh. He rubbed Marissa's shoulders and pointed through the crowd. "See there, my love. That's Phineas Van Kellen."

"It is?" Marissa asked. "Who is Phineas Van Kellen?"

"A very smart man. I've just agreed to build a place for him downtown. And he's just agreed to do it my way."

"Oh, I'm so very glad, Ian!" Marissa declared happily.

He flashed her a smile, and for a moment she thought they shared the world.

If only she could tell him the truth about herself! She had almost done so that night in the carriage house. But it wasn't just her own life she held together with a lie—she had Mary and Jimmy to consider, too. And if Ian did despise her for the lie, no matter what their lives had become together, then the others might be hurt.

"See, Marissa?" Ian was saying. She had missed something, and she didn't know what. "Here—"

He had rolled over on the blanket, and Jimmy and Mary were doing likewise, she in her fresh white cotton dress and stockings, he in his light beige suit and handsome new Italian shoes. Bemused, Marissa joined them and laughed as Ian showed them the proper way to construct buildings with blades of grass. "Now see, when the earth shakes, you need a building with some sway. You must have pilings, and you must have steel, but you must also be careful to have that sway!"

He was so passionate about his creations. Marissa loved that in him. She smiled.

"Does the earth really shake so badly?" Mary asked Ian, sitting up.

He looked at her, but never replied, because Grace Leroux was standing over their blankets. "Ian, and dear, dear—oh, I am sorry! It's dear little Myrtle, isn't it?"

Ian had risen and helped Marissa up. "My wife's name is Marissa, Grace. And Mr. and Mrs. O'Brien, you must remember them."

"Oh, yes! Of course." Grace knew their names, Marissa was sure of it. But she could be so very rude with such an innocent demeanor!

Marissa forced herself to smile as Grace sweetly told Ian about certain men he needed to see. Then someone else called Ian, and he excused himself and stepped away from them. He turned back to point out the way to the tea garden.

Mary and Jimmy started toward the garden, and Marissa was momentarily left alone with Grace.

"You think that you've won, don't you?" Grace said. Her smile was gone and her eyes were hard and there wasn't a thing pleasant or innocent about her. "Well, mark my words, little girl, you haven't even begun to play."

There was such venom behind her words that Marissa felt a tinge of unease, but she managed to smile. "Grace, should you forget my given name again, please feel free to call me Mrs. Tremayne."

And then she stepped past the startled woman and hurried after Mary and Jimmy, her smile growing all the while.

Grace was wrong, she thought. She had won. And she won because Ian had allowed her to do so.

BUT LATER that night she wondered if she had been right after all. She had won for the moment.

But if she was caught, living out her lie?

That lie and the way she had to live because of it were the only things marring what was quickly becoming an otherwise perfect life.

And Ian had to wonder what she was doing with the allowance when he signed the papers for her each week. She lived in his house and, other than her excursions with Mary, it would seem she really had little to do with the money. He knew that she was still helping Mary and Jimmy, but he had no idea of just how much money she was sending home, and he certainly knew nothing about the long letters she wrote to Uncle Theo.

Ian did know, however, that she was making a contribution to the Orphan's Fund, although he didn't know that she had discussed it with Mary first. There was one little rascal, Darrin MacIver, of whom she had grown very fond during the Sunday meals at the emporium.

He was ten years old with the street wisdom of a hardened

adult, huge brown eyes and long lashes, and a gaunt, haunted face that might one day be very handsome. Father Gurney had told her that his mother had been "a poor fallen angel" in the Barbary Coast area, and the poor wee lass had died there, leaving Darrin on his own. The child knew every vice game in town, played poker and could swear like a sailor. He had sassed Marissa one day, and all the training of the lady who had become Mrs. Tremayne had fallen from her shoulders and she'd given him a brisk talking to in turn. He'd grown quiet, but on his way out that morning—sweet rolls stuck into his pockets—he had paused to tell her that she was "an all right fellow."

She had spent some money buying Darrin a new suit of clothing, a corduroy cap, flannel breeches, two cotton shirts, long socks, vests and shoes. His delight at the presents had brightened his eyes like lamps, but then the shine had faded and he had pushed the boxes toward her.

"Don't need no clothes, Miz Tremayne."

"But you do need clothes, Darrin. You've holes in your britches, young man!"

"I can make it on what the old man gives me."

"Father Gurney, you mean."

"Yeah. The old man."

"Father Gurney."

"Weren't never a Catholic," he said stubbornly.

"Well, we English are not customarily Catholics, either, Darrin, but I respect such a man sincerely, and therefore he is Father Gurney!"

"Father Gurney," Darrin agreed at last. "But I'm not a charity case!"

If ever there was a charity case, it was Darrin, Marissa thought. But no matter how sweet life had become, she would never forget the taste and smell and feel of coal dust, and she understood him in a way that he must never know.

"Darrin, I need letters mailed every so often. And I'd like

them kept quiet. The clothes don't need to be charity; you can mail the letters for me in return. You can start this Tuesday—meet me around the corner from the entrance to the emporium at about ten o'clock.''

He still didn't trust her, but at last he agreed. Just in time, it seemed, for Ian was coming toward them, interested in the boy who had seemed to capture so much of his wife's attention.

''You like the lad, eh?'' he asked her.

''Yes, I do, very much.'' She smiled at Ian. ''Don't you like him?''

''Yes, I most certainly do. He reminds me of you. It's in the eyes.''

He was teasing her. ''Ian, Darrin has very handsome brown eyes. Mine are green.''

''Yes, that's true. But upon occasion, it seems that you both have a very haunting shade of gray within them.'' He walked by her without further comment, and she watched him.

He was not going to persist, she realized. He had just reminded her that he had not forgotten that he had many questions he might still want to ask her.

That night she was nervous through dinner, and uneasy when he came to her room.

But he didn't ask her any questions about her past. She stood looking out the windows in the turret of her room, her silk nightgown touched by the moonlight. He came to her there, and swept her into his arms, then carried her to bed.

And again, the night passed in magic.

SHE AND Mary met Darrin by the emporium the next Tuesday, as she had planned.

The scamp was there, waiting for her in his new outfit. She greeted him, then handed him a letter for Uncle Theo.

He stared at the letter. ''You could mail this yourself, you know. Quite easily.''

"Maybe. But I'd like you to."

He shrugged. "Sure." Then Marissa realized that he was looking over her shoulder, and that a hostile expression had come to his face. "It's the wicked witch, it is!"

She turned to see that Grace Leroux had just come around the corner. The woman stopped, surprised to see them.

"Darrin!" Mary said, startled by his comment.

"She's someone to keep a firm eye on!" Darrin warned Marissa.

"I can't stop her from shopping in the emporium," Marissa told him. She realized that Grace was watching her intently, with a curious and cunning expression. Then she smiled suddenly.

Darrin was right—it was a wicked smile.

But it was a smile. Grace liked to play social games. Fine. Marissa waved. Grace hurried on.

"She is a wicked witch!" Darrin insisted.

"Darrin, she's so involved with the Orphan's Fund—" Mary began.

"She's involved to impress people, and that's all!" Darrin insisted. "Well, I'll be on with my business then, ladies. Good day to you."

Darrin walked on, and Marissa suggested lunch.

They dined at Delmonico's, and Marissa ordered champagne. Sipping it, Mary looked around the restaurant at their fellow diners, the women in their beautiful gowns, the men in their frock coats and morning suits. She smiled and leaned closer to Marissa.

"Can you believe this, that we've come to be here? And everything is so wonderful."

"Yes, things are wonderful."

"I have never seen you happier," Mary told her. "But then, I've never seen you in love."

Marissa flushed and Mary laughed. "All right, so I have never been happier!" she agreed with Mary. Yet even as she spoke the words, she felt a chill settle into her spine. "And sometimes I'm frightened," she murmured.

Mary set down her glass. "You've got to tell him the truth."

"I can't tell him the truth! I don't dare."

"You must."

Marissa shook her head. "There have been times when I wanted to tell him. Times when the words have been right on the tip of my tongue. But then I remember that I cannot. Mary, I must think about all our lives! About you and Jimmy and Uncle Theo! Oh, Mary, what if he would not tolerate the truth?"

"He loves you!"

"He has never said that he loves me."

"But he does love you! Oh, Marissa! It's in his voice when he talks to you, it's in his eyes when he looks at you. And dear Lord, Marissa! He has proven himself to be such an extraordinary man! Strong and ethical, and so very handsome and sure of himself!"

Marissa smiled. Oh, he was sure of himself! And they could still argue themselves silly, for she was jealous and he wouldn't lie....

And there was still the fear that he might find her out.

"Shall we order?" Marissa suggested, giving her attention to the menu.

"Mmm. But what if he catches you? Wouldn't it be better to tell him yourself?"

"Yes, and if I can just find the right moment somewhere along the line, then I shall do so." She looked at Mary, and saw that her friend still seemed to have a keen sense of excitement. "What is it?" she demanded.

"Oh, Marissa! Jimmy and I are going to have a baby."

"A baby!" Marissa cried with delight. Mary had so much love to give. She and Jimmy were wonderful together. They would love a child and give it so much!

"Oh, Mary!" she cried, grabbing her friend's hand. Then she gasped. "Oh, Mary, what has the doctor said? Are you well enough to have a baby?" She couldn't forget how sick Mary had been in England.

"Yes, I'm quite well enough, and—I'm having a baby one way or the other, Marissa! Oh, Marissa, be happy for us!"

"I am happy for you, so very happy!" Marissa promised her. She squeezed her friend's hand again, then lifted her glass and offered a toast.

But when she lowered her head to the menu again, she realized almost bleakly that she couldn't tell Ian the truth now. More than ever before, she had to protect the secret they all shared. Mary was going to have a baby.

Mary had said that she felt well, but the next Tuesday when Marissa called upon her to come downtown, Mary was still in her nightdress, not feeling at all well.

"It's morning sickness, and nothing more! You and Jimmy must stop worrying!" Mary told her.

Marissa was worried, but she had to go downtown anyway. Darrin would be waiting for her.

Lee was upset that she wanted to go alone. "John can drive you downtown. You should not go alone."

Marissa was surprised. "Lee! I know the area very well now. I'm going to ride down by myself, and I'll be just fine!" The last thing she needed was to have John Kwan with her, wondering what she was doing!

Lee was still unhappy, but Marissa smiled and ignored her. She was touched that Lee seemed to care, and pleased with the affection that had risen between them now that Lee knew that Marissa loved her husband—and Marissa knew that Lee did not!

She rode the small black mare, Jet, that she had taken over for her own. She left Jet in the livery stable by the emporium and visited the store. Ian was not in, she learned. He was due soon, but he was visiting a building site. She stopped by to see Jimmy, and was pleased to see how happy he was among his coworkers and how well he was doing as a buyer and manager. She left him to hurry down and have morning tea with Sandy, and was thrilled when Sandy told her that plans were afoot to open the cafeteria on several early mornings during the week for the orphans.

It was nearly ten o'clock when she kissed Sandy's cheek and hurried out to the corner. She glanced nervously up and down the street, hoping that Ian would not come upon her. Then she saw Darrin hurrying toward her along the walk. She smiled and waved. A minute later, he was with her.

"You're all alone, Mrs. Tremayne."

"Yes, Mrs. O'Brien is not feeling very well."

He frowned, and Marissa was both annoyed and amused. "Darrin, I'm quite able to take care of myself, you know."

"Sure, I know." He shrugged. "I put your letter in the post within half an hour last time," he told her proudly.

"Then here's the next."

He took the letter from her. "You've still got kin in England, huh?"

"I—I've people back home, yes."

"That must be nice," he said. Then he quickly corrected himself. "No, I guess not. Kin lie to you and betray you—and leave you. It's better just to be on your own, that it is. If there's anyone you can believe in, it's yourself, and that's that, I do say!"

He took the letter from her. "Good day to you, Mrs. Tremayne." He walked on and then stopped and turned back. "Take care of yourself, Mrs. Tremayne. We're not far from the Barbary Coast."

She nodded and waved, her heart breaking. She wanted to talk to Ian about the boy. He was such a prickly little lad. Maybe they could find something for him to do up at the house. They could feed him well and give him a good home without offending his pride.

She started walking idly, unaware that she had turned from the main street into the quiet alleyway behind the shops. She was so preoccupied with thoughts about Darrin that she didn't pay much heed to the sound of footsteps behind her.

Then she sensed that she was being flanked. She glanced quickly to the left and right. On one side was a tall man with a dark mustache and a bowler hat worn low over his forehead. On the other was a clean-shaven blond man with a smile that made her skin crawl.

Too late, she realized that she was in danger. She opened her mouth to scream, but before a sound escaped from her, the mustachioed man caught her around the waist and shoved a soaking handkerchief over her face. She breathed in a sickly sweet smell, and the world began to spin.

She fought desperately for reason, fighting the drug that assailed her senses. She had always fought so very hard! And now she could not kick or claw or scratch. She was powerless, and her body was very, very heavy. She could not even scream.

The street careened before her as she started to lose her grip upon consciousness. She could not even feel the arms of the men who held her.

She had fought so long and so hard, and now that happiness was hers…

She could fight no more.

Her last conscious thought was that there had been no one to see her. She would leave behind no sign of a struggle. No sign at all. She had wandered off alone.

Then she could think no more. All the world was black.

But she was not as alone as she had thought.

Darrin MacIver, suspicious street-smart child that he was, had not walked away.

He hadn't thanked her for the clothes, he told himself. Then he muttered out loud that he didn't need to thank her for the clothes, he was working for her now, wasn't he?

But there was something about her that he liked. She was young, and she didn't seem so awfully much older than he and some of the boys. Yet she seemed to be a real lady, not like that Mrs. Leroux. When Marissa Tremayne talked to him, he felt that she really wanted an answer. He felt she cared.

And she had changed *him,* too. Tremayne, the man with the money. Not that he had ever been mean or anything to any of the boys. It had just seemed as if it hurt him to look at them now and again. He'd lost a baby when he lost his wife, Darrin had heard. Funny, life was. A nice rich man with good intent like Mr. Tremayne, and his wife and kid up and die. And down in the brothel, the prostitutes had kids like him in the squalor every damned day.

He felt a sudden guilt at his language. Neither the good priests nor the brothers had ever made him feel guilty. "I'll bet she knows a few swear words herself!" he thought, kicking a rock in his path. Oh, she probably knew a few, all right. Just like she seemed to know him, what was in his mind and what was in his heart. And she was so pretty, so beautiful, with all that golden red hair of hers, and those huge green eyes. He liked her. He liked her a lot. She had changed his life.

He turned, suddenly determined to say something. Thank you, maybe. Something.

He started to follow her.

He was just in time to see the two men sweep up Mrs. Tremayne in her elegant green riding habit and shove her into the rear of small black carriage.

He stood dead still in the street, his mouth open. Then he shouted, "Hey! Hey, you let her go! Hey!"

The carriage moved into the street. He started to run, then

he realized that he would never catch it. He stopped again and looked around blankly.

He saw the large sign. Tremayne's. He started to run again. Mr. Tremayne had to be in. He just had to be in by then.

He started running to the store. He hesitated only once.

And that was when he saw her, the wicked witch, Leroux. He didn't know why he paused. He just wanted to know what she was doing where she was, on the sidewalk, coming around the corner. Pulling a glove up her wrist, and smiling. Oh, smiling. With such great pleasure.

Darrin couldn't worry about her. Not at the moment. He shoved past her. "Mr. Tremayne!"

He was shouting the man's name long before he burst through the doorway.

CHAPTER FOURTEEN

IAN HAD JUST settled into the swivel chair behind his desk. He was congratulating himself about Jimmy O'Brien—the Irish lad had proven himself to be an invaluable asset already. In time, he could take over a great deal of the management. And the more management Ian could hand to others, the more time he had left for architecture and building.

And Marissa, and a personal life that had suddenly become very important.

"Hey, there, young sir! You can't just go barging in on Mr. Tremayne! What's the matter with you, lad?"

Ian frowned. His secretary, Arthur Mount, had shouted the words. Through the frosted glass of his office window he could see the silhouette of Mount holding a squirming youngster by the collar.

"I've got to see him! Let me go! It's an emergency! You let me go or I'll—"

Mount groaned with pain. The youngster fell to the floor, then came crashing through Ian's door. It was the orphan boy, Darrin. He rammed his cap down hard over his forehead. Ian stood, coming around his desk just as Arthur Mount limped in, following the boy.

"I tried to stop the little hoodlum, Mr. Tremayne, I did! Give me just a minute and I'll box his ears and—"

"No, no, that's all right, Arthur," Ian said, somewhat amused by the belligerent boy and the indignant, limping secretary. "There must be some serious problem for Darrin to be so anxious. What is it, lad? Can we help you?"

"They've got her!" the boy burst out. And suddenly the

toughened street kid was stuttering. "They—they've taken her. Mrs.—Mrs. Tremayne. Two men. Outside on the street corner. I met her like I was supposed to, and I turned away. And they had her. Two men. They rode off in a carriage."

Ian stared at the boy blankly for a moment, unable to assimilate and unwilling to comprehend his words. "What?" The single word exploded from him like a rocket; he gripped Darrin's shoulders in a vise, staring at him hard. "What?"

"Two men." Darrin was thinking fast, desperately. He still trembled inwardly, but he gritted his teeth. "One tall with a handlebar mustache. Dark. Pin-striped suit, red vest. The other was blond, not as old as the other guy, maybe about twenty-two. No hat. No whiskers. They took her in a small black one-horse carriage pulled by a small bay, and rode down from the corner eastward—"

"Barbary Coast," Arthur supplied.

"Chinatown, I think," Darrin said, his wide eyes solemnly on Ian.

Ian dropped the boy's shoulders and headed for the door. "Call the police, Arthur. Get someone here quick. I mean quick!"

He went out onto the street, ran the length of the store and tore around the corner. There was no sign of anyone there. No sign of a scuffle, nothing. Frantically he stared down the alleyway, feeling as if cold fingers had clamped down hard around his heart. The boy had made the whole thing up, he tried to tell himself. But he hadn't. Darrin was beneath her spell, Ian had seen that easily enough. The lad adored her.

He swung around. Darrin was there now, he had followed behind him, close, hopeful.

"From here?" Ian demanded. "They took her from here?"

Darrin nodded.

"All right," Ian said. "Get my horse from the livery stable. Then wait at the store and tell the police everything that you told me. Everything. Any little detail might be important."

Darrin fled to do as he had been told. Ian stepped out into the street. There were tracks everywhere, but he could just barely discern where a small carriage had been pulled in close to the buildings in the alleyway. Chinatown. He knew where they were heading. Into the brothels and opium dens, where beautiful women definitely had a price.

Darrin was already coming down the street with his horse. He stared at the boy and he knew they both realized something.

Marissa had to be found quickly, or she would never be found at all. That was the way when a woman was shanghaied.

"Meet the police," he told the boy. "And find Mr. O'Brien in the store. Tell him to get hold of John and Lee Kwan. Perhaps they can discover something. I'll be in Chinatown." He leaped quickly upon his horse. With a nod, he raced down the alleyway, heedless of traffic.

THE NEWS of Marissa's kidnapping spread like wildfire. She was the wife of one of San Francisco's most prominent, affluent and respected men. Also, one of its most popular and charming, for in his days as a widower he had both shocked and excited the mamas of the society belles who would have gladly become his wife by his escapades in the dance halls of the Barbary Coast. Wickedly handsome in evening attire, he was apt to leave an opera for a late show and more decadent companionship. He was loved for his passion for certain ethics—and his total ignorance of others.

In her mansion on Nob Hill, Grace Leroux heard the news from a neighbor with shocked distress.

Then she turned into her doorway and smiled.

Down near the waterfront, in the Barbary Coast, Lilli Reynolds heard the news, and her heart went out to Ian. Few people knew how deeply he had already been hurt.

She called a special employee to her room.

He was a man with a long scar down the left side of his face. He had small eyes, a cavernous face, and was surely as ugly as sin.

But no one knew the dens of the Barbary Coast as well as he. His name was Jake Breed. He'd been in the Barbary Coast as long as anyone could remember. He didn't work for Lilli because he needed money, but because she was the only person he had ever loved.

From her settee Lilli lit a long cigarette and indicated the outside world. "Mrs. Tremayne has been taken. The police seem to imagine that she's in Chinatown somewhere. She was taken by two men." Lilli gave him the description Darrin had so meticulously given to Ian and then the police. "Find out what you can." Lilli hesitated only a moment. "I have a feeling that this was no accidental job."

"I won't come back without something," Jake told her.

Lilli offered him one of her warm smiles. "I know that."

MARISSA awoke very slowly, the drug seeming to take a long, long time to fade. She was aware first of a sweet scent in the air. Then she came to realize that she was lying upon silk. She could feel the elegance, and the softness, and for long moments, the feel of that silk was deceptively comforting.

It was difficult to open her eyes. When she finally managed to do so, she was stunned to realize that she was looking up a very long way at a very fat man.

His hair was straight and black, and he had a long, straight black beard, and a mustache that fell over the beard with the same astounding length. He wore a Chinese coat and dark trousers, and he studied her, rubbing his bearded chin so that the long strands of hair shook.

"Green eyes," he murmured. Then he turned to someone behind him. "Yes, she is worth much. But you are over-

anxious—and greedy. We will discuss the price. I will send
for tea and a pipe, and we will finish our business.''

The price. They were talking about her. She wanted to leap
up and rip out that black beard by the handful. She still
couldn't move. She could barely keep her eyes open.

She decided to close them and try to fight off the sick dizziness that remained. She heard whispers.

''The price doesn't matter! We've already been paid!''

''Right, damned right, so whatever we make now is pure
profit, and I want some of it!'' came the response. The first
voice had been deeper. Marissa was certain that it belonged
to the dark-haired man who had seized her. The second voice
had been higher, more youthful. The blonde.

And then the large Chinese man returned. She heard him
ordering someone around, and heard the sound of liquid being
poured into cups. She smelled something, a cloying, sweet
scent, and she wondered if it was opium.

The Chinese man gave her two abductors an offer for her.
Apparently, it was shockingly low. ''You must be insane! Not
only has she green eyes, but she has golden hair! She's young
and beautiful. She has superb lines, wonderful breasts—'' the
blond man began.

''And the word is on the streets as to who she is. The police
are seeking her already.''

''Ah,'' interrupted the darker of her abductors. ''But you
have the resources to get her on a ship within the next hour.
And once she is gone…''

The Chinese man haggled. Marissa slitted her eyes, desperate to survey her surroundings.

She was in the corner of a large room. There were only
two windows, and those were beyond the men who were hag-
gling at a low round table. Straight across the room from her
sat a woman, her head low, her back bowed in absolute sub-
mission. She was beautiful, a little China doll. She was there
to serve the tea, to light the opium pipe, Marissa thought.

She would not be difficult to elude....

But the men were there. If she tried to rise, to escape, they would be down on her in seconds. Carefully, unobtrusively, she tried to gain strength, flexing her fingers, then her toes. The feeling was coming back to her. She stiffened an arm, then a leg, then relaxed them. She started to inch over to the window. They weren't paying the least bit of attention to her. If she were not too high up, perhaps she could jump out. And if she were high up...

At least she could scream. She had to do something!

They had come to some kind of an agreement. The men were rising. "They will take her to the ship right now. You will wait for your payment below until she is safely on the ship," the heavy Chinese man said.

Now...right now. They were coming for her now. They might drug her again, and she would be helpless, unable to protest.

Marissa could afford no more finesse. She leaped to her feet and raced for the window.

The blond man shouted and jumped. He was almost upon her. She turned and kicked him with all her strength. He bellowed in pain and fell to the floor. Marissa reached the window. She tore open the drapes.

She was high, very high. On the third floor. If she jumped, she would kill herself.

But the streets were crowded. The citizens of Chinatown pulled their little wagons through the street, or walked quickly, some with their papers, some with carts of vegetables and meats.

Some were criminals.

And some were good people.

A hand touched Marissa's shoulder.

She leaned out the window and screamed. "Help! Help me! Oh, dear God, somebody help me!"

She was wrenched into the room with such force that she fell, stunned, upon her back.

"Perhaps we should renegotiate, gentlemen," the heavy-set Chinese man said. "You neglected to inform me that she is an incredible amount of trouble!"

IAN HAD toured the streets, one by one, stopping to ask questions, growing ever more determined and desperate. Passing by a market, then a known opium den, Ian saw a man called One-Eyed Charlie who was a notorious—and extremely slippery—criminal. Charlie dealt in hashish, the best, and in female flesh, the most pathetic. He'd been taken downtown to jail a score of times—he had always managed to avoid conviction. Evidence disappeared, just as women disappeared.

Seeing Charlie, Ian didn't hesitate. He shouted the man's name. Charlie cast his one good eye in Ian's direction, then started through the narrow alleyways, plunging through the crowds. Ian shouted again, leaping from the horse, and racing after Charlie.

He caught up with him in the middle of a narrow alley where clothing and animal carcasses hung in profusion. He catapulted onto the man's back, then dragged him to his feet, nearly strangling him as he shook him by the collar. "Where is she, where the hell is she, Charlie? If she's gone, you aren't going to get off this time! I'll break your neck here and now if I don't get something!"

Charlie burst into a spate of Chinese. Ian shook him, and Charlie switched to English as he began to turn blue. "I don't know, I don't know what you're talking about—"

"My wife, Charlie! The whole damned city knows, and you're going to tell me that you don't?"

"I don't have her, I swear, but I'll find her! Put me down, I'll find her. She could be in a few places. I'll find her—"

"Ian!"

He heard his name shouted as he held Charlie by the throat.

He looked at the street and saw Lee Kwan coming toward him quickly. "Ian, we've got something. Drop Charlie. We've got something!"

Ian looked at Charlie then dropped him. Charlie sprawled on the ground, then picked himself up and dusted his loose trousers, staring at Ian suspiciously.

Then he bolted and ran like a rabbit.

"Lee, what?" Ian demanded anxiously.

"Lilli called. She said she sent feelers out, and she was able to get an address. She said to warn you that it could be dangerous."

"The address, Lee, give me the address."

"I've called the police—"

"And they might be too late! Give me the damned address!"

SHE HAD scratched, she had clawed, she might have cost a few of the heavy Chinese man's helpers a new dynasty of children, but in the end it had done her little good.

Marissa was carefully trussed and wound into a carpet. She could scarcely breathe, and she was afraid that she would lose consciousness when she most desperately needed her senses.

She was thrown over the shoulder of a man who bore the imprint of her nails from his brow to his chin. She could see nothing. Her arms were caught to her sides by the carpet, and she thought she would die if she couldn't breathe soon. But she could hear clearly.

Her assailants were gone, and she had been left to the mercy of the Chinese flesh merchant. She could understand nothing of the language, but she knew that she was being sent to a ship. She was leaving the house in Chinatown, and the man she had so ignominiously wounded was making no effort to be gentle as he carried her downstairs. Her face, wound in the heavy carpet, thudded hard against his back again and again. She could not brace herself for she could not move her arms.

She heard the shouts as they reached a rear alley. She was pretty sure the man who carried her was flanked by three others, wiry, strong young men who carried sharp knives and knew how to use them. She had fought them all until she had felt the blade of one of those knives at her throat. And the heavy Chinese man had warned her then that her value would not decrease too dearly should she bear a scar or two here or there in discreet places.

It was impossible to contemplate what was going to happen to her. She'd been warned but she hadn't wandered into any dangerous neighborhood. She'd been taken anyway. And now God alone knew where she would end up, she thought bleakly.

Did it matter? She would lose everything of importance to her. This life, Uncle Theo, Mary, Jimmy...

Ian. Love.

All her life she had been searching. Even when she hadn't known it. And she had finally found everything. God had given her not just a way to survive. He'd given her far more than gowns and beautiful things. He'd given her Ian. He'd given her love.

Perhaps this was justice. Perhaps she'd been given too much. Perhaps, like Icarus, she had wanted to fly, and so God had seen to it that her wings were melted and that she came crashing to the ground.

No! Tears stung her eyes. She could not accept defeat so easily!

She began to slam her body back and forth. Someone had to notice the movement! The carpet began to loosen around her.

"Stop!" Hands clamped down upon her brutally. She ignored them, squirming like a worm. It would do her no good, she thought desperately.

Then she heard the voice.

"You! You there! Stop this instant."

It was Ian. She could have sworn it. Her heart began to hammer, and she writhed with greater determination to make the package of carpet and herself move more visibly.

The man carrying her did stop. Marissa felt him whirl around, and then she was dropped carelessly to the ground. There was a challenge spoken, and then she heard a thunder of footsteps.

Frantically, she rolled out of her carpet and staggered to her feet.

They were in the alleyway, Ian, the man who had held her and the others. The others, with their horrible, wicked knives.

The man who had carried her roared like a lion. Then he bore down on Ian like a steam engine. Marissa screamed, but Ian paid no heed. He was assessing his enemy. He stepped aside just before the man could butt him, then slammed his joined fists down upon his attacker's back. The man crumbled at his feet.

But the others were encircling him now. The eternal fog was settling upon the city, and the streetlights were winking on. The knives were caught in that glow, twinkling as their owners twisted and turned them in warning.

There was another cry and one of them broke from the group, leaping for Ian, his knife high and poised. Marissa screamed a warning again. Perhaps she was in time; perhaps he had already known. He caught the man's arm. They plummeted to the earth together and began to roll. The two other men ran after them. Marissa gathered up her tattered skirts and did the same. In the fog, she could see nothing but the entwined figures thrashing upon the ground.

And then one man was up.

Ian.

"Ian!" She shouted his name.

"Get out of here, Marissa! Get the hell out of here!" he shouted to her.

She couldn't go. The other two men were taking no chances. They were approaching him together. He backed away, a careful eye on the deadly knives. One rushed him. The second started to do the same.

"No!" Marissa shrieked. She ran forward, leaping upon the man's back. She grasped his face, blinding him. She heard a growl burst forth from him. His hand was upon her, groping, trying to dislodge her.

His knife went clattering down to the cobblestones. She felt herself wrenched free. In the night she saw his murderous dark eyes. And then it was as if she was flying as he hurtled her aside to deal with Ian.

Somewhere in the night, she heard a police whistle. She tried to rise, and she staggered against a wall. She heard a gasp, and the sound of steel ripping into flesh. She screamed, doubling over.

Ian!

Then there were footsteps everywhere. The police had arrived.

Suddenly arms wound around her, lifting her swiftly. She cried out, then her eyes widened. Ian, his face blackened with the grime from the street, blood streaming from a cut near his eye, looked at her. "My God!" she breathed, "I thought it was you!"

"No," he said softly. "Don't look back."

But she had already done so. One man lay in a hideous arch over his own knife. Police officers were hurrying around his body and the others.

"Mr. Tremayne!" One of them called after him. "Mr. Tremayne, we've questions—"

"And you can ask them tomorrow!" Ian answered. "I'm taking my wife home now."

She smiled and leaned against his chest. He carried her out to the street. Lee and John Kwan were in a carriage there. Lee helped her up, and Marissa leaned against her while Ian tethered his bay to the rear of the carriage. Then Ian held her again.

"How did you ever find me?" she asked.

"We moved quickly. Darrin saw them take you. Still, I would never have known where to look if it weren't for Lilli," he admitted.

Marissa nodded. "Then I must thank her," she murmured.

The rest of the ride home was made in silence. It didn't matter. Marissa felt so very comfortable. So loved. She was home with John and Lee.

And she was cherished by Ian. He had fought for her. Risked his life for her. Killed for her. She would never question his feelings or his past again.

Darrin and Lilli were waiting outside the house. Marissa descended from the coach and hugged the boy first. Then she looked at the woman.

"I just wanted to see that Ian brought you home safely," Lilli said. Her dress was subdued. She wore no makeup. She had carefully chosen her attire to come to the house, and now she was speaking very shyly.

Behind her, Ian didn't say a word.

"Lilli, I can never thank you enough. Please, come in," Marissa said.

"Oh, but I can't—" Lilli began. "It wouldn't be right—"

"You're always welcome," Marissa assured her. She glanced at Ian, who looked at her approvingly. "There is no way that it could not be right."

Both Lilli and Darrin were pressured into coming in. Marissa described the house, her assailants and the day, and Ian commented that in the morning, she would have to tell the police. Lee served cold meats and fresh bread and lemonade.

Ian insisted that Darrin take a room in the house for the night, and called the orphanage to say he would be with them. Lilli bid Ian good-night, but Marissa walked the woman to the door.

"Thank you," she whispered again.

Lilli touched her cheek. "No, thank you. I was never your enemy, my dear. I never could have competed. I won't come again. It wouldn't be right. But I am your friend. If you ever need me."

"Thank you again," Marissa told her. "And we will see one another again."

Marissa closed the door on her. Lee was waiting, and insisted on making her a hot toddy, and setting her into a warm tub. And when she was there, Ian, freshly bathed and in a smoking jacket, came for her.

For the very first time, he brought her through the doorway and made love to her in his bed. She lay beside him, sated, miraculously content, feeling so very cherished, and so very blessed.

His arms were strong around her. His lips brushed her forehead. She inhaled the rich scent of his soap and his warmth, and snuggled more closely against the crisp hair of his chest. She closed her eyes and savored the rugged feel of his hair-roughened legs entwined with hers. Thank you, God, thank you! she repeated in silence over and over again.

And she knew then that she had to tell him the truth.

"Ian?" She whispered his name.

But to her surprise, he was asleep beside her. Deeply, contentedly asleep. His face was strikingly young in repose. And very, very peaceful.

Marissa bit her lip. There would have to be another time. She could make him understand, she could tell him that she loved him too much to live a lie anymore.

And she had to believe that he would love her enough for it not to matter.

She smoothed his hair. She couldn't wake him. Her time would come.

Or so she serenely believed that night.

Fate was destined to betray her again.

CHAPTER FIFTEEN

THREE DAYS LATER Ian was at his office in the store, looking over the police reports. The Chinese flesh dealer, Lau Wang, had been closed down. One of his men had been killed in the fight; two others were in jail. But the men who had originally kidnapped Marissa were still at large, and once she had been with him in safety for the night, she had remembered the curious conversation that had gone on between the two men.

"They said something to the effect that they had already been paid, Ian. That whatever they made from Lau Wang would be pure profit."

Lilli hadn't been able to help her. Her man had only been able to discover that Marissa was being held at Lau Wang's. She had promised, though, to have her people keep their eyes open.

Ian had let it be known on the street that he'd pay well for information regarding the kidnapping. It might have been a mistake. He'd already entertained a number of drifters and seedy characters in his office. When Arthur told him he had another visitor, Ian sighed and assumed the man had come seeking some reward.

He leaned back in his chair as the newcomer entered the office. Surprise touched him briefly, for this man was decently, conservatively dressed in a bowler and a suit.

"Mr. Tremayne?" As soon as the man addressed him, he heard in the words the man's English accent, so similar to his wife's, and his curiosity was aroused.

"Yes, I'm Ian Tremayne. Have a seat, sir." He indicated the chair across from his desk. "How can I help you?"

The man cleared his throat. "My business was really with your wife, you see, but there's a very handsome Chinese woman at your home who is guarding the door like a lion."

Ian smiled. Lee did have the heart of a little lioness, and she was extremely loyal to Marissa. More loyal to Marissa than she was to him these days, he thought in wry reflection.

"We've had some trouble recently," Ian told his visitor. "Miss Kwan is understandably nervous."

"Yes, of course. I understand. But for the sake of your wife's uncle, it's imperative that I reach her."

"Her uncle!" Ian said with surprise.

"Theodore Ayers."

Ian shook his head. "I'm sorry, I've no idea what you're talking about."

The man seemed as confused as Ian. "Let me introduce myself. I'm Lawrence Whalen, curate of St. Giles's parish."

"And?"

The stranger shook his head. "I can't understand that Marissa has never said anything to you, she is so very devoted to Theo. And to her home. You must know that she is supplying funds to the parish."

"No, I didn't know," Ian said quietly. He wondered why he was experiencing such a bitter sense of unease. It seemed that a huge rush of water was spilling by him, a cacophony in his ears. "Please, explain."

"It's imperative that Marissa come for Theo, Mr. Tremayne. He joined with certain men in a strike against the mine owners, and he's being held by the law right now."

Ian still didn't understand who in hell the man was, but he asked, "If he's being held by the law—"

Lawrence Whalen, his face mirroring his unhappiness with the situation, leaned toward Ian. "There were men killed during the riots that followed the strike. The mine owners intend to prosecute Theo for murder unless Marissa will take custody of him." He was quiet for a minute, then he sighed. "And have her swear that she'll keep Theo out of England for the rest of his life.''

Ian stared blankly at Whalen. ''Are you quite sure you know what you're talking about? My wife has no living relatives.'' He knew that for certain. That was why the squire had been so determined Ian should marry his daughter.

It was Whalen's turn to look surprised. ''Well, sir, Theo was Marissa Ayers's only living relative.''

''Ayers? My wife's maiden name was Ahearn.''

''Oh, no, sir! The squire's name was Ahearn.''

He was losing his mind, Ian thought. ''Right. Squire Ahearn's daughter, Marissa, is my wife—''

''No, no, sir. The squire's daughter's name is Mary. Katherine Mary Ahearn. I had quite a time tracing them both to you, Mr. Tremayne. Seems Marissa never told her uncle she had married, only that she had come to the States with Miss Ahearn. Indeed, this has been a headache that has cost us a great deal of time, but a man's life is at stake, a good man's life, and Marissa has certainly given her all to the parish, and therefore the vicar was especially concerned. I'm sorry; I seem to have given you quite a shock. If we had not cared so deeply—''

''No, no. It's quite all right,'' Ian interrupted him quietly. He held a pencil and it snapped in his hand. Lawrence Whalen jumped, startled. Ian gave him a bloodless smile. ''If my— my wife's—uncle is in danger, then something must be done. Perhaps, Mr. Whalen, you will be good enough to accompany me to my home. The handsome lioness who greeted you at the door is also an exceptional cook.''

''Well, I'd be quite delighted, sir,'' Mr. Whalen agreed.

Ian excused himself and went out to speak with Arthur, telling him he'd be gone for the rest of the day. He returned for Lawrence Whalen and rented the man a horse from the livery stable when he went for his bay.

Ian was amazed to discover that he could point out certain

of the city's sights to the man. A glance at his own fingers upon the bay's reins showed him that his fingers were shaking. Inside and out he felt the staggering heat of his rage taking hold of him. It seemed incredible that he could still function normally.

Well, he had known she kept some secret in her heart. He had even suspected that she had lied. He'd never realized just how great her lie, that she had managed to make a complete fool of him. Nothing in his life seemed real anymore. He'd been a fool to trust her. A fool to let her into his heart in any way.

A fool to love her.

They reached the house. John Kwan, as always, seemed to have anticipated his arrival. He ran outside, ready to take the horses into the carriage house.

Ian preceded Lawrence Whalen up the steps to the foyer. Lee opened the door, looked suspiciously at Whalen, then at Ian. "It's all right, Lee. Mr. Whalen has come on important family business. Would you call Mrs. Tremayne down, please. Mr. Whalen, the parlor is to the left, if you would join me there. May I interest you in a brandy?"

Lawrence Whalen thanked him and accepted the brandy. Ian offered him a sweeping smile and said, "Can't join you in brandy, no, I think not. I'll have a whiskey. No, maybe I'll just have the bottle."

He was pouring a drink when she entered the room. She was in white, beautiful, eyelet white, a dress with a high collar and sleek lines, a straight skirt except for the very small bustle at her rear. Her hair was drawn up with just a few ringlets to curl by the side of her face. Her eyes, those fascinating emerald eyes with their curious blazes and flames, were on him. Wide, interested, innocent. So damned innocent, his wife.

But was she his wife? He wasn't even sure about that anymore. What the hell was legal and what wasn't?

It didn't matter. What mattered was that his hands were

still shaking. It felt as if the whole of his body was on fire. The witch. Entering his life so completely. Listening to his dreams. Wedging her way into the hearts of the orphans. Captivating his employees. Stealing his heart, making him think he could live again.

He'd been better off with whores.

He smiled icily. "Hello, dear."

"Ian, what—"

And then she saw Lawrence Whalen, and it was apparent that she must have realized that the gleam in Ian's gaze was absolute fury. She fell silent for a moment, then she quietly greeted Whalen.

"Mr. Whalen. What—what has brought you all the long way to America?"

"It's your uncle, Marissa. I've explained to your husband."

"Oh, my God!" The color drained from her face. If anything could be said to her credit, she loved this uncle. That much was true. "Mr. Whalen, is he all right? Has something happened? Oh, dear Lord—"

"Now, now, don't distress yourself, Miss Ayers. I'm sorry, Mrs. Tremayne. Marissa." Lawrence Whalen was on his feet, patting her hand. She was going to fall, so it appeared.

But then she was such a wonderful actress.

Ian used a foot to drag a chair up behind her. "Sit, my love. Do take a chair. Mr. Whalen will explain." She stared at him for a moment, aware of the edge to his voice even if Mr. Whalen was not. She had to be wondering just what course he would take now that her deception was discovered.

He didn't blink. He wanted her to worry.

And at the moment, he didn't have the least idea of what he wanted to do. All he knew was that he was more furious than he could remember being in all his life.

And hurt.

Damn, but why hadn't she told him?

Because everything between them had been a lie, from the very beginning to the bitter end.

And he was so damned angry because he was so damned hurt. He wanted to reach out and shake her. He wanted to hear her cry, just as he wanted to cry out even as he stood there, staring at her.

She tore her eyes from his at last and gave her attention to her guest, and she seemed to understand a great deal more than he about what was going on.

"Please, Mr. Whalen, what happened? Uncle Theo was not supposed to be working! I left him plenty of money—"

"I'm sure you did," Ian commented dryly. He saw her color, but she did not look at him.

"It was a matter of his friends, Mrs. Tremayne," Whalen told her quietly. "They were striking against conditions. Theo joined them. He wouldn't have it any other way. He's one of their leaders, always has been, working or not. You know your uncle. That Mr. Lacey had been terribly hard on the miners, you see. He cut the wages. Well, you know what those wages were to begin with!"

"But what did Uncle Theo do?" she asked. She sounded like a lost girl, Ian thought. She could so easily have drawn his sympathy. He stiffened. No, she had done that already.

"Lacey had brought in men, and there was a scuffle, and some of the men were killed. He wants to charge Theo with murder." He was quiet for a minute. "And ask for the death penalty."

"No!" Marissa cried.

And Ian almost reached out to her. Almost.

"The vicar went to Lacey, Mrs. Tremayne. And Lacey will drop the charges if you'll just come for Theo—and swear that he'll not set foot in England again."

"But he couldn't have been guilty. Uncle Theo is not a murderer—"

"Mrs. Tremayne!" Whalen interrupted very softly. "You've

been gone awhile now. But have you forgotten the power Lacey wields?''

She stood, clenching her fingers into fists at her side. ''There is no problem, Mr. Whalen. I'll come for my uncle immediately. Mr. Lacey has nothing to fear from us,'' she added bitterly.

''No,'' Ian said flatly, leaning against the cherrywood liquor cabinet. ''You won't be going anywhere.''

She stared at him, startled, her eyes growing very wide. He could almost see the desperation washing over her. ''Ian, I'll do anything. I'll—I'll do anything,'' she repeated. It must have been very hard to talk with Mr. Whalen there. ''I must go for my uncle.''

''I repeat, my love,'' he said with an edge. ''You'll not be going anywhere. I—''

''Ian, for the love of God, please!''

''Well!'' Mr. Whalen said, nervously twisting his hat with his fingers. ''I can see you need some time alone. Mr. Tremayne, I can leave—''

''You've been invited to dinner, Mr. Whalen, and you must not leave. However, my wife and I do have a few matters to discuss. If you'll excuse us...?''

''Of course!'' Whalen said.

Ian looked at Marissa, then indicated the door to the foyer and the stairway. She stared at him blankly for a moment, refusing to accept the fact that he was going to force them into an immediate confrontation.

''Ian—''

''Marissa, if you will, please?'' The last was not a request in any way, but a sharp command. She swallowed sharply, lifted her chin and excused herself to Whalen. Ian smiled to the man. ''Please, make yourself at home. Have another drink—there's a daily paper in the rack by the door. This discussion just might take some time,'' he said pleasantly. Then he followed Marissa as she hurried through the foyer.

"That was very good, Marissa," he commented as they reached the stairs.

"What was good?" she hissed.

"Your manner with Whalen. You're beginning to believe that you were born a lady yourself, aren't you?"

She swung around, a hand raised. He caught it before she could begin to strike. "Aren't you worried about Uncle Theo?" he queried her sharply.

A deep blush colored her cheek and she wrenched her hand free and hurried up the stairs. She stood still in the hall, and he shoved open her door. She didn't move, and he pushed her through the doorway none too gently. She almost stumbled, straightened, and took a seat regally at the foot of her bed, staring straight ahead.

He leaned against the door for several moments, then exploded. "My God, don't you have anything to say to me yet?"

She stared at him. "No! No, you're not going to believe or understand anything I have to say anyway!"

"Try me."

She leaped up, staring at him. "Don't you see? There was no other way. We had to lie to you, Mary and I. There was no other choice."

"Because you had to have the money."

"Yes! Oh, God, how can you be so angry? You always knew I married you for the money."

"Yes," he said softly, deceptively softly. "But before, it was your money!"

"It's Mary's money."

"No, no, it's not!" he exploded. "You made me a party to fraud! She's married to James O'Brien, and I'm married to you. Hell, am I? I don't even known if we're legally married or not!"

Marissa lowered her head suddenly and walked to the turret window. "It's legal," she muttered.

"What?" he thundered.

"It's—it's legal." He was staring at her, and she looked at him at last. "The squire had seen to it that you had a license, but there was nothing filled in on it. I signed my own name."

He swore and hit the wooden door. "Thank you, madam! You have made me as guilty in this little scheme as you are yourself. Why the hell didn't you tell me?"

"You wouldn't have married me!" she exclaimed.

He leaned against the door, hands crossed over his chest. "You're the maid," he commented suddenly. "The maid with the tea tray and the burning eyes. How in God's name did I miss that?"

She swung around on him. "Because I was a maid! Just a maid! No one for the rich and wonderful American Ian Tremayne to bother about!"

He started to laugh, a dry, humorless sound. And the laughter was directed against himself. "And you weren't just the maid, were you? Oh, no! Had I begun to imagine such a deceit, I'd have known so easily. Ah, yes! You knew all about the hardships in the coal mines! You were the little girl all dressed in white who fell into the mud. There are no other eyes like yours, none other in the world. You've known me for a long, long time—"

"I'm amazed that even now you could associate the coal rat with your wife!" she cried out.

He shook his head, earnest, still furious. "Madam, the prejudice has been yours, not mine! I couldn't care in the least where you came from. Coal dust washes away. But lies and deceit do not!"

Marissa barely heard what he said. She heard only the condemnation in his voice. "I had no choice!" she cried.

Ian continued to stare at her, the depth of his fury evident in the coldness of his eyes. "So you knew me, you knew me all along. And you knew why you looked so familiar to me!" He started walking into the room, closing in on her. He could see the fury of her pulse beating against the beautiful flesh of her throat. "You knew all along. And you never, never said a word to me."

"I couldn't—"

"Yes, damn you, you could!" he thundered. "You had chance after chance."

"No! You don't understand!"

He had reached her. Maybe if he hadn't been stricken anew by her beauty he wouldn't have been quite so angry. He reached for her arm, pulling her against him. Her eyes rose to his. Her emerald eyes. Dazzling, green, damp and appealing even now. He wanted to throw her from him. He had longed so desperately to believe in her.

"You scheming little liar! My God, did you use me!"

She tried to wrench free from him. "No! Let me go, Ian. I couldn't—"

And then he did push her away, with a force that sent her flying onto the bed. Stunned, she stared at him. Her eyes were damp. He gritted his teeth, trembling, and he strode to the door, anxious to leave her.

"Ian!" She cried out his name and rose. "Ian, I know you hate me. And I know you want me gone, and I know I owe you a fortune. But please, please—"

"Please what?" he snapped, spinning around.

"You—you have to let me go for my uncle!" she told him. "He's not guilty of any of this. You must let me go—"

"No."

"Ian!" She raced to him. He caught her wrists. Her hair was tumbling free, falling down her back. He wanted to run his fingers through it, bury his face in the red-gold cascade and breathe in the fragrance. "Ian, please! I'll do anything."

"Anything? You do sell out easily," he told her coolly.

"Bastard!" she whispered, and the tears were hovering on her lashes. He could see her grit her teeth. "Anything!" she snapped again.

The tension between them sizzled. He didn't know when the fury and the hatred had turned to desire, he only knew that he would have sold his own soul at that moment. And she was repeating the word to him.

"Anything…"

He drew her hard and tight against him, and he gave his fingers free rein to thread through the hair at her nape. He tilted her head to his and found her lips. Angry, he ground his mouth to hers. Still furious, he forced her lips apart, and kissed her.

She started to protest, but he lifted his mouth from hers briefly and stared into the glistening green inferno of her eyes. "Anything!" he repeated.

She inhaled sharply and stepped away from him, those hypnotic green eyes were still upon his. She tossed back her head, pulling a pin and freeing her hair. And she loosened the pearl button at her throat. And then another, another, watching him with a heated defiance all the while. With elegance, with grace, she dropped the white gown. It fell to her feet in a swathe of innocence. With dignity still, with mesmerizing grace and beauty, she dropped her chemise upon the dress, her petticoats, her silk drawers. And she stood before him, challenging him, taunting him. She was like some goddess as she stared at him then, her eyes liquid and emerald and undauntable, the shimmering sweep of her hair evocative as it curled over the marble rise of her breasts.

"Anything," she murmured.

He smiled slowly and removed his coat, tore at his tie and ripped buttons from his shirt. Shoes and trousers were quickly abandoned and he set his hands upon his hips. Her gaze flicked just once, and he laughed aloud.

"Anything," he agreed, and he swept her off her feet and carried her to her bed. And then his mouth found hers again, found it with hunger and need and fury…

From somewhere deep within, he tried to control the tumult

rising with the rush of his blood, the heat of his body. But it suddenly seemed that there was no need, for she was meeting his kiss with a fury and passion of her own. Her fingers tangled in his hair, her lips sought his. Her hands moved down the length of his naked back, light, delicate, haunting, over his spine, kneading his buttocks, soft as a whisper as they stroked his flesh. He deserted her lips to press his mouth against her throat, and he left that soft white column to caress her breasts with the heat and moisture of his lips and tongue. She arched to his touch, cradling his head to her. He drew soft, fascinating trails down the soft flesh of her abdomen, and he stroked her thighs with his fingertips, whispering against her flesh.

He loved her, he knew then. He loved her still, no matter what she had done. He couldn't sweep away the anger, but he loved her. Loved the beauty of her flesh, the fragrance of her. Loved the spirit, and loved the taste of her kiss. Loved the way she moved against him.

And her eyes, open, clear when she made love to him. Challenging and innocent. Framed by the magic sunburst of her hair. He caught her gaze and moved lower against her, bringing his body against her, bringing his kiss intimately upon her.

Sweet cries escaped her, and she touched him in her turn, her fingers closing upon the hardness of his desire. Molten, hot, trembling, they came together. He made love with a rhythm that was fast and furious still, the culmination of all the love and hatred and anger simmering between them.

The end came quickly, explosively. He shuddered fiercely, felt the heat and fury and passion seep from him in a little shower of his seed, deep into her body. And he felt her trembling beneath him, and he knew that she, too, had found a physical release, even if there was nothing that could bridge the gulf that stood between them now.

He eased his weight from hers and sat on the edge of the

bed for a moment. Then he rose and padded silently to the turret windows. The fog was rolling in, thick, rich. He felt as if his thinking processes were rolling with that fog. He still loved her. He was still furious. He could feel his muscles knotting anew with the tension.

Watching him, Marissa bit softly upon her lower lip, wishing that she dared rise and walk to him. She wanted to whisper that she loved him, but it was probably too late. She pulled the sheets to her breast and fought tears. His anger was so great she had felt it in his touch. And yet she had been glad. She had wanted him with an equal desperation. It had been all she had to hold on to.

His shoulders squared, straightened, fell. "Well, it seems that I must say that I'm sorry again," he muttered, his back still to her.

He had told her that once before. And it hurt more deeply now.

"You needn't be sorry," she whispered.

"Indeed, I must," he said coolly.

"Ian, damn you!" she cried, and she hesitated and added softly, "I love you!"

He swung around, naked, masculine, and suddenly very terrible in his anger. "You, madam, needn't conjure up such a pathetic lie. It doesn't become you."

She gasped, feeling as if she had been slapped. "Oh, you—bastard!" she hissed. She was going to burst into tears. She had dared to bare her heart, and it meant nothing to him at all. She had to hold on to something.

"Is that a way to talk when you still want something from me?" he demanded sharply.

She tossed back her hair, hating him very much at that moment. "I'm going for my uncle. If I beg on the streets or steal, I'm going—"

"You are not!"

"Dear God, they'll kill him! How can you be so cruel?" she demanded. He couldn't mean it. He had to let her go.

"No one is going to kill him."

"Don't you understand? I have to—"

"You're not leaving San Francisco. I'll go for your uncle."

"But your work—"

"You're not leaving. God knows where you might wind up, and for the moment, you're still my wife. If you want to help your uncle, you can follow a few simple rules until I get back. You don't leave this house alone. Ever. Lee or John must be with you. You are limited to the store, the carriage house, and an occasional social function in my absence. Is that understood?"

He was going for Theo. That was all that she could allow to matter. But the cold way he spoke to her cut into her heart, and she was still afraid that she would break down if he did not leave her soon.

And she wouldn't even mind burying the very last vestiges of her pride, except that it wouldn't matter. He wasn't going to believe anything she had to say to him.

"Yes, I understand," she said flatly, staring at the sheet.

"Then get dressed. Mr. Whalen will surely miss us soon enough. And I intend to leave with him on the evening train. I want this done."

"Tonight? You're leaving tonight?"

"Yes, it might quell my urge to throttle you."

She flushed, still staring at the sheet. "You can start divorce proceedings," she murmured, "and be plagued no more." Then she gasped, raising her eyes to his. "None of this was Mary's fault. It was my idea, solely my idea. She—she's going to have a baby. You wouldn't—"

"No, Marissa, I wouldn't cast Mr. and Mrs. O'Brien out on the streets," he said.

"You won't fire Jimmy?"

"Jimmy has proven himself useful," he said, a definite edge to his voice.

She stiffened. "And I have not, I take it?"

"Oh, no, Marissa. You have proven yourself useful enough, too. But then, so have other women."

She forgot that she was completely at his mercy and leaped to her feet. But she had barely slammed her hands against his naked chest before he caught her arms and held her still against him. She felt again the masculine heat of his body against her own, and she wanted so desperately to lay her head against his chest. To make love again. To be held.

Cherished.

She cast her head back and met the cold blue ice of his gaze.

He would never cherish her again.

"Remember Uncle Theo, love," he reminded her. He smiled and touched her cheek. "You really are so beautiful, love. A fool's undoing, so it seems." He smiled bitterly, and his fingers tightened around her arms. Then he released her and started for the connecting door.

"Ian!"

He turned back.

"What are we going to do?" she cried.

"I don't know, Marissa. I just don't know," he told her. "Get dressed so that we can get this fiasco of a meal over with, and I can be on my way."

He didn't bother with the clothes on the floor, preferring to stride over them and through the door.

He closed it behind him with a very definite slam.

In misery, Marissa sank down upon the foot of her bed and bit down hard against the threatening onslaught of tears. What was going to happen?

He had already told her.

He didn't know.

CHAPTER SIXTEEN

"MARISSA! It's a telegram for you!"

Sitting at the tea table in the little terrace at the caretakers' cottage, Marissa felt her heart begin to pound quickly. She leaped up and hurried through the sunny kitchen and parlor to meet Mary at the doorway. A young uniformed man tipped his hat to her. "Mornin', Mrs. Tremayne. I went up to the big house, but I was told you were down here, so I came on to find you. Hope that's all right."

"That was very thoughtful of you, thank you," Marissa murmured, eager to snatch the telegram from him. It was mid-April, and Ian had been gone over six weeks, and she had received only one message from him, that having come about three weeks ago. It had been short and terse. "Theo fine, in my custody. Leaving soon. Ian."

Her fingers shook as Mary bid the telegram man good day. She tried very hard to hold the paper steady enough to read this message.

"Arriving San Francisco evening train on April sixteenth. Have John at station. Ian."

"What does it say?" Mary demanded.

Marissa read the message out loud and sank down in one of the needlepoint chairs that flanked the door. "Oh, dear Lord, Mary. He'll be home tomorrow night!"

Mary knelt beside her, covering her hands with her own. "Well, that's wonderful!" Marissa didn't comment.

"Marissa, it is wonderful, things will be all right!"

No, things would never be all right again, Marissa thought.

She could still remember the night he had left. They had both sat through dinner very politely with Mr. Whalen.

Afterward she had tried to speak to him; she had tried to tell him that she appreciated the fact that he was going for her uncle. But her words had been stiff, and Ian had been cold, and it had been alarming to realize just how desperate he was to be away from her. One minute it seemed that he wanted to strangle her, the next he wanted nothing to do with her. He didn't want to hear her voice.

It was the distance that frightened her. The coldness.

During his absence, she had clung to little things. She had been bitter at first that Ian had clearly ordered John Kwan to follow her everywhere she went. She could only assume that he didn't trust her in the least. But when she had assured John one day that it wasn't necessary to trace her every step, John had solemnly assured her that it was.

"No one knows what happened, the day you were kidnapped, Mrs. Tremayne. I have given my solemn word that nothing will happen to you while your husband is gone. I am not the only one that watches."

She had been startled by his answer, and then she had begun to tremble—with pleasure that Ian had at least been concerned about her physical well-being.

He might have been anxious for some enterprising soul to shanghai her now.

But then again, he was a man of certain ethics, and perhaps those ethics would not allow him to let evil fall her way.

But his two messages to her had been very cold and terse. It didn't seem his feelings had softened one bit since he had been gone. And it seemed that she had lived on pins and needles since that night.

Not that the days and weeks had passed in any outside torment. Society had discovered her. The wives of many of San Francisco's most influential men had come to call on her. She had been very careful at first, but it seemed that the women's interest in her had been natural and real. It had made her uneasy, however, to realize that she was beginning to move in a circle with Grace Leroux.

And she had felt like a fraud with every movement she had made in Ian's absence. It had been Mary who had insisted that she must keep up his social front for him while he was gone. Whatever he chose to do when he returned would be his decision.

Marissa remembered now with what assurance she had told Grace that she had won. Well, the game had changed.

But at least it seemed that she had not taken them all down with her.

Ian had contacted his secretary, Arthur, before he had gone, and Jimmy had been given a great deal of the management power in Ian's absence. Marissa had taken to spending a great deal of time at the emporium, helping with the breakfasts. She and Darrin had formed a fast bond, and she spent many afternoons with him. She'd tried to coax him into living at the mansion on Nob Hill in the servants' quarters on the third floor, but Darrin had steadfastly refused. He wouldn't do so until Mr. Tremayne had returned, and only maybe, then. He wasn't beholden to anybody, really, and he liked Mr. Tremayne really fine, but he wanted to know Mr. Tremayne's mind before taking on a job or a room at his place.

Marissa had to swallow hard on that one. She wasn't sure if Ian intended to keep her at the mansion, much less let her make any of the decisions regarding life there.

Sometimes she tried to mask her fear and heartbreak with anger. He wanted nothing to do with her now because he had discovered the humiliating fact that he had married a servant girl. The maid. The coal-miner's brat. She told herself that Ian was a snob, a member of the American aristocracy, and that she should hate him for the arrogance she had discovered that first time she had seen him.

But his arrogance was in his boldness, and in his temper,

and in his passion. And they were all things for which she had come to love him.

There was no easy way to hate him. Especially when she lay awake and dreamed by night of that last evening between them.

And especially when she was slowly becoming certain that that particular evening had led to certain results. She hadn't said a word to anyone yet, not even Mary. She told herself that she wasn't sure, even though she was. And then she wondered somewhat bleakly just what she should do, and what it would mean. She couldn't tell Ian, not until they had come to some kind of an understanding about their future. If he meant to divorce her, she wouldn't stop him with the news that she was expecting a child.

And it frightened her, too, to know that his first wife had died in childbirth. That she was alive and well and expecting might make him despise her all the more, and surely he would draw comparisons between his beloved Diana...

And the English maid who had tricked him.

"Marissa," Mary murmured, her voice concerned, "you can't worry so much! You've gone absolutely white. I'll bring you something. You just stay there for a moment!"

Mary disappeared into the kitchen and returned with a small glass of sherry. Marissa took it from her gratefully and swallowed it. "Sorry," she murmured.

"Don't be sorry, just don't be so nervous," Mary told her. "I'm sure that he won't take my—our!—allowance from the bank anymore, but Jimmy's income at the store is quite sufficient now. And—"

A wave of cold had come over Marissa. "Mary, don't you understand? We all fooled him. What if he fires Jimmy?"

"Why would he have put him in charge of so much if he meant to fire him?" Mary demanded with serene wisdom. "And he left word with Arthur to make sure that he had good seats for four to see Caruso."

"Ah, but what four?" Marissa murmured. "He might be intending on taking Grace—"

"Oh, no! He's taking us, I know it. He told Jimmy."

"Maybe he's taking you and Jimmy and Grace," Marissa murmured.

"He's not going to ask for a divorce," Mary insisted. "He simply wouldn't."

"Because of his social position?"

"No." Mary laughed. "He'd snap his fingers at his social position, surely you know that."

"But if he doesn't divorce me, it just might be a greater hell," Marissa said. She stood and paced nervously. "I couldn't endure living the life I once thought I wanted. I couldn't stay with him in name only and watch him head off to the Barbary Coast or to the opera or theater with his good associate, Grace, on his arm."

"You must stop being such a pessimist, Marissa," Mary insisted with a sigh. "It's not like you at all." She smiled. "You're the fighter, remember. You definitely put up a fight when Jimmy and I were down."

"It was easy to fight then," Marissa said.

"Because you weren't in love then," Mary told her. "But being in love, Marissa, you must fight for him even harder."

Marissa smiled after a moment, the glitter of the challenge coming to her eyes. "You're right, Mary. I am in love with him, and I will fight for him. I'll even fight him, if that's what it takes."

Mary smiled serenely. "Things will work out. Have faith."

Marissa tried to have faith. She kissed Mary and hurried to the house. She had just called John to make him aware that they must be at the train station the following evening when Lee came to tell her that she had a visitor.

"Eda!" she said warmly when Lee brought her into the parlor. She wasn't sure if she had wanted a visitor or not, but maybe it was best not to be alone. "How lovely to see you," she told the woman. "What can I get you?"

"Not a thing, dear." Eda stared at Lee pointedly and then waited for the beautiful Chinese woman to leave the room. Marissa offered a barely discernible shrug to Lee. Lee smiled, quickly lowered her head and left the room.

"What is it?" Marissa asked.

Eda Funston was not the type of woman to beat about any bush. "Marissa, you've suddenly become the talk of the town."

Her brows shot up. "More so than Mayor Schmitz and the arrival of Caruso?"

"Indeed, I'm afraid so. I imagine I know where this rumor started, and it's simply abhorrent, but still, the rumor is around, and I thought you should be warned."

"What is the rumor?" Marissa asked her.

"That Ian Tremayne's wife is not the daughter of an English squire. That she is a fortune-digging little maidservant who tricked him into marriage."

Marissa felt cold. As cold as ice. She folded her hands and stared at them, then looked evenly at Eda. "I *was* a maid, Eda." She couldn't admit that the rest was the truth as well.

To her surprise, Eda waved a hand impatiently. "This is America, San Francisco more precisely. There's nothing wrong in being a maid." She smiled. "Half the occupants of this hill come from good old robber baron stock! Don't you let any of this get to you, not one single bit! I'm quite sure I know where this all started!"

Where? Marissa wondered, and she felt ill, wondering if Ian hadn't told someone himself.

"It's that wretched Grace Leroux. She was always asking questions about you. She must have hired an investigator to dig into your past."

Had Grace done so? Or had Ian told her himself, because he was tired of his wife?

"Keep your chin high, my dear," Eda told her. "I didn't mean to upset you, merely warn you. Forewarned is fore-armed, so they do say!"

Marissa smiled. "Thank you, Eda. I do appreciate your coming to forewarn me. Please, won't you stay for dinner?"

"Oh, no, thank you. Freddie will be expecting me. But you take care. Ian is due soon, isn't he?"

"Tomorrow night."

"Well, he'll soon set things straight. Whatever you were, dear, you're his wife now."

Eda gave her a hug and hurried out in her efficient way.

Marissa stood in the foyer and suddenly felt that she was not alone. She looked up and saw Lee watching her.

"It seems there's quite a rumor about me," Marissa mur-mured.

"I've heard," Lee told her.

Marissa quirked a brow, but she wasn't really surprised. San Francisco was a big town, but news traveled very quickly.

"Well, it's true, Lee. I am no lady."

Lee cocked her head and smiled. "You speak to John and me as politely as you speak to your friends. You tend to the children because their lives matter to you. I would say, Mrs. Tremayne, that you are indeed a lady." She turned and dis-appeared through the dining room door, leaving Marissa in the hallway to ponder her words.

Finally Marissa smiled, then wearily climbed the stairs to her room. She stood in the turret, staring out the window at the fog blanketing the city.

She had been there a few seconds when Lee tapped on her door. She had brought a message. "There's a boy outside awaiting your reply if there is any."

Marissa thanked her and ripped open the note.

She smiled as she looked at the words, then she laughed.

The note was from Lilli, and it warned her that a smear campaign had sprung up against her. And Lilli, too, told her that she must snap her fingers at the rumors and keep her chin high. "Someone else is on your side, Marissa. It seems that a few well-aimed tomatoes were thrown at Grace as she walked out of her favorite hat shop the other day. Thought you might appreciate that. Oh, and I thought you might also appreciate the information that the little scamp who hurled the tomatoes was not caught."

"Is there any answer?" Lee asked her.

"Yes!" Marissa told her, still smiling. She penned out a thank-you to Lilli and sent it with a tip for the messenger.

Then she stared out at the city again. The city she was coming to love so much for its raw beauty and its recklessness. She had friends here. Good friends. From all walks of life.

And it was Ian's city.

She started to tremble, then she willed her hands to be still. Mary was right. She was a fighter, she had been born a fighter.

And she was going to fight for Ian.

THE NEXT night she stood on the platform at the station, waiting for Ian's train.

The train was late, and she tried to still her nerves by reading the paper. There was trouble in Russia again; the czar had put down a revolt. And a reader's poll showed that most people were convinced that the automobile would never be an alternative to the horse-drawn buggy. She tried to read further but she couldn't give anything her full attention. She was fooling herself. She couldn't give the paper any attention at all.

There were a large number of people waiting for the train. Marissa recognized a few of the matrons who lived not far from her on Nob Hill. Mrs. Nancy Masterson was down the platform from her. She had heard that her son was coming in from his college in the east. She caught the woman's eye and started to smile, but Mrs. Masterson turned from her quickly.

She was doomed, Marissa thought. Hold your chin high, she reminded herself. And she did so. Then she heard the train's whistle. She had to brace herself to keep from shaking.

The great brakes squealed and steam rushed around the wheels.

And then she saw Ian, standing by the rear of the third compartment, waiting to detrain. And behind him was Uncle Theo, looking tall and gaunt but dapper. And Marissa held her breath, waiting to see what would happen.

Please, Ian, please! she wished in silence. Don't ignore me before Mrs. Masterson! Then she realized that she didn't give a damn about Mrs. Masterson; she just didn't want Ian to ignore her. Should she rush to him? She didn't know what to do. It didn't matter. She seemed incapable of movement, as if her feet had been nailed to the platform.

It didn't matter. "Marissa!" She heard her name shouted with Theo's soft, slurring accent and she didn't have to run because he was running to her. Then she was crushed in his arms, and she hugged him fiercely, feeling tears running down her cheeks. Whatever else happened, she would be grateful. Theo was all she really had, and Ian had saved him for her. She looked into his eyes and saw the happiness there and the glistening of tears and she cried out and hugged him again.

"Marissa, oh, my God, love, but it's good to see you again! Thank you, thank you, girl, for sending that young man of yours. I owe the both of you my life," Theo murmured, holding her closer.

"You're here, Uncle Theo, safe and sound, and that's all that matters," she said softly in reply. But he had slowly slid her to her feet, and now she could see over his shoulder and she knew that that was not all that mattered in her life, not anymore.

Ian was almost upon them, tall and striking, and drawing attention within the station as greetings were called to him. He responded, but his eyes remained on Marissa.

Then he did seem to hesitate, and Marissa saw a frown darken his brow. And she realized to her horror that Mrs. Masterson was talking about her to someone, talking loudly.

"Why, she's nothing but an upstart, so they say. The downstairs maid. Tricked him into marriage, seduced him, I dare say."

"Oh, my, no!" came an outraged reply from a tall, heavy-bosomed dowager in dove gray. She looked down a very imperious nose at Marissa. "And our own Mr. Tremayne was such a prize!"

"Perhaps he'll find a way to rid himself of her," Mrs. Masterson said firmly, in her whisper that carried halfway through the station.

And despite her staunchest resolve, Marissa could feel the color flooding her cheeks. She prayed that Uncle Theo hadn't heard the things being said. If he did, he pretended not to.

And suddenly Ian was walking again, a slow smile curving his lips. He paused by Mrs. Masterson and took her hand. "Nancy!" he greeted her pleasantly, brushing a kiss over her hand. "How nice to see you. Edgar is due home for the break, eh?"

"Oh, yes, Ian!" She was positively tittering, Marissa thought.

"That's good, Nancy. He's a fine lad." Ian tipped his hat to the dowager at Nancy's side. "Edith, how are you? A fine evening to you, ladies." He started away, but then he turned back. "Oh, by the way, Nancy. My wife did not trick me into marriage. Anyone has only to look at her to discern why I was quite determined to marry her from the moment we met. Good evening, then."

He walked away, leaving the women to gape after him. And it was only when he had almost reached her that Marissa could see the sparks of anger flying in his eyes. Eyes that touched her with hostility still, when she would have greeted him with so much gratitude. Indeed, she had almost thrown her arms around him in happiness.

But seeing his gaze upon her, she held still. "My love!" he greeted her loudly for other ears. And he set an arm around her shoulder, and kissed her cheek.

His lips were cold.

She looked at him. "Welcome home, Ian."

"You needn't have come to the station."

He was playing out a charade for the ladies, Marissa thought. And all she wanted was to go back to that brief time of complete happiness when she could have thrown herself against him, breathed in his cologne and the clean masculine scent of him, rubbed her cheek against the texture of his coat. Well, appearances mattered. He was playing for them. She could do the same.

She faced him with a radiant smile, running her fingers over his lapel. "I'd not have dreamed of it! I had to see you as soon as possible!"

"And your uncle, of course."

"Oh, yes, and Uncle Theo, of course!"

She looped one arm through Theo's, and the other through Ian's, and she allowed her voice to slip huskily low for the benefit of Nancy Masterson. "Do let's hurry home, Ian. Dinner will be waiting, and you must feel that it's been a long, long time since you've slept in your own bed!"

"Mmm," he agreed, placing a hand upon her arm. "Do let's get home." There was a definite edge to his voice.

As they left the station, Marissa swallowed hard. They had escaped Mrs. Masterson, but Uncle Theo was an intuitive old soul and could surely sense the sparks between them. What would he think?

But what anybody thought didn't really matter at all.

Ian mattered.

And Ian was home.

UNCLE THEO stood in the doorway of the house in Nob Hill and stared, jaw agape, at the chandelier and the marble flooring and the staircase rising high to the second floor. Marissa swallowed hard, thinking that Ian must be very aware of her roots now. But then he had to be aware of her past already—he had been to pick up Uncle Theo, he had seen the tiny cottage, he had breathed in the coal dust.

"Uncle," she murmured, urging him forward. Then she was ashamed of herself for having been ashamed of him. And she was suddenly furious with Ian for making her feel so miserable.

Not that Ian had done anything, or indicated in any way that Theo was awkward in his rich surroundings. He walked in and called to Lee that they were back. Then he turned to Theo. "May I take your coat, sir?"

"What? Oh!" Theo let Ian take his coat. A new coat, Marissa saw. Ian must have bought it before they left London. Theo seemed unhappy to let the fine woolen garment go, but then Marissa realized that the men had done a great deal of shopping. Theo was newly clad from head to toe. He was wearing handsome black leather shoes, and a dove-gray suit with tiny charcoal-gray pinstripes. His shirt was white with a pleated front, and his vest was a charcoal gray that matched the pinstripes on the suit.

She realized suddenly that her uncle was a handsome man, tall, gaunt, very dignified.

"This—this is your house?" Theo said to Ian.

Ian smiled at him. "Yes, and I think you'll find it comfortable enough in time. John will see your trunks up to your room, and after dinner you can settle in."

Theo took his hand and shook it heartily. "Thank you, Mr. Tremayne. Thank you so very much."

"Ian, Theo, Ian. Please."

Theo turned to Marissa and swung her into his arms, trembling. He looked over her head at Ian. "My God, I cannot believe you, sir! I am so grateful for Marissa, that this is her life. Ah, Marissa, but you did well.''

"Indeed," Ian murmured dryly. "Very well."

She stiffened, but then Lee came and said that dinner could be served immediately.

It was the most difficult meal of Marissa's life. She tried to comment on things that had been happening. Ian replied stiffly. Theo stared from one of them to the other.

At last the meal was finished. Ian suggested that Lee show Theo to his room. Suddenly unwilling to be alone with the man she had waited so desperately to see, Marissa jumped up and said that she would show her uncle up.

And upstairs, when Theo had seen the space that was to be his and his alone, he hugged her fiercely again and whispered, "Marissa, but this is fine. You've found yourself a fine, fine man. And all this, too! But God has smiled upon us. And bless God, girl, for you've deserved this!''

No, this was God's irony for the deceit she had practiced, Marissa thought. But she laughed and hugged her uncle in return. She had to give him this first night in San Francisco. Whatever Ian chose to do, Theo would at least have this night.

But when she started for the door, he suddenly called her back.

"Marissa."

"What is it, Uncle?"

"Whatever is wrong, you can solve it. I know you can."

"Nothing is wrong, Uncle Theo."

"Ah, but I can see it, girl! I can see it in your eyes. But you mustn't be disturbed. You mustn't let some little quarrel upset you. He loves you, lass."

"Did he say that, Uncle Theo?" she asked.

He shrugged. "No, no, he didn't so much as say it, but then I've spent some time with the man. He came to the jail and I was made to understand just who he was. You might have told me that you had married, Marissa," he said, wounded.

"I'm sorry, Uncle Theo. I really thought I knew what I was doing. Good night, now, Uncle. I love you. And I'm glad to have you here."

"Marissa, we'll get on, you and I. We always have."

"Yes, Uncle, we always have." She ran to him and they hugged tightly once again. Then she left him, still staring around his room, and retreated to her own.

She sat on the foot of her bed and bit hard into her thumb and waited. Ian would come; he would have something to say to her soon.

He didn't come. She stood and began to pace the room. She sat down on the foot of the bed again, and then she stretched across it. Maybe she should try to find him. But it seemed that he didn't want to see her.

She closed her eyes, and she must have dozed for a while. She checked the time by the clock on her mantel and was startled to realize that it was four-thirty in the morning.

She stood and pulled the pins from her dishevelled hair. In front of the mirror she brushed it out, fighting tears and a feeling of desperation. He hadn't even wanted to talk to her.

He hadn't wanted to touch her, even in anger. That was the most frightening. If she had lost his passion, she had lost everything.

She stared at her reflection, her eyes wide and haunted, her hair flowing thick and free down her back and framing the pallor of her cheeks.

Then she started, aware that John Kwan and Ian were outside in the hall.

"I can't imagine what's gotten into them!" Ian was saying.

"I've never seen the beasts so restless, sir," John agreed. "But it does seem that you've got the bay settled down for the night. Thank you. I'm sorry you were disturbed on your first night back."

"Curious night, John. I noticed the dogs barking downtown when we came in tonight. Oh, well, maybe the stars are aligning in a peculiar fashion or something. Who knows. Get some sleep, John, whatever you can."

He was still awake. Marissa waited, holding her breath. But he entered his room from the hallway, and she could hear him shedding his coat in his room. She waited longer, hearing nothing but silence. And then she couldn't stand it anymore. She burst through the connecting doors to accost him face to face.

He was stripped down to his black trousers and white pleated dress shirt. It was open at the throat. He stood at the window, staring out at the night, or at the coming morning. Very soon, the first hint of dawn would streak across the sky, and the misty beauty of the city below them would be visible.

"Marissa," he murmured, and his mouth took on a crooked, taunting smile. "What a time for a visit. And when your uncle is already here, and you've nothing left to bargain for."

She gasped, stunned. "Oh, how dare you!" she snapped in fury. Fists clenched at her sides, she strode across the room to stand before him. "How dare you! I came here to thank you for what you did for him, and that's all. I can promise you, Ian Tremayne, I'll never come for anything more! I'll never touch you again, I—"

She broke off as his fingers shot out and circled her arm, dragging her to him. "But you're my wife, Marissa. Just where you wanted to be."

She was so close to him. She felt the bitterness and the tension that had not died. She wanted his fingers to move across her cheeks with tenderness. She wanted a whisper of love, and if she could receive it, nothing else would matter.

But she wasn't going to receive it.

"You didn't want a wife, Ian. You made that clear enough. But then it seemed to be all right until you discovered that you married the maid. Not good enough for a scion of Nob Hill!''

''Why, you little witch!'' he snapped heatedly, and she was jerked closer against him. The warmth of his breath fanned her cheeks, the scent that was inherently his filled her with the rampant heat of his body. ''You lied to me! I gave you every chance, and you just kept lying and lying. You married me to climb a ladder.''

''I didn't—''

''You married for money. We both knew it. It was just that I thought it was your own damned money.''

''Then let us both out of this! I don't want your money, I never wanted your money. I just want out. And then you won't have to worry about what people think or say—''

''I don't give a damn what people think or say.''

''Then go ahead—divorce me!''

''There will be no divorce.''

''But you just said you don't give a damn about propriety, about the things people say—''

His vise around her arms was so tight that she nearly cried out. His eyes were the silver-blue of a dagger as they pierced into her heart.

''There will be no divorce, Marissa. And it hasn't a thing to do with others, it has to do with a vow. Till death do us part.''

''So you will let us live in this agony!''

''I would let us live in hell, madam!''

She stared at him in silence for a second and then she cried out. ''I cannot! I cannot! I cannot live with you when you—''

''You will live with me. And as a wife!''

She trembled with hate and fury and excitement, and with love and hope. At least she could still anger him, still arouse him. She could have his touch this moment if she so desired. No.

"No! I can't live this way because I cannot bear it!" she told him. "I—I love you—"

"Liar!" he thundered.

But he seemed so startled that his hold on her loosened, and she wrenched free from him. They stared at one another for a moment, and then she cried out and ran from his room.

"Marissa!"

His voice bellowed after her. She ignored him, and tore down the stairway. She burst outside, knowing that he would be after her.

And now she didn't want to see him. She had bared her heart and soul once again to try to convince him that she loved him. He didn't believe her, or else it didn't matter. She couldn't endure his mockery right now.

She raced to the carriage house and into her mare's stall. The animal bolted, nervous, skittish. "Oh, please, what is the matter with you!" she whispered to the horse. What was wrong with all the animals? She soothed the mare quickly, then bridled her and leaped upon her back without bothering with a saddle.

The first streaks of dawn were becoming apparent in the far east as she trotted out of the carriage house. Ian was on the lawn.

"Marissa!"

She nudged the animal into a canter, knowing that he would follow her soon. She'd had no plan, but now she realized that she could race for the store. It would be open because Sandy and others would be preparing for one of the orphans' breakfasts today.

She raced recklessly through the streets, seeing the city as she began to come to life. Most people would still be in their nightshirts, but several grocers were setting up their produce. Newsboys were already on the streets. Some sleepy soul swore at her as he jumped out of her way.

Feeling guilty, she plowed on, and soon reached the store.

She jumped from the mare and tethered the animal. She looked up the street to see that Ian was already thundering down upon her.

She quickly flung open the door and nodded to the security guard who greeted her retreating back. Then she hurried down to the basement, anxious to be with others.

Across the room she could see Darrin. His freckled face broke into a broad grin and he rose to greet her. He began to frown, taking in her wild hair and disheveled appearance.

She couldn't hide behind children, she thought. If Ian was angry enough, he'd drag her out of the basement and demand a confrontation. She had no right to be here. She should have faced him, no matter what.

"Mrs. Tremayne!" Darrin called to her.

And then there was a rumbling beneath her feet.

"What the—" someone cried.

"Shaker!" Darrin shouted. "Shaker! It's a shaker! A big one."

The rumbling became a cacophony, and it seemed as if the world began to crumble and break.

CHAPTER SEVENTEEN

THE MOST AMAZING THING to Ian was that he saw the quake. Saw the way it ran up the street, tearing the ground apart, saw it rend the earth asunder.

There was the sound, a rumbling, a moaning.

The bay reared, nearly unseating him, and Ian leaped quickly from the animal's back. Even as he soothed the horse, he looked down the street. And he could see it.

The great buildings, waving, undulating, engaged in a macabre dance. And the rip...the rip itself, slashing its way down Washington Street, undulating, sweeping, cascading, coming toward him like the massive and powerful waves of an ocean.

''Marissa!'' he screamed. The desperate urge to protect her, to see her, to hold her, at all costs, assailed him. But it was too late. The street was ripping in half. Steel pipes were bending and snapping. Wood, cement, concrete, metal...everything buckled beneath the gigantic tear...

It reached him. The bay screeched as it was picked up and hurtled toward the building. Ian could give the horse no comfort for he was suddenly flying himself, picked up as if he were no more than an ant, thrown in a high arc then slammed down flat. He braced himself against the wall he touched. It was the brick wall of the emporium.

He stared across the street. Facades were crumbling, buildings were falling. He braced himself as the world continued to shiver and shake. Marissa! She was inside the building...

The building would hold! he promised himself. His grandfather had built it well, and he had personally seen to all the modifications over the years. The store would hold.

Before him, a wall came crashing forward. Great chunks of cement came hurtling through the air, and he rolled just in time to avoid being crushed. A wood frame building came crashing down as if it had been wrecked by dynamite.

And the street continued to undulate, the buildings to dance.

Ian heard screams, horrible screams.

And then suddenly, the earth went still.

The bay was down; he ignored it. Screams were rising from all around him. He barely heard them. Picking himself up, he ran to the emporium entrance.

Only one thing gave him pause.

He could hear a hiss. A slow, almost lazy hiss.

But he knew what it was. Gas. The pipes beneath the city had been split by the quake. At any moment, explosions could start up.

"Marissa!"

He tore into the store and found a security guard on the floor. Ian stooped beside the man and quickly noted the smashed display case by his side. It was Bobby Harrison, a young Irishman who had been with the emporium since his sixteenth birthday.

The latest in French pottery had downed him.

Ian lifted him. The man began to blink. "Mr. Tremayne. I'm sorry, sir. There was a shaker. Oh." He grimaced. "You must know that. The case fell. I—"

"Yes, Bobby, it was a shaker, a bad one. My wife just ran in here, before the quake. Where did she go? Who else is in here, and where?"

"Just the folks down in the basement. No one's been up to the offices, and no one's come to work on the floor. Only some of the kitchen folk to cook, and—" he paused, his eyes opening wide "—the kids. There's about ten kids down there already. Two cooks, a priest, er, Sandy is in, and that's it, I'm sure." He stared at Ian. "You needn't worry, she's going to stand, sir. I'm sure of it. Some merchandise went flying around, to be sure, but the building, she's as good as gold.''

"We've got to get them out of here, Bobby," Ian said. "The gas mains are broken. We've got a sprinkler system, but if the pipes blow..."

Bobby understood. Despite the jagged cut on his forehead, he was quickly on his feet. "I'm right with you, sir." Ian was already racing along the corridor for the elevators. He pressed the call button, then realized that the elevators might have been hurtled off their tracks. He turned and started for the stairs to the basement.

"You need to do something about that shoulder, sir," Bobby told him.

"What?" He hadn't realized he was bleeding; he hadn't felt a thing. He looked down to see that blood was bright and very red over the white cotton of his shirt sleeve. "It's all right," he said briefly.

He threw open the door to the stairs and ran down them. He started to press through the door to the cafeteria and discovered that it wouldn't budge.

"Dammit, give me a hand here, Bobby," he said. He threw his shoulder against the door, but nothing happened. Bobby joined him, and together they threw all their weight against the door. Nothing happened. "What the hell?" Ian demanded, his anxiety growing.

"Ian!"

Softly, faintly, he heard Marissa's voice.

"Marissa!" He thundered against the door, calling her name.

"Ian, we're trapped! A beam has fallen, and brought down some of the roof." Marissa sounded calm, and she sounded unhurt.

"All right! I'm going to get to you. Is everyone all right? Has anyone been hurt?"

"Ian, you must hurry. Sandy was struck by a cart. She's bleeding very badly. We've a few other injuries, too."

"Are you hurt?"

She hesitated, then said, "I'm fine."

He hoped she really was. That she wasn't just being brave, as she knew so well how to be.

She'd handle what was happening in there. She'd bind up the wounds and keep the others calm. Not because she was his wife.

Because of the person she was. The proud and beautiful downstairs maid from the coal mines who had learned all her lessons the hard way.

"Ian, do hurry, please!" He could hear that she was trying hard to stay calm. Things were clearly worse than she was letting on.

Much worse. He could still smell the gas.

"I'll hurry," he promised vehemently. And he added a silent prayer. Dear God in Heaven, let me be swift!

SHAKER. Darrin had called it a shaker. It couldn't have lasted for more than half a minute, but it had changed the world.

Ian was alive, he was near, and he was going to get them out. Those simple facts meant everything to her. They almost made her stop the trembling that had begun in her with the quaking of the earth. She had never been so terrified in her life.

In the basement, all hell had broken loose. Tables and chairs had seemed to jump and leap around with minds and purposes of their own. Shelves of china and glassware had crashed and shattered. Plaster had cracked and beams had fallen. For a split second she had looked up at the roof and she had been terrified that the entire building was going to cave in. But it did not cave in. Even as the walls trembled and shook, they remained firm. Screams and cries littered the air as the shaking continued.

And then the shaking had stopped, but the cries had not.

Trembling, jerking, she had dragged herself from the spot where she had fallen by the door, just two feet from the fallen beam. Ian! she called silently. She wanted to scream in raw, blind panic. She had left him on the street. Anything could have happened to him. Oh, dear God, dear God, she was going to shriek and scream hysterically...

She couldn't! She knew that; she couldn't. Some of the youngest of the little boys had been screaming, and she had tried to call out assurances to them. All the lights had gone, and darkness permeated the basement. "It's all right, it's over now, it's going to be all right!"

Was it over? She didn't know! she thought with a growing panic. If only she hadn't run, if only she was with Ian, she wouldn't be so afraid. He would know what to do.

"I'm cut!"

"Me foot's broke, I know it is!"

"Oh, Marissa, I'm bleeding! I'm bleeding badly!" That call was from Sandy.

"We've an emergency lantern, Mrs. Tremayne," one of the cooks, a heavy man named Ralph, told her.

"Wonderful—" she began, and then she broke off, for the smell of gas was slowly becoming obvious around them. "No, no! Ralph, don't."

"Oh! Yes, you're right."

She could not panic! And she could not lose all sense and logic worrying about Ian. She couldn't imagine that a building might have fallen, that the earth might have opened...

"It's going to be all right!" she said.

The slightest bit of daylight was beginning to filter in through the slim grates that were at street level. Her hands still shaking, she called out to the boys, asking who was hurt. Then she heard a deeper voice.

"'Tis Father Donohue, Mrs. Tremayne. I'm little help for

the làds. I'm caught beneath a table here, and I cannot move. I think me leg's crushed.''

There was only a slight quiver to the good Father's voice, and Marissa bit into her lower lip, applauding his bravado.

''All right, then, my good young fellows, I'll get to you one by one!'' Marissa promised them.

''We're all going to die!'' a lad babbled hysterically. It was Tiny Grissom.

''Tiny! We are not all going to die. I'm not going to die. I've still a great deal ahead of me to do!'' she assured him.

And she did have a great deal ahead of her, she realized. She knotted her fist over her stomach and began to shake again. She was going to have a baby. And so help her, she was going to live to have that child. Ian's child. ''We're going to be fine, Tiny. Just fine. Now you remember that, every one of you!''

''I'm—I'm here!'' Darrin suddenly called out. ''I'll keep to the left side, Mrs. Tremayne.''

And so between them, she and Darrin reached the boys one by one, and those who were not trapped by some piece of fallen furniture or debris she grouped together. One of the youngest lads definitely seemed to have suffered from an injured foot, and she carefully wrapped it in a bandage she made by ripping up one of the tablecloths.

Sandy was the one who scared her. A food cart had fallen upon her, and there was a great pool of blood soaking her skirt. Feeling ill and praying for courage, Marissa ripped up Sandy's skirt and created a tourniquet for her leg just above the thigh. The trickle of blood seemed to stop, but Marissa still felt ill. Teddy Nichols, Ralph's assistant, arrived at her side with a large bottle of cooking sherry, and they encouraged Sandy to drink.

It was then that she heard Ian's voice. And in the first few seconds she couldn't even answer him, she was too busy whispering prayers of gratitude. He was not only alive, he was coming to their rescue.

"See? We're all going to be fine. They'll be with us any minute."

She hoped so. The scent of gas was still very strong on the air.

And only seconds later she began to smell smoke.

IAN FOUND the emergency equipment in its slot in the wall and seized the ax. Bobby followed him, and he began to hack at the door. The wood gave easily enough, but once he had managed to slice through it, he realized that there was more than a beam blocking him. Tables had overturned, plaster had fallen, and some bricks had come loose. There was a high pile of debris between him and the people he was so desperate to reach.

"We dig through, I guess," Bobby said.

"Maybe there's help in the street," Ian murmured. "I'll be right back."

But there was no help in the street. There was the most curious mixture of panic and absolute detachment going on. People, some ready for work, some half dressed and some almost naked, wandered around aimlessly, almost like sightseers.

And still, the screams were rising. Two of the city's horse drawn fire carts were racing down the ripped-up streets.

The face of San Francisco had changed within seconds. Some buildings still stood; many did not.

And the screams were going on and on.

Someone was shouting orders, a policeman perhaps, trying to gather what folk he could to lift the debris of a rooming-house. He was managing to find some support. It wasn't that the people weren't willing to help, Ian knew. They were still in shock.

The firemen were shouting warnings to evacuate the area.

Ian was well aware that he wasn't going to get any help, and he could understand why. The firemen were using everybody they could recruit to rescue the people caught in the tangle of fallen buildings.

Down the block, Ian could see the flicker of flames rising from a downed wooden structure.

He breathed out a silent prayer, then he felt a renewed soaring of hope.

The bay was up. His handsome horse was up and standing, bleeding only slightly from a wound on the fetlock. And despite the panic, the horse hadn't fled. Marissa's mare was nowhere to be seen, but the bay was standing firm and waiting.

"Good old fellow," he murmured, patting the animal's neck briefly. "Wait for me, I may need you."

Then he hurried into the emporium. "Bobby, it's you and me. We're going to have to arrange some kind of a pulley and lever system. Let's dig and get to it, eh?"

Bobby looked panicked for a minute. Then he smiled. "Sure, Mr. Tremayne. Let's dig, shall we?"

They started digging. In a while, Ian called out to Marissa again. "We're coming. How's everyone doing?"

Horribly, Marissa thought. Sandy was no longer conscious, and she hadn't heard from the Father in a while. The boy with the injured foot was softly sobbing.

"We're—we're holding out," Marissa said. But they weren't holding out, not well at all. Her eyes stung terribly. Darrin was coughing every other second. So were the others. Ralph was complaining that he couldn't breathe.

"Almost to you!" Ian called.

Marissa bit her lip. She could see them working. The door was down, and there was more light peeking in. Ian and Bobby were dark silhouettes against that light, silhouettes in constant motion.

And still, the time went slowly. So slowly.

They could hear the shouts in the streets. The warnings to evacuate the area.

And they could hear the screams, too.

"Marissa!" Ian called to her. "We've created something of a tunnel here. I need a boy to volunteer to crawl through first."

She looked at Darrin. He shook his head, his eyes watery, his breath a wheeze. "I'm not coming out until you come out, Mrs. Tremayne."

"I'll go," a lad named Peter told her bravely. His voice only quavered a little.

"Good boy, that's grand," Marissa told him. She found his hand. His palm was wet in hers as she brought him to the debris in front of the doorway. Once they were there, Ian started shouting instructions to him. He had to keep his weight upon the beam. When he was close enough, Ian would grab him and carry him through.

"You all right with that, young man?" Ian asked.

"Yes, sir, Mr. Tremayne!" Peter promised.

And so they all watched him crawl atop the broken table and plaster chunks and make his way to the beam. He moved slowly, carefully and with a natural agility. It still took him endless minutes to reach Ian.

But then Ian's strong arms grabbed him, and the entire room cheered.

"That's my lad!" cried Father Donohue.

But Marissa knew that they were still in very deep trouble. Father Donohue was trapped. And Sandy could never make such a crawl. She wasn't conscious.

"Billy! Billy Martin. You're next now!" she called out cheerfully. Then she backed away and found Ralph and Teddy.

"We've got to free the Father," she said. "Maybe with the boys out there, they'll be able to dig a larger opening. But we have to free him while they're trying."

The two cooks looked at one another. Ian was shouting to her, wanting to know what was going on. She hurried to where he could see her and tried to put the truth of the situation into her voice without alarming the boys.

"We've just got to move a few things to reach Father Donohue, Ian. Darrin will be here. I've got to help Ralph and Teddy."

She could see him looking at the little boy who had just made it through. "Peter, now you're on the safe side, lad. I need your help. Take up that broken spade there and help Bobby start digging again, eh?"

"Yes, sir, Mr. Tremayne, sir!" Peter promised.

Marissa, hearing him, smiled, but she blinked quickly. She was very close to tears, and she couldn't afford to cry.

She hurried to Father Donohue. At his side, Ralph and Teddy were surveying the huge oak table that trapped the Father along with a tangle of broken chairs. She saw their dilemma. If they shifted the table the wrong way, it could fall upon him and crush his lungs.

"Mrs. Tremayne," Teddy told her. "You get down there by the Father. When Ralph tells you to, pull. And pull fast. It's the only way we can see to clear him."

Tiny, the boy with the hurt foot, limped his way over to her. He was a small boy, thus the name, but he had a certain wiry strength about him. "I can help you with Father Donohue's shoulders, ma'am."

"Tiny, you could be hurt here," she warned. She wondered if Father Donohue was going to make it. His blue eyes were closed; his fingers rested upon the cross that lay on his chest.

Tiny was no longer caught up in his own fear. He offered Marissa a crooked smile. "He's been Mom and Dad both to me for a lotta years now. Can't see's how I'll have anything much left myself were I to lose him, too."

Father Donohue's eyes opened. "Ye've a lifetime ahead of you, me lad, and don't ye forget it! Now the two of ye take grave care there, for I've a fondness for me Maker, and I'm certain he's a fondness for me, so if I leave ye this day, it'll be fittin'.''

"Father, enough blarney!" Marissa told him with forced cheer. She looked at Ralph and nodded. Tiny and she each took hold of an arm.

"Yea, though I walk through the valley..." Father Donohue began.

And then there was a screeching sound as the two men shifted the desk. The sheared portion would come flying down in seconds, Marissa knew. She and Tiny pulled and pulled hard, and there was a thunderous crashing just a split second after they freed Father Donohue's legs.

Again, a rousing cheer went up in the basement. But when Ralph tried to help Father Donohue to his feet, the man buckled with a cry.

"'Tis no use. Me leg is definitely broken," Donohue said.

"We'll get you out," Marissa insisted. "Bring him some of the sherry, Teddy. I'll check on Sandy."

Sandy, stretched out on the floor, her head laid upon Ralph's apron, was still unconscious. Her breathing and her pulse were irregular. She needed help, and needed it soon.

"It's going to be all right," Marissa whispered close to the girl's ear. She knew Sandy couldn't hear her. It didn't matter.

"Mrs. Tremayne," Teddy told her. "The boys are almost out. We've got to do something about Sandy and the Father."

"Yes, of course," she murmured. They were looking at her to know what to do. She glanced toward the doorway. With a number of the boys helping from the other side, the tunnel through the bricks and beams and plaster was widening. She looked quickly at Ralph. "I need two tablecloths. We'll rig stretchers for the Father and Sandy. Between the three of us, we can get them to the opening, and Ian will have to pull them through."

"There's not enough space—" Ralph began.

"Then they'll have to keep digging," she said stubbornly.

She hurried to the opening. She could see Ian's silhouette, dark now against the full light of day. What time was it, she wondered? The quake had lasted only seconds, but it seemed that hours had passed. She was tired and thirsty and her throat was growing harsh and dry as the smoke in the basement steadily increased.

"Ian!"

"Yes. Can you come now, Marissa?"

"No, I can't. We're trying to rig stretchers. We've got to have the opening a little larger. Can you keep at it?"

He was silent. Silent so long that she knew they were all risking their lives.

And she didn't want to die. She really, desperately didn't want to die. And she didn't want the tiny life within her to expire without ever having had a chance.

For the first time she realized that a child would be a part of them both. She could have a tiny son with his father's ink-black hair and striking blue eyes, and their baby could even mimic his smile.

And dream his dreams of a better world.

"We'll dig, Marissa," Ian said, but then she heard him turning to a number of the boys who were already out. "There's no reason for you lads to hang around here. You, Billy Martin, you're in charge. Take the lads out of here. Ask a fireman which way you should be heading. But move quickly now. Stay together, and get away as soon as you can."

"Yes, sir!" Billy told him, and then Marissa could hear Billy taking charge, lining up the boys from the youngest to the oldest.

And she could hear the sounds of digging again.

"You get out now, Mrs. Tremayne," Darrin told her. "I can help with Sandy and Father Donohue."

She shook her head. "No, I've got to see everyone out,"

she told him, and she hurried to Sandy's side. "We need to take care getting her on the tabletop, Ralph. We'll have to carry them to the hospital like this, too, so we might as well make sure we've got it right to begin with." She started to tell them how to roll Sandy, then how to see that she was tied properly on the tabletop. Ralph stared at her curiously.

"I've been around a mine disaster or two, Ralph," she told him with a rueful smile. "Do trust me, please. I know what I'm doing."

"I never doubted it," Ralph told her. "Teddy, grab that tablecloth like Mrs. Tremayne told you."

Soon they were ready with Sandy. Ralph and Teddy lifted the makeshift stretcher, and Marissa watched nervously as they moved to the tunnel.

"Can you do it, men?" Ian called to them.

"Yes, Mr. Tremayne. Teddy and I and the boy can get her to the opening. We're fine on this end."

And so they began. Trying to get their burden over their heads was difficult and demanded the men's concentration. Sandy almost started to slip once, and Marissa caught her breath. But the stretcher evened out high above their heads, and then Ian cried out. "We've got her! Get to the Father, and quickly."

It was just then that the ceiling sprinklers, triggered by the thick smoke in the basement, burst into action. Water spewed down upon them.

Startled, Marissa cried out.

"Marissa!" Ian shouted.

"I'm—I'm all right! Just surprised!" she called back. Drenched, she turned quickly to Ralph and Teddy and the stubborn Darrin. "We've got to get Father out, now!"

Quickly, nervously, their wet fingers slipping over fabric and wood, the four set to work on Father Donohue.

Despite the odds against them, they managed to secure him

to a stretcher. Father Donohue groaned with pain as they lifted him.

"Stop!" Marissa said. "His leg, we should have splinted it first—"

"No, ye'll not stop! I'm firm to this stretcher and ye'll get me the hell out so that ye'll get yerself the hell out, excuse me, Lord!" Donohue insisted with thunder in his voice.

Marissa and Darrin smiled at one another, and Teddy and Ralph repeated the procedure with Donohue. She heard a soft moan, and she knew how desperately he was fighting the pain.

"Got him!" Ian called.

"Mrs. Tremayne—" Darrin said.

"After you, my boy, and I mean it!" Marissa insisted. "I'll be right behind you, and then Teddy and Ralph."

Darrin agreed at last, climbing nimbly. Within seconds, he had crawled up to the tunnel and passed through. "Come on, Mrs. Tremayne!"

"I'm coming!" Marissa called.

But she never got farther than taking the first foothold of her climb.

An aftershock suddenly seized hold of the earth, and she lost her balance and fell to the ground.

There was a ripping sound, and a shard of wood from the beam came loose.

"Marissa!" She heard someone scream her name, and she tried to roll away from the falling missile. She moved quickly, but not quickly enough. She felt a searing pain as the chunk skimmed by the back of her head.

"Marissa!" She heard her name again. It was Ian's voice, she was certain, and yet the sound too quickly faded. She closed her eyes, and fought the void that was opening to welcome her.

"Marissa!" Arms closed around her. She opened her eyes. He had climbed through the tunnel to reach her. She wanted to smile. She wanted to touch his face and tell him that he was always noble, even if he couldn't begin to love her anymore.

But she couldn't do anything at all.

Outside, fires were beginning to burn with a red and regal splendor.

But in her world, there was nothing but blackness.

CHAPTER EIGHTEEN

IAN DARED TAKE NO time to ascertain Marissa's condition while they remained within the building.

The Tremaynes had built a fortress, but not even a fortress could stand in the path of the ferocious gas blaze surely eating its way to them.

There was no time for anything; he could only carry her through the tunnel space, locked to his body with one arm, while he used his feet and his free hand to drag them along. When he came to the end of the tunnel through the debris, Darrin was waiting to help him. He allowed Marissa to collapse into Darrin's arms, then slipped free himself, calling to Ralph and Teddy that they must hurry.

He jumped clear and swept Marissa into his arms, leaving the others to deal with Sandy and Father Donohue as he carried her fleetly from the building and into the daylight.

There was not much of it. The smoke was a blanket upon them now.

She inhaled and exhaled on a shaky note. Her eyelids flickered open, and she offered him a feeble smile. Then her eyes flickered shut once again. He set a finger upon her pulse and found it steady. He whispered her name and leaned closely over her, listening to the pattern of her breathing. It, too, was steady and deep. She was going to be all right.

"Mr. Tremayne!" Ralph was behind him, carrying the Father with the help of one of the lads. The other boys had already fled to safety, except for Darrin. And Darrin was never going to leave Marissa, Ian knew that.

"How's the lady, sir?" Ralph asked. Darrin had already come around beside him.

"She'll make it," Ian said. He rose, carrying his burden. No, no burden, ever, he thought. Her weight was easy to hold.

They hadn't made it, though. Not yet, he thought. The street was filled with refugees, fleeing the threat of fire. Some were dressed, some were not. Some carried belongings. And some abandoned them along the way.

"Mr. Tremayne!"

He heard a shout and turned to see that a horse-drawn hospital wagon was coming to their side of the street. Driving it was one of Dennis Sullivan's fire lieutenants, Matthew Montague.

"Matthew!" he called in return. The wagon came to a halt at his side. "Sir, you're needed down the street. A man with building experience. They've got to rig up some kind of a system to lift a roof. There's twenty people trapped. Can you help them?"

"My wife—" he murmured, looking at Marissa. Her clothes were sooty and bloodied, her face was blackened with smudges of dirt. She was so still, and so beautiful, in her dishevelment. So vulnerable. They couldn't ask him to leave her.

"I can take your injured to the hospital, sir. Your wife will be well tended, I swear it."

"I cannot leave her," Ian said.

Darrin stepped up behind him. "I'll stay with her, sir. I'll never leave her. I'll tend her, I promise."

Bobby touched his arm. "I'll come with you, sir."

Ian wanted to scream out against the injustice. He had crawled through hell to reach Marissa, and now they wanted him to abandon her.

But she was going to be all right. He knew it. And there were twenty people caught beneath a roof, and he could help.

He couldn't let them burn. The death toll would be high enough today.

"All right, Matthew."

Darrin leaped into the wagon and Ian crawled up behind him. There were already injured aboard. People with hollow eyes and bloodied bandages. Ian glanced their way, then laid his wife down, her head cushioned gently upon Darrin's lap. With guilt he realized that Father Donohue and Sandy were in far more dangerous shape, and he helped to bring them to the wagon.

"Where is Chief Sullivan going to form his fire line?" he asked Matthew.

"I'm sorry, sir. I don't know much of the plan yet. I'm afraid the chief is in the hospital. He went to reach his wife and fell through the floor." He was quiet for a minute. "I'm afraid they don't think he's going to make it, Mr. Tremayne."

Ian felt ill. Dennis Sullivan had been the one man in the city truly aware of its strengths and weaknesses. A good man, who had fought for more.

"I've got to get going, Mr. Tremayne," Matthew said nervously. He looked at the flames that were clearly visible behind them.

Ian stepped back. Darrin looked over the side. "Take care of them!" he called to Matthew.

The wagon rolled away. Terror struck his heart.

He might never see Marissa again. He was going to walk in the direction of the fire.

He had to see her again. They had survived thus far; they had to weather the fire.

She had never understood him. When he had tried to tell her she hadn't listened. He didn't give a damn if she was the daughter of the greatest sinner or the finest saint, a child of riches or a waif born in poverty. He had fallen in love with her, and neither time nor distance had changed a thing. He had been angry because she had lied, and kept on lying. She hadn't trusted him. Even when he had cradled her in his arms and spun out his dreams for their future, she hadn't trusted him.

She had never said that she loved him. Not until she had needed him. And then he had been angrier still because it had seemed that she needed to buy his help. He would have gone for her uncle whether she had loved him or despised him. She should have known that.

But that was the only time she had said she loved him. Until this morning.

And then she had run away from him.

Away from him...

And into the fire.

"I'm with you, sir," Bobby said, clearing his throat and tapping Ian on the shoulder.

"No, you're not," Ian told him. Bobby was a young man and there were surely enough willing hands by the downed roof. Only a fool walked toward a fire.

"See that bay there, Bobby? He's my horse, a darned good one. Take him and follow the wagon. Make sure that everyone is taken care of. Do what you can. I'll meet you at the hospital."

"But, sir—" Bobby protested.

"Would you get the hell out of here so I can get where I'm needed?" Ian demanded impatiently. Then he turned and started walking into the stream of people. The going was hard. People, some half dressed, were surging down the street. They carried what they could, or dragged carts of household belongings. Some held nothing, and some looked dazed. Some wore bandages, and some chatted as if they were tourists out for a stroll. And some had eyes that seemed already dead.

Ahead of him, he saw the fallen roof, and half a dozen firemen and civilian volunteers trying to help. One of the men recognized him, and they all made way for Ian to survey the situation. He called for rope and pulleys, and explained that they were going to lever away a section with what equipment they had. Everyone set to work.

To Ian's amazement, he realized that the coming fire was casting light across the darkening street. Twilight was coming.

And the fire was coming closer and closer. And with it, a continual stream of humanity.

San Francisco was under military law, someone told them. Funston had taken over at about four in the afternoon.

Looters were being warned that if they were caught, the police and the military would shoot to kill.

There had been tremendous bravery.

And there had been events to shock humanity. Thieves chopping away fingers to steal rings from corpses. Scalpers demanding huge amounts of money for the use of their wagons. Grocers demanding fortunes for a loaf of bread.

And always, there was the fire.

By early evening, the roof was cleared away. They were able to pull three women, six children and seven men from the wreckage. Three men were dead; they had been crushed by the falling walls. And one woman had been suffocated by the plaster. They had probably died immediately, Ian thought. And he breathed a prayer of relief, for he had been hearing other tales, horrible tales. Stories about men and women trapped, and rescuers trying to help them but not being able to. Stories about people running from the blaze, hearing the screams of the trapped behind them.

There was one story about the man who had begged an army officer to shoot him before the blaze could reach him.

Ian stayed with the firemen and the volunteers as the dusk became darkness, and only the ferocious fire was left to light the city.

It was out of control. It didn't take a trained eye to see that. The fire was entirely out of control.

And so, it seemed, was the city.

HE HAD been holding her. Holding her, looking down into her eyes. And his gaze had been blue-gray with anguish, filled with concern. He had held her, and she had known that things would be all right...

But even as she awoke, she sensed that he was no longer with her.

Everything around her was white. Incredibly white. She blinked and realized Darrin was sitting in a chair by her bedside. He saw that her eyes were open and leaped to his feet.

"Mrs. Tremayne! You're awake. The doc said you'd come to soon enough. Promised me that you'd be fine, he did. I couldn't believe him, I was so scared. Well, no, I wasn't really scared, you know—"

"It's all right, it's all right!" Marissa acknowledged with a weak smile. She tried to sit up. She felt a fierce pounding, but it quickly subsided. "Ouch!" she murmured.

"Oh, you are still hurt—"

"Darrin! I've a knot on the head and a bit of an ache, but I'm sure the doctor was right and I'll be just fine. I was never badly hurt."

"Well, you had us frightened enough!" Darrin told her. "You were out cold."

"But I'm awake now," she said gently. "Darrin, what about Father Donohue and Sandy?"

"They set the Father's leg and gave him some brandy and sent him on. Sandy is not doing so well. She lost an awful lot of blood, they say. But they've sewn her up, and they're crossing their fingers. Now, you hold on, Mrs. Tremayne. I'm going for the doctor—"

"Wait!" she called. "Darrin, what—what happened to Mr. Tremayne?"

"Oh!" He came back to her bedside. "They needed him. He had to stay."

"What?" she cried with alarm.

"Seems they needed somebody who knew something about the structure of a building to lift up a roof. Mr. Tremayne had to go back with them. I promised him, though, that I would stay with you.''

Marissa nodded, feeling dizzy. He'd gone on. He'd pulled her through, but then he'd gone on. And she must have dreamed that he held her in his arms with such anguish and tenderness.

Darrin returned in seconds, but not with a doctor. One of the nurses, a black-garbed nun, accompanied him into the room.

''Ah, Mrs. Tremayne, I'm so glad that you're back with us. Dr. Spencer. says you'll be fine, just as long as you take it easy. Except that I'm afraid you won't be able to take it quite so easy. We're evacuating the hospital.''

''What?'' Marissa gasped.

The nun grimaced. ''I'm afraid the fire is coming our way, and doing so quickly.''

''The fire has come this far?''

''Indeed, I'm afraid so. We're under martial law, and officers have just come to warn us that we must be out.''

''Has anything been heard of my husband, Sister?'' Marissa was already crawling out of the bed.

''Mrs. Tremayne,'' the Sister said with a frown. ''Where are you going?''

''I've got to find my husband—''

''Mrs. Tremayne, there is no way to find your husband. He is working with the rescue crews, and he is a very smart man, I've heard. He'll find you when he's able. Don't you see!'' she added with some frustration. ''There's no way for you to find him! Mrs. Tremayne! There's looting going on out there. And police and army traveling the streets. Looters have been shot dead in the streets. Children have been beaten. Thievery and abuse goes on. You cannot find your husband, and he can take care of himself. He will find us, I promise you.''

''But we're moving—'' Marissa began.

"To the park, Mrs. Tremayne. He'll find us. Now, get back in bed until we've got the evacuation arranged."

Marissa shook her head. "No, Sister. I can't find Ian, but I'm not sick. And others are. I can help, and so can Darrin. Give us something to do."

"Mrs. Tremayne—"

"Sister, we can carry things!"

The Sister sighed, then smiled. "Fine! I can use some volunteers! Those who can walk will. We've wagons outside for those who cannot. Come, I'll assign you to patients to watch!"

IAN THOUGHT it had been the longest day of his life. He stayed with his crew, connected with what was going on in the city through messages from the policemen, the firemen and occasionally one of the army officers.

The main thrust against the fire had been the use of dynamite.

But the firemen had never really been trained to use dynamite. Though the rumor was subdued, it was out there that they were causing more damage than good. Improperly laid, the explosions were sending sparks on to untouched dwellings.

But they needed a good fire wall. A solid stretch of space with nothing to feed the flames.

Mayor Schmitz was calling meetings and forming a committee of civilians to help make decisions. People were saying that Freddie Funston had had no right to place the city under martial law.

But terrible stories were running rampant. Stories of men shot for looting, and left in the streets with placards attached to their bodies. "Punishment for looting! Thieves take care!"

There were stories about cowardice and wretchedness. Stories about the average man, and stories about the rich and famous.

Word had already come in from Oakland that William Randolph Hearst, the great native-born San Franciscan now living in the east, had sent out early morning editorials minimizing the damage and change to the city.

He would definitely be changing his editorials in his New York and Chicago newspapers. When the San Francisco *Examiner* started up print again, there would be nothing left to minimize.

There was terror in the streets, but there was also the greatest heroism.

Ian, so tired that he didn't even feel it any more, just kept on working. He moved along with the fire wagon, his pick thrown over his shoulder, traveling from site to site, wherever he was needed. Bobby had come back to him with messages. Marissa was fine, safely in the hospital. Bobby had ridden to the house on Nob Hill, and Theo and the Kwans and Jimmy and Mary O'Brien were fine. The house had stood well, and none of the animals had been injured.

Darrin was still with Marissa, and a Dr. Spencer had said that she would suffer no aftereffects. It was really just a bump on the head.

Bobby rode back, and Ian felt at ease.

Until he heard that the fire had come licking dangerously close to the hospital. Then he knew that he had to hurry. He felt desperate to reach Marissa.

He was afraid he might lose her forever.

By then, they were into the second day of the fire. Marines had been ordered in, and orders came down that the crew had to break for a few hours of sleep at the very least.

Ian didn't sleep.

He left the others and hurried through the streets to the hospital. He'd had a perfectly good horse, he reminded himself. He'd given the bay away, and now he'd have given everything to have him back.

He started to run, feeling that he wouldn't make it in time.

He didn't. The last wagon was drawing away as he reached the hospital.

The first lick of fire was touching the roof.

Ahead, Ian saw a man on foot, following the wagon. Ian raced after the man.

"Wait! Where have the patients gone? Where are they being taken?"

The man stopped and turned to him. He looked as weary and worn as Ian felt.

"They've all gone, sir. They've all gone."

"Yes, I know, but where?"

"The Golden Gate Park. They're setting up the hospital and more. There will be tents for those left homeless, and food lines." He paused for a minute, looking at Ian. "Hope you find who you're looking for, sir. I sure do."

"Thank you," Ian said. "I'll find her."

Exhausted, he started walking toward the park.

He just wanted to see her face.

THE HOSPITAL had almost been cleared when Marissa ran into Dr. Spencer in the hallway.

"I heard you were up and about, Mrs. Tremayne." He caught hold of her and led her beneath one of the lamps, inspecting her eyes. "Well, it seems that you look all right. Are you still dizzy? Nauseated?"

She shook her head. "I'm fine, really."

He sighed. "There's nothing much I could do about it if you weren't. Too many broken bones and bleeders and burn victims. Still, you ought to be taking it easy during the next few days."

"I—I need something to do," she told him.

"All right, then. I've got a broken ankle left down in the ward. A society belle, and I haven't the medical staff to deal with her. The ankle is splinted and set. She'll have to hobble along. She's the last to be moved except for a few of the critical patients, and I need to get her down to the wagon as quickly as possible. We're out of crutches, and we haven't a spare person to try to fashion anything makeshift at the moment. Want to take her on?''

Marissa nodded, and Dr. Spencer pointed down the hall. "Left door. You're on your own.''

She wasn't exactly on her own. Darrin, her little shadow, was waiting for her even as she spoke to Dr. Spencer. Marissa grimaced to him as the doctor walked on to tend to his more serious patients. Then she started down the hall to the ward.

A woman was sitting propped up on the bed. She was clad in day clothes, with her dove-gray skirt split so that the ankle could be attended to properly.

She looked at Marissa as Marissa walked into the room, and then both women froze.

"You!'' Grace Leroux whispered.

From down the hall came a scream. "The fire! My God, it's caught the roof.''

"Hurry! It's catching fast.''

Marissa saw the fear that flicked through the other woman's eyes. She clenched her jaw and walked into the room, Darrin following her.

"Come on. We've got to get you out of here,'' Marissa told the woman. And to her surprise, Grace started to laugh. There was something very near hysteria in the sound. "You're going to help me? I don't believe it. Don't you know that this place could incinerate at any minute?''

"Yes, I know, so let's hurry.''

"Oh, aren't you just so kind!''

"Grace, let's go,'' Marissa urged.

And then the woman was quiet. "You're really going to help save me, after everything?''

"You spread rumors about me, Grace. That's not exactly murder.''

Grace kept looking at her. It was Darrin who spoke. "Don't

you understand?'' he said softly. ''Grace is the one who set you up. She paid those men to kidnap you, to take you to Chinatown. To sell you across the ocean.''

Marissa inhaled sharply. Staring at Grace, she knew it was the truth.

''So what now, Mrs. Tremayne?'' Grace mocked softly. ''Are you still so willing to save me?''

Marissa took hold of her arm and pulled her up. ''Yes, I hate the stench of burning flesh. Now, for the love of God, can we go?''

Darrin supported one shoulder, Marissa the other. It was very slow going, but she and Darrin eventually got Grace down the stairs and into the wagon.

Dr. Spencer came riding up to the wagon then. ''Get in with the patients, Mrs. Tremayne—'' he nodded to Darrin ''—son.''

''I don't think that there's room—'' Marissa began.

''You're still my patient. Get in.'' He rode up close to her. ''You're a reckless young woman, Mrs. Tremayne. Brave. But do you really want to risk the child you're carrying?''

She felt a flush cover her cheeks. Darrin had heard the man. She didn't know who else had. And she didn't know if it mattered or not. They were living in disaster. Who would even remember the doctor's words?

And she didn't know if Ian would come back so she could try to tell him herself.

Without a word, she crawled into the wagon.

But when they reached the park, she discovered she couldn't dwell on any of her own worries. People were streaming in from all over the city. Food lines were set up, and they needed people to man them. Children were running around, lost and terrified. There were minor injuries that needed attending to.

Help was on the way. A train was coming in from the east laden with doctors and nurses. They would come soon.

But for the moment, she was needed.

Even Nob Hill had been threatened. The great mansions were catching on fire. A new worry awoke in her as she feared for Uncle Theo, Mary and Jimmy. She had to believe that they would get out all right.

Marissa found the woman in charge of the food lines. The heavy-bosomed matron had no difficulty putting her straight to work. She and Darrin were assigned the lost children.

Marissa immediately began to make plates for them, and bind up little injuries, and try to make them believe that everything would soon be all right.

She was holding one little toddler when she looked up to see Bobby. He was staring at her, as pleased as could be. "Found your uncle, Mrs. Tremayne. And the Chinese folks and your friends down the hill. And the horses are going to be all right, well, I think they are, they were confiscated by the city. Better than burning up for nothing, right? Anyway—"

He stepped back, and there was Theo. She leaped up with a glad cry and hugged and kissed him. Theo was fine; his eyes were bright. He was ready for this new battle. He took the toddler from her while she went to see Mary.

Mary was already ill. Rounded now with her baby, but pale, she was lying on an army cot in one of the little tents. Pale and beautiful. Marissa felt her heart go out to her friend.

Mary cried out when she saw her, trying to rise to embrace her. Marissa hurried to her side and sank down beside her. "Oh, Mary, I'm so glad to see you safe—"

"And you! Bobby told us you'd been hurt, and we were so worried, but here you are."

"We've survived it, Mary. And we're going to keep surviving."

"You're so strong. Always so strong. I don't know what I would have done without you through the years."

Marissa looked at Mary and smiled wryly. "Me! Oh, Mary,

you've always been the one with the optimism, certain that things would work!''

''The weak one. So useless now.''

''Mary! You're not useless. You're about to have a baby. Very soon. Oh, Mary! Strength isn't in anything that we can or can't do. It's in the heart! And you've the strength of a tiger, I promise you.''

Mary smiled, her lashes low, not quite believing Marissa, but not about to argue with her. Marissa told her to sleep, that she needed to get back to the children.

When she returned, she realized that her group was growing. Someone had handed Darrin a six-month-old child for her to tend to, so now her charges ran from that babe to a sweet fifteen-year-old girl who was doing her very best to be helpful. There were about thirty in all. And all of them frightened and missing their parents.

Marissa made sure that they were fed. She set about tending to their little wounds again. It was easier now. She and Darrin weren't alone. Bobby was there to do her bidding, and Jimmy split his time between seeing to his wife and helping her with the children.

And she had Uncle Theo, too, and between them they got the children settled down for some sleep, despite the fact that it was still daytime. And between them, they sat in the large tent allotted them all, and spun out fairy tales to take the children's minds off of the disaster.

Toward the end of the night, she looked up to see that a man was leaning against the post at the entrance. She stared harder and she realized that the tall, blackened creature was Ian.

Her heart slammed hard against her chest, and then seemed to fly. He was alive.

And he was watching her. She didn't know how long he had been standing there. She thought that it might have been awhile.

She almost cried out, almost leaped up and rushed to his arms. But she was suddenly afraid. Maybe his wife shouldn't be here. Maybe she was showing the circumstances of her birth, both she and Theo, so at home in such conditions.

He was alive, she told herself, and nothing else mattered.

But Ian didn't move, and she didn't move. She stared at the little girl tugging on her ragged skirt, and she finished her story with a faltering voice.

And then she rose. She tucked the little girl into a cot. "Your husband's come, Marissa," Uncle Theo said. "I'll see to the rest. With Darrin, me fine lad. And then I'll be tucking him in, too. This has been way too much for a boy this one's age."

"Thank you," Marissa murmured. She smoothed her hands over her skirt and stared at Ian. They were a pair. He was black with soot from head to toe, his white shirt barely recognizable, his hands charred, his hair whitened with ash. And she was still in her blackened white, too, her skirt torn for bandages.

And then he walked slowly toward her. The blue of his eyes was startling against the darkness of his face.

"Ian!" she murmured awkwardly. She smoothed her hands down her skirt again. "I'm so glad that you're alive!" she whispered, and then she kept talking. Too swiftly, and defensively. "I shouldn't be here, I imagine. If you'd married a real lady, she wouldn't be among the bread lines and the waifs. I'm sorry, I—"

"Ian!" Jimmy burst into the tent. "Ian, can you come quick? We need some help."

CHAPTER NINETEEN

A NEW WAGONLOAD of injured had just come in, and every available pair of hands was being put to use to carry the burned and wounded into the tents.

Doctors and nurses were arriving in the city now; medication had arrived from Oakland, and from every town close enough to render quick assistance.

Ian carefully lifted and carried men, women and children. He had just laid down a small child suffering from smoke inhalation when he looked up to see a familiar figure bent over a woman toward the rear of the tent.

For a moment he was puzzled. Then he realized that the man was Lilli's employee, the very questionable and homely Jake.

He felt a tinge of unease sweep down his spine, and he hurried along the row of cots to reach him.

As he had feared, Jake was bending over Lilli.

The stout, ugly man looked up and saw Ian. He seemed relieved, and quickly left his place at Lilli's bedside, motioning for Ian to sit. Ian hesitated, and the man said, "Please sir. It'd mean so much to her."

Ian knelt down carefully by the cot and took Lilli's hand. He fought hard to keep from shuddering, thinking of the pain she must be suffering.

Half of her beautiful face had been hideously burned.

He curled his fingers around hers. She opened her eyes and saw him.

"Oh, Ian!" she whispered. She twisted to hide the disfigurement.

"Lilli, Lilli," he murmured. "They're going to help you." He glanced at Jake. "Have they given her something for the pain? I heard that they were very low yesterday on anesthetics—"

"She's had morphine. I saw to it," Jake told him.

Thank God. She wasn't suffering. But something about Jake's voice told Ian that the man didn't think Lilli was going to make it.

"Ian…" It seemed very difficult for her to speak. "You shouldn't…have seen me so. You'll remember me like this."

"Lilli, I'll remember that you were always there for me. A beautiful heart in a beautiful person. But I won't need to remember anything, Lilli. This is your city, just like it is mine. You're going to pull through. I'm telling you—you're going to pull through. And we're going to walk arm in arm down the waterfront again. We're going to watch the ships, and buy shrimp from the peddlers, and tea in the garden. Do you hear me, Lilli?"

She squeezed his hand. "You're a good man, Ian," she said. "I always loved you so. But she loves you, too. You know that."

"Does she, Lilli? It's what she says. How can you tell?"

"It's in her eyes, Ian. You'll walk on the waterfront with your wife, Ian. Not with me."

"We'll all live to see it grow again, Lilli."

She didn't answer him. Her hand no longer squeezed his. He leaned close to her. He could still hear the soft beating of her heart.

"The morphine," Jake said.

Ian nodded.

"If there's any change, Mr. Tremayne," he said, "I'll come find you."

"Thank you, Jake," Ian said.

Wearily, he rose. He was on his way out of the tent when

he nearly plowed into one of the doctors. The haggard-looking man paused, watching him.

"You're Tremayne, Ian Tremayne. Not that there's much likeness now, but I've seen your picture in the paper often enough with your buildings and your political stands. They should have listened to you and Sullivan. The quake didn't destroy the city—the fire did."

"So it seems," Ian murmured. He was anxious to get back to Marissa. "Doctor, er—"

"Spencer. Adam Spencer. I saw your wife this morning."

Ian's interest was renewed. "They assured me that she was fine. Is there something I don't know?"

Spencer smiled. "I'm not really sure."

"What's wrong with her? If the bump was not a bad one, why did you let her up? Why is she—"

"Mr. Tremayne, please. The bump was not bad. And a garrison of soldiers couldn't keep her down once she determined she wanted to be up. But she should watch out for herself."

"Why is that?"

"Unless I miss my guess, sir, your wife is about two months pregnant."

Ian stumbled, as if he had been struck.

"You didn't know, I see," Spencer murmured. "I'm sorry, she surely wanted to tell you herself. Well, she might not have done so. And I'm sure she's still up. She has such an affinity for those children. Maybe it's for the best that I told you. The both of you need some sleep. I hear you've been trying to save the entire city. It can't be done. Get some sleep, Mr. Tremayne. And see that your wife gets some, too."

Ian nodded, numbed, elated, stunned, all in one. And frightened. He couldn't bear to lose her.

And he knew what the risks were. He'd already lost one wife and child.

"Thanks," he told Spencer, and he turned and strode

through the barrack-like tents that flourished like spring flowers in the once green park.

He got lost once, turning into a large tent where a number of the elderly had been brought. He realized that he was exhausted. He hadn't slept in forty-eight hours. He started out again.

Marissa. He wanted to throttle her. Shake her and throttle her. She was pushing too hard.

And he wanted to hold her. He wanted to crush her against him and hold her forever.

He was too tired to throttle or kiss her, he realized, but he kept on going, searching for her.

"Ian!"

He paused, aware that he had headed in the right direction this time because Theo was standing before him. "Ian, 'tis glad I am to see you back. I've managed a few extra blankets, and I've bound two of those army cots together in the rear of the tent—I know she won't leave the children, you see. But there's room for you both to get some rest, and that you must do. You look like hell, boy, if you don't mind me saying so."

"Thanks," Ian murmured dryly. "What about you? Where are you going?"

"Oh, I'll be here. There's just a shortage of cots at the moment. I've got the lad, Darrin, set up with blankets inside, and I'll join him. Him and me, we aren't so used to anything too comfortable, you know?"

"Theo, you're not a young man—"

"And don't you go making me an old one. I know you'll fix me up nice and fancy again soon enough. The ground's good enough for me tonight." His voice grew gruff. "I don't want that niece of mine on the ground, and you're the only one's going to get her to sleep tonight on a cot."

Ian smiled and clapped Theo on the back. Then he ducked into the tent.

Marissa was just tucking the baby into a makeshift crib. He

walked over to her and touched her shoulder. She turned, startled.

"You've done what you can for the little ones tonight, Marissa. They'll need you again in the morning. Come on, now. You've cared for these babies, now give a care to our own."

Her eyes opened wide. She was surprised that he knew, but he intended to offer no explanations that night, and she was too weary to start demanding them. Indeed, she didn't say a word.

"Marissa, we need some sleep," he said firmly. He caught her hand and led her to the bed that Theo had made for them.

She was as grime-covered as he. As disheveled, her glorious hair blackened with soot and ash. Tonight none of it mattered.

He swept her up, laid her down and sank beside her. And setting his arm around her, he pulled her against his chest, holding her close.

And there they both slept.

When Marissa woke, she was alone. It was very early, still dark. It must have been about five o'clock. It was almost three days since the quake had struck.

There was activity all around her. The children were up and awake. Darrin was playing with the baby, and Uncle Theo and Bobby were handing out pieces of bread.

Ian was nowhere to be seen.

"He's gone out, Marissa," Uncle Theo said, stopping by her side with a bucket of milk. "They've fixed one of the main water pipes—there's some water again."

Even as he spoke, they heard a thunderous explosion, muted by distance, but still painfully clear.

"They're still dynamiting."

"Dynamite and cannons. They're trying to save the docks. If they can do that, well, then, maybe it will be over," Uncle

Theo said. The city had burned for three days, Marissa thought. What could be left?

"Come on, lass. We need to get these little ones fed. They're going to be ferried over to Oakland this afternoon."

She smiled, because she could tell he wanted her to. Inside she felt a wall of misery building. San Francisco was nearly gone. These poor children would be lost.

And after she had helped to get something into them, she learned from Bobby how bad matters really were. Some of the streets were empty now. The magnificent Palace Hotel had burned, despite all the planning and care that had gone into it. Great mansions on Nob Hill had burned. The firefighters, too busy to deal with those already lost, had been told to cast the deceased into the flames of the burning buildings.

The Barbary Coast had burned, along with its Dead Man's Alley, Murder Point and Bull Run Alley.

Some thought it for the best.

There was a fear of the rats. Doctors were warning people that they could be looking toward an epidemic of bubonic plague.

But until the fire was put out, that had to be the primary concern.

Within an hour, the children were all off on the ferry, except for the baby. Marissa had decided to keep her until her parents could claim her. She was so very little. And she had finally offered Marissa a tenuous smile, and that smile had nearly broken Marissa's heart. Dr. Spencer had seen to it that she had proper milk for the little girl, whom she had decided to call Francesca.

There were many births there, in the open air, and at the hospital barracks at the Presidio, she heard. And many parents were naming their children after the circumstances, names as wild as Golden Gate, San Francisco and Presidio.

Francesca, the feminine of the saint after which the city had been named, did not seem so bad.

Darrin was with her. Darrin still wouldn't leave her, and Marissa was glad of it. She didn't know what the future would bring, but she wanted the boy to be loved and cared for. Surely, Ian would allow her to bring Darrin home.

If they had a home.

She was vaguely wondering about the fate of their house when Darrin returned from a trip for milk. "Marissa," he told her, accustomed at last to using her given name, "the lady from the, er—from the Barbary Coast is here. The one who helped find you. And she was hurt awful bad."

"Lilli?" Marissa said, startled.

Darrin took the baby and showed Marissa the way. She hurried to the tent. One of the newly arrived nurses pointed her toward a cot in the rear, and she hurried toward it.

Then she froze, for the cot was empty.

"Oh, my God!" The cry of horror escaped her in a whisper. Lilli was dead.

Lilli might have been the best friend she had in San Francisco.

Then someone touched her shoulder, and she turned. It was a gnarled, ugly man, but he had interesting eyes. "You're Mrs. Tremayne."

"Yes. Yes, I was—looking for Lilli."

"The doctor is seeing to her, changing her bandage."

"Oh! Oh, thank God! She's going to make it?"

Even as she spoke, a nurse came in, leading a heavily bandaged Lilli to her bed. Most of her face was swathed. Marissa hurried forward, nodding to the nurse. "Lilli, it's me, Marissa Tremayne. I'll help her," she told the nurse.

The nurse was busy and glad to hand Lilli over to Marissa. "Marissa!" Lilli murmured softly. She touched her face. "You're here, and well. I'm glad for you. For you and Ian."

"You're going to be fine, too, Lilli."

She sat Lilli down on the cot. Lilli groped for something, and the ugly little man took her hand. "I'm going to live, yes.

But I'm going to be horribly scarred." She laughed softly. "And in my business…oh, I'm sorry. I didn't mean to offend you."

"You haven't offended me, Lilli. I just feel that you—that you deserve better!" she said softly.

And Lilli laughed, squeezing her hand. "I'm going to get better, Marissa. Seems it took a fire and a dreadful burning to find out that Jake here loves me. And he's been saving every penny I ever paid him. He's going to marry me, and I'm going to set up regular housekeeping. Of course, we'll never have respectability. No one will ever call on me. San Franciscans have long memories. But I'm staying. I am a San Franciscan."

"Oh, Lilli, I am so very glad!" Marissa said. "And someone will call on you. I will call on you."

Very little of Lilli's mouth showed, but her smile was radiant. "I believe that you will. But I think that you should hurry back now. When I was being bandaged, I heard all kinds of shouting and excitement. I think they quelled the fire on the docks." She was quiet, then added with exasperation, "Ian will be coming back."

"You knew that he—went out?"

"He came to see me last night and this morning," Lilli said. "Oh, for heaven's sake, Marissa! He loves you. He's just the kind of man who doesn't forget old friends, even when they are scarred and ruined and hideous."

"Lilli, you'll never be hideous," Marissa told her. She rose and very gently kissed the top of her head. She turned to Jake. "Congratulations!" she told him.

And then she hurried out.

People were shouting. Crying out, jumping up and down. A stranger suddenly swung his arms around her. "They beat it! They beat the fire! Seven-fifteen exactly, they say. They beat the fire from the piers around East Street, and beat it back to the area south of the Slot! Where it was born, lady, there it died! The fire is out!"

Stumbling, she hurried to the tent where she had spent the night.

And as Lilli had suspected, Ian was back.

His face was nearly as black as his pants and the boots that he wore, but he was talking to Uncle Theo and doing so animatedly. His teeth and eyes flashed handsomely against all the darkness around him.

Then he turned and saw her.

It was over, she thought. It was true. The fire had died, and it was really over. She lost all thoughts of inhibition, and she cried out and raced over to him.

She saw his brow shoot up and for a moment she was afraid. So afraid that he would not open up his arms to accept her. But he did. She flung herself against him, and she found herself lifted and held, held so very close.

And then he gently let her slide down against his body.

"It's out?" she whispered.

"Pray God it stays out," he said.

She heard a motion behind her and turned to see that Jimmy and Mary were standing behind Theo with Darrin and little Francesca.

"I think that we should give these two a moment alone—" Mary began.

"Oh, no, no, no, wait, just wait a little minute," Ian said. His arms remained around Marissa.

"I think you've all been wondering and waiting. All the time that I was gone...and then nothing seemed to matter while the fire burned. But as long as we're all gathered here now, we should discuss a few things."

Jimmy cleared his throat. "We were guilty, Mr. Tremayne. Just as guilty as Marissa. More so. She'd have never done what she done if she hadn't loved Mary so much like a sister."

"Yes, you are guilty," Ian agreed flatly. "All of you. And

you made me guilty of fraud, taking all that money. So here's what we're going to do."

Marissa felt a cold chill sweep over her even as he held her. A fear as icy as the fire had been hot. She fought it desperately. Lilli had said that he loved her, and Lilli knew him well. And he had cared, she knew that he had cared. Last night he had insisted on holding her while she slept...

Last night he had known about the child.

He had come riding after her the fateful morning of the quake. And he had dug through rock and rubble and wood to get to her. And he held her so securely now.

He had refused to think of divorcing her. She knew that. But the marriage wouldn't mean anything anymore, not unless she had his love.

"I'm going to put back all the money that has been taken out of Mary's trust fund. I don't think that people are lining up to prosecute us, but we are all guilty of fraud. If we repay the fund, then I will, at least, feel that we've not defrauded the squire, and if anything should happen in the future, we will only be guilty of having borrowed the money."

"But, Ian!" Mary gasped. "What will you have? The emporium is burned to the ground, Nob Hill has burned—"

"I've a lot of insurance, and all with very reputable companies." He smiled. "And haven't you heard? The world is helping San Francisco. Money is already pouring in from New York and Chicago and Boston and countless other cities. And I've been told they're collecting across the globe. This city will rebuild.

"And I will rebuild with it. Jimmy, you and Mary should survive very nicely on the salary that I intend to pay you until Mary reaches the legal age to receive her inheritance. Theo, you're one of the most admirable men I've met, and I'm delighted to have you continue on with us. Of course, you're the one innocent party in this group, aren't you?"

"Innocent as a babe," Theo said smugly. Marissa wanted to kick him.

"There's only one stipulation to all of this, of course," Ian continued.

"Oh, Ian! You've been far more generous than we'd any right to expect," Mary told him. "We'll do anything."

"You might want to think about it, after the past few days," he advised her. "Because this is the stipulation. I'm not leaving here. San Francisco is my home. There's going to be a lot going on when they sit down and try to figure out how to rebuild properly. I want to be a part of that building. You've just weathered an earthquake and a fire to rival the worst. Are you sure you want to raise your child here? This is my home—it isn't yours."

Theo spoke up quietly. "It is now, Ian Tremayne. Home is where you build, and where you hope, and where you dream. We've nothing left behind us. So here we are, and here we stay."

"Indeed," Mary murmured. "Here we stay."

"Then so be it," Ian said. "I've finished with all I've got to say to you all about the matter."

"Oh, Mary!" Marissa burst free from Ian to hug her friend. Mary hugged her back, but almost immediately, Ian had his hand upon her arm, pulling her back. "I've finished with them, my love. I did not finish with you."

Startled, and chilled once again, Marissa stared into her husband's face. She squared her shoulders defensively, meeting his bright blue gaze. It was fathomless, and far from reassuring.

"You'll all excuse us?" he said to the others.

"I've got the little one, sir," Darrin told him.

Marissa thought he winked at Darrin, but she was being pulled out of the tent. And then Ian had her hand and he was walking toward one of the ponds, far from the area where all the refugees were camped. And then he suddenly swung around and stared at her.

"And what about you?" he demanded.

"What—what about me?" she whispered.

"I'm well aware that you did what you did to help Mary. And Theo. And I know now about your school in England. But I also know that you were seeking a better life. You dreamed of a big house, of an easier life. Well, my love, I may not have a house anymore. So, what about you?"

She jerked her hand free, furious that he could still think so little of her. "Ian Tremayne, how dare you. I have had all that I can take! I—"

"Marissa, love, there's nothing wrong with wanting to soar!" he told her softly. "One of the reasons I love you so deeply is your determination to seek something better."

"I married you for money, yes, but I—" She stopped dead still, suddenly certain that she hadn't heard him right at all. "What?"

"I said, one of the reasons I love you—"

"You love...me?"

He smiled, the slow, lazy, taunting smile that had once so easily seduced her. "Yes, Marissa Ayers Tremayne. I love you. I wanted you from the very beginning. I started to love you because of that haunted quality in your eyes. Because of the mystery, the determination, the spirit. I fell so deeply in love with you that I couldn't stand the fact that you hadn't trusted me. Marissa, you little fool! It never mattered to me where you came from. I love what I've learned about your past. And I'm glad that you can't bear to see lost children without taking them under your wing. I'm glad that you can't be licked by catastrophe or fire. You are everything I could have ever wanted."

"Oh, Ian!" she whispered, staring at him, unable to believe his words, or the tenderness within him. But there was truth, wonderful truth in his eyes. And as he smiled at her, blackened and haggard, she still thought she had never seen a more striking man. There was strength in his tired form, in the set of his shoulders, in the handsome contours of his face, strength, courage, determination and love.

She threw her arms around his neck, rising on tiptoe to kiss him.

"Well?" he demanded. Even now, she thought wryly, disheveled and worn as he was, he carried that arrogance about him.

"Well what?" she whispered.

"You didn't answer me. What about you?"

"Ian Tremayne, I love you. I never deserved you, because I did lie and cheat to get you. And I did hate you. I hated you because you saw so many things in me too easily. But I wanted you, too. And then I saw how good you were to Mary and Jimmy, how good you were to all of us. And when I came here at first I was so very jealous, and so I was so furious! And I wanted to hate you. I wanted so much to hate you so that I wouldn't care about Grace and Lilli—"

"There wasn't anyone once I had met you," he told her.

She smiled. "Thank you for that. But there was. Diana."

"I'll always love her a little in my heart. But you even allowed me to let her go, Marissa. Can you understand?"

Her eyes glimmered with the threat of tears, and Marissa prayed that it was all right to be so happy when a great city lay in ruins beyond them. But God would understand, she thought.

She intended to help rebuild that city.

"Ian, I love you! So much!" Then she added, "Oh! Ian, I saw Lilli, and—"

"And she's going to marry Jake and live happily ever after," he told her.

"Yes, and I'm so glad."

"You don't mind her so much anymore?"

"She probably saved my life. No, I don't mind Lilli anymore. I promised her that I'd call on her, and I will."

Ian smiled. "Yes, I think that you will."

"But Grace—"

"Grace is taking her broken ankle and leaving the city," Ian said flatly.

Marissa's eyes widened. He knew what Grace had done. "Ian, how—"

"Darrin told me that Grace had arranged to see that you disappeared. I spoke to her this morning, briefly. She's not interested in staying. Not really. And after I had a talk with her...well, she can inflict herself upon Chicago or New York for a while."

Marissa laughed. "Oh, Ian, I do love you so very much!" she told him, her arms wrapped around his neck. He held her close against him.

"So you'll stay."

"I'm your wife, Ian. Of course, I'll stay. Like Theo said, it's my home now, too. It's where I can hope and dream and build. It's where I can be with you. Oh, Ian! It's the first real home I've ever had. Oh! There's just one thing. It's Darrin. Could we—"

He started to laugh, interrupting her. "I knew, my love, that we weren't going home without Darrin. And I'm beginning to imagine that we might also be going home with an infant we're calling Francesca."

"It's just that she's so very little, Ian. We'll keep her just until her parents can come for her."

"And then we'll have our own very soon," he murmured, stroking her cheek.

"Oh, Ian, do you mind?"

"I'm delighted, Marissa. So very delighted. A year ago, my love, I was a bitter and angry man, alone. And now I am surrounded by love and loyalty. And it is all because of you."

His lips touched hers at last. With warmth, with tenderness, with a fervor that defied the very world. His kiss held passion; it held promise; it held all the desire that she could ever imagine. And it held love.

And it went on and on.

"Mr. Tremayne! Mrs. Tremayne!"

Dimly, she became aware that someone was calling to them in a voice that was becoming more and more frustrated. It was Bobby.

Marissa broke free from Ian's kiss and turned quickly.

Bobby was mounted upon Ian's bay. His uniform was torn, and he had smudges of soot on his face.

But he was smiling.

"Your house, sir, it's standing! More than half the hill is burned clear to the ground or gutted, but your house is standing."

"I don't believe it!" Ian gasped.

Bobby leaped down from the bay's back. "Go on, sir, and take a look. There's not much else to do here, help is pouring in from all over. If you want—"

"If I want!" Ian exclaimed. He swept Marissa into his arms and sat her upon the bay's back. Then he leaped up behind her.

They moved slowly as they left Golden Gate Park. But then Ian gave the horse free rein, and they moved swiftly through the burned streets, cantering all the way to the hill, then up the length of it.

And there, as Bobby had told them, the house still stood. Around them, mansions had burned. The walls were scorched and blackened, but the beautiful house still stood.

Ian eased down from the bay and reached for Marissa. Laughing, she fell into his arms. "We've even a home to come home to! A place for this ragtag family you've created!" he exclaimed.

And then he kissed her again, and while he kissed her, he

lifted her into his arms and headed up the pathway to the house.

"We've got to go back for the others," she reminded him, breathing the words against his kiss.

"Bobby will see that they come here," Ian told her.

Then he paused at the front step.

"I have everything," he said. "What more could God grant?"

He kissed her, and as he kissed her, he suddenly discovered what greater blessing there could be.

It began to rain.

Sweet, cool rain began to fall. And he lifted his eyes to hers, and they both began to laugh with delight.

His lips touched hers once again as the cleansing rain continued to fall, running down their cheeks, clinging to their lashes. Mingling with their kiss.

And then he hurried up the steps to the house.

Miraculously, they had both come from fire, and found their way home.

SEDUCTIVE STRANGER
Julia Justiss

To Catherine
My sweet, lovely and talented daughter.
Strive always to be the best
And accept nothing less.

PROLOGUE

Sudley Court
Spring, 1808

APOLLO WAS RIDING down her drive.

Or so it seemed to Caragh Sudley, hand over her eyes and breath seizing in her chest as she squinted into the morning sun at the solitary horseman trotting down the graveled carriageway toward Sudley Court.

She was returning to the manor after her early-morning ride when the sound of hoofbeats carrying on the still morning air drew her toward the front entrance. At first merely curious about the identity of the unexpected visitor, as the man grew closer she was stunned motionless by the sheer beauty of horse and rider.

The pale sunshine threw a golden nimbus about the gentleman's hatless head, making his blond hair gleam as if the sun king himself were arriving in regal pomp, his chariot exchanged for the gilded beauty of a palomino. The brightness behind them cast the rider's face in shadow and silhouetted in sharp relief the broad line of shoulders and arms that were now pulling the stallion to a halt.

She shook her head, but that dazzling first impression refused to subside into normalcy. The tall, powerfully built beast tossing his head in spirited response to his rider's command, creamy coat rippling, was magnificent, the man now swinging down from the saddle no less so.

A dark-green riding jacket stretched across his shoulders and fawn breeches molded over saddle-muscled thighs, while up closer she could see his blond locks had tints of strawberry mingled with the gold. His eyes, no longer in shadow once he'd dismounted in her direction, were a shade of turquoise blue so arresting and unusual she once again caught her breath.

The chiseled features of his face—purposeful chin, high cheekbones, firm lips, sculpted nose whose slight crookedness added an intriguing hint of character to a countenance that might otherwise have seemed merely chill perfection—only confirmed her initial perception.

'Twas Apollo, Roman robes cast aside to don the guise of an English country gentleman.

Should she behold him, her sister Ailis would surely be calling for her palette and paints.

Caragh smiled slightly at the thought of her imperious sister ordering the man this way and that until she'd posed him to her satisfaction. And then realized this paragon of Olympian perfection was approaching her—plain Caragh Sudley who stood, jaw still dropped in awe, her face framed by limp wisps of hair blown out of the chignon into which she'd carelessly twisted it, the skirts of her old, shabby riding habit liberally mud-spattered.

She snapped her mouth shut, feeling the hot color rising in her cheeks, but as the visitor had already seen her, she would only make herself look more ridiculous by fleeing. How unfortunate, the whimsical thought occurred as she tried to surreptitiously brush off the largest clumps of mud and summon a welcoming smile, that unlike Daphne, she could not conveniently turn herself into a tree.

"Good morning, miss," the visitor said, bowing.

"Good morning to you, too, sir," she replied, amazed to find her voice still functioned.

"Would you have the goodness to confirm that I have reached Sudley Court? I need to call upon the baron."

"That would be my father, sir. You will find him in the library. Pringle, our butler, will show you in."

He smiled, displaying just a hint of dimples. "Thank you for your kindness, Miss Sudley. I hope to have—"

Before he could complete his sentence, her sister emerged from the shrubbery of the garden behind them, a lad laden with an easel and paintbox trailing in her wake. "Caragh! Did that package from London arrive for me yet?"

Caragh waited a moment, but her sister paid no attention to the newcomer. "Well, has it?"

Caragh's delight faded in a spurt of resentment she struggled, and failed, to suppress. With the arrival of Ailis, her all-too-short exchange with the Olympian would surely come to a premature halt.

Wishing her sister could have intruded a moment earlier or five minutes later, she replied, "If it has, Thomas will bring it when he returns from the village." She steeled herself to glance at the stranger.

Who was not, as she expected, staring in open-mouthed amazement at her stunningly beautiful sister, but rather observing them both, his expression polite. For a moment Caragh wondered about the acuity of his eyesight.

"Blast!" her sister replied, still ignoring the newcomer. "I only hope I have enough of the cerulean blue to last out the morning."

Blushing a little for her sister's lack of manners, Caragh motioned her head toward the visitor. "Ailis!" she said in an urgent undertone.

Her sister cast her an impatient glance. "You show him in, Caragh, whoever he is. I cannot miss the light. Come along, Jack." She motioned to the young lad carrying her supplies and walked off without even a goodbye.

Caragh's blush deepened. "M-my younger sister, sir. As you may have guessed, she's an artist—quite a good one! But very—preoccupied with her work. She's presently engaged upon an outdoor study requiring morning light.''

''Who are we mere mortals to interrupt the inspiration of the muse?'' he asked, his comment reassuring her that he'd not been offended by her sister's scapegrace behavior. ''But I mustn't intrude upon your time any longer. Thank you very much, Miss Sudley. I trust we shall meet again.''

Before she could guess his intent, the visitor took her hand and brought it to his lips. After that salute he bowed, then led the stallion off toward the entry.

For a moment Caragh stood motionless, gazing with wonder at the hand he'd kissed. Her fingers still tingled from the slight, glancing pressure of his mouth.

When she jerked her gaze back up, she noted the visitor had nearly reached the entry steps, down which one of the footmen was hastening to relieve him of his horse. Quickly she pivoted and paced off toward the kitchen wing. She'd not want the stranger to glance back and find her still staring at him.

Once out of sight, her footsteps slowed. The handsome visitor had bowed, kissed her hand and treated her as if she were a grand lady instead of a gawky girl still a year from her come-out.

Best of all, he had not been struck dumb when Ailis appeared. He had actually managed to continue conversing intelligently after her sister left them. Nor had his gaze followed Ailis as she walked away, but reverted back to Caragh's much plainer face.

The few remaining pieces of her susceptible heart that had not already surrendered to warmth of the stranger's smile and the bedazzlement of his blue-eyed gaze, succumbed.

But of course, in the London from which he must have come, he probably met beautiful ladies every day, all of them elegantly dressed in the latest fashion, and so had schooled himself to maintain a polite conversation, no matter how distracting the circumstances.

Briskly she dismissed that lowering reflection. The thoroughness of his training did not diminish the excellence of his behavior. Indeed, he was a *Vrài* and *Gentil Chevalier, beau et courtois,* straight from the pages of an Arthurian legend, she concluded, freely mixing her literary metaphors.

But who was he? Suddenly compelled to find out, she headed into the house.

Creeping past the library, where a murmur of voices informed her the visitor must still be closeted with Papa, she slipped into the deserted front parlor, hoping to catch one more glimpse of the stranger before he departed.

Perhaps when I make my come-out in London next year, I shall meet you again. Only then, I shall be gowned in the most elegant design out of the pages of La Belle Assemblée, *my hair a coronet of curls, my conversation dazzling, and you will be as swept away by me as I was by you today…*

She was chuckling a bit at that absurd if harmless fantasy when the closing of the library door alerted her. She flattened herself against the wall until footsteps passed her hiding place, then peeped into the hall.

Once again, sunlight cast a halo around the stranger's golden head as he stood pulling on the riding gloves the butler had just returned to him. Caragh sighed, her eyes slowly tracing the handsome contours of the visitor's face as she committed every splendid feature to memory.

After retrieving his riding crop, he nodded to acknowledge the butler's bow and walked out.

Resisting a strong desire to scurry after him and take one last peek through the fanlight windows flanking the entry, Caragh made herself wait until the tramp of his boots descending the flagstone steps faded. Then she ran to the library, knocked once, and hurried in.

"Papa," she called to the thin, balding man who sat behind

the massive desk, scribbling in one of the large volumes strewn haphazardly about his desk.

Making a small moue of annoyance at the interruption, her father looked up. "Caragh? What is it, child? I must get back to this translation before the cadence escapes me."

"Yes, Papa. Please, sir, who was your visitor?"

"Visitor?" her father echoed, seeming to have difficulty remembering the individual who had quit the room barely five minutes previous. "Ah, that tall young man. Just bought Thornwhistle, he told me. Wanted to pay his respects and inquire about some matter of pasturage. I suppose you shall have to consult with Withers about it before he returns. I simply can't spare the time now to bother with agricultural matters, not with this translation going so slowly."

Apollo would be calling again. Delight and anticipation buoyed Caragh's spirits.

"Very well, Papa. If I will be meeting with him, however, perhaps you had better tell me his name."

"His name? Dash it, of what importance is that? I expect he'll announce it again when he returns. Now, be a good girl and take this breakfast tray back to the kitchen. It's blocking my dictionary."

Inured to her father's total disinterest in anything not connected to his translation projects, Caragh suppressed a sigh. "Of course, Papa." Disappointed, she gathered up the tray and prepared to leave.

"Goodbye," she called from the threshold. Already immersed in his work, her father did not even glance up.

Then a better idea occurred, and her mood brightened. Depositing the tray on a hall table to be dealt with later, she hurried in search of the butler, finally running him to ground in the dining room where he was directing a footman in polishing the silver epergne.

"Pringle! Do you recall the name of the gentleman who just called? He is to be our new neighbor, I understand."

"Lord Branson, he said, Miss Caragh," the butler replied.

"And his family name?"

"Don't believe he mentioned it. But he left a card."

"Thank you, Pringle!" Caragh hurried back into the hallway. There, sitting in pristine whiteness against the polished silver tray, was a bit of pasteboard bearing the engraving "Quentin Burke, Lord Branson."

Smiling, Caragh slipped the card into her pocket. Her own Olympic hero come to earth now had a name. *Quentin.*

CHAPTER ONE

Sudley Court
Early Spring, 1814

GIVEN WHAT a Herculean endeavor getting them to London was turning out to be, 'twas small wonder it had taken her more than five years to manage, Caragh thought, gazing into her sister's stormy face. Indeed, loving animals as Caragh did, she would probably have preferred mucking out the Augean stables.

"Ailis," she said, trying to keep the aggravation out of her voice, "you know you promised me last week that we would surely be able to leave this Friday. The boxes have been packed for days, Aunt Kitty is expecting us, and quite probably has set up appointments for us in London which it would be very rude to break with so little notice."

"Oh, bother appointments," Ailis responded, with a disdainful wave of one paint-spattered hand. "What difference does it make when we leave? The shops will still be there, as will the endless round of dull parties hosted by acid-tongued old beldames interested solely in dissecting the gowns, jewels, lineage and marriage prospects of their guests. Besides, you know I agreed to leave only after I complete the painting."

Stifling her first angry response, Caragh took a deep breath. After reminding herself that at least one of them must remain reasonable, she said in a calm voice, "We had a bargain, Ailis! I will allow you to visit the galleries, continue your own work, and even take lessons—but you must do your part, and conduct yourself with the modesty and propriety expected of a young lady embarking on her first Season. Behavior which would not include embarrassing our aunt by compelling her to cancel obligations at the last minute—or issuing blanket condemnations of individuals you've not yet even met.''

"Who will, I daresay, turn out to be exactly as I've described them," Ailis retorted. "Were I not so anxious to have the benefit of Maximilian Frank's tutelage, I would never have agreed to go at all. 'Twill be a waste of time and blunt, as I've warned you times out of mind. I've no desire whatsoever to marry."

The anxiety always dormant at the back of Caragh's mind returned in a rush. "Ailis, Papa won't live forever. How do you intend to exist if you don't marry?"

"Since you seem so enamored of the estate, why don't you marry? I could come live with you, and everything could continue as it's always been."

Which might have been a perfectly acceptable alternative, except that the only man Caragh could envision marrying still saw her only as his good neighbor and friend. "Believe me, you would find it much more comfortable to be mistress of your own establishment." *Where you can order people about with full authority,* Caragh added silently.

Even so, she had to compress her lips to keep a smile from escaping at the thought of the havoc her temperamental sister would wreak in the household of some hapless brother-in-law, should she ever become a permanent guest in his home. No, 'twas still best to try to find Ailis a complacent husband of her own.

"You know when Cousin Archibald inherits, he'll move his family here," she reminded Ailis. "Though he would, of course, offer to let us stay, I am sure he would prefer not to have two female dependents hanging about. There's little chance of going elsewhere, since Aunt Kitty hasn't the room to house us permanently, and with our inheritance tied up in dowry, we'd not have the funds to set up a household of our own. Surely you don't see yourself hiring out as a governess or companion! 'Tis unfortunate, but if you wish to continue living in the style you do—and keep on with your work—you shall have to marry. At least London will offer a broader choice of potential husbands.''

Although Caragh had delivered more or less the same speech on several occasions over the last few weeks, for once her volatile sister's eyes hadn't glazed over. Indeed, Caragh noted with a spark of hope, Ailis actually seemed to be paying attention this time.

''I suppose you are correct,'' Ailis replied, her expression thoughtful. ''I shall hardly be able to work in peace here at Sudley with Cousin Archibald's five little demons roaming about.''

Caragh exhaled an exasperated sigh. ''That is just the sort of comment you must cease voicing aloud, if you do not wish to spoil all your prospects! Beauty is well enough, but a gentleman of breeding will want his bride to display courtesy toward others and moderation in her speech. And besides, Cousin Archibald's children are quite charming.''

Ailis shrugged. ''If you like loud, sticky-fingered, impertinent nuisances. The last time they visited, the eldest drove me to distraction, following me like a ghost everywhere I went, while the younger ones burst in whenever they chose, and the squinty-eyed smallest swiped my best detail brush to sweep her doll's house. She's lucky I didn't break her arm when I found she'd stolen it.''

Before Caragh could remonstrate once more, Ailis disarmed her by breaking into a grin. ''Come now, Caragh, you know you were as happy as I was when the grubby brats finally departed! And I concede that you have a point. I shall have to give some thought to my future. *After*,'' she said, rising from her chair, ''I finish this painting. I must get back to it before the light shifts. I just wanted to let you know I would not be ready by Friday.''

"And if you might grant me the boon of revealing such confidential information, when do you expect to finish it?"

Oblivious to Caragh's sarcasm, Ailis paused in her march to the door. "Perhaps by the middle of next week. I shall let you know."

Closing her eyes, Caragh uttered a silent prayer for patience. She would have to dispatch an immediate note to Aunt Kitty delaying yet again their arrival in London. She only hoped their aunt hadn't already arranged the tea with the patronesses of Almacks she'd mention in her last letter. Cavalierly missing such a meeting would doubtless strike a serious blow to her sister's chances of a successful Season.

As she had so often as her sister grew to adulthood, Caragh wished she might consult their long-dead mother. Reputed to have been a headstrong beauty, she might have known better how to successfully handle the equally beautiful and tempestuous offspring who so closely resembled her. At least, Caragh thought the two strikingly similar, based on the miniature she'd tucked away in her desk, the sole image she retained of the mother who had died when Caragh was seven. Her grief-stricken father, unable to bear gazing on the portrait of a lady he'd lost so tragically young, had had the full-length portrait of his wife that once hung in his library removed to the attics.

"Never mind, Pringle, I'll show myself in."

As the voice emanating from the hallway beyond the salon penetrated her thoughts, Caragh's eyes popped open and her heart leapt in her chest.

Over the last six years, her own London Season had been put off for one reason after another—Papa's episode of ill-health, a disastrous fire in the stable wing, the necessity to take over managing all the estate business when their manager Withers died unexpectedly, and most recently, Ailis's reluctance to leave Sudley Court. The shy, awkward girl who'd nervously discussed pasturage agreements had become an as-

sured young woman whose competent hand kept the household and estates of Sudley Court running smoothly.

In that time she'd learned, with no great surprise, that
Quentin Burke was not an Olympian, but a flawed and mortal
man like any other. She'd even, over the course of managing
their horse-breeding operation, encountered among the aristocratic clients who came to Sudley Court, men as handsome
as Lord Branson.

But one thing remained constant. The gentleman who had
captured her sixteen-year-old heart one fair spring day still
held it in as firm a grip as when she'd first lost it to the
stranger riding down her drive. And he was just as unaware
of possessing it as he'd been that long-ago morning.

She felt her lips lifting of their own volition into a smile.
A swell of gladness filled her chest as the man whose face
was dearer to her than sunshine, whose friendship had come
to be as essential to her existence as air and water, strolled
into the room.

"Oh, famous, Quent!" her sister said, meeting him at the
door and offering her fingers for the obligatory salute. "You
can natter on to Caragh about London while I get some work
done."

"Lovely to see you, too, Ailis," he replied as she drew her
hands back and skipped out. He turned to Caragh, a twinkle
in those arresting turquoise eyes that, despite the passage of
years, could still make her dizzy.

"A lovely surprise to see you, Quentin," she said. "I had
no notion you'd be stopping at Thornwhistle this soon after
your last trip. When did you arrive?"

She caught her breath as he kissed her fingers, even that
slight touch setting her whole body humming. She struggled
to resist the impulse to close her eyes and savor the sensation.

"My estate business finished up early," he replied, dropping into the wing chair beside her. "So I thought I'd spend
a few days at my favorite property—and stop by to see if my

favorite neighbor would actually manage to coerce her beauteous baggage of a sister into London this Season. No, I shan't stay for tea—'' he waved her off as she headed to the bell pull ''—but I should not refuse a bit of conversation.''

Sighing, Caragh reseated herself. ''I believe we shall eventually make it there. Though I had to resort to bribery, and only succeeded because Maximilian Frank fortuitously returned from Italy to set up a studio in London. Ailis is mad about his paintings, which are…not in the usual style.'' She paused to take a deep breath before continuing, ''I-I've agreed to let her have private lessons with him. And I trust you'll not bandy that fact about!''

''Lessons!'' he echoed, clearly astounded. ''A gently-born maiden taking drawing lessons from the illegitimate son of an East India merchant? Da— Merciful heavens, Caragh!'' He shook his head. ''With the chit cozening you into permitting behavior as questionable as that, do you really think you'll manage to marry her off?''

Although Quentin's query only echoed what she often asked herself, nonetheless Caragh felt herself bristle. ''You can't deny her stunning beauty, and her dowry is quite handsome as well. In addition to that—''

''She's reached the age of twenty still lacking even the most rudimentary of domestic skills and her manners are… uncertain at best. Now, now,'' he said, waving off her sputtering attempts to remonstrate. ''You know I'm fond of her, and freely admit she is amazingly talented. But even her doting sister must acknowledge she's certainly not the sort of meek, biddable, conventional miss most society gentleman seek in a wife.''

Caragh sighed again. ''No,'' she admitted. ''I just hope to find for her a gentleman whom she can like and who will treasure her for what she is—not what she isn't.''

''If you can bring her to notice one. Is she still spurning all her would-be suitors as imperiously as ever?''

Caragh had to grin. "Oh, yes. The squire's son brings her flowers once a week, which she can't be bothered to accept, and crossed and recrossed sheets of Darlington's turgid poetry arrive in nearly every post, which she tosses in the fire unread. Even the Duke of Arundel's youngest son, having apparently heard tales of her storied beauty from his Oxford classmates, found a pretext to stop by and see Papa on some spurious mission from his classics professor. Ailis either ignores them completely or treats them with a contemptuous disdain that seems to inflame them to further protestations of ardor. Perhaps they think of her as a challenge, as the suitors of Ithaca did Penelope."

"Only she paints instead of weaves?" Quentin asked with a grin. "Speaking of classical scholars, how does your father? Should I call on him now, or is he currently so lost in versifying he will resent any intrusion?"

"I believe he is revising today, so you may enter the library with impunity. It must be going well, for he actually joined us for breakfast and conversed with Ailis for almost half an hour."

Apparently Caragh was less successful than she'd thought at keeping the bitterness out of her tone, for the look Quentin fixed on her was sympathetic. "Caragh, you know that in the depths of his heart, your papa values all you do to keep Sudley functioning. Even if he seldom expresses his appreciation."

"A gratifying if entirely fictional notion, though I thank you for it," she replied drily, having long since given up hoping her father would notice her or anything she did. Nor did she feel guilty any longer for the stab of resentment that pierced her at witnessing his sporadic demonstrations of affection for the one living mortal he occasionally did pay attention to—her beautiful sister, who could scarcely be bothered to converse with him and had never lifted a finger to assist him.

Caragh shook herself free of those ignoble thoughts. "I trust you found everything at Thornwhistle in order?"

"In excellent order, as you well know. Let me once again commend your stewardship! Manning told me you'd taken care of having the north meadows reseeded after the heavy rain earlier this month. With you already so encumbered with the burden of managing Sudley and arranging a removal to London, I certainly appreciate your taking time to oversee my paltry affairs!"

A flush of pleasure warmed her cheeks at his approval. "'Twas nothing. I promised I would keep an eye on things, so I did. Friends assist friends, after all."

"So they do indeed," he confirmed, reaching over to press her hands...and setting her tingling once again. "What should I do without my good neighbor? In fact, I think 'tis about time I did something for you."

An electrifying vision flashed into her mind—Quentin hauling her into his arms and kissing her senseless. Her cheeks firing warmer still, she beat back the image, mumbling something disjointed about there being no obligation.

"I don't feel 'obligated,' I *want* to help. That is, I expect your father is not accompanying you to London?"

She barely refrained from a snort. "No."

"Given the shambles the estate was in when I inherited, I've not previously felt I could afford to be away for any length of time. But now that everything is finally in good order, I believe I can safely allow myself a respite."

"An excellent notion," Caragh said. "These last few years, we've scarce been able to persuade you to pause long enough to celebrate the Yule season with us."

"Quite wonderful celebrations, and I cannot thank you enough for including me. I even concede," he added with a hint of a smile, "that from time to time I've longed for a break. But the hard work has been worth it, Caragh. It's taken eight long years, but I'm proud to say I've just returned from our bankers in London, having redeemed the last of Papa's debts. Branson Park is unencumbered at last!''

"Quentin, that's wonderful!'' Caragh exclaimed. "How proud you must be!''

"I knew you, more than any other, would understand what that means to me. And so, though I had no real need to visit Thornwhistle, I simply had to come and share the news with you.''

Those breath-arresting blue eyes paralyzed her again while his handsome face creased in an intimate smile that made her long to throw herself into his arms. She dug her fingers into the armrest of her chair, fighting to squelch the desire and remain sensible. *A friend,* she reminded herself urgently. *He sees me as just his good friend.*

"I'm so pleased that you did,'' she managed to reply at last. "But I can't imagine you lapsing into idle dissipation. What task shall you take on next?''

"I've just completed the other major task dear to my heart—the refurbishing of Branson Hall. A project for which you have been a major inspiration, by the way.''

"Indeed? How so?''

"I don't suppose I ever told you what a profound impression Sudley Court made on me during my first visit—the beauty of its design enhanced by loving and meticulous care. I vowed that very morning that one day, I would restore Branson Park to a similar level of perfection.''

He shook his head and laughed. "If you could have seen my home as it was then, you would know how truly audacious a dream that was! Oaken floors dirt-dulled, carpets threadbare, window hangings in tatters, half the rooms missing furniture or swaddled in Holland covers!''

Caragh shook her head dismissively. "Whatever its state when you began, having seen the improvements you've installed at Thornwhistle, I have no doubt the house is now magnificent!''

"It is," he acknowledged in a matter-of-fact tone that held not a trace of boastfulness. "I should love to show it off to you—but first, you've a Season to manage. And since I've decided I deserve a reward for finally completing two such major projects—and have just purchased a property outside London which will doubtless require a period of close supervision—I've decided to go to Town for the Season myself. Now, what do you say to that?"

He would be in London, where she might see him and ride with him and chat with him, not just for the few weeks of his periodic visits to Thornwhistle, but for an entire Season? "That would be wonderful!" she exclaimed.

He smiled, apparently pleased by her enthusiastic response. "So I thought as well. I can be on hand to squire you about when you have need of an escort, and perhaps help you corral Ailis, should she fall into one of her…distempered starts. Besides, with Branson now restored to its former glory, I suppose it's time for me to complete my duty to the family and look about for a wife."

Alarm—and anticipation shocked through her. Before she could dredge up a reply, he patted her hand. "You, my good friend, could advise me on the business. Since females know things about other females no mere male could ever fathom, you could be of excellent help in guiding me to make the right choice."

She could guide him. In choosing a wife. As his good friend. Her half-formed fantasy dissolving, Caragh sucked in a breath and somehow managed to force a congenial smile to her lips. "O-of course. I should be happy to."

His smile deepening, he squeezed her hands. "I knew I could count on you! Now, if you think it safe, I'll go pay my respects to your papa. When do you expect to depart for the metropolis? Must you supervise the rest of the planting?"

Thrusting her agitated feelings aside to be dealt with later, she forced herself to concentrate on the immediate question.

"No, Harris can handle that and the repairs on the tenants' cottages. 'Tis Ailis I'm waiting on. She refuses to depart until this current painting is complete, which should, God willing, allow us to depart by the end of next week." Caragh couldn't help another exasperated sigh. "If she doesn't redo the blasted thing yet again."

"Excellent," Quentin replied. "Since, given your skillful care, I'm sure I will find nothing of importance requiring my attention at Thornwhistle, I should be ready by then as well. Perhaps we can travel to the metropolis together. Only think how diverting it shall be! Two workhorses like you and me, pulled from our traces and forced to concentrate on nothing more compelling than what garments we shall wear or which entertainment we shall attend! I declare, after a period of such frivolity, we shall scarcely recognize ourselves!"

After bringing her hands up for a salute, he released them. "Shall we ride tomorrow morning? Good, I shall see you then." Sketching her a bow, he walked out.

Caragh watched him go, her lacerated heart still twisting in her breast.

If having his company here were not already delightful torment enough, she was now to suffer through a Season watching him search for a wife? No, even worse—advising him on that choice!

A mélange of misery, outrage and hurt swirled within her at the thought. Sternly she repressed it.

Enough bemoaning, she reproved herself. She would do what she must, as always.

But even as she girded herself to endure the unendurable, from deep within her came unbidden the girlish fantasy she'd thought to have long ago outgrown. The image of a beautifully gowned, impeccably coifed Caragh Sudley whose elegant appearance and sparkling wit shocked Quentin Burke into finally realizing that his neighbor was no longer just an engaging and capable girl, but an alluring woman.

A woman he wanted.

'Twas not so impossible a fantasy, she thought, a renewed sense of purpose filling her. *Mayhap London will hold more surprises than you imagine, Quentin Burke.*

CHAPTER TWO

HALF AN HOUR later, after listening politely to a monologue about the latest progress of his host's magnum opus, Quentin escaped into the hall. Ascertaining from Pringle that Caragh was closeted with the housekeeper, he resigned himself to waiting until tomorrow's ride to speak further with her and headed down the entry steps to collect his bay gelding from the waiting groom.

Fresh and eager for a gallop, the horse danced and fought him for the bridle, so he'd proceeded some distance down the carriageway before Quentin got the beast settled down. He turned in the saddle then to look back one last time at the graceful Palladian facade of Sudley Court.

In the bright noon sun, the weathered stone walls glowed a soft gold beside the dazzling white of the columned portico, whose pristine classical lines always stirred his soul. The scythed lawn, the clipped shrubs and neatly tended flower beds complemented the well-maintained appearance of the structure itself, conveying an impression of timeless order and serenity. As did the rest of the estate, from the stables that housed the famous Sudley horses to the sturdy stone outbuildings to the recently rethatched tenants' cottages.

His own Branson Park was now its equal, he thought with a surge of deep satisfaction. His only regret was that his dear mama had not lived to see it. Still in all, he had much to celebrate, and as he'd told Caragh, good reason to indulge himself with a few months' dissipation.

Especially since doing so would enable him to repay in part the loyal friendship Caragh Sudley had extended him since he bought Thornwhistle, the first of his investment properties, nearly six years ago. Though a Season in London might allow her a welcome break from her myriad duties at Sudley, Quentin thought it unlikely that anyone who'd charged herself with trying to steer the Beautiful Baggage through the social shoals of a Season was likely to have much time to relax. He could help her shoulder that burden, and see she took some time for herself.

What an intriguing assembly of unusual talents his good friend possessed! One of the most skilled estate managers he'd encountered, she could converse knowledgeably about agricultural matters in one breath and in the next, offer an allusion from the classics so beloved by her papa. An absolute genius at handling any beast with four hooves, she was a better rider and as fine a shot as he and could speak about the bloodlines of a horse or a hound with authority. From the first, he'd found her altogether as easygoing and companionable as any of his male friends.

Indeed, around her he could relax and almost forget she *was* a female. She never bored him prattling on of gowns and gossip and would rather challenge him to a game of whist or billiards than sit over her embroidery or tinkle the keys of a pianoforte. Best of all, she alone of the unmarried females of his acquaintance employed not a particle of the annoying flirtatiousness to which most gently-bred maidens, particularly since the radical improvements in his fortune, were wont to subject him.

He chuckled, remembering how she'd appeared the first day he'd ridden down this drive to call on her father. While still at a distance, he'd taken the small lass in the shabby gown for a maidservant. Once he drew nearer, he'd amended that impression, deciding with her slender figure, her pale face haloed with wisps of golden-brown hair and her great hazel eyes raised up to stare at him, she more resembled a wood sprite.

That whimsical first impression changed to irritation when he returned two days later to consult with her father—and was received by her instead, declaring *she* would discuss with him the leasing of the Thornwhistle pastures. Believing it a novel but no less blatant ploy to gain his notice by a chit barely out of the schoolroom, he'd uttered a repressive setdown. Only to be handed his head on a platter when she flashed back that since she, and not the baron, handled the disposition of agricultural matters at Sudley Court, he could work with her, or leave.

He stayed. He quickly came to admire her competence, and over the intervening years always consulted her about estate business during his frequent visits to Thornwhistle. From the first she'd offered to oversee the solution of any small problems that occurred between his periodic inspection trips, and occasionally he'd taken her up on that offer, with excellent results.

He smiled again at Sudley Court's stately facade, knowing well how many hours of Caragh's toil were represented in its timeless beauty. For years, she had shown herself a shrewd manager and a staunch friend. He would indeed, he thought as he urged his horse back in motion, prize her opinion on the necessary but uninspiring business of acquiring a wife.

He only hoped he could be of equal assistance in her quest to find a suitable husband for her sister. Despite Ailis's dazzling beauty, he was certain the hunt would not be easy, and keeping the baggage from committing some irretrievable social faux pas until they'd accomplished the matter harder still. Caragh might well have need of his steadfast support.

It was likely to be the only support she received. Lady Catherine Mansfield, the aunt with whom the sisters would be residing, he knew to be silly and rather feather-witted, unlikely to offer much resistance if the strong-willed Ailis set her mind to something, no matter how ill-judged. And despite his conciliatory words to Caragh, Quentin privately thought

Baron Sudley shockingly remiss in his duty to his family—not unlike, he thought with a bitter twist of his lips, his own sire.

Though Caragh handled the mulitiplicity of duties it entailed magnificently, still the baron should never have pushed the heavy burden of running the estate off on his daughter's slender shoulders. Neither had Sudley ever, as far as Quentin could tell, attempted to exert a father's steadying influence over his headstrong younger daughter.

Reaching the end of the lane, Quentin turned his mount back toward Thornwhistle and kicked him to a gallop. He could not in good conscience be too severe with the baron for neglecting his duties, however, when he himself had for several years been putting off one of his own.

With his debts paid and Branson Park refurbished, he had no further excuse to delay finding a wife who could maintain the splendor he'd so painstakingly restored and breed the next generation of Bransons to carry on the name.

Which was why, despite any problems Ailis might cause, knowing his dear friend would also be in London made him view the upcoming Season with much greater enthusiasm. With Caragh nearby to visit and ride and confer with, to brighten even the most insipid of ton parties with her dry wit and stimulating conversation, perhaps the dull business of finding a wife might not be so tedious after all.

CARAGH PEERED OUT the fanlight windows flanking the front entry to find Quentin riding away. She'd hoped to catch him before he departed and invite him to remain for nuncheon, and perhaps discuss further what appeared would be their joint venture in London.

He was already beyond hailing distance, however. Just as well she'd missed him, she told herself, sighing. She must take these papers in for Papa's signature and get a letter written to Aunt Kitty so James might ride it into town to be posted this afternoon.

After lingering until Quentin disappeared around the corner of the carriage drive, Caragh headed off to face her father. Best to catch him straightaway, before he became reabsorbed in his work, and thus annoyed by her visit.

She knocked once and waited, then knocked again. When a third rapping on the heavy oak panel still had not produced a response, with a resigned shake of her head, she pushed the door open and walked in.

"I'm sorry to disturb you, Papa, but there are some documents you must sign."

Her father started, then looked over, his expression distracted. "Caragh?" He glanced out the window at the sunny afternoon garden before turning back to her. "As 'tis still light out, it cannot be time for dinner. So what is the matter now, child?" He drew his brows together, frowning. "You know I detest interruptions when I am nearly at the end of a chapter!"

"I regret the intrusion, Papa, but I must mail back immediately the authorization the lawyers sent you to allow them to set up an account for us in London." When he continued frowning, she added, "You do remember Ailis and I are to leave next week?"

His frown faded, leaving him thoughtful. "Yes, I recall your mentioning it. You've arranged to have matters here at Sudley taken care of in your absence, I trust?"

Suppressing her aggravation, she took a deep breath and began to repeat once again the information she'd conveyed to him at least three times already. "Naturally, Papa. The spring planting is nearly complete and the colts from this year's foaling are already bespoken. Pringle and Hastings have instructions for managing the household, and Harris will inform me of anything requiring attention on the farms, so," she concluded, her tone turning a touch acerbic, "you need not fear some domestic disturbance will disrupt your work."

He nodded, apparently satisfied, and bent to sign the papers she extended. But after he'd affixed his seal, as she reached to pick them back up, he caught her hand. "I suppose, much as I despise London and all the memories it holds, I...really ought to be accompanying you there."

She looked up, startled. His eyes, usually bright with fervor for a distant time and people long dead, had misted over.

Caragh knew the tragic tale—the Quorn country hunt at which the handsome young baron and London's reigning belle had fallen in love, marrying as soon as the banns could be called and then retiring to the country. Her mama's triumphant return to the metropolis six years later, where, despite her long absence and the presence of younger beauties, she soon reclaimed her mantle as Queen of the Ton. Her untimely death from a fever a bare two months afterwards, upon which her father quit the metropolis, vowing never to set foot in the city again.

Tenderness rose up to penetrate her resentment. "It's all right, Papa. Aunt Kitty will take good care of us, and you should almost certainly find the busyness of a Season tedious. Nothing but dressmakers and social calls and parties, and the city so noisy that working would be difficult. You wouldn't wish your progress to be slowed now, not when you're so close to finally finishing the first draft."

Her father straightened, the sorrow leaving his eyes. "You are right, of course. Did I mention I'd received a letter yesterday from Briggs at Oxford? He thinks the university might be interested in publishing my translation, and asked that I send him a copy once it's complete! Though it's not nearly ready for that—I've scarcely finished the draft, and there's much, much work remaining. Still, his interest was very heartening."

"'Twill be a magnificent achievement. We're so proud of your scholarship, papa."

"Thank you, my dear. You will...watch over Ailis? There

are so many dangers and temptations in the city, and unlike you, she's not very...practical. She doesn't always realize what is best for her.''

Ever Ailis. Once again suppressing that lingering sense of hurt, she replied, ''You may trust Aunt Kitty and I to keep her from harm.''

''I expect I can. And—keep yourself safe, too. You've been a good daughter to me, Caragh. Better than I deserve, probably.''

A lump formed in her throat, preventing reply, and ridiculous tears gathered at the corners of her eyes. He might not be the most considerate of papas, but Caragh still loved him, and his rare praise touched her deeply.

''Here, then,'' he said, handing over the documents. ''Enjoy the idle gaiety of the metropolis. And with this, I trust you will not have to interrupt me again? Having just read them over, I'm not entirely sure I've caught the rhythm of the last cantos correctly, and I cannot quit now until I've rewritten them. I shall not manage it before midnight if I'm compelled to stop every hour to attend to some trivial household matter.''

Their tender moment of tenuous connection was obviously at an end, Caragh thought, suppressing a wry grin. ''I shall endeavor to see there are no further interruptions.''

''Good. Have Cook send my dinner in on a tray, won't you? Between Quentin's visit and all these perturbations, I've lost so much time already today, I shall have to work straight through the evening.''

After his jovial and unusually attentive presence at breakfast, Caragh had assumed her father, who on most days barely noticed the dishes placed before him, would for once appreciate a well-prepared dinner. To the Cook's delight, she'd instructed her this morning to prepare a meal more elaborate than their usual simple fare.

The kitchen would already have begun upon the menu she'd chosen, a fine roast with several removes and Ailis's favorite cherry tarts for dessert. Upon learning her efforts for her master were to be reduced to a covered plate upon a tray, Cook was likely to suffer palpitations.

"If you insist, Papa. What time should you like it?"

But her father, having evidently expended the full measure of time his self-absorption would permit for something not directly connected to his work, had already returned his gaze to his manuscript. Knowing any attempt to wrest his attention away would likely be greeted with a sharp rebuke and a rec-ommendation that she do what she thought best, Caragh made no attempt to repeat her inquiry. Silently she gathered up the papers and left the library.

Though the task awaiting her in the city might be no less thankless than the duties she was leaving behind at Sudley, as Caragh looked down at the document that would fund their visit, she felt her spirits lift.

In London there would be bookshops, theatres, exhibitions, entertainments the likes of which she had never before ex-perienced. She'd have a whole Season's worth of time to en-joy, as Quentin described it, an existence devoted mostly to frivolous dissipation.

And one last chance to dazzle open the eyes of Quentin Burke.

CHAPTER THREE

ON A FOGGY morning three weeks later, Quentin pulled up his lathered mount at the far reaches of Hyde Park and turned to Caragh, who was reining in her equally spent mare beside him. "That was marvelous!" she cried.

A profusion of gold-brown tendrils peeping out from beneath her riding hat, her cheeks becomingly flushed from the wind, she favored him with a smile so brilliant he was doubly glad he'd hit upon the happy notion of stealing her away while the fashionable world—including her sister and aunt—were still asleep. "It was indeed," he agreed.

"Thank you so much for insisting we come! I've been so busy since arriving, I've scarcely had a moment to myself, and have dearly missed a daily gallop."

"Then you must resolve to take one with me every morning, no matter how busy you are. I hope your campaign to launch Ailis is going well, for you've been quite neglecting me the last two weeks. Whatever happened to our plan to spend the Season in frivolous dissipation?"

"And here I've tried to be courteous and not place demands upon your time!" she replied indignantly, nudging the mare to a walk. "Besides, I *have* been frivolous. Ailis and I have indulged in a positive orgy of shopping, expending funds whose total I refuse even to estimate, though I am quite certain the sum could fund seed and repairs for Sudley for the whole of next year. We've visited Hatchard's, been to Gunter's for ices and had a splendid evening viewing the feats of equestrian daring at Astley's. Anyway, with Tattersall's and

Gentleman Jackson's and your clubs to visit, I take leave to doubt you've felt neglected.''

Signaling his gelding to keep pace beside the mare, he grinned at her, pleased to have roused her fighting spirit. Yes, these morning rides were a good first step, but he'd have to think of other ways to detach her from Ailis and ensure she didn't waste her entire Season in London playing duenna to the beauty. ''You must take care that your impractical sister doesn't tow you down River Tick before the Season even begins.''

''Oh, 'tis not Ailis who likes shopping—it's our aunt. Although it seems we've purchased enough clothing to outfit seven women, Aunt Kitty assures me we've acquired only the barest essentials. Ailis considers an excursion to the dressmaker more curse than enjoyment, and told me yesterday she refuses to stir another step from the house if our destination requires her being measured, pinned or basted.''

''How go the plans for her presentation?''

''Well enough, I suppose. These first two weeks we've been laying the groundwork, Aunt Kitty says, having suitable gowns made up to allow us to pay calls on the most important hostesses.'' A mischievous sparkle glinted in her eye. ''Indeed, 'tis a good thing my aunt sleeps until noon, for she would have apoplexy were she to know I'd gone riding in this old habit! And I must admit, we have spent a good deal of time visiting galleries, meeting with Mr. Frank and setting up Ailis's lessons.''

Quentin frowned. Nothing that tied Ailis to the middle-class world of working artists was likely to advance her marital prospects among the ton. ''You were not able to dissuade her from that?''

Caragh threw him an exasperated look. ''You sound like Aunt Kitty. No, I couldn't dissuade her. Considering her main reason for agreeing to come to London was to further her artistic education, I thought to have a better chance of winning her cooperation on social matters if I first allowed her to begin lessons. I've made it quite clear that if she doesn't honor her part of our bargain and participate in the ton activities Aunt Kitty considers necessary, I am prepared to cancel the sessions and return with her to Sudley.''

Quentin chuckled. ''Ah, blackmail! And how did she receive that bit of news?''

Caragh grinned back at him. ''Without throwing a tantrum, if that's what you're implying. I think I've finally managed to bring her to realize that with Cousin Archibald in line to inherit, she simply must make plans to secure her future. Since, for a woman, marriage to an agreeable partner is the only practical way to achieve that, 'tis best to act now, while she is still young and lovely enough to have a real choice. In any event, my genteel threat seems to be working. Aunt Kitty had the Almack patronesses to tea, and Ailis was on her best behavior, at once demure and charming. Lady Jersey and Countess Lieven both pronounced her a handsome, pretty-behaved girl and promised vouchers.''

''Ailis, demure? Now *that* I'd like to behold!''

''Give her some credit, Quentin,'' Caragh protested. ''She can behave when she wishes to.''

''Ah, but how long will she wish to?''

As soon as the teasing words left his lips, Quentin regretted uttering them, for the sparkle faded from Caragh's eyes. The thought that her sister might not choose to contain her high-spirited and rather unconventional nature until she was safely affianced would have to be his friend's chief worry.

Before he could think of some light comment to bring the smile back to her face, Caragh shrugged, as if shaking off whatever unpleasant thoughts his remark had aroused. ''The first of the new evening gowns is to be finished by tomorrow, so Aunt Kitty intends to present us to a select circle of friends at dinner before going on to the Duchess of Avon's ball. And so, if you will not be too *busy*—'' she stressed the word, giving him a darkling look, ''may I count on you to attend?''

''Of course. And I'd be happy to escort you to the Duchess's ball as well.''

She made him a little bow. ''Thank you, my gallant knight. There shall also be the small matter of Ailis's presentation ball the end of next month. Aunt Kitty is already awash in fabric samples, trying to decide whether to deck out the ballroom in white netting and baby's breath or pink satin and roses.''

''Now that's a charming image: Ailis in white satin and ostrich plumes, or pink silk and rosebuds, launching off to snare a mate.'' Quentin tried to picture Caragh, currently wearing a shabby, outmoded riding habit all too typical of her wardrobe, dressed to the nines and gliding into a ballroom. He couldn't. ''Which of the two garments shall you choose?'' he asked, suppressing a chuckle.

She swiped at him with her whip. ''Neither, as well you know! Ailis shall be in pearls and white satin, and would doubtless darken your daylights if she heard you describe her as intending to 'snare a mate.' Why should she bother, when suitors flock to her quite willingly? I'll wear something in green, probably, as befits the elder sister. It is to be my presentation as well, you know.''

Although after his father's death Quentin had been too preoccupied tending to the business of restoring his estates to visit London, he'd assumed that Caragh must have had the obligatory Season at eighteen and returned to Sudley by choice. ''You were never presented?'' he echoed, incredulous. Though the baron was an indifferent parent at best, Quentin could hardly believe he would have neglected so important a responsibility.

''No. With one thing or the other, there was never time.'' She glanced away from him, faint color flushing her cheeks. ''Are you going to say *I* am off to 'snare a mate?' ''

Quentin felt an unpleasant jolt, such as he sometimes experienced when picking up an iron poker after walking across the thick Axminster carpet in the library to tend the fire. "Certainly not!" he blurted without thinking, distracted by the intensity of the disagreeable sensation.

When Caragh looked over sharply, eyebrow raised, he hastily continued, "Not that you wouldn't be perfectly capable of attracting a desirable offer, but—well, surely you cannot focus on anything else until you get Ailis riveted, which should take the Season at least. Nor can I imagine your father wishing you to stir far from Sudley."

"Perhaps not. But at some point, I shall be forced to 'stir' from Sudley, unless I'm willing to be reduced to the status of superfluous dependent in the household over which I was formerly mistress."

She was right, he realized suddenly. This Season she really ought to concentrate on finding a husband not just for Ailis, but for herself as well.

Unsettled by the dismaying consequences that possibility engendered, he protested, "But your father is in excellent health. There's no reason to believe your cousin will inherit anytime soon."

"Lord willing, Papa will be baron for a good many years. But that makes it no less important for me to settle my future now, for the same reasons I've argued to Ailis," she pointed out.

"I suppose so." But even as he agreed, Quentin was conscious of a strange sinking sensation. Although he realized Caragh was no longer the shyly charming young girl next door but a woman grown, somehow he'd vaguely assumed she would stay on at Sudley for the indefinite future. That their friendship would continue unchanged, as warm and vital a presence in his life as it had been these last few years. Surely she wished for that, too!

"Make what plans you must," he said at last, giving her

his most charming smile, ''but I absolutely forbid your taking any steps that might endanger our friendship!''

She smiled sweetly. ''Perhaps my eventual husband will be a friend of yours. Then we could all be friends together.''

Somehow that solution didn't seem particularly appealing. Unwilling at the moment to examine any more closely the reasons behind the sour feeling that had settled in his gut at the prospect, he was glad to seize upon a diversion.

''I thought you said Ailis always slept late. Isn't that her, riding toward us now?''

Caragh swiveled in the saddle. ''Why, yes, it is!'' Her initial expression of surprise turned grimmer when a tall young man on a flashy black stallion rounded the corner of the bridle path in her sister's wake.

The man caught up with Ailis, who slowed her horse and turned to him. Though they were too far away for their conversation to be intelligible, Quentin read in the flirtatious arch of the girl's neck, the sinuous bend of her body as she leaned toward the man—and the arrogant confidence with which the newcomer inclined toward her—that the two were more than chance-met acquaintances. He squinted into the sun, trying to identify the vaguely familiar male figure.

''Who is the gentleman?'' he asked, giving up the task.

Caragh's lips had thinned and her expression was eloquent of disapproval. ''Viscount Freemont. He's something of a patron of the arts, I understand. He was at Maximilian Frank's studio the first day we visited, so of course, the artist introduced us. Since then, he's 'happened' to drop by several times just as Ailis was finishing her lesson, escorting us home on the first occasion and insisting we accompany him to Gunter's for ices on the second. Although she received him, Aunt Kitty confided that his reputation is rather—fast. You know him?''

''Not personally, although he's a member of White's. Family is impeccable, but the talk in the clubs holds him to be wild indeed. Certainly not the best sort of companion for an innocent maid entering upon her first Season. Particularly,'' he added as they approached, "a young lady riding at dawn with nary a groom in attendance.''

Caragh gasped in consternation, but as they urged their horses nearer, Quentin's guess was soon confirmed. Freemont and her sister walked their mounts side by side, their heads as close together as Ailis's position in the sidesaddle would permit. Her groom, unlike the man who trailed Quentin and Caragh at a discreet distance, was conspicuously absent.

They made a striking pair, Quentin had to admit. Ailis, her dazzling blond beauty displayed in a form-filling habit of pale-blue velvet, mounted sidesaddle on her gray, and Freemont with his Adonis-handsome face and blue-black hair, his tall, broad-shouldered figure all in black on his midnight-hued stallion.

Caragh exhibited no appreciation whatsoever of the picturesque tableau. "I shall have to have a chat with Ailis,'' she muttered, her jaw set.

When they reached the couple, Ailis hailed them cheerfully, no hint of guilt or embarrassment in her manner as she presented the viscount to Quentin. However, Freemont's quirk of the lip and raised eyebrow as he returned the acknowledgement showed clearly, Quentin thought, anger stirring, that the gentleman was quite conscious of the impropriety of his actions.

"Do ride along with us,'' Caragh invited. Picking up on the urgent look his friend threw him, Quentin sidled his mount up to Freemont's, while Caragh cut her mare in between the viscount's stallion and her sister's horse.

The viscount grinned at the maneuver, but signaled his horse to drop back. "The dragon protectress?'' he drawled.

Quentin gave him a stone-faced look. "As the *lady* is a particular friend, I'd advise you to mind your language.''

"No offense intended. I suppose so luscious a damsel has need of protecting.''

Quentin found any desire to engage in socially innocuous conversation deserting him. "From you, perhaps?" he retorted.

"Most definitely," the viscount agreed with a laugh. He eyed Quentin up and down with a mockingly assessing look. "You're an ally of the protectress, then. Should I expect a challenge?"

Restraining the desire to pull the viscount from his saddle and plant a fist in the middle of that arrogant face, Quentin replied, keeping his voice carefully even, "Not if you remember the maiden in question is a young lady of quality and treat her accordingly."

"Ah, but a damsel not at all in the common way, you must admit. An amazingly good artist, for one. Such drive! Such fire! It quite compels a man to wonder where one might *lead* such a passionate creature."

Curbing his temper, Quentin forced himself to ignore the man's baiting. "If you wish to wonder about it while enjoying the young lady's company, I'd advise you to curtail any... inappropriate conduct that might *lead* her family to cut the acquaintance."

Freemont laughed out loud. "You think she would be governed by the dragon, should her inclinations run otherwise?"

Quentin glanced at Caragh, who was leaning toward her sister, speaking in tones too low for them to hear.

"I wouldn't underestimate her influence."

Freemont followed his glance and raised an eyebrow. "Perhaps you are correct. Although certain gentlemen might consider that just adds spice to the challenge."

Quentin clenched his teeth, wishing furiously he had the authority to ban Freemont from calling on Ailis then and there. "Certain *gentleman?*" he grated out, his voice dripping scorn. "I wonder, Freemont, do you box?"

"Occasionally," the viscount replied, turning back to him with that irritating smirk Quentin longed to smack off his face.

"We should have a go at Jackson's some day. You look to be almost up to my weight."

"Perhaps. Although in general I prefer to protect my pretty face. Makes it easier to entice the ladies, you know. Branson," the viscount nodded a dismissal and spurred his mount to a trot.

Ailis had broken away, riding ahead of her sister, and once again the viscount brought his mount beside Ailis's sidesaddle. "Shall I escort you home, my angel?"

"You need not put yourself to the trouble," Caragh called out quickly. "Lord Branson and I will take her. We couldn't invite you in for refreshments in any event, for we shall have to depart again almost immediately."

"I'm sure Holden would not consider it a trouble," Ailis said, giving the gentleman in question a provocative glance from under her long lashes.

The viscount seized Ailis's hand and brought it to his lips. "No service I could render you would ever be a trouble, Miss Ailis."

"There, you see?" Ailis nodded toward Caragh, then turned back to the viscount. "Let's have one last good run. Race you to the chestnut copse!"

Before Caragh could protest, both riders spurred their horses and galloped off.

Doubtless realizing that tearing after the pair, like a nursemaid chasing her recalcitrant charge, would only make her appear ridiculous, Caragh did not, as Quentin had feared, go in pursuit. Instead, she reined in, letting him draw up beside her.

"I worry about her," she said quietly.

As well you should, Quentin thought. "Would you like me to make further inquiries into the viscount's character?"

Her face cleared and she looked up at him, her eyes shining with gratitude. "Would you? Yes, I should very much appreciate it! Naturally, of all the admirers she's had fall at her feet, she has to notice the only one whose behavior I fear may not match the level of his breeding. And she's such an innocent, she has no notion how easily an unprincipled black-guard could ruin her reputation and her prospects.''

By the time they'd cantered to the far side of the park, there was no sign of her sister or Freemont. Caragh sighed. ''I shall have to speak to her again, more forcefully, once we're back at the house. And then drag her off for one last fitting, which means she's likely to be in a tearing ill-humor the rest of the day.''

Quentin curbed his first, bitter retort. Blast the baggage! Could Caragh not have even one morning's respite from dealing with her troublesome sister?

''Let's get you back, then,'' he said, keeping his tone light. ''And when you go for those fittings, I hope you'll be getting yourself something pretty, too.'' He reached over and squeezed her hand.

And felt another small shock—but this time, a pleasant one. Startled, he released her hand. ''Shall we be off?''

FOR A BRIEF MOMENT, Caragh left motionless the hand Quentin had squeezed. Faint tremors reminiscent of the first, strong jolt that had pulsed through her at his touch still throbbed through her fingers. Surely he had felt it too, that…force that surged between them?

But Quentin was already riding off, seemingly oblivious. Well, perhaps not. With a small sigh of disappointment, Caragh wrapped the reins back around the hand and kicked the mare to a canter.

During their short ride together, she'd refrained from taking Ailis to task about her conduct in coming unchaperoned to the park, not wanting to trigger her volatile sister's temper or spur her to an ill-judged and probably public reaction. But once they arrived home, the jobation Ailis urgently needed to hear could not be put off.

Bless Quentin, who apparently did intend to support her in dealing with Ailis, just as he'd promised. Although, if he turned up anything truly salacious when he investigated the worrisome viscount, she wasn't sure how she was going to induce Ailis to give Freemont up.

Well, no point worrying over that now. At the moment, she had the more pressing, if no less disagreeable task of delivering a lecture to her probably unreceptive sister.

As expected, she found Ailis in the sitting room they shared between their two chambers. She entered upon her knock to find her sister gathering her painting supplies in preparation for the afternoon's lesson.

"Oh, hullo, Caragh. Be a dear, and buy me another package of this yellow pigment while I work with Max today, won't you? I'm sure I won't have enough to complete the sunset study he's helping me with."

Her thoughts concentrated on marshalling her arguments in a way most likely to make an impression on her sister, Caragh absently accepted the packet Ailis extended. "Did you enjoy your ride?"

"Yes, 'twas very pleasant. Put this thinner in my box, won't you?"

Caragh stowed the tin Ailis handed her. "I was surprised to see you, though. I didn't realize you'd planned on riding this morning."

"I hadn't planned on it, until Holden came by this morning and invited me. He is a handsome devil, isn't he? Such a countenance! I told him I should like to do his likeness." She sidled a glance at Caragh. "Bare-chested, in Greek draperies."

"Ailis, you didn't tell him that!" Caragh gasped.

Her sister merely grinned. "I shall have to talk to Max about arranging it."

"Perhaps you should concentrate on finishing the sunset study first," Caragh countered quickly. "Indeed, you must take care not to let Lord Freemont act the devil he looks. This isn't the country, Ailis, and the more…casual manners we practice there will not do in London. You really shouldn't address him as Holden on such slim acquaintance."

Ailis shrugged. "'Tis what Max calls him. I should feel rather foolish 'my-lording' him in the studio."

"Perhaps such familiarity might be permitted there, but certainly not among the polite world. And if you ride with him, you must bring a groom along."

Ailis stopped in her packing and looked up. "A groom?" She tossed her blond head back and laughed. "Is he supposed to rob me of my virtue in broad daylight within the confines of Hyde Park? Or beside some merchant's cart on some busy London street? Such a feat of equestrian skill would be worthy of Astley's!"

"I agree, the likelihood of him compromising you on horseback is slim. Still, as nonsensical as the rules of behavior seem to you, Ailis, to flout them brings discredit not only upon you, but also upon Aunt Kitty—and me." Caragh smiled, trying to soften the reprimand. "And although I certainly would never bother with it in the country, in town I take a groom even when I ride with so good and longtime a friend as Quentin."

"Which is both ridiculous and unnecessary, since Quent would hardly try to compromise you, even had he a perfect opportunity," her sister retorted.

Caragh bit her lip against the pain of her sister's tactless words. "True enough," she allowed. "Still, we've only just met Lord Freemont, and know little of him. Surely you'll agree that the character of the gentleman with whom you might spend the rest of your life is vitally important."

"Who said I have any intention of marrying him? It's just that he alone, of all the so-called gentlemen I've met thus far, does not bore me senseless reciting bad verses in praise of my eyebrows, or turn cow-eyed and speechless when I enter a room. He admires my *work,* Caragh—and he's quite knowledgeable about painting, as well being a major patron of Max and several other artists. He talks to me of things that matter, treats me like a *woman*—not some celestial being upon a pedestal to be gazed upon with awe."

Caragh could well understand the appeal of a gentleman treating one like a woman. "I can see how refreshing that would be. But we've hardly arrived. Once we begin attending parties, I imagine you will meet any number of handsome and well-spoken men who will admire both your beauty and your intelligence."

"Society gentlemen?" Ailis sniffed. "Not if they are like the coxcombs whose portraits Max has done."

"Since Mr. Frank meets them as employers, his relations with them would naturally be...different than that of a lady they wished to court, or marry."

"Indeed?" Ailis raised her eyebrows. "I should think their treatment of an employee—although to treat someone of Max's genius as a mere servant is preposterous!—would be much more illuminating of their character than their behavior as suitors."

As Maximilian Frank made no secret of his often contemptuous opinion of the aristocracy, Caragh wasn't surprised to hear that the man's impressions of some of his employers were less than complimentary.

"I suppose you are correct. Still, Mr. Frank is known as something of a radical. I'd be a bit cautious about accepting without question his rather Jacobean views on the equality of man and the abolition of the monarchy."

Ailis grinned. "I shall not go that far...yet."

Caragh gave her a severe look. "There are certainly men of true character among the nobility—is not Quentin Burke an example of that? I just ask that you be open to meeting them. And that you be a bit more...circumspect in your dealings with Lord Freemont. Here in London, the code of behavior for unmarried ladies is very strict, and with your presentation—''

''Bother my presentation!'' Ailis exclaimed, tossing down the paint case and rounding to face Caragh. ''I've told you all along that it matters little to me whether I'm a success with the ton or not, as long as I achieve *my* goals in London. I like Holden and I intend to continue seeing him, so you might as well accustom yourself to it.''

Caragh struggled to keep her anger in check. ''And you, dear sister, had better 'accustom' yourself to the fact that if you wish to *remain* in London, you will honor our agreement and not do anything to embarrass Aunt Kitty.''

Caragh braced herself for an explosion, but to her relief, Ailis held up both hands. ''Come, let's cease quarrelling over trivialities. I'll agree to try to remember the rules of dull propriety, if you will cease preachifying on the virtues of virtue.''

Although Caragh wasn't sure she ought to concede the point while Ailis still referred to the serious matters under discussion as ''trivialities,'' her sister was offering to compromise—a rather unusual occurrence. At any rate, 'twas probably the best she was likely to wangle from Ailis at the moment. ''Agreed. Now, at the risk of immediately breaking our truce, I must remind you that we have one last fitting this morning on the gowns for Friday's rout.''

''Not today!'' Ailis groaned. ''I must finish the sketches for the sunset study by this afternoon!''

Once Ailis immersed herself in her art, she was as hard as papa—and even less congenial—to pry loose. ''Do the fitting immediately,'' Caragh cajoled, ''and I promise I'll occupy Aunt Kitty so you may have the rest of the day to work on sketches.''

Ailis gave her a reluctant smile. ''Blackmailer.''

''Revolutionary.'' Caragh linked her arm with her sister's. ''Let's be off to battle tape measures and straight pins.''

And so Caragh was able to bear her sister off to the mantua-maker. While Ailis, a long-suffering expression on her face as they stood being pinned and prodded, doubtless used her time to contemplate her sketches, Caragh found herself wondering if Quentin was merely being kind in recommending that she buy herself something pretty.

Well, she thought, taking a nervous breath as she regarded her image in the glass, if this gown didn't inspire him to see her in a new light, nothing ever would.

CHAPTER FOUR

As it turned out, Quentin did not join Caragh for dinner at Lady Mansfield's townhouse, nor did he escort them to the Duchess of Avon's ball. What he'd expected to be a short visit to his new property outside London turned into a day-long marathon of dealing with disgruntled tenants and trying to assess how best to remedy the damages wrought by years of mismanagement on the part of the estate agent, whom he dismissed upon the spot.

Knowing by midmorning he would not be able to get away, he dispatched a servant with his regrets and a note promising Caragh he would seek her out upon his return and lend her his support for whatever remained of the evening.

Night had long since fallen when he galloped back to his lodgings. After downing a platter of cold meat and a tankard of ale while his valet helped him into his evening clothes, he hurried off again, arriving in time to be presented to the duchess along with the last of the guests waiting in what must have been an endless receiving line. That duty completed, he went off in search of Caragh, his progress slowed by a number of hopeful mamas determined to add his name to their blushing daughters' dance cards.

Recalling with sardonic amusement the scant attention such ladies had paid him eight years ago, when all he possessed was a modest title, a heap of debts and a crumbling estate, Quentin noted at the corner of the ballroom a large gathering of gentlemen. As he struggled closer through the crush, he saw Ailis at the center of a milling group of admiring swains.

Who had, he noted in fairness, a great deal to admire. In a

pure-white gown of simple cut that emphasized the classical perfection of her profile, her blond curls threaded through with pearls, matching pearls at her ears and throat, she looked the portrait of innocent maidenhood. Though he might privately deplore her rag manners and the cavalier manner in which she took advantage of her sister, he could not deny Ailis possessed beauty enough to dazzle even the most jaded palate.

The throng vying for her attention included not just younger and more impressionable men, but a number of older, cultured gentlemen as well. Also among the group, he noted, were those of the dandy set who, although they themselves had no intentions of becoming leg-shackled, always wished to be seen among the court of the latest Incomparable. An indication that Ailis was well on her way to becoming the diamond of the Season.

He devoutly hoped Caragh could harness that attention to lure her sister and some unsuspecting victim into matrimony before the ton discovered how drastically the lady's character varied from the appearance of docile, well-bred loveliness she currently presented.

Nearby, its wearer obscured by the press of gentlemen, he saw a tall nodding ostrich plume in cherry red, which must denote the presence of Lady Catherine. He did not as yet see Caragh.

Having elbowed and pushed his way through the crowd, he maneuvered past the current contender for Ailis's attention to present his compliments. The slight raise of her brows as she rose out of her demure curtsy told him that, for the moment anyway, she was finding the role of Innocent Virgin highly entertaining. For Caragh's sake, Quentin prayed that amusement lasted long enough to get the chit safely riveted.

Reassured that the unpredictable Ailis seemed to be on her best behavior, Quentin relinquished his place to the next eager gentleman and backed out of the crowd, still searching for

Caragh. As he scanned the vicinity, a flash of light from the corner snagged his attention.

The crowd shifted and once again the glitter of what must be candlelight reflected by golden fabric caught his eye. A moment later, a dark-coated man moved aside, revealing first the gilded silk of a lady's skirt, then the lady herself. As Quentin's appreciative gaze moved upward, he felt his lips curve into a smile.

The fluid gown gave an alluring hint of its wearer's hips and molded closely over a very fine bosom, its décolletage low enough to entice, but high enough to thwart all but an arousing glimpse of what lay beneath. Aroused in truth, Quentin's eyes wandered slowly over shoulders showcased in a teasing puff of gold-dipped fabric, up a graceful neck where curly tendrils of honey-gold hair escaped from a loose topknot of Grecian curls. And finally came to rest on lips curved in a half smile in a heart-shaped face that was…Caragh's?

Shock made his jaw drop and halted him in mid-step. Suddenly dizzy, he closed his eyes and shook his head. But when he opened them again, the vision hadn't changed. The alluring woman in the enticing gown truly was his neighbor and friend, little Caragh Sudley.

He'd never again be able to consider her "little." The thought sputtered through his head before he jerked his gaze from that slither of gown and tried to reassemble his scattered wits.

Before he managed that feat, she spotted him. In a flutter of gilded skirts, she approached. "Lord Branson, I had about despaired of you!" she said, extending him her hands.

For a long moment he stood staring at her, oblivious to her outstretched hands as another bolt of entirely unplatonic appreciation sizzled through him. He couldn't seem to tear his gaze from the soft, never-before-viewed skin of her neck and shoulders and collarbones, that shadowed cleavage that positively dared a man to tug the silk bodice lower and feast his eyes and lips on the treasures just teasingly out of view....

Desperately he tried to channel his errant thoughts back to properly fraternal channels and summon some intelligent reply. "C-Caragh, how...how lovely you look tonight. L-like a glimmer of candlelight!"

Tantalizing. Seductive. He clamped his lips shut before he could add the words, while Caragh raised her eyebrows, no doubt surprised by his stammering enthusiasm.

Feeling himself flush, he stumbled on, "A very...stylish gown indeed." *And how intriguing the view!* "If this is an example of the new wardrobe you've been accumulating, I heartily sanction the expense."

A soft blush tinted her cheeks and her clear eyes sparkled. "It is, and thank you. Aunt Kitty will be quite thrilled to know it meets with your approval. Though you needn't empty the butter boat over me—or do you mean to practice your wife-wooing wiles?"

"Are they working?" he asked as he belatedly bent over her fingers she still offered.

She uttered that throaty gurgle of a laugh that always brightened his spirits, made him want to chuckle in return. *Relax,* he told himself, trying to calm his still-agitated mind. *Despite the gown, it's just Caragh.*

"As I expect the mamas of the young ladies you decide to court will soon be drenching you in quite enough flattery, I shall not answer that," she replied.

He did laugh then, before brushing his lips against her knuckles. A faint, heady scent of honeysuckle enveloped him and a low hum seemed to resonate between their joined fingers. He straightened slowly, finding himself strangely reluctant to let her go.

Don't be a clutch, he rebuked himself. *This is* Caragh, *not some demi-mondaine.*

While he struggled to order his disturbing and unprecedented reactions, Caragh stood quietly, her face tilted up to his, an expression of puzzlement—and something else he couldn't quite place—in her eyes.

Finally, her blush deepening, Caragh gently detached the fingers he'd forgotten he still held and placed them on his arm.

HE CERTAINLY SEEMED dazzled, Caragh thought hopefully. And surely...surely he must have felt it too, that little shock when he kissed her hand. That sort of quivering that still vibrated between them, her gloved fingertips resting where she could almost feel the pulse beat in his wrist. Surely such a reaction could not be all one-sided?

Or was he just confused at seeing her out of her drab outmoded garb and in this form-revealing ball gown? *Find out,* a little voice whispered.

"Is the gown the height of fashion?" she asked. "The mantua-maker swore 'twas so, but we are so newly arrived, I have nothing to base my judgment on. You've visited London often enough. Would you say the décolletage is right—neither too daring nor too matronly?"

His gaze drifted down to her chest and lingered there. He opened his mouth, closed it. The intensity of his stare made her skin heat. Then, cheeks reddening, he abruptly raised his glance back to her face. "It is...attractive. But you might wish to have the bodice cut a trifle higher in future. You don't wish men to gape at you."

"Would they gape?"

"They will if you show them much more," he muttered.

He *had* noticed! Caragh exulted. Having been achingly aware of *him* from the moment he first rode down her drive, excitement buoyed her spirits at this confirmation that, for the first time, it appeared Quentin was finally seeing her not as his helpful little neighbor, but as a woman.

Just what did he mean to do about the realization? Heart

pounding with recklessness and hope, Caragh vowed to find out.

"Did your business prosper today? I hope the problem was resolved."

He was still staring at her as if he didn't quite recognize the woman addressing him. But given the din in the ballroom, perhaps he hadn't heard the question.

She leaned closer, close enough to see the shades of blue shimmer in his turquoise eyes, to denote each separate golden lash that framed them. From inches away, he exuded the heady fragrance of shaving soap and virile male. Her glance lowered to his firm lips, and for a moment she couldn't remember what she was supposed to be asking.

Now or never, she thought, and took a deep breath, trying to slow the trip-hammer beat of her pulse. "Ailis is dancing this set, which should keep her out of mischief for the moment. It's too noisy and crowded here for conversation. Come out on the balcony with me and get some air." She tugged at his arm.

To her alarm and delight, he nodded and led her out of the ballroom.

The breeze on the balcony was chilly. After closing the doors behind them, Quentin turned back to Caragh and noticed her shiver.

"You don't have your shawl! Perhaps we should go back in. I don't wish you to catch a chill."

With him standing this close, her blood was more apt to boil, she thought. "No, the cold is…refreshing."

"Stand here in front of me, then. I'll block the wind." He maneuvered her a step closer into his warmth.

Lift her head, and she could feel the breath from his lips… "How did you find matters on the new estate?" she managed to ask.

"In a muddle, I'm afraid. I have, by the way, set some

further inquiries abroad about the matter of Lord Freemont. I hope to have a full report for you soon.''

"I'm relieved that he hasn't appeared this evening. Perhaps he views such ton entertainments as the duchess's ball too tame.''

"Quite possibly."

"In any event, I can only be glad for his absence. It frees me of worrying that he might tempt Ailis into doing something improper.''

As she was tempted, she thought, her glance once again lingering on Quentin's lips. If she were to brace a hand on his shoulder and raise up on tiptoe, she could brush her mouth against his....

He was staring down at her, gaze focused on *her* lips. Did his blood pound like hers to the pulse of her nearness? Was a voice shrieking in his head, as it was in hers, for him to lean through the small distance that separated them...and kiss her?

Past the lump the size of a crumpet that had somehow lodged itself in her throat, Caragh managed to whisper, "Though sometimes, being improper is...quite tempting."

Time seemed suspended, breathing ceased, and with every nerve braced in anticipation she thrilled to his mouth's gradual descent. Her eyes fluttered shut.

The first brush of his lips was sweet and so intoxicating she immediately hungered for more. Her hands rose of their own volition to grasp his lapels and she leaned into Quentin, deepening the kiss.

He clutched her shoulders and opened his mouth, gave her the ardent wash of his tongue against her lips. Her pulse leapt, something heated and urgent tightened within her, demanding release.

But before she could think to seek his tongue with her own, he stepped back suddenly and pushed her away. Already nearly boneless, she would have fallen had his strong grip at her shoulders not kept her upright.

"Your...your aunt will be missing you," he said, his voice uneven. He steadied her on her feet and then, with an insistent hand to the small of her back, propelled her back into the ballroom.

In his haste he half pushed her across the floor until they located her aunt, whereupon he quickly removed his hand. "I think I need a glass of the duchess's excellent champagne," he said, avoiding her glance. "May I bring each of you ladies one?"

Nearly weeping with disappointment, Caragh clamped her lips, still fired by his touch, tightly together to keep them from trembling and nodded.

He set off immediately. Around her, bejeweled dancers whirled like colorful tops through a waltz, Aunt Kitty's high-pitched voice babbled a falsetto note over the chorus of a hundred conversations. Caragh saw them, heard them, but comprehended nothing.

Well, she thought despairingly, the daring ball gown had done its work. Quentin Burke now realized that Caragh Sudley was a woman, with a woman's desires. And, she noted, watching him struggle with obvious impatience through the crowd, the knowledge thrilled him so much he couldn't wait to get away from her.

QUENTIN DOWNED a glass of champagne in one gulp, his hand trembling, then seized another.

What had come over him? Kissing Caragh Sudley on the balcony as if she were some...lightskirt out of the Green Room!

He was lucky he'd come to his senses before she fainted or struggled free and slapped his insolent face. True, she'd looked so impossibly lovely, so—seductively female, 'twas little wonder that shock had made him overreact. She shouldn't have surprised him so!

Of course, he realized she was now a woman grown. Still, he didn't appreciate having the fact brought home as blatantly as it had been by that demirep's excuse of a gown! Any man seeing her in it would instantly conceive thoughts just like his, which meant he'd better snap up the champagne and get back. And here he'd expected his escort tonight would protect *Ailis* from importunate suitors!

He paused to take a long, slow sip. He'd have to make it clear to Caragh that she must never wander out onto deserted balconies with gentlemen. Some other man with more muscle than morals might have taken advantage of her innocence, imprisoned that slender body against his chest and tasted much more than that tempting mouth.

Though it would have been the last thing the bounder tasted for a fortnight, once Quentin's fists got done with his lecherous lips.

Still, Caragh's suddenly changed appearance was…troubling. Not that he grudged her the frivolous, flirty gown, but he certainly preferred seeing in her familiar, sensible, Caragh-type garb.

Did he indeed? his still-simmering body instantly riposted. Could not passion add a spicy zest to what was already a deeply enjoyable friendship?

Not before a tolling of wedding bells, his mind answered. The implications of that conclusion shocked him anew. Though he'd never before conceived of marrying Caragh— any more than he'd considered marrying Alden or any of his male friends—the idea, now that he did consider it, wasn't without appeal. He might keep his good friend permanently close…and indulge in every fantasy that golden gown had evoked.

The idea fizzled for a moment, but then like champagne left too long in a glass, went flat. For one, he had no idea if

Caragh would be interested in proceeding in such a direction. More important, though he'd never made the attempt before, he knew instinctively that though they might be able to travel the road from friends to lovers, there would be no coming back.

Growing up with all male cousins, he'd not had any female playmates. Caragh was the first and only woman with whom he had ever developed a true friendship, except for his mother. He certainly didn't see Caragh in that guise, however deep had been the affection he bore for that sainted lady. As for his other relationships with females...

There'd been the blond charmer right after he left Oxford, with whom he fancied himself violently in love until she informed him that, as he stood to inherit only a debt-ridden barony, she must not let him dangle after her any longer. Stung by that dismissal, he'd willingly let his Oxford mates introduce him to females of another class, who were pleased to settle for well-paid pleasure of the moment and no promises for a future.

But even such uncomplicated relationships had the potential to become disruptive. He recalled with a grimace a well-endowed opera singer whose coloratura shriek and unerring aim with a wine bottle had rendered the ending of their affair singularly unpleasant. And three years ago, there'd been Alden's younger sister, with whom he thought he'd established a teasing, older-brother rapport. Until his friend, in some embarrassment, asked him to stop visiting him at home for the present, as his sister was fancying herself in love with the still-ineligible Quentin.

When he examined the matter, he had to conclude that every dealing he'd had with women since coming of age had been complicated—except for his friendship with Caragh. In that bond alone had he managed to combine the easy camaraderie he shared with his male friends, the exhilaration of discussing matters of importance he found at gatherings of estate managers, and the stimulation of intellect he found when debating his scholarly acquaintances. It was, in sum, a relationship like no other. A relationship he valued like no other.

A relationship he would go to great lengths to preserve and had no wish to risk losing by trying to overlay it with the tantalizing but dangerous and unpredictable elixir of passion.

No, far better to rein in his overactive imagination and over-eager body, lest he stumble into a situation that led not to marriage and happy-ever-after, but to heartache and the permanent loss of one of his dearest friends.

His troubled mind settled by that sage decision, he drained the last of the second glass and motioned the waiter to hand him two fresh flutes. Straightening his shoulders, he paced purposefully back to the ballroom, ready to banish all thoughts evoked by provocative golden gowns and keep Caragh Sudley firmly where she belonged—as a dear *platonic* friend.

CHAPTER FIVE

SEVERAL MORNINGS later, Quentin awaited Caragh in her Aunt Kitty's parlor. Too concerned and restless to take a seat in the chair to which the butler conducted him, he stood by the hearth, gazing into the fire.

The facts he'd just confirmed about the character of Ailis's favorite admirer, Viscount Freemont, were disturbing enough that he'd felt compelled to bring a report of them to Caragh without delay. The urgency of his mission had succeeded, at least for the moment, in relegating into the background the discomfort he still harbored after that incident with Caragh on the balcony at the Duchess of Avon's ball. Feelings that, he admitted, had led him to avoid her for the past several days.

Resolving to keep his relationship with Caragh platonic was certainly wise. However, acknowledging a decision as wise and managing to carry it through were two entirely separate matters, a fact he'd been forced to admit as soon as he'd walked back into her golden proximity that night and handed her the champagne. Neither his imagination nor his body proved easy to restrain, leading to an awkwardness that had marred the rest of the evening.

He must do something to alleviate that subtle tension, restore them to the easy relationship they'd always enjoyed...though as yet he had no idea what. However, years of focusing on only the first step in solving what might otherwise seem nearly insurmountable problems had allowed him to bring his estate back from the brink of disaster. Perhaps he should use that technique here, put aside for the moment these disturbing new impulses and concentrate instead on the most pressing concern—the matter of Ailis and Viscount Freemont.

The news he must impart was sure to distress Caragh, confirming as it did that the viscount was most definitely not a fit suitor to a maiden of her sister's tender years. Especially one as volatile and heedless of convention as Ailis.

Caragh's appearance at the parlor door a moment later distracted him from his musings. And disturbed him, he admitted with exasperation and an almost wistful annoyance, far more than it ought.

Her fashionable muslin morning gown, in a soft green that complemented her gold-burnished curls and hazel eyes, was neither low-cut nor especially form-fitting. Yet once again Quentin found himself instantly, intensely aware of the swell of her breasts beneath the modest round neck, the curve of shoulder that seemed to emphasize the graceful lines of her throat, the lips, now curving into a welcoming smile, that had yielded so bewitchingly under his own.... He jerked his gaze upward.

Damn and blast! he swore silently, his neckcloth now choking his suddenly overheated neck. Subconsciously he must have been hoping, he realized, that time and the prosaic light of day would dissipate the disturbing alchemy that had surrounded them that night at the ball.

Obviously it had not. Working to stifle his body's instinctive reaction, he watched her approach and wondered whether the tantalizing physical appeal that now struck him so forcibly had bonded itself inseparably onto the strong fraternal attraction he'd always felt for his easygoing, intelligent neighbor. After that scene on the balcony, would there be no way to separate them again?

"What a nice surprise, Quentin," she said, extending her hands.

"Hullo, Caragh." Cautiously he took them, steeling himself for the zing of response that raced through his nerves when he touched her.

She jerked her hands free and turned aside, as if she, too, had been scorched by that brief contact.

"I'll have Evers get us some tea," Caragh said, breaking the uneasy silence. "Is this a social call, or does some business bring you here? Whatever it is, I hope 'tis nothing that requires my going out. With Ailis's come-out ball in just a week, the household is in an uproar, Aunt Kitty is all flutters, and I've a thousand details still to attend before we go to Lady Cavendish's rout tonight." She looked up at him inquiringly.

Dropping his gaze from her too-compelling eyes, Quentin gathered his disjointed thoughts.

"I'll be brief, then, and we can dispense with tea. But I felt you ought to hear this as soon as possible."

"What is it?"

"I'm afraid I have some rather disturbing information to impart concerning Lord Freemont. Perhaps you'd better sit down."

"Oh, dear. Should I call for brandy?" she asked wryly as she seated herself on the sofa and motioned him to a place beside her.

"Perhaps. And ready a gag and some restraints for Ailis."

Caragh sighed. "I was afraid it would be bad. So, tell me the wretched whole."

Despite her unprecedented behavior on the balcony, for which he must surely be somehow responsible, Caragh had always been a calm and rational individual, so best to just tell her directly, he decided. Without further preamble, Quentin began, "To his credit, I can report Freemont is indeed a knowledgeable patron of the arts and a generous supporter, particularly of talented newcomers. The rest is not so positive. I regret to confirm that the rumors of his taking under his protection a number of the highest flyers are quite accurate. Worse, however, it appears he has also made mistresses of females outside the demi-monde, all of whom have borne him illegitimate offspring. One of them was even gently born, though whether or not he seduced her into ruination with false promises of marriage I could not ascertain. His club mates report he is quite proud of his prowess among the ladies and frequently boasts that no female, be she duchess or drudge, will ever leg-shackle him into marriage.''

With a soft exclamation of distress, Caragh closed her eyes. For an instant, Quentin worried she was about to faint. After all, stalwart she might be, but she was still a lady bred, and his news must have shocked her.

"Damn him!" she exclaimed, relieving him of concern for her maidenly sensibilities. "Why, of all her suitors, did Freemont have to be the one to entice Ailis? I shall have no choice now but to forbid him the house.''

She shook her head and sighed. ''As his rogue's reputation is more likely to enhance his appeal to Ailis than lessen it, keeping them apart is going to be the very devil. Especially as I've no doubt the wretch will attempt to see her during her lessons with Max, once I refuse to receive him here.''

''I suppose there's no chance of suspending those...?''

She jumped to her feet and paced to the window, her speaking glance rendering a verbal response to that question unnecessary. ''She's already contemptuous of the rules that govern proper behavior, unconcerned about the judgments of society and since she evinces no desire to marry anyway, certain to be furious at my banning her from seeing Freemont. I wouldn't dream of trying to ban her lessons as well.''

''If she has so little inclination to marry, are you sure you're right to more or less force her into it?''

''How else is she to survive if she doesn't marry?'' Caragh demanded. ''Make her living as an artist? Oh, I don't expect you to understand! Even when your estates were crumbling, you had the freedom to choose your course of action! You might have sold off some land, sought employment in the

church or the army, or even abandoned everything and emi-
grated to the Americas. But we have no funds not tied up in
dowry and no authority to manage even those! There is no
choice, no chance, for a woman outside marriage. It's Ailis's
whole future at stake here, and I can't stand by and let her
ruin it, even if I must push her to it against her will.''

She looked so fierce, he wanted to applaud her—and so
desperate, he wanted to take her in his arms.

But, remembering what had happened the last time he'd
done that, he'd better restrict himself to verbal support.

''You know I'll help in any way I can. Would you like me
to break the news to her? I'm the one who confirmed the truth
of Lord Freemont's behavior, after all. Perhaps she would take
it better were the information to come from an impartial outsider.''

Her fierceness faded, leaving her looking weary and discouraged. Once again, Quentin resented the thankless effort
Caragh expended on her sister's behalf.

''I appreciate the offer, but no. She'll doubtless rail and
complain and weep. I won't subject you to that.''

Having observed a few such scenes with Ailis, Quentin
shuddered. Unable to force himself to face that daunting prospect again, he said instead, ''Then how can I help?''

''If you could escort us tonight? Perhaps you could amuse
and distract her on the journey, occupy her until her other
admirers bear her away—and keep Lord Freemont at bay,
should he happen to be present. That is...'' she colored and
looked away, ''if my...behavior the other night didn't give
you a disgust of me.''

She knows I've been avoiding her, he thought with a hot
flush of guilt. ''No, of course not! I...expect 'twas much more
my fault than yours. It was just...a surprise.''

''An unpleasant one, apparently,'' she said dryly, her
cheeks still rosy as she reached over to adjust the perfectly
straight pleats in the window curtains.

"No! That is, not...exactly." As uncomfortable as this abrupt shift in conversation made him, perhaps 'twas best to address the problem head-on. Oh, that they might resolve it now, banish the lingering awkwardness that had grated at him these last few days and recapture the pleasant relationship he so prized!

Doggedly he made himself continue. "But...I've never thought of you in...those terms. We've been friends, good friends, for years, in a relationship that has been straightforward, congenial, and as enjoyable for you, I hope, as it has been for me. Proceeding down the road we dallied near that night would...complicate it."

With a gusty sigh, he ran a hand through his hair. "Usually, everything about dealing with women is difficult! That's why I found you so different, so delightful. What we've shared over the years is unique in my experience. I...I just don't want to do anything that might ruin that."

"I see," she said softly, toying now with the curtain tiebacks. "But...isn't it possible that taking that...road might lead to a relationship even more enjoyable? And if so, would that not be worth the risk?"

"I don't know, Caragh," he said, determined to be as honest as possible. "This whole matter is beyond the realm of my experience. I do know your friendship is very special to me. And I know that if we try to make it...more, things between us will have to change. If...what happened then wasn't pleasing to us both, I fear we'd not be able to turn back and recapture what we have now." He shrugged his shoulders, helpless to explain it any more clearly. "And what we have now is too precious for me to chance losing."

For a long time she said nothing. Quentin sat motionless, terrified he might have already said too much and offended her beyond repair, furious at himself for not having avoided the conversation.

Finally, when he thought he would have to either babble

something else or bolt from the room, Caragh eased his anxiety with a smile. "You could never do anything that would destroy what we have." She took a long, unsteady breath. "I shall be your friend 'til my last breath."

Everything would return to the way it had been before the ball. His spirits soaring on a burst of euphoria, he sprang up and strode to the window. "As I will be yours," he promised, seizing her hand and bringing it to his lips.

A charged awareness sizzled through the hand that held hers, burned in his lips as they brushed her fingers. Startled, he released her.

Yes, everything would return to the way it had been…as long as he could ignore this disconcerting, and annoyingly automatic physical response to her.

HER PRECIOUS DREAMS turning to cinders, Caragh watched Quentin's troubled brow clear, unmistakable relief lighting his eyes. Sternly repressing a missish desire to burst into tears, she finished the prosaic business of setting a meeting time and place, then walked Quentin to the door and bade him goodbye. Her chest felt hollow, her heartbeat echoing within its hope-deprived space like Quentin's retreating footsteps in the empty hallway as she listened to him depart.

She'd tried to reassure herself when, instead of calling on her the day after the ball, Quentin had sent a note. Tried to buoy her sagging spirits as one by one the days slipped past with no further word from him, telling herself that her radically changed appearance had surprised Quentin—she had wanted to shock him, hadn't she? Of course he would require some time to adjust to the new and startling fact of their mutual attraction. Once he did, he would want to at least cautiously explore this new development.

But she knew now her instincts on the night of ball had been right. The speech he'd just delivered proved beyond doubt that attracted to her Quentin might be—but he wasn't happy about it. He had no desire whatsoever to attempt to take their relationship to another level. Indeed, he'd practically begged her to allow them to go back to the way they'd always been.

She stifled a bitter laugh. She supposed her female vanity should be gratified that he wasn't repulsed by her physical charms, though, as the end result was the same, it made little difference.

No, Quentin Burke was not willing to admit the physical connection that whispered between them. All he wanted was for them to remain platonic friends.

Friends.

Could she bear that now, knowing he had responded to her touch? When she hungered for so much more?

It appeared that, unless she were prepared to do without him entirely, she would have to endure it. He was not prepared to offer her anything more—and she'd just given him her word she'd accept that decision.

Until this moment, she hadn't realized how much her heart had counted on persuading Quentin Burke to follow a very different path. The stark truth that he would not hurt more than she could have believed possible.

Blinking back the tears that stung at her eyelashes, for a few minutes she allowed herself to grieve, to acknowledge the devastating depth of that sweet and painful longing. Then she took a long, ragged breath and forced herself to walk from the room.

Like other unpleasant facts about her life she couldn't do anything to change, she would think no further on it now. Besides, she had a pressing duty to perform that was just as unpleasant.

Telling Ailis she must give up Holden Freemont.

SINCE Lord Freemont sometimes stopped by to escort them to Ailis's art lesson, Caragh first summoned Evans to inform him that the viscount would no longer be received by their household. Then she mounted the stairs to her sister's chamber.

Her head throbbed with an ache almost as sharp as the one piercing her heart. But, despite her personal anguish, she must somehow summon words convincing enough to persuade her volatile sister to end her friendship with Lord Freemont. She could only hope that desperation would make her eloquent—and pray that for once, Ailis would prove reasonable.

She stood for a moment before the door, girding herself for the combat to come. Then, putting her own unhappiness aside, she knocked on the door and entered.

Ailis looked over in surprise. "Caragh—I was just about to summon you! I wish to go to the studio early today. Max said it would not disturb him to have me there while he works and I need to complete underpainting the background before today's lesson."

"I've no objections. But first, I need your agreement on a matter of much graver importance."

Occupied in packing her art supplies, Ailis didn't even look up. "I can't imagine anything more important than getting the background right. But if you will allow me to go to the studio early all *week*, I'll agree without discussion to participate in whatever tiresome social ritual about which you're preparing to harangue me. Only please, no more teas with that pack of old harridans that govern Almack's."

"Really, Ailis, that description is as unflattering as it is inaccurate, and is just the sort of imprudent comment I would have you refrain from voicing, even to me! Lady Jersey—who, I must point out, is barely older than I am—is known for her wit and charm. Countess Lieven and Princess Esterhazy both combine a lively intelligence with a vast—"

"'Silence' Jersey would rather skewer with her wit than charm, and the others do not enjoy discussing anything outside their narrow little aristocratic experiences. But come, let us not pull caps. What do you wish from me now?''

For an instant Caragh wavered, tempted to let herself continue lecturing Ailis on a breach of propriety much less contentious than the one she'd come here to discuss. But she knew she'd best harness the limited span of attention her sister spared to anything not directly connected to her art for addressing the problem of Lord Freemont.

Letting the easier topic go, she took a deep breath. "I'm afraid what I must ask will be difficult, and you may not understand or agree with the necessity of it. Nonetheless, it is crucial that you obey me in this. Ailis, you must cut your acquaintance with Lord Freemont.''

A tin of mineral spirits suspended in one hand, Ailis looked up, her eyes wide with surprise. ''Cut *Holden*'s acquaintance? But he's the only man of our class in London who understands art and is not crushingly, boringly conventional. Why should I avoid him?''

Briefly Caragh recounted to her sister the litany of transgressions the viscount had committed. However, as she'd feared, Ailis appeared unimpressed.

''A penny-press tale of rumor and innuendo,'' Ailis said with a wave of her hand as she returned to packing up her brushes and paints.

''So I had hoped. But concerned about your deepening friendship with him, I asked Quentin to investigate the allegations. He did—and what I've just related is fact, not rumor. I'm sorry, Ailis, but surely you see you cannot continue to associate with a man who has shown himself to possess so reprehensible a character.''

Ailis shrugged. ''So he keeps opera dancers and actresses. If that offense renders a gentleman unacceptable, I should have to give the cut direct to half the men of the ton.''

''He did more than that, Ailis. Making mistresses of women of a certain class is regrettably all too common, but there is a code of behavior to which even such gentlemen adhere. 'Twas offense enough that Lord Freemont dallied with servant and shop girls, but when he trifled with a girl of his own station, he transgressed beyond redemption. To seduce such a girl and not marry her—to make her an outcast among her own class and a disgrace to her family, is just not done, Ailis!''

"How do you know *she* did not pursue *him?* I, for one, have no trouble imagining a girl finding him fascinating enough to willingly forfeit her family's good opinion and her place in society. And how many 'gentlemen' would refuse a comely woman if she threw herself at his head?''

"Even if it transpired as you describe—though I take leave to doubt that any gently-born girl, no matter how lovestruck, could be heedless enough to actively seek her own ruination— a true gentleman *would* have refused her. And quietly returned her to family. Besides, there's the matter of the…illegitimate children he's sired.''

"Once again, a natural and certainly not uncommon oc- currence among gentleman who take mistresses. As long as he provides for the brats, I cannot see what all the fuss is about.''

Exasperated and alarmed, Caragh stared at her sister, trying to understand the girl's seeming acceptance of actions she herself found unforgivable. Was Ailis dismissing Caragh's ar- guments simply because she resented being ordered to give up her friend? Or could she honestly excuse Freemont's prof- ligate and irresponsible behavior?

Shrinking from that disturbing conclusion, she persisted, "Even if it is as you say, do you really see no harm in the viscount's having allowed a girl to ruin herself and her child, subjecting the innocent babe—his *own* innocent babe—to the lifelong shame of illegitimacy?''

Ailis shrugged again and resumed packing her supplies. "The girl was most likely content. And if she did regret it later—though I can't imagine why anyone would regret being excluded from a society as vain, boring and hypocritical as ever I predicted before coming to London—'twas her own fault for not knowing what she wanted.''

At least at this moment, Ailis was not going to be brought to admit Freemont's guilt, Caragh realized. Submerging her distress over what that might say about her *sister's* character, she shifted her focus to the more pressing task—getting Ailis to shun the viscount.

''If you cannot see his culpability, I am sorry. But society considers his character flawed, and so do I. Holding that view, I cannot allow you to associate with such a man and put at risk your own reputation and your chances to make a good marriage.''

Caragh paused, bracing for the reaction, but intent upon packing her supplies, Ailis did not even glance up.

''I've instructed Evers,'' she continued after a moment, ''that we will no longer receive Lord Freemont. I expect you to respect that decision. I further expect you to refrain from seeing Lord Freemont, or speaking to him should we chance to encounter him—even at the studio.''

With that, she had the dubious pleasure of knowing she had once again captured her sister's full attention.

Ailis set down a vial of paint and turned to face Caragh, her eyes narrowed. ''*Society* may do as it likes, and so may you. But Holden has been a friend to me—a friend who understands and shares the things *I* consider important! How dare you forbid me to see him? Is not attending these endless social functions punishment enough? Do you wish to make me totally miserable?''

''What I wish,'' Caragh replied, trying to hold on to her temper, ''is to secure you a future that allows you to continue doing what you want. You know the only way you'll be able to pursue your artistic ambitions is to marry a congenial man who will approve of that goal! Destroy your reputation by associating with Holden Freemont and you'll destroy any chance of achieving that.''

"Smile sweetly, say nothing of substance, and marry, marry, marry! Faith, how *sick* I am of that refrain!" Ailis retorted as she flung her last brush onto the case and then flounced to the window.

Her own temper dangerously near a boil, Caragh stalked after her. "Then perhaps you'd better remember that if you don't marry, marry, marry, after father's death your dowry will become a part of the estate—to be dispensed, along with all funds, at Cousin Archibald's discretion. Papa has always indulged your passion for painting—but how willing do you think our dear cousin will be to spend money on canvas, paint or lessons? Be sensible, Ailis!''

Though her sister's rigid jaw, flashing eyes and rapid breathing spoke of a fury that might already have galloped far beyond the reach of reason, Caragh grabbed her sister's arm and forced her to turn around. "You *will* listen to me! Papa's lawyer already agreed to make your having sufficient funds to continue your painting a part of the settlements when you marry. I hope and trust you will find a gentleman with whom you *wish* to spend your life. But even should you not, surely you can see it would be easier to cajole some starry-eyed contender for your hand to agree to those terms than to try to persuade Cousin Archibald to do so! Is giving up Lord Freemont so much compared to safeguarding your artistic future?''

"Cousin Archibald,'' Ailis hissed through gritted teeth, "can go to devil!" Jerking her arm free from Caragh's grasp, she once again stormed away.

At this last evidence of intransigence, Caragh's reserves of patience finally ran out. "Very well,'' she said to her sister's retreating back, masking her anger and irritation behind a veneer of calm. "But heed this, and heed it well. We made a bargain before we left Sudley that you could pursue your painting while I found you a husband—which, if you continue to associate with Lord Freemont, will become impossible. If you refuse to give him up, there is no point in our remaining here. Defy me in this, and we will return to Sudley at once.''

Ailis stopped in mid-stride, then slowly turned to face Caragh. ''You would stop my lessons and drag me back to Sudley?''

''I don't wish to do so. But if I must, I will.''

Her face contorting in rage, Ailis grabbed the nearest object—a small vase from the bedside table—and hurled it at Caragh, who, with years of experience in dealing with her sister's wrath, ducked out of the way.

As the vase shattered against the far wall, Ailis shouted, ''I hate you! And I hate this shallow, useless society you keep pushing me to move in! I won't give up Holden, I won't give up lessons and you cannot make me!'' Tears beginning to spill from her vivid blue eyes, she crossed her arms and glared at Caragh.

Shaken and near tears herself, Caragh glared back. ''No, I cannot make you behave. But I can restrict your actions until you've calmed down and had time to think. I'm sending word to Mr. Frank that you are indisposed and cannot come to your lesson today. Perhaps you can use the time to envision what your life will become if you refuse to comply—and end up losing your lessons forever.''

''You wouldn't!'' Ailis gasped.

Caragh strode to the bell pull. ''I'll have Mary take him a message at once.''

Tears flowing freely now, Ailis stared at Caragh. ''Get out!'' she cried at last. ''Get out and stay out! Oh, how I h-hate—'' her words ended in a sob.

''I know,'' Caragh said softly as her sister flung herself on her bed, weeping, ''how you hate me.''

Heartsick and weary, knowing she could accomplish nothing else until Ailis calmed, Caragh left. The pain in her throbbing head now so intense she feared she might be sick, Caragh stumbled back to her room by blind reckoning, jerked on the bell pull and sought her bed.

Numbly she waited for the maid to bring her cold compresses and headache powder. She could only hope after the storm of fury had passed, Ailis would recognize the truth of her arguments and honor their bargain—so that Caragh would not have to carry out her threat.

CHAPTER SIX

LADY CATHERINE'S townhouse seemed uncommonly quiet when Quentin arrived that night to escort the ladies to Lady Cavendish's rout, a circumstance soon explained when the butler conveyed to him that neither his mistress nor Miss Ailis intended to go out. Only Miss Caragh awaited him in the salon, the butler explained.

Surprised and a bit concerned, he followed the servant down the hall, curious to hear Caragh's explanation for her missing relations.

His concern intensified the moment he walked into the salon. So pale and drawn was Caragh that alarm overpowered that punch-to-the-gut physical awareness that hit him now whenever she came near.

"What is it, Caragh? Are you ill?" he asked as soon as Evers withdrew.

"I must look wretched indeed for you to greet me thus," she answered wryly, motioning him to a seat. "I've a bit of the headache still, but otherwise I'm quite well, thank you."

"Evers told me your aunt and sister would not be down. Is the malady contagious? Or," he guessed, reading the tension lingering in her eyes, "did Ailis treat you to a scene that left both her and Lady Catherine prostrate?"

For a moment the pain in her eyes intensified and she sighed. "I suppose there's no reason to mask the truth—not from you. Yes, I'm afraid it was rather wretched. Just hearing about it second-hand was enough for Aunt Kitty to take to her bed."

Anger at Caragh's supremely self-absorbed sister shook

Quentin again. "You told her she must no longer receive Freemont…and she took it badly?"

"About as badly as you could imagine. Not only does she refuse to admit his unsuitability, she vows she will not give him up. To which I threatened to remove her from London and her precious art lessons. To demonstrate how seriously I meant that, I cancelled her lesson today and compelled her to remain at home. Whereupon she locked herself in her room and now refuses to admit anyone."

Once again Quentin felt that deep compulsion to take her in his arms. He settled for grasping her hand and squeezing it. "I'm so sorry, Caragh. It must have been awful for you."

To his horror, her chin trembled and tears welled up in her eyes. Before he could think of some comment to avert the impending flood, she pulled her fingers free of his and swiped at her eyes.

"It…it was, but you needn't worry that I'm about to turn into a watering-pot. Between Ailis and Aunt Kitty, I've had enough of scenes and sobbing! Still…I—I only wish Ailis realized I'm trying to do what is truly best for her."

"She blames you."

Pressing her lips together again, she nodded.

Once again, Quentin yearned to gather her against his chest, offer the comfort of a sympathetic shoulder. But he dared not, any more than he could give voice to his furious opinion that Ailis should remain in her room on bread and water until it finally penetrated her single-mindedly selfish skull that Caragh not only had her best interests at heart, but for years had submerged her own needs and wishes to care for her supremely unappreciative sibling.

Caragh took a shuddering breath, pulling him from his mental recriminations. "Maybe you were right," she said softly. "Perhaps it is wrong of me to try to force her to marry when she has so little inclination. But neither can I give her free rein to ruin herself and bring scandal down on poor Aunt

Kitty's head! Perhaps I should just pack us up and head back to Sudley—even if I have to drug Ailis and lash her to the carriage to get her there.''

"I'll bring the laudanum and the rope.''

Her unexpected gurgle of a laugh surprised him—and warmed him to his toes.

"Oh, Quent, I'm so glad you stopped by! But I mean to release you from escorting me tonight. As Ailis will not be in attendance, I won't need reinforcements to head off potential disaster. And since I myself shall be doing nothing more dangerous than attempting to explain Ailis's absence to her hordes of disappointed suitors, I believe I can manage on my own.''

"Perhaps you ought to stay home and rest as well,'' he replied, giving her tired face another inspection.

"Here?'' She gave an eloquent shudder. "After Ailis's tantrums and Aunt Kitty's swooning, even the vestiges of a headache aren't enough to keep me in this abode of lamentation! No, a few hours of ordinary conversation with individuals not in the process of railing or fainting sounds quite appealing! However, since I imagine you consider such entertainment rather tame, I acquit you of the duty to come with me.''

Though Quentin had been tempted at first to accept Caragh's offer and hie himself off to the more congenial surroundings of his club, he decided upon the spot to squire Caragh—and make sure she enjoyed herself.

For one evening at least, he vowed, still furious with Ailis on her behalf, someone would make *Caragh's* happiness a priority. Unfortunately, he had a hard time keeping his mind from contemplating ways of distracting her from her familial troubles that had little to do with ballrooms or society banter.

Firmly squelching such thoughts, he replied, "On the contrary! I'd been looking forward to it.''

At her raised eyebrow, he grinned. "Looking forward to spending time with you, then,'' he amended. "And supporting you, as you have so often supported me. That's what friends do for each other, after all.''

Her eyes lifted to his, then roved his face before stopping to linger on his lips. ''Yes...friends do,'' she said, almost in a whisper.

The intensity of her glance was as potent as a touch. Quentin's lips burned from it, and suddenly from deep within him boiled up a fierce need to pull her into his arms, to feel her lips, rather than her gaze, upon his own.

Before he could decide whether or not to commit such insanity, Caragh turned away and called for her wrap. Shaken, Quentin wasn't sure whether to be relieved or regretful.

AMUSING CARAGH turned out to be much easier than Quentin had expected, given the tumultuous day she'd suffered.

By the time they climbed into her coach, she'd masked her troubles behind her habitual calm. With a few well-informed questions about the problems he had encountered at the new property, she soon launched a conversation about pasturage and tenants that outlasted the wait in their hostess's receiving line.

After that, he stood aside while she greeted and consoled a crowd of gentlemen disappointed at the absence of her sister. Still, Quentin noted that several discriminating men in the group lingered after the others wandered off, evidently as interested in Caragh as they were in her more striking sister.

Garbed in another new gown of pale green that brought out the hazel of her eyes—and whose simple, unadorned style once again emphasized the ample curves of her body—she was lovely enough to engage any gentleman's interest. Concern over her distress had at first muted his awareness of her as a woman, but by the end of their carriage ride, he was once again uncomfortably conscious of her strong physical allure.

The orchestra struck up a tune, and one of the gentlemen led Caragh off. A number of other couples left for the dance floor, thinning the company around him until he was rather too visible to matchmaking mamas for comfort. Not wishing to fend off any who might approach, Quentin strolled after Caragh into the ballroom.

She was dancing with Lord Sefton, an affable baron a few years Quentin's senior. And though that gentleman appeared to be making proper conversation, Quentin noted his eyes frequently dropped to the attractive décolletage beneath his nose.

He would be tempted, he thought, eyeing the man with distaste, to stalk over, pull Sefton aside, and demand that he stop ogling Caragh as if she were some Covent Garden ballerina. Except that he suffered from a similar fascination himself.

Nor was he the only gentleman watching her. Sir Desmond Waters, one of the group that had surrounded her after they left the receiving line, had also drifted into the ballroom and stood near the dance floor, his attention fixed on the graceful lady in the pale-green gown.

Unsettling as it was to see her the object of masculine attention, Quentin knew it was nonsensical to allow that to irritate him. After all, as she'd pointed out back at Sudley, no less than Ailis did Caragh need to marry, and nowhere else would she find a larger selection of potential husbands. Though Quentin would prefer that they go on as they always had, at least in his head he understood how prudence demanded that Caragh take advantage of her time in London by fixing some worthy gentleman's interest—a development, he reflected gloomily, that would inevitably bring about changes in their relationship.

Unless…he could insure their friendship changed as little as possible by promoting a match between Caragh and one of his friends!

His spirits rebounded as he considered the advantages of such a plan. If Caragh chose a friend of his as husband, since the man would already be assured of Quentin's honorable character, he was unlikely to be jealous or mistrust Quentin's long-standing relationship with his bride. Quentin, in turn, could be assured that Caragh wed a man worthy of her. Melding the two separate friendships into a single, comfortable whole would be much more feasible were he already on intimate terms with both parties.

In addition, knowing she was his *friend's* wife would reinforce his efforts to ignore her physical appeal.

Yes, he decided, promoting such a marriage for Caragh offered his best chance to see her suitably settled while preserving their relationship with as few alterations as possible.

To devote full concentration to this delicate matter, he'd have to put off his own search for a spouse. But since he'd prefer to have Caragh's assistance in that, and she would be unable to focus on his affairs until her troublesome sister was safely riveted, he'd most likely have to wait on that anyway.

Besides, he was in no hurry to get leg-shackled. Unlike a maiden who needed to marry in her tender years, he was just coming into his prime. And as long as his refurbished fortunes, if not his looks, remained intact, he thought sardonically, there would be no shortage of eager aspirants to the honor of becoming his wife.

After subjecting his catalog of unmarried friends to a rapid mental review, he set off through the ballroom to hunt down the most likely contenders. To his satisfaction, he spied the man at the head of his list, Lord Alden Russell, in conversation with their hostess.

Waiting until Russell extricated himself from that garrulous lady, he waved his friend over.

"Quentin, well-met!" Alden said as he approached. "Have a glass of champagne with me in honor of my escaping Lady Cavendish without promising her a dance!"

"Since it's that lady's champagne, it hardly seems fitting," he said, grinning. "Besides, I'm about to entreat you about something myself."

"Please, no accompanying you to inspect some weed-infested acreage in the wilds of the country!"

"It was just outside York and the inn where we stayed had, as I remember, a very superior claret," Quentin countered. "But this request should be a pleasure. Are you acquainted with Miss Sudley?"

Alden groaned. "Please don't tell me you need me to dance with some squinty-eyed ape-leader dear to the heart of your sainted mother! Perhaps I should throw myself on our hostess's tender mercies after all."

"She's hardly an ape-leader," he assured Alden, accepting the glass his friend snagged for him from a passing servant. "Miss Sudley is the lady in green—dancing over there."

Alden lifted his quizzing glass in the direction Quentin indicated. After subjecting Caragh to a head-to-toe inspection, he let his gaze linger, as Sefton's had, upon her bosom.

"My apologies for maligning you," he said, turning back to Quentin with a grin. "I'd be happy to dance *that* little lady into a dark corner."

Although Quentin had often traded such assessing remarks with his friends, with Caragh the female being assessed, he found Alden's comment unexpectedly irritating. "That *little lady*," he replied rather stiffly, his enthusiasm for Alden as a potential suitor dimming, "is a good friend of mine."

Alden's grin widened. "Wouldn't mind making her a good friend of *mine*—that is, if you've not already put your bid in?"

"My 'bid?' This ain't the Cyprian's Ball," Quentin replied, his irritation increasing. "Miss Sudley is a lady, you'll remember."

"And a particular friend, you said? Meant no disrespect, as you should know." He cocked an eyebrow and studied Quentin. "Sure you haven't an interest there yourself?"

"Only in seeing that, as she is newly come to London, she

meets gentlemen of the better sort. Though I begin to doubt my wisdom in including you in that number,'' he added.

"Quentin, you wound me!'' Alden protested, clapping a hand to his heart. "I'm the soul of gentility.''

"See that you demonstrate it. Miss Sudley, you might remember, is my neighbor at Thornwhistle. I imagine you've heard me speak admiringly of her on any number of occasions. An intelligent and charming girl.''

"Then I should be delighted to do the pretty. You'll introduce me?'' He placed a hand on Quentin's elbow and urged him forward.

By now Quentin was beginning to regret he'd approached Russell, but having come this far, he couldn't fob the man off without truly offending him. Reluctantly he allowed himself to be led onward. "I suppose so. But I must warn you to treat her...gently. She's had a rather agitating day, and for once does not have to chaperone her younger sister. I want her to enjoy the evening.''

Alden snapped his fingers. "Now I recall the name! *She's* the elder sister of the new blond Incomparable?'' He halted and subjected Caragh to another long look. "Lovely enough, though she can't hold a candle to the chit, which is why I didn't recognize her, I suppose. The duenna's night to play the belle, is it? Well, we shall just have to see that she does.''

Alden picked up his pace, angling for the edge of the ballroom floor where Caragh had just made her final curtsey. Quentin had no choice but to trot in his wake, already questioning the wisdom of what he'd just set in motion.

"Thank you, my lord, for a delightful dance,'' they heard her say to her partner as they approached.

Lord Sefton patted her hand. "'Tis me who should thank you, m'dear, for having the courage to allow such a heavyweight to guide you about the floor.''

Caragh laughed. "Nonsense! I've seen you in the field, my lord, and there's not a better rider to the hounds at any weight.

I'd not otherwise have allowed you to buy one of Sudley's best colts last spring.'' As she gazed up into her partner's face, she spied Quentin approaching, and a smile leapt to her lips.

"Coming to claim a dance, I hope, Lord Branson?''

A shaft of delighted gratification warmed him as he bowed to her. "Miss Sudley, Lord Sefton. I believe you know my friend, Sefton, but allow me to present him to the lady. Lord Alden Russell, Miss Sudley.''

Caragh murmured a polite greeting and curtseyed. While Russell's salute of her fingertips was entirely proper, Quentin felt he retained her hand a tad longer than necessary. And need he stand quite so close?

"I've been eager to meet you, Miss Sudley,'' Russell said. "Branson tells me you are a most accomplished lady—a fair Athena, able to train any horse to bridle.''

Sefton shook his head approvingly. "Indeed. The Sudley stables breed the best hunters in England!''

"Hardly the 'gray-eyed Athena,''' she said, looking at Alden with heightened interest. "You are a student of the classics, Lord Russell?''

He shook his head, an engaging smile on his lips. "Not a scholar of your father's caliber, I fear.''

"Fair Athena'' indeed, Quentin thought, throwing Russell a disgusted look. "Miss Sudley inherited her grandfather's eye for horseflesh,'' he said, determined to fix the conversation in more prosaic channels. "In the course of stocking my properties, I've inspected the best animals on the market, from Devon to Yorkshire to Coke's at Norfolk, and I've seldom seen a farm produce such consistently superior beasts.''

"The colt I purchased has certainly proved superior, m'dear. I hunt with three mounts now—switch from one to another to keep 'em from tiring, carrying my twenty stone over a good long chase! Though that horse of yours has such heart and speed, I swear he'd go the distance and none the worse for it—not that I mean to let him, of course. Dash it, I'll offer you a thousand guineas if you'll promise to sell me another come spring.''

''A generous offer, my lord, but I'm afraid all the foals for this spring are already bespoken.''

''You must promise me one next year, then. Truly, you should persuade your papa to expand your operation. You've a steady customer in me, and I daresay I know a dozen more who'd leap at the chance to purchase Sudley stock.''

Caragh shook her head regretfully. ''Though I've often dreamed of doing so, I fear we haven't sufficient pasturage at Sudley to expand.''

''Perhaps Sudley should buy more acreage, ma'am,'' Russell said. ''It so happens that I have a farm that might be suitable—prime fields, but rather at a distance from my other holdings. Since the tenant chose to emigrate to the Americas when the lease ran out, I've decided to sell it rather than seek a new occupant. I should be happy to offer it to your father— and gain myself such a delightful new neighbor.''

To Quentin's irritation, Russell accompanied that speech with a beguiling smile that caused Caragh, innocent of dalliance as she was, to blush. ''Thank you, my lord. I shall certainly keep the possibility in mind.''

As the orchestra tuned up, couples filtered past them to the floor. ''If I might have the honor of the next dance, Miss Sudley?'' Russell asked.

Did Quentin only imagine her directing a brief, longing glance toward *him?* After that short pause, she replied, ''I'd be delighted, sir.''

As Russell walked past him to claim her, Quentin stayed him with a hand. ''She's an innocent, remember,'' he murmured in Alden's ear. ''Rein in the flirtation.''

''I'll be artless as an altar boy,'' Russell promised, a gleam in his eye as he pulled free and offered Caragh his hand.

Damn, it would turn out to be a waltz Alden had purloined.

Disgruntled more than he wished to admit, Quentin could do little but remain at the edge of the floor making desultory conversation with Lord Sefton, who soon sought out a more encouraging audience.

Watching Caragh dance with Russell, Quentin found himself noticing small details he'd never particularly noted before. Such as how a man was permitted to clasp his partner so closely, 'twas virtually an embrace. That when danced energetically—and Russell was certainly energetic—the waltz's spiral patterns allowed a man to spin his lady in circles dizzying enough that she cried out in mingled alarm and exhilaration, while her breasts, temptingly displayed by the low décolletage of her gown, rose and fell rapidly with exertion.

Gritting his teeth, he looked away from the sight. Russell couldn't seduce her in a single dance, after all. Quentin would do better to stop watching their progress around the floor like a hound held back from the hunt and concentrate on conjuring up other, more suitable prospects for Caragh.

Though he tried to keep his mind on that important matter, his glance strayed with lamentable frequency back to the floor. Alden's gaze seemed to be focused where it should be, on Caragh's *face*. Still—wasn't he clasping her rather *too* closely, even for the waltz? And continually inclining his lips to her ear, as if murmuring some intimacy?

Two actions in which Quentin could not permit himself to indulge, he thought with some indignation.

He took a deep breath and tried to soothe away his annoyance. Just because he must restrain himself around her, surely he wasn't…jealous of Alden's ability to act freely.

He had about succeeded in calming himself when the dance ended. However, rather than escorting Caragh back to where he stood waiting, Alden took her elbow and began to walk her away from Quentin.

Puzzled, Quentin stared for a moment at their retreating figures before an explanation occurred. That blackguard better not be attempting to take her out into the garden! With a flash of indignation, he sprinted after them.

Instead of guiding Caragh to the tall glass doors leading onto the balcony, though, Alden turned aside and disappeared with her into the hallway.

A deserted anteroom would be just as bad as the shadowy garden, Quentin thought grimly, as he dodged through the crowd after them. Before his temper heated any further, though, he burst into the hall—and saw they were still strolling down the passageway.

As he quickly narrowed the distance between them, Alden glanced over his shoulder. The amused twitch of his friend's lips told Quentin he wasn't at all surprised to find him in rapid pursuit.

"You seem in a bit of a hurry, Quent," he drawled. "Hunting someone?"

"We were about to partake of some refreshment," Caragh said. "Would you join us?"

"I'm sure he would," Alden said. "Branson does like to remain close to his *friends*."

"My pleasure, Miss Sudley," Quentin replied, throwing Alden an annoyed glance over Caragh's head.

After tussling over who would procure Caragh champagne and a plate of fine slivered ham, the threesome moved to a small table. "Miss Sudley, you must tell me more about the horses you raise—before I claim my second waltz," Russell said.

"Unfair," Quentin found himself objecting. "I've not yet had the pleasure of even one waltz with Miss Sudley."

Caragh looked up at him, her eyes widening with surprise and her cheeks turning pink. "I should be happy to waltz with you, Lord Branson."

Then he remembered the implications: Caragh in his arms, her soft brown ringlets teasing his chin, her rounded curves almost but not quite touching him. The mere idea of holding her that close tightened his body and made his senses swim. Which was exactly why, he belatedly recalled, he'd meant to avoid waltzing with her!

But he couldn't fob her off now, leaving the field to Russell...or disappoint the eager anticipation he read in those great hazel eyes.

Take her home, he decided. If he could persuade her to leave now, he could avoid both the danger of waltzing with her himself and the threat inherent in allowing Russell to do so.

"But how thoughtless of me!" he exclaimed. "I should rather have asked if you were feeling up to it. Though you've done an excellent job of masking it, with the heat and candle smoke so thick in here, your head must be paining you more than ever. Allow me to escort you home instead. I know you must be anxious to check on your aunt and your sister." Quentin turned to Alden. "Miss Sudley's relations were a trifle...indisposed this evening."

Even as imperative as it was to part her from Alden, Quentin felt guilty for the worry that immediately shadowed her eyes.

"Perhaps you are right," she conceded. "I do still have the headache a little, and I should like to check on...my relations."

"Allow me to escort you," Alden interposed quickly. "You could console me for the loss of that second waltz by giving us an opportunity to become better acquainted. I'm entirely trustworthy, as Branson will attest! You can rely on me to get you home safely."

Over Caragh's head, Russell gave him a disingenuous smile. Quentin felt a sudden urge to slap it off his erstwhile friend's lips.

"I'm sure I can," Caragh was replying, "but I'm afraid Ailis would not be able to receive you tonight. Tomorrow, however, if you wish to call, I trust she will—"

"Miss Sudley, when I call, it won't be to meet your sister," Russell interrupted softly.

Lips still parted, Caragh stared at Alden, confusion on her face until the import of Russell's words finally registered. Once again her face colored and she lowered her eyes, stuttering some inarticulate reply.

Quentin had to grudgingly concede his friend some credit for making Caragh, accustomed to being relegated into the background by her sister's dazzling beauty, realize that a man might find her desirable, not just as a conduit to her sister, but in her own right.

Credit he might give, but not to the point that he'd allow Alden the prize of escorting her home. "Kind of you, Russell, but there's no need for you to go out of your way. I'm concerned myself about Lady Catherine, who is a dear friend. As I'd planned to stop in to check on her in any event, I will escort Miss Sudley."

Once again, Alden's sardonic grin told him his friend didn't believe a syllable of his excuse for dispensing with Alden's presence. "Based on your greater acquaintance with the ladies, Branson, I will relinquish my claim—this time. Miss Sudley, I look forward to becoming as great an intimate of...your *family* as my Lord Branson."

With a flourish, he caught Caragh's hand and brought it to his lips. "You may count on me to call tomorrow, ma'am. Quent—many thanks for your diligent efforts on my behalf." He executed a cocky bow and walked away.

"Ass," Quentin muttered. "Ask," he repeated hastily as Caragh looked over. "Must ask the butler for your cloak. Shall we go?"

Her gaze lingered on him a moment as if she, too, found his behavior odd, but he was thankful that she did not take him to task for it.

"Very well," she murmured. "I must admit, I am rather weary. I shall be very happy to fall into my bed."

Oh, that I might fall there with her. The thought escaped before he could quell it. Perspiration breaking out on his brow, Quentin seized Caragh's elbow and hurried her down the hall to the entrance, where he hailed the butler and requested their wraps.

It was more than past time to see his ''good friend'' safely home.

CHAPTER SEVEN

BUT ONCE they'd entered the carriage for the ride back to Lady Catherine's, the anxiety he saw in her eyes once again held his physical impulses in check.

"You fear Ailis will still be angry?"

Caragh sighed. "Yes. I've never seen her in such a temper. She's grown ever more…independent-minded since we've arrived in London. I increasingly worry that at some point, she will cease to pay even a modicum of attention to my advice and do something truly rash. And if she should, with the interested gaze of the ton fixed on her, there will be no hiding it or explaining it away, as I might to our friends and neighbors back at Sudley."

"Very likely she shall do nothing more rash than indulge herself in a good cry," Quentin said, trying to set Caragh's mind at ease and hoping his words proved true. "In any event, should you need me to contain any potential damage, I hope you know you have only to ask."

She gave him a tremulous smile. "Truly, Quent, I don't know what I should do without you!" Gazing up at him with tear-sheened eyes, she squeezed his hand.

An instant of her touch reheated all his simmering desire. Neither did he know how he could do without her—without the soft, trembling lips that, with just a slight downward bend of his head, he might claim. Without caressing the curves he knew lay concealed beneath her cloak, without turning the troubled shudder of her sigh into agitation of quite another sort.

Surely she must be as aware as he of currents flashing between them! As if responding to his thought, her eyelids fluttered shut and she leaned those seductive, barely parted lips closer.

Even as his rational mind screamed at him to tear himself out of the magnetic pull she exerted, he inclined toward her, until he could feel the warmth of her breath on his own lips—

With a jolt, the vehicle stopped, jerking him away from her. The rush of cold air admitted as the carriage door was opened swept him back to sanity.

With more force than he'd intended, he pushed Caragh toward the open door. After a shocked second of immobility, during which he couldn't seem to summon a word of explanation or apology, she scrambled off the seat, leaving him gazing into frigid night air.

Damn and blast! he swore silently, his hands shaking as he gathered his hat and cane to follow her. If he couldn't manage to maintain better control over himself than this, he *was* going to ruin everything.

Furious with himself, he remained a few prudent paces behind her as they mounted the entry stairs. Better bid her good night immediately, before midnight and moonlight led him into doing something even more foolish.

When Evers met them at the threshold, he waved away the butler's offer to relieve him of his coat and hat. And for the first time since the...he couldn't come up with a word to adequately describe the madness that had seized him back in the carriage, Caragh looked at him.

Her face seemed as serene as ever, though the light from the hallway sconces was too dim for him to be certain.

"Will you not stay while I see about Ailis and Aunt Kitty?" she asked, her voice calm and unrevealing.

"No. Upon reflection, both ladies are probably already asleep. Don't disturb them on my account."

He should apologize, and he would—later. In his still-muddled state of mind, he couldn't think how to do so without

opening the way for a discussion of the whole incident, something he was too fog-brained to handle now.

"Very well," she replied after a slight pause. "I'll bid you
good night, then."

"I must go out of town again tomorrow, but expect to be
back by nightfall, so if you have need of...anything, send me
a note. I will call as soon as I return." He swept her a bow.
"Good night, Caragh."

She stared at him another long moment, her expression un-
readable, and then dipped a curtsey. "My lord. Thank you for
your escort, and may you have a safe journey."

HAVING TURNED DOWN the footman's offer to find him a
hackney, Quentin paced off into the chilly night. A brisk walk
would steady his nerves and help him sort out how to end,
once and for all, this irrational behavior.

If he had been able to practice the years of self-discipline
necessary to restore his fortunes, surely he could manage the
far simpler task of controlling his physical appetites!

Except that thus far, it had not proved all that simple. Since
he knew he possessed willpower in abundance, it appeared he
must be consistently underestimating the strength of Caragh's
allure.

That troubling conclusion stopped him in mid-stride.

If his response to her was proving impossible to prevent
and very difficult to control, perhaps remaining platonic
friends was not so wise a policy after all.

A flare of excitement flashed up from deep within him at
the prospect of allowing his frustrated impulses free rein.
Ah—to be able to touch her, taste her, follow this fascination
as far as it took them!

But she was not a Cyprian with whom he could amicably
part once the initial excitement of an affair faded, he reminded himself. Touching Caragh meant springing the trap of
wedlock.

Which might be a joyous bond, if passion cooled from its first, fast boil to a permanent simmer while leaving every other facet of their relationship unchanged. But if, after the initial fever of lust chilled, they were confronted with the wreckage of a friendship, wedlock would become a prison of life-long regret.

Was the gamble worth the risk? For a moment Quentin teetered on the edge, enchanted by the prospect of what might be, daunted by the threat of what might be destroyed were he to act on his desires.

In the end, once again he could not quite persuade himself to chance losing the precious and familiar by taking that bold, irreversible leap.

Better instead, he decided, to first give one more go to finding a suitable suitor for Caragh—someone, he thought, recalling with resentment Alden's subtle digs, less insinuating than Russell about Quentin's interest in Caragh and more cognizant of the privilege Quentin was offering in allowing him to court her.

Someone, too, that he could stomach seeing dance with and woo and touch Caragh as he himself could not.

Quentin couldn't at this moment envision such a man.

But enough reflection for one night. Tomorrow, while on the road to and from his property, with his mind and body freed from the witchery Caragh's presence seemed to work on him, he would think further about the matter.

Feeling suddenly weary, he summoned a link boy to find him a hackney. Yes, tomorrow he'd be able to make sensible, responsible decisions that would keep the treasure of their friendship undamaged. But just for tonight, as he drifted to sleep, he would allow himself to remember again the thrill of her lips almost touching his while her sweet honeysuckle scent filled his head.

HER EMOTIONS and impulses still in turmoil, Caragh silently watched Quentin walk out. After dismissing Evans and the footmen, she went into the salon, poured herself a glass of port and took it up to her chamber.

Dispensing with her maid as soon as the girl had assisted her into her night rail, Caragh dropped wearily into the wing chair before the fireplace. A few sips of the fortified wine warmed her throat but could not banish the chill in her heart. Telling herself sternly that she would not weep, she rested her head in her hands.

For a while she'd almost let herself hope. There'd been between them the same simmering urgency she always felt, but tonight Quentin seemed acutely aware of it as well. For all that he'd introduced her to Lord Russell, he'd loitered close by, watching them, and she was certain, had whisked her away from the party to avoid letting his friend waltz with her. And then in the hackney—just when she was certain Quentin would kiss her at last, he'd brusquely pushed her away.

As if revolted by her behavior and, most likely, his own.

She might as well face the fact squarely. Quentin Burke would not be drawn against his will into acting on his attraction to her. And he had a stronger will than any man she knew.

Are you sure? a little voice asked. Could she force the matter, exploit the heat flaring between them to push him beyond control?

Seductive as the idea was, after brief consideration she dismissed it. Given his behavior tonight—and she had no reason to believe his reactions were likely to change—should she succeed in seducing him, he wouldn't thank her for it. No, he'd likely be even more revolted than he'd seemed tonight—and angry with her besides, for breaking her word and tricking him into something he didn't want. Rather than gain a lover, she might very well destroy what remained of their friendship.

Friendship. With what she really wanted just out of reach, the word had a bitter, almost taunting resonance. Did Quentin's friendship mean enough that she was willing to endure being with him, longing for so much more than he was willing to offer?

She took another sip of the wine, considering. But the ache of wanting him and the ache of losing him were so intertwined, she gave up trying to decide which would be worse. She was too weary and disheartened, and besides, she had other problems to face.

She should tiptoe in and check on Ailis. Aunt Kitty must be asleep already, else she would have left word for Caragh to come up when she returned and relate every detail of the party she'd missed. Although her sister might be sleeping also, Caragh could at least gauge her current mood by seeing if her door was still locked.

She finished the last warming sip of port and fetched her wrapper. Quietly she slipped from her chamber and walked down the hall to her sister's door.

The latch, when she tried it, was still locked fast. She hesitated, but as she could see no light emanating from beneath the heavy oak panel, she decided not to call out her sister's name.

Ailis had evidently gone to sleep still nursing her anger, so there was no point rousing her now. Perhaps, Caragh thought without much conviction as she returned to her own chamber, by tomorrow morning, after a refreshing night's sleep, her sister might be more reasonable.

She herself slept poorly, disturbed alternately by dreams of an angry Ailis pelting her with paint jars and an aloof Quentin avoiding her. Soon after dawn she gave up the attempt and summoned a startled maid to help her dress.

Annie, the girl her aunt had assigned to serve both sisters, confided as she helped Caragh into her morning gown that Miss Ailis had remained in her room all evening, refusing to grant admittance to anyone, even the kitchen maid who brought up her supper tray.

Caragh descended to the breakfast parlor where, owing to the early hour, she was able to dawdle over tea and buttered toast in blessed solitude. Her head still hurt, her heart still ached, and she really would prefer not to have to deal with another of Ailis's tantrums.

But delaying the confrontation would only wind her nerves tighter. After lingering in the library until the hour was sufficiently advanced, contemplating possible ways to reason or bribe or charm Ailis out of her temper, she squared her shoulders and purposefully mounted the stairs to her sister's room.

The latch, when she tried it, was still locked tight.

Irritation stirred. 'Twas more than time for her sister to stop acting like a selfish, spoiled child who considered only her own wishes and needs. Ailis must start recognizing the realities of the society in which they lived and realize that her conduct affected not only her own position, but Caragh's and Aunt Kitty's as well.

She rapped sharply on the door. "Ailis, it's Caragh. Open the door, please! I'll ring for your chocolate and we can talk."

She waited, but neither a reply, nor the soft pad of approaching footsteps answered her demand.

She knocked again, harder. "Ailis, wake up! If you wish to be ready for your lesson, you must rise now. Be quick about it and we might even be able to arrive early. While you prepare, we can discuss that...other matter like calm and rational beings."

Still no response. Anger rising, she pounded on the oaken panel until she felt certain even a heavily-sleeping Ailis could not possibly ignore the ruckus. "Ailis, open the door now!"

But when the echo of her rapping died away moments later, she was left with nothing more than raw knuckles and a swiftly rising sense of grievance. "Very well, Ailis," she said to the stubbornly closed portal. "I'm going to fetch the housekeeper's keys. Whether you wish it or no, talk we must, and we will do so *now*."

Caragh stomped away. By the time she'd tracked down the housekeeper and borrowed her keys—an easy task, as that lady was more than happy to be spared the risky job of disturbing the tempestuous beauty—her anger was tempered with a niggle of worry.

Surely Ailis hadn't become so incensed that she'd done herself a mischief? No, 'twas nonsensical, Caragh reassured herself, damping down a sudden spiral of fear. More likely she'd open the door to find nothing more alarming than a roomful of splintered crockery.

Despite that soothing thought, her fingers trembled as she turned the heavy key in the lock. "Ailis, I regret having to invade your privacy," she called out as she walked across the threshold, "but you've left me no…"

As Caragh glanced around the chamber, her heart leapt in her chest and the rest of her words were washed from her lips, as if by water spilled over newly-inked parchment.

The heavy window curtains were still drawn, leaving the chamber dimly lit. But even in the shadowy half light, Caragh could see the room was neat as a nun's cell, the assortment of painting supplies that normally cluttered the dressers and tabletops vanished. The bed linens were drawn up and tucked in, appearing already made up for the day…or never slept in the previous night.

Propped against the pristine pillows reposed a note in her sister's scrawling hand, addressed to Caragh.

CHAPTER EIGHT

HER HEART POUNDING in cadence with her throbbing head, Caragh tore open the folded piece of vellum and scanned it. The message was predictably brief.

> Caragh, I am off to do what I must. I shall be taken care of, so don't worry.
>
> A

Her first shock giving way to a sick numbness, Caragh drew open the drapes and methodically surveyed the room.

Ailis must have left sometime the previous evening. Never concerned about tidying up after herself, Ailis would not have smoothed the bed linens had she rested even briefly.

As Caragh expected, the wooden chest in which her sister transported her art supplies was gone, along with all the brushes, paints, oils, and varnishes that filled it. Were she embarking on a journey of any length, Ailis would sooner leave naked than without her paints.

Next Caragh threw open the clothes press. Missing were the old gowns her sister had brought with her from Sudley, as well as her new day and afternoon gowns and her riding habit. Missing also were her warmest pelisse, an assortment of kid half-boots and her sturdy walking shoes.

Nearly all the dinner and evening garments still hung in isolated splendor to one side of the half-empty wardrobe, the crystal beading on the gown nearest her winking in the dim light like a mocking eye.

Caragh closed the door on it and walked over to the bureau.

A few spangled scarves and some mismatched gloves lay scattered like driftwood at ebb tide on the bleached wood of the empty drawers that had previously been stuffed with her sister's garments.

Her last hope that her sister's flight might have been an impulsive, short-lived exercise in pique expired. Ailis had taken all the belongings she needed to live a life outside society—permanently.

As that dismaying conclusion shocked through her, on legs gone suddenly rubbery, Caragh sank into the chair beside the untouched bed. Choking down the nauseating panic rising in her throat, she seized her sister's note and read it again.

Going to do what I must... Which would mean painting without restrictions, of course. *I will be taken care of...*

Smoldering anger revived to displace the panic. Caragh knew of only one person likely to "take care of" her sister while allowing her artistic bent free rein. That notable rake and patron of the arts, Holden Freemont.

Caragh leapt up, her momentary weakness banished in a swell of grim determination. Her most urgent task was to trace her sister and drag her back home quickly, before word of her disappearance leaked out. Whether or not to press Ailis to continue with their original plan of finding the girl a husband was a decision that could wait until her sister was recovered, though Caragh's first inclination was to give up what increasingly seemed to be a nearly impossible, and certainly thankless, endeavor and take the girl back to Sudley.

But first, she owed it to Aunt Kitty to find Ailis before her sister's typically heedless and self-absorbed action not only ruined the girl's reputation, but humiliated her innocent aunt as well.

That Ailis had obviously thought nothing of repaying all Caragh's efforts on her behalf with the worst sort of scandal cut deeply, but she damped down the hurt to be dealt with later. Squelched too were the guilty recriminations already whispering at her that somehow she should have foreseen this…that she had obviously been too indulgent and should, over the years Ailis had been in her charge, have worked harder to mold her sister's headstrong nature to conform to their society's standards.

Briskly she exited the room and relocked it. She'd likely have a lifetime to regret the path that had brought her to this moment. She must focus now on finding Ailis before anyone in the household discovered she'd fled.

Setting her mind to work on that problem, she paced back to her chamber, sending a passing footman to summon Annie and carry a message to the stables.

A pity Quentin was out of town, she thought as she pulled her riding habit from the wardrobe. His discretion was unquestioned and his assistance would certainly have proved useful. But with every moment carrying her sister farther from London and closer to a scandal that could ruin them all, Caragh didn't dare await his return.

By the time the maid knocked at her door, she'd concocted a plausible, and partially truthful, story. "Annie, help me into this habit, please."

"Of course, miss." The maid hurried over to attack a row of tiny buttons. "Beggin' your pardon! If'n I'd a knowed you was to ride, I woulda had the habit ready."

"'Tis my fault. I, ah, neglected to mention earlier that Lord Branson requested my assistance at his new estate outside London." Quentin *had* said he'd appreciate her advice on the choice of a new manager there—sometime.

"Don't worry," Caragh added hastily to quell the look of distress coming over the girl's face, "I know carriage travel makes you queasy, and in any event, 'tis so slow that I prefer to ride there." Also true—though his new estate was not her destination today. "I'll take a groom, so you may remain comfortably here in London."

"Why, that be right kind of ye, miss! Are ye sure ye'll not be needin' me?"

The fewer who observed this little errand, the better, Caragh thought. "No, I shall be perfectly fine. Rob will watch out for me."

The buttons accomplished, Annie went to fetch the riding hat while Caragh pulled on her boots and gloves. "I'm not sure how long I shall be away," she continued. "Please explain to Lady Catherine when she wakes that since I'll have Rob's escort, and probably Lord Branson's as well for the return journey, she needn't worry if I'm late."

"Yes, miss, I'll tell her when she rises."

"And Annie, I've had...communication with Miss Ailis this morning." Which she had, in a manner of speaking. "She's not...recovered from her agitation, so I've relocked her door and ask you to insure that the household leaves the room undisturbed until my return."

"But what of meals, miss? She had no dinner last night."

"When my sister takes a notion in her head, eating loses all importance."

Annie looked dubious, but nodded her compliance. "Very well, miss. I'll have Evers inform the household."

Nodding a dismissal, Caragh gathered up her crop and strode from the chamber. Though she was nearly certain Holden Freemont was a party to her sister's flight, she should first make sure. So, although propriety dictated that a single lady never called upon a gentleman, as she ran lightly down the stairs, she decided to go first to Lord Freemont's townhouse. If he had indeed run off with Ailis, she thought acerbically, the small detail of Caragh's paying him a call unchaperoned would be more than lost in the furor over that much larger scandal.

As she exited the house, she found her mare and Rob the groom awaiting her at the foot of the entry stairs. Bidding the man to follow her, she set off immediately.

As she rode that short distance, her mind flitted though a tangled undergrowth of possibilities like a mouse pursued by a hawk. If Freemont *had* gone off with her sister, were they headed to Gretna Green? Surely even a rake of Lord Freemont's ilk wasn't so lost to decency as to aid a gently-born maiden to flee her home without intending to marry her.

He'd not flinched from such a thing before, she recalled. But that girl was a member of a rather obscure family. Though the ton accorded its privileged males much more leeway than the females, surely if Freemont were to compromise one of Society's newest Diamonds and then not marry her, he would find himself as ostracized by the ton as her sister.

The scandal would be bad enough even if they wed over the anvil. However, much as she loathed the idea of calling such a scoundrel "brother," the consequences to the whole family if the two did not wed were so dire that for the present, Caragh didn't wish to even contemplate them.

Moments later, they arrived before Lord Freemont's house on Mount Street. Now to bluster her way in. Taking a deep breath, Caragh dismounted and handed the reins to her groom, who went wooden-faced once he realized at whose dwelling they'd stopped—and what his mistress meant to do.

She turned and walked purposefully up the entry steps, the disapproving stare of her groom burning into her back. No matter how this turned out, she thought with a sigh, he'd have quite a tale tonight with which to regale the residents below stairs.

Having been mistress of a large estate for ten years, Caragh soon overcame the initial reticence of Freemont's butler to part with any information concerning his master. A few moments later she walked back out on shaking knees, having confirmed that Holden Freemont had indeed left London in his traveling chaise the evening previous. Bound not for Scotland, or so he'd told the servant, but for his estate in the country.

Which meant ruination for them all, if Ailis had in fact left for *Berkshire* in Freemont's company. Once remounted, Caragh sat with the reins slack, dread a cold lump in her gut as she fought down a paralyzing sense of helplessness and forced herself to concentrate on determining what she should do next.

Would Ailis have journeyed with the viscount, even after determining he had no intention of marrying her?

For several moments Caragh sat pondering the question, eventually concluding with chagrin that, tempted by the freedom to paint without restrictions and a strong infatuation for the handsome aristocrat, her sister would probably not be overly upset to discover that Freemont's destination was not Gretna. Ailis had ever protested she had no interest in marrying.

Still, the viscount, though wild, was older and more knowledgeable than her heedless sister. Upon further reflection, Caragh simply could not believe that Freemont would throw away his own standing in the ton to run off with her sister without intending marriage.

Perhaps, she tried to rally herself, Ailis had warned Freemont that her family was going to forbid her to see him, prompting the viscount to suggest they elope. Wishing to delay any pursuers who might seek to stop them before the couple could reach Gretna and be safely wed, he might have deliberately given his butler erroneous information.

Caragh could only hope 'twas so. Armed with that hope and the detailed description of Lord Freemont's carriage she'd bullied out of a footman, she decided to ride out of London and check for news of the fugitives at the first few posting stops along the Great North Road.

A crested, red-lacquered coach with its wheels picked out in yellow should be notable enough that some tollgate keeper or posting-inn groom would remember it.

"Miss, which direction do ye wish to ride? The horses be gettin' restless."

"North, Rob," she replied, wheeling her mount around. "We ride north."

Her goal was Islington, first stop on the road toward Gretna. The nature of her quest making it impractical to withhold the information any longer, during the ride there Caragh confided to the groom the barest outline of what she suspected. The shock and censure she'd steeled herself to see did indeed flash through his eyes. But Rob made a quick recovery, generously offering to do anything he could to help her recover her missing sister.

Taking him up on that pledge, as they neared the town, Caragh sent Rob to canvass the establishments on the left while she stopped at those on the right. Between them, they questioned landlords and stable boys at every inn and hostelry along the main road. But even with a small coin as a prod to the memory, no one recalled seeing a coach matching the description they gave.

Thanking heaven that they had set out early, with the stoic groom in her wake, she pressed on toward Barnet, stopping now at each of the villages along the way. By the time they reached this second major junction, Freemont should certainly have needed to change horses.

Whatever hope she still cherished of catching up with a sister bent on a runaway marriage slowly died as, one by one, they interviewed the landlords and stable masters of all the posting inns around Barnet. Not a single one recalled servicing such a vehicle or speaking with its commanding, aristocratic ebony-haired owner.

Freemont might have avoided stopping at a public inn by changing horses at the home of some friend along the route, but such a possibility was slim, and she knew it.

In any event, Caragh did not have sufficient funds, baggage or retinue to continue pursuing the fugitives up the Great North Road. If she wished to check the main road to Berkshire and still return to London before nightfall, she would have to turn back south now.

HOURS LATER, a weary, heartsick Caragh rode back into London. Her exploration along the road to Berkshire had been as fruitless as her trek north. It seemed that her sister and Freemont, if she indeed had left the city in his company, had taken neither route.

Fear, worry and anger roiled queasily in her empty stomach. Though she'd urged Rob to fortify himself with meat pies and ale at several of their stops, she herself had been able to stomach only some strong, hot tea. Especially since, with afternoon waning, she'd been forced to turn their horses once again back toward the city. Though she knew better than to commit the folly of continuing to search until nightfall caught them alone and unprotected along the London road, it went against every feeling and instinct for Caragh to return to Aunt Kitty's with her sister's whereabouts still unknown.

But as she jolted toward Mayfair on the last of the ill-gaited job horses they'd hired that day, a new inspiration revived her flagging spirits. Calling Rob to follow, with a last, desperate surge of hope she urged the placid beast to a trot and headed east toward the City.

Maximilian Frank's studio was located on the top floor of a building near Covent Garden. Keen as her sister was about her lessons, there was a chance that, even if Ailis had peremptorily decided to leave the city, she would have somehow contacted her mentor to let him know her plans. And if she had, Caragh prayed she might have informed the artist where she meant to go—and with whom.

Looking startled and a bit embarrassed, Frank's maid ushered Caragh to the small downstairs parlor. Her master was working and could not at the moment be disturbed, the girl said, resisting Caragh's demand that she be allowed to speak with the artist at once.

Not until Caragh threatened to bypass the girl and go up unannounced did the maid finally concede to allow Caragh to follow her, muttering darkly that Mr. Frank was going to be that put out. Reaching the top-floor studio, she banged on the door, announcing in strident tones that Miss Sudley was without and insisted on speaking with him *immediately*.

After a long pause, during which the maid threw Caragh a resentful glance, the door finally opened. Pressing her last coin into the maid's hand, which brightened the girl's face considerably, Caragh walked past her into the studio.

Clad in a velvet dressing gown, his hair in disarray, the artist surveyed her with a glance that was half-irritated, half-amused. "Miss Sudley? To what do I owe the honor of this...unexpected visit?"

On a divan half-hidden behind a screen adjacent to the easel at the center of the studio lounged a very beautiful and nearly naked woman. Her cheeks heating, Caragh realized just what sort of work had been in progress.

Refusing to let embarrassment hinder her, she said, "Mr. Frank, I apologize for bursting in upon you in so unmannerly a fashion, but the matter is urgent. May...may I speak with you in private, sir?"

The maestro's thin lips quirked in a smile. "Since I've already been...interrupted, I suppose you may. Florrie, fetch more wine, won't you, love? This shall take but a moment."

In a languid uncurling of limbs, the girl rose, arranging about her a diaphanous wrap that did little to conceal charms the artist was still observing with obvious appreciation. Seeming fully conscious of the effect she was having on half her audience, the girl glided over to them, letting her body brush against Mr. Frank as she passed. She tossed a dismissive sniff in Caragh's direction before she exited, as if to imply she had no worries that this mud-spattered, hollow-eyed aristocrat would distract her paramour for long.

After the beauty's departure, the artist at last focused on

Caragh. His bemused smile changed to a look of genuine concern.

"You seem upset, Miss Sudley. Please, take a chair. Can I offer you some refreshment?"

"No, thank you, I shall stay but a moment. I must question you on a matter of some delicacy, sir. I trust I can rely on your discretion?"

At his nod, she continued, "I...I am looking for my sister, Mr. Frank. She left my aunt's house sometime last evening and we have had no word of her since. I have reason to suspect she may have gone in the company of Lord Freemont. As you can imagine, it is imperative that I find her and bring her home as soon as possible."

"Did she leave you no indication of her intent?"

"There was a note, saying she was doing what she must and for me not to worry. As you can see, 'twas much too vague to be of any use in discovering her whereabouts. Would you happen to have any idea where she has gone?"

"As a matter of fact, I believe I do. That is, I was aware of your sister's ultimate plans, though I did not realize she intended to put them into effect this soon. Please cease worrying, ma'am! I'm sure your sister is quite well. Indeed, it was very bad of Ailis not to be more forthcoming, but if my suspicions are correct, you will find her not three streets from this very house. Where, you see, she has set up her own studio."

For a long moment, Caragh stood stunned. During this long day of searching and soul-searching, she had considered many possible explanations for her sister's disappearance—but never this. She could not have been more astounded if the artist had told her Ailis had decided to tread the boards at the nearby Theatre Royal.

"Her own studio?" she echoed, finding her voice at last. "But—why? How? How could she have arranged such a thing?"

Maximilian Frank shrugged. "Your sister is a painter of great talent, Miss Sudley. She told me her chief ambition is to make her living as an artist. I, for one, believe she can do so. For particulars of the actual arrangements, you'll have to ask Ailis, but I believe Holden helped her find a flat and negotiated the terms."

Worse and worse! "Lord Freemont is k-keeping her?" Caragh asked, barely able to choke out the words.

The artist raised an eyebrow. "As to that, I couldn't say. Why don't you talk directly with Ailis? Unless I'm much mistaken, I believe you will find her at 21 Mercer Street, top floor."

At that moment, the dark-haired model opened the door. In the sudden silence engendered by her reappearance, she walked back through the room, hands cupping a crystal decanter of wine. As she bypassed Caragh, she allowed the belt of her robe to slip, gifting the artist with a full view of her naked torso. "Don't be long," she murmured.

Frank licked his parted lips, his gaze riveted on the girl's hip-swaying progression. After watching her rearrange herself on the divan, he finally recalled Caragh's presence.

"You now know everything I do," he said, motioning Caragh to the door. "Mercer Street, top-floor flat. Now, if you'll excuse me, Miss Sudley?"

"Of course. Thank you, Mr. Frank, and I apologize again for disturbing you."

"No trouble, Miss Sudley. I can understand a sister's concern." His glance sympathetic, he paused to pat her hand. "You mustn't be too angry with Ailis, my dear. When her head is full of a project, she forgets everything else, a common failing among artists, I fear."

After an exchange of goodbyes, Caragh walked out, the door closing behind her practically before she cleared the threshold. Numbly she descended the staircase.

And she'd thought that Ailis running off to the countryside

was the worst thing that could happen! With a laugh that bordered on the hysterical, she almost wished her sister had left with Freemont. Better flight to the rural fastness of Berkshire than Ailis ensconced, probably with her lover at her side, right in the middle of London under the soon-to-be fascinated gaze of the ton.

Even worse than ruination in Society's censorious eyes would be Ailis's apparent intention to set herself up as an artist. Falling victim to a fatal passion could be understood, if still condemned. Betraying her birth and class by sinking to the level of a hired workman would be neither understood nor forgiven. If Mr. Frank's supposition were in fact true, Ailis would become an outcast shunned by all.

The social damage to the rest of her family would be almost as dire. Caragh uttered a groan. How was she to break the awful news to Aunt Kitty?

Though all she wished was to return to her chamber, lock the door, and pull the pillows over her aching head, she must first discover the truth of Mr. Frank's information. Mustering the last of her strength, she steeled herself to pay a call at Mercer Street.

CHAPTER NINE

TEN MINUTES LATER, Caragh stood before the door of a top-floor apartment, her stomach churning with a mixture of eagerness and dread. Feeling in her bones the ache of every mile she'd ridden this endless day, she knocked.

The door opened—to reveal a girl in the gray gown and mobcap of a maid. At least it wasn't Freemont, she thought, trying to quell a sudden lightheadedness as she released the breath she'd not realized she'd been holding. "Is...is your mistress Miss Ailis at home?"

"Who should I say is calling?"

So Ailis *was* here. Relief at finding her sister safe warred with the dread of realizing that the devastating scandal she had ridden all day in hopes of avoiding was now almost certain to overtake them. "Her s-sister," Caragh replied, her voice breathy as she struggled to get the word out. "But you needn't announce me. I'll show myself in."

Brushing past before the maid could protest, Caragh crossed the room, which contained a sofa and several armchairs buried under a quantity of boxes, to the door at the far side.

Hand on the latch, she paused briefly, squelching an hysterical bubble of laughter as she wondered what she could dredge up to say to the girl she'd nurtured and loved for years. The girl she'd discovered today she did not know at all.

Slowly she pushed open the door—to discover her missing sister within, arranging art supplies on shelves that lined one wall.

"Oh, Caragh, it's you," Ailis said, giving her a brief

glance. "Now isn't a good time to visit. I must get these paints organized so I can resume work tomorrow. Do you recall whether the order I placed for brown ochre was delivered last week? I can't seem to find it."

Her sister's tone was light, conversational—as if they'd parted only a few hours ago after a cozy tea. As if Caragh had been fully cognizant of Ailis's plans and location. As if she had not spent the whole of a very long day galloping around greater London, half out of her mind with worry over her sister's safety, reputation and future.

Fatigue disappeared, incinerated by a blistering rage that flamed up out of every weary pore. For a moment she was too incensed to speak.

"Well, don't just stand there," Ailis said, looking her way again. "Since you're here, do something useful. There's another box of paints on the workbench—be a dear and start unpacking it for me."

"Ailis, I didn't come here to help you unpack!"

"No?" her sister replied, too intent upon her task to spare Caragh another glance. "Then why did you come?"

"Because I've been in the saddle since near dawn this morning, riding over the best part of two counties trying to find you!"

This time when Ailis looked up she met Caragh's gaze, eyebrows raised quizzically. "How could you possibly think I would leave London? My teacher, my work, are here."

"If you'd been a bit more specific in your note, I would have been spared an anxious and exhausting day!"

"Did I truly not mention where I was bound? Well, I was a bit rushed when I wrote. How did you find me, then?"

"I finally thought to pay a call on Mr. Frank, who directed me here...to your—*studio?*" With a sweeping hand motion, Caragh indicated the open room with its wide, north-facing widows, shelves filled with painting supplies, rolls of canvas stacked against the wall and to one side, a screened-off area containing a bed and dresser.

Ailis drew herself up proudly. "Yes. *My* studio."

"Ailis, do you really intend on…living here?"

"Of course. I hadn't thought to move in just yet, but then you enacted me a Cheltenham tragedy over Holden and I just couldn't tolerate any more. Fortunately, I already had the key for the flat, but it took all evening to pack my clothing and most of today to have the furnishings delivered."

"Was taking this studio *Lord Freemont's* idea?"

"He did suggest it, but I had planned on something of the sort from the very beginning."

It took a moment for the import of that statement to register. As comprehension dawned, Caragh said slowly, "You…decided to do this before we ever left Sudley?"

Her sister nodded. "Why else do you think I agreed to come to London?"

So Ailis had allowed Caragh to draw in Aunt Kitty and organize a Season in which her sister had intended all along to participate only until her true goal could be realized. As that incredible conclusion struck her, Caragh's saddle-weakened muscles seemed no longer adequate to support her.

She tottered to a chair. "Ailis, how could you deceive us so?"

Her sister shrugged. "Would you have arranged for me to come here had I confided my true intentions?"

That question being rhetorical, Caragh addressed another pressing concern. "But how shall you live? You cannot think Papa will frank you."

Her sister gave an airy wave of the hand. "Oh, I shall be quite all right. Before we left, Papa authorized me to draw on his bank for a considerable sum."

"Papa sanctioned *this?* I don't believe it!"

"Well, he didn't precisely sanction it," Ailis replied, a mischievous twinkle in her eye. "You know how he is, Caragh.

I simply drew up the draft and presented it, telling him it was a matter of estate business. He signed it without looking up from his dictionary. I've already obtained one lucrative commission, with a promise of others. Holden has been a darling as well, helping me last night after I left the house and using his carriage to transport all my things. I don't know how I would have managed without him.''

"Has he offered you carte blanche?" Caragh asked bluntly.

"He offered, but I declined." Ailis smiled—a satisfied, cream-pot, knowing smile. "He *is* my lover, though, a thoroughly delightful one! Though so indiscreet, the rogue, that I imagine soon everyone will know:"

Ignoring Caragh's gasp, Ailis sighed and pronounced in theatrical tones, "I fear I am quite *ruined*—just as I intended. Now you will have to cease pestering me about a ton marriage and leave me alone to pursue my art."

Stung to the quick, Caragh retorted, "All I ever wanted was to secure your future so you might do as you wished!"

"Then you accomplished your aim, for I am doing so now."

Anger surged once again to the fore. "Ailis, did you even consider what doing—" she waved her hand to encompass the room "—this will mean to Aunt Kitty? To me?"

Ailis sniffed. "'Twill be a seven-day's wonder, no more. I expect Aunt Kitty can visit some friend or other until the gossip dies down. As for you, Caragh, I suggest you stop trying to live vicariously through the triumphant Season you've been pushing me toward since I was in short skirts and do something with your *own* life. And I don't mean tending Papa. Haven't you learned by now he will never notice or appreciate anything you do for him?"

Sentence by sentence, her sister's brutal, hurtful words piled like stones on her chest, making breathing difficult and response impossible, even had she been able to think of anything to say.

But Ailis didn't seem to expect a reply, for before Caragh could begin to dredge from her shattered emotions some sort of rebuttal, she continued, "It is rather late. If you aren't going to make yourself useful, you might as well go back to Aunt Kitty's and let me finish. I must begin work at first light."

Beyond words, almost beyond movement, Caragh stumbled to her feet and mutely walked to the door. Behind her, her sister had already resumed unpacking her boxes. "Higgins, put this tin of varnish on the shelf next to the oil. Careful, you clumsy girl! Don't drop it!"

A few moments later Caragh found herself back on the street with no memory of having descended the stairs. Rob met her at the door, his tired face lined with worry. "Did you find Miss Ailis? Is she all right?"

"Yes, Rob, she is here, and quite well. I'm afraid I dragged you about all day on a fool's errand."

Obviously not knowing how to respond to that, without comment Rob assisted her to remount. So drained was Caragh that she could barely support herself in the sidesaddle.

Yes, she'd been a fool, a pathetically blind, complacent fool! She would have laughed, had she not feared if she did, she would end by cackling uncontrollably—or dissolving into tears.

The stark fact was that Ailis was lost to Society—and her family—by her own choice. She'd made it clear she neither expected nor wanted anything further from them.

Somehow Caragh was going to have to break the news to their aunt—and figure out what to do with herself next.

After practically falling out of the saddle before Aunt Kitty's house, sustained by pride alone, Caragh steadied herself and walked up the stairs. Sore of heart and body after the day's ordeal, all she wished for was a long soak in a hot tub and the oblivion of sleep.

But she knew she must first speak to Aunt Kitty, slim as her reserves were for dealing with the hysterics her revelations were likely to produce in her excitable aunt. Having no idea where Ailis might have jouneyed today while in the process of moving her belongings, and therefore no idea who might have seen her in Holden's carriage, it was imperative that Caragh warn her aunt of the scandal about to descend upon them—*before* some saccharine-toned acquaintance delivered the news with sweetly false commiserations.

She half expected to find the house already in an uproar when she returned, but apparently her sister's mercurial disposition was well-enough respected by the staff that no one had ventured to interrupt her self-imposed isolation.

By now, Rob was certainly being grilled by the other servants on his day-long absence. Though she'd asked him to return noncommittal replies until she'd had time to acquaint her aunt with the facts, she knew the news couldn't be hidden much longer.

After passing her sister's still-locked door, Caragh found her aunt with her maid, completing her toilette for whatever entertainment she'd chosen to attend that evening.

"Caragh, dear, you're back!" Her opening smile faded as she took in her niece's bedraggled appearance. "My, you look…well-aired. If you hurry, you still can bathe and change in time for Lady Standish's rout."

"I'm rather tired, Aunt Kitty. I should prefer to stay home."

"I thought you might, after riding about all day. So energetic! Well, did you help Lord Branson accomplish his tasks?" Lady Catherine threw her an arch look. "Such a dear boy! I do hope he appreciates all you do for him."

Emotion clogged her throat when she considered Quentin's probable reaction to today's fiasco. She wasn't sure which would hurt more—his outrage at Ailis's actions, or the sympathy he was certain to offer her.

One heartache at a time, she told herself, fighting back the tears. Having reached the limits of her emotional endurance for today, she would *not* think about Quentin.

"Aunt, I must speak to you on a matter of grave importance."

A look of apprehension came over Lady Catherine's face. "Grendle, would you fetch my gold-spangled shawl? I left it in the library, I believe." As soon as the maid left the room, she turned to Caragh.

"It's Ailis, isn't it? I did knock at her door this afternoon, thinking certainly by now hunger would have overcome temper, but she refused to answer. She…she hasn't done herself an injury, has she?"

"Not exactly. You might rather say she's done *us* an injury." Caragh motioned her to a chair. "You'd better sit, Aunt Kitty."

"Dear me!" her aunt cried, sinking into an armchair. "I knew I should have removed that Meissen vase from her room! Your uncle brought that back from India for me, and 'twas one of my favorites!"

"I'm afraid 'tis worse than broken pottery." Caragh sighed deeply. "There is no gentle way to phrase this, so I'll just say it directly. Ailis left your house in secret last night. I discovered her missing this morning. Fearing she might have eloped with Lord Freemont, I concealed her absence and spent all day riding about, trying to trace her."

"Lord have mercy!" Lady Catherine wailed. "Please, tell me you found her and brought her safely back!"

"She is safe," Caragh said, patting her aunt's hand. "But…but I could not convince her to come home. Aunt Kitty, I'm afraid she's rented a flat near Covent Garden and set herself up as an artist. She intends to support herself by painting."

For a long moment Lady Catherine stared at Caragh as if she were speaking in tongues. As the full import of the news slowly penetrated, the look on her aunt's face went from anxious to horrified. "Ailis intends to *w-work?*" she asked, her voice wobbling. "As an…artist? Here in *London?*"

Fortunately, Caragh had already located her aunt's vinaigrette, for, after uttering those awful words, her aunt's shocked face slackened and she fainted dead away.

Calling for the maid, Caragh caught the lady before she slid from her chair. Some ten minutes later, after a copious application of hartshorn and burnt feathers, with reinforcements from Lady Catherine's maid and two footman, Caragh managed to get her distraught relation to bed.

But the scene that unfolded before her aunt finally exhausted herself into sleep, filled with sobbing, lamentation, and calls upon a merciful Providence to send her to an early grave, was as awful as Caragh had imagined.

When at last Caragh was able to seek the solace of her own chamber, the tisane she'd ordered for her headache steaming at the bedside, she felt wretched enough for the grave herself. The soothing concoction dulled her headache from a hammer's pounding to a sharp ache, but though she was exhausted in body and desolate in spirit, her mind kept circling round and round the same path like a mouse trapped in a feed bin, making sleep impossible.

Ailis was correct about one thing. Regardless of what Caragh decided to do in future, there was no point in remaining in London for the present, to be talked about and pointed out by the curious every time she and Lady Catherine left the house. Aunt Kitty would probably suggest they retreat to the home of her good friend in Bath to weather the initial storm of gossip.

For a moment, a ghost of anger stirred. Lady Catherine loved her life among the London ton. For her aunt's sake, Caragh prayed that Ailis's iniquities would not be permanently laid at the door of the kindly relation who had had no hand in her upbringing and had sheltered her only briefly.

Her own situation was more problematic. The sister of Disgrace, she would never again be invited to the functions of the highest sticklers, lest she bring into some proper home the taint of Ailis's wrongdoing. It was quite probable she'd be shunned by most other hostesses as well, at least until they ascertained whether Society's leading ladies had decided Caragh might still be bid to their less-select assemblies.

If she wished to elbow her way back into Society, her best course would be to return to London before the end of the Season and face down the gossip. Her chances of making a good marriage—perhaps any marriage—had vanished with the departure of her sister from this house. But since the only man she wanted had no wish to marry her, the fact that she would no longer be considered worthy of wedding a member of the ton didn't trouble her overmuch.

And what of Quentin? He'd promised to call when he returned to London. Fortunately for Lady Catherine's peace of mind, he must have been delayed, for his paying her aunt a visit earlier today would have exposed Caragh's excuse for leaving this morning as the lie it was.

Which meant he'd most likely be by sometime tomorrow. Probably, if Lord Freemont were as indiscreet as Ailis indicated, directly after he'd visited his club and heard the appalling news.

Her heart ached at the very thought of his handsome brow creased in anger and concern. Though after the events of today every other soul she knew in London might give her the cut direct, she knew he would stand her friend.

Tears she made no attempt to stem began to slip down her cheeks. How her battered spirit yearned for the words of solace she knew he'd offer!

Seeing her distress, would he put aside cautious constraint and take her in his arms, let her lean against his strength and draw comfort from his steadfast affection?

But should he allow that, with her reserves of will and strength so low, could she trust herself not to trespass beyond the bounds of friendship? Could she feel his arms about her, and not seek the touch of his lips? What if her body ignored the commands of her weary mind…her fingers pulling him closer, her lips and tongue probing for entry? Would he shove her away in revulsion, as he had the night of the ball?

A wave of remembered pain and humiliation swept through her. No, she could not bear that again! Until she had recovered from the shock and hurt of today's events, sorted out her future and was certain she could once again greet him with the cool friendliness that was all he desired from her, she had better not meet Quentin Burke.

With that bleak realization, a sense of calm descended on her troubled spirit. Yes, she would leave London—but not in Aunt Kitty's company. Her aunt, along with delivering further lamentations Caragh had no wish to hear, would press her to do the socially sensible thing and return to London as soon as possible. Right now, Caragh wasn't sure what she wished to do.

She needed peace and solitude to determine what that might be. First thing in the morning, Caragh decided, she would begin packing, and as soon as Aunt Kitty awoke, inform her that she was returning home to Sudley.

CHAPTER TEN

IN THE LATE AFTERNOON two days later, the carriage transporting Caragh on the last stage of her journey from London pulled up before Sudley Court. Her sister's harsh words a goad driving her beyond sleep, she'd risen before dawn her last morning in the city to begin preparations for her departure. By the time a yawning servant tiptoed in to stir the coals on her hearth, she had her trunk already packed. Waiting only long enough to force down a Spartan breakfast and confer with her tearful aunt, before noon she'd collected her maid and departed on the mail coach.

Everything at Sudley Court looked soothingly familiar, she thought as the steps were let down. One of the footmen came to help her alight and immediately called out for Pringle, who was shocked to discover that the Young Person who'd just emerged from the hired carriage was in fact his mistress. Reassuring him as he escorted her into the hall that both her aunt and her sister were in perfect health, she promised to apprise him of the reasons behind her unexpected arrival as soon as she'd conferred with her father.

With his daughters no longer in residence, Pringle told her, the baron seldom left the sanctuary of his library. He'd even taken to having his meals there, instructing the staff not to disturb him except to deliver his tray. Which often remained untouched on a side table, the butler said with a disapproving shake of his head, until its successor appeared hours later.

After dismissing Pringle outside the library, Caragh eyed the firmly closed portal with misgiving. She'd had a long journey in which to ponder what to say to her father, her staff and the neighbors. Knowing there was no easy way to tell the tale, and anxious to get the painful matter over with, she'd decided to confront Lord Sudley immediately. Even if "immediately" were not, she thought with a flash of resentment as she remembered her sister's words, a time her father might deem convenient.

After rapping loudly enough, she hoped, to penetrate his fog of scholarship, she entered the library.

Her father remained oblivious to her arrival, his eyes on the manuscript in front of him, his lips silently mouthing the translation he was doubtless in the process of formulating. Caragh took a moment to observe the thin, intelligent face and perpetually sad eyes of the man who had sired her.

A swell of affection rose out of the turmoil of grief, anxiety, resentment and fear to warm her briefly. She noted that the finger tapping at his manuscript was ink-stained, and as usual, his coat didn't match his waistcoat and the knot of his cravat was slightly askew.

"Papa!" she said in a loud voice. "I must speak to you about Ailis."

His brow knit briefly in annoyance, Lord Sudley glanced up. "Caragh?" he asked, only mild surprise in his voice at discovering in his library a daughter who should have been still in London. "Is it time for dinner already?"

Her absence had apparently been just another of daily life's mundane details, relegated by her father to the back of his consciousness, she realized with a pang. Quelling it, she continued, "Not quite, Papa. But I've just returned from London and I have urgent news. About Ailis."

"Ah, I recall. You took her to Kitty's for the Season. Urgent news, eh? She's received an offer from a worthy young man? Excellent!"

Anxiety over her father's reaction sharpening the dull headache that had plagued her for the last two days, Caragh slipped into the only armchair not stacked with books.

"N-not exactly, Papa. Ailis...decided to settle her future in another way entirely. You recall how passionate she is about her art? She...she has renounced wedlock and Society and intends to become a professional artist. I left her in London at her new studio."

Having decided these facts were upsetting enough without adding any reference to her sister's relationship with Lord Freemont, Caragh sat back to await her father's response. She had no idea, she thought with an odd sense of detachment, whether he would greet the news by weeping, tearing his hair, and accusing her of having been grossly remiss in her duty to her sister—or nodding politely in acknowledgement and returning to his work.

As understanding registered—of both the bare facts she'd recited and the implications she hadn't, Lord Sudley looked stricken, his dark eyes turning more mournful yet. Much as she'd tried to armor herself against it, at this evidence of her father's distress Caragh felt her initial guilt and anguish well up again. Desperately she blinked back tears.

After a long silence, her father swallowed hard. "She's lost to us, then?" he asked softly.

"I'm afraid so. I tried to reason with her, Papa, but she was adamant. Establishing a studio and living for her art are all she wants to do. All she intended to do in London from the first, apparently." She sighed. "The resulting scandal is going to be rather dreadful."

After that observation, silence stretched between them. Guilt stabbed Caragh again.

Angrily she pushed it away. She would not apologize to Papa for failing to instill in her sister an adequate appreciation for her position in life and the duty she owed her family. A failure that was also, after all, at least partly her father's.

But rather than calling her to account, her father continued to gaze mutely into the distance. "The ancients would say

that we must each of us do what the gods within compel us,"
he said at last. "Regardless of the dictates of Society."

"Ailis is certainly doing so."

Her father nodded. "Is she happy?"

Startled, Caragh realized she'd not thought to ask herself
that question. "Yes, Papa," she replied, recognizing the truth
of the answer as she pronounced it. "I believe she is."

Her father lifted his hands in a helpless gesture, as if to
indicate there was no more to be done. "Will you go back to
London?"

"I-I'm not sure, Papa." Even knowing her father's detachment from everyday life, she was surprised to find him resigning himself to so irreversible a change in her sister's circumstances without further exclamation or argument. "I
haven't yet had time to decide what I wish to do."

He nodded again and picked up his pen—a signal that their
interview was at an end. "I suppose you'll inform me of your
decision. Now, if you don't mind, I should like to finish this
passage before dinner."

He will never notice or appreciate anything you do...
Shaken by the force of the angry resentment seizing her, Caragh rose swiftly and fled from the room.

Having ascertained that his darling Ailis was settled and
happy, her father had voiced not a single expression of concern over the scandal that a normal papa would have realized
had blighted any matrimonial hopes his remaining daughter
might have cherished. Nor had he offered a word of sympathy
or understanding about how Ailis's unilateral decision had
destroyed Caragh's sojourn in London and severely restricted
her choices for the future.

Biting her lip to once again quell a drip of tears, Caragh
went in search of Pringle.

First she'd brief the butler on the situation, that the staff
might be prepared to offer appropriate but vague responses to
the uproar of questions—and no doubt, criticisms—sure to

erupt once the news of Ailis's disgrace reached the county. Finally, she would write a note explaining events to Lady Arden, the squire's wife and grande dame among county society.

She smiled a little bitterly. Would the neighbors among whom she'd grown up shun her or treat her with the same icy disdain she knew she'd be receiving in London?

Once she finished the note, she would at last be free, free from the responsibilities, the questions, the inquisitive eyes. She'd escape to the stables, saddle her favorite mare and ride.

Riding had always calmed her, quelled the headaches that built in her temples when the never-ending chores of running the estate and dealing with Ailis pressed too heavily upon her.

She'd ride now to ease the tension that had coiled tighter and tighter since the brutal interview with her sister. In blessed solitude, she would at last have the leisure to examine the accusations that had fermented like a boil in her heart, lance them with the cold steel of reflection and determine which held truth, which reflected only her sister's self-absorbed view of the world.

And come back prepared to turn the conclusions she reached into a new direction for her life.

THE NEXT MORNING, Quentin rode back into London. The pesky matter of breaking in the new estate manager had taken far longer than the single day he'd predicted to Caragh. Feeling somewhat guilty for leaving her to cope alone with the ticklish task of cajoling her tempestuous sister, he wished to call on her as soon as possible to see how matters were progressing.

So, instead of heading for St. James Square, he directed his mount to Upper Brook Street. Pulling up his horse before the entry, still mentally rehearsing an amusing anecdote from his trip to cheer a possibly distressed Caragh, he was surprised to find a servant removing the knocker from the door.

Curious, he waited for a servant to take his mount. Although he supposed the butler might have felt that, with the quantity of callers visiting daily, the brass stood in need of polishing, he still felt a tremor of unease. Surely Ailis in her pique hadn't done anything so scandalous the family thought it necessary to make an abrupt departure!

His foreboding turned out to be justified, however, when a more than normally wooden-faced Evers replied to his request to see Caragh with the information that Miss Sudley was not at home. Quentin's concern deepened to alarm when the man added, after a significant pause, that none of the ladies were presently in residence.

"Good heavens, man, what has happened? And don't try to fob me off with whatever innocuous and uninformative reply your mistress directed you to offer! I'm well enough acquainted with the family to know the truth."

Ever's impassive facade creased into a worried look. "Aye, my lord, I expect you're that. 'Tis not my place to divulge, nor do I know for certain, all that occurred. I suggest you seek out Lady Catherine. Her dear friend in Bath, Miss Quimbly, has taken ill and requested Lady Catherine's assistance."

So the ladies had fled to Bath! Ailis must have done something truly awful, he thought grimly. After subjecting the butler to intense scrutiny, he concluded the man had indeed told him all he knew, or was permitted to impart.

"Very well. But should any of the ladies contact you, please convey to them my concern, and inform them I shall call on Lady Catherine as soon as possible."

"Very good, my lord. I expect as how my lady would welcome a visit."

Having unbent enough to offer that opinion, Evers resumed his impassive butler's demeanor and escorted Quentin out.

He'd lunch at his club, Quentin decided. Any action of Ailis's scandalous enough to require them to leave London just as the Season was reaching its height would likely still be the subject of conversation there.

Pausing in St. James Square only long enough to change into suitable clothes and down a tankard of ale, Quentin took a hackney to White's. The hour being rather early, the rooms were still thin of company. But among the octogenarians reading their newspapers, he hoped to find at least one acquaintance who could fill him in on the happenings in the city over the last three days.

He was thus relieved to see in his customary chair overlooking the bow window an older gentleman who'd been a friend of his father's—a fact Quentin had never held against the easygoing, genial old bachelor. Lord Andover was also an inveterate gossip, a trait Quentin had hitherto deplored, but which on this occasion should prove useful.

"Quentin, my boy, good to see you! Back from rubbishing about on your farms again, are you? Stap me, I cannot see how you abide all that rural rustication. Your papa would have expired from breathing a tenth of that country air."

"I'm sure he would, sir," Quentin replied, motioning a waiter to bring him a glass of wine and taking the seat adjacent to his lordship. "I trust you are well." He tapped the newspaper. "Events in town keeping you amused?"

"Indeed! There's just been the most interesting and unusual scandal! Concerns that beautiful Sudley chit that was making her bow this year. I say, don't you own some property in their county? Though from what I hear, you own property in nearly every county of England now. Going to become a regular Golden Ball of the Grasslands, aren't you, lad?" Lord Andover chuckled at his own turn of phrase.

"Not quite, my lord," Quentin replied, smiling gamely. "I do know the Sudleys, though. A scandal, you say?"

"Unlike anything I've ever experienced in my forty years in the ton!" Andover confirmed.

"What exactly transpired?" Quentin asked, curbing his impatience as he tried to lead the old man to the point.

But Lord Andover was not to be rushed. "I've seen a few faux pas in my day, slips of omission or commission that earned the lass who made them a trip home in disgrace. But ah, this!"

"Was the girl sent home in disgrace?"

Lord Andover grinned. "Indeed not. In fact, you being an intimate of the family and all, if you'd like the full story, I expect you could catch up with the little charmer over by Covent Garden. She's opened a studio there, I understand. Intends to paint portraits—a girl of gentle birth! Have you ever heard the like?"

"Miss Ailis Sudley has opened an artist's studio?" Quentin echoed, horrified to his bones. If this were true, such a breach of conduct and good breeding was more than serious—it was irreparable.

"So I hear. However, I also hear Freemont spends a lot of time there, so if you pay her a call, you'd better knock loudly, if you take my meaning." The baron wagged his eyebrows suggestively.

"Lord have mercy," Quentin murmured. No wonder poor Lady Catherine had rushed out of London.

The damage to the reputation of a widow well established among the ton was likely to be bad enough. But what of Caragh? His first shock gave way to a second as he pondered the impact Ailis's unforgivable behavior would have on her sister.

It took but an instant to realize that, for an unmarried country girl with neither great wealth nor the highest of rank to protect her, the results were likely to be catastrophic—and permanent.

Though after his morning ride, Quentin had looked forward to a snug lunch at White's, he found his appetite had vanished.

Caragh would have to be devastated. He must go to her at once.

Delaying for the moment his second-strongest desire—to seek out Ailis Sudley and strangle her on the spot—he finished his wine, listening with as good an appearance of interest as he could contrive while Andover went on to describe the lesser contretemps currently taking place among the ton. Then, excusing himself from lunch, he sent a footman to summon a hackney and gathered his things.

With luck and fast horses, he could be at Caragh's side by tomorrow.

The only bright note in this whole sorry situation, he thought with gallows humor as the hackney bore him back to St. James Square, was that for the foreseeable future, there would be no need to come up with a new list of potential suitors for the now-ineligible Caragh Sudley.

Within an hour he was back on the road, headed for Bath. Pushing on despite a steady rain, he managed to arrive, saddle-weary and mud-splattered, only a few hours past his original estimate. While thankfully availing himself of a bath, a hot meal, and the comfort of dry clothes at one of the city's best hostelries, Quentin sent a footman to ascertain Lady Catherine's location.

That task accomplished, he set out once again, sure Caragh would appreciate his diligence in speeding to her side, his anxiety to see her and ascertain her state of mind sharpened by three days of worry.

The butler who admitted him seemed doubtful of his reception. But after calling upon his most imperious manner to insist the man announce him anyway, then cooling his heels in the parlor for nearly half an hour, he was informed that Lady Catherine would in fact receive Lord Branson. Not until he'd supported that lady through a noisy spate of tears did he at last discover, to his extreme disappointment, that Caragh had not accompanied her aunt to Bath.

Nor, Aunt Kitty confided, still dabbing at her eyes with her saturated handkerchief, had her niece given her any word about when she meant to rejoin her, that they could begin repairing to the extent possible the damage Ailis had caused to the innocent Caragh's reputation. Which, Lady Catherine admitted, the conclusion bringing on another burst of weeping, was probably not going to be very much. Her poor Caragh was ruined almost as effectively as her scandalous sister!

Having ascertained that Caragh had chosen to flee to Sudley, Quentin exhausted the last of his limited reserves of patience, remaining for nearly another hour at Lady Catherine's side, inserting soothing murmurs during each pause in that lady's long lamentations about the situation. So eager was he to escape and ready himself to set off yet again, he did not even attempt to disabuse Lady Catherine of the erroneous conclusion she obviously drew about the nature of his affection for Caragh, after he let slip his intention to leave immediately for Sudley. At last, with Lady Catherine's arch blessing for being so *devoted* a supporter of her dear niece, he was finally able to break away.

Thoughtfully he considered the situation during his transit back to his lodgings. Knowing the ton's abhorrence for unconventionality, Ailis's behavior had likely dealt a death blow to any matrimonial hopes Caragh might have entertained. Sooner or later, he needed to take a wife—Society's opinion of whom did not particularly matter to him. Perhaps, he concluded as the chair men set him down at his destination, it wouldn't be such a bad idea to turn Lady Catherine's erroneous conclusion into reality.

By offering to marry his best friend, Caragh Sudley.

CHAPTER ELEVEN

TWO AFTERNOONS LATER, with a rising sense of ire, Caragh sat at the desk in the bookroom re-reading the missive the butler had just delivered to her from the squire's wife, Lady Arden.

My dearest Caragh,
I can only imagine how Distressed you must be at such Shocking Behavior by one of your Own Blood! So unfortunate That Girl's Infamy must needs cast a Shadow over your own hitherto Stainless Honor!

Rest assured, were I not at the moment Wholly Encumbered by my Duties here at the Hall, I should fly to your Side to support you in your Hour of Need.

However, there is still much to be done preparing for my Jenny's Come-Out next Season. Indeed, in view of that Important Event, and given the Tender and Impressionable Sensibilities of a Young Girl of her age, perhaps it would be best if you did not call here for the Present.

I have spoken to Mrs. Hamilton and we both feel that it would also be Advisable if you were to refrain for a Time from participating in the Parish Ladies' Benevolence Association. Naturally, as the Works of that Organization reflect back upon the Church, its Members must be Exemplars of Unimpeachable Virtue. We will of course notify you when, after a Suitable Interval, we feel it Proper for you to resume your Activities with us.

In the meantime, believe me your Most Sympathetic Neighbor and Friend!

Some friend, Caragh thought in disgust, tossing the letter onto the desk. Perhaps the note wasn't the cut direct she'd likely be receiving from her acquaintance were she still in London, but given that she'd just been politely banned from calling on her neighbors and participating in their association, it constituted her rural society's nearest thing to it.

Closing the ledger she'd been perusing, she stretched her tired shoulders. Lady Arden's reaction, though disappointing from one whom she'd previously believed to be truly a friend, was not unexpected. And if such was the response she was to receive even from people who had known her from the cradle, the tentative conclusions she'd drawn during her long ride two days ago were justified.

She had little desire to ''earn'' her way back into a Society that would ostracize one individual for the actions of another. Or for that matter, one that would condemn a lady simply for defying its conventions.

She'd also come to terms with her sister's accusations. Ailis had been right in asserting that Caragh had wanted social success for her, but not so she could revel in her sibling's reflected glory. She had only wished for Ailis to be sought after so that she might have the largest court of suitors from which to select her life's partner. Though Caragh had enjoyed the variety of entertainments London had to offer, with her main purpose for going to the city no longer achievable, she had little interest in remaining a part of the ton.

After much painful soul-searching, she had to concede there was, however, truth to her sister's allegation that for years, Caragh had assisted her father in the vain hope that he might someday notice and appreciate her. Worse, she recognized that she had acted in a similar fashion with Quentin—with similar results. Well, she would be Little Miss Do-Good-for-Everyone no longer.

Her sojourn in London, though short, had demonstrated that both the estate and her father could manage quite well without her. Quentin could hire an assistant for his manager at Thorn-whistle, if the current agent proved unable to complete all his duties without her assistance.

Nor would she feel bereft at being excluded from the local benevolent association. Her main function at its meetings had been to keep the peace between Lady Arden, who considered herself the ranking female of the county, and Mrs. Hamilton, who boasted kinship with an earl and, as vicar's wife, thought her opinions should take precedence. Caragh had often returned from their meetings with a headache as severe as if she'd been dealing with one of Ailis's tantrums.

Papa had asked if Ailis's new life made her happy. Caragh had not previously had the luxury of embracing a task simply for the joy of it, but now, set free by circumstances from most of her former responsibilities, for the first time in her life she was considering what she truly wished to do.

Surely an upheaval in her life as dramatic as that caused by Ailis's disgrace meant the Divine Being must be impelling her to some new purpose. And, borrowing from the ancients, she recalled Aristotle's definition of happiness as the full use of one's powers along lines of excellence.

Frightening as it was to think of being cast adrift to make her way alone, still the notion of using her talents to build a new life caused a thrill of anticipation.

Since girlhood, only in one place at Sudley had she been truly relaxed and happy—with her horses. Some of her fondest childhood memories were of the long hours she'd spent with her grandfather in the barn he had built to house his broodmares. His good friend and hunting crony from Quorn country, Hugo Meynell, obsessed with producing a new generation of faster hounds capable of hunting foxes on the run, had urged the late Lord Sudley to experiment with breeding horses with the speed and stamina to pace his dogs. Her grandfather had devoted the last portion of his life to meeting that challenge.

Her parents, who had met on the hunting field, had actively assisted her grandfather's endeavors. Caragh remembered vividly the day when she, as a six-year-old, had proudly pointed out to a visitor the attributes of a Sudley colt. Her parents and grandfather had praised her lavishly afterward for her precocious expertise—one of the few instances when she could remember receiving her father's unqualified approval.

By the time her grandfather had died the following year, the Sudley stables had become known throughout the neighboring counties for producing quality mounts.

After Mama's death, however, her father withdrew from working with the horses his wife had loved so dearly, leaving the day-to-day running of the breeding operation to his agent and increasingly, to Caragh. She found it fascinating to evaluate the foals and decide which to retain for the program, which to sell. Exciting to see the young horses put through their paces. Exhilarating to experience the results of the careful mixing of bloodlines in the fleetness and strength of the horse carrying her across the field at a gallop.

So great had grown the demand for Sudley mounts that for the last several years, all the foals expected in the spring were bespoken even before their births. As she had told Lord Russell, for some time she'd longed to be able to expand their program, but that portion of the estate at Sudley that could be devoted to pastures and horse barns was already filled to capacity.

And so she would follow her talents and turn calamity into opportunity by purchasing another, larger property to devote solely to the breeding operation. She would establish her residence there—and leave behind the family and Society that neither needed nor valued her.

As she had already been exiled by the ton, taking the radical step of living alone and earning her own bread could do her no further harm. She was confident that the Sudley stock's

superior reputation would bring clients flocking to her, regardless of her social standing.

She would seize this chance to make her life over in a
fashion she, and she alone, chose.

She ran a fingertip down the ledger. Under her careful stewardship, Sudley was doing well. Having worked hard for ten
years to generate it, she felt justified in allotting a portion of
Sudley's income to fund her plans. Quentin's friend, Lord
Russell, had already indicated he had a suitable property for
sale. She would send her estate manager to inspect it, and if
he approved the land, she would make an offer on it.

And Ailis had even shown her how to do it. Present Papa
with legal documents—such as a bank draft and authorization
to move the horses and equipment—and he would sign them
without question, just as he had countless times over the years.

She would, of course, need one more thing to complete her
happiness. But since making Quentin Burke love her was beyond her control, she'd also decided to limit her dealings with
Lord Branson.

He was in London to find a wife, a task with which she
had no desire whatever to assist him. As his marrying would
inevitably put limits on their friendship and possibly lead to
awkwardness between them, it was just as well that she intended to relocate away from Thornwhistle, where she would
have few opportunities to torture herself with the thrilling,
agonizing temptation of his presence.

For her own well-being, when she left her old life behind,
she would leave behind also her friendship with Quentin
Burke.

Dismissing the little voice that insisted turning her back on
him would prove impossible, she focused once more on her
accounts, intent on determining the largest sum for which she
could responsibly write the draft. She had, she told the little
voice firmly, cried all the tears she ever intended to cry over

Quentin Burke. It was time to exchange girlish dreams for a woman's reality.

She turned a page, creating enough breeze to stir Lady Arden's letter and sent it drifting to the floor. Automatically Caragh bent to retrieve it, then stopped. *Coward,* she thought, *you hadn't even the courage to deliver your rebuff in person.*

Instead of picking the letter up, she trampled it under her foot.

Her first act of defiance, she thought with a giggle as she returned her attention once more to the ledger. Ah, how good it felt!

Just as Caragh finished adding the totals for the last entries, Pringle interrupted to announce she had a visitor.

Lord Branson awaited her in the parlor.

QUENTIN LOOKED UP to see a coolly self-possessed Caragh walking in. "Quentin, what a surprise!" she said, holding out her hands for him to salute. "How kind of you to stop by."

Relieved to find her much like her normal self, still, he had to applaud her sangfroid. Her greeting was as conventional and her tone as calm as if she had never undergone the catastrophe of taking Ailis to London.

Despite her brave front, though, she was too intelligent not to know just how dire her circumstances had become. Indeed, tucked beside his admiration for her fortitude lurked a touch of disappointment that she hadn't run, sobbing, into his arms.

"I didn't expect to see you here at the height of the Season," she continued as he brought her hands to his lips. "Was there some emergency at Thornwhistle?"

Surprised, he dropped her hands and stared at her. "Caragh, you must know I didn't come all the way here to inspect a farm! I want to help in any way I can. I'm so sorry I was away when...all this occurred. I came as soon as I learned what had transpired. Have you determined yet...what you mean to do?"

"Should you like tea?"

Carrying on in the face of disaster was one thing, but she was taking this business of maintaining appearances a bit far, he thought, exasperation nibbling at the edges of his concern. "If you wish. All I truly want is to tackle the problems Ailis has left you with."

"I do have a plan," she replied as she waved him to a chair and seated herself opposite. "In fact, your visit will save me writing to inform you of it. Since I intend shortly to remove from Sudley permanently, I shall no longer be able to watch over Thornwhistle. Its management is something for you to decide, of course, but I would recommend that you keep Manning on."

"Don't trouble yourself about Thornwhistle! Where do you mean to go? Joining Lady Catherine in Bath for a time would probably be best, so that she can assist you in planning your reentry into Lon—"

"Do not even speak of that!" her raised voice cut him off. Her face coloring, she lowered her tone. "I had only ever intended to remain in London long enough to see Ailis established. Since, in a manner of speaking, she now is, I have no desire to return."

"Surely you don't mean to live in permanent exile from Society? Come now, Caragh, I've never known you to run from difficulty! I admit, 'twill be rather uncomfortable at first, but once the scandal dies down, persons of breeding and sense will realize that you cannot be held accountable for your sister's actions. I grant you, vouchers to Almack's are probably out of the question, but I think that…" His voice trailed off as, smiling, she shook her head.

"Quentin, I'm not *afraid* to go back. I don't *want* to go back. There is no longer anything for me to accomplish in London."

So she did despair of marrying. She expressed that dismaying conclusion with such serenity that Quentin's chest tightened, tenderness at her bravery laced with anger at her sister's brutal theft of her hopes.

Before he could turn his muddled emotions into speech, she continued, "For a long time I've wanted to expand our breeding operation, but there simply wasn't sufficient space here at Sudley. So I've decided to purchase another property, move the breeding stock there and devote myself to running it. Alone."

"You intend to manage a horse breeding farm—by yourself?" he echoed, astounded. For a lone female to direct an enterprise whose primary clients were gentleman would be only slightly more respectable than opening an artist's studio. "You cannot be serious!"

She gave him a look of hauteur and raised an eyebrow. "I assure you I am. I thought you would appreciate my expertise enough to approve."

"I'm not questioning your competence—heavens, Caragh, I know better than anyone that it wasn't your Papa who solidified Sudley's reputation for producing superior horseflesh! But operating the farm with your father as ostensible manager, living under his roof, is a very different matter from running it openly while residing alone! You would doom yourself to being permanently ostracized by Society, with no hope of redemption should you later come to your senses!"

Her expression turned frostier and her eyes flashed. "I am in full possession of my faculties right now. I love working with horses, and as you yourself admit, I excel at it. What else would you have me do? Stay on at Sudley until Cousin Archibald inherits and wrests control from me? Live with Aunt Kitty on the fringes of Society, expected to be grateful for invitations to the larger parties and less exclusive routs? Dwindle into an old maid waiting for some gentleman, down enough on his luck to ignore scandal for the privilege of spending my dowry, to honor me with an offer of marriage?"

"Of course not," Quentin snapped, exasperated. "You can

marry me. It's certainly a better solution than running a horse farm!''

She grew very still, her eyes on his face. "I see," she said slowly. "You would sacrifice yourself to keep me from becoming a permanent exile from Society? How very...noble of you."

"Caragh, I didn't mean it like that!" Having shocked her—and himself—by rushing his fences, Quentin ran a hand through his hair, trying to redeem what even he recognized to be an ineptly-worded proposal. "I hadn't meant to blurt it out in so ramshackle a manner, but I have thought seriously about both our situations. I came here with the intention of making you an offer—and that was *before* I knew anything of your plans."

She studied him for a moment. "Why would you propose to me?"

He shrugged. "There's no point denying we both know your chances of making a match with any other gentleman of comparable birth and fortune are slim. And I, too, must marry sometime."

Watching her face, he could tell that un-lover-like speech was hardly convincing. Time to abandon caution and bring to bear the persuasive power of their attraction. He rose and came to her side.

"We've been friends for years, Caragh, the best of friends," he said, taking her hand. "I'd hate to see your bright mind and passionate spirit wasted in spinsterhood. I believe we could make a comfortable and congenial life together. Do you not think so as well?"

"I...I don't know. What has been between us as of late has not been...comfortable."

"Ah, *that*," he said, visions of Caragh in his arms—in his bed—sending a thrill through him. "It could be, I promise you, a delight." He bent to trace his lips across the top of her hand.

She jerked away as if scalded—and in truth, his lips sizzled from the heat of that contact as well. Jumping up, she paced to the window and stared out. "And what if you later met a lady who engaged your emotions—as more than a friend?"

"Since I have gone two-and-thirty years without finding such a lady, I have no expectation of doing so in future. Besides, I would never play you false, Caragh. Surely you have more faith in my honor than that."

She turned to smile at him, though her eyes remained pensive. "Yes," she said softly, "I have never doubted your honor."

Quentin felt an answering smile bloom on his face. He'd surprised her with his unexpected offer at a time when she was still upset and unsettled—and who could fault her, given the upheaval in her life? Once she'd had time to consider it, surely the affection between them would persuade her he was right.

Besides, Caragh was too sensible to refuse. He knew his value on the Marriage Mart, and for Miss Sudley to bring Lord Branson to the altar would have been accounted a triumph even before Ailis created her scandal.

And once she did accept him—ah, then he could sweep her into his arms and kiss her with all the passion he'd been restraining for what seemed an age.

She cleared her throat. He jerked his attention from that pleasing prospect back to her face.

"Honored as I am by your proposal, Lord Branson, I cannot permit you to make so great a sacrifice. I don't mean to be ungracious, but I have accounts to complete this morning." She walked to the door and tugged on the bell pull. "Pringle will show you out. I hope you have a pleasant journey back to London."

Before Quentin divined what she intended, she curtseyed and slipped out the door.

For a few moments Quentin waited, before his brain sifted

through the meaning of her words to arrive at the incredible conclusion that his good friend had just...walked out on him.

He'd been...dismissed! Dismissed as if he were some casual acquaintance paying a morning call, rather than a worried friend who'd spent three days tracking her down—and had just made her an offer of marriage. No, he thought, growing more incensed by the moment, dismissed as if he were a lackey interviewing for a position she had decided against offering him.

He had galloped all the way back to Thornwhistle before his first floodtide of anger—and hurt—receded. Reviewing their interview over a glass of wine and in the cooler light of reason, though, he had to wince. True, he'd never delivered a proposal before and the idea of her running a farm had shocked him into an unrehearsed and premature delivery of it, but he really should have done a better job of explaining his desire to wed her.

He was no expert on females, but he knew even one as sensible as Caragh probably wanted to be courted about so important a decision. Yet he'd included none of the sweet words of affection or tender vows of devotion a lady probably expected to accompany a proposal of marriage.

In fact, he'd botched the whole meeting rather badly. Coxcomb that he was, had he really expected Caragh to jump at his offer simply because he was Lord Branson of Branson Park? Surely he should have known such a consideration would not weigh heavily with her. And, since he had broached his proposal as a means to salvage her reputation, she would, of course, return that gesture of nobility with one of her own, by refusing to accept his sacrifice.

By the time he'd finished off his dinner and a good bottle of claret, he'd decided he must return in the morning with a carefully written and well-rehearsed apology, followed by a much better worded proposal. One he felt confident that this time, she would accept.

He wouldn't mind letting her purchase a property and expand her breeding operation. No more than Caragh was he inclined to the idle life of the London ton, preferring the sense of accomplishment that came with hard work well done. As good as she was with horses, Caragh was sure to make a success of such an endeavor, and he would be proud to support her—as long as he was present to supervise when potential buyers came calling.

Just imagining the ribald jokes and suggestive innuendoes to which she would certainly be subject were she to pursue that absurd notion of running a farm alone made his temper rise and his hands clench into fists with the desire to pummel the yet-to-be-determined offenders.

Yes, he'd return tomorrow and be much more convincing—once he got her to hear him out. He frowned, a niggle of doubt shaking his certainty.

Caragh might be wary of receiving him, fearing an uncomfortable repetition of his arguments. Perhaps he should begin by ignoring the matter entirely, instead urging her to take him to the stables and explain her plans for expanding the Sudley operation. And then, while she was relaxed and in her element, once again the warm, witty, welcoming Caragh he knew so well rather than the wooden stranger who had occupied the Sudley parlor today, he would deliver his much-improved proposal.

Which, he devoutly hoped, *his* Caragh would promptly accept. For now that he truly considered the matter, to his surprise, he realized he'd grown entirely too fond of his dear friend's company to let her exile herself far from him in some remote rural village.

The following day, just before noon, Quentin set out for Sudley. By this hour, Caragh should have completed her morning duties and be amenable to a stroll to the barns. Then if his mission were successful, he could utilize her father's noon break to ask for Caragh's hand.

That formality completed, he could whisk Caragh back to the parlor to celebrate their new engagement with a glass of champagne and some even more intoxicating kisses.

Concentrating on that happy outcome quelled the unexpected nervousness that slowed his step and tightened his neckcloth as he handed over his horse and mounted the entry stairs. His attention distracted by mentally rehearsing his proposal, he only half heard the butler return his greeting.

Until the man startled him out of polishing his pretty phrases by saying that Miss Caragh was no longer at Sudley.

She had, Pringle regretted to inform him, departed this morning—for London.

CHAPTER TWELVE

IN THE AFTERNOON several days later, Caragh climbed the stairs to her room in Aunt Kitty's London townhouse. She'd sent word by messenger to Lady Catherine, begging leave to stay in the house during her sojourn in town.

To her surprise, rather than informing the servants of her arrival, her aunt journeyed from Bath to greet her personally. Though Lady Catherine did not judge that sufficient time had yet elapsed for them to attempt reentering London Society, still she wished, she tearfully assured Caragh, to lend her support through whatever trials had forced her poor maligned niece to return so soon to the metropolis.

Deciding there was no point in further upsetting her kindhearted aunt by divulging her real reason for consulting with Sudley's lawyer, Caragh had allowed Lady Catherine to believe she had come merely on a matter of estate business for her papa. Before the end of this visit, though, she thought with a sigh as she entered her chamber, she would have to inform Aunt Kitty of her real plans—a confession likely to evoke an attack of hysteria only slightly less severe than the one brought on by the news that Ailis had set up her studio.

Poor Aunt Kitty, Caragh thought, her affection for her gentle aunt tinged by no small amount of guilt. What social millstones her nieces were proving to be!

Aside from that one regret, she judged the rest of her trip an unqualified success. Tossing aside her reticule, she smiled as she set down the folder of documents she'd brought back from the office of their lawyer. Mr. Smithers, having long known that Caragh and not her father directed estate business at Sudley, raised not an eyebrow at her request that he make an offer on a tract of land being offered for sale by Lord Russell. Though even the lawyer, she suspected, would be shocked at the notion of her being so unconventional as to move from beneath her father's roof to openly manage the enterprise.

She'd learned an hour ago that Mr. Smithers was now negotiating for the property and foresaw no difficulties in completing its purchase. As soon as the transaction was finalized, Caragh would return to Sudley to begin moving her livestock and equipment to the new property.

Which she hoped would be soon. She knew her brusque refusal of his suit and immediate departure must have wounded Quentin, but maintaining a cold distance—and escaping at the first possible instant—was the only way she survived their meeting. The urge had been far too strong to soothe her troubled spirit by throwing herself into his arms—where, for the first time, he seemed quite willing to receive her.

But only, she reminded herself bitterly, to use the power of their attraction to seduce her into accepting his...sympathy proposal. Oh, to have him change his mind about attempting to combine friendship and passion, not because he'd found her too enticing to resist—but out of *pity!* She still writhed at the thought. Her pride and self-respect would never forgive him that betrayal of their friendship.

Especially since, despite the lowering terms in which he had phrased it, she had been all too tempted to accept.

Her eyes stung and her heart twisted at the memory. His willingness to ''sacrifice'' himself for her might be noble, but she'd thought he knew—and appreciated—her capabilities better than to expect she would let Ailis's action reduce her to helpless dependence on Society's—or some well-meaning friend's—goodwill.

She'd thought she knew *him* well enough to expect his

support and encouragement for her continued independence, rather than a mouthing of conventional proprieties.

If he were her Apollo, she'd better take care not to become Icarus, foolishly flying closer to the object of her fascination until he destroyed her.

Enough! she told herself, putting a hand to her forehead. She would think no more on that painful and humiliating interview.

But one thing she must not forget: Quentin Burke had not brought his fortunes back from the edge of ruin by being easily discouraged. If, after further reflection, he still believed her plans ill-advised, he would be back—with perhaps even more devious and seductive tricks to dissuade her.

She had better leave the City before he returned—or have her defenses primed to resist him.

The other decision she must make was less clear. Sighing, she picked up and reread the note Evers had brought her today—from Ailis.

Heard from Holden that you are in town.
Please come to see me.

For a moment, she stared at her sister's distinctive, boldly-formed letters as if they held the key to the puzzle that was Ailis.

Caragh's first impulse upon receiving the note had been to crumple it up and cast it into the fire. She'd been at the point of feeding it to the flames when a more considered reaction stopped her. Sighing, she returned to the desk and smoothed it out.

Ailis's cold dismissal of Caragh's loving care as mere self-interested manipulation had cut so deep, Caragh still had no words adequate to express the pain. Nor had she any desire to expose her lacerated spirit to more of her sister's barbed commentary.

And yet…they were sisters. The bonds of affection, on her side at least, were strongly forged—stronger, it appeared, than the hurt. Ailis might have wrenched responsibility for her future out of Caragh's hands, but despite the casual cruelty of her sister's methods, Caragh could not so easily turn off a lifetime's habit of watching out for her.

She ran a finger over the note once more. Ailis had added an atypical "please," which in her sister's cryptic way was tantamount to an apology. And Caragh did genuinely want to know how Ailis was doing, whether the promised commission had come through and whether she would, in fact, be able to support herself. The sum she had drawn from Papa's account, far less than her dowry, would not pay the rent or keep her in paints for long.

In her current state of social isolation, Caragh would likely receive neither hard news nor gossip about her sister's situation. Knowing that at this delicate juncture Aunt Kitty would not welcome a visit, even should her sister be moved to make one, if Caragh wished to know how Ailis was doing, she would have to go to Mercer Street.

She smiled ruefully, knowing her decision was already made. And despite what *some* people seemed to think, she did not shrink from facing difficult, even painful tasks.

The early spring afternoon's light was already fading. Ailis would be finishing her day's painting, putting up her oils and cleaning her brushes. If she intended to visit, now would be a good time to call.

Still arranging your schedule based on Ailis's needs, Caragh thought, her smile turning bitter. How long-ingrained habits persist!

But Aunt Kitty would be resting in preparation for dinner. Caragh might slip out and back without having to explain where she'd gone.

That fact swaying the balance, she drew on her gloves, caught up her pelisse and strode from the room.

Some half-hour later, Caragh stood with her hand poised to ring her sister's bell, already regretting her impulse to visit and wondering if it were too late to recall the hackney that had conveyed her here.

Deciding that it was, and that she'd come too far to turn craven now, she gathered her courage and rang the bell. Still, nausea churned in her gut as she waited for the maid to answer. The wound was still too fresh, her tears too close to the surface.

Ailis herself pushed the door open with an elbow, her hands occupied in pulling off her painting smock. As she turned to see Caragh, her fingers froze on the ties.

Abandoning an attempt to smile, Caragh opened her lips to offer a greeting, but no sound emerged.

For a moment they stood staring at each other. Then Ailis tossed her apron aside and seized her sister in a rib-bruising hug. "Caragh! Oh, I'm so glad you came!"

In all the years they'd been growing up, her undemonstrative sister had rarely embraced her. As Caragh hugged her back, tears welled up and fell despite her best efforts to restrain them, catching in her sister's hair where they glistened like crystals set in a golden frame.

Finally Ailis pushed her away, her own eyes moist. "Here we stand like a pair of doltish watering-pots! Come in!" Tucking Caragh's hand in her arm, she pulled her into the room. "Higgins!" she called in the direction of what must be a small kitchen. "Bring us tea in the studio, you lazy girl!"

While Caragh removed her wrap, Ailis swept aside paint cloths and brushes to clear her a seat on the small divan, then dropped into the overstuffed chair beside it. She fastened her brilliant blue-eyed gaze on Caragh.

"You got my note, then?" At Caragh's nod, she continued, "I know I'm often oblivious to an individual's feelings, but I do know I hurt you. I'm sorry, Caragh. I didn't really mean what I said about…well, you know. When I'm angry, my tongue runs faster than my wits. But sooner or later I needed to make the break, and there was no easy way to do it. When the contretemps over Holden erupted, it seemed the perfect opportunity. I knew I must do something so…beyond the pale, that even someone as tenacious as you would have no hope of 'redeeming' me. And at least for a time, you would be too angry to try.''

Caragh managed a watery smile. ''You certainly succeeded.''

Ailis grinned. ''I don't mean to apologize for *everything*. It *is* time that you stop trying to smooth everyone else's life and get on with living your own.''

''You'll be happy to know that I've come to agree with you. Not, however, without some painful reflection, so don't think to be absolved of all guilt.''

''I quite refuse to accept any. Would you have ever ceased playing Wise Older Sister and Dutiful Daughter if I hadn't forced you to?''

''Once you were settled, I believe I should have reached that conclusion on my own.''

''Perhaps. But you must concede my actions hastened the event. So, what is it you've decided to do?''

''Purchase more land and expand our breeding operations. You know I've had my eye on a new pair of Irish thoroughbreds for the past year, but lacked the means—and space—to acquire them. With the addition of those bloodlines, within a few years Sudley foals should be the most sought-after hunting stock in England.''

''So you don't intend to remain here and play the fatuous Society game? Famous! I must have Holden obtain some champagne so we may toast our new lives!''

Putting the fact that the viscount was apparently still involved with her sister aside to deal with later, Caragh said, ''You've obtained the commission, then? You will be able to manage on your own?''

"Not just manage, but prosper." Her eyes taking on a sparkle, Ailis gave her a mischievous look. "Of course, it's not quite the sort of commission you are probably envisioning."

"Is it not portrait work?"

"In a manner of speaking. 'Tis a series of life studies that will be bound in a folio. I excel at figure drawing, you know. Lord Wolverton commissioned one set, but Max tells me that quality work of this sort is so rare, he is certain that once Wolverton's friends see it, I can expect a number of other commissions to follow."

"Ailis, that's wonderful! I'm so proud for you." Caragh had to admit to surprise, tinged with a bit of awe. She hadn't really believed that her sister would actually be able to earn a living at her art.

Ailis's smile widened. "While it isn't what I should like to do as a life's work, Max can sell the folios for so astronomical a sum that I shall have a tidy income to sustain me until I start winning commissions in oils. Besides, the drawings are rendered from life, so they are good practice, and doing them is quite…stimulating. Come, let me show you."

"I should love to see them." Rising, Caragh followed her sister to her work bench.

"This is the sketch that Lord Wolverton saw first—a study I'd done that Max liked well enough to hang in his studio. Originally I called it *Longing*."

Ailis held out to her a drawing of a young girl, her face tilted up and her misty eyes gazing into the distance with a mingling of sadness and desire. The girl's expression sounded so immediate a chord of recognition deep within her that, for a moment, Caragh ceased to breathe. "She looks as though she just lost her true love!"

"Perhaps. But Lord Wolverton thought she might have just found him." Ailis passed her a second sketch.

In this study the girl's expression had turned shy but focused, her eyes gazing out at the viewer as if mesmerized by someone beyond the picture's frame. She had loosened the wrapper she'd been wearing in the first sketch, leaving her bare shoulders exposed and telegraphing a seductive promise that caused a familiar tightening in the pit of Caragh's stomach. "Oh, my!" she said faintly.

Ailis passed her the next sketch. Only a trace of shyness remaining, the girl's eyes smoldered over her slightly parted lips while she held the robe together—just beneath her bare, taut-nippled breasts.

Caragh knew she should tell her sister to stop, but sound seemed to have dried in her throat. While she looked on mutely, Ailis presented the next.

Shy waif had disappeared, replaced by knowing Eve. The girl gazed out with confidence, wrapper sleeves at her forearms, the robe hanging open to display the whole front of her nude body, from full breasts down her rounded belly to the length of her slender legs. With her hip arched and one leg slightly bent, she held the fingers of one hand poised at the junction of her thighs, as if about to reveal the treasures within.

A flush of heat flooded Caragh's face, and she lifted a trembling hand to fan herself. "H-how many m-more?" she stuttered.

Ailis grinned. "Several. But perhaps you should sit down."

Caragh sank onto the stool Ailis pushed toward her. Which was fortunate, for her knees would probably have given way had she been standing to view the next sketch Ailis handed over. In this, the girl's unseen lover at last appeared, kneeling naked with his side to the viewer, his tongue reaching within the folds she had parted for him, his large member stiff and proudly erect.

Caragh's chest grew hot, her nipples tingled and a tight pressure coiled at the base of her thighs...at that point which the girl's lover was so assiduously stroking with his tongue.

Shocked, appalled and fascinated, she watched spellbound

as Ailis displayed the rest of her sketches...the lover with his erection probing between the girl's thighs while he suckled her breast; the girl kneeling before her lover, filling her mouth with his penis; the two side by side, the lover's tongue buried in the girl's mound while she licked his taut member; and finally, the girl with her legs drawn up, her head lolling back and her hands clenched on her partner's shoulders while he thrust himself between her parted thighs.

"I now call the series *The Seduction*," Ailis said as she reassembled the sketches.

For a long moment Caragh sat stunned. She had seen sketches of nude classical sculpture in her father's library and as a country girl, knew the rudiments of how animals coupled. But never before had she been made aware, in graphic terms, of the way in which a man and a woman could use their bodies to give each other pleasure.

When her stupefied brain finally resumed functioning, her first thought was to wonder how *Ailis* knew about it. "*Y-you* sketched these? But...but how could you?"

Ailis laughed. "Oh, Caragh, you're such an innocent!" Still chuckling, she walked over to pour a steaming cup of tea from a pot the maid must have brought while Caragh was sitting mesmerized. Handing it to her, she said, "Holden wasn't my first lover. Several years ago—"

"S-several *years?*" Caragh gasped.

"—when I became fascinated with figure study, I noticed a farm boy in the fields north of Sudley who possessed quite a magnificent physique. For a few pennies, I persuaded him to model for me. And, as I'm sure you can now understand, viewing his...attributes elicited a heated curiosity as to just how he might employ them. I now know he wasn't particularly skilled, but on the whole, the experience was both enjoyable and instructive."

"But the risks you took! What if you'd conceived a child?"

Ailis shrugged. "I didn't. At any rate, I know to take the proper precautions now."

Dizzy from trying to assimilate such a barrage of revelations, Caragh did not pursue that point. "But afterward? Were you not embarrassed to encounter the boy?"

"For a few more pennies, I had him promise not to approach Sudley land again." Ailis smiled. "He seemed rather dazed by the experience. Were he literate, I expect he would have claimed he was but a poor mortal seduced and abandoned by Aphrodite, disguised as an English gentlewoman."

"I can imagine," Caragh murmured, still astounded.

"One of the benefits of residing in London is the ease of obtaining models. As you can understand, it's better for the study of technique to work with a live model—"

"You sketched a model doing…that?" Caragh asked, her voice rising to a squeak.

"The girl was a prostitute, of course, so I expect she's performed acts more inventive than those. I haven't yet found a male model, so to compose some of the sketches, I posed myself and Hólden before a mirror." Ailis chuckled again. "The darling boy was quite willing to participate."

Rendered once more bereft of speech, Caragh thought for the first time that it was perhaps beneficial that Ailis had left her family to set up her studio. If Aunt Kitty had ever discovered such sketches in Ailis's room, the poor lady would have expired in a fit of apoplexy.

Caragh wasn't entirely sure her own heart, still thumping wildly against her ribs, was strong enough.

"I can see you are quite overwhelmed, so I'll say no more for now. Besides, there's something else I wanted to ask. If you've decided to run your farm instead of clawing your way back to a place among the ton, you must have given up the idea of making a Society marriage. So what do you mean to do about Quentin?"

From lust to Quentin wasn't a far leap in Caragh's mind,

but her still-overheated senses were making speech difficult. While she fumbled for words, Ailis waved a hand impatiently. "You needn't try to deny you're smitten by him. I may be absorbed in my work, but I'm neither blind nor dumb. Do you mean to marry him?"

That question effectively doused Caragh's ardor. "After your disgrace, he made me an offer. A noble sacrifice to save me becoming a spinster."

"Am I to understand you've refused this gallant gesture?"

"Yes. I hardly wish to marry a man inspired to wed me out of pity."

Ailis raised her eyebrows. "I would wager 'pity' has little to do with it, but 'tis your own affair. Marriage is a rather dismal business in any event. But love-play—ah, now that is a different matter altogether. If you lust for Quentin as I think you do, then make him your lover."

Remembering her pathetic efforts already in that vein, Caragh laughed out loud. "Let me assure you, Ailis, I have no skill whatsoever in enticing a man! Besides, Quentin will always see me as his virginal, gently-born maiden neighbor. Should I succeed in seducing him, his honor would demand that he marry me afterwards. Which is almost as revolting a reason to propose to me as pity."

"You must do as you wish. But I still say if you want him, do what is necessary to get him." Ailis winked at her. "I can give some advice, if you like."

Before Caragh could decide whether or not she wanted to avail herself of that offer, from the room beyond she heard a clock strike the hour. "Heavens!" she gasped, "I completely forgot the time! Thank you for the tea, but if I'm not to be late for dinner, I must get back."

With a shrewd look, Ailis waved her toward the exit. "Yes, better return before Aunt Kitty misses you. Higgins will summon a hackney. Wait a moment before you walk down, though. I have something I think you must have.'' Ailis jumped up and strode to her workbench.

Moving by rote, Caragh put on her pelisse and gloves. Her body still tingled and her thoughts stopped and stuttered as she tried to assimilate the incredible information—and images—revealed to her over the last hour.

Ailis caught up with her by the door, surprising her with another quick, fierce hug. ''I'm glad we've reached an understanding.''

''So am I,'' Caragh replied, and meant it. After tonight, she would carry with her a radically different image of her sister. No longer the strong-willed, selfish child who needed her sister to tend her, Ailis had become a self-absorbed but independent woman with, Caragh realized with a touch of humility, a worldly experience far greater than her own.

''For you,'' Ailis said, handing her a folded piece of drawing paper.

Caragh would have thought she'd received too many jolts already this evening to be moved by anything else, but as she unfolded the gift, a bolt of surprise—and desire—flashed through her.

The pencil drawing, apparently a study for one of her sister's commissioned works, featured a naked man reclining on his side—displaying an impressive full erection. A man who smiled seductively at her from Quentin's face.

''Ailis, how could you?'' she cried, torn between outrage and amusement.

''Oh, it took me but a moment to alter it to Quent's features,'' her irrepressible sister replied. ''Keep it—and dream about him.''

At that moment, Higgins skipped up the stairs to tell her the hackney had arrived.

Ailis tugged the drawing free and refolded it, then held it out. ''Come visit me again.''

After a half-second's hesitation, Caragh took the sketch back. "I will."

Bemused and unsettled, Caragh followed the maid to the waiting hackney. After the great blow her sister had dealt her, her affection for Ailis would be forever altered. But the gaping breach between them that had so blighted her spirit was a fair way to being healed.

Caragh felt a warm expansiveness, a new hope flooding her. Anything was possible, she thought jubilantly. Perhaps even—her thumbs caressed the drawing—seducing Quentin Burke.

CHAPTER THIRTEEN

LISTENING with half an ear to her aunt's chatter, Caragh sat through dinner, her mind still churning over the events of the late afternoon. But after the footman came to clear the plates, her aunt's cheery voice wavered, recalling Caragh's attention.

Obviously thinking about the variety of entertainments which, several weeks previous, she would have been readying herself to attend at this hour, Lady Catherine put on a brave smile. "Should you like to try a hand of whist in the parlor, dear? If not, I have that chair cover I've been meaning to finish this age."

Guilt jabbed at Caragh. Now that her mission here was nearly accomplished, she really must stop putting off a discussion of her future and reveal to the kind relative who had supported her so valiantly what a viper she was still nurturing in her bosom.

"Let's just have a comfortable coze, shall we?"

Lady Catherine's face brightened. "I should love it! I understand how...distressing this whole affair must have been for you! Your hopes for Ailis so cruelly dashed, and as for your own..." Her aunt heaved a sigh. "I hadn't wished to press you into discussing it until you were ready, but I think it an excellent idea for us to begin redesigning your future."

Knowing how her aunt was likely to feel about her plans, Caragh's resolve almost wavered. But her dear aunt deserved better of her than to learn her intentions at the last moment. "Shall I bring us more wine?"

Lady Catherine nodded. Girding herself, Caragh poured two glassfuls and followed her aunt into the parlor.

"I know we've suffered some…reverses, but you needn't be too cast down," Lady Catherine said as she seated herself. "I am still Somebody, after all, and more important, I can count at least two of Almack's patronesses as bosom bows. What we must do first—"

"Aunt Kitty, I know you would willingly trade upon your well-deserved reputation to ease me back into Society, but I really feel I must take a…different path."

"Oh, dear." Her aunt's smile faded and she took a quick sip of wine. "I'm not going to like what I'm about to hear, am I?"

Caragh smiled, her eyes misting. "I'm afraid not—at least, not initially."

Lady Catherine took a larger gulp. "You'd best open the budget and tell me the whole, then."

"You know Papa has given me free rein to manage both the house and estate at Sudley for years. Since a husband would probably wish to take over my finances and my stables and relegate me to household affairs, I believe I prefer to remain unwed. I'm happiest working with my horses. In fact, I'm about to expand the breeding operation. I came back to London to arrange the purchase of additional land."

"But Caragh, you were hardly in town long enough to meet anyone before Ailis…well, my dear, let me assure you, when you make the acquaintance of the right gentleman, all thought of who manages what will go right out of your head! Please, give it more time before you convince yourself that marriage will not suit you."

Caragh offered a rueful smile. "I'm afraid the rub is that I've already met such a man, Aunt Kitty, but…but he does not return my regard. With my feelings already fully engaged, I cannot envision developing a *tendre* for someone else. So it's best I resign myself to spinsterhood."

"My poor darling! But you mustn't give up! There are

ways to…move such a situation along. An intimate tête-à-tête unexpectedly interrupted—''

"Oh no, Aunt Kitty!" Caragh cried, torn between amusement and gratitude. "If he does not wish to wed me willingly, then there is an end to it."

"Few gentleman ever wish to wed *willingly,*" Lady Catherine countered with some exasperation. "Most have to be…assisted to that decision! I promise you, taking a husband will be infinitely more pleasing than residing with your father. And though I was never so blessed, there is always the possibility of children. Besides, what shall you do after Archibald inherits? You cannot imagine that he will leave you in charge of the Sudley stables."

"No." Fidgeting with her wineglass, Caragh took a deep breath. "I expect I didn't make myself perfectly clear. I do not intend to remain at Sudley with Papa. I shall be moving all my horses to the land now being purchased—of which I shall be sole owner. So Cousin Archibald inheriting Sudley will have no effect on me."

Her aunt's eyes widened as she comprehended the full implications of that speech. "Y-you will live there without your Papa? And operate—a breeding farm? But Caragh, your clients will be almost solely—gentleman!"

"Yes, I suppose they will."

"Once word of this gets about, your reputation will be ruined almost as effectively as Ailis's!" Lady Catherine wailed.

"It won't be quite that bad," Caragh tried to appease her. "I shall be immured in the country, and you know the ton cares little for anything that occurs outside—"

"Breeding *horses!* Oh, this must be all your mama's doing!" Aunt Kitty burst in. "But how? I screened the letters you received most particularly, just as I promised your Papa!"

"Mama's doing?" Caragh echoed. Had the distress of envisioning a second social disaster overset her poor aunt's mind? "Now Aunt Kitty, you know that…"

As she watched her aunt's indignant face, the incredible suspicion crystallizing in her head made her lose track of her sentence. "You can't mean Mama is…still alive? But…but I thought she died of influenza when Ailis was in short skirts!"

"Would that she had, the unnatural creature!" Lady Catherine said crossly. "Especially as it appears she has inspired both her daughters to behave almost as badly as ever *she* did!"

"Mama truly is alive, then? Does Ailis know?"

Her irritation fading, Lady Catherine looked suddenly uncertain. "You mean Aurora…has not contacted you?"

"No! Until this moment, I thought her dead these fifteen years."

"Oh, dear," Lady Catherine said faintly. "Then I'm afraid I have been vastly indiscreet. Your Papa will be so vexed with me!"

Caragh waved an impatient hand. "He will never learn of it. So tell me, where is my mother? Where has she hidden all these years? And what did she do that caused everyone to tell us she had died?"

Lady Catherine took another sip of wine. "I suppose it is too late to insist I know nothing about it?"

"Much too late. Granted, she figures in my memory only as a beautiful lady who occasionally deigned to visit her grubby offspring, but still, I'm curious. And I *am* her daughter, little acquainted with her as I was. Do I not have a right to know?"

Lady Catherine sighed. "I suppose you do. But I fear there will be quite a dust-up when Michael discovers what I've let slip."

"Unless the details have somehow become embedded in the original Greek of the *Iliad,* you have nothing to worry about. Have another sip of wine and tell me everything."

As if in need of more than just a sip, Lady Catherine

drained her glass. Setting it down, she began, "Aurora was stunningly beautiful, you know—Ailis is her image."

"Which is why Papa has always favored Ailis," Caragh said drily.

"Michael was just down from Oxford, a hopeless scholar, his head stuffed full of poetical nonsense. What must he do but take one look at Aurora Wendover, riding neck-or-nothing to the hounds at some hunt, and tumble head over heels! The most frivolous chit in the ton, and he's declaring her to be the very embodiment of some heathenish deity."

"Aurora, goddess of the dawn? Or the huntress Diana?"

Lady Catherine waved a hand. "Goodness, how should I know? Since Michael was handsome and his verses celebrating her perfection quite superior to the drivel generally spouted by her court, she deigned to consider herself in love with him, too—for a time."

"It didn't last?"

Lady Catherine uttered an unladylike sniff. "I tried to tell my brother how unsuitable a match it was! But he wouldn't listen—and Aurora had long since learned to manipulate her papa into allowing her whatever she wanted. They married and Michael bore her off to Sudley, eager to craft a new folio of verses in her honor. I suppose for a time, with their mutual love of horses, they may have been happy. But Aurora Wendover was not created to live quietly in rural obscurity. As soon as she recovered from her confinement with Ailis, she began pestering your papa to take her back to London. The spring before Ailis turned five, he finally did."

"Where she once again conquered the ton."

Lady Catherine nodded. "Yes, despite being a mother and quite old! Between the court of dandies hanging about her drawing room and the crowd trailing her wherever she went, she drove poor Michael to fits of jealousy, especially over some count in the Italian ambassador's retinue. When the Season ended and Michael insisted they return to Sudley, there was a dreadful row. The next thing I knew, Michael was at my door virtually incoherent, and Aurora had run off to Italy with her count!''

''Did she divorce Papa to marry him?''

''I don't believe so. As a papist, the Italian couldn't have married a divorced woman—and he may have already had a wife, for all I know! In any event, Aurora didn't remain with him long. Ever skilled at manipulating, she managed to coax her heartbroken papa into settling a handsome income on her. I understand she hired a villa in Rome and bought a country estate in Tuscany. She lives there now, spending the season in town, patronizing the arts—and taking lovers half her age.''

''She sounds fascinating!''

''She has a most unsteady character and I am heartily sorry that you and Ailis share her blood.'' Lady Catherine said roundly. ''My poor brother never recovered. He found what solace he could in his books, gradually withdrawing from the world until now I believe he scarce notices anything that did not transpire some ten or twenty centuries ago.''

Suddenly Caragh was arrested by the memory of her father's melancholy face. No wonder his eyes were always sad, his thoughts turned from a painful reality to an inner world he could order and control. ''Poor Papa.''

''Well, now you know the whole. If you are set on burying yourself on this horse farm, I suppose I can comfort myself with the knowledge that, though you are bidding fair to be as unconventional as Aurora, at least you'll not create quite so public a scandal.''

Impulsively, Caragh reached over to hug her aunt. ''Thank you, Aunt Kitty! For taking me on to begin with, given my history. And for loving me despite my faults.''

Her aunt hugged her back. ''I might deserve your thanks, if only I'd managed to get you respectably settled. But if you will not allow me to attempt that, at least promise me you'll be happy, child.''

"I shall certainly try to be."

"Now, if you'll excuse me, dear, I believe I shall go up to bed. I'm feeling a bit...overwhelmed."

"I'll take you up."

After leaving her aunt with another hug, Caragh continued on to her bedroom. She let the maid help her into her night rail, but once the girl departed, her mind racing with too many ideas and observations to find sleep, she abandoned her bed and curled up in the wing chair by the fire.

Never in the wildest flights of fancy could she have imagined what she'd learned this day! That Ailis, who had taken a lover at sixteen and seduced Lord Freemont, would be earning her living—sketching erotic art! That their mother, very much alive, was leading a still-scandalous existence in Rome. Though her sister—as she had bitter reason to know, Caragh thought with a muted pang—seemed to place scant value on familial ties, she still ought to tell Ailis their mother was not, as they'd grown up believing, among the Dearly Departed. But since her sister had little interest in anything that did not directly touch on her art, there was no urgency in conveying the news.

Caragh shook her head and laughed. At least she and Ailis came by their unconventional behavior honestly.

She stilled, listening carefully to confirm all was quiet and the household abed. Then she went to the desk, unlocked the top drawer, and drew out the drawing Ailis had given her. A wave of heat that had nothing to do with the fire in the grate washed over her as she studied it.

What if Quentin were here with her now, lounging nude on her sofa? She grinned at the possibilities. How would his... endowments compare with what Ailis had sketched?

Make him your lover, her sister urged. Being her scandalous mother's unconventional daughter, perhaps she should.

THE FOLLOWING DAY, Quentin set out for London. After Caragh's refusal of his suit and her unexpected departure, he'd returned to Thornwhistle to take the one rational action he'd managed to filter from their turgid confusion of an interview. Though he had not yet given up hope of dissuading Caragh from her disastrous notion of running a farm, it was high time he ensured his property was being properly run by his own estate manager, without benefit of advice from his neighbor.

But though that work kept him occupied for several days, it did nothing to soothe the queasy mix of uncertainty, anger and concern that still troubled him. Until Caragh had disappeared, some alien spirit taking her place within the outwardly familiar body of his friend, he'd not realized how much he depended upon her level-headed intelligence, how much he enjoyed her wit and warmth.

To put it simply, he missed her.

His immediate reaction, of course, after having been rebuffed in absentia that second time, was to let her go her own way if she valued his opinions so little. But by the second day after her departure, the pride-driven desire to hold himself aloof began to crumble. By the time he'd assured himself of Manning's competence, he'd decided to set aside his hurt and seek her out.

Perhaps, he told himself as he journeyed back to London, her unprecedented behavior was merely the product of shock and distress after being pitched so unprepared into Ailis's scandal. Quite understandable under the circumstances, and a lapse he'd willingly forgive.

To determine how best to approach her, he needed to ascertain how serious she was about carrying through this plan to expand the Sudley breeding farm. Then he could figure out how to persuade her that marrying him would be the right choice, whether or not she went through with it.

For he'd found, once he got himself over the hurdle of actually framing a proposal, that he rather liked the idea of contracting a sensible, practical marriage of convenience with his best friend. Or at least he had until that stranger back at Sudley had coolly rebuffed him.

Surely, having had time by now to recover her normal composure, the Caragh he called upon in London would be the same Caragh he knew and valued so highly. They could discuss the matter of a future together rationally, and with the addition of the right lover-like words, he would induce her to agree it was in both their best interests to combine their resources in marriage.

Combine their bodies as well. But he'd best put that distracting thought out of mind until he'd obtained her consent to his proposal.

He had another, previously postponed reason for returning to the metropolis. At his first opportunity, he intended to seek out Ailis Sudley and tell just what he thought about her self-centered lack of appreciation for her sister's efforts and her callous disregard of Caragh's feelings and reputation.

He reached London in the late afternoon and, still uncertain whether to seek out Caragh immediately or send a note announcing his return to town, he decided instead to call on Ailis. He felt no uncertainty whatsoever about what he needed to tell *her*. Besides, Ailis might have some news about Caragh that would give him a hint about how to approach her.

As soon as he refreshed himself from the journey, he set out for Ailis's studio, where a maidservant led him through a small anteroom to an open chamber whose large north-facing windows telegraphed its purpose as eloquently as the clutter of paints, canvas rolls and brushes that dotted every level surface. Clad in an outmoded day gown, her sleeves pushed up, Ailis sat on a sofa to receive him.

"Quentin, how kind of you to come visit."

A note of irony colored her voice. He cast her a sharp glance, but she was smiling pleasantly. Though the words of the diatribe he'd come to deliver pressed heavily upon his tongue, he ought to be civil and exchange a few pleasantries before launching his attack.

"What a handsome studio! I imagine the morning light is splendid."

She nodded. "It is, and holds well into afternoon. I've been able to make great progress since moving here."

"You've obtained work?"

"Yes, I'm just finishing a very lucrative commission." Her smile deepened. "I shall have to show it to you sometime."

"Caragh approves?"

"She was a bit shocked at first, but I believe she enthusiastically supports it now. She has visited me here, you know, and I'm pleased to say we are once again in perfect charity."

"I don't doubt it—Caragh being ever generous to those she loves." Unable to keep the edge out of his voice, Quentin continued, "I do wonder, though, after Caragh championed your art for years and attempted to arrange your future to accommodate it, how you could have played so low a trick on her. I grant that you are young and blinded by your muse, but surely you've noticed how hard she works at Sudley, always putting everyone else's needs before her own. Was it really too much to ask to let her have a whole Season to enjoy herself before you did this—" he gestured around the room "—and destroyed it all for her?"

While he spoke, his voice rising in volume as he proceeded, Ailis's smile faded and her eyes turned hard. She listened to his jobation in silence, making no attempt to reply until he stopped for breath.

"Have you finished yet?"

Her coolness, her total lack of remorse, incensed him. "No, I have not! How could you hurt her so? You do at least understand that you hurt her, I trust! She's been looking after you with a mother's devotion since she was barely more than a child herself, and how did you repay her for that loving concern? With deceit, scandal and disgrace!"

Ailis arched an eyebrow. "My, my, and who appointed Quentin Burke judge and jury? Before you become too assiduous about examining the log in my eye, perhaps you'd better look in the mirror and examine your own."

"And just what do you mean by that?"

She rose from the sofa and walked over to glare at him. "Just that it isn't only at Sudley that Caragh worked hard all these years. I seem to recall her traveling quite often to Thornwhistle, too. Rearranging her schedule to accommodate your calls when you deigned to visit, toiling late to finish her own tasks after you'd left. If I selfishly received the care she freely gave without offering a return, have you done any better? Did you ever look beyond the obliging friend to determine what the woman beneath might wish? Perhaps, my lord, you should answer *that* question before you accuse *me* of taking advantage. Now I must change. Higgins will show you out."

Without giving him a chance to reply, she turned away and, as Quentin stared after her in disbelief, for the second time this week, a Sudley female walked out on him.

Rising to his feet with such vehemence that his chair rocked on its legs, he stalked to the door.

How dare Ailis accuse *him* of selfishness and insensitivity! he fumed as he pounded down the stairs. Caragh had assisted him on many occasions, it was true, but he helped her as well. They were devoted friends who always sought the best for each other!

At the echo of Ailis's strident question, Quentin's pace faltered. Out of memory bubbled up Caragh's soft voice asking if it might not be possible to add passion to their relationship—a possibility he had firmly rejected.

An uneasy feeling settling in his chest, he continued down the stairs. Could there be at least a germ of truth to Ailis's accusation? Had he ever truly asked himself what *Caragh* wanted from their relationship?

Or had he only considered how to maintain their friendship

in the fashion most acceptable to *him,* arbitrarily accepting as a given that Caragh wanted the same thing he did?

By the time he reached the street he'd slowed to a walk, his anger muted to a slow burn. Perhaps he had been a little...forceful...in insisting on the terms of their relationship. For the best of reasons, of course—to keep that precious bond intact. But he had decided on that course rather...unilaterally.

And he could have seized more opportunities to express his appreciation for the care she expended on Thornwhistle, as well as his admiration for her intelligence and wit.

Frowning, he paced down the street. Surely he could discount most of Ailis's speech as merely a way of parrying his verbal onslaught by mounting a counterattack of her own.

Caragh couldn't think of him selfish and dictatorial...could she?

Still, the possibility that Caragh might entertain even a muted version of the opinion of him expressed by Ailis was deeply troubling. An even more unpalatable thought followed hard upon that.

Had she refused his suit not out of the confusion and distress engendered by the scandal, but because she found him in his own way as selfish and unappreciative as her sister?

He simply couldn't believe it. But little as he credited it, the notion was too disturbing to dismiss out of hand.

He must call upon Caragh first thing tomorrow and lay that anxiety permanently to rest.

CHAPTER FOURTEEN

AFTER A RESTLESS NIGHT, awakening at intervals from vivid dreams in which she and Quentin replaced the models in Ailis's sketches, Caragh awoke, her body still tingling, a dull throb pulsing between her thighs.

She pushed herself to a sitting position, the friction of the night rail's linen against her taut nipples sparking a thrill of sensation. Ah, if that glancing caress had come from Quentin's fingers!

She fanned her heated face. Could she overcome modesty and upbringing and find the boldness that would put his hands there? Equally important, could she trespass upon their friendship to trick Quentin to it? For if she were sure of nothing else, she knew beyond doubt that Quentin Burke would expire from lust before he would bed a gently-born virgin.

Her mother had destroyed a family to pursue what she wanted. Caragh would never go that far, but with her reputation already lost and the man she desired unmarried, she could follow her desires without hurting anyone.

Except perhaps herself. But could the anguish of Quentin leaving her after lying in her arms be any worse than the anguish of living without him, forever bereft of his touch?

If she succeeded in seducing him, she would have the memory of that closeness to cherish. She would have relief from the fire smoldering within her and a personal knowledge of the powerful, inexplicable force that bonds men and women together.

And she would have been very clever in disguising her identity, for if Quentin ever succeeded in uncovering her ruse, his anger and his honor would force him to coerce her into marriage. The only outcome she could envision that would be worse than her current misery would be to trip herself into wedlock with a man who didn't truly love her.

Was a night of Quentin's love worth taking that risk?

Caragh leaned back against the pillows and drew Ailis's sketch from beneath her pillow. Her body flamed anew as she traced a fingertip down the outline of the bare shoulder and torso, across the length of the taut erection.

To have her hands touch not cool parchment but warm flesh, her fingers—and lips—explore not an artist's sketch but the man out of her dreams, would, she decided, be worth every risk.

She would have to be very careful. But before she left London to begin her new life, she would seduce Quentin Burke.

Laudable audacity, she thought with a sigh as she carefully refolded the sketch and rang for her morning chocolate. She still hadn't the faintest idea how she could bring it about.

But Ailis might. So this evening, Caragh would pay her sister another visit.

Shivering against the morning chill, she threw on a wrapper and drew a chair close to the hearth. After the maid delivered a tray, she warmed her hands over the steaming brew and glanced at the morning paper.

Sipping chocolate, she read in a desultory fashion, her thoughts frequently distracted by flashbacks to last night's torrid dreams, speculation about how she could engineer a seduction, and curiosity over how her sister had produced those amazing…figure studies.

She'd skimmed the political news and several pages of society gossip when a small advertisement caught her attention—the announcement of a Grand Masquerade Ball to be held at Vauxhall Gardens on Friday next, with Refreshments and a Superior Orchestra to Delight the Discerning Guest.

A masquerade ball! As her mind focused on the possibilities, a knock sounded at the door.

"Beggin' your pardon, miss, but Lord Branson is waiting below to see you. Will you receive him?"

Though she could have wished for more time, the outlines of a plan were already forming. "Tell Lord Branson I will be down directly."

HEARTENED when the maid returned to inform him that Caragh would receive him—for he'd half feared, if Ailis's accusations had any merit, that she might refuse to see him—Quentin rehearsed once again what he intended to say.

Avoiding any mention of his previous offer, inquiring about her plans and expressing once again his appreciation for her efforts on his behalf would do for a start, he decided. He would then take his cue from Caragh on where to proceed next.

Hearing voices approach, he straightened and wiped his suddenly damp palms on his pant leg. Oh, that the lady who walked through that door would be *his* Caragh, rather than the chilly stranger he'd encountered at Sudley!

A welcoming smile on her face, Caragh came toward him, hands extended. "Quentin, what a delightful surprise! I thought you still at Thornwhistle."

Joy and a relief so intense he felt momentarily light-headed washed through him. *His* Caragh was back.

He seized her hands in a punishing grip and kissed them fervently. The immediate punch of contact as their gloved hands met, as his lips grazed her knuckles, rocketed through him. For a moment, all he could think was how much he'd missed her—and how much more he craved of her touch.

Finally pulling his mind back to the moment, he said, "I've only just arrived. I regret that our...visit at Sudley was so short. You must tell me how your plans are progressing."

If she wished to make some explanation—or apology—for

the manner in which she had received his proposal, he'd just given her a perfect opening.

He braced himself, but with no discernable constraint or embarrassment, she answered, "Quite well, thank you. And I am doing much better, too, so you'll have no need to amuse me with absurdities, as you did that day at Sudley."

"Amuse you?" he asked cautiously.

"Yes—with that spurious offer of marriage! I must admit, you fooled me at first into thinking it a legitimate offer, which made me quite angry, until upon reflection I realized your intent. After all, you couldn't have truly called yourself my friend and made a serious offer."

"I...I couldn't?"

She laughed. "Of course not! To suggest, after all the years I've managed Sudley, that I was not capable of suitably handling the masculine attention inherent in expanding the farm—most of which would come from clients who are already well acquainted with my family—would have been insulting, to me and to them. And to offer marriage because you felt sorry for my situation would have been unsupportable...had you been in earnest, of course."

"Of...of course."

"If I've learned anything about you over the years of our friendship, Quentin, it is that you judge by what you know to be true, not by the artificial dictates of Society. You've assured me on several occasions that you admire my skill at estate management and respect my independence. How silly of me, even for a moment, to think you would suddenly begin to question either! I can only attribute it to the...distress I was experiencing at that moment."

"Yes, I could see you were...distressed."

"After all, had we not, just a bare week previous, decided that—" she turned her head away, her cheeks coloring "—that passion and friendship would not mix? To have taken it upon yourself to alter those terms unilaterally, without consulting *my* preferences, would have been arrogant, presumptuous and insensitive.''

"Arrogant, presumptuous and insensitive?'' he echoed, inwardly appalled. "I suppose you could say that.''

"And I know you are none of those,'' she affirmed, pressing his hand warmly.

Once again, as her fingers lingered on his, that immediate connection between them fired his senses. He fought the effect, knowing he dare not risk another blunder.

"I hope you also know,'' he said, struggling to find the proper words, ''that however…unfortunately I may have expressed myself, all I ever sought was your happiness.''

Her breezy smile faded and her face grew almost…sad. "I know,'' she whispered. For a moment she let her fingers rest in his. Then, withdrawing her hand with a slow, lingering caress that he felt down to his toes, she said in a bright tone, ''Now, let me tell you where things stand on the expansion of my enterprise.''

Arrogant? Insensitive? Presumptuous? Shocked to discover how Caragh had viewed his offer, Quentin only half heard the details she rattled off about her land purchase. Though he had certainly not intended to be any of those things, after examining that ill-fated proposal from her perspective, he had to reluctantly admit there might be some justification for her viewing it that way.

He *had* rather blindly proceeded according to the social convention that proclaimed an unmarried maiden must always be gratified by a proposal of marriage, regardless of its reason or wording. Nor had he accompanied his offer by avowing any tender feelings. And were Ailis to once again pose her pointed question, he would have to admit that in this instance, as the first time he'd discussed the nature of their relationship with Caragh, he had failed to consult her opinion, presuming to decide for them both that marriage was the best course.

"I did wish to ask for one favor, Quentin.''

He jerked his attention back to the present. "A…a favor? Ask what you will, and if 'tis within my power to give, it is yours."

For an instant her glance caught his. "Would that it were," he thought he heard her murmur. But before he could ask her to repeat the comment, she seized his arm, once again rattling his concentration.

"Nothing too arduous, I assure you," she continued. "It's just…well, as you know, my social schedule is rather…restricted at present, and soon I shall be back in the country, where entertainments are even more limited. I should very much like to attend the masquerade ball at Vauxhall Friday, but of course, I could not go to such an affair without an escort."

A deep wave of sympathy welled up to war with the sensual pull. Of course, banned from balls and parties as she was, she would pine for some amusement. "I should be happy to escort you. Will Lady Catherine go also?"

"I don't think so. She, ah, does not care for masquerades. I'm to meet with the lawyers that afternoon to finish details of the land purchase, so I may need to meet you directly at Vauxhall—I'll send a note. Speaking of which, I have an appointment with them shortly, so I must bid you good-day."

She rose, once again giving him her hands to kiss. He covered them with his own, relishing the contact and loath to break it. "Until Friday, then."

She curtseyed. Reluctantly he released her and bowed. As he reached the door, she called his name. He turned back with an inquiring look.

"Thank you for being my friend."

He smiled, his blood still humming at her nearness. "You can count on me," he assured her, and walked out.

That had not gone too badly, he told himself as he climbed into the hackney Evers summoned for him. He'd avoided a repetition of the disaster at Sudley and, he hoped, moved them further down the path of restoring to their friendship its previous comfortable intimacy.

He looked down at his still-tingling fingers. Well, almost comfortable.

Though he was nearly certain she'd known his proposal to be genuine, she'd pretended otherwise, allowing them to proceed beyond her refusal with a minimum of awkwardness and recrimination. She'd even given him a way to retreat from the shoal-filled waters of renewing his suit.

All he need do was continue to acquiesce in the charade that his proposal had been merely an attempt to amuse her out of her distress, and he had every reason to believe they would eventually recapture the same warm and easy relationship they'd shared before the upheavals that occurred after Caragh brought Ailis to London.

There remained the thorny problem of dissuading her from abandoning her father and moving to her new farm alone, but since he'd evidently offended her so deeply by suggesting a marriage of convenience, perhaps that too could be finessed under the guise of friendship.

Which should have relieved and pleased him—except that by now, he was almost sure a platonic friendship with Caragh Sudley was no longer what he truly wanted.

JUST AFTER DUSK, after sending Aunt Kitty into palpitations by informing her she meant to visit Ailis, Caragh arrived at her sister's studio. To her relief, her sister had already finished her day's work and reclined on her sofa, a glass of wine in hand.

"Sorry to burst in on you unannounced," Caragh said as she walked in, "but I must tell you—I mean to do it! And I shall need your advice on how to make my plan succeed."

Ailis's eyes lit with comprehension. "You propose to seduce Quentin? Bravo! Let's drink to that resolve, and you shall tell me how I can help."

While Ailis called for another glass, Caragh paced, too nervous to sit. "There's to be a masquerade ball at Vauxhall Friday, and I've obtained Quentin's promise to meet me there. Now I must determine where to meet him, in what disguise I should appear, and how I shall convince him to...to ravish me."

"Must you be disguised?" Ailis asked, handing her the wine.

"Certainly! Should I succeed in making us lovers, and he somehow recognized me, you know what that would mean."

"Ah, yes, the gentleman's sense of honor. He'd have you riveted as soon as a special license could be bought. We cannot have that! One of my models is an actress at Drury Lane—she can help with the disguise. And we must think where you are to take him. Though trysting in the open can be delightful—" Ailis winked at her "—Vauxhall is much too public for you to be comfortable seducing him there."

"Indeed not!" Caragh cried, her cheeks pinking at the very idea of performing the acts shown in Ailis's sketches in a location, however dimly lit and secluded, into which other people might at any moment wander. "What do you suggest?"

"Let me think about it. Surely Max or one of his friends will know of some suitable place."

Her embarrassment deepening, Caragh took a sip of wine. "What I most need you to advise me about, though, is how I...get him to that point. I have no experience with men, you know. If I can't entice him, arranging the disguise and the rendezvous will be wasted effort."

"True, although I doubt you will have much difficulty persuading him—he's a man, isn't he? But you must know more than just how to entice." Ailis looked at her thoughtfully. "Whatever persona you choose, for your deception to succeed, you shall have to appear experienced in the giving of pleasure. In fact, it would be best if you were to inflame his senses and then satisfy him so exquisitely, he will cease to think at all, much less have the wit to connect the siren who seduced him with the proper, virginal maiden she vaguely resembles.''

The notion of bringing Quentin Burke completely in thrall to her sensual control made her dizzy with delight—and desire. ''That sounds wonderful. But how can I learn to do that? Do you,'' she could feel her blush deepening, ''have more... more...sketches I could study?''

Ailis grinned. ''Though I consider myself fairly skilled, I think for this, you need the advice of a master! I've just contracted to do a portrait of Lady Belle Marchand. Do you know of her?''

''Lady Belle? Isn't she the courtesan Lord Bellingham has had in keeping for years? The one the Duke of York offered him ten thousand pounds to relinquish—and he refused?''

''The same. If her reputation is any indication, I wager she knows more about bewitching a man than any female living. And she really is a delightful lady.''

''You've met her?'' Caragh gasped, scandalized to think of her little sister actually consorting with this most infamous of the Fashionable Impures.

''How else could I decide whether or not I wished to paint her likeness? I shall send her a note asking her to come by early tomorrow evening. Rachel can stop by before her performance as well. So let us toast to tomorrow, sister dear. With our expert assistance, you shall soon give Quentin Burke the most erotic night of his life!''

CHAPTER FIFTEEN

AILIS ANSWERED the door the next evening upon Caragh's first knock, glass of wine in hand. "Let the transformation begin!" she cried, passing the glass to Caragh and sweeping her into the room.

Already nervous about the undertaking, Caragh downed a large gulp. "Have my...tutors arrived?"

"Rachel is here. Lady Belle shall not stop by until later, once we've perfected the disguise. You shall need to be wearing it when she gives her instructions, to insure you can follow them while garbed in different dress." Ailis laughed and whirled Caragh around. "This shall be so entertaining!"

"Let's hope it's not a farce," Caragh muttered, downing another gulp of wine.

"Nonsense, you shall be perfect. That is, you are still sure you want to do this, aren't you?"

Caragh smiled wryly. "Do I want to? Yes. Am I sure I can manage it? No. Am I frightened out of my wits about failing? Absolutely!"

As they walked into the studio, a curvaceous brunette rose from the sofa. "Fail to seduce a man? My dear, 'tis almost impossible! Seeing that most of 'em think of little else, a smile and a wink is usually enough."

"Caragh, meet Rachel DuVollet, currently of Drury Lane. Rachel, my sister Caragh."

"You are performing with Edmund Kean, are you not? I thought your Lady Macbeth particularly fine."

The actress looked at her with heightened interest. "I'm

flattered that you noticed. With Edmund on the stage, the rest of us have a tendency to be ignored.''

''Is he very difficult to work with?''

Rachel laughed. ''We thespians are a rather selfish breed at best. If Edmund weren't so remarkable an actor, I doubt he could induce anyone to take the stage with him. Speaking of acting, what role shall you play to bedazzle your gentleman?''

''It will be dark, you will be masked and Rachel will help us alter your appearance, but you shall still need some convincing persona if you wish to avoid his recognizing you,'' Ailis said.

Caragh crossed her arms and struck a woeful pose. ''Ah, *chérie,* I am but a poor widow, forced to flee *la France* with my darling Phillippe, who later gave his life *en combattant* Boneparte, that monster Corsican.''

''Magnifique!'' Ailis cried, while the actress clapped her hands. ''Since you can hardly accomplish this mute, I worried he might know your voice. But your French is excellent and that accent delightful. He shall be charmed—and completely taken in.''

''I sincerely hope so,'' Caragh said with a sigh.

''Widow's black is a good choice for gown and veil,'' Rachel said. ''Especially at night, 'twill mask your features better than any other color. Muffle your voice, too. Add a wig, and your own sister won't know you.'' She waved Caragh toward the sofa. ''I brought several wigs and an assortment of gowns from the theatre. Let's see which become you the best.''

Before Caragh could utter another word, Ailis and Rachel began stripping her out of her afternoon gown. For the next hour, the two women dressed and undressed her like a manikin, finally deciding on a black velvet gown with matching cloak, a soft velvet toque with a figured black veil to mask her face and a wig of short black ringlets. Having chosen the ensemble, they made Caragh walk, kneel and lie down on the sofa to make sure the wig would stay in place.

"The wig feels secure, but I cannot say the same for the gown," Caragh said. "Are you sure the bodice isn't too low?"

"Dearie, you want the gent to be thinking of bedding, right?" the actress asked. "Give him an eyeful of you in that ensemble and trust me, the only thing he'll be wondering is how fast he can peel off that last inch of cloth." She looked over at Ailis and giggled. "Worked for me with the Earl of Gresham, anyways."

Ailis grinned at Caragh. "You can't dispute proven success." Taking Caragh's arm, she marched her over to the cheval glass. "Behold, I give you...Madame LaNoire! The Black Lady," she added for Rachel's benefit.

Through the obstructing veil, Caragh peered at herself in the glass. "Oh, my!" she said weakly.

Gazing back at her stood a slender woman, dusky curls escaping beneath her jaunty toque, her face tantalizingly obscured by a mist of black veil. With the cape pulled behind her shoulders, even she had to catch her breath at the dramatic contrast between the midnight velvet of the gown and the ghostly paleness of her skin. The high, tight waistline pushed up and accentuated the voluptuous roundness of her nearly-bare breasts, which did indeed appear as though they might at any moment burst free from the extremely brief bodice.

"He won't be able to take his eyes off you," Ailis promised.

"Nor will any other man that gets a peep, so you'd best keep the cloak fastened until your gent arrives," the actress advised. "Now, I must go. Don't want to be late getting into makeup and give Edmund the Ego a reason to shout at me."

While Ailis walked her guest to the door, Caragh stared at herself in the glass, then held up her arms and made a slow pirouette. Though the material was heavier than the silks and muslins to which she was accustomed, it draped beautifully and the nap was as soft as a caress against her skin. Seeing herself peeping naughtily through her veil, dressed like an enchantress, made her feel like one.

I shall actually be able to do this! Giddy at her boldness, she threw back her head and laughed. As she doffed the bonnet and cloak, Ailis walked back.

"First, the disguise. Next—" Ailis went over to scoop something off her work bench "—the key to your pied-à-terre." With a flourish, she presented it to Caragh.

"Where? And whose is it?"

"Darling Max suggested it—I knew if love-play were the purpose, he would know how to arrange it! An artist friend of his, now traveling in Italy, has a flat nearby. Before Friday, I'll take you there so you can familiarize yourself with it— and rearrange things if you like."

"Italy!" Caragh exclaimed. "I nearly forgot! Ailis, did you know that Mama is still living?"

"*Our* mother? I thought she died of a fever ages ago."

"So we were told, but Aunt Kitty let slip last night that the story was a ruse to cover up the fact that she ran off with an Italian gentleman when you were still a babe. Did you truly not know?"

Ailis shook her head. "No, why would I?"

"Aunt Kitty said she's become quite a patroness of the arts. I thought perhaps Mr. Frank might have met her on his travels."

Ailis burst out laughing. "If she supports galleries in Rome or Florence, he's probably seduced her!"

"From what Aunt Kitty says, she probably seduced him," Caragh said drily. "I expect she goes by some other name now, so he wouldn't have made the connection."

Ailis clapped her hands. "Famous! While you're enticing a gentleman into the artist's rooms here, our long-absent mater may be enticing its owner into her suite in Rome. You see?"

She flung an arm out at Caragh, as if closing the argument. "With such blood in your veins, how can you fail?"

Ailis laughed again. "No wonder Aunt Kitty never wanted to let me of her sight!"

"I think Papa understood. When I told him about your studio, he said something about the inevitability of doing what the gods within compel you."

Ailis shrugged. "Well, I think we would all have been much better off if, instead of burying himself with his books in the countryside grieving, he'd have found another wench to replace her."

Could she find another buck to replace Quentin when their stolen night was over? Caragh wasn't so sure. "I think, in spite of everything, he still loves her."

"'Tis his life to waste," Ailis said with a sniff. "I would have chosen to move on."

She would have no choice but to move on, Caragh thought with a flash of sadness. But before then—she would have the magic of her night with Quentin.

Provided she could, in fact, entice him to the rooms—and escape undetected. "How shall I manage it if...if I can persuade him to escort me there? I don't suppose we could...you know, still fully clothed."

"It can be done," Ailis said with a grin, "but I don't recommend it. Skin to skin is so much more...satisfying."

Her words softened to a sigh and she closed her eyes, obviously remembering. Caragh felt a tremor of desire, just imagining the feel of Quentin's skin—hands, lips, body—against hers.

"I shall have to leave the lamps low—or dispense with them—to keep him from recognizing me."

"Light just one lamp when you arrive and insist on blowing it out before you remove your veil. We'll make sure the room is arranged so you'll not be caught in the moonlight. And require him to leave you in darkness. You are Madame LaNoire, *n'est-ce pas?*''

Caragh looked down at the low bodice of the wicked gown that emphasized the proud thrust of her breasts. ''*Oui, c'est vrai.* Now—what do I do to ensure this is an evening he will never forget?''

''Let us defer to the expert. I believe I hear Lady Belle at the door.''

They walked to the entry as the maid ushered in their visitor. Growing up with her sister, Caragh had become inured to physical loveliness, but the woman who glided with sensual elegance into the room was beyond doubt the most beautiful creature Caragh had ever beheld.

Her face, a profile of Grecian perfection framed by ringlets of purest gold, her skin the smoothness of white marble, she turned toward them a bow-shaped mouth that smiled in greeting, while eyes of an intense gentian blue inspected them.

No wonder, Caragh thought, her mouth agape, rumor reported that gentleman had offered enormous sums to lure this woman from her long-term protector.

''Lady Belle, thank you for visiting on such short notice,'' Ailis said.

''One must humor the whims of so talented an artist,'' Lady Belle replied. ''And this is your sister, I presume?''

Surprised to hear in the woman's husky voice the cultured tones of a gently-bred lady, Caragh found herself sinking into a curtsey deep enough to do honor to a royal. And truly, this woman held herself with the noble bearing of a queen.

''Lady Belle, I only wish I had half Ailis's beauty! But thank you for agreeing to come.''

Lady Belle nodded, handing her pelisse over to the maid, along with a coin the startled girl pocketed with alacrity before hurrying off. The evening gown revealed once her wrap had been removed—of a deep blue silk almost the color of her eyes—was cut in the latest fashion and obviously expensive. Yet the bodice, unadorned by jewels, lace or furbelows, was only moderately snug and almost modestly cut, higher than those sported by most of Society's ladies and much higher than that of the gown Caragh currently wore.

Of course, as the lady's bust and shoulders were as perfect as her face, she had no need to display them nearly naked to rivet the attention.

"Won't you join us in here, Lady Belle?"

The courtesan took a step, then halted. "Oh, dear!" she said in vexation. "I wished to ask you about the preliminary sketch you made, but I've left it in my reticule. Could you fetch it, please?"

Ailis nodded. "I'll be right back. Please," she said with a wink to Caragh, "make yourselves *comfortable*." She waved them toward the sofa in the studio.

Which was obviously a jab at how *un*comfortable she was likely to find this interview, Caragh thought, tempted to stick her tongue out at her sister as she took a chair opposite Lady Belle.

Caragh's composure wasn't helped by the penetrating gaze the courtesan focused on her. "So, you wish to seduce a particular man?"

Caragh found herself blushing. "Y-yes, ma'am. But I fear I am woefully ignorant of how to go about it."

"You are a virgin, then?"

Caragh's blush deepened. "Y-yes."

"You are sure you wish to do this? You will likely ruin your chances of wedding, should you succeed. It would be…infamous for you to be coerced into it."

The almost bitter intensity of her tone distracted Caragh from her embarrassment. Was that how this woman, who looked every inch a lady, had ended up a byword for carnality?

Intriguing as the answer might be, she couldn't possibly make so personal an inquiry of a stranger. "I am sure," she said, returning to the original question. "The man I would bed is also the man I love. But as he feels for me only a tepid affection, marrying him would end in misery. I should, though, like just one chance to lie in his arms."

With a graceful gesture, Lady Belle indicated the wig. "Hence the disguise?"

"Yes. Should he recognize me, he would insist that we wed, and I couldn't bear that."

"You have some means of support if you do not marry?"

"I manage a horse-breeding operation—in my own name."

Lady Belle nodded. "That should provide you a good income. Very well, I shall help. First, you must take precautions against conception. A vinegar-saturated sponge is best. I expect Ailis can get you a supply. Now, what do you wish to know?"

"I'm told this gown will focus his interest. What else can I do to...attract him?"

"You will be veiled?"

Caragh redonned her toque and wrapped the figured veil over her face. "I shall meet him at a masquerade ball in Vauxhall Gardens, dressed like this."

"Good. Night, shadow, a bit of aloofness will add to the allure, challenge him to master your mystery. You'll wear that cape?"

Caragh plucked the cloak off the sofa arm and tossed it on, tucking it behind her shoulders as Ailis had instructed. "Like this."

Lady Belle studied her for a moment. "The whiteness of your skin under the torchlight will capture his attention, entice his eyes to linger. You can further inflame him by leading his gaze on the journey his hands and mouth will already be thirsting to follow. Come here, please."

After Caragh obediently approached her, the courtesan picked up one of the tasseled cords that tied the cloak beneath her chin. "With him watching you, retie the cloak and then release one of the cords like so."

Beginning at the hollow of Caragh's throat, she slowly traced the silken tassel down the naked skin of Caragh's chest, over the swell of her bosom, then whisked the soft bristled tip over Caragh's breast before releasing it.

Caragh caught her breath, feeling her nipple stiffen in response to that subtle caress. Heat sparked in her stomach, pooled between her thighs. "Oh, my!" she gasped.

Lady Belle smiled. "A squeeze of his arm when he offers it to escort you down the path, a brush of your torso against his in a waltz—and he will be more than ready, my dear."

"I shall contrive an excuse to have him escort me to the apartment. But…how do I—persuade him to come in?" She felt her face heating again.

"You are presenting yourself as a married lady?"

"A widow."

"A *French* widow," Ailis said, returning with the sketch.

"Ah, then he will be prepared for some boldness. Simply tell him you want him."

"That's…all? It's that simple?"

At Caragh's incredulous tone, Lady Belle laughed. "Generally—yes."

"But…but I'm not a beauty like you or Ailis."

"My dear, sheer physical attractiveness often has little to do with sensual allure. If you have done all I have described, you can be sure he will want you. That is, you have no reason to suspect he finds you…unappealing?"

"No. Quite…quite the contrary."

"Then he is yours for the taking."

"Well…I shall need some assistance there as well. I want this to be a night he will never forget."

"Do you know how intimacy progresses?"

"In general terms."

"She has seen my 'Seduction' series," Ailis inserted.

Lady Belle nodded. "That would be a good sequence to follow. You remember each phase?"

Caragh smiled. "I assure you, each pose is etched into my brain!"

Ailis grinned. "I don't doubt it. I'm quite a superior artist."

"Nonetheless, it would be well to review the process, if you could fetch the sketches, please?" While Ailis went to the work bench, Lady Belle turned to Caragh. "If you have never been with a man, you must prepare your body as well. Since some women bleed the first time, to maintain your pose as an experienced woman, you will want to avoid that. And depending on his size, the stretching necessary for your body to accommodate his may be painful."

"I have the solution!" Ailis said. Handing Lady Belle the portfolio, she walked over to rummage in a side table, returning with a large, smooth piece of solid whalebone—in the shape of a male member. "Many women use a dildo to obtain satisfaction in the absence of their partner, but using it—as a lover would use his—will accustom you to the size and feel of a man."

Her cheeks on fire, Caragh took the object gingerly. "So I prepare myself in advance. But Friday night, how do I... begin?"

"Disrobe for him...or let him disrobe you, as he prefers," Lady Belle advised.

"He will find watching your pleasure stimulating," Ailis said. "While you experiment with the dildo, touch yourself to see which areas of your body are most sensitive, how much pressure is most pleasurable." Taking the portfolio, she flipped to the sketch of the girl standing naked before her lover, her fingers at the junction of her thighs. "With the lamp still lit and your veil in place, let him watch you touch yourself like this. It will fire his blood, do you not think, Lady Belle?"

"Assuredly. Most men find it titillating for the lady to take charge. Forbid him to touch you until you give him leave. Explore his body first, using your hands and lips to find his most sensitive places.''

''Then take him in your mouth,'' Ailis said, ''like this.'' She displayed the sketch to Caragh.

'''Tis very effective,'' Lady Belle agreed. ''Do you think you can do that?''

The idea of baring her body to Quentin, touching him intimately, *tasting* him, made Caragh's mouth dry and her pulse race with eagerness. ''Oh, yes.''

''Sliding your tongue along the length of his member, then suckling it gently, especially here—'' she pointed at the sketch ''—where the tip joins the shaft, will create the most exquisite sensations for him. Massaging him here at the same time—'' she indicated the plump sacks suspended below the rigid shaft ''—will intensify the sensations even further.''

''He will probably wish to do the same for you,'' Ailis said, indicating the sketch in which the couple pleasured each other.

Imagining Quentin doing that to her, while she did the same for him, effectively deprived Caragh of speech, even had she been able to think of something to reply.

''When you are ready, let him recline against the pillows and mount him from above,'' Lady Belle advised. ''Watching you taking him within you, being able to fondle your breasts and touch the point of your joining while you move with him, will also heighten the experience for him.''

''And when the act is completed,'' Ailis added, ''let him linger beside you, reliving and savoring each moment.''

''I shall certainly do that,'' Caragh said. Indeed, if intimacy with Quentin proved to be as exquisite a sensual and emotional experience as she anticipated, it was going to be very difficult to send him away at all. But she would worry about that later.

''Anything else I should do?'' she asked.

''That should be sufficient for the first time. After all,'' she added with a touch of self-mockery, "you are a widow—not a courtesan."

"Lady Belle, I know you have an engagement, so we will not keep you longer. Caragh," Ailis said with a wicked grin, "you should review the sketches again while I discuss Lady Belle's portrait with her."

As the two women moved to Ailis's work bench, Caragh flipped through the drawings, recalling with each pose the advice she'd been given. Imagining herself and Quentin in those positions soon had her skin sheened with dampness, her pulse throbbing and her body quivering in a low buzz of anticipation.

She wished their rendezvous were tomorrow rather than Friday—and yet, at the same time she wished the time might never arrive, that she might savor this delicious sense of anticipation forever. For after the searing crucible of union would come the devastation of parting.

But first, she promised herself, she would experience the full height and depth of love's ecstasy—and transport Quentin Burke to that heaven with her.

CHAPTER SIXTEEN

AFTER CHECKING his pocket watch, Quentin once again scanned the throng of merrymakers strolling through the colonnade before the Vauxhall Gardens orchestra. Queens, knaves, jesters and medieval knights mingled with patrons dressed in more normal fashion, their only concession to the masquerade the dominoes worn over their faces.

Although it was not yet late, there were already a number of tipsy gentleman swaggering about, loudly accosting an assortment of "ladies" in scandalously brief gowns, who, after much giggling and tapping of fans, accompanied them into the shadows down one of the infamous Dark Walks.

Viewing the increasingly rowdy behavior of the crowd, Quentin could well believe Lady Catherine had no taste for attending the masquerade here. He was somewhat surprised that she was allowing Caragh to come, even with his escort. Probably that kind lady had allowed compassion for her niece, so unfairly barred from more conventional amusements, to overrule her caution, a lapse Quentin could readily understand. Nonetheless, he'd already decided that once he found Caragh, after a few dances and a taste of the Arrack punch and wafer-thin ham, he would hustle her back to the safety of her aunt's house.

It was now almost half an hour later than the time she'd indicated for their rendezvous, he noted uneasily. The note she'd sent him indicated that, with the session at the lawyers expected to run late, she intended to bring her costume with her and meet him directly at the Gardens. She'd assured him

Smithers would dispatch one of his clerks to watch out for her until she found Quentin.

He was wishing he had insisted on meeting her at the lawyer's offices when he caught sight of a lady of Caragh's size and height, standing by the orchestra with her back to him. A second look confirmed she was gowned in the black Caragh had written she'd be wearing.

He sprinted toward her, his immediate relief succeeded by vexation. Neither the promised clerk—nor any sort of escort that he could see—appeared to be hovering in the vicinity to protect her. He would certainly send a few sharp words to her lawyer!

Coming up from behind, he placed his hands on her shoulders to turn her toward him. "Caragh, I'm so relieved—" he began, only to release her and spring back when the lady uttered a little shriek.

"Monsieur! Qu'est-ce que vous faites, alors?"

"Excuse me, ma'am!" he cried. "I thought you were…"

As his gaze swept down the figure of the woman he'd inadvertently accosted, the rest of his apology went straight out of mind. From the back, this slender lady might have resembled Caragh, but from a hand's breath away, he could see that the curls tumbling from beneath a jaunty toque were not a soft golden brown, but deepest ebony. And though the lady was garbed in black, never would Caragh have worn so scandalously—and enticingly—revealing a gown.

In fact, his body, unconcerned about the true identity of the lady possessing such delicious curves, was already rising in enthusiastic appreciation. Even his more responsible brain was having difficulty ordering his eyes to cease devouring the visual delight spread beneath them and lift instead to the veiled lady's face.

"Je m'excuse, madame!" he said, recapturing the power of speech. "Pardon me, please! I…I thought you were someone else."

She appeared to regard him through the veil for a moment, then nodded. "Since you were gentleman enough to release me *immediatement,* I accept the apology, monsieur."

At that moment, a boy approached Quentin. "You be Lord Branson, sir? A lady from Mr. Smithers's office done sent me with this message fer ye."

Quentin took the note and slipped the lad a coin. Squinting in the flickering light of the flambeaux, Quentin scanned Caragh's message. By the time they'd completed their transactions, she wrote, she'd developed one of her headaches and felt compelled to return straight home. She ended with profuse apologies for having inconvenienced him.

A bit annoyed at having wasted his time, Quentin refolded the note. Still, with this gathering already bordering on the disreputable, he was really rather relieved he'd not have to shepherd Caragh through it.

When he looked up, the veiled lady was still facing him. He thought again that, except for that display of bosom, somehow she reminded him strongly of Caragh.

"It was not distressing news, monsieur?"

"Not at all, madame. Just that the friend I was to meet will not be coming after all."

He was about offer a final apology and bid the veiled lady good night when one of the revelers staggered over and seized her by the shoulder. "How's about a kiss, sweeting?"

With an inarticulate cry, the woman tried to twist out of the drunkard's grasp. Incensed, Quentin seized the man's arm, jerked his hand off the lady's shoulder and forcibly returned it to the ruffian's side. "The lady isn't interested. Be on your way, man."

For a moment, it seemed the drunkard would protest his intervention. But after owlishly noting Quentin's height from head to boot tips, he apparently decided against it. "Meant no harm," he muttered, backing away.

The lady put a hand to her bare throat. "*Mille fois merci,* sir!'' With a little shudder, she readjusted the silken cords that held her cloak in place. In spite of himself, he could not help watching as she tightened the knot, then smoothed the tasseled ends down the front of her bodice, across the peaked tips of her breasts... He stifled a groan as heat flushed through him.

"It isn't my place to say so, madame, but you shouldn't be in Vauxhall alone." *Certainly not in that gown,* he added silently.

"*Vraiment,* I did not wish it, monsieur! I was walking with my friends, there—" she pointed a slender hand "—when a large party pushed past us. Almost they knocked me down! When I found my balance, my friends had disappeared. So I wait here for them. This place, *il me fait énervée*—how you say? It makes me nervous."

For a gentleman, there was but one reply. "Since I no longer need to wait here, let me help you find your party."

"*Comme c'est gentil,* monsieur! But I cannot ask it."

"Nonsense. I could not have it on my conscience that I left so pretty a lady unescorted in the midst of so unruly a crowd."

Once again, the lady studied him from behind her veil. "I should not, sir, for I do not know you. But you have twice been the gentleman, and truly, I cannot like to stay here alone."

"My word as a gentleman, madame, I will not take advantage. Though 'tis not exactly proper, allow me to introduce myself. Lord Branson, at your service." Quentin bowed, trying not to notice as he bent down how close that action brought his lips to her enticing bosom.

She bent her head and curtseyed in return. "Madame LaNoire, milord. Many thanks for your noble rescue." Tentatively, she offered her hand.

More conscious than he wanted to be of those warm fingers resting in the curve of his arm, Quentin led the lady along a circuit through the Gardens. But although they checked in every gathering spot, they did not find her friends.

At length they returned to the area by the orchestra. "So dark it is, I fear we missed them. But I cannot keep you longer. Surely, they will come back for me."

"No more than before could I abandon you now, madame. Should you like a glass of punch? Perhaps by the time we have some refreshment, your friends will return. No, truly it is no bother!" he said, forestalling her protest.

"You are sure? *Eh bien,* then I accept with gladness, milord."

Keeping an eye on her to make sure she was not accosted again—and really, 'twas no hardship to keep an eye on that luscious display—Quentin obtained punch and some sandwiches of slivered ham. A few more coins given to the attendant, and he was able to lead the veiled lady into a box with a clear view of the passing crowd.

"You are French, Madame?" he asked after they had sipped some punch.

"*Oui,* monsieur."

"But your English is quite good."

"*Merci,* monsieur. I have had years here to learn it. *Mon cher* Phillippe was a royalist, so we were forced to flee our home. His dearest wish was to see that monster Corsican driven from *La France.* And for that—" her voice softened "—he gave his life."

"My condolences, ma'am. Have you no family here?"

She shook her head and gave a soulful sigh "Some friends only. I do not go out often, *moi,* but tonight, they beg me. They say the music here is lovely and ah, I do so adore *la danse.* But it was mistake to come."

The melancholy of her tone touched him. Despite the riveting display of bosom, she seemed a proper matron. Bereft of support from the men of her family, cut off from her world…in truth, her circumstances were very like Caragh's.

He wouldn't be able to offer his neighbor some diversion

tonight. But perhaps he could give this sweet lady a brief respite from her grief.

Quentin put down his mug. "You must dance with me."

"Milord, I could not!"

"Why? You just said you came here for the dancing. You must know by now I shall not harm you, and in any event, this is the most crowded, well-lit place in all of Vauxhall. You can still watch the revelers, and I promise to release you the instant your friends return."

"*Vraiment,* milord, I should not."

Sensing her resolve weakening, he made her a deep bow. "Would you honor me, madame?"

Though she shook her head at him, she held out her hand. "You are very bad, monsieur."

"On the contrary," he said, smiling as he lead her onto the dance floor, "I am very good." *Oh, that I might show you how good,* the thought flashed through his head before he could suppress it.

She seemed to enjoy the first dance so much, he immediately asked her for a second. Which, since it turned out to be a waltz, was probably a mistake.

She fit a bit too nicely in his arms. He couldn't stop thinking of her nearly bare breasts brushing his chest, separated from his flesh only by the linen of his shirt and a flimsy bit of velvet. His fingers itched to see if the ivory skin glowing in the dimness would be as soft as the plush of her gown. And the subtle pull of that fabric as the nap dragged against his coat and trousers as they danced, heightened his unwanted arousal.

By the time it was over, his breathing was labored and sweat beaded his forehead. He had, he told himself grimly, been much too long without a woman.

His partner, mercifully in ignorance of his heated thoughts, clasped his hand fervently. "Ah, monsieur, that was *magni-*

fique! Not since the last ball with my dearest Philippe have I danced so! *Merci, merci encore!*''

Quentin bowed. ''My pleasure, madame.'' *Both more and less than I would have liked to give you.* ''I take it you have not yet seen your friends. Shall we make another circuit of the grounds?''

''No. Perhaps they are still here, but *moi*, I am *fatiguée.* I would go home. But ah, milord, I cannot say enough how *gentil* you have been! I…I had forgotten what it is like to be with a true gentleman.'' She made him a deep curtsey, then turned to go.

''Wait!'' he cried, catching her arm. ''You cannot mean to travel at night alone! I don't wish to be presumptuous, but you must allow me to escort you.''

She shook her head. ''No, I already trouble you too much.''

''No trouble, I assure you. After all, I too must cross the river and find a hackney to convey me to my lodgings. It would be no trouble to drop you on the way.''

She hesitated, looking toward the river, then back at him. ''I would feel safer, I cannot deny. You are sure it is no bother?''

''Not a bit.'' He offered his arm. After another moment's hesitation, she took it.

Quentin walked her to the quay and engaged a boatman to oar them across. But once they were seated side by side on the narrow seat, the sway of the boat rocking them together, he grew all too conscious of her slim figure tucked beside him.

It was even worse in the hackney. In that closed space, the scent of her perfume teased his nostrils, her dusky curls tickled his cheek…and he simply couldn't stop thinking of those outrageously tempting breasts beneath her cloak, a mere brush of his hand away.

Being French, she probably did not realize what havoc that lavish display of skin played with English sensibilities, he thought, surreptitiously tugging at his over-tight neckcloth. He was both relieved and sorry when the jarvey pulled up before the address she had given him.

When the carriage stopped, she looked over at him. "I...I should not ask, but...my hallway is very dark. Could you walk up with me?"

"Of course." Giving the driver a coin to wait for him, Quentin followed her up.

Inside the entry, she located a candle and matchbox, then lit a taper. Carrying it to illumine the gloom of the stairs, she led him up to an apartment on the top floor.

Moonlight from a tall window on the landing outlined her figure in silver, cast in relief the figured pattern of the veil covering her face as she drew a key from her pocket and unlocked a door.

Quentin watched her, wondering with a touch of whimsy how the rest of her life would treat her, this gentle widow cast adrift so far from her homeland. Suddenly he wished he might pull aside the veil and kiss her goodbye.

She pushed the door open, then turned back to him. Hesitantly she put a hand on his arm. "I...I wonder if—but no, I must not. You will believe me...wanton."

A frisson of excitement zipped through him at the word. "N-not at all," he stumbled. "What is it?"

"It is just...I am widow, *vous savez.* I miss, ah so much, the loving with my Philippe. *C'est curieux,* but you...very much resemble the man I love. So much, I ache to leave you."

His heartbeat leapt as she took a ragged breath, her voice quieting so he had to lean closer to hear her words. "Just for tonight, I wish not to be alone. Just for tonight, I wish to know again what love is. Ah, *mais, c'est impossible!*" She dropped his arm and stepped away. "You have a wife, *oui?*"

"No!"

"A lady you are promised to?"

He shook his head. "There is a lady I wished to marry, but she…she refused me."

She remained silent, as if pondering that revelation. "Foolish lady!" she murmured at last. "Just for tonight, we console each other, eh? You will…stay with me?"

Desire swelled in him, restrained by a touch of guilt. But as he'd told her, Caragh *had* refused him. There were no promises between them, no bonds but friendship.

So how could he refuse this sad, sweet lady?

When she once again took his hand, he let her lead him within.

SHE SET the candle down inside and lit a single lamp, then beckoned him to follow her through several shadowy rooms. His pulses leapt again when beyond the threshold of the next, she halted—beside a large canopied bed.

Setting the lamp down on the bedside table, she turned to take him eagerly into her arms. But when he raised his hand to grasp her veil, she caught it.

"No, my love. Now I show you all of me but my face. Later, when the light is dim, I remove the veil."

"Why?" he whispered. "You know I will not harm you."

"I know. But with my Philippe gone, I must work to survive. I teach French and music to the children of your ton. One who influences innocents must be, as you say, 'above reproach.' If you know my face and see me later, on the street—"

"I would never betray you!"

She put a finger to his lips. "Ah, *non*. But seeing you, knowing what you know, I might betray myself. Now if I see you, it will be for me a secret joy."

"A joy I may not share?"

"You have another life. For us, there can be only tonight. You…understand?"

He nodded reluctantly. "If I must."

"Then, let us begin."

She shrugged out of her cape and tossed it on the bed, then turned her back and indicated the tapes to her gown. *"S'il vous plâit, monsieur?"*

CHAPTER SEVENTEEN

OH, DID IT please him! *"Certainement,"* he murmured. Fingers clumsy with eagerness, he loosened the tapes, then struggled to free the long line of tiny buttons securing the back of the gown. As the fabric released, he lifted it away, drawing the sleeves down her arms, letting the heavy full skirts fall to her ankles.

Beneath the gown she wore stays and ruffled petticoats over a thin linen chemise, through which peaked nipples now, at last, showed clearly. He wanted to rip the linen aside, view with no further impediment those full plump rounds that had titillated him all evening, but she gently pushed his hands away.

While he watched each movement, she slowly dropped one strap, then the other. He heard himself groan as bit by bit she peeled down the remaining inch of cloth. Cupping her hands beneath her breasts, she lifted them, massaged them, rubbed the stiffened nipples with her thumbs. "Do you like what you see, milord?"

"Yes." His voice sounded hoarse, guttural.

"You would see...more?"

"Yes. More. Everything."

She laughed softly as she unlaced the stays and tossed them aside, then stepped out of the petticoats. Straightening, she stood before him, breasts bare, the fine linen now barely veiling her body from stomach to calves. She ran her hands down her sides, over her belly, letting them come to rest on her thighs, her thumbs grazing the dark triangle at her center. "More?"

He was nearly frantic with the need to touch her, taste the pale skin and dark puckered nipples, but this slow unveiling was too enrapturing to resist. "M-more."

She wrapped her fingers in the linen beneath her breasts and drew it down her ribs, tugged it an inch at a time over her belly and hips, little by little revealing the tight dark curls beneath. "More?"

"Ah, yes!"

She turned her back to him and teased the fabric lower, let it whisper down her legs. Bending over, she gave him the arousing vista of her naked back and buttocks as she dropped the chemise to her feet and kicked it away.

Languorously she straightened and turned back to face him. "More, milord?"

Beyond speech now, he nodded.

She eased her bottom up onto the bed and sat back, then drew a leg up, gripped garter and stocking and pushed them down, arching and withdrawing her foot. While he stood, breathless at the glimpses she allowed him, she removed the other stocking. Leaning back, she parted her thighs to give him a fuller view and ran a fingertip over the nub at her very center.

Over the roaring in his ears, he heard her say, "Come to me."

But when he rushed to the bedside, his eager fingers reaching for her, she sat back up and once again caught his wrists. "*Pas encore,*" she murmured. "Not yet."

Placing his hands back at his sides, she wrapped her legs around him and drew him close, until his straining breeches were pressed to the spot her fingertip had caressed. "Now, let *me* see *you.*"

He wanted to indicate his approval, but his voice seemed to have stopped functioning. Apparently taking his silence for approval, she loosened the knot of his cravat, unwound the cloth and tossed it aside, then plucked open the buttons of his shirt until she had bared him from throat to chest.

"Comme c'est beau," she murmured, running her fingers from his breastbone up to the hollow of his throat and back while he stood motionless, in thrall to her touch. She clutched him tighter with her legs, bringing him even closer into her heat while she struggled to free him from his tight jacket. After stripping him of his shirt with the same teasing slowness with which she had removed her chemise, she set to work on his bare torso. Using fingertips and the pads of her thumbs, sometimes barely touching him, so that the tiny hairs of his skin bristled in electric response, sometimes massaging with deep and powerful strokes, she caressed every inch of skin.

By now he was ablaze with need, desperate for her to remove the rest of his garments and subject his lower body to the same thorough exploration she had given his arms and chest. And once again, she drove him nearly to madness with her slow deliberate pace. Yet so exquisite was the torment, he could not bring himself to disobey her command that he remain motionless, submissive to her control.

One by one she unhooked the buttons of his trousers, until his throbbing erection sprang free. Nestling him against her moist warmth, she leaned forward until her breasts just grazed his chest, then inched his breeches down his backside, caressing his buttocks with her fingers as she went.

By now restraint was almost pain. Every instinct urged him to seize her and plunge himself deep within the slick canal so excruciatingly close. When she bent to tug his breeches lower, her face near enough to his rigid shaft that he could feel the warm breath through the veil, he nearly lost control altogether.

Fortunately she seemed to sense how close to climax—and collapse—he was hovering. She untangled her legs and slipped off the bed. Urging him up on it, she tugged his boots and then his breeches off, treating him to a wonderful view of bare backside and bouncing breasts.

After she'd stripped him completely, she ordered him to recline against the pillows. Once more stilling his hands, she climbed back up on the bed and straddled him, positioning herself so his rigid erection almost touched the cleft between her parted thighs. "Would you see more, milord?" she whispered.

"Y-yes," he gasped, beyond anticipating what she might do next, carried away by wonderment. And so he watched as this time, she traced her hands from his forehead down his nose, teasing apart his lips and pausing to allow him to suckle her fingertips, then trailing her moistened fingers down his chest, circling his nipples, slowing her pace as her hands descended.

His breathing erratic and his heartbeat thundering in his ears, he watched her fingers trace down the now acutely sensitive skin of his abdomen, pausing just above the point he most wished her to stroke, then flaring her hands out to his hips, fluttering them over his buttocks.

Nearly growling with equal parts of gratification and frustration, he struggled to keep still. A few moments later his patience was rewarded when, while still caressing his backside, she moved her other hand up and slowly, so slowly anticipation squeezed his chest until he could no longer breathe, with the barely perceptible pressure of one fingertip, stroked him from base to tip.

He shuddered violently, his penis leaping beneath her finger. She encircled him with her hand, steadying him, then drew her hand down his length and back once, twice.

"*Parfait,*" she murmured. "*Absolument parfait.*"

He wanted to tell her she was perfect, absolutely the most divinely perfect lover he'd ever known, but his words seemed like wild creatures fled before the coming of the earthquake, unable to be recalled into speech. He could not articulate, he could only feel. And watch.

"You observe still, *mon cher?*" she asked. Despite the veil that obscured her face, she must be able to see that though his tongue was mute, his eyes remained riveted on her hands...which gently caressed him. And, at last, guided him to that place he most longed to be.

He gritted his teeth and closed his eyes, groaning with the effort to hold back as her wetness dewed the tip of his erection until, unable to stop himself, he thrust into her.

She gasped, her arms going rigid on his shoulders. Alarm restoring his control, he withdrew. "Did I hurt you, *ma belle?*" he whispered.

"N-no, *mon cher,*" she whispered. "Only...it has been so long, *vous savez.* Almost it is like the first time again."

"Then we will take it slowly," he promised.

And so he did, though the slowness was almost torture to him. She moved her hips to take him in a fraction at a time, until at last she'd drawn his length completely within her moist warmth.

"It is good now for you, my sweet?" he asked.

"*Vraiment,* it is h-heaven," she said, her fingernails biting into his shoulders as she rocked herself forward.

That bold movement unraveled the last of his control. With a hoarse cry, he seized her buttocks and drove deep. She cried out as well, matching his rhythm and meeting him thrust for thrust until, with an inarticulate wail, she shattered around him.

Satisfaction at her pleasure swelled in his chest before his own climax erupted within her, robbing him for a few heart-stopping minutes of breath and sight.

He awoke to find her slumped against him, their bodies slick with sweat, her heartbeat rapid against his chest. For a long time he was too full of delicious satiation to be able to move or speak. Finally, with a supreme effort, he found her hand and managed to bring it to his lips.

"You, *ma belle dame,* are perfect."

She murmured and with a languid movement, pushed to a

sitting position astride him, setting off a series of exquisite aftershocks. Raising her hands above her head, she arched her back and stretched, angling her full, high breasts close to his face.

Catching her shoulders, he eased her forward until he could capture one pink nipple. She moaned as the captive hardened under his tongue and her inner muscles contracted, sending another burst of sensation through him. With one hand he circled and massaged her other breast, brushing his thumb over the tip, as she had shown him earlier.

By the time he had thoroughly sampled each breast, her breathing had gone ragged again and he could feel himself hardening within her. She began to rock, small, gentle thrusts that soon brought him back to full erection.

He observed only her this time, listened as her breathing turned from pants to gasps, noticed as her arms went rigid and her hands clutched on his shoulders, suckled in rhythm with her increasingly rapid thrusts. Just as he felt his own control unraveling once again, she arched into him and cried out. Her body spasmed around him, demolishing the last of his resistance, and once again, his world exploded into a soaring starburst of sensation.

Afterward they both dozed. He awoke languid, conscious of the pleasant burden of her soft body cradled against his chest. Awe and amazement welled up in him, and unable to resist the temptation to peek at the face of the lady who had brought him twice to paradise, he tugged at her veil.

She jerked awake at once and caught his fingers. "*Pas permis,* my naughty one," she reproved. Disengaging from him, she slid off the bed and stood beside it, beautifully naked but for her veil, her breasts dappled pink with the marks of his possession.

He sat up on his elbow, and for a few moments she allowed him to feast on the sight of her. Then she blew out the lamp, leaving the bedchamber in inky darkness, silent but for a soft rustling he realized must be madame at last removing her veil.

Excitement swept through him. He leaned forward in the darkness to meet her, pulled her onto the bed beside him and back against the pillows. "At last I shall see you," he whispered, and felt her lips curve into a smile as she allowed him to trace first his fingers, then his lips over her naked face.

But when he moved his mouth lower to nip at her tender neck, she pulled away. "*Pas encore,* milord," she said, urging him once again back against the pillows. "You have seen. Now, you shall feel."

And before he could imagine what she intended, she began her slow journey of exploration again, this time using her tongue.

ANOTHER BLISSFUL interlude later, he awoke again. Smiling into the darkness, he stroked the shoulder of his dozing lover, wondering which had been more intense—his pleasure when he'd watched as well as felt her guide him to completion, or the pleasure produced when he was focused only on her touch?

While he pondered that sweet dilemma, she stirred beside him. He bent down to capture her lips—lips whose contours he wished to memorize, that should his lady not permit him to see her unveiled, he might still be able to recognize her should they pass by chance on the street.

As if suspicious of his intent, she drew away. "*C'est tard, mon amant,*" she whispered. "Much too late. You must go before the sky lightens. I cannot risk that anyone see you here."

He wanted to protest, but she had already slipped from the bed. By the sibilant sounds in the dark chamber, he knew she must be gathering up their clothing. A moment later he dimly perceived the pale outline of his shirt as she guided it over one hand.

Soon, too soon, he thought. Though, given the circumstances she'd described, he understood her caution, still he sought to put off the moment of parting. Interrupting her with a long slow kiss, he ran his hands over her peach-soft skin, interfering with her determined efforts to get him into his shirt, then distracted her by bending to suckle those firm, sweet breasts.

"Méchant!" she groaned, pushing him away. "No more delay." But though, whether from the chill or to escape temptation, she threw on a thick satin dressing gown, she showed herself not quite as committed to hurrying as her words might indicate.

After fastening him into his shirt, she paused to once again caress his buttocks before tugging up his breeches. Then she kissed his spent member so enticingly he nearly insisted they linger longer before, with a sigh, she drew away and firmly rebuttoned his trouser flap.

When she brought him boots and jacket, he stayed her with a hand to her shoulder. "Will you let me see you?"

She caught his hand and kissed it. "Nay, love, I dare not."

Disappointed, but not surprised, he asked, "Will you let me see you again?"

She hesitated, making his heart leap. "That, too, would not be wise."

Sensing her waver, he pressed harder. "But you will allow it? I beg you, *ma belle dame,* please say yes."

Without answering him, she moved away into the darkness. A few moments later he blinked against the sudden brightness and jerked his gaze to her face.

She stood beside the candle she'd just lit holding his jacket and boots—her face once again obscured by the veil. Swallowing his disappointment, he walked to her and ran his finger over the soft patterned fabric that masked her features. "You still do not trust me?"

"Please, you must go now."

She seemed already a bit distant. Sensing that pressing her to reveal her face would only make her withdraw further, he did not persist. Instead, he let her assist him into his jacket and boots and lead him to the door, where she dropped him a curtsey.

"Thank you, milord."

She rose, clearly expecting him to walk away. Yet he could not seem to make himself take the first step. What sorcery she had worked on him, he marveled as he dawdled on her doorstep? Never before had he been so reluctant to end a romantic interlude.

"Can I return here tomorrow?" he found himself asking.

He tensed as he awaited her answer, suddenly realizing he desperately needed her to agree, not sure what he would do if she refused.

Finally, with a shuddering sigh that rippled through her slender frame, she whispered, "*Oui. Vraiment,* 'tis madness, but yes. Come at midnight."

His drooping spirits revived on a surge of delight and wild anticipation. "I promise to make it a madness you will never regret. Until tomorrow at midnight, then."

She opened the door and after peeping into the hallway, motioned him through it, allowing one last kiss to her hand before shutting it behind him.

For a long moment after that portal closed, he stared at it, listening as the soft pad of her footsteps retreated, lost in awe, curiosity and wonder.

Finally he forced himself into motion. After tonight, he must concede the French deserved their reputation as masters of seduction. If only he could see her! How he thirsted to look upon the face of this lady with the tragic past and the magic touch!

But even should she never permit that, the splendor of the night they'd shared far surpassed his craving to view her features. And he had tonight still to anticipate. How many hours until midnight?

Smiling in the dimness, he fingered his pocket watch and with an eager step, trod down the stairs.

HOURS LATER, Caragh sat on the divan in her sister's studio, sipping hot chocolate. After dismissing the maid with an impatient wave of her hand, Ailis turned to Caragh. "So, did I not tell you 'twould be delightful?"

Caragh smiled. "Aye, you did."

"And viewing him in the flesh after having studied the drawing did not...disappoint?"

Caragh chuckled. "Oh my, no!"

Raising her eyebrows, Ailis laughed too. "I think I shall have to have him model for me—if only so I may make you a more accurate sketch to remember him by!"

"I'm not ready to be reduced to memories just yet. The reason I called—beyond thanking you again for all your help—is to beg more...supplies. I've asked Quentin to return to the flat tonight."

Ailis's amusement faded. Regarding her sister thoughtfully, she sipped her tea. "Are you sure you are not committing more of yourself to this than you ought?"

Caragh gave her a wistful smile. "I'm not sure of anything," she replied, mastering the wobble in her voice before it told Ailis far more than she wished to explain.

Her midnight excursion, so much more magnificent than anything she could possibly have dreamed, seemed to have dissolved the careful hold Caragh had been maintaining over her emotions. During those stolen hours in a borrowed room, the lust, curiosity and wistful need to hold Quentin close that had driven her to that outrageous masquerade had both strengthened and evolved into something almost beyond her ability to control. Physical rapture had deepened her love for him, while love in turn, she suspected, had intensified her physical pleasure. Sending him away had been nearly impossible.

Her resolve not to see him again, one of the fundamental tenets upon which she'd permitted herself this rash undertaking in the first place, had faltered upon the mere repetition of his request that they meet again.

Other emotions she'd not anticipated assailed her as well. Guilt at deceiving Quentin, using his body under false pretenses and eliciting his ready sympathy for a creature who did not exist. Shame at probing the depth of his allegiance to her, though—mercifully or not, she wasn't sure—she'd been too cowardly to pursue the matter to its end and baldly ask if he loved the girl who'd refused him.

If he loved *her*.

"Foolish lady" indeed!

"Are you going to tell him the truth?"

Ailis's inquiry startled her back to the present. "No!"

"If your activities last evening were as vigorous as I imagine, you are probably lucky that the wig—and your anonymity—survived the night intact. How much longer do you expect such luck to hold? If you would keep Quentin as your lover, 'twould be much simpler to abandon pretense."

"You know I cannot. If Quentin discovered I am Madame LaNoire, he would insist that we marry." She took a deep breath, voicing aloud the truth that had become more painful minute by rapturous minute of their time together. "Delightful though it be, the...arrangement cannot become longstanding."

Ailis shrugged. "If you enjoy him that much, I don't see why not. Simply refuse to marry him. 'Tis what I do every time Holden pesters me about wedlock. He cannot force you, after all."

For a moment, Caragh was diverted from her own predicament. "Holden is pressing you to marry? The confirmed rake, brought to his knees at last? Famous!"

Ailis waved a nonchalant hand. "I daresay he only asks because he's so certain I'll refuse. I like him well enough and he's a charming lover, but no man is charming enough to persuade me to trade independence for the iron trap of matrimony."

Matrimony with Quentin could be heaven, not trap, Caragh thought wistfully. But only if he truly loved the lady who'd refused his suit—and he'd given Madame LaNoire no hint that he would have affirmatively answered the question she'd not been brave enough to ask.

Caragh wanted only what he willingly offered her—or rather, Madame LaNoire. One more glorious night.

"Well, sister, is advice all I can pry from you? Or may I take more of those clever little sponges as well?"

"Both, of course." Ailis set down her wineglass and went behind the screen that concealed her bed, returning a moment later with a small pouch. "Remember to use them properly," she said as she handed it over. "I still think it best for you to reveal the truth—I know, you won't," she said before Caragh could protest. "Should your disguise somehow slip, however, don't say I didn't warn you."

Caragh took the pouch and tucked it in her reticule. After one more stolen evening, she would let Quentin go, then get on with her life and refuse to look back. "Nonsense, 'tis but for one more night. In so short a time, how could anything go wrong?"

CHAPTER EIGHTEEN

TWO DAYS LATER, Quentin sat at the desk in his London study, staring sightlessly at estate documents he'd ostensibly been reviewing for the past hour. Instead of the prosaic details of materials purchased and funds expended, though, in his mind shimmered indelible images of the two nights he'd spent with Madame LaNoire.

She'd not allowed him to remove her veil during their second evening either. But, after extracting his promise not to touch that forbidden item, she had agreed to his request that, reversing roles, they repeat the love-play of their first night. He had thoroughly enjoyed inspecting every inch of her body in the lamplight, driving her to the brink of ecstasy with the same extreme slowness with which she had tortured him, before plunging them both over the edge to fulfillment. And knowing this time, *she* watched *him* as he explored her, from the curve of her toes to the velvet folds beneath the dark curls at her center to her pink-nippled breasts, made the journey even more erotic.

Or had his senses been more stimulated the second time, after he extinguished the lamp, removed her veil, and retraced that journey with his tongue, both of them enveloped in a cloak of darkness that intensified every touch, every scent? Certainly he'd been able to tantalize her to climax several times before finally heeding her ragged pleas that he sheath himself within her.

A knock on the door interrupted that arousing speculation, plummeting him back to the uninspiring vista of the estate ledgers stacked atop his desk. Even after he dealt with this tedious array of paperwork, the evening stretched bleakly before him. Though he'd pleaded with all the persuasion he could muster, the bewitching Madame LaNoire had sadly but firmly refused to let him return.

With a catch in her voice, she'd asserted that despite the certainty of delight they might share, his visiting again would be too risky—for them both.

Knowing thoughts of her had already monopolized far too much of his time and attention, he had reluctantly bowed to her decree. It appeared likely he would never see her again— without ever having really seen her.

Should they chance to pass on some Mayfair street, would he recognize her? Or, as she had predicted, might she pause to gaze covertly at him, recalling the rapture of those nights, while he walked on oblivious?

A mingling of protest, regret and something disturbingly like dismay stabbed in his gut.

The knock sounded again. "Enter," he barked.

"Begging your pardon, my lord," his butler bowed himself in, "are you intending to dine at home? Cook was not given instructions."

Was it as late as that? He glanced at the mantel clock, startled to find it late afternoon. Yesterday, in sated splendor he'd slept through most of the daylight hours. Inspecting the nearly untouched stack of papers on his desk, he realized he had daydreamed away the better part of them today.

"No," he said, suddenly restless and weary of his own company. "I shall dine at the club as usual. Summon me a carriage in half an hour."

The end of so unexpected and magical an interlude was bound to leave him feeling somewhat melancholy. A few convivial hours of wine, political commentary and companionship at White's would be just the thing to restore his spirits—and distract him from recalling that tonight, no veiled lady waited to enrapture him.

He entered the club an hour later to find it as bustling as he'd anticipated. Lord Andover, seated in his usual spot by the bow window, spotted him as he entered and waved him over.

"Been rusticating again, old fellow? Haven't seen you at dinner of late."

"No, sir. Busy, I expect," he replied noncommittally, the knowledge of the sort of rusticating in which he had been indulging burning like a bright flame within him.

"Come, sit down! You'll broach a bottle and share a few moments with an old man, eh?"

Regretting the quest for information that had led him to ingratiate himself with his father's friend the previous week, Quentin took the seat indicated. Though a recitation of the latest society gossip no longer appealed, he couldn't see a way to refuse without slighting the old gentleman, who had, in truth, proved helpful.

Andover looked him up and down, eyes shrewd in his wrinkled face. "Now you have the appearance of a man who's been well-satisfied." The old gentleman cackled. "Been calling on your old neighbor, that Sudley artist chit?"

Irritated, Quentin ignored the first remark to concentrate on the second. "Yes, I did call on Miss Ailis. Despite what rumor claims about artists, I interrupted no orgiastic revels-in-progress. Nor did I find a lover hiding in her armoire—just a quantity of canvases and paints, and a rather unconventional lady set upon using them to make a living."

"Make a living—bah!" Lord Andover dismissed that pronouncement with a disparaging wave of his hand. "A real Diamond, they say, and living alone now?"

"She is a beauty, yes. But not quite alone—there's a maid-servant in residence."

"I'd wager the cost of Prinny's next extravagance that she'll never earn enough to fill a teapot. Since she's betrayed her birthright and given up any claim to gentility, stands to reason she'll soon be taking a protector. I hear Freemont's already dangling after her, so what are you waiting for?"

The old man poked Quentin in the side. "Being a close friend of the family, you have a decided advantage in winning her favors, if you make your move quickly!"

"Being a close family friend," Quentin said stiffly, "I couldn't consider such a thing. Damme, Andover, I've known the chit since she was in short skirts."

"Think how much better she will look in—or out of them—now," Andover said, chuckling at his own witticism.

Quentin wasn't amused. "I hardly think her aunt, Lady Mansfield, or her sister, Miss Sudley, would appreciate such conduct toward their near relation by someone they trust to be both a friend and a gentleman."

"Lady Mansfield's above reproach—courted the gel m'self, years back—but the elder Miss Sudley had better look to her own reputation," Lord Andover said. "I hear she's been visiting the artist chit and mixing with her low-bred friends. Siblings and all, I understand, but if she does that overmuch, Miss Sudley will find herself featured alongside her sister in the latest print shop broadsides. Both fillies bred from the same mare, eh?"

Before Quentin could make a sharp rejoinder about the unfairness of slandering the Sudley daughters because of their mother's ancient scandal, a voice from behind him said, "What is this about Miss Sudley?"

Quentin turned to see Alden Russell approaching.

"Russell, pray join us," Andover invited. "Know the Sudley chits, do you?"

"Never been introduced to the Diamond-turned-artist," he replied, taking the chair offered, "but Branson presented me to the elder—a lovely, intelligent lady. Quite a knowledgeable estate manager too, as he can also attest. In fact," Russell said, turning to Quentin, "my solicitor has just completed the sale of some land to her family—that parcel I mentioned to her.''

''Caragh—Miss Sudley is buying the old Reynolds farm?'' Quentin echoed.

''Wants to expand their horse-breeding operation, my lawyer said. I'm delighted to see the land go to a purpose for which it is so well-suited—especially when I hope it will frequently bring the lady herself there to oversee it!'' He grinned at Quentin. ''Of course, I shall have to call frequently to offer my assistance whenever she visits the neighborhood.''

The hot light in Russell's eye as he announced that intention, added to Quentin's knowledge of just how often—and just how well-chaperoned—Caragh would be at the new property, nearly made him choke. Bad enough that, should she proceed with this mad intention of running the farm alone, she would leave herself open to just the sort of speculation and innuendo Andover was already bandying about, as well as potential insult from the clients who patronized the operation. But to know his erstwhile friend, who'd already offended Quentin by making randy remarks about the lady, would be able to lie in wait for her not five miles outside her gate was outside of enough!

He must, Quentin swore with a murderous glance at Russell, immediately begin redoubling his efforts to persuade Caragh not to relocate there alone.

Before he could master his irritation to make a reply light enough not to engender Russell's suspicions, several newcomers joined them and the conversation became general. Although Quentin normally would have enjoyed the heated discussion that ensued about the several bills just introduced into Parliament, he soon found his attention wandering. Restlessness claiming him again, as soon after dinner as possible without arousing comment, he took his leave of the club.

Eschewing a carriage, he elected to walk. His mind needed clearing, and with the whirlwind of events the last few days, he had neglected Caragh. Indeed, so caught up had he been in his interludes with Madame LaNoire, after scanning the note of apology Caragh had sent for failing to meet him at Vauxhall, he'd not thought about her since.

The unwelcome information that the property she had bought for her new enterprise adjoined Russell's land had swiftly cleared what remained of that sensual distraction. In its wake remained the troubled uncertainty that had plagued him ever since a coolly distant Caragh had refused him at Sudley Court.

He had missed her acutely after that episode, missed the easy camaraderie of their friendship. Not until it was suddenly withdrawn did he fully realize how much his emotional well-being had become anchored to the deep abiding warmth of their relationship. Indeed, he was fast coming to believe that persuading Caragh to marry him was imperative not just to protect her future, but to secure his happiness.

Especially when he considered the unappealing possibilities inherent in her having Alden Russell as her nearest neighbor.

As for his most recent source of pleasure… A pang of guilt touched him. At the time he'd succumbed to Madame La-Noire's blandishments, there had been no commitment between Caragh and himself—at Caragh's own insistence. He had not broken her trust. Had matters already been settled between them, he would have resisted the veiled lady's entreaties, however tempting.

What was he to do about that lady, whose sad plight still whispered at the edges of his consciousness? If he were not contemplating a future with Caragh, he might be tempted to woo for his mistress the lady who had, silhouetted by moonlight that first night, seemed so hauntingly like his good friend.

Who was she, this lady so fiercely driven to hide her face? A governess as she claimed—or the actress from the Green Room her masquerade costume seemed to indicate? Whatever her true identity, it seemed clear she lived in precariously straitened circumstances.

Despite the subtle physical *something* about her that reminded him of Caragh, in character there could hardly be two women more dissimilar.

While Madame LaNoire eked out a bare subsistence in a private household, Caragh directed a lucrative breeding operation in the public arena. A refugee from her own world, the French lady seemed fragile, in need of protection, whereas Caragh, after being rejected by her class, had with courage and spirit decided to forge a new future of her own design. One lady was reticent and submissive, the other independent and self-assured.

Though they did share one characteristic. As he'd lately come to appreciate, Caragh possessed a sensuality as deep as Madame's own. In fact, at the hands of a sensitive and knowledgeable tutor, Caragh might well become a lover as creative and responsive as the veiled lady.

That conclusion burst into his brain with the attention-riveting power of an exploding fireworks, halting him in mid-step. Faith, what an amazing amalgam that would be—to have in one woman the courage, strength and competence that was Caragh wedded to the passionate sensuality of Madame LaNoire!

Add sensual power to the hold Caragh already had on his affections and he'd be in imminent danger of falling completely under her spell. One lazy trace of her finger along any part of his anatomy could reduce his rational mind to mush. And her lips—a spiral of desire coiled through him at the mere thought of what Caragh's lips, trained in Madame LaNoire's sweet witchery, might do.

Caragh had already shown that she would prove a willing pupil. Indeed, had she not once tried to urge them down this very path? An overture he—fool that he was!—had firmly rejected. Since he'd never known her to fail in mastering any skill she attempted, could he but convince her to marry him and perfect her in this new art, she might make them both deliriously happy for a very long time.

Wooing her to such a course entailed risk, for once they changed the terms of their friendship, there could be no going back. But as he was fast becoming convinced that they must marry, which would alter the parameters of their friendship in any event, the prospect of gaining a best friend who was also his warmest erotic dream of a lover seemed to far outweigh any possible loss.

Especially after having just experienced the glimpses of heaven given him by Madame LaNoire. The idea of experiencing such delights with Caragh filled him with both joyful anticipation and a sense of awe.

Mille fois merci, madame, he said silently, *for opening my eyes to the possibilities within my grasp.*

As he entertained visions of that exalted future, the uneasiness that had plagued him dissolved, along with the last of his lingering reservations about marrying Caragh. Once he persuaded her to it—and he intended to persevere until he did—he could proceed to turning those enchanting visions into reality.

Grinning, he picked up his pace. Although another tiresome visit to that pesky new estate outside London would prevent his calling on her tomorrow, he would reply to her previous note this very night, begging leave to visit her the day after. And then begin his new campaign to swamp her objections and sweep her into his arms.

But as he paced along, a lingering concern nagged at the edges of his euphoria. Though he'd known her but a few hours—and still did not know the truth of her story—Madame LaNoire had touched him deeply. Was she truly the widowed governess she claimed, her employment uncertain and her financial reserves almost nonexistent?

If so, it didn't seem proper, somehow, that while he confidently proceeded toward a bright future with Caragh, the woman who had inadvertently led him to conquer his doubts remained so unprotected and at risk.

If she were who she claimed, he ought to repay the gracious gift she'd offered him by rectifying her precarious situation—and insure, should her capricious employer dismiss her, that she was not forced to choose between compromising the virtue she seemed to prize so highly by taking a protector, or starvation.

Outright financial assistance she would most certainly refuse. But surely she would not reject an offer of a legitimate, but more secure, position. Among his network of relations and business associates there should certainly be someone who could employ as a companion or governess a foreign widow of gentility and refinement.

After a few moment's reflection, he recalled hearing from his solicitor that his mother's Aunt Jane, an elderly spinster, had requested that he find a replacement for her recently-deceased companion. A sweet-tempered, gentle woman esteemed by both friends and servants, Aunt Jane suffered from poor eyesight and particularly missed, she told the solicitor, having a companion to read to her.

With her governess's background and quiet melodic voice, Madame LaNoire might be the ideal candidate for Aunt Jane's new companion. Such a position, at his relation's house just outside London, would offer permanent security without requiring the lady to move far from the few friends she had in England. And its salary, discreetly augmented by Quentin, would permit her to accumulate a modest sum for her retirement—or as dowry for another marriage, should she cease grieving her lost husband and wish to wed again.

Of course, before promoting her for such a position, he would have to discover the truth of her circumstances. Regardless of the debt he might feel he owed her, he could hardly in good conscience seek to introduce into his great aunt's household a woman of whom he knew for certain only that she was apparently French, seemingly genteel, and supposedly widowed.

The easiest way to discover it would be to call upon Madame LaNoire herself. So it appeared he would have to go against that lady's wishes and visit her again—though not this time, he acknowledged with a pang of regret impossible to squelch, with midnight interludes in mind.

A few minute's conversation with them both concentrated on the matter of legitimate employment should establish whether she was in fact a virtuous widow—or an actress who'd toyed with playing an amusing new role.

It would also obviate the need for secrecy. He would finally be able to view her in full light—without the veil.

His curiosity fully piqued by that prospect, he halted again and pulled out his pocket watch. Was it too late to stop by tonight?

A glance at the timepiece confirmed that the evening was not yet far advanced. Visiting now might well offer his best chance of catching her at home, for he must be out of the city tomorrow, and in any event, she most certainly spent the daylight hours at her employer's residence.

He would try it, he decided.

As he hailed a hackney, he had to admit that however platonic his intentions, a fever of anticipation was licking through his veins. Committed as he now was to claiming a future with Caragh, some indefinable *something* still bound him to the veiled lady, drew his thoughts back to her plight and person like a lodestone seeking north.

Probably, he assured himself, 'twas merely the same rigid sense of responsibility that had led him to toil for eight years to redeem his heritage. Naturally, until he knew Madame LaNoire to be safely situated, he'd be unable to dismiss her from his thoughts. Once that task was accomplished, he could focus solely on Caragh.

By the time he'd reached the landing outside her door, his heart was pounding, not just from the exertion of half running up three flights of stairs. Holding his breath, he rang her bell.

When she opened the door and spied him, would she gasp, her eyes wide with shock? Would she shut the door in his face, seeing his intrusion as a breach of her trust and an unwarranted invasion of her privacy? Or hold out her hands and welcome him warmly?

Though he sought to squelch it, another enticing possibility kept squirming back into his consciousness. If Madame LaNoire was as moved at seeing him as he expected to be at seeing her, might she suggest they share one final night of intimacy before forever severing their connection?

His mind alternately rejecting and entertaining that prospect, he waited. After several minutes, during which no sound of approaching footsteps emanated from behind the door, he rang again.

His excitement dimmed as the minutes passed and the door remained stubbornly barred. Might she be already abed and asleep? She'd told him she rarely attended evening entertainments. Surely by this hour she should be home.

Knocking again, he called out her name until, not wishing to rouse the neighbors, he felt compelled to cease. Still there was no response from within.

A sharp disappointment scalded him. Short of breaking the lock, which he would rather not do, there was no way for him to enter and ascertain whether she was in fact within.

Loath to give up on his purpose, he lingered, administering several more sharp raps. Eventually, though, he had to acknowledge that Madame LaNoire was either not at home, or sleeping too soundly to rouse.

As he descended the stairs, he cheered himself with the reflection that he could still accomplish one bit of business tonight. As soon as he arrived back to his rooms, he would pen Caragh that note.

CHAPTER NINETEEN

My dear Caragh,

I regret the business that takes me from town, robbing me of the delight of your company.

I hope you suffered no recurrence of the headache that plagued you the night of the masquerade, and look forward to calling on you as soon as I return.

Until then, I remain

Your very devoted Quentin.

FINGERS TREMBLING, Caragh set the note, which retained a faint lingering scent of his shaving soap, back on the breakfast tray beside her hot chocolate. Seizing the cup, she took a gulp, but the savory brew seemed to have turned to chalk.

Quentin was coming to see her. Soon. Panic rose in her chest. Thrusting the tray aside, she hopped to her feet and began pacing the room.

He would lounge on the sofa in Aunt Kitty's drawing room, expecting her to pour him tea and sit beside him while they conversed about the continuing problems at his new estate or plans for moving her stock or her sister's shocking career.

Sit. Beside. Him. Heaven have mercy! she thought, putting hands to her hot cheeks.

She now knew how Pandora must have felt, trying to stuff back into that box all the unexpected devils her rashness had allowed to escape.

How could she look at Quentin and not remember seeing every inch of his skin as she slowly undressed him—as he had seen hers? Or hand him a teacup without their fingers touching—fingertips that had caressed *his* body colliding with fingertips that had explored *hers?*

Not that she regretted a second of the two glorious nights they'd spent together. Indeed, so splendid were those interludes, it had been terrifyingly difficult to resist his pleas for yet another night. Her palms still showed the crescent marks of the nails she'd dug into them to keep herself from turning that "no" into a "yes."

Though this note did put an end to her secretly entertained and impossible hope that the bond between them was so strong he had somehow recognized the veiled lady to be her—and now realized beyond doubt that they belonged together. Having deliberately played upon both his chivalrous instincts and his masculine desire, she couldn't fault him for succumbing to the seduction of this supposed stranger. 'Twas ridiculous to feel disappointed—had she not deliberately created a persona so unlike her own that it would be nearly impossible for him to connect the two?

For the best of reasons. Should Quentin Burke discover his midnight lover was not the experienced widow he'd been led to believe, but his previously virginal neighbor, she'd find herself quick-stepped to the altar by a man whose keen sense of honor would not allow him to do otherwise, no matter how furious he'd doubtless be when he discovered her deception.

Given the depth of her love and the beauty of the intimacy they'd shared, she could not bear to contemplate living with the enmity such a forced marriage must create.

How stupidly innocent and blindly arrogant she'd been when she chose to proceed down this path, thinking to assuage her curiosity and indulge her senses with a few stolen nights of pleasure.

By that second night, their minds and bodies had become so well attuned that she and Quentin were able to anticipate, savor, prolong each other's enjoyment. The power of their mutual attraction seemed to create an almost audible hum between them.

How could she sit beside him in a drawing room and deny that pull? How could they be close enough to exchange teacups, and he fail to perceive it?

For nearly half an hour she paced, trying to think of some arrangement by which they might meet and maintain sufficient physical distance. She could not. When he called, he would surely take her hands as she entered the room, would expect to sit beside or directly across from her as they conversed.

And when he did, she simply could not carry off the pose of congenial friend. Not with the memory of his hands, his mouth on her, the feel of him sheathed within her still so vivid. The very hairs on her skin prickled at the thought of being near him.

Perhaps later, given time for the intensity of these feelings to fade—and surely, if God were merciful, they would!—she could manage to cobble back together the pieces of the serene demeanor she'd been able to present to him the previous six years. Teach herself to accept his arm or his hand and not yearn for more.

But not by tomorrow or the day after.

What reason could she invent to delay his visit?

She paced to her desk, thinking rapidly. She'd signed the deeds this morning, completing the final step in the purchase of her new property. She could write Quentin a reply and claim that, as she'd already sent instructions for Sudley's manager to begin the moving process, a complicated business that would likely require all her time and attention for the foreseeable future, she was on the point of leaving London. She could ask him to call on her at her new farm, delaying the visit until she'd finished setting up the operation so she might be able to show it off to him proudly.

He would honor such a request—wouldn't he?

Walking to the window, she stared out at the gray dawn

and examined the plan, searching for potential flaws. After several minutes, she concluded it offered both a reasonable excuse for quickly departing the metropolis and her best chance to delay Quentin's inevitable visit until she was better prepared to deal with it.

Though the idea of fleeing shamed her, that humiliation paled beside the dire consequences of having her deception uncovered.

Feeling a bit calmer, she strode to the armoire to withdraw her portmanteau. She'd pack the essential items, let Aunt Kitty's maid finish the rest and be on the road to Sudley by this afternoon.

Moving stock, equipment and personnel would indeed keep her too busy to fret over the dilemma she'd created. Then, while she set all to rights at her new property, she could begin once again armoring her heart against Quentin.

Against his kindness and caring. The engaging sense of humor that always lifted her spirits, the exhilaration of racing their mounts across a meadow, or vying over billiards, or debating the best way to resolve some problem on one of their estates.

Against the touch that had awakened her body to desires and responses she'd never dreamed she possessed, a pleasure that had liquefied her bones and swept her away on a floodtide of delight, to subside in ecstasy later within the safe harbor of his embrace.

Against the devilishly seductive thought that her great love for him, combined with his genuine liking for her, would be enough to make a marriage work.

She took a ragged breath, the irony of it forcing her to a rueful smile. It appeared Quentin had been right to resist attempting to add passion to their friendship.

With her loss of innocence had come a vastly magnified physical awareness of Quentin, a knowledge of how addicting was the pleasure he could produce in her. Denying that hold was shattering her heart and reducing to splinters the stout defenses behind which she'd previously managed to resist him.

Tears stung her eyes. Angrily she swiped them away.

She would not, she vowed, become like her father and play Orpheus, who, when his bride was stolen from him by a viperous seducer, shut himself away from the world, forever mourning his loss.

Every man had flaws—even Quentin. Perhaps while she toiled to assemble her new enterprise, she could create a list of his faults, use it to school herself into considering it fortunate they would never marry. Let dispassionate reason pry loose the hold Quentin had established over her heart and soul, a hold she'd stupidly allowed passion to strengthen.

Once she had the farm running well and could demonstrate how successful and content she was as a single lady in control of her life, he would see there was no need for him to "salvage her future" by making her his wife.

And perhaps by then she would be able to meet him and feel only the tepid platonic friendship that was all Quentin Burke wanted from Caragh Sudley.

QUENTIN RETURNED to London in the early evening to the news, conveyed to him in a note from Caragh, that she once again had left the city. In fact, she requested that he not visit her until after she'd finished the move to her new property and had the farm functioning properly.

In addition to disappointment, a vague sense of…hurt pierced him as he read the note. Urgent as her business was, could she not have lingered just one more day and delivered her message in person? That emotion was swiftly succeeded by a niggling sense that perhaps Caragh was avoiding him.

But the facts didn't truly support such a suspicion. She'd been completely open and cordial at their last meeting. Excited as she was about her plans for the new venture, it was hardly surprising she was impatient to begin carrying them out.

Much as he burned to follow her immediately, as an estate manager himself, he understood both the complexity of the task facing her and the pride that had her urge him to postpone visiting. No more than she would he relish a friend calling at one of his new properties until he'd had time to staff, organize and begin running it efficiently.

Since the farm was located in a rural corner of Hampshire, it was unlikely anyone in the ton would discover her new venture for some time. With her reputation safe for the moment, he had little excuse not to honor her request.

It appeared he must contain his impatience for a few weeks at least.

The only sweet note in that otherwise sour conclusion, Quentin was confident after last night's discussion, was that Russell did not realize how soon his new neighbor intended to take up residence. Even so, in his current state of frustration, Quentin wasn't sure he could maintain a suitably friendly demeanor toward the man if he happened to encounter him over dinner at the club. He decided to stay home and order a cold collation.

Rather than brooding over what could not be changed, he told himself as he made short work of a beefsteak and ale, he should instead concentrate on settling a matter that could. Directly after dining, he would pay another call on Madame LaNoire.

A hot flash of anticipation washed through him, followed by another wave of guilt. He had to admit, this lingering…fascination with the veiled lady was a bit disturbing.

'Twas merely an attraction based on sympathy magnified by a healthy dose of lust, he reasoned. Once he married Caragh, with whom he shared a much deeper bond, and had *her* in his arms to beguile his senses, memories of Madame's allure would fade to the insignificance of a candle's glow beside a raging bonfire.

The sooner he secured Madame LaNoire's future, the sooner he might focus all his efforts on settling his with Caragh. After instructing a footman to summon a hackney, he allowed his valet to help him into his greatcoat.

A short drive later, he found himself once again mounting the stairs to Madame LaNoire's apartment, his nerves simmering with anticipation and grimly suppressed desire. Once again he knocked repeatedly, to no avail.

This time, however, he had come prepared. Squelching the protests of conscience, he produced from his pocket a long iron key. He had noted on his previous visit that the heavy oak door sported an old-fashioned lock. Before leaving his rooms tonight he'd rooted through his belongings to unearth a key the blacksmith at Branson had fashioned to open some long-neglected storage rooms for which, they'd discovered during Branson Park's renovation, the original keys had somehow become lost.

It was still early enough that he was certain Madame was away from home rather than asleep. Since finding her in residence was proving more difficult than anticipated, if the key chanced to work, he could leave her a note explaining his purpose and begging the favor of a reply.

He'd not yet decided what he would do, should he leave such a message and she fail to contact him.

Dismissing that thought, after peering down the staircase to insure he was not being observed, he inserted his key into the lock. After some jiggling, he managed to turn it and heard the latch click open.

Heartbeat speeding, Quentin pushed open the door and entered the apartment.

Calling her name as he walked, he proceeded from the small antechamber through the sitting room into the bedroom.

Given the lack of response to his knock, he was not surprised to find no one at home.

What did surprise him, as he retraced his steps more slowly through the deserted rooms, was the palpable sense of emptiness that struck him, sharp as the click of his boots on the bare floor. Not only was Madame LaNoire not at home, it appeared she had not been home for some time.

The parlor hearth was cold, containing neither ashes from a previous fire nor the kindling necessary to start a new one, while the table beside the wing chair before it was barren of newspapers or needlework. No dishes cluttered the dry sink in the small kitchen; no cooking pot sat ready on the stove. Even in the bedchamber of which he had such warm memories, the bed linens were cold and creaseless, as if no one had lain upon them in a long time.

He wandered across that dim chamber, to halt beside a dressing table in the opposite corner. Recalling the clutter of bottles that had always adorned his mama's, he noted with surprise that not a single vial of perfume or box of powder sat upon the table's surface—not so much as a brush or a hairpin.

In growing dismay, he hurried to the armoire and jerked open the door. The space within was as bare as the dressing table.

Impossible though it seemed, the conclusion was inescapable. Madame LaNoire was not just out—she was no longer in residence.

Dismay intensified, laced with an edge of panic. Had their tryst been discovered and she dismissed, compelling her to abandon her lodgings? Given her lack of resources, where could she have gone?

Surely nothing so dire could have occurred in the space of just a few days! But whatever the reason that had led her to leave home, Quentin felt compelled to find her, make sure she was safe—and verify that it was not their stolen interludes that had brought her to harm.

Unable to explain even to himself the urgency that drove him, he hurriedly relocked the door and trotted down the steps. As expected, what appeared to be landlord's apartment occupied the ground floor.

His knock was answered by an unkempt older woman, straggly gray hair escaping from beneath a stained mobcap. The surly look with which she opened the door faded as she took in his fashionable dress, and she belatedly dropped a curtsey.

"What kin I do for ye, m'lord?"

"I'm sorry to disturb you, ma'am, but I'm looking for one of your tenants, a Madame LaNoire?" Improvising rapidly, he continued, "My sister, who has engaged her services as a governess, sent me to fetch the lady, but she doesn't appear to be in. Might you know of her whereabouts?"

The matron peered at him, frowning. "Don't have no tenant by that name, m'lord."

So the name she'd given him was false, Quentin thought without surprise. That fact, added to her insistence on retaining the veil, only reinforced the likelihood that she was exactly what she claimed—a virtuous widow intent on keeping her reputation free from any taint of scandal. Which would make it all the more likely that his hopes of placing her in Aunt Jane's care would be realized.

After, of course, he found her.

"Perhaps I did not get the name aright—my sister's handwriting is sometimes difficult to decipher. Surely you've seen her, a slender, dark-haired lady with a pronounced French accent? My sister assured me she lived in this building."

The matron shook her head, setting the tattered lace of her cap bobbing. "B'ain't never had no furriners living here. Be ye sure ye've got the right house?"

His clandestine inspection of Madame LaNoire's flat left

him certain of that, though he hardly wished to confess that excursion to the landlady. Since he knew beyond doubt this was the correct building, why did the landlady disavow all knowledge of her? Could it be Madame LaNoire's accent had been false as well?

"I believe I am correct," he said slowly, his mind still scrutinizing possibilities. "I am quite certain my sister indicated she resided on the top floor."

The lace fluttered again with another denial. "Got no lady on the top floor. In fact, 'tis nobbit up there now. Flat is let to an artist gent, but he's off traveling in some rubbishing place—Rome, I hear."

Quentin shook his head, trying to make the disparate pieces fit. One explanation occurred, so awful he felt compelled to ascertain forthwith whether it might be true.

"Does that gentleman have a w-wife," he stumbled over the word, suddenly realizing the bitter implications should it turn out his veiled lady was *not* a widow, "who might have returned before him?"

The lady shrugged. "I wouldn't know, m'lord. Long as a tenant pays the rent on time so's I can turn it over to the owner and keep me own flat, I don't put my noggin in nobody else's business."

He took a ragged breath, relieved to at least not have that possibility confirmed. "Do you know when the artist plans to return?" he persisted.

Once more the mobcap bobbed as the lady shook her head. "He didn't say, but the rent's paid up until autumn."

Which left Quentin exactly—nowhere. Unable to think of any further questions that would not arouse still further the curiosity of the matron, who already showed signs of suspicion about his interest in the artist, he judged it prudent to retreat. Regardless of what she might know—and unless she were a better actress than he could credit, it appeared she knew little—he would learn nothing further about Madame LaNoire's whereabouts from her.

"I must have misread my sister's note after all. Pray excuse me, ma'am," dropping into her hand a coin that elicited a gap-toothed smile and a flurry of assurances that Mrs. Jeffries be ever at his service.

Trying to stomach his second major disappointment of the day, Quentin wandered to the street to summon a hackney, his mind awhirl with speculation. Could Madame LaNoire be the artist's errant wife? She must have some association with the man, or she would not have had a key to his flat.

A more palatable possibility presented itself as he journeyed back home—that she was a friend asked by the artist to watch over the property during his absence. Who, when she determined upon seducing Quentin, decided to further protect her identity by borrowing the premises for their tryst.

How much of what she had told him was real, how much invention? With her face masked and the dwelling she'd taken him to belonging to someone else, he had to acknowledge that her name, her story and even her voice might have been equally false.

The only thing he knew to be true was the intensity of the passion they'd shared.

Given his determination to wed Caragh, that was hardly a memory on which he needed to dwell. He would do better to wash his hands of the mystery that was Madame LaNoire and get on with his own plans. The care with which she'd obscured the truth of her circumstances argued that she felt in no need of his assistance.

And yet…if her story were true, she might well be in difficulty, possibly because of their brief liaison. Unable to rid himself of that persistent worry, he decided to allow himself one more evening to ponder how he might discover her current whereabouts before abandoning his efforts to assist her.

The idea came to him just as the hackney reached his lodging.

The artistic world was a small one. Possibly Ailis or her mentor Mr. Frank knew the painter who'd rented the rooms Madame LaNoire had borrowed. At the least, he should be able to determine that man's identity, perhaps discover whether a friend—or wife—was watching the property.

He might even learn the identity of his veiled lady.

Once again, excitement and an irrepressible desire stirred at the prospect.

Would he find her to be a virtuous governess in real need of his assistance? Or an artist's model, an actress or courtesan who had amused herself by weaving a tall tale to hoodwink a gullible gentleman?

It hurt to consider that his lovely veiled lady might have been laughing up her sleeve at him the whole time they'd spent together. And yet, as he forced himself to face the possibility, when he recalled her air of gentility, her voice, her carriage, he simply couldn't believe her to be less than a lady born.

In any event, learning the truth about her was fast becoming such an obsession, he suspected he would never rid himself of this fascination unless he followed the trail to its end, whatever that turned out to be.

The hour was now too late for social calls, he decided, regretfully refraining from banging on the roof to redirect the jarvey. But first thing tomorrow, before she became enmeshed in her work, Quentin would drop by the studio of Ailis Sudley.

CHAPTER TWENTY

QUENTIN WOKE EARLY, driven by a sense of expectation. Today he might finally unveil his mystery lady!

He jumped from bed and strode to the window, pulling aside the heavy curtains. The dawn appeared clear, with just a glaze of high clouds—the sort of day that would provide the steady north light in which an artist preferred to work. Doubtless Ailis Sudley would be up and at her easel early to take advantage of it. If he wished to speak with her, he'd best snare her before she began painting, for he knew she wouldn't hesitate to have her maidservant send him away if she were deep in the throes of artistic creation when he called.

As soon as he felt she must be awake and about, he presented himself at her studio.

Fortunately, he caught her still at breakfast. Accepting her offer of coffee, he took a chair in the sitting area she'd screened off from the open workroom. Ailis lounged on the sofa, clad in a thin wrapper that accented her ample curves.

Odd, he thought, noting dispassionately the voluptuous outline of her bosom as she raised her arm to drink her coffee, that her striking blond beauty left him unmoved, while her less conventionally pretty sister inspired in him a deep physical attraction.

Would Madame LaNoire turn out to be a beauty, once he was finally able to gaze upon her face?

"To what do I owe the honor of this early visit?" Ailis asked, pulling him from his reflections. "Whatever it is, be quick about it, for I mean to be at work within the hour."

So much for a gracious hostess's manners, Quentin thought,

grinning. ''Perhaps I just wanted a few moments of scintillating conversation.''

''Then you would certainly not have sought me out,'' Ailis returned, not at all offended. ''Come, Quent, cut line. What is it you want?''

''Some information. I'm trying to trace an artist and thought you, or Mr. Frank, might know him.'' Now that he was so close to possibly solving the mystery, Quentin had to work to keep his tone light and mask the urgency that stretched every nerve trigger-tight.

Ailis raised an eyebrow. ''And what need would you have of an artist?''

Having anticipated the question, he replied smoothly, ''Now that Branson Hall is restored, I'm looking for still life paintings to adorn some of the rooms.''

''Fortunately, neither I nor Max do still life, else I should be much insulted that you did not consult us first. This artist specializes in them, then?''

''So I've been told.''

''Ah. Who recommended him? One of your aristocratic acquaintances?''

''Really, Ailis, does it matter?'' Quentin replied, exasperation cracking his calm facade.

''A bit impatient, are we?''

Controlling himself with an effort, he replied, '''Tis you who wished to conclude the interview quickly.''

She nodded, though her eyes sparkled with an amusement he had learned over the years to mistrust. ''So I did. What is this esteemed individual's name?''

''I'm afraid I don't know. When I admired the work and asked the owner, he could not recall.''

As he'd hoped, this lack of appreciation for the artist succeeded in diverting her from speculating about his interest in the matter.

''How typical of the rich!'' she exclaimed, her eyes firing

up. "Completely oblivious to the importance of the genius who creates the masterwork!"

"Lamentable, I know," he soothed. "He did, however, recall the location of the man's studio—a top-floor flat on Maiden Lane, not far from here."

"Maiden Lane?" Her indignation subsiding, Ailis grew thoughtful. "You're quite certain it was Maiden Lane? I don't know of any artist of repute living there, but I'm newly come to London. If you wish, I can ask Max."

So he must leave no more knowledgeable about the veiled lady than when he'd arrived. Once he'd controlled his disappointment—which was far keener than it should be—Quentin replied, "Yes, I should appreciate that."

"He's away at the country home of a client now, finishing up a portrait, but I shall ask him directly when he returns."

He clenched his teeth to prevent an oath of frustration from escaping. "When do you expect Mr. Frank back?" he said instead.

Ailis gave a graceful wave of her hand. "I'm not certain. Completing the final details should occupy several weeks, I should guess. It's fortunate I have a commission of my own to finish up, for which he's already approved the preliminary sketches, else I should sorely resent his absence."

Several weeks! After spending the last few hours in ardent expectation of perhaps learning the identity of his veiled lady today, several weeks seemed an eternity. Fuming inwardly, Quentin rose to his feet.

"I've taken up enough of your time for today, then. Thank you for the coffee."

"Should you like to see some of the sketches before you leave?" Ailis asked, rising as well.

Despite the choking sense of frustration that made him want to pound a fist into the studio wall, it would only be polite to agree. Besides, he was curious to see what commission Ailis, as both a fledgling artist and a female, had managed to wangle.

"I should be honored."

She led him around the screen to the workbench. "The initial sketch was a figure study I'd done for Max, which he thought handsome enough to hang in his studio. One of his clients liked it so much he commissioned a series."

"Does the patron know you are the artist?"

"Max told him it was the work of his most promising student," she told him as she opened a leather portfolio and leafed through its contents. "The client was thrilled, apparently thinking to purchase the series for much less than he would have expected to pay Max. But being the exceptional mentor he is, Max secured a very fine price for it. I shall have no need to draw upon my reserve funds for quite some time," she finished, a note of pride in her voice.

"My congratulation, Ailis! It sounds as though you've made a fine beginning." Having long considered her to possess a superior talent, Quentin was genuinely happy for her. And it dampened somewhat his still-smoldering anger toward Ailis to learn that the career she had wounded her sister and ruined Caragh's future to secure at least showed promise of being successful.

"I decided not to include this sketch in the series, so you may have it. In fact, thinking I might one day offer it to you, I recently made a few changes." She held out the parchment, a little smile playing at her lips.

"Thank you, that's very kind. I shall treasure it."

Ailis chuckled. "I'm sure you shall."

As Quentin glanced down at the sketch Ailis handed him, shock sucked the air from his lungs and the conventional compliment he'd been about to utter evaporated off his lips.

His eyes riveted to the drawing of a slender woman reclining on her side, one arm masking her face, a tumble of dusky curls cascading over her shoulders and down to frame her breasts. Her naked breasts.

The utter relaxation of her limbs and the sheen of perspiration glistening on her nude body conveyed the impression of blissful satiation. Indeed, her lover reclined behind her, his face in shadow as he kissed her shoulder, his arm over her hip, his hand on her belly, his fingers resting possessively over the curls at the juncture of her thighs.

Shocking as it was to realize the creator of this erotic tableau was the little girl who'd grown up his neighbor at Thornwhistle, what stole his breath was the woman's startling resemblance to his veiled lady.

Memories came flooding back—of lying tangled in the bedclothes after lovemaking, his lady reclining just so, satisfied and pliant in his embrace. The sketch's suggestion of the subtle stroking by which he could rouse her responsive body and begin the magic spiral again sent a blast of desire and longing through him.

He must have been staring for some minutes before he managed to pry his gaze from the image and his mind from the memories, for when he at last looked up, Ailis was smiling broadly.

"You like it, I can see."

"I...it...confound it, Ailis, how could you—" he broke off, heat flooding his face, nothing in his previous experience equipping him to discuss so intimate a matter with a female, much less a gently-reared, unmarried one.

She laughed, her voice rich with amusement. "Honestly, ton gentlemen are such hypocrites! They think nothing of reveling in the embrace of courtesans or mistresses, but are rendered speechless by viewing the *image* of such pleasure when in company with a female." She shook her head. "Even Holden, as wicked as his reputation is, was shocked when he first saw the sketches."

He wanted to argue something about a gentleman's discretion and the need to protect a lady's tender sensibilities, but couldn't quite get his tongue around the words. Besides, such a speech was probably wasted on the creator of this startling drawing.

"Are…all the sketches in the commission like this?" he managed at last.

"Oh, no! Most are much more explicit…but I didn't wish to shock you overmuch."

Quentin could only be glad she'd decided to refrain. The very suggestion of what else she might have drawn propelled his thoughts back to Madame LaNoire's bedchamber, tightening his body with another flush of need, leaving him once more speechless.

She laughed again at his obvious befuddlement. "Come now, Quent, don't be such a rustic. 'Tis considered quite normal for a *man* of my age to have experience. Indeed, had I been wife these last five years to some complacent husband and had already produced the requisite heirs, you must admit that your compatriots would now be vying to put *me* in just such a position as the girl in the sketch."

Quentin opened his lips to object, then closed them. Recalling the bawdy comments already being tossed around concerning her at the gentlemen's clubs, he could not with veracity protest that assessment.

"Thank you for not insulting my intelligence by attempting to deny it," she said, patting his hand before taking his arm to lead him to the door.

She halted with him before the entry. "You will take good care of it," she said, a naughty gleam in her eye.

"Of course," he replied a bit stiffly, still striving to regain his shattered composure.

"I'll be in touch with you when Max returns," she said as she plucked his greatcoat from the clothes tree. As she pulled the heavy garment off, though, it snagged on the adjacent pegs, knocking several items to the floor.

Ailis exclaimed in annoyance. Before she could reveal any more of her charms by bending over in her flimsy wrapper, he thrust the sketch into her hands. "Allow me," he said, kneeling down to retrieve the fallen garments.

"Thank you, Quent," she said as he straightened to offer her a pair of gloves and a long trailing scarf.

Something about the touch of the latter item caught his attention. Grabbing the end, he drew it back and stared. For the second time that morning his breath suspended.

The long, filmy rectangle fashioned of black velvet had a pattern of fleur-de-lis burned into its surface—the same design he'd traced with his fingertips, trying to map the features of the face hidden behind it.

"Wh-what is this?" he gasped, his heartbeat now loud in his ears.

Ailis raised an eyebrow. "Quite evidently, 'tis a lady's scarf."

"Yes, yes," he said impatiently, "but where did you get it?"

"'Tis Caragh's. I thought the pattern so pretty, I asked her to lend it to me to use as a drape in my figure studies."

Caragh's? Incredulity, delight and consternation pulsed through him. But 'twas preposterous! Patterned scarf or no, Caragh could not possibly be his veiled lady. Still...

"How long have you had it?" he demanded.

Ailis's eyebrow lifted higher. "Two days. I kept it when she came by to tell me she was leaving town to begin the move to her new property. Oh, she did tell you she's bought land to expand her farm—"

Quentin scarcely heard her after the first riveting words. *Two days...* As he ran the veil through his fingers, the soft fabric whispered under his thumbs in patterns he'd memorized in the lamplight and traced lovingly under the erotic spell of darkness. He took a deep, gasping breath. "Y-you are sure it is *Caragh's?*"

Ailis gave him an odd little smile. "Positive. Why do you ask?"

He shook his head. In character, experience and conduct the two women could not be more dissimilar. Surely there was some other explanation. "I...I've seen something similar. Lovely, isn't it? It must be quite a popular style in the shops."

Ailis shook her head. "As it happens, I was with Caragh when she bought it and can attest we saw nothing remotely like it. The pattern is burned into the velvet by hand, so even should others have been produced, I don't expect any two could be identical. Does it matter?"

"N-no, not especially." Numbly he handed it back.

While he shrugged into his coat, Ailis folded the scarf neatly—and inserted the sketch in it. "Since you seem to like it so much," she said, holding the items out to him, "keep the scarf, too. Or return it to Caragh when next you see her. When will that be, by the way?"

"I'm...not sure. She asked that I wait to visit, ah, until— later." Like a river at flood tide, his thoughts were boiling over each other in a mad chaotic rush of speculation, making it extremely difficult for him to concentrate on conversing with Ailis.

He needed to get away, examine the scarf more closely, consider the implications of this startling development.

Mercifully, the traditional courtesies of leave-taking fell automatically from his tongue. And then he was alone, walking back down the stairs, clutching against his chest the velvet scarf—and Ailis's scandalous drawing.

In the brighter daylight of the street, he gave the scarf a minute inspection. After studying the graceful swirl of pattern, closing his eyes and tracing his thumb across the plush crests and silken valleys of its surface, his conviction intensified that this was indeed the covering that had veiled his lady's face those two nights.

The conclusion made him dizzy, as if he were standing at

the end of a long tunnel, watching his life spiral away from him, out of control. He took a steadying breath.

He'd return to his rooms, pour a strong brandy and ponder this again, slowly.

But the facts as he examined them in the unhurried privacy of his chamber led him back to the same conclusion, absurd and impossible as it first seemed.

He must take a trip to Bond Street and make a survey of the ladies' scarves. If that visit confirmed Ailis's contention that the scarf was indeed one of a kind, it must inevitably follow that...*Caragh* was Madame LaNoire?

As he tried to get his mind around the enormity of that conclusion, other details floated up out of memory.

When he'd first approached the veiled lady at Vauxhall, he recalled suddenly, he had mistaken her for Caragh. Even after two nights with her, something about the soft, fluid sound of her French syllables, her carriage, the angle of her body as she moved continued to whisper to him of Caragh.

And it was Caragh who'd begged him to attend the masquerade, Caragh whose failure to appear had left him alone and unoccupied—at the precise moment he encountered Madame LaNoire.

Coincidence? Or calculation?

Yet, convincing himself that Caragh was his veiled lady appeared absurd on the face of it. How could a gently-born virgin—for he would stake his life on the fact that Caragh was an innocent—have played the knowing widow?

The answer occurred, so simple he wondered why it had taken him so long to make the connection. Caragh might be innocent, but, he thought grimly, gazing at the sketch Ailis had given him—her scandalous sister was definitely not.

If Caragh were indeed Madame LaNoire, it was certainly Ailis who had helped her plan and execute the deception.

Anger welled up. How dare Caragh abuse his trust by perpetrating such an outrage? The heedless, unconventional Ailis he could well believe capable of it, though his mind boggled at imagining her actually instructing her sister in the arts of seduction.

He recalled the veiled lady's curious mix of carnality and hesitance, especially on their first night together. At the time, bewitched by her, he'd accepted without question her explanation that, having been celibate so many years, she was experiencing again the ways of a man with a woman as if for the first time.

Experiencing again—or for the *very* first time?

Into his mind flashed the image of the coy little smile Ailis had given him as she handed him the sketch—the *recently altered* sketch—of the sleeping woman who so closely resembled Madame LaNoire. His suspicion of her duplicity strengthened.

Who else might so easily access the key to another artist's studio? Or have at her disposition, given what she'd inferred to be in the rest of her series of sketches, a veritable pictorial guide to seduction with which to tutor an innocent?

If his suppositions were correct, Ailis had known all during their meeting this morning what he really sought. No wonder she'd drawn out the questioning, delighting in his discomfiture. *She knew of no artist of repute in that studio,* indeed!

He gritted his teeth against a choking swell of fury. If the infuriating wench had been to hand at this moment, he'd have been seriously tempted to strangle her.

And yet, as he gazed back at the sketch, some of his emotion shifted into burgeoning desire as, against his will, the deft lines of her drawing elicited vivid memories of those two evenings in Madame LaNoire's bed.

How could he murder someone who'd helped to produce two of the most glorious nights of his life?

Another thought occurred, and he slammed his glass down in agitation. No wonder Caragh had fled London before his return! Confronted face-to-face, she'd never been good at dissembling. If she were truly Madame LaNoire, she might have managed to fool him with an opaque veil and an untraceable accent, but after what she had done to him in candlelight and darkness, she would never be able to meet his gaze squarely in the unrelenting light of day without blushing. Nor, had *she* been his midnight lover, would she be able so much as to enter the room without them both becoming immediately conscious of the powerful physical bond created by two nights of thorough and passionate lovemaking.

Though he still could not truly believe it, if Caragh *were* Madame LaNoire, what was he to do about it?

Fury and desire to repudiate her friendship forever for deceiving him warred with exhilaration at the notion that the inventive, passionate lady who'd so captured his mind might be the lady who already held his affections.

He'd have to marry her, of course, but as he'd already decided on that course some time ago, that would hardly be a sacrifice. At the notion of having a lifetime of Caragh to titillate his mind and Madame LaNoire to inflame his senses, a delighted anticipation filled him.

Except…a strong stirring of caution quelled his delight. Would it not be folly to wed a woman who had behaved like a veritable hussy? Having shown herself capable of planning an elaborate seduction, how could he be sure after they were wed that Caragh might not take the notion into her head to entice some new lover?

Still, even if events proved she was indeed Madame LaNoire, Quentin simply couldn't believe Caragh a wanton. Every instinct told him she would never have permitted such intimacies, much less sought them out, were her emotions not completely engaged.

Which brought him to the perplexing corollary. If Caragh *were* Madame LaNoire, *why* had she done it?

Despite his anger, he had to feel flattered at the great lengths to which she'd apparently gone to make him her lover.

Still, the whole charade had been unnecessary. He'd already asked her to marry him. She had only to say yes, and his body would be hers. Permanently. Why concoct this elaborate deception?

He took another fiery sip of the brandy, struggling to understand the impenetrable labyrinth of female reasoning. She'd professed herself insulted that he would offer marriage merely to salvage her reputation, although that was an eminently sensible reason to marry. Also practical and logical was the desire to wed someone for whom one already entertained a warm affection.

Unless… The only reason he could imagine to explain why a virtuous lady would sacrifice her honor and perpetrate such a ruse was that Caragh didn't just like, but loved him. Loved him too much to agree to marry for merely practical or logical reasons. She wanted his love in return—or nothing at all.

Convinced mild affection was all he had to offer her, had she decided to sample how glorious passion could be before devoting herself to her horses and turning her back on marriage forever?

Glorious it had certainly been!

He jerked his mind back from the temptation to focus once again on recalling those arousing interludes. He needed to decide what he meant to do now.

First and foremost, before he wasted any more time in uninformed speculation, he must determine whether or not Caragh was in fact his veiled lady.

He might return and baldly ask Ailis—but she'd had ample time this morning to reveal what she knew. Since she'd not chosen to avail herself of the opportunity, even if it were true, she was likely to deny the connection, after extracting the maximum entertainment value from mocking his delusion.

Better instead to follow the trail of the veil. Once he was able at last to confirm or refute the incredible notion that Caragh might actually be Madame LaNoire, only then would he confront the puzzle of what to do next.

CHAPTER TWENTY-ONE

THREE WEEKS LATER, Caragh leaned back in her chair in the small library she'd taken for her office and flexed her tired shoulders. The east-facing window before her desk looked out over a pleasing vista of scythed lawn, behind which stretched the newly erected fences of the paddocks for her stallions. The west and north sides of the small manor house were also surrounded with verdant pastureland partitioned off by fencing to contain the herd of mares.

She'd found the stone buildings of the original farm in excellent condition. Not having to expend funds on repairs, she noted with a pleased glance at the ledger, would leave her the necessary capital to construct all the additional barns she'd planned this very first year. There was even sufficient cash remaining to update the manor house and put in a new cook stove, which was certain to delight the few servants she'd brought with her from Sudley.

The move itself had required a full week, and she'd spent the next two with carpenters, stonemasons and grooms supervising the beginning of the additions and inspecting the new stock she'd had sent over from Ireland.

So serene were the vast meadows now dotted with grazing horses that she'd decided to call her new venture Hunter's Haven. The horses here would breed strong; her clients would find the stock so superior that the Haven would indeed become the refuge of choice for those seeking the finest in horseflesh.

She hoped it would prove a haven for her as well.

Her days were long, intense and exhausting. But as satisfying as it was to guide her longtime dream into reality, the best part of the move thus far was that the hectic pace kept her too busy to think about Quentin.

Most of the time, she amended with a sigh. In odd moments between tasks, as now, his image persisted in muscling its way out of the background of her mind to seize center stage, however much she resisted thinking of him and the halcyon hours she'd tricked him into spending with her.

She still vacillated between cherishing those evenings and regretting she'd ever conceived the bacon-brained idea of making him her lover. But she now knew with absolute certainty that fleeing London had been wise.

Beyond the difficulty of meeting him with the knowledge of their intimacy burning like the illicit secret in her breast, the ache of missing him was so acute that, were he still near enough, she knew she would break down and seek him out, however great the danger that he might uncover her deception.

Stronger still was the hunger for his touch, for the incredible sensations he could summon with his cunning hands and knowing tongue. Her will would certainly not be strong enough to resist the temptation to redon her veil and, in the guise of Madame LaNoire, summon her lover back for yet another night of bliss.

Passion, she was discovering, was a Pandora's box indeed. The powerful need he'd unlocked in her refused to be contained, clamoring instead for additional fulfillment.

As she had each previous occasion when thoughts of Quentin refused to be subdued, Caragh drew from beneath her ledger a now-worn sheet of vellum. Upon arriving at Hunter's Haven, she'd followed through on her London resolve and begun a list of Quentin's faults. A list she was supposed to review until she overcame her useless unrequited love for Quentin Burke.

"Managing" had been the first entry. He was certainly that. But like her, his intentions when he took on a project—or a person—were always pure. He wished not to control or subdue, but to improve, and he usually succeeded. His bringing his estate back from the verge of ruin was proof enough of that.

She ended by crossing it off the list.

"Arrogant" was the second item. But after pondering the matter, trying to recall when he had imposed his will or opinions on her, she concluded he had never tried to dictate her agreement or disregard her feelings. Certainly he was an ardent advocate for what he believed, but he had always sought, and listened patiently to, her opinions. Occasionally he even changed his views in favor of hers.

She'd drawn a long dark line through "Arrogant."

And so it had gone with "Insensitive," "Conceited" and "Humorless." The only item she'd penned on her list that she had not eventually crossed off was "Does not love me."

She touched her fingertip to the words again, her eyelids stinging. Even that was hardly a failing. As she knew only too well after living for more than two decades with her father, even with the deepest desire and after the sincerest of efforts, you could not *make* someone love you.

Perhaps she should just concede defeat and tear up the list. It seemed that rather than convincing her how lucky she was to escape Quentin's spell, reviewing it only made her ponder him and his qualities at greater length, leaving her missing him all the more keenly.

Enough self-pitying nonsense, she told herself crossly, thrusting the paper back under the ledger. List or no list, as her memory of the seductive pleasures of his body faded, the hold he had over her mind and heart would dissipate, too. Then she would finally master this unacceptable weakness for him, extinguish once and for all the pathetic longing for his touch.

She had better, she thought grimly, make progress in that direction quickly. She'd already penned him two notes, chatting of her progress and referring vaguely to when she expected to have Hunter's Haven presentable. She couldn't hope to stave off his visit much longer.

And how she wanted him here, despite how dangerous his nearness would certainly prove!

A knock at the door set her heart racing.

Idiot! she told herself as she bid the supplicant enter. It would surely not be Quentin, too impatient to wait any longer in London for her summons. Silently chastising herself for her fixation on the man in terms crude enough to have impressed her stable boys, she turned toward the door, struggling to master her hopeless hope.

Standing behind the butler on the threshold was not, of course, Quentin. Instead she saw his London friend and the former owner of her new property, Lord Alden Russell.

"Your nearest neighbor, Lord Russell, Mistress," the butler intoned.

Smiling, Lord Russell walked past the servant and swept her a bow. "The very warmest of welcomes to our county, Miss Sudley! Had I known you intended to take possession of the property so quickly, I'd have been much more gracious about bowing to Mama's wishes that we return to Hillcrest Manor for a short respite from town."

It was quite impossible not to smile back at his open friendliness. "Thank you, Lord Russell," she replied, curtseying. "Please, do come in."

"I'm not interrupting?" He gestured to her desk with its stack of account books.

"Not at all. I needed a break—" *from more than just account books,* she thought "—and was on the point of ringing for some tea. Won't you join me?"

"Alas, I cannot stay. I was on my way to do an errand for Mama when I saw your sign and felt compelled to discover if the new owners had yet arrived."

"Another time, then," Caragh replied, nodding a dismissal

to the butler, who left them with a bow. "You will stay a few moments, I hope?"

"Finding you at home, I cannot deny myself that pleasure," he murmured.

Surprise and a warm gratification flowed through Caragh as she walked to the wing chair before the fireplace. Since Ailis's debacle, she had spent so much time armoring herself for criticism and rejection that Lord Russell's warm friendliness fell like soft rain on parched ground. "So your mama is a lover of country living, but you are not?" she asked, gesturing him to the sofa.

Before seating himself, he caught her hand and brought it to his lips. "I am now," he murmured.

A subtle current flashed between them. Before her masquerade as Madame LaNoire, she might not have noticed—or identified—what the pressure of his fingers, the tenor of his voice, were telegraphing. *He's attracted to me,* she realized in surprise.

That novel thought was followed immediately by a new and rather gratifying sense of feminine power. Not sure what she meant to do about it, she ignored the innuendo under his words.

"I should think you would be, given the beauty of the land hereabouts. By the way, I'm very grateful to you! I found the property in just as excellent a condition as you and your lawyer described it. It shall do wonderfully for my enterprise."

"'Hunter's Haven,' the new sign said," Lord Russell replied, accepting her tacit rebuff of his flirtatious overture. "You specialize in that breed?"

"Yes, as I believe I told you when we first met. Sudley produced some excellent horses, but with insufficient pasturage to maintain them, I was forced to sell all but a few. An impediment to expansion of the breeding operation that shall no longer hinder me, given the vast amount of prime pasturage here. With the addition of the superior Irish stock I've just purchased, I'm quite excited about our future."

"It sounds promising indeed. I always thought this would be a perfect property for horse-breeding. Once you have the operation organized and running to your satisfaction, I should love to tour it."

"I shall be happy to show you around. But if such an enterprise interests you, why did you sell the farm?"

Lord Russell shrugged. "I haven't the talent for horses I understand you possess, and I've enough other acreage to manage. Now, I've interrupted you long enough," he said, rising. "I just wanted to extend a welcome and assure you that, should you need anything while you're settling in, please don't hesitate to call at Hillcrest."

"That's very kind," Caragh replied, rising as well.

"When do you expect your father?" he asked as she walked with him to the door. "By rights, I should have postponed my call when your butler informed me he was not yet in residence, but I must confess, I was too impatient to heed the proprieties. Oh, and Mama bade me invite you to dinner tomorrow, just a small gathering. She plans a more formal affair to introduce you and Lord Sudley to the neighbors once you've settled in."

Heat rose in Caragh's face. She might return an evasive answer, put off revealing that her father would not be coming to join her. But it would be shabby to bask in the warmth of the hospitable gestures of her new neighbors while leaving them in ignorance of her true status.

She cleared her throat. "My father is a classical scholar of some note. I'm afraid he is far too immersed in his studies to have time or interest in supervising a farm. He...he intends to remain fixed at Sudley."

His bright smile dimmed. "Now that is a disappointment! Not only will we be deprived of his acquaintance, but I had hoped you would be making your residence more or less permanently among us. However, an enterprise as vast as you envision will surely require you to make frequent visits." Winking, he gave a theatrical sigh. "I shall have to content myself with that, I suppose. Please do join us for dinner tomorrow, even without your father." Reaching for her hand, he said, the caressing undertone back in his voice, "I must make the most of my opportunities."

She allowed him to kiss her fingertips, noting once again that small quiver of physical attraction. He was quite a handsome gentleman, she thought dispassionately.

All the more reason to set him straight from the outset. "Lord Russell, before I accept your mama's obliging invitation, you should know that my visits here will be more than frequent. I...I intend to reside here. Without Papa," she added, once more feeling the color rise in her cheeks but determined to make sure there could be no misunderstanding.

His eyebrows winged upward, and for a moment he stood silent.

Even without Quentin's warning, she'd known that by flouting convention, as a single woman living alone she would leave herself open to criticism, ribald conjecture, perhaps even dishonorable offers. She braced herself for the appraising look, the intensifying of his sexual innuendo once he realized the full implications of her disclosure.

Faced for the first time with actually dealing with that potential reaction was more humiliating and distasteful than she had ever imagined. Grimly she set her teeth and lifted her chin.

"What an immense undertaking!" he said at last, bowing with perfect propriety. "Mama and I shall certainly look forward to your telling us all about your plans when you come to dine."

Caught off guard, she let out a gusty breath she hadn't realized she'd been holding and looked up into his face. Could it be he had *not* understood? But no, he would have to be dim-witted indeed not to have comprehended her meaning. Both from Quentin's descriptions and her own dealings with him, she knew him to be quite intelligent.

"You...you are sure? I should not wish to embarrass your lady mama."

He laughed. "Mama is made of sterner stuff than that—as are you, I'll wager. Or so Quentin has led me to believe. 'Flashing-eyed Athena, wise and fair' indeed! Until tomorrow evening, then?"

He did understand...and meant to befriend her anyway. Gratitude and humility brought her shockingly close to tears. "You are both indeed kind, then. Until tomorrow."

Once more he kissed her hand, his lips lingering on her bare knuckles long enough for the current running between them to intensify.

Pulling her hand away, she wondered if she should revise her previous impression. Was friendship all he was hoping for from a woman who'd just announced herself gentry-born but not gentry-behaved?

And what coercion would he have to exert over his poor mama to keep her from withdrawing her invitation once she learned the shocking truth about her new neighbor?

"I'm deeply indebted to Lord Branson for introducing us," Russell said, pulling her from her thoughts, "and I hope to become much better acquainted."

She curtseyed in return to his final bow, then watched him walk out, an odd mix of feelings—gratitude, suspicion, uncertainty—jostling within her. Just what sort of acquaintance did he wish for with his unconventional new neighbor?

Although inviting her into his home to dine with his mama argued against his harboring any ignoble intent, she didn't yet know him well enough to be sure.

Ailis would probably say his intentions were irrelevant, advise her to use the attraction he obviously felt to smooth her way in the neighborhood. Perhaps even take him for her lover.

That would certainly be one way to distract herself from longing for Quentin and quiet the body still clamoring for his touch. She felt a surge of warmth within at the thought.

But her stolen nights with Quentin had taught her several hard truths. She had no intention now of taking another lover, even were she to develop a warm enough friendship with Lord Russell to envision such a step.

She was having difficulty enough coping with the first experience. Loving Quentin as she did, their intimacy, for her, had truly been a merging into one flesh. Having to send him away had been like ripping her soul in two. She didn't think she could survive a second such experience.

Besides, she was discovering, she was not as much her mama's daughter as, in the throes of hurt and heartache, she'd originally assumed.

The social upheaval which still buffeted her had been Ailis's doing. She herself had no real wish to defy the ton's rules by spurning wedlock and traipsing from lover to lover, as her mother—and Ailis—seemed inclined to do. Nor, after nearly a month of isolation at her new farm, was she finding it quite as much a blessing as she'd envisioned to live totally removed from society.

From her girlhood, she'd assumed the reins of a large household and taken up corresponding responsibilities in her rural society. In addition to her work with the Benevolent Association, she'd participated in a continuous round of calls and consultations with her neighbors. At home, she had her father and Ailis to look after, their company at meals and in the evenings—even if the company of two such self-absorbed individuals was often less than stimulating.

Though her work here was satisfying and occupied nearly every minute, for the first time she was living totally cut off from both family and local society.

She was, she had to admit, lonely.

She missed the almost daily business of calling and receiving calls. She'd grown to dread the silence of meals where she dined alone but for the attending footman. And after dinner, on some evenings where the only sound in the room was her even breathing and the hiss and pop of the fire, she even missed the fractious ladies of the Benevolent Association.

And what of holidays? With whom was she going to share the warmth of the Yule log, the excitement of Boxing Day or the festivities of midsummer?

It appeared Quentin had been right when he'd urged her not to hastily make so irreversible a decision as cutting herself completely off from society.

Having, in addition to a successful farm, a home that included not just servants but also friends, a husband and eventually children on whom she could lavish her love had, she now realized, a deep-seated appeal.

It wasn't pride that would keep her from confessing this discovery to Quentin when he finally made his visit. She dare not admit it to him, lest he be quick to suggest it was not yet too late to have both her farm and the family she longed for—by accepting his offer of marriage.

Even now, the desire to do so pulled at her with frightening strength. After her nights as Madame LaNoire, she knew they would share passion as well as friendship. Would such a union be so impossible to bear?

But she knew her world too well. Ton couples often went their separate ways once the necessary heirs were conceived. Indeed, it was thought odd for a married couple to live in each other's pocket. As long as a husband supported his wife and children and treated them with courtesy—sometimes even when he did not—society considered it acceptable for him to pursue relationships elsewhere.

When the initial fiery heat of Quentin's passion for her faded to the tepid warmth of companionship, would he be able to resist the temptations their world would inevitably present to a handsome man of his wealth and position?

Discovering that the husband she loved with such intensity had lain with another woman would devastate her.

Her only real chance of avoiding that fate would be if the friendship Quentin felt for her were buttressed by a love as deep and abiding as her own. A love he had, up until now, shown no signs of harboring.

And if, after knowing her these six years, he had not yet developed such an attachment, it seemed unlikely he ever would.

The misery of that conclusion was a familiar one. Before melancholy overwhelmed her, though, a more cheering thought occurred.

She couldn't marry Quentin. But if, despite her status, Lord Russell persisted in befriending her—and that friendship proceeded into courtship—might she envision wedding him, should he turn out to be as kind and honorable as he seemed?

Not in the near term, of course. Her heart and mind were still too full of Quentin. But perhaps once she'd had time to extinguish that love, the yearning for a family might permit her to foster affection for someone else.

Considering that prospect, she suddenly understood why Quentin had felt confident about pressing her to marry him. She now saw the appeal of pledging one's troth to a partner for whom one felt nothing more intense than shared respect and friendship. Such a union might not engender heights of bliss, but it was also unlikely to plunge one into valleys of despair as deep as those she'd recently been plumbing.

Sighing, she turned her gaze out the window in the direction of Hillcrest Manor.

Regardless of his ultimate intent, the attentions of her new neighbor had already brought warmth and a glimmer of hope into her isolation. Perhaps Lord Alden Russell would prove just the antidote necessary to cure herself once and for all of the malady of loving Quentin Burke.

IN THE EARLY EVENING, Quentin sat at the desk in his London study, idly flipping through a stack of invitations. After three long weeks of attending functions ranging from Venetian breakfasts to dinners to musicales to come-out balls, none of the delights promised tonight by London's hostesses held the slightest appeal.

When they'd first arrived in London and he'd wanted to be available to offer Caragh his escort and support, he'd been pulled away repeatedly to address a continuous stream of small concerns at his new property. Naturally, he thought sourly, now that he most needed work to occupy his mind, no further problems had occurred. Even his paperwork had slowed to a trickle.

Yesterday, desperate for some activity, he'd ridden to the estate outside London to find, as he expected, that the new manager he'd just installed was doing splendidly. Indeed, upon his departure, after thanking him for the visit, the man had rather pointedly remarked that as he had matters well in hand, my lord needn't waste any more of his valuable time traveling out from London.

Without the Sudleys' affairs and his own business to distract him, he'd been experiencing for the first time the full measure of attention Society accorded a bachelor considered by the ton to be an extremely eligible parti.

He had to admit, he'd reveled a bit at first in the triumph of being sought out by matrons who, before his transformation of the Branson fortunes, would have steered their precious daughters well clear of him. For a few evenings he'd found it rather amusing, wondering if the ambitious mamas had all studied the same course at their female academies on "Pushing Eligible Daughters to a Gentleman's Attention."

As his connection to the scandalous Sudleys was well known, he was now finding the performance increasingly distasteful. After Lady So-and-So cornered him over dinner or dancing or cards and prevailed upon him to let her present her "darling Marianne," she would invariably opine that, given the distress he must have suffered over those "unfortunate girls," he would doubtless find it refreshing to meet a young lady whose breeding was as matchless as her countenance. She would then gesture toward the daughter, who, after lowering her eyes demurely behind her fan, would glance up with an unmistakable "come-hither" look.

He was having a hard time of late restraining the strong desire to cut off Lady So-and-So's effusions about her progeny by informing her just what he thought of a "lady" who would malign persons not present to defend themselves.

Perhaps Caragh was wiser than he'd thought in deciding to forego Society.

Ah, Caragh. Longing, confusion, impatience and the bite of repressed desire scorched him anew whenever his thoughts strayed to her, as they did all too frequently.

Impatience that had chafed him every moment since he'd made a thorough search for velvet scarves, from the elite establishments on Bond Street to the peddlers crying their wares on the streets, without finding another similar to the one draped around his bedpost.

He was now virtually certain that Caragh had to be Madame LaNoire.

After three weeks of wallowing in a most atypical stew of indecision, he was still uncertain what to do about it.

His first thought had been a fierce desire to disregard her wishes and ride to see her immediately, to confront her before she had a chance to prepare herself for the meeting. If she reacted with awkwardness and hesitancy, her cheeks rosy with embarrassment at the memory of their intimacies, surely that would prove her to be the innocent he wanted to believe her.

He had nearly convinced himself of the gratifying notion that love for him must be what had driven her to such unprecedented conduct. Desire to claim the man she loved without obligating him to marry her had spawned the deception.

To convince her to admit the truth and come to him openly, he would have to avow his own love in return.

Could he offer her that?

Just imagining Caragh's dear face on Madame LaNoire's responsive body caused powerful emotion to bubble up from deep within him, a fiery amalgam of desire, affection and tenderness. Awe and euphoria swelled his chest.

What an amazing woman! Intelligence, courage, honor he'd already known she possessed. But the outrageous impudence that would lead her to create a deception of this magnitude and the passionate audacity with which she'd carried it off illumined a side of his good friend he'd never suspected.

Small wonder he'd had such a difficult time trying to get the veiled lady out of his mind and senses! He could envision no more exciting a prospect than sharing his life with a woman who could in the space of a single day ride, shoot and manage property like a man, keep house, entertain guests and attire herself with the elegance of a lady—and in his private chambers, drive him delirious with the skill of Madame LaNoire. He was likely to become completely besotted by such a creature.

In fact, he conceded, most likely he already was.

Recalling the joy she brought him, he was hard-pressed not to summon his horse and ride to her farm this instant.

Hunter's Haven, she was calling it.

Heaven, he would name it, if the two of them might be there together...

Which was the crux of the problem.

Every time he told himself to dismiss worries over her possible wantonness and abandon himself to anticipation of their imminent union, the image of the cuckolded husband—a fabled figure of fun in both literature and society—rose out of mind to give him pause.

He couldn't really believe Caragh would serve him such a turn. Every instinct and years of association argued that, in deciding to seduce him, Caragh had acted out of love rather than lechery. But then, he would never have predicted that the Caragh he thought he knew so well could have masqueraded as Madame LaNoire.

Innocent or doxy, he was honor-bound to marry her. The only question was whether he could do so with a full and open heart, or still harboring an unsettling suspicion.

The simple truth was he missed her, and even with his worries about her character, he wanted her.

Hoping time would resolve his doubts, he'd swallowed his frustration and impatience and remained in London awaiting her summons. Waiting, and wasting his time on these damned idiot entertainments.

A wave of frustration welled up, escaping the rapidly fraying bonds of his patience. With an oath he swept the trayful of invitations to the floor.

To hell with matchmaking mamas! He would spend the evening at his club. And give Caragh exactly three more days before, bidden or not, he would go to her.

Suitably re-attired, an hour later he entered White's to find old Lord Andover already at his favorite post by the window. Having little desire for company, Quentin bit back an oath. Resigning himself to the inevitable, he pasted a smile on his lips and approached.

"Ah, Branson, good to see you!" Lord Andover hailed him, waving his cane in salute. "Been missing you. Engaged in cutting a swath through this Season's young lovelies, I hear."

"Not nearly as large a swath as you would, my lord, should you ever decide to thrill the ladies by abandoning this masculine stronghold."

Andover chuckled, his cheeks pinking with pleasure at Quentin's remark. "Damme, I'm much too old to trouble myself doing the pretty! Now, there was a time in my youth…ah, but I've never been much in the petticoat line. Not like you!"

The old gentleman poked his finger at the paper on his lap. "*Morning Post*'s society column asserts that 'a certain Lord B, too regrettably absent of late on his estates about London, returned to set several feminine hearts fluttering with his assiduous attentions at Lady L's come-out ball last night...'"

Quentin waved a deprecating hand. "I'm merely the latest raw meat being offered the Society hostess wolves."

"Yes, several of their usual favorites have decamped," Andover agreed. "Russell, for one. Smoke of the city bothers his mama's lungs, he told me. Said Lady Russell was insisting he take her to the country to recuperate."

Quentin, who had been only half listening until he might politely take his leave, suddenly whipped his gaze back to Andover. "Russell has gone out of town, you say? To Hillcrest Manor?"

"He didn't specify, but 'tis his mama's favorite property, so I expect that's where she dragged him. He was kicking up quite a dust over it..."

Russell was at Hillcrest Manor—a mere five miles from Caragh's new property?

"...not like you," Andover was saying. "The Russell lad prefers London to some rubbishing rural backwater full of livestock and bumpkins. I expect he'll not remain long."

If Russell had gone to Hillcrest, he would soon learn through the infallible network of servant's gossip that the new owner of Hunter's Haven had taken up residence.

The lovely new owner, whom he'd already ogled on several occasions, would certainly soon become the object of his assiduous attentions. Attentions that, Quentin thought, a surge of fury rising in his breast, he would not bet on remaining honorable once he discovered that Caragh intended to live there alone and unchaperoned.

The very idea of Russell luring a lonely and responsive Madame LaNoire into his arms and her bed flamed Quentin's long-smoldering frustration into fury, curled his fingers into fists he hungered to clasp around Alden Russell's throat. He jumped up, nearly knocking over his chair.

"Excuse me, my lord, but I must leave on the instant," he said, sketching a bow. "Urgent business." Ignoring the astonishment on the old man's face, he strode away.

He'd pack his bag tonight and be on the road to Hunter's Haven first thing tomorrow.

Not that he didn't trust Caragh. But if she felt as lonely and dissatisfied as he did, if her body ached for his touch as much as his did for hers, she might be vulnerable to a handsome, charming devil like Russell.

Wanton or innocent, she was *his* lover and would soon be his wife. Doubts be damned, it was past time for Quentin to claim the lady who had stolen his heart as completely as she'd bewitched his senses.

Having gone to such lengths to conceal her identity, Caragh might well, at first, deny the deception and reject his suit. But if she should prove a little slow to believe in his love or to accept the proposal he was more eager than ever to tender, he now had a few more tools in his arsenal of persuasion.

Fortunately, he thought, his lips curving in a smug grin, he knew just where Madame LaNoire was most vulnerable to his touch. Should Caragh prove resistant to reason, he would simply lure her into his arms where, if he repeated his offer at the right moment of intimacy, she would be helpless to refuse him.

Besides, the cardinal rule in assuring that a woman of passionate temperament was not tempted to find another lover was for her current lover to keep her well satisfied.

A task to which Quentin was looking forward with great enthusiasm. Even if he had to strangle Alden Russell first.

CHAPTER TWENTY-TWO

PEERING INTO the dull tin mirror as he shaved five days later, Quentin reflected he'd been right to set out without his valet. Not only would the modest accommodations, much less exalted than the man would deem fitting for a gentleman of Quentin's stature, have pained him, the journey had been an exercise in frustration from start to finish.

After exchanging his own mount for a job horse at a busy inn the first afternoon, he was halfway to the next posting stop when the animal threw a shoe. He'd led the lame beast for over five miles, only to discover at the first hamlet he encountered that the town smith was gone for the day and the inn had no mounts for hire.

Not until nearly noon the following day, having with a liberal infusion of gold coins persuaded the smith to put aside his other tasks, was he back in the saddle. Soon after, the dull gray clouds dissolved into steady rain which intensified to a ceaseless torrent, turning the road to a river of mud and limiting visibility to within a few feet. Though every delay rubbed his ragged patience like a burr beneath a saddle, he knew 'twas insanity to try to gallop his mount through dense fog along an unfamiliar road in hock-deep mud. He spent his second night drying his sodden clothing before a smoking fire at a modest inn, still far from his destination.

He made better progress the third day, but it was not until late afternoon of the fourth day that he finally turned the last hired mount into the streets of the village nearest Hunter's Haven. Rather than ride up to Caragh's gate bone-weary and mud-splattered, he decided to endure one final night apart and stay at the inn in the village.

In addition to rubbing his temper raw, the dawdling pace of his journey had given him entirely too much time to worry over what Alden Russell might be doing with *his* lady.

With a sigh, he put the shaving water aside and rang for a servant to remove it. Taking up one of the clean cravats the inn's maidservant had just pressed, he set about tying it.

In the first heat of jealousy, he'd unfairly suspected his friend might take advantage of Caragh's unusual circumstances. Upon more reasoned reflection, he'd decided that, regardless of Caragh's situation, Alden was unlikely to make improper advances toward a lady he knew to be gently born.

However, despite her assertion that she intended to renounce Society—and her rejection of his suit, for which he thought he now understood the reason—he did not believe someone as loving as Caragh would be content to spend her life alone. She might not, he sincerely hoped, easily succumb to the blandishments of a man who wished to *seduce* her, but she just might be persuaded to *marry*, should some other eligible and presentable gentleman press her.

A handsome, charming, persuasive gentleman like Alden Russell. A man who'd been attracted to her from the outset, who had heard Quentin sing her praises, who was intelligent enough to weigh her excellence of character more than her sister's indiscretion.

A man not blinded by years of friendship, who had seen immediately upon meeting her that the girl Quentin held in such esteem had become a desirable woman.

At that conclusion, he gave one end of the cravat such a tug he nearly ruined the knot.

Still, though Caragh might eventually decide she had erred in deciding to remove to Hunter's Haven, she probably hadn't yet had sufficient time to begin regretting her self-imposed isolation.

And, Quentin reassured himself again, dropping his chin to crease the cloth into perfect symmetrical folds, as far as he knew, Russell wasn't hanging out for a wife. Most likely he'd only be interested in engaging Caragh in an agreeable flirtation to pass the time while his mama held him captive at Hillcrest.

How likely was he to have fallen in love in the short space of...a week?

It had only taken Quentin two magical nights.

Just thinking of Alden discovering love the way Quentin had was enough to bring his rational musings to a halt and fire the primitive jealousy smoldering beneath.

He gave a final nod to the scuffed mirror and strode from the room. If Alden had become enamored of Caragh, that was regrettable. But if Quentin discovered Russell had been hovering about her—or daring to lay hands on *Quentin's* lady— he was going to murder him.

Now to find Caragh and persuade her to finish the unfinished business between them with a wedding.

Once on the road, desire and impatience to see her swelled to such a pitch of anticipation he had difficulty refraining from kicking his horse to a gallop.

He hoped the shock of his unexpected arrival would send Caragh running to him before she remembered all the paltry reasons she'd used to convince herself to keep him at arm's length. And once he had her there—ah, he'd give her no opportunity for regrets! He intended to kiss her until she had just breath enough to say "yes" to his proposal of marriage.

Thoroughly warmed by envisioning that happy scene, he turned his horse in through a stone gateway bearing the sign Hunter's Haven and spurred his mount down the drive. After a few moments, the wooded border of the carriageway gave way to newly-fenced pastureland. Then the manor itself appeared in the distance, mullioned windows sparkling in the morning sun.

In just a few moments, he thought, heedless of his clothes as he kicked the horse to a gallop, he would be kissing her hands, her lips…

Reaching the manor, he turned his horse over to a servant and hurried up the entry stairs, heart pounding and hands trembling with eagerness. His enthusiasm was checked by the butler, however, who informed him Miss Sudley was not in the house, having departed at first light to supervise the ongoing construction of some new barns.

Stifling a curse at this further delay, he swallowed his disappointment and followed the footman the butler summoned to lead him to the construction site.

He'd hoped to bribe her butler into letting him come into her presence unannounced. It was unlikely, with him approaching down an open lane, that he'd now be able to use the element of surprise.

With her forewarned of his approach, he feared he'd probably need to apply some intimate persuasion to get her to admit her deception and accept his hand—which he could hardly do in the middle of an open field full of interested workmen. Fortunately, his guide informed him the new barns were being constructed beside an existing structure. He would have to persuade her to give him a tour, then look for an estate office or tack room—given the height of his impatience, even an unoccupied box stall would do—for the privacy in which to press his argument.

Once he confronted her, might she admit everything and fall into his embrace, as eager to be back in his arms as he was to have her there? Or would she have used these weeks of separation to armor herself against him?

Rounding a curve in the lane, he saw straight ahead a knot of workmen around a frame structure, masons at its base setting a first course of stone. Unable to wait any longer, he paced past his escort, searching for her.

As he trotted by a stack of lumber and building stone, a

flash of light blue caught his eye. He slowed, then skidded to a halt.

On a cloth spread on a bench of stone blocks sat Caragh, gesturing toward the toiling workman. Pressed close behind her, his hand on her shoulder—was Alden Russell.

He must have uttered some sound, for Alden glanced over. In his eyes, Quentin saw the same desire he felt welling up within himself.

The gladness flooding him at the sight of her steamed immediately into rage. For a moment he couldn't trust himself to speak or move, so strong was the impulse to charge over, rip Alden's hand off Caragh's shoulder and plant him a facer.

While he struggled to master it, Caragh turned toward him. Through the red haze clouding his vision he saw her eyes widen, a smile of delight spring to her lips. She half rose, only to sit back at the restraining pressure of Alden's fingers.

Quentin's gaze narrowed to the hand that prevented Caragh from coming to him. He was going to break every bone in it.

"Quentin, what a surprise!" Russell said, his unwelcoming tone and the unfriendly glint in his eyes confirming Quentin's suspicions that his friend was as little delighted to see him as he was to see Russell.

"Y-yes," Caragh echoed, her voice uneven, "I was not expecting you. Have you other business in the area?"

Even then, he might have carried off the meeting with some aplomb, had not Russell stepped in front of Caragh, as if to deny Quentin access to her.

The courtly veneer of civilization disintegrated under the primal hostility of a man who sees his mate coveted by another. Sidestepping Russell, he grabbed Caragh's arm and pulled her to her feet. "I have business with *you*," he all but snarled.

"Quentin, what in the world?" she exclaimed.

"See here, Branson, that's no way to greet a lady!" Russell protested, seizing his sleeve.

Quentin jerked his arm free and gazed into Caragh's eyes. "Come with me, please, Caragh! It's important."

Russell stretched a warning hand toward Quentin. "Miss Sudley, if you wish me to send him to the right-about, I'd be happy—"

"Thank you, Lord Russell, but that will not be necessary. I...I'll rejoin you in a moment."

After one speaking glance, Caragh followed Quentin silently as he led her toward the stone barn. He knew he'd annoyed her, rushing in like someone demented, but the feel of her flesh under his fingers at last, following swiftly upon the shock of finding her with Russell's hands on her, was making it very difficult for him to think.

Her docile silence ended the second they entered the barn. "Quentin Burke, what in blazes was that all about?" she demanded, shaking her arm free of his grasp.

He opened his mouth, then closed it. The clever little packet of an address he'd intended to deliver seemed to have smashed itself to bits on the unexpected shoal of Russell's presence, leaving him at a loss for words.

After all, he couldn't shout "How dare you let him touch you?" or "Why did you keep me away so long?"

Instead, he fumbled in the pocket of his waistcoat, dragged out the figured veil and flung it at her. "This!"

She gasped, her eyes widening and her face going pale, then crimson. Having given him all the proof he needed, Quentin stepped toward her, eager to sweep away every misunderstanding in the heat of the passion they'd shared.

She sidestepped his advance and backed away toward a stall, her arms crossed before her. "I fail to see what *that*—" she jerked her chin at the scarf that had come to rest on the stable floor between them "—has to do with you dragging me off like a Bedlamite."

"Come, Caragh, you can't mean to deny it!"

"Deny what?"

"Vauxhall! Madame LaNoire!"

She sniffed, the picture of hauteur. "Not having gone to Vauxhall, I have no idea what you are talking about."

"Come now, haven't you tortured me enough, practically nestling in Russell's arms? Need I remind you what you did to me that first night at Mercer Street? Then again, I should be delighted to show you." He stepped closer.

"N-no!" she cried, holding up a hand. A tell-tale crimson came and went in her cheeks, but her glance didn't waver. "What nonsense are you spouting? Indeed, I begin to believe you *are* a Bedlamite."

"If I am, 'tis you who've made me one!" he nearly shouted. Grasping for control, he exhaled a gusty breath. "Faith, Caragh, I know I'm making a hash of this, but I've never known you to tell an untruth. Surely you don't mean to start now by denying that, under the guise of Madame La-Noire, you lured me from Vauxhall to Mercer Street and made me a gift of your virtue—and what a beautiful gift it was! But you must agree, sweeting, 'tis now imperative that we marry."

For a long time she made no reply, merely gazing at him, her breath coming quickly, her face guarded. He longed to cross the space separating them and pull her into his arms, assure her everything would be all right as long as they were together, but her hostile stance warned him not to attempt it.

Hugging her arms more tightly about her, she said at last, "Even if...what you said were correct, I see no reason to marry. A man does not feel obliged to wed a woman just because they shared...intimacies. Why should I?"

"That sounds like your sister speaking. Has she had the tutoring of you? Caragh, I'm not that sly cur Holden Freemont, and you're not Ailis!"

"Indeed I am not!" she flashed back. "If I were, I'd have my servants haul you off my property for embarrassing me in front of my friends and staff, dragging me from my work and then verbally harassing me!"

"I don't mean to harass you!" He groaned and ran a hand through his hair. "I admit, I suppose it seems I am. But if ever a matter needed settling speedily, this—"

"Enough!" she broke in, shaking her head rapidly "I'll not hear another preposterous word."

With that, she straightened her shoulders, jerked her chin up and marched past him, treading the velvet scarf into the mud of the stable floor.

He snatched up the crumpled material and shook it off, then ran to grab her arm. "Caragh, we are not done yet!"

She ripped her arm free and whirled to face him. "How dare you presume to dictate to me?"

He reached out a hand, desperate, appealing, but she batted it away.

"Touch me again," she said, her low voice trembling with emotion, "and I *shall* have you evicted."

"Because you can't ignore what happens between us when I do?" he threw back.

In response, she turned her back on him. "Good day, Quentin," she said as she walked away. "Kind of you to stop by, but I'm still too busy to entertain company. I hope your business in the neighborhood prospers."

For an instant he considered calling her bluff, but the reason struggling to emerge from the chaos of jealousy, hurt, disappointment and anger warned him trying to hold her by force would only alienate her further. Better to let her go, for now at least.

He'd chosen his ground poorly and then made mice-feet of his advance. Caragh was too much a fighter to succumb meekly to what she saw as an attack—even if she secretly agreed with him—as, despite her stance today, he knew she must. Why else would she not trust herself to allow his touch?

He'd not been able to detain her long enough to reconstruct

the pretty, persuasive speech that his rage at Alden Russell had driven out of his head. He would have to come back later, apologize, plead with her to listen to him one more time.

How he was going to lure her into meeting him after having just blundered so badly would require some ingenuity. But he hadn't pulled himself up from near-poverty to impressive wealth by quailing at a challenge.

He wasn't about to give up the woman he loved either.

Slowly he walked from the barn. Caragh stood beside a stonemason, her eyes focused on the workman's face, nodding as he talked. The surrounding laborers listened silently, their approving glances and respectful attitudes showing she had already won the local craftsmen over to the novel idea of working for a woman, a significant achievement in the few weeks she'd been at Hunter's Haven.

Pride in her character and abilities washed over him, cresting to a swell of love and admiration.

Gently he brushed the drying mud from the tufted scarf and slipped it back into his waistcoat.

He thought at first she would ignore him as he walked by. But with admirable graciousness, considering the rancor of their brief meeting, she stayed the stonemason in mid speech and turned to him.

"Good day, Lord Branson. Thank you for your visit." Though a subtle blush stained her cheeks, her cordial tone gave no hint she'd threatened to have him forcibly ejected just a few moments previous.

"Miss Sudley," he replied, bowing to her and nodding at Russell. The triumphant gleam in Russell's eyes nearly overset Quentin's resolve to retreat with whatever dignity he could muster. But knowing he must not further prejudice his case by giving in to the desire to mill down his erstwhile friend, he managed to keep his back straight and his feet marching away from her.

As he trudged, he raised his hand to touch the crushed

velvet inside his waistcoat. No, by heaven, he would win her. The consequences of a future without Caragh were so bleak he refused even to contemplate them.

A LONG, chore-filled day later, Caragh finally reached the sanctuary of her office at the manor. After weeks of wrestling with the problem of her love for Quentin, she'd developed a real appreciation for Hercules's struggle with the nine-headed Hydra.

Just when, under the soothing balm of Lord Russell's attentions, she felt she was at last making progress in her attempt to cut off and cauterize the many threats Quentin Burke posed to her emotions, the immortal center of the beast—the man himself—arrived, overthrowing all her efforts. Instead of dismissing him from her mind as speedily as she'd dismissed him from her property, she'd been impatient all day for the privacy with which to contemplate how she meant to deal with his unexpected reappearance—and unprecedented behavior.

She drew from its hiding place beneath the ledger the crinkled list that she had not, in the end, been able to make herself destroy. Shaking her head in bemusement at her folly, she read through the familiar words again.

After his performance at the building site, she ought to restore ''Arrogant'' to the list—and add ''Presumptuous'' as well.

But given that he'd evidently discovered the truth behind Madame LaNoire's disguise, what could she expect? Tempted as she'd been to refute his assumption, he'd been correct in believing it went too much against the grain for her to lie. Though she'd not actually confirmed his assumption, he would surely construe her evasion for the admission it was.

Perhaps what had impelled him to seek her out was the possibility that their interludes might result in a child. Since she now had evidence it would not, she could put to rest that argument for forcing a ring on her finger.

Despite the wording of her dismissal, she knew quite well that one paltry reverse wouldn't send Quentin Burke scurrying back to London. Sooner rather than later, he'd be returning for another skirmish.

Hopeless gudgeon that she was, an immediate surge of anticipation filled her at the thought.

What good would it do to meet him, talk with him any further? Seeing him only meant taxing her mental reserves by pretending herself indifferent to his appeal, as well as courting the danger that he might use her physical yearning for him against her.

After all, he'd given her no indication that anything else had changed between them. He'd certainly not vouchsafed the declaration of undying love she secretly craved—and without which she refused to marry him.

Sighing, she started to thrust the paper back under the ledger when another memory stilled her hand. Quentin had given no sign his feelings for her had changed, except...there had been a *look* on his face when she first saw him. His eyes narrowed on the fingers Alden Russell was resting on her back, that look had said he would derive great pleasure in separating Lord Russell from those digits.

Passing in review both his words and his actions, her startling suspicion wavered toward certainty. Slowly a smile curved her lips, and for the first time since Madame LaNoire had watched the lover she adored departing, she felt a stirring of hope.

Taking up her pen, she scrawled "Jealous" on the list.

A flaw, to be sure. But perhaps, if she were clever enough to manage the matter of Lord Russell, one that might at last bring her more joy than she had ever believed possible: having both her enterprise and Quentin Burke on his knees, delivering a *heartfelt* declaration.

LATE THAT EVENING, Caragh finally transferred the last of the week's totals for labor and materials from the craftsmen's bills into her ledger. Closing the leather journal with a thump, she sighed and stretched her tired shoulders. She'd sent the servants to their beds hours ago, so after lighting a single candle to guide her to her chamber, she blew out the rest and headed for the stairs.

She was, she had to admit, just the tiniest bit disappointed that Quentin had not come back to spar with her again today. She really was hopeless, she thought with a despairing shake of her head, when even the idea of clashing with him sent a burst of energy and excitement flowing through her. But the sooner he appeared—particularly if he encountered Lord Russell when he did—the sooner she could begin testing whether Quentin's apparent jealousy sprang from a paternalistic desire to protect his "innocent" friend from a man's carnal advances—or because he wanted no man but himself to make such advances.

As she entered her chamber and set down the candle, a shiver of delight escaped the prudent hold she was trying to maintain over her emotions. Oh, that she might drive him to distraction with jealousy! If he truly feared she was tempted by another man, perhaps that shallow emotion could be the catalyst to transform his affection into a deeper, genuine love.

She was smiling at that happy prospect when she was seized from behind and a thick gloved hand clapped over her mouth.

Unable to scream, she struggled like a madwoman, twisting and lashing out with hands and legs. But hampered by her skirts and a long cloak that protected her assailant from her blows, she found herself being pushed inexorably toward the bed.

She landed face-first on the soft surface and tried to twist free, only to have her attacker sit down and swivel her into his lap. As he did, she caught a glimpse of a tall figure swathed in a black cloak, his face obscured by a black domino.

"Ah, *cherie,* listen to me! *Vraiment,* you must not struggle so," a deep masculine voice in a lilting French accent breathed into her ear.

A *familiar* deep masculine voice.

"Quentin!" she shrieked, the sound muffled by his glove. "Let me go!"

"But I dare not liberate your lips, *ma jolie,* unless it is to cover them with my own. Only hear my sad tale, *je vous implore.*"

"Madness," she muttered into his glove, amused in spite of her anger at him for frightening her. But since she was clearly no match for his strength, better to cease struggling and allow him to say whatever he wished—before the heat of his body against hers melted will and resistance into nothing more protective than a puddle beneath his boot.

Though she went still, he bound her even more closely, as if he wished to meld them into one body. A possibility that, acutely conscious as she was of his hard chest behind her and startlingly prominent male member beneath her, did nothing to improve her ability to concentrate on outwitting him at this game, whatever it turned out to be.

"I was a man given a great gift, *ma chère,* the gift of a young girl's love. Yet foolishly, I was too blind to see the gem she offered. Even when the girl changed before my eyes, her loveliness enhanced by a woman's passion as a diamond cut by a master jeweler takes on brilliance, I was too cautious to claim this prize. Now I may have lost that which I have come to love so deeply. Please, will you not end my suffering, *bien-aimée,* and tell me it is not too late?"

At last he removed his gloved hand, but before she could utter a word or even take a breath, he jerked her chin up and covered her mouth with a kiss.

At first his lips on hers were hard, demanding, as if to stifle protest before it began and channel any anger into fire of another sort.

But by the time her greedy senses rallied in response, fogging her brain and robbing her of any desire to object, the kiss gentled, became coaxing, almost reverent, as if she were a priceless object too delicate to be roughly handled. At the tenderness of the slow, lingering brush of his lips against hers an ache of love and longing swelled in her chest. *This is where I belong,* her heart whispered.

In spite of the dizziness afflicting her when at last he released her lips, she could feel his heart thundering in his chest beneath her. *As rapidly as my own.*

"Quentin," she groaned as she sagged against him, "that was not fair. And how dare you invade my chamber in the dead of night and scare me witless?"

"Who are you to talk of fair?" he demanded, cupping her face in his hands. "You took what you wanted, hid the truth from me, then disappeared before I had a chance to say what *I* felt or wanted. After my stupid jealous fit this morning, I feared you might never do so. I had to come up with some way to insure you'd let me speak to you."

"Well, you now have my full attention," she replied wryly, "so say what you wish." *And quickly, before the joy of being in your arms again makes it impossible for me to refuse whatever you might ask.*

From the pocket of his long cloak, he drew out the black velvet scarf. "You *were* Madame LaNoire?"

Since there was no longer any point in denying it, with a sigh, she nodded.

"Why did you do it, Caragh?"

"Because...because I longed to be close to you. But just because I pretended to be Madame does not mean anything must change between us. Certainly you don't need to marry me! No one but we two—and Ailis, of course—knows of this and there…'' she felt her face heat in the darkness. ''I know for sure there will be no…consequences.''

''Ah, but there have been—exceedingly grave consequences, my sweet. For if an audacious and lovely lady had not embarked upon so scandalous a course, I might have drifted along forever, too complacent to recognize the truth.''

He resettled her closer into his embrace and continued, ''You were little more than a child when we first met. Not until I finally put the puzzle together and figured out that the friend I valued so highly was also the Madame LaNoire who had so bedazzled me did I realize that you are the one woman, the only woman, I shall ever want. Surely you love me, too, or you would never have embarked on so outrageous a course. That is, you're not going to make a practice of seducing innocent Vauxhall revelers?''

Incensed, she jerked away from him and attempted a punch to his jaw, which given her proximity and the poor angle of its delivery, merely glanced off his chin. ''Certainly not!''

Chuckling softly, he captured her hand and kissed it. ''You relieve my mind. So you *do* love me, my dear Caragh?''

''Since that first morning you rode down our drive,'' she admitted. Oh, how liberating it was to say those words at last! Still, she must be wary. ''But you say Madame 'bedazzled' you. Is it truly a life with Caragh you want—or simply more nights in the bed of Madame LaNoire?''

''You doubt that what I feel is love? I confess I was slow to recognize it myself, nor can I put my thumb on the precise moment when I decided that marrying you was essential to my happiness. But if love is wanting to spend the rest of my days with you, a joy that wells up whenever I am near you, and a hunger to take you here and now and never let you go, then I swear by my sacred honor that I truly love you.''

''You…you are that certain?'' she whispered, not daring to believe it.

He nodded. ''I came here intending to persuade you into

accepting my proposal by seduction, if necessary. But that wouldn't be a proper way to begin a life together. You must accept me willingly, with a clear mind—not befuddled by passion—much as I long to befuddle you again.''

His ardent eyes compelling her gaze, he held out his palm. "Caragh, will you give me your hand?"

When without hesitation she placed hers on his, his face lit in a smile. He lifted her fingers to his lips and kissed them tenderly, then laid her hand against his heart.

"Caragh Sudley, will you marry me and make my life a joy for the rest of my days?"

He wasn't down on his knees, but given the strength of the commitment evident in his eyes, the passion of his tone—and the hardness of the anatomy pressing so invitingly against her bottom—it was good enough.

"As long as you haven't any stuffy notions about waiting to act on this—'' she rubbed her derriere against him, eliciting a groan "—until after the vows are formalized, then I accept. After all, I am my mother's daughter."

"So long as you agree to become my wife as well as my wanton, there is nothing I'd like more. After all, I did come prepared."

At that, he nudged her off his lap and stood. Swiftly he began unfastening his cloak to reveal first his bare throat, then his naked chest...

He stopped, the cloak still masking him below his waist. *"Il vous plait, Madame?"* he murmured with an exaggerated French accent.

"Tu me plais beaucoup," she replied, laughter in her voice. And then sought his lips as, tugging the cloak from his shoulders, she dragged it free and pulled him back into bed.

*Please turn the page for an exciting
sneak preview of Julia's next book
WICKED WAGER
Available in November 2003*

CHAPTER ONE

As Lord Anthony Nelthorpe, lately captain in the Seventh Hussars, stepped across the threshold of his London town house one foggy fall morning, a giggling, mostly naked woman burst onto the upper landing and fled down the stairs. A balding, half-naked man followed, eyes focused owlishly on his hand clutching the rail as he maneuvered the steps and then lurched off after her.

"So, Neighbors," Tony remarked to the retainer in threadbare livery who had opened the front portal for him, "I see my father is engaged in his usual pursuits."

"Yes, my lord," the man replied, his age-spotted hand trembling as he struggled to close the heavy door. Tony turned to assist him, remembering only at the last minute that this wasn't the army anymore, where a man in battle helped another man, regardless of rank. Neighbors would be as embarrassed as he was shocked, should his master's son and heir lower himself to assist the butler.

Curling the fingers he'd extended toward the servant into a fist, Tony turned away. "I expect the earl will be too... preoccupied to receive me this morning. At a more opportune moment, would you tell him I've arrived—and have some beef and ale sent to the library now, if you please."

The butler bowed. "At once. On behalf of the staff, may I say 'welcome home,' Lord Anthony."

"Thank you, Neighbors." At his nod, the old man shuffled down the hall in the direction of the servants' stairs.

Mouth setting in a grim line, Tony watched him retreat, noting the hall carpet was as worn as the butler's uniform, and dirty besides. Shifting his weight painfully, he limped toward the library, noticing as he went the layer of dust that veiled the few pieces of furniture and the ornate arches, which in his youth had sheltered exquisite Chinese vases set on French marquetry tables. Long gone now, of course.

Evidently Tony's esteemed father, the Earl of Hunsdon, still preferred to squander whatever income could be wrung from his heavily mortgaged estates on liquor and the company of lovelies such as the one who'd recently tripped down the stairs.

Welcome home, indeed.

Gritting his teeth, he made himself continue the rest of the way down the hall, sweat popping out on his brow at the effort. The surgeons who'd put the pieces of his shattered knee back together had predicted he'd never walk again. He still wasn't very good at it, he admitted as he reached the library door and clung to the handle, panting. Thank God riding was easier.

A high-pitched squeal interrupted him, followed by a rapid pad of footsteps. The bawd ran into view, pausing with a shocked ''Oh, lah!'' when she spied him.

With matted hair dyed an improbable red that matched the smeared paint upon her lips and nipples, powder caked in the wrinkles of her face and beneath her sagging breasts, she was not an enticing sight, even had he been in better shape to appreciate the appeal of a mostly naked female. But then, with his ugly limp and post-hospital pallor, he was none too appealing himself.

Still, he'd seen his father unclothed, and Tony was twenty-five years younger besides. Not wishing to give the tart an opportunity to change targets, he ducked into the library and slammed the door behind him.

Well, Tony, despite the carnage of war, you made it home, he thought. No longer a captain, but once again Viscount Nelthorpe—whoever the hell that is.

Certainly not the self-absorbed, vain aristocrat so confident of his position in the world who'd fled this house one drink-hazed night three years ago. He'd left England one step ahead of the duns, with little more than the clothes on his back, his horses and a commission in Wellington's Fighting Fifth Infantry—won in a card game.

Nothing like privation, terror, hunger and pain to give one a fresh perspective, he observed wryly.

Though he wasn't sure yet what he was going to do with that hard-won wisdom. The pain in his knee having finally subsided to manageable levels, he shifted his leg and hazarded a glance around him. Now that his eyes had adjusted to the gloom within the curtain-shrouded room, he noted the library was as dusty and unkempt as the hallway. Lord knows, he thought, puckering his brow in distaste, there was work enough to be done here.

A knock interrupted his reflections, followed by the entry of Neighbors. The butler presented him a tray containing a foam-topped tankard and a covered dish, from which emanated such appealing odors that for the moment Tony forgot everything except that he'd not eaten since last night. Fool that he was, thinking to reach London before nightfall despite the slower pace necessitated by his recovering knee, he'd not had enough cash when darkness overtook him to pay for his dinner, the inn room he'd been forced to take, and breakfast, too.

Grimacing, Neighbors set the tray down at the edge of the desk, then pulled a handkerchief from his pocket and hastily wiped a spot clean. "Begging your pardon for the conditions, Master Tony, but last winter his lordship let go all the servants but me, Betsy and one parlor maid—a good girl, but she can't manage so big a house all alone. Betsy's as fine a cook as ever, though, so you needn't be worrying about your dinner. She sends along her welcome, too, by the way."

As he spoke, Neighbors removed the cover on the dish,

sending Tony a drool-inducing waft of beef-scented air. "Tell Betsy that, after what the army ate—or more often didn't eat—in the Peninsula, with meals like this she shall soon make me her slave for life. As for the estate—I know you have done your best. I mean to do something about…conditions." Though heaven knew what, as he was nearly as pockets-to-let now as the night he'd run away.

But instead of returning the skeptical lift of brow a Nelthorpe's promise of improvement should merit, the old man's somber face brightened. "We know if anyone can turn it around, you will, Master Tony. After all, you be one of the Heroes of Waterloo!" After giving him a deep bow, as if he deserved the highest respect, the butler left him to his meal.

Hero? he thought as he gazed at the man's retreating back with a half scornful, half despairing curl of his lip. *If you only knew.*

But surviving such a battle made one practical as well as philosophic. No sense letting the bleak memories spoil what appeared to be an excellent breakfast and some fine English ale. He'd wait until after he tucked in to it to begin pondering his future.

After years of the constant giving and taking of orders in the army, followed by the harrowing day-by-day struggle to recover from his wounds, he found it disconcerting rather than relaxing to admit he had no plans whatever.

He must talk with Papa and determine just how grim their financial condition was—though judging from what he'd already seen this morning, that looked to be grim indeed. Given the scene he'd happened upon as he arrived, any such conference would have to wait until this afternoon at the earliest.

With the ease of long practice he submerged the sense of hurt that, despite his having sent a letter informing his sire of his imminent arrival, his father couldn't be bothered to remain sober and presentable long enough to personally greet the son he'd not seen in three years. So, what to do next?

He could write a note informing Mama that he was back in England, but as she'd not corresponded with him in all the months he'd been away, he wasn't sure at which of Papa's remaining estates the countess currently resided. Probably the one with the handsomest footmen, he thought sardonically.

He'd ride to the park, he decided. The exercise of the knee muscles required for riding was beneficial, the doctors had told him, and paradoxically seemed to ease rather than aggravate the aching, as long as he didn't keep at it too long. And though this late-morning hour was still unfashionably early for anyone in the ton to be about, he might spy an acquaintance with whom to share a drink at Whites—where, he presumed, he was still a member.

His spirits lifted as soon as he'd climbed awkwardly into the saddle and set off into the mist. The army must have changed him more than he knew, he thought with a grin, when an excursion into the lingering smoke haze of a London morning had more appeal than remaining in a cozy, if admittedly dusty, library with a snug fire.

Pax, the gray gelding given him by a grateful infantry officer whose life he'd saved at St. Jean's Wood, was proving to be an easy, even-gaited mount, though he lacked the spirit a cavalry officer preferred in his steed. If God had any mercy to spare for the battered carcass of one Anthony Nelthorpe, he thought with a shudder, he'd never again have need of a good cavalry horse.

As he rode down Upper Brook Street toward Hyde Park, a tepid sun began to break through the remaining haze. A happy omen for his return, perhaps.

Then he saw her—a slender figure in a black habit mounted on a showy chestnut mare. Having watched her from a distance through innumerable marches from Badajoz through

Toulouse, he recognized her immediately, even though he was still half a street away.

For a moment he let the reins fall slack, admiring as always her erect carriage and perfect form. Even on a sidesaddle, she rode as one with her horse, looking as if she naturally belonged there. Which, having spent the greater part of her life in the saddle, he supposed Jenna Montague did. Lovely Jenna—unattainable, unapproachable, his first colonel's daughter and the woman he'd tried to coerce into marriage.

Except for when she found him on the field and tended him after Waterloo, Tony hadn't seen Jenna, now Lady Fairchild, up close since that ill-fated encounter. His fingers reached automatically to touch his throat, where beneath the starched linen of his cravat he still bore the scar from the knife wound she'd inflicted while successfully resisting the less-than-honorable persuasion he'd threatened to employ.

The mark she'd left on his mind and heart had proved just as indelible.

As always, though he felt immediately drawn to her, he hesitated. Then he remembered that the man she'd chosen to marry instead no longer stood watch, his steely gaze promising dire retribution if Tony dared to so much as approach his wife. Colonel Garrett Fairchild had died of wounds sustained at Mont St. Jean.

However, given that he'd once more or less threatened her with rape, Tony thought Jenna was as unlikely to respond to him favorably as the now-departed Garrett. Should he try to hail her, he'd probably receive at best a cold nod, at worst the cut direct.

Which would it be? he wondered. But before he could decide whether or not to try his luck, she pulled up her horse before a handsome town house and handed her reins to the waiting servant who ran up to help her dismount. No chance now of reaching her before she slipped inside—once more beyond his reach.

He watched until she'd ascended the stairs and disappeared beneath the Grecian-porticoed entry. How differently might his life have turned out had he secured her hand nearly three years ago? Her hand, the enjoyment of the curves concealed beneath her pelisse—and the rich dowry that would have allowed him to pay off his debts, abandon his nascent army career and return to comfortable decadence in London?

Instead, he'd spent the following two and a half years sleeping on hard ground or in vermin-infested billets and foraging for meager provisions, his mind and heart branded with the searing iron of a dozen successive battles. Nightmarish vistas of smoke-obscured chaos, the smell of hot gun barrels and fresh blood, the screams of dying men and horses amid the din of rifle and artillery haunted him still.

But over those years he'd also witnessed countless episodes of selflessness and self-sacrifice—for one's company mates, the army, for England. He no longer believed, as his father had preached, that honor was a concept only for schoolboys and fools. And he himself was no doubt a better man for having met the challenge of that hard, bitter, yet inspiring trial.

Better, perhaps, but not of course the equal of Colonel Garrett Fairchild and the other truly noble heroes who had died in the woods and fields of Waterloo.

He kicked his horse into action and rode up to the gate. "Whose house is this?" he called to a young man in livery loitering at the foot of the steps.

"Viscount Fairchild's, m'lord," the boy answered.

So she was staying at the home of her late husband's family, Tony thought. Perhaps, even though she was likely to greet him with scorn, he ought to call on her. Garrett Fairchild had been a dedicated officer and an exemplary soldier, and Tony did regret her loss. Besides, by the time he'd been lucid enough to carry on a conversation, he had been moved to another hospital, so he had never had the opportunity to thank her for her care after the battle. Given the debt he owed her for that, he should deliver his thanks in person, even if she took that opportunity to administer a well-deserved snub.

Yes, he decided, urging his horse back to a trot, he would definitely pay a call on Jenna Montague.

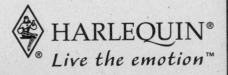

NICOLA CORNICK

became fascinated by history when she was a child and spent hours poring over historical novels and watching costume drama. She still does! She has worked in a variety of jobs, from serving refreshments on a steam train to arranging university graduation ceremonies. When she is not writing, she enjoys walking in the English countryside, taking her husband, dog and even her cats with her. Nicola loves to hear from readers and can be contacted by e-mail at ncornick@madasafish.com and via her Web site at www.nicolacornick.co.uk.

HH659-TR

GAIL RANSTROM

was born and raised in Missoula, Montana, and grew up spending the long winters lost in the pages of books that took her to exotic locales and interesting times. That love of the "inner voyage" eventually led to her writing.

She has three children, Natalie, Jay and Katie, who are her proudest accomplishments. Part of a truly bicoastal family, she resides in Southern California with her two terriers, Piper and Ally, and has family spread from Alaska to Florida.

LIZ IRELAND

is the author of both contemporary and historical romances. She became fascinated by the pioneers who settled on the prairie by reading such great women writers as Laura Ingalls Wilder and Willa Cather. A native of Texas and a recent immigrant to the wilds of Portland, Oregon, Liz lives with her husband, two cats and two dogs.

CHARLENE SANDS

resides in Southern California with her husband, Don, and two children, Jason and Nikki. Her love of the American West stems from early-childhood memories of story time with her imaginative father. Tall tales of dashing pirates and dutiful sheriffs brought to life with words and images sparked her passion for writing. When not writing, she enjoys sunny California days, Pacific beaches and sitting down with a good book. She loves to hear from her readers. Contact her at charlenesands@hotmail.com or visit her Web site at www.charlenesands.com.

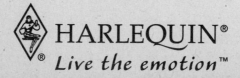